Queen of Shadows

Volume Two in the Shadow God Trilogy

By Kathe Todd

I0562522

Chapter 1

Leila sat at her desk and gazed out the window toward Pleasance Street, her mind wandering. Spring had come at last to Parat, and she was finding it hard to concentrate. "Ouch!" she cried out, her reverie shattered, as one of the kittens sank his needle-sharp claws into her leg through her black robe, trying to climb up into her lap.

She grasped the furry little miscreant by the scruff of the neck and held him aloft, inspecting him. The twin cubs were very nearly identical, but Hanzi had a light dusting of black hairs edging his ears and the tip of his tail. This one was Ion. Long before winter had released its icy grip on the imperial capital, Kathal had come into her second heat. Before Leila had even been aware of it, the canny cat had slipped away. She'd been gone for two days, and returned smugly pregnant.

As Leila and Tevo became aware of the situation, they'd half expected to find her delivering a litter of mongrel kits fathered by some particularly ambitious tomcat. But somewhere in Parat she had managed to find a true Nima pard to sire her brood. Thank the Eight pards' litters were not large!

The kittens were six weeks old now, and utterly adorable. Not to mention a huge nuisance, destroying everything they touched. Maks and his mother Marcelina had been entranced, and they had already promised Maks that Hanzi would be his. What they were to do with Ion, they had not yet figured out. Perhaps they could find a home for him among the Nima who would be here at Parat's gathering ground a few months' hence.

Leila snuggled the baby to her, wrapping him up in her arms and planting a kiss on his head. Then she tucked him into her lap, admonishing "Curl up and go to sleep, will you?" before getting back to the stack of paperwork before her. Leila and Tevo had vacated the two upstairs bedrooms in favor of the master bedroom downstairs, now that they were lovers. The upstairs spaces had been converted to offices for temple business.

Oh, and what a lot of it there was! The Shadow God Betsalel's return to the pantheon of the Gaspari Dominion had been

3

witnessed by a throng of thousands. His resurrection of Tevo at Leila's command had launched an entirely new aspect to his character as a god. His province was darkness and shadows, sleep and dreams, and the refuge that death could bring – but added to that was now the hope, the expectation, that if you worshipped him fervently enough he might bring your lost loved ones back to life.

Betsalel himself was none too happy about that, pointing out privately to Leila that it was only the fact that Tevo's soul had still hovered nearby that had allowed the resurrection to be possible. Once a soul had gone into another living body, or joined with the One, his divine powers might reanimate the flesh but the person who had once inhabited it would be gone for good.

"You couldn't just wrest the soul back?" Leila had asked, curious. Being on conversational terms with one of the eight principal deities of her world had gone from being a bizarre and astonishing thing to something quite commonplace.

"If the soul had joined The One, no," Betsalel explained. "No more than you could extract a glass of water from the pond into which you had poured it. But if the soul had taken a new body, it is possible you could coax it out – especially if the imprint of the body in which it had until recently lived was still in effect."

Realistic or not, the new expectation that worship of Betsalel might at some point down the line result in a chance to recover one's deceased beloved had unleashed a flurry of new worshippers. Donations had poured in, and construction was already well underway on the new Temple of Betsalel in Parat's southwestern quarter. After the old one had been razed to the ground two centuries before, no one had ever wanted to build on the site. Until now.

Tevo had been promoted from acolyte to high priest, an unlikely occupation for the teenaged former thief. But he had done as much as Leila had, in the end, to return the Shadow God to his place in the pantheon. More, really, since he had actually given up his life. The responsibilities accompanying this post were something he was still getting used to, but he'd proven to have an unlooked-for aptitude. Once the donations had begun coming in (and after consulting with the High Archon) he'd arranged for the reborn Church of Betsalel to have a bank account.

They'd broken ground on the new temple in early autumn, and the very first addition to the site had been an idol of Betsalel, placed on the same pedestal from which the previous one had been wrested, and destroyed, during Emperor Fernand's pogrom against the dark god's believers.

Leila had been astounded. "You make it *yourself?*" she'd asked disbelievingly. She'd assumed that, just as the gods themselves were shaped by human belief and worship, so the idols through which they manifested in the physical plane were carved by the hand of man. When they'd decided to begin work immediately on the new temple, she had begun looking for sculptors.

"My idols are not just statues," the dark god explained with a hint of amusement in his voice. "They are conduits, power points around the world that permit me to take form in the physical plane. Have you not noticed that all of the gods' idols, other than differences in size, are identical?"

Leila had visited the Temple of the Seven in Marsine a few times in childhood, as well as the much grander one in Parat – and six of the individual deities' temples here as well. He was right. "How are they formed, then?" she asked, mystified.

For answer Betsalel, who was standing before her in a physical form slightly taller than the average human man, grew a little. The standard height for the idols in Parat's Temple of the Eight, foremost power nexus on the planet, was twenty feet. But once manifested, the gods could appear at whatever size they liked. He glanced down at his torso, and pulled a handful of his substance from his side as if gathering up a handful of clay. The "flesh," if that is what it was, closed up and became unblemished. There had been no blood.

The dark god cupped his hands and held them out to Leila with the wad of his substance cupped within. As she watched, fascinated, it writhed and became a perfect miniature of Betsalel's idol. He handed it to her. It felt slightly warm, but was as stiff and unyielding as any statuette of stone or metal might be.

The high priestess was awestruck. "This," she said hesitantly, turning the perfect miniature over in her hands, "is you?" It even had a miniscule glowing red gem for the never-sleeping third eye.

"It's not me, it's a gateway for me," Betsalel said softly. "It's hard to explain – I exist, alone, in a plane beyond the physical. But my power there is sustained by the belief and worship of humans on this plane. And the more of that there is, the more I can do."

"This is awfully small for the new temple," Leila remarked as she continued to examine the newly budded idol. Betsalel smiled at her, once again no more than six feet high, and rested his hands on her shoulders.

"Place it on the pedestal," he promised, "and I'll manifest there and make it whatever size you think is right. With the new strength you have found for me, such a thing is no trouble at all."

That their gods were human enough to tell lies had been a shocking revelation to the thousands of onlookers who had beheld the confrontation between Lucia, Goddess of Light, and her seven siblings at the Temple of the Eight last summer. But to Leila, at least, Betsalel could speak only the truth. She held within her body a fragment of his idol from the temple in the Blackwald, and through this conduit she knew his soul.

So it was no surprise to her, when she and Tevo worshipfully placed the tiny idol atop the pillar they'd excavated, to see it come alive and grow before their eyes as the Shadow God smiled down at them. "Whoa," Leila had said, as the god continued to grow. "I think eight feet should be about right. You want to be bigger than human, but not so frighteningly large that worshipers will fear to approach you."

Now walls were beginning to rise around the pillar. The new temple would include living quarters for acolytes and priests who wanted to devote their lives to the Shadow God's worship; but Leila and Tevo, the nucleus of Betsalel's new priesthood, intended to keep living at their comfortable and private residence on Pleasance Street.

The symbols of Betsalel remained, now painted on the front and back doors and carved into the frames of each window. The frustrated thief taker, Cyryl Kubasz, had attested to their effectiveness at warding the house from hostile intrusion. But the "Palamban" décor of the house's living room had been replaced with conventional, and far more comfortable, upholstered furniture. It had become home, and they now affectionately called the place "Shadow Manor."

The kitten ceased his painful kneading of Leila's lap, and dropped off to sleep in a warm ball. Sighing contentedly, the high priestess pulled another piece of correspondence from the pile on the desk and began studying it again, as she considered her reply.

Chapter 2

Usafi stirred in his cradle, his murmurs soon becoming a wail. His mother Uzuri turned from her weaving and hurried across the room to scoop him up. This beautiful baby boy was a gift from Mulia, and though Uzuri had brought shame on her family by bearing him out of wedlock, he was the joy of her life.

Now in her middle forties, Uzuri had been married for many years but her prayers for a son had gone unanswered. Then her husband had died, and she had gone to live with her brother and his family, as was considered fitting. She had become little more than a servant here, but it would not have been thought respectable for a woman to live alone. Mauaji controlled her finances, as well, for under the laws of the kingdom of Palambo an unmarried woman's nearest male relative was responsible for her upkeep.

Yet Uzuri had managed to escape her prison, falling into an affair with a man a decade younger. She had experienced more passion, more rapture in this relationship than she had ever felt during her fifteen years with the late, unlamented Wazee. But her paramour was married to someone else, and it was only Palamban royalty who took multiple wives.

Suckling her son, the tall, dark woman thought with wistfulness of that affair. It had been worth the disgrace to have this perfect little person to love, she thought. And she felt vindicated as a woman. Presumably it had been Wazee, not herself, who was to blame for her former inability to conceive.

Clean and dry and replete, Usafi was once again sleeping soundly and Uzuri had returned to her weaving when Mauaji came in. Her sister-in-law Faradhi had been away this past week in an outlying village, nursing her ailing mother; and her nephew Imbaso had been gone for more than three years studying abroad. So they were alone in the house.

Uzuri turned from her loom to eye her brother uneasily. As usual these days he was clad all in black, a cowled robe that covered him from head to toe. There were rumors of evil goings-on at the temple where Mauaji had become an acolyte when he was in his teens, but bad things tended to happen to those that spoke out against the worship of Betsalel.

It was said that the Shadow God's worship had been completely banned in the vast Gaspari Dominion to the north hundreds of years before, due to these same dark rituals. But rumors had now reached the kingdom that Betsalel himself had appeared in the Temple of the Eight in Parat and reclaimed his position among the gods and goddesses of the pantheon. Uzuri hoped that didn't mean worse was to come.

Uzuri bowed her head slightly, showing respect for the head of the household, and murmured "Good evening, my brother. You are well?" She hadn't seen him in a couple of days, as he was often busy on temple business. Over more than thirty years of service he had risen to become the arch-priest of the Temple of Betsalel in Namei, generally acknowledged to be the dark god's foremost temple within the kingdom.

Mauaji nodded curtly, unsmiling. He seemed to be in the grip of a powerful excitement coupled with grim determination, and his sister quailed back from him as he approached. He was eight years her senior, but still in his strength. He walked, not to her, but to the cradle where Usafi slept.

He bent to lift the baby up, careful not to wake him, and Uzuri's heart rose into her throat. "What are you doing?" she hissed. Her misbehavior in bearing a bastard child had reflected badly on Mauaji's stewardship; and while he had not thrown them out on the street, he had never shown the least sign of affection for his nephew.

The sleeping child started, then drifted off again as his uncle held him snugly in the crook of one arm. "Fear not, sister," Mauaji said with a hint of fondness in his voice, "It is time for the little one to be dedicated to our lord. If he is consecrated to Betsalel early in life, he will grow up lucky." The boy's mother greeted this explanation with doubt, but she had been told that her brother had also undergone this ritual as a baby. Long before she was born, of course.

"Am I to hold him while you perform the rite?" Uzuri asked, making to rise and fetch a cloak. Still holding Usafi in the crook of his right arm, Mauaji waved her off with the left.

"If the child were a girl, you would hold her and the rite would be performed by a priestess," he explained quietly. "As we know not who the boy's father is, I will be standing in for him. Go back to your weaving."

"Very well," she said softly, and seated herself at the loom once more. "Don't be too late." Rites of Betsalel of course had to be performed during the hours of darkness.

"No need to wait up," Mauaji replied, as he let himself out of the house without waking the baby.

Hood up to hide his face, the arch-priest made his way around the curving road and up one level to the Temple of Betsalel. One of the major trading hubs in this part of the kingdom, thanks to traffic on the Pana River running between the far-off Talj Jabal mountains and the Western Ocean, the city boasted temples to all eight of the major deities and several minor ones as well. Only in Iskand, the nation's capital, was there a temple to all of the Eight such as one might see in Parat.

Usafi fussed briefly at the motion of Mauaji's rapid progress along the stone-paved streets, but settled again as his uncle held him more closely. The arch-priest let himself in through the temple's rear entrance. The main doors of the temple were kept wide open through the night for the convenience of the Shadow God's casual worshipers – those who were not a part of the secret cult within the church.

As Mauaji carried the sleeping baby down the stairs to the underground complex where true worshipers of Betsalel held their secret rites, his thoughts were desperate. His entire adult life, he had followed the rituals as prescribed by the Secret Scriptures. He'd been initiated into the church while still a teenager, and for decades they had prayed, and sacrificed, and done everything they had been instructed to do. But the god had not come.

The idol of Betsalel in the inner sanctum of his temple in Namei was a true one, they knew – formed from the original in the

Temple of the Eight at Parat in the Gaspari Dominion, where the worship of the Eight had begun. Legend had it that in centuries past the prayers of worshipers, particularly of those higher in the priesthood, had induced the god to manifest within his idol and grant their wishes. But for all of Mauaji's lifetime, and for generations before him, this idol had remained inert. Were they doing something wrong?

During his tenure in the priesthood that was a long-standing family tradition, Mauaji had tried everything. But no matter how vile or perverted the rituals, no matter how fervent the prayers of the flock and their leaders, they had failed to raise a response. Clearly their god was not satisfied with their efforts.

This was his last hope. Always before the sacrificial victims had been chance-caught strangers, the children of prostitutes stolen while they tumbled their customers, visiting foreigners. But was the death of such truly a sacrifice? Now he had in his hands a victim of substance – a child of his own blood. Admittedly the baby was an embarrassment to him, and he would not be sorry to see the boy disappear; but the familial repercussions would certainly be a trial. Betsalel would almost *have* to come!

Mauaji found a robed and hooded acolyte awaiting him outside the basement level's inner sanctum, to which the idol of Betsalel had been removed centuries ago. "Is all in readiness?" he murmured.

The acolyte replied, "They await you within." As he passed the entrance to the stone-lined chamber, Usafi spasmed as if he'd been pierced with a needle and began squirming in his uncle's grasp – screaming his little head off.

The arch-priest moved down the central aisle, flanked on either side by black-clad initiates where they knelt to the black idol near the back wall of the room. Torches lined the walls on either side, providing a dim flickering light as Mauaji approached the altar.

The stone platform was massive, more than six feet long and four deep, its top around three feet off the floor. At the rear was a large semicircular recess, beyond which stood the pedestal on which the idol was set. Deep red flames flickered up from the hole. They were supposed to be "black flames," as mentioned in the Secret Scriptures; but those must have been a gift from the god himself and had not been granted to them. The best they'd been able to come up with was the true red color (matching Betsalel's all-seeing third eye) created from adding certain chemicals to the charcoal fueling the fire.

Usafi was shrieking uncontrollably now, as if he had somehow intimated what was about to be done to him. Mauaji's attempts to calm the boy had no effect, and he hastened to get on with the ritual. He laid the baby on the altar as if he were about to change his diaper, and began removing the cloth with which he'd been wrapped. Usafi was not walking yet, so was clad in a single length of colorful cotton cloth imprinted with the designs popular in most parts of Palambo.

Now the child was naked, the cloth cast to the floor, and his uncle held him aloft to the multitude of initiates who knelt waiting in fervent anticipation of the ritual to come. "Here is our sacrifice!" Mauaji declared, "A child of my own blood. Call forth our master now, call to him with all your hearts!"

The throng began chanting in unison, "Lord Betsalel, come to us! Accept our sacrifice!" over and over again as the arch-priest turned his back on them and held the screaming child up to the black idol.

"Lord Betsalel, Shadow God, Dark One, Prince of Darkness, Deliverer of Death, hear our prayers!" he beseeched the silent idol. There was no response.

None from the idol, at least; but suddenly the baby's frantic wailing ceased and he lay inert in his uncle's arms, gasping for breath. His black eyes were wide and staring. Mauaji laid the suddenly quiescent child down on the altar and picked up the sacred knife, which had been prepared for this ceremony. Its razor-sharp, curved blade was eight inches long, etched with mystic symbols, and it had been dipped in a sacred oil that contained the same chemical as that used on the altar fire.

The arch-priest grasped the knife and thrust it into the ruddy flames, and it burst into fire itself – red flames licking along the blade. "Accept our sacrifice, Dark One!" he cried, and plunged the knife into the baby's throat – pulling down to split him from breastbone to crotch. The chanting of the initiates rose to a fever pitch.

As Usafi's soul fled his frail body, ripped asunder by his uncle's knife, it quivered in terror. There were no nearby, unsouled bodies into which it could flee, but being alone in the void was an incomprehensibly horrifying experience. This soul had sprung to life within the body of the child born to Uzuri, created by it – not transferred there from another, dying body. It had no prior experiences to guide it, and it desperately sought a home.

Nearby, so close he could reach out and touch it, was a being. Yet not a being – a construct of belief, created by two centuries of human psychic energy and worship – and soulless. It offered knowledge, and power, and form, and the soul of Usafi fled to it.

As Mauaji consigned the infant's body to the fire at the back of the altar, the flames suddenly leapt up to twice their former height – and they were black! The torches all around the room flared to scarlet, providing a baleful light to illuminate the scene. The arch-priest and his fellow worshippers watched in half-horrified fascination as all of their hopes and dreams came true.

The idol of Betsalel writhed and changed by before their eyes, transforming. The shape, while essentially still that of a man, became more bestial. The third eye winked out and two golden ones opened – enormous slit-pupiled eyes in the face of a black leopard. It opened its mouth to reveal blood-dripping white fangs, and raised its arms to show that each finger was tipped with a curved, razor-sharp claw.

"Betsalel, Betsalel, Betsalel!" the assembled worshipers chanted in ecstasy. They had done it, they had awakened their dark god at last! The now-animated and changed idol leapt down off of its pillar to stand on the blood-stained surface of the altar. The loincloth was gone, revealing insignificant genitalia, and the feet were seen to be clawed as well. Behind, a long black tail switched.

"Silence!" the god roared, and in a second all there were struck dumb. "You will mention the name of Betsalel no more!" he commanded. "Henceforth, you will address me by my true name. I am Kivuli, the Death Who Comes in the Night. Serve me, or die!"

Chapter 3

Leila awoke with a flaring of fire in the middle of her chest, eyes wide in the darkness as she lay in Shadow Manor's enormous master bed with Tevo slumbering beside her. What was *that*? She recalled no bad dream, and the pang had lasted for only an instant so it wasn't indigestion. As she lay there wide awake, an irresistible urge came over her. She needed to go to the temple and consult with Betsalel, now!

No point in disturbing Tevo. She hastily donned some pants and a black priestess robe, along with her favorite comfortable boots. A glance at the clock on the living room mantelpiece revealed it was nearly two in the morning. Too late to find a cab, and the Temple of the Eight was only a little more than a mile away – not worth the trouble of getting Nimble ready to ride. She could jog it in a few minutes.

Over the past few months, southern-bred Leila had discovered much to her surprise that there were aspects of winter in Parat's northern climate that she actively enjoyed. Playing in the snow was fun, and the city boasted an enormous, shallow lake that was given over to ice skating in the winter months. A natural athlete who'd been trained in agile pursuits for years, she quickly picked it up and had found the vigorous physical activity a wonderful antidote to hours spent in paperwork and religious outreach. She was now as fit as she'd ever been, and she hadn't been running long before she found herself arriving at the temple.

The main sanctuary was available to casual worshipers at all hours, and Leila wasn't surprised to see Betsalel already manifested in his idol – shrunken to the 6-foot height she preferred for conversing with him, and anxiously waiting for her to appear. As she hurried inside, he stepped to her and enfolded her in a gentle embrace.

"What is wrong, master?" she asked worriedly. Something earth-shaking must have happened, to cause this reaction in a god.

"Sit, child," the Shadow God commanded, and the two of them sat facing one another on two of the sanctuary's carved stone benches. Leila looked up at him, her brows knit with concern.

"It has been stolen from me!" Betsalel announced, sorrow and loss in his deep voice.

"It?,,," Leila prompted.

"My idol, one of the foremost of my idols in Palambo. And others as well, I believe, though I am blind there and can't say for sure." The high priestess was confused.

"Didn't you say that the Palamban church had begun worshipping their own evil natures in your name, and you were no longer able to manifest in your idols there?"

The dark god nodded sadly. "True," he said. "Probably within a generation after Lucia's coup in the Gaspari Dominion a movement swept through my church in Palambo, with human sacrifice and black rituals turning my worshipers from me and breaking my connection with them. Yet my idols were still true scions of my idol here, parts of my being – just as the one that stands in my new temple is, here in Parat. Now another entity has stolen them and made them its own."

"Lucia?" Leila gasped. Ever since her defeat of the Light Goddess here in this very room last summer, she'd been half-fearing divine retribution or at least a counter-maneuver. Betsalel shook his head.

"My sister's attributes are too far removed from mine for her ever to have the power to manifest within one of my idols, no more than I could take over one of hers. We are polar opposites. No, I fear that someone, presumably the arch-priest and his followers within my church at Namei, has created a djinn."

Leila was a voracious reader, and she was familiar with djinns. They were a supernatural being that featured prominently in the mythology of the eastern parts of the kingdom of Palambo, usually considered to be fearsome and deadly. Men might bend them to their will, but they were in constant peril of being devoured by their servants. "I thought djinns were mythical?" she asked. While the dark god's high priestess might be well ahead of the average worshiper in her understanding of the supernatural world, it was clear she had more to learn.

"Djinn is just a name people use. Another is demon, or those of a benign nature are usually called angels. Overall, these supernatural beings are called daemons," the shaken god explained patiently.

"And they're not imaginary?" Leila asked.

"Oh, they are," Betsalel said sadly. "They are constructs of human belief, sprung from the human imagination and given substance as more and more humans grant them credence and attention."

"But how could an imaginary being steal your idol?" Leila asked. "I just don't understand."

"What makes a daemon real, what gives it divine powers – perhaps equal to those of any god – is when the belief construct is inhabited by a human soul," he explained. In answer to her questioning look, the Shadow God went on, "Daemons, usually in a benign form as angels, are what permit mages in the Dominion and elsewhere to perform their feats of magic. Their elaborate rituals serve to beguile the angel – and there are many of them, each with their own specialties – into doing what would otherwise be impossible."

Leila gazed at him open-mouthed, in astonishment. "You told me human souls either take another body or join with The One," she said.

"Almost always that is the case," the god admitted. "But there are other options. Some souls wander lost, untethered, and haunt the places familiar to them in life. And some enter artificial entities created by the belief of man and make those entities real. It is possible, thus, to become something like a god."

"So, this corrupted image of you as a figure of evil has acquired a soul and taken over your Palamban church?" Leila asked. The concept of a real deity intentionally created by men to be anyone's worst nightmare sounded like a very bad idea. The Shadow God nodded sadly.

"I fear that is the case," he said softly. "And I need you to go and stop him, if you can."

What?! Again?! "Me? I'm busy reestablishing your church here in Parat," Leila objected. For a god, her master Betsalel seemed awfully needy.

"Tevo is doing a wonderful job," the god pointed out. "He should be able to do without you for a few months. But I have no one else I can call on. Nowhere in the southern half of the continent is there one of my altars that has not been corrupted."

Leila was already becoming resigned. If there was anything she could do to stop a malign version of the dark god from running rampant in the land of her father's birth, she had to make the attempt. Such vileness must be stopped. "But how am I to travel to Palambo, to this… Namei, did you say?" Betsalel nodded. "I don't suppose you could just magic me there?"

The god seemed to consider. "If I had power in Palambo, which of course if I did you wouldn't need to go there, I believe I could carry you with me from this temple to another there, through the dimension in which I normally reside. But that's a moot point. You will have to take a coach, or ride your horse, south past the Antels to the coast of the Center Sea, and take a ship from there. Namei is far to the south, beyond the desert that spans most of the Center Sea's southern shore."

Now that she was no longer on the run, Leila had been able to ride Nimble for pleasure whenever she had time; so the horse was in good condition and probably up to the task. It would be faster and likely more enjoyable than riding in a coach, except for the possibility of foul weather. But she was a small young woman, and though she was well able to take care of herself the need to be constantly fending off predatory males would be a colossal nuisance.

"If I have to leave Tevo to run the church, and Kathal has to stay here and raise her babies, who will I take as a guardian?" she asked. The Shadow God gave a small smile.

"I could fetch Yeil back from the Blackwald for you, if you like." He knew full well how little the girl and the raven had enjoyed each other's company.

Leila snorted. "Why not just provide me with a talking polecat, instead?" she suggested. Betsalel remained silent for a few moments, thinking.

"How would you like it," he asked, "if you could be your *own* companion?"

"What, split myself in two?" she asked, puzzled.

"I can give you the power to be an army of people," the god replied. "Only one of them a time, of course – but were you, say, a well-muscled thug standing over six feet tall, with a sword at your side and a few well-placed scars, might that not work to ward off unwanted attention?" He smiled again, showing surprisingly white teeth in his coal-black face.

At her questioning look he went on, "It is in some ways similar to the Shadow power I gave you last year. You have only to picture in your mind who you wish to appear to be, and all who behold you will see that person – or creature. This includes clothing and armament. You can seem so formidable that none will dare to attack you. It might also be useful for you in creating disguises so that you can go among the people of Namei."

"Will I really be six feet tall and armed with a sword?" the girl asked.

"No," the god replied a little apologetically. "It will all be an illusion, but a strong one. Should you strike an adversary with one of your daggers, he will be convinced that the six-foot man has cut him with the sword. He will even see his blood on its blade. And when you speak, he will hear a voice appropriate to the visual image."

"That should work well," Leila said, hiding a secret smile. Oh, the fun she could have with this ability! It almost made all she was going through on behalf of the Shadow God worthwhile. "If I am illusion-clad as a Palamban, will the Palambans then understand my speech?"

"No," Betsalel answered. "But I can easily give you the power to be fluent in Kiswa, the principal language of that kingdom. I did the same for the raven last year, you will recall."

The two of them arose, and as before the god rested his hands gently on Leila's shoulders, kissing her on the forehead. "Child of Shadows, take this power of illusion and use it to protect thyself. The Kiswa tongue is yours as well," he continued in that language. She understood it seamlessly.

Betsalel stepped back, looking down at his shadow child. What an amazing little creature she was! Then in another instant, he was looking at himself! The little imp had immediately used her new ability to mimic the appearance of the god who had granted it to her. They smiled at each other, seemingly eye to eye – though in reality Leila was peering up at him from ten inches closer to the floor.

The illusory Shadow God reached out his hands and clasped those of his model. It even truly felt as if he were holding hands with a man of his size! Betsalel was well-pleased. He had spent two hundred years, a tiny fraction of his lifetime but recent and fresh in his mind, unable to do much beyond light a candle with his divine powers. It was good to know he hadn't forgotten how to be a god.

Leila became herself once again, smiling broadly. "Thank you, master!" she declared. "This is going to be a *huge* help!"

"One more thing," Betsalel replied. As he had done months ago, he grew slightly before taking a tiny pinch of flesh from his side. In his palm it flowed into the shape of a miniature idol, no more than two inches in height. "Keep this with you always," he said, handing it to her. "With this, I can come to you at need. Together we will drive this djinn from my temples."

"Thank you," Leila said, tucking the tiny idol into a pocket of her robe. She stepped forward and gave the Shadow God a hug. "It will take me a few days to get ready to go. I guess I'll have plenty of time to talk with you, now I've got you in my pocket." With a gamin's grin and a cheery wave, Leila exited the temple and began jogging home.

Chapter 4

By the time Leila had returned to Shadow Manor the combination of running nearly three miles and being up in the middle of the night made her tired enough to sleep again – though her mind was buzzing with excitement. She stripped off, and examined herself in the room's stand mirror before climbing back into bed, pressing herself up against Tevo's back. He stirred but didn't wake.

As dawn light came spilling in through the drapes, Tevo rolled over, prodding his bed partner in the behind with his morning erection. Mmm, her rear was so nicely rounded, so smooth. He brushed the hair aside so that he could kiss her shoulder. Not long after Betsalel's return to the pantheon last year, the god had kindly restored his priestess and her acolyte to their original skin tones and grown their hair back in a moment.

It felt odd, silkier somehow. Tevo opened his eyes to see a fall of straight golden hair lying against skin as pale as porcelain. "Augh!" the young man shouted and in seconds he was standing at the side of the bed, erection rapidly falling, as he stared in consternation at the stranger he'd been sleeping with. She was lovely, and he had never seen her before in his life.

"Who the hell are you?" he demanded, hands held over his crotch. The girl (she looked no more than sixteen) sat up in bed, her shapely full breasts delicately tipped with pink winking at him as her enormous cornflower blue eyes widened and she smiled at him sleepily.

"Why Tevo," she said mischievously, "don't you recognize me?"

Angry now, Tevo snapped "No! I never saw you before in my life. And where's Leila?" His lover relented, and in another second the familiar face and figure of his beloved was sitting there in the bed. The young priest realized then that there had been quite a resemblance between Leila and the blonde girl. The shape of the face and the figure were nearly the same, though the coloring was very different. Was he losing his mind?

"I'm sorry sweetie, I couldn't resist," Leila apologized. "Come on back to bed and I'll tell you all about it." Tevo slipped in beside her, and she threw her arms around him. "Are you sure you don't like me better as a blonde?" she purred. "I can be any woman you've ever wanted..."

"You already are," he replied, and kissed her firmly.

A considerable time later they got up and dressed, and continued their discussion over the breakfast table. Marcelina had baked them a sort of coffee cake, and it was still warm and delicious as they sat sipping hot, sweetened tea. "I'm not happy about you going," Tevo said.

He knew full well he was not Leila's boss. Hell, Betsalel was a *god* and Leila was just as likely to argue with him as with anyone. But having all of the responsibility for the church while she was gone would be a headache. Missing her from his bed would be an agony – after all, he was only eighteen. And she was going on an unbelievably long, perilous journey with an even more perilous, maybe impossible task at the end of it. Oh Leila, don't go! He said nothing more.

"I'm not happy about it myself," she replied thoughtfully. "I'll miss you so much! But I can't just sit here while some demon from the pits of the hell inside twisted men's minds ravages its way through Palambo. They're killing babies, Tevo! And now that their 'god' has become real, with real powers, it will be getting much worse. I have to go. Anyway, with Betsalel at my beck and call, I shouldn't meet anything I can't handle."

"I wish you could carry *me* in your pocket," her lover replied gallantly. She grinned at him. Whatever he might say about her being the only woman he'd ever wanted, their lovemaking this morning had been particularly hot after the revelation of her new power.

It was only after she put on the illusion again later and stood before the mirror, nude, that she realized she had recreated her childhood image of her mother – though not the mother she truly remembered. This version of Miriam Sampson was more innocent, younger. She felt a pang at seeing her as she had probably looked before she had been done in by her love for young Vandao.

A thought came to her, and in a moment Tevo was facing himself across the dining table – right down to the black priest robes he was wearing. He started, then studied the image carefully. "That is seriously creepy," he said.

"Yeah, I know," Leila replied. "But whenever I'm really missing you I can stand in front of a mirror and see your face."

It took another two days for Leila to prepare for her journey. Funds for the trip were taken from the church coffers, which were burgeoning. Not a great deal remained of the gold the two young thieves had stolen from the old fence in Kohl, and as full-time employees of the church it was their prerogative to use the church's money for their needs.

The high priestess called her god to his tiny idol in the back yard at Shadow Manor one midnight. The thumb-sized figure burgeoned in an instant, and at her behest he laid hands on the dozing Nimble. The young gelding was imbued with the power of tirelessness, able to run all day without flagging. With speed of critical importance, Leila needed every advantage she could get.

Other, more mundane measures were taken to assure that Leila would arrive at her destination swiftly and in good condition. She bought a hooded oilskin cloak that would cover her from head to foot and provide some protection for her mount, as well. Springtime was rain time in most parts of the Dominion, though there might still be some snow in the mountains. Thank the Eight (or perhaps, the Dominion's Department of Highways) that broad, well-paved roads ran throughout its borders!

Leila still had her prized daggers, a souvenir of her time with the Night Guild in Marsine. She also had an excellent bow she'd bought mostly as a piece of misdirection as she was fleeing toward Parat the previous year. It was a fine weapon, but she judged that the need for long-distance weaponry was slight on this trip. Nor did she expect to need to hunt for food, as she'd be traveling on the main highways and staying in inns.

Yet in the spirit of being prepared she couldn't resist taking a tour of Parat's armorers to see what other useful items of lethal intent might be added to her arsenal. In the guise of a tall young bravo she roved the shops, seeing some pretty unlikely items. There were the curved scimitars of Palambo, the pikes favored by castle guards throughout the Antels, intricate items like the little spring-loaded bolt gun she'd had when she was younger (before deciding her daggers were more useful). These, she passed by.

But one thing she saw, she couldn't resist. The weapon resembled a pair of brass knuckles, beloved of tavern bouncers and street toughs. But these were made of shining nickel steel, and between the knuckles four curved, razor-sharp blades like claws were tucked away. Press the lever with your thumb, and the spring-loaded claws popped out to lock in place. They were only a couple of inches long so unless you used them to rip out your enemy's throat they were unlikely to be lethal – but they sure as hell would discourage an attacker. And leave them wondering what had hit them, afterward.

Now all was in readiness, and Leila said her goodbyes to Tevo in the privacy of their home. When she left, mounted on her tireless horse bearing his heavy packs of supplies, it was as a six-foot-tall man in his late twenties. He was carrying a sword.

Chapter 5

Wolfgang Schultz made it to Skiern the first night, retracing the journey of last spring's half-Nima siblings in reverse. Nimble was fresh and frisky, feeling as well as he ever had in his six-year life after running at an easy gallop all day. He ate an enormous quantity of oats in the inn's stable – while his rider downed a large quantity of stew and bread in the inn's common room before retiring, limpingly, to his bed.

Augh, Leila thought, dropping the illusion and peeling off her clothes before collapsing on the feather mattress. What was I thinking? Everything from the waist down felt as though it was carved out of wood, yet somehow alive with pain. Ugh. It had been years since daily hours in the saddle had been part of her routine, and she just wasn't used to it yet.

The temptation was strong to pull Betsalel's tiny idol from the pouch in which she kept it, and ask her god to perform a healing on her such as he'd done for her and Tevo both after they'd freed his idol from its prison last year. But a stubborn part of her didn't want to do that. Tough it out, she commanded herself, and fell into a dreamless sleep.

In the morning, feeling somewhat better, Leila performed some stretching exercises before donning the semblance of Wolfgang Schultz and going downstairs to eat breakfast. Having been looked down on most of her life for her dark complexion, Leila had been unable to resist the temptation to become a blond.

It was not that she bought into the notion that having blond hair and blue eyes made you better than someone with dark skin. Put this guy out under the hot sun for a few hours, and he'd be a boiled lobster. But it was interesting for Leila to take note, not only of the different reactions Wolfgang got for being a member of the dominant race in these parts, but also of those he got for being a man.

Whenever Leila took on a disguise she always built at least a minimal back-story for the character, trying to inhabit the imaginary person as fully as possible. As the muscular, six-foot Wolfgang, she not only had to move differently and speak differently, she had to leer at the barmaids. And this created a problem for her, early in her second night's stay at an inn in Kalze. Wolfgang and his tireless horse were making double the time Rolf and Gerde Petulengro had managed with this same horse pulling a cart, last year.

Leila had removed her clothing after supper and crawled beneath the sheets, eager for sleep to take her. She was already feeling a bit less achy than she had the night before, and was hoping that in another day or two she'd be back to her former fighting trim. But before her mind released its grip and she drifted away, there came a rattling at the door's latch. It was being opened with a key!

Seizing one of her daggers from the nightstand, Leila hastily donned the semblance of Wolfgang. The clothes piled on the chest of drawers were hers, far too small to be the leather traveling garb the young Dutcher had been wearing. But the room was lit only by a candle. And of course, if this was an intruder intent on robbing Wolfgang, they'd shortly be dead and wouldn't be noticing anything.

The door opened to reveal the young barmaid Wolfgang had been admiring earlier. She looked to be perhaps eighteen, a well-rounded and handsome young thing, and she was clad only in a flimsy robe. "Sorry to bother you, Herr Schulz," she dimpled, "but I was concerned that you might not have enough blankets. Nights can be cold in Kalze, even in the spring."

She was indeed carrying a blanket folded over her arm. I'll be damned, Leila thought. Evidently her natural preference for beauty in men had led her to make Wolfgang too handsome for his/her own good. "Um, uh... Ilse, is it?" the muscular blond stammered. She smiled encouragingly at him, making her way toward the bed. The robe fell open a bit to reveal her plump charms beneath.

Wolfgang fended the barmaid off gently. "Ilse, you are delightful and delectable. I am very honored that you thought so kindly of me. But I'm afraid I, uh, am not able to perform at this time." She looked at him big-eyed, wonderingly. How could this gorgeous hunk of a man be unable to perform? "It's... I'm so embarrassed to say this... I seem to have picked up a dose of the clap."

Ilse recoiled. Gonorrhea, while not deadly, was certainly an annoyance – and the cure for it was extremely unpleasant. What sort of girl had this handsome Dutcher been rolling with, then? Actually it was precisely *her* sort of girl, having a man one night and then never seeing him again while she moved on to the next, who kept such infections constantly spreading. But that had not occurred to her, as yet.

"I'm sorry," she said shyly, hastily dumping the blanket onto the bed and then, gathering her robe around her, fleeing from the room. Phew, Leila thought. Nothing like growing up in a whorehouse to give you an edge in the battle of the sexes. Releasing the illusion, she dug some wedges out of her pack and inserted them under the door's edge, making sure that there would be no further intrusions.

Thereafter Wolfgang became less a paragon of young Dutcher manhood. He grew a decade older, developed a large nose and several facial scars, and wore a wedding ring. He was still an imposing-enough figure that he was not troubled by highwaymen or bar toughs; but neither did any more barmaids attempt to enter his chambers in the middle of the night.

Two nights later Wolfgang came to Kohl, arriving fairly late and taking a room at the same inn where the half-Nima siblings had stayed. Magda was considerably less friendly to the forbidding-looking man than she'd been to Gerde, serving him his supper without any idle chitchat. Hardly aching at all now that her young body had accustomed itself to days on horseback, Leila went out exploring the town afterward – clad not in the illusion of Wolfgang, but in her shadows.

She found Bohdan's pawn shop boarded up, a "for let" sign on the door. Leila and Tevo's robbery must have been the final straw that convinced the old man to pack up and retire, she hoped. That he might have died later of brain injuries inflicted when she'd conked him with that heavy art object was something she preferred not to consider.

From there it was Ceske, then Salz. The long days of travel were wearing, but they no longer left Leila feeling completely done in. Now she was starting to feel horny, to long for Tevo's arms around her. They had lost their virginity together, but over the months since then they'd gotten quite good at making love. She missed him desperately, but there was nothing to be done about it.

Wolfgang, a lonely soul who rarely spoke more than a dozen words with anyone from day to day, turned onto the main road heading west after passing through Rosen without stopping. He skirted the Blackwald on its southern border, then picked up the road coming south from Munch before too many hours had elapsed. While Leila was no longer physically devastated by her journey, she was once again beginning to feel the emotional starvation of being too long without a friend. She longed for Tevo, and not just for the pleasure of their lovemaking.

Now that she was not simply falling into an exhausted sleep each night, Leila had begun spending her evenings studying some of the books she'd brought with her. There was a world atlas, with detailed maps of the entire continent shared by the Gaspari Dominion, the kingdom of Palambo, and the multifarious realms of the Hando. Though men had been sailing in boats and ships for thousands of years, no one had ever found any other major land masses.

Scholars had figured out hundreds of years ago that the earth was a globe, one of many circling the sun. Since the invention of telescopes a couple of centuries before (polished lenses, like so much else, having originated east of the Killtops but then been eagerly adopted and improved on by the clever and industrious Gasparis), five additional worlds had been identified – and the possibility of life on these globes had captured the popular imagination.

Over the centuries numerous mariners had attempted to circle the globe, going west from the Dominion or east from the furthest shores of the kingdom of Hanshu – foremost of the Hando realms. Some of them had been blown back to shore, complaining of hideous storms, of nowhere to restock their supplies of food and water. None had every completed the journey. And it was not surprising. The continent was some seven thousand miles across – and if the scholars were right, the planet itself was nearly four times that size in circumference.

A few scattered islands had been mapped within a couple of days' sailing of the continent in most directions, but no one had yet found land with unknown people living on it. Betsalel had mentioned that there were other worlds in the universe, some of them with thinking creatures living on them. But he'd said nothing about people living elsewhere on this world than the continent on which Leila stood. Likely that meant there were none.

Besides refreshing her knowledge of geography Leila delved into some books of Palamban history she'd bought. After all, half her heritage came from that land even if she had never visited the place before. Despite the direness of her errand, she was looking forward to seeing that exotic place, full of people with dark skin like her.

Much as had been the case in what was now the Gaspari Dominion, the kingdom of Palambo had begun small and gradually annexed its neighbors. It had only achieved its current size a little over a hundred years ago, however, and had never really been entirely at peace. There were many different ethnic groups on the southern part of the continent, and most of them were not all that happy to be under the rule of the Amhari aristocracy.

The Amhari were the dominant racial and cultural group of the original kingdom of Palambo, from whom Leila's own father had sprung. They were tall, slim, very dark-skinned, with prominent, straight, narrow noses and lips of a similar thickness to those of most Dominion natives. Their eyes were black or dark brown, their hair black and very curly but not as wooly as that of the natives from further south. And their culture had once been very warlike, as evidenced by their long history of successful conflicts.

They had even subdued the fearsome Daregs, the lighter-skinned, hawk-nosed nomad tribes who had roamed the deserts south of the Center Sea and west of the Talj Jabal for millennia. The ancient ancestors of the Daregs had settled along the northern reaches of the valley of the Azraq, the mighty river that drained the central part of the southern continent into the Center Sea. There a civilization had arisen, one of the foremost of ancient times.

The conquering Palambans had captured that land's capital city, Iskand, which stood on the shore of the Center Sea at the mouth of the Azraq, and had made it the capital of their new empire some two hundred-fifty years ago. Unsurprisingly, the Palambans did not base their date system on the consolidation of the Gaspari Dominion as the Gasparis did – but modern dates were easy enough to pin down.

Wolfgang spent the night at an inn in Wena, then galloped on in the morning and reached Milos before nightfall. Nimble seemed to be perfectly fine with their days of relentless travel, recouping his energies during each night's rest (though stable staff remarked on more than one occasion of his prodigious appetite). Leila hoped it wasn't going to cause problems when they finally got where they were going and he was stuck, standing around a stable, for weeks at a time.

The grim-looking, middle-aged Dutcher hopped onto his fresh and frisky gelding in the stableyard at Milos after an early breakfast, and set a course along the main road leading south. But on an empty stretch of highway some twenty miles from that city, the horse abruptly became ridden by a man in his later fifties – a hawk-nosed, shrewd, olive-skinned trader's agent from Miradil who went by the name of Suleiman Abaza.

Leila could extend the illusion to include the horse while she was riding him, she knew. She could easily have appeared as a fairy maiden riding on a unicorn, had she wished. The thought made her smile. Unicorns were mythical, of course – and if they'd been real, she would no longer have been able to catch one. When she was younger she'd been given to making heartfelt vows, but nearly all of them had fallen by the wayside in the years since.

She had sworn to kill Madam Droma, the evil brothel keeper who had made life hell for Leila's mother and the rest of her "girls." Yet so far as she knew, the madam was still alive and well and ruining young women's lives back in Marsine. She had at least taken a little revenge, though, rolling the brothel's customers for their valuables when she'd been running with Tomas' gang of street urchins at age nine.

She had sworn never to touch alcohol, and when she'd broken that vow at age thirteen the evening had ended in tragedy. And she had vowed that she was going to remain a virgin for life. Until Tevo had come along. She had no regrets on that score, other than the regret that he was not accompanying her so they could be making love every night. And she quite enjoyed a glass of wine with dinner. No harm came of it, if you used good sense and moderation.

She had vowed never to worship any gods, and look how *that* had turned out – she wasn't just a worshiper, she was a priestess. Well, she still had her vow to kill her father Vandao in revenge for abandoning her mother (and her, in utero) to a cruel fate. Maybe she'd get the opportunity soon.

Her mind circled back around to the question of whether she should have Nimble appear as a fiery desert stallion, or something. Nah. A middle-aged trader's agent wouldn't likely chose such a mount, and there'd be no way to maintain the illusion once she and the horse had parted ways at the inn. The road began to climb a hill, vineyards as far as the eye could see on either side, and Leila caught a whiff of the sea. They had come to Jena!

Chapter 6

A couple of years before, desperately lonely after roaming the central Dominion by herself with only Kathal and the horse for company, Leila had decided that what she really wanted to do was set herself up in Jena under a new identity – one that would last her for the rest of her life, and with enough money that she would never need to steal (or work) again.

She had never been there, but it seemed as though its location would make it ideal. It was almost three hundred miles from Marsine, far enough away that it was unlikely anyone from the Night Guild would ever discover here there. Yet the climate and setting were similar.

That dream had led to Leila's theft of five thousand florins' worth of the Count of Oester's historical treasures, and to a relentless pursuit that had hounded her all the way to Parat – via the Blackwald and the ruined temple where Betsalel had captured her for his own. She had been terrified and angry at the time, having her life taken over by a god; but now she had learned to accept it, somehow. Were not the rewards worth the cost?

Now she was riding down the road into Jena in the middle of springtime, and it was every bit as beautiful as she had dreamed. Houses of stone or white-painted adobe brick climbed the hillsides on either side of the road, their tile roofs glinting terra cotta red or glazed blue. An amazing panoply of flowers was in bloom, like brilliant confetti scattered among the houses and trees. A light, salt breeze came in off the water from the harbor below, preventing the sun from making the day too hot.

For a moment Leila was seized with the urge just to chuck her quest and spent a few weeks here in a rented villa, enjoying the ambience. But no. Suleiman needed to get his grizzled butt onto the next ship leaving for Halath, the major port on the southern coast of the Center Sea. From there a road led south, across the desert, to Namei.

Suleiman booked a room in the Sleeping Shepherdess, an inn far enough away from the harbor district that it boasted a stable for his horse. Nimble remained an ordinary-looking chestnut gelding, but he'd now acquired a name more in keeping with his owner's eastern ethnicity. "Please give Wapesi as much food as he wants to eat," the robe-clad trader's agent told the stableboy. "Soon he will have plenty of rest, but he has carried me far." The boy nodded, accepting a silver shilling as his tip, and went on about his business.

As a major seaport centrally located along the Center Sea's northern shore, Jena saw its share of foreign travelers. After securing his room from the innkeeper and locking his belongings therein, Suleiman set off with a step that some might have thought remarkably spry and jaunty for a man in late middle age. He soon found himself walking along the waterfront, throwing back his head and taking a deep breath as the scents filled his nostrils.

Not all of them were pleasant, of course – most rather the reverse, in fact. But to seaport-bred Leila, they were the scents of home. She hadn't been on a pier, scarcely even within sight of the sea, since she had fled Marsine nearly four years earlier. Salt, rotting fish, tar, a hint of sewage. The cries of the gulls, the sounds of sailors calling to each other in Gasparto and Kiswa and the tongues of the Hando. They filled her senses and sent her back to her childhood.

Near at hand, beside a long pier where the fishing fleet docked, fish fresh from the nets was being gutted, battered and fried beneath a canopy that sheltered a couple of small tables with chairs. It smelled absolutely wonderful! Suleiman hurried over and gave the girl a few coins in exchange for a small wooden plate heaped with hot, crispy fish pieces. The flesh was firm, white, and delicious, and there were few bones to worry about.

The fish stand offered only water to drink, and Leila was a little leery about drinking water from a place with an unknown source. While no one in her world had yet figured out the link between polluted water and epidemic disease, common sense dictated that you tried to find water that was pure and clear. Suleiman handed the plate back and went across the broad street fronting the harbor to one of the many taverns serving the maritime trade. He tried to select one that at least looked clean, and ordered a bottled beer to wash down his early supper.

The barmaid (or possibly, the proprietress; she looked to be around Suleiman's age) took his money with a smile. At this hour of the afternoon business was quiet. "You just in off a ship?" she asked. A great deal of the trade around the shores of the Center Sea arrived by boat.

He smiled at her. "No, actually I hope to be leaving on one soon," he explained. "I've been traveling on horseback from Miradil across the width of the Dominion, scouting trade goods and negotiating deals for my employer." Hands busy washing mugs, she raised her eyebrows.

"That's a long journey," she said conversationally. "I'll bet you'll be glad to be sailing back, then."

Suleiman took a swig of his beer and sighed. With a rueful smile he replied, "I *wish* I were sailing back to Miradil! I can only hope that my wife will not have had me declared legally dead by the time I return. From here my horse and I journey to Halath, thence across the desert to Namei where I will begin my travels again – eastward through Palambo, eventually taking ship again for home when I reach Iskand. By then, I should have established enough trade contacts to keep my employer and his entire company busy for the rest of my life."

The woman smiled. "I don't envy you that! Doing business here at the harbor and talking to sailors every day I've often thought I would like to travel. But what you're doing sounds more like punishment." The hawk-nosed man shrugged.

"Ah, I think it is just that I'm getting too old for this life. I loved it in my youth. But it's well-paid, and I will share in the profits. Likely I will be able to retire before long, and my wife and I can just sit around and enjoy our grandchildren. Our son and his wife are expecting their second."

After a moment he added, "Well, they were… Likely the child will be walking and talking before I get the chance to see him or her." He finished his beer, and handed the empty bottle back over the counter. "I'd best be about looking for a ship to take me to Halath, then."

The bartender leaned over the bar a little, pointing off to her left. "Just go down that way, it's about three blocks, and you'll see the Jena Municipal Shipping Office right across from the main pier. They're open most hours, and every ship in the harbor has to go there and register when they arrive – what they are, what their business is, how long they're staying, and so forth. It's a plus for them, because their customers can find them, and convenient for would-be travelers or shippers. I'm sure they'll help you find what you're looking for."

Suleiman made a light little bow and performed a sort of rolling salute in her direction. "Thank you, lovely lady. You have been most kind and helpful to this tired old man." With that he left the tavern and headed in the direction she had indicated. Leila didn't recall Marsine having anything so well-organized as what the woman had described, but then she had never been seeking passage or arranging to have goods shipped. A child's perception of the world, even a child as canny as Leila had been, was often incomplete.

A clerk in her early twenties greeted the eastern gentleman on his arrival at the Municipal Shipping Office. Suleiman, who after all had been a professional traveler since long before Leila had been born, showed no nervousness or hesitation as he approached the unfamiliar situation. There were half a dozen stations along the office's front counter, but at this hour only the one he stood at and another, where a man he took to be first mate on some vessel or another was filling out a form, were manned.

"How can I help you, sir?" The young woman asked politely. She looked to be a local, with dark brown hair and eyes to match. She might have passed for Tevo's older sister, giving Leila a pang.

"I am in need of passage for myself and my mount on a ship for Halath," Suleiman replied.

"Bringing a horse, eh?" the clerk asked, glancing up at him for confirmation. In the Dominion horses were the most common mounts, but they were by no means the only animals on the planet ridden by man. And this was a busy, cosmopolitan port.

"That's right, dear," he said with a slight nod.

"Just a moment," she said, and got down off her stool.

Behind her on the wall was an enormous chart, evidently showing every available slip in Jena's extensive harbor. She carried a notepad with her and made a couple of notations on it with a pencil, then pulled a large book from a rack below the chart and brought it back to the counter.

"I have the *Maria Elena* out of Baricel leaving for Halath with a stopover in Ruza next Mulday. Or there's the *Kaskazi,* homeported in Halath itself, leaving on Delday. That's a smaller vessel, only a hundred-fifty feet, but they have indicated that they have some space for livestock." The bigger the better, Leila thought. She had no idea what to expect on a sea voyage, but she was about to find out.

"That first vessel sounds good," Suleiman said. "Can you tell me where she's docked?"

"You'll find her out along the main pier there," the young woman said with a gesture toward the front door. "Berth four and five, on the left side." She smiled at him, pleased to have been able to assist him. Like the proprietress of the tavern, she had always dreamed of traveling to exotic lands. But working in this job and meeting people from all over the world was almost as good!

"Thank you, dear," Suleiman said with an answering smile and tipped her for her service. Leila wasn't sure whether this was customary, but the girl didn't object. There was something about inhabiting the persona of a grandfather that her thinking of a woman four or more years her senior as a "girl."

The well-upholstered trader's agent made his way across the broad, crowded street to the largest of the harbor's many wharves. This one jutted out hundreds of feet into the deep basin that had been carved, in antiquity, out of the broader bay on which Jena sat. It was reserved for larger vessels, and the *Maria Elena* must be one of the largest of them if she was occupying two berths.

Leila knew that ships floated on water and usually were moved across it by the power of wind pushing against their sails. That was about the extent of her nautical knowledge, and it had not occurred to her to bring along a book on the subject. So she was utterly ignorant of what she saw as Suleiman walked down the pier, looking for the *Maria Elena.*

Immediately to the left was a smallish vessel. Large, certainly, by the standards of the one commercial boat ride taken by the High Mysterion Laleihala last year. But none too big to be sailing across the vast Center Sea. The journey to Halath was nearly a thousand miles. It had a pair of masts, both with triangular sails.

Another, slightly larger vessel was moored beyond it. They must need to use rowboats or something to pull these ships out from the pier and get them pointed in a direction where they could begin moving under the power of their own sails, Leila realized. Similarly, boats must have been used to push them sideways so that they could have been moored in the first place – or so she guessed.

Beyond that one was an enormous tall ship twice the length of the first one. It had a high prow and stern in the style of Catal (the county of which Baricel was the principal seaport), four masts with square sails plus a triangular one running from the frontmost mast to a sort of mast-like thing sticking out at the front. Beneath that was a handsomely carved and painted figurehead of a dark-haired woman modestly clad in classic blue robes. Leila would be willing to bet that was Maria Elena, and that she was married to the ship's owner.

The vessel was a hub of activity, with sailors and porters scurrying around using portable cranes to load bales and crates of cargo into the ship's holds through enormous hatches on deck. Leila noted that many of the sailors had black hair and dark eyes, though most of them had skin paler than hers. "Pardon me young fellow, is this ship the *Maria Elena*?" Suleiman asked of a teenage boy who was standing, watching, as the crate he'd just help boost up off the pier was maneuvered into the hatch by his teammates.

The boy turned and saw a middle-aged-pushing-elderly man dressed in a once-fine but now worn robe over his trousers, in the eastern fashion. He tipped his cap respectfully and said "Aye, sir, she is." Suleiman smiled avuncularly at him, and handed him a small coin. If you had the coin to spare, Leila had already learned in her short life, being a good tipper could ease your way immensely.

"Thank you, son. I'm in need of passage for myself and my horse to Halath."

"You'll be wanting to see Señor Rodriguez, the purser. Just go up that gangway over there and tell the mate standing at the top of it that you want to book passage. He'll direct you further." With that, and a wave in the direction of the gangplank, he turned aside as a cart brought another crate of cargo forward for him to secure to the crane.

Suleiman made his way to the gangplank and walked up it. Leila found that it was not as stable as she had expected, but Suleiman was careful not to show surprise. On the deck of the ship he found a man in his early thirties wearing a uniform of some sort. "May I help you sir?" The man asked politely.

"Apparently I need to see Señor Rodriguez," Suleiman said. "I need to book passage to Halath for myself and my horse."

"Ah," the man replied. He gestured across the deck to where a man sat at a small portable desk. There appeared to be a couple of people in line waiting to speak with him. "Just go over there and get in line. He'll see you shortly."

While he waited to speak with the purser, Suleiman looked about him curiously. But while the eastern gentleman had been on ships many times and was not impressed, it was all Leila could do to keep from gawking like an untutored child. Senior Rodriguez assisted the two people in line ahead of Suleiman, and soon it was his turn.

"Passage for me and my horse to Halath?" He asked.

"I assume that you want fodder for the horse, and to take meals with the crew?" the purser responded. Suleiman nodded, but there was a hint of question in his eyes so the man went on to explain, "We are principally a cargo vessel. We do have half a dozen passenger cabins and there is plentiful space below for your horse, but we are not set up to provide entertainment or lavish meals."

An old hand at sea travel, Suleiman nodded. "How long will the voyage take?" He asked, as if that had been all that concerned him.

"We stop over in Ruza for a little more than one day. We will arrive in Halath fifteen days after departing from Jena."

"That sounds satisfactory," Suleiman said. "And the fare?"

"All together, that will be fifteen florins," Rodriguez said. Leila winced internally. Fifteen florins was a princely sum, and she had not brought a fortune with her. On the other hand, with her new ability stealing any extra funds she needed should be child's play. Fun, too, she had to admit. Suleiman handed over the money and the purser took his particulars, which he entered on a ledger. "Please be here with your horse and baggage no later than eight in the morning on Mulday. We sale at 11:42 with or without you."

Chapter 7

By the time Suleiman had finished booking his passage the sun was almost down and he returned to his inn. The Sleeping Shepherdess, despite its somnolent name, was a lively place in the evenings. And now that Leila was no longer on the road, no longer seeking to avoid attention, Suleiman was able to stay up late enjoying the ambience.

He drank a bottle of excellent wine, washing down some delicious local seafood, and chatted happily with his fellow inn patrons on a wide range of subjects. The trader's representative further embroidered his personal story, and picked up gossip from all parts of the Dominion. He retired to his bed far later than Wolfgang had done during the long trip from Parat.

Leila had two whole days in which to enjoy staying in Jena; and while she was getting rather fond of the old trader's representative, she had the urge to just be herself in this city she'd been fantasizing about for years. So, shortly after Suleiman had left the inn, he ducked into an alley and Leila emerged.

She was not without artifice, however. Her hair looked nicer than it had in years, her dress was a copy of one she'd seen on a local matron and admired, and though her feet were clad in her favorite pair of comfortable walking boots, she appeared to be wearing fine sandals.

On the first day she was once again on the wharves, enjoying the sights and smells and having some more of that wonderful fried fish for lunch. She toured the colorful market square, dazzled by a variety of fresh fruit she hadn't seen in years, and bought herself a lovely lace shawl. In the later afternoon she became Suleiman again and went to visit with Wapesi in the stables behind the Sleeping Shepherdess.

After the horse's amazing performance during their journey here, Leila had feared that spending a day cooped up in a stall would have him ready to jump over the moon. But it appeared that the god's gift only supplied him with extra energy when he needed it. He seemed calm and content.

The next day the "new and improved" Leila, wearing her new shawl, got a little extra exercise wandering far up among the houses in the hills overlooking the harbor. She didn't want to admit it to herself, but secretly she was looking for the villa – the one she had dreamed about in her fantasy of two years before. The breeze was warm and pleasant, the little houses lovely, and she saw half a dozen that might have been made just for her.

But, she also realized, she was not the same person she had been two years before. Her horizons had expanded, she had found love, and she had also found a purpose in life – one beyond stealing everything that wasn't nailed down, at least. Perhaps Jena could become a destination for her and Tevo after they'd retired from the priesting business. Assuming, of course, she didn't end up killed by the evil djinn on this particular adventure...

Needing to be down at the dock boarding his ship early tomorrow morning, the trader's agent took to his bed earlier than he had the night before. In the morning he settled his account; but rather than have his horse saddled, he led the beast – laden with his baggage and the horse's tack as well – as they walked together down toward the harbor.

Wapesi was led up the gangplank and down a wooden ramp into an area of the cargo hold set aside for livestock. He was confined in a narrow straw-lined stall, helping to ensure that he could keep his feet when the going got rough. Leila recalled that Nimble had been none too thrilled with his brief journey along the river leading to Parat last year. What was the poor beast to think, spending more than a fortnight in these cramped quarters? But there was no help for it.

Suleiman patted his mount on the nose, saying "Be of good cheer, Wapesi. I'll be back to see you before long." There were hours yet before the ship would sail, but the crew were busy as could be preparing for it. Fascinated, the trader's agent walked around the decks watching them work. Leila's heart was pounding with excitement.

Chapter 8

The *Maria Elena* was not far out from the harbor at Jena when Leila began to feel queasy. She was thankful that the need to be on board so early, coupled with the midday departure, meant that her breakfast had long since been digested. She found that she was able to resist the urge to retch, though it was a close thing – and she had no desire whatsoever for lunch.

Suleiman retreated to his cabin. The *Maria Elena's* passenger cabins were located on the next level down from the main deck – three on either side with a narrow corridor running alongside each set of cabins, and more cargo space in between. Thus each cabin had its own little porthole, which Leila found a lifesaver. By pulling the small sea chest provided with each room over underneath the porthole, she was able to stand and put her head out the small round window. The chill sea breeze, laced with spray, helped to drive the feeling of nausea away.

Hours later, Leila found that she was becoming accustomed to the motion of the ship as it sped across the waves. She was thankful that she'd been able to take passage on such a large vessel, as she suspected that one the size of that first ship she'd seen on the pier would have been rocked twice as much.

Now, she was beginning to feel hungry. But lunchtime had been hours ago, and she doubted that any food would be available to her. She was anxious that no one should think Suleiman would have been so affected, so she resolved to offer some excuse for his failure to appear at lunchtime and make the most of dinner – whenever that might be. Time to go exploring!

Suleiman left his cabin. The accommodation was not bad, really – a sturdy wooden bed covered with a feather mattress, the little chest on which Leila had been standing, a small wardrobe, a washstand, and a sort of privy stool. That last item featured a cover for when it was not in use, and apparently a pipe running down to discharge whatever you put in it to the sea below.

He went first to visit his horse, who seemed a little uneasy about the motion of the ship and the many creaking noises that surrounded them. He offered what comfort he could, then climbed the stairs to the deck above, where a stiff breeze pushed the ship along at a fair clip. Sailors were all over the place, adjusting the rigging to their officer's commands, going about whatever mysterious business was required to keep the ship sailing along. Apparently, all was going well. Leila hated being so ignorant, yet unable due to her disguise to ask all the questions that were boiling in her mind.

Suleiman had seemed like a good idea at the time, a harmless fellow who would have good reason to be traveling this great distance yet would not be carrying enough money to make him worth robbing. Or so Leila had hoped. Now she kind of wished she'd selected some other disguise, one that would have let her admit that this was her first sea voyage. Ah well.

The old trader's agent wandered around the deck and stood looking over the rail, watching dolphins swim alongside. Leila had never seen dolphins before. She loved how graceful they were in the water, how much enjoyment they seemed to be taking as they leapt and dived in the *Maria Elena's* slipstream. She wished she could become one of them – but while she might appear as a dolphin easily enough, she herself didn't even know how to swim. No sensible person would have attempted swimming in Marsine's polluted harbor, and she had never had the opportunity to learn.

Dinner was served late, at what appeared to be around seven in the evening. The ship had a large mess hall, centrally located on the same deck as the passenger cabins. Only five of the six were occupied on this voyage, and the paying passengers shared a dining table with the captain – a singular honor, Leila supposed.

This soon after leaving port, there was plenty of fresh food aboard and the meal was delicious: braised beef with mushrooms in a wine sauce, wilted spring greens, a grain pilaf. Leila had to restrain herself not to fall on her food like a starving weasel, it had been so many hours since she'd eaten breakfast. She chided herself for having failed to include some food supplies in her pack before leaving Jena.

The captain, Julio Flores, proved to be an urbane and charming host. The diverse group at the table were made to feel at home, and Leila found the conversation stimulating though Suleiman didn't have all that much to say. There was a very dark-skinned Palamban woman in her early fifties, one Surimba, accompanying a lovely and innocent-looking teenage girl. Linda Cervantes was the youngest of the Count of Catal's three daughters, and Surimba was escorting her from Baricel all the way to Iskand (the *Maria Elena's* next port of call after the ship arrived in Halath) to be married to King Omali of Palambo – Surimba's elder brother.

Suleiman congratulated the girl on her fine marriage alliance even as Leila was fuming with rage at this poor child (two years her senior, but far behind her in life experience) being sent off to the ends of the earth to marry a man nearly old enough to be her grandfather. Linda appeared to have no objections, though. She'd been raised from birth with the expectation that she'd have no say in who she married, and if anything she was regarding the experience as an exotic and exciting adventure. Leila hoped she would still think so a year from now.

The two were being escorted by a pair of fierce-looking and heavily armed palace guards, their protectors as well as their chaperones; but those were dining with the crew at another table. The other two passengers dining with Suleiman and the women at the captain's table were Mfanya, a Palamban trader out of Halath; and Imbaso, a handsome young man in his early twenties with gleaming dark brown skin and flashing black eyes. He had been studying in Wena for the past three years, learning the ways of the Dominion, and was clad in the sort of clothes worn by upper-class young men of that city.

Imbaso was very taken with Linda, who like many people in Catal (unlike further south in that part of the Dominion) had green eyes and blonde-streaked light brown hair. Her skin was a sort of honey tone, and she looked as though she might be able to get a tan. No doubt she'd soon have the opportunity to do so, assuming that King Omali's wives were ever allowed out of doors.

Linda's chaperone Surimba was seated between them, however, and she was not amenable to the young man spending much time in converse with her charge. So he chatted with Suleiman, sitting on his left, instead. "It was my father's idea in the first place for me to go to the Dominion for study," he was explaining. "I couldn't believe how cold the place could get, that first winter! But I really came to enjoy it, after a while. There's much less strife there, and you can really devote yourself to scholarship."

"And lots of pretty girls, I suppose, as well?" the grizzled trader's agent asked with wink. Imbaso flashed a gleaming smile, startlingly white in his dark face.

"A bit of that as well, I must admit." They were speaking in Gasparto, and the young man spoke it well but with a slight, drawling accent that Leila found charming.

"So, are you finished with your studies then?" Suleiman asked. Imbaso's face fell.

"Unfortunately, no," he said. "I had another year to go to receive my degree, and was looking forward to achieving it. But my father sent word by fast messenger that I must return home to Namei. Something has arisen, though he wouldn't say what. I suppose I will find out when I get there."

Namei! So they were going to the same place, then. "You will be going by caravan from Halath to Namei? I too am going that way."

"Yes," Imbaso replied with a smile. "It's really the only safe way to cross the desert. The highway is a good one, almost up to the standards of the Dominion, and there are oases or watering holes at intervals along it. But the Dareg have never been completely subdued, I fear. Many of them have turned to banditry, and the highway is their hunting ground."

"I expect we'll be in each other's company for some time, then," the older man replied. "I look forward to it." The captain was on Suleiman's left, and Mfanya, was chatting with him as if they were old friends.

"Do you make this trip often, Bwana Mfanya?" Suleiman asked the trader. The man, a sober-looking fellow in his middle thirties, nodded.

"This is my third trip in the past two years, Sayyid. My wife would be much happier if my work kept me closer to home, but my father is getting too old for these voyages. And there is a big market in Palambo for the manufactured goods of the Dominion."

The older man nodded sagely. "My wife, too, wishes that I would stay at home. And as I am likely as old as your father, I think this trip will be my last." And so the talk went around the table, as the *Maria Elena* sailed on through the night. Her beam was broad and her cargo was heavy, so she didn't move all that quickly despite her acres of canvas aloft. But unlike a man on foot, or a horse-drawn carriage, she could keep moving along at her steady pace twenty-four hours a day – as long as the wind kept blowing.

The weather continued fine, and Suleiman spent most of his daylight hours walking around the decks, enjoying the sea air and the feel of the enormous ship as it lifted him up, then gently let him down on the breast of the waves. As enjoyable as the trip had been so far, though, Leila had no illusions about wanting to go to sea as a permanent lifestyle. Being out here on the sea was pleasant, and peaceful; but it was also a bit like being stuck on a very small island.

One early morning she exited Suleiman's cabin cloaked in her shadows, and climbed the mainmast to the lower of its two lookout platforms. She'd been getting a fair amount of exercise walking around, but she longed for something more athletic. She'd watched the sailors go up and down, crawling around in the rigging like a troop of monkeys; and it looked like fun.

Whoo! The view was much better from up here. But the ship's motion was much more pronounced, as well. The platform swayed from side to side with the mast it was attached to, and in just a few minutes Leila was beginning to feel a little queasy and climbed back down. Later, Suleiman ate less heartily at the breakfast table than was his usual wont.

Six days out from Jena the ship docked at Ruza, on the southernmost tip of Cilit: the Center Sea's largest island. There were dozens of them dotting the sea, and all of the bigger ones had people living on them. The population of Ruza was a mix of people from around the shores of the water that surrounded them, and it was the capital of the independent state of Cilit. In ancient times both Gaspar and Palambo had claimed the island, but three hundred years ago both empires had decided it wasn't worth fighting over.

They arrived in mid-morning and didn't depart until early afternoon of the following day, giving Leila a chance to do some exploring. Suleiman took Wapesi out of his stall inside the ship and galloped him all over the island, to the horse's utter delight. He hadn't seen the sun in the better part of a week, and was loath to return to his confinement.

When they left Ruza, the captain quietly warned his passengers that they had now entered dangerous waters. "The pirate Mgondi has been seen in this area recently," he said. "I learned in Ruza that he and his fleet of marauders captured a Palamban merchantman on her way back from Roma late last week. They set the captain and his crew adrift in a lifeboat and carried off the ship, along with two wealthy passengers, for ransom."

There was a murmur of excitement around the table. "What will we do if he comes after us?" Surimba wanted to know.

"We're too slow to outrun him, I'm afraid," Captain Flores admitted. "But we are well-armed. All of the crew have bows and cutlasses, and there are a dozen ballistae on either side of the ship. Mgondi has no ships as large as this one, and he would find boarding us a challenge. In any case, Memsahib Surimba, he is no wanton murderer. Should we be captured, you and your charge would be kept unharmed and ransomed back to your brother."

The conversation at the table that evening was all about pirates and fighting. The illusory trader's agent partially unsheathed an illusory scimitar from an illusory scabbard hung from an illusory belt on his illusory robe, and assured the Memsahib that if fighting came he was no stranger to it. She favored him with a grateful glance.

Chapter 9

The pirates did not come. But a storm did, buckets of rain lashed by gale winds coming out of the northwest. The passengers huddled in their cabins, puking their guts out into their privy stools, and for the first time on her maiden voyage Leila discovered what it truly was to be seasick. She had abandoned her illusion. While she could hold the basic appearance of Suleiman even as she slept, it was too much effort to maintain as she retched in misery, clinging desperately to her privy stool to keep from being rolled across the cabin floor to smash into the wall or the bed.

Just as Leila had determined that she had now rid her stomach of everything she had eaten today, yesterday, and probably the day before, an earsplitting "crack!" came from above followed by a crunching, rending sound. The ship, which had been tossing wildly, lurched sharply and began listing slightly to the right. What had just happened?

Her terror driving away her nausea for the moment, Leila put on her waterproof cloak and then swathed herself in shadows as she crept from her cabin and went up on deck to see what was going on. It was early afternoon, she thought, but outside it was as dim as the hour of dusk except for occasional bolts of lightning.

Black clouds filled the sky, though you could hardly see them for the driving rain that was lashing the decks. Forward of the stairs up which Leila had crept, pandemonium reigned. Lightning had struck the mainmast, it seemed, cracking it from top to bottom and setting the tightly furled sails ablaze. The fire had gone out almost immediately, but on its way down the mast had smashed the railing on the starboard side of the ship (Leila *was* beginning to pick up a few nautical terms) and fallen into the water.

The sailors had cutlasses out, hacking away at the rigging as they struggled to free the downed mast before the ship foundered. Waves were surging over the sides, threatening to sweep them away. Then with a snap the last line parted, and the broken mast with its crossbars, sails, and rigging fell quickly behind as the ship was driven on toward the Palamban shore.

The captain was on deck, also wearing an oilskin cloak, shouting to be heard above the storm. "Hard aport!" he called to the helmsman, who was fighting the large wooden wheel. The wind seemed to have come about and was now blowing from the northeast, threatening to wreck them. Should they survive, they'd find themselves on a desert coastline many miles from the nearest town or village.

Leila bolted back down the stairs and returned to Suleiman's cabin, then pulled out her tiny idol of Betsalel. "Master, I beseech you, come to my aid!" she cried, placing her left hand over her heart (where, the Shadow God had told her, a part of him resided beneath the flesh) and holding the statuette in her right. It squirmed in her hand, and she quickly bent to set it down on the bed. In seconds Betsalel grew to around five feet tall, then looked around him at the close quarters and decided not to grow any more.

"What is happening, child?" he asked, puzzled. Yeil had told her that her connection with the dark god enabled him to see out of her eyes, but perhaps his attention had been elsewhere.

"We're on a ship, almost to Palambo I think," she said anxiously. "There's a storm out there and one of the masts just broke off. Now it seems like the wind might be going to drive us onto the shore. You need to save us, but in some way that's not going to draw a lot of attention."

Betsalel climbed down off of the bed and then sat on it, his hands resting on his knees and his two "normal" eyes closed as he sent his senses out to assess their surroundings. "I see," he said softly. "Hold my hands, Leila. Give me your belief." She seized his two utterly black hands in her own. They were one of the least human things about him, as she and other dark-skinned people did not have the dark pigment in the undersides of their hands and the soles of their feet.

Even at this size, less than Leila's height, the dark god's hands were somewhat larger than hers. He was male, after all. The girl knelt before him, his hands tightly clasped in hers, and closed her own eyes. "You can do anything," she breathed, and in a moment she felt the wind begin to slacken. It had changed course, now blowing almost due east, and already the rain was ceasing as the clouds began to break up and the wind fell further – from a gale to a stiff, gusting breeze.

Betsalel rose to his feet, drawing Leila up with him, and she threw her arms around him. It was so strange, having him almost her size! "You've done it!" she cried.

"I think that no one noticed my intervention," the dark god mused.

"I suppose you had better go back, then," Leila said reluctantly. Betsalel was not Tevo, but he truly knew her – and she'd had no one with whom she could be herself in weeks.

"Have you spoken with Tevo?" she asked, "How is he?" The Shadow God smiled into her eyes – a little disconcerting, since his were glowing red in the cabin's dim light.

"I speak with Tevo daily," he assured his little high priestess. "And with many other worshipers as well. He misses you greatly, of course. As do I. Why have you not called me sooner?"

Leila dropped her eyes. "I've wanted to," she admitted, "but I didn't want to bother you without cause." Betsalel embraced her gently.

"Do not ever imagine that your call would be a bother," he assured her. "You are the first and foremost of my worshipers alive on earth. Call me whenever you like, to report your progress or just to talk. I am here for you, Leila."

"All right, I will!" she promised, returning his embrace. "Tell Tevo I love him!" Then she stepped back and the dark god shrank once more to thumb size before becoming inert once again. Leila scooped it up off the bed and brought it to her lips for a kiss before tucking it back into its pouch. Then she lay down on the bed and surrendered herself to an exhausted sleep.

Chapter 10

Two days later, near mid-morning, the *Maria Elena* limped into the harbor at Halath. She lowered two boats carrying lines that were tied off to the pier. Then her capstans warped her in until she was tied up beside it. Aside from the offloading of cargo, they would need to step a new main mast and make major repairs to her rigging before the ship could continue her journey to Iskand.

All of the passengers disembarked, and Suleiman accompanied young Imbaso to the office of a caravan agent to learn when they might be able to set off on the journey to Namei. The horse Wapesi was loaded down with the old trader's agent's baggage, and was being led by his halter. He seemed very glad to have seen the last of his dark confinement below decks – though having less imagination than the human passengers, he had not suffered as much as they had during the storm.

"It has been so many years since I was last here," Suleiman remarked as they made their way through a warren of streets leading away from the harbor, "I can scarcely recognize any landmarks." Leila had studied a map of the city, which was one of Palambo's foremost Center Sea ports. But looking at a map and navigating an actual city were two different things.

The young man smiled indulgently. "It's changed a lot just within the past ten years," he said. "I think there are even some buildings that have been put up since I was last here, taking ship for the Dominion to begin my schooling." They found the office after wandering for some time, and learned that a caravan was gathering north of the city and was scheduled to depart two days hence. They could book places on it now, if they wished; but they would need to speak with the caravan master at the mustering site in any case.

"Might as well go out there and do it in person," Imbaso said, and Suleiman nodded in agreement. "What do you say we have some lunch, first? I know a pleasant café nearby."

"An excellent idea," the old trader's agent replied. "I'm thinking about taking a room in an inn for a couple of nights until it's time for the caravan to leave," he added. "These old bones would just as soon have a bed under them, and there'll be plenty of nights spent sleeping in a tent once we're on the road."

"Not a bad idea," his young companion replied.

There were many horses in the streets of Halath, most of them the small, graceful desert breed. It appeared that the city didn't offer much in the way of public sanitation, and as it seldom rained here manure was piled in the streets everywhere. It was hotter than blazes, a dry heat, and Leila was thankful that she was able to be dressed in a short-sleeved shirt and lightweight trousers while Suleiman appeared to be clad in a woolen robe – as were most of the men that they saw around the city.

Wapesi was tied to a hitching rail in the shade of a spreading acacia tree, while Suleiman and Imbaso went into the café. Its walls were more than a foot thick, whitewashed adobe brick, and it was relatively cool inside. A couple of young black boys with enormous palm fans were employed keeping the air moving. They both ordered a richly flavored stew with chicken and vegetables in it, served over finely-chopped and cooked wheat that soaked up the sauce delightfully.

"Most delicious," Suleiman said as they were sipping from little cups of kaf after the meal. Making idle conversation, he went on "So, is your father dragging you back home to join in the family business?"

Imbaso smiled. "He didn't really say why I must return, only that all in the family are well but that the matter was urgent. I doubt it has anything to do with his 'business.'"

"Oh?" the trader's agent asked, after taking another sip of the thick, bitter drink. "Why? What's his line of work, then?"

Imbaso smiled again. "My father," he said – pausing a bit for dramatic effect – "Is the arch-priest of Betsalel at one of the dark god's main temples in Palambo." Leila was riveted. All this time Suleiman had been enjoying the young man's company, and Leila hadn't realized that she had before her the very person she needed to make friends with, if she was to infiltrate the temple and learn the nature of the djinn who had stolen her master's idol. And she didn't want to do it as an elderly trader's agent, that was for sure!

Suleiman raised an eyebrow. "Quite a shocker for the Dominion, up until recently," he remarked. Imbaso nodded.

"I thought it best not to mention that detail to anyone while I was studying at Wena," he admitted. "But the events at the Temple of the Eight in Parat last year certainly changed things. Now that it's no longer forbidden to worship Betsalel, I can come out of the closet."

"So you are a worshiper of the Shadow God as well?" Suleiman asked. Imbaso nodded, but waved a hand in a gesture that said "more or less."

"It's a tradition in my family," he said. "At least one member of the male line has been involved in Betsalel's priesthood for quite a few generations. I'm not what you'd call devout, though. All that religion stuff just seems like a bunch of mumbo jumbo once you've had a university education, I'm afraid."

Leila had the sinking feeling that she knew more than Imbaso did about his father's plans. Now that the dark god they were worshipping in Namei was real again, he probably expected his "not-devout" son to become an initiate. Finishing his kaf, Suleiman rose to his feet. "Thank you for suggesting this place, it's been most pleasant. I suppose I had better go to the shipping office to see if there are any messages for me. My employer has a list of my stops, so that he can reach me if there is any important news. Then I'll get a room, and I suppose I'll see you later today out at the mustering ground?"

Imbaso stood and clasped the older man's hand. "See you then," he said with a smile. Suleiman led Wapesi out of sight. The horse had been sampling acacia leaves but had not found them to his taste. Time to get that inn room and put the horse into a stable where there was something for him to eat.

Ducking into a narrow alleyway, the elderly Eastern trader's agent quickly transformed into a Palamban girl of around sixteen. She was in essence Leila, except that her skin was darker, her eyes were black instead of deep green, and her hair was curlier. And she was clad in a garment that was a duplicate of several Leila had seen on women in the marketplace they'd passed during their journey through town.

I hope it's not going to be a problem being a woman alone, Leila thought as she made her way in search of a hostelry with stable facilities. Time to be an orphan again, I imagine. I am Usiku, only survivor after my family's farmstead was raided by bandits. I successfully fled with the horse, and am now seeking to make my way to Namei so that I may put myself under the care of my uncle and his family. The Thabban River, which flowed into the Center Sea at Halath and helped to form its harbor, did have many farms along its banks.

Leading the horse, she made her way back to the souk they'd passed through earlier, and approached a motherly-looking woman tending a stall selling spices. "Good day to you, mother," Usiku said in flawless Kiswa.

"Good day," the woman replied, eyeing the girl curiously. Unaccompanied young women in the marketplace were not an uncommon sight, but you didn't usually see them leading what looked to be a foreign horse.

"I am new in town, and I was wondering whether you could direct me to a hostelry where it would be safe for a woman alone to stay?" the girl asked. The stallholder looked sympathetic.

"For how long?" she asked.

"Just a couple of nights," Usiku replied. "I'll be taking a caravan for Namei soon, traveling to stay with relatives."

From the woman's expression she was burning with curiosity – but she didn't ask, and Usiku didn't volunteer any more information. "Go to the Temple of Mulia," the stallholder suggested. "The sisters there operate a women's hostel."

"And do they have a place for my horse?" the girl asked. The woman nodded.

"Many women travel some distance to pray to Mulia," she said. "They can provide you with some shelter and fodder for your animal. I assume you've bought him to take you on the journey to Namei?"

"That's right," Usiku replied, revising her cover story on the fly. "I got him from a trader's agent who had been going to take him to Namei. Then apparently he had to leave in a hurry, and no longer needed the horse. The animal was quite cheap – I hope he's all right."

The woman eyed her. Her father had been a horse trader, and while the oversized horses of the Gaspari Dominion were generally considered to be inferior to the desert breed, this one looked like a young and healthy specimen. "I'm sure he'll be fine for you, assuming you know how to ride."

Usiku winced. "I've been on a horse a couple of times before, but I'm hoping I'll get the hang of it during the journey to Namei."

"You might be better off getting a ride on one of the wagons," the stallholder suggested.

"We'll see, I suppose," the girl said cheerfully. "At least he can carry my baggage. Which direction is the Temple of Mulia?"

"Follow this main street down four blocks, turn right, then three more blocks and a left," the woman gestured. "The temple is on your left, a big building covered in yellow tile with a mosaic of Mulia as the Mother on the façade out front. You can't miss it."

"Thank you kindly," Usiku called, and set out on her way. At the temple's women's hostel, she saw to Wapesi's comfort and arranged for a room for herself – a small cell with a cot in it, actually, similar to the acolytes' rooms she'd seen at the ruined temple of Betsalel in the Blackwald. Then she went out again.

Resuming the appearance of Suleiman in yet another unoccupied alley, Leila headed for the harbor and found something that was close to being the local equivalent of the Municipal Shipping Office in Jena. The place was considerably less impressive, but it did hold at least one clerk who seemed to know what he was doing. Speaking in Kiswa, the old trader's agent told him "I am most anxious to go to Iskand as quickly as possible. Are there any ships leaving today?"

The harbormaster's clerk studied his ledger. Along with full fluency in spoken Kiswa, Leila had been granted the ability to read the Palamban script. It looked like there was one possible vessel, if it hadn't left yet. "I'm sorry, sir, but there is only the coaster *Pepo* sailing today. They are leaving in a little more than an hour, and it is a very small vessel. I doubt they will be able to accommodate a passenger."

"I'll sleep on the deck if I have to!" Suleiman declared. "I must get to Iskand at once! Where is she moored?" The clerk shrugged. The would-be passenger did not look like the sort of fellow who was going to enjoy sleeping rough, but it was up to him. He stepped around from behind his desk and walked the older man to the door, then pointed off to the left.

"You see the slips down beyond the main harbor here? The *Pepo* is moored down along in there. It's an old ship, a dhow, painted faded blue. You'll need to talk to Adebi, he's the first mate. Good luck!"

"Thank you!" Suleiman cried, and scurried off in that direction.

As soon as he'd moved beyond easy sight of the shipping office, the old man ducked into an alleyway and vanished from sight. Clad in shadows, Leila made her way back up through the streets of Halath. As she went, she collected a new wardrobe. She wanted to be dressed more appropriately for the desert, in truth as well as in illusion.

Leila made her way to her tiny room in the women's hostel before releasing her shadows. She'd accumulated two or three outfits and some fresh underwear, rather than go to the trouble of laundering what she had with her. There'd been no opportunity for any washing, the last week of the voyage on the *Maria Elena*. She had some paper, pen, and ink with her; and after changing into some of her new clothes she sat at the tiny table in her room, and began to write.

Chapter 11

Imbaso had walked from the café where he and Suleiman had lunched to the gathering ground where the caravan led by Jammal Hassan was being assembled. He'd had the use of a horse at the stables kept by his university in Wena, but hadn't brought a mount of his own on the long journey to the Dominion. He did have his own horse back home in Namei, of course, a pretty little dappled grey Hisan mare that had been a gift to him from his father on his sixteenth birthday.

Father had had her bred to a local stallion of note a couple of times while he'd been gone, and had written that the first colt showed promise. He would only be two now, though – old enough to begin training but years away from fulfilling that promise. Horse racing was a popular sport in the area around Namei. Imbaso hoped he'd be able to borrow or rent a horse from the caravan, rather than having to buy one. He detested riding on camels.

The gathering ground was an immense fenced area beyond the outskirts of Halath, alongside the well-paved main highway running south toward Namei. With only two days before the caravan was to depart, the scene was chaotic. Horses, camels, and oxen ate and drank, bellowed and shat everywhere. Wagons were being loaded, tents folded and stored, casks of water and foodstuffs being brought in. Quite a few tents, probably belonging to the caravan company, were still pitched and would remain so until it was time to leave.

The area was reached by a pair of large gates, which stood open now in early afternoon. A caravan guard stood duty on either side of the opening. Imbaso greeted the one on the right, who appeared to be a Dareg. The Palambans might have beaten the desert tribes at their own game, but they were still the masters of the desert. The majority of the caravan operators in this part of the world were of Dareg descent.

"Salaam," Imbaso said, bowing slightly. "I am here to sign up with the caravan. To whom should I speak?" The man eyed him impassively. There was still a little racial tension between Daregs and the Amhari people of Palambo. "Are you a paying customer, or are you hoping to enroll as a guard?" he asked. Imbaso had exchanged the Dominion clothing he'd been wearing aboard ship for desert garb – with a sigh of regret – but he did find it somewhat flattering the Dareg would think it possible he was a guard.

Flashing a white-toothed smile, the young man replied "Paying customer, though I know how to use a blade if the occasion arises." Among the Palamban upper classes, weapons training for males was practically compulsory. And Imbaso had spent much time during his years of study in Wena sparring with Gaspari-style sabers.

"Do you see the large white tent over there?" the guard asked, pointing. Imbaso nodded. "Go there, and speak with Jammal Hassan. It is he who decides what additional people we take on this caravan." Thanking the man, Imbaso headed for the tent – far larger than any other in the enclosure, and centrally located. As he went he was looking around. He had traveled with a similar caravan as he was on his way to the Dominion three years before, and the sights were familiar enough. But he was looking for the tall chestnut gelding, the horse belonging to Suleiman Abaza.

Surprisingly he had found that the liked the old fellow (older than his father by several years) quite a lot, and he was looking forward to continuing their curious friendship during the trip to Namei. Once they arrived there, of course, the trader's agent would be on his way along the course of the Pana heading east while he would be learning what earthshaking event had occasioned him missing out on his senior year at the university in Wena.

There were many horses about, most of them tied up and eating from feedbags though a few were carrying riders on errands. But all were of the smaller, lighter Hisan breed, ideally suited to the desert. That Wapesi of Suleiman's might have a desert name, but he was clearly of Dominion stock. The trader's agent had probably purchased him in Miradil before setting off on his journey.

Hoping his friend hadn't encountered any difficulties obtaining lodging, Imbaso found himself approaching the caravan master's tent and stepped inside. The heavy white fabric reflected much of the sun's heat, and it was marginally cooler inside. Good old blazing-hot Palambo, he thought. Winters in the Dominion had been hard to get used to, but he was now wishing for the cool breezes of the southern slopes of the Antels that were so delightful in late spring.

There were several people in the tent, including a young man Imbaso took to be a clerk. The older man who sat at a large table in the center of the space, clearly a Dareg, he guessed was the caravan master – Jammal Hassan. The Daregs could be fierce-looking, with those prominent hooked noses and jet-black eyes set in faces far lighter in color than those of the Amhari; but Hassan looked friendly enough.

"What can I do for you, Bwana?" he asked, using the Kiswa term of address since Imbaso was obviously an Amhari. The younger man grinned at him.

"Jammal Hassan?" he asked, and received an answering smile and a nod. "I'm here to sign on to the caravan as a paying customer," he said, and the caravan master's smile broadened.

"You wish to go to Namei?" he asked.

"That's right, Sayyid," he replied. The Dareg seemed to appreciate the courtesy. "Will you be bringing your own food, or do you want us to provide it?" Hassan asked. Juggling the needs of an open-ended number of people, animals, and cargo wagons in a caravan was a skill that took years to perfect.

"I'd prefer to have the caravan provide my food," Imbaso said. He'd been through the same routine on his trip here from Namei. "I'm also hoping you can lend me or rent me a horse, as I'd prefer not to ride a camel." The caravan master's dark eyes glinted.

"We can certainly lend you a horse, provided you are willing to be part of the armed response if we are attacked by bandits. You seem to be a capable young man…" It was not quite a statement.

Imbaso flashed his dazzling smile again. He pulled the gleaming scimitar at his side (a weapon that had been at the bottom of his trunk for most of the past three years) a little way out of the scabbard, by way of indicating that he was ready and able to come to the caravan's defense.

Hassan returned the smile, and nodded slightly. "Anyone else in your party?" he asked. Imbaso hesitated.

"A friend of mine, an elderly trader's agent from Miradil, is also traveling with this caravan to Namei. Suleiman Abaza. Has he arrived yet?" The caravan master gestured to his clerk, who produced a ledger book and scanned it. He'd apparently been following their conversation, for after around a minute he reported.

"No Abaza, no trader's agents, as yet."

"Perhaps he's been delayed," Imbaso said. "In any case, he'll be paying his own way. But you might want to hold a place with him in mind. He's bringing his own horse."

"No matter to me," Hassan said. "If he arrives, we will sign him up. The fee for you to travel with us, eating our food and riding our horse, is ten asand, or the same in Gaspari florins if you have them."

Imbaso handed over the coin, in florins. The letter calling him home had come bundled with a bank note enabling him to draw funds from the Bank of Parat, Wena branch. Father had kept him on a short leash while he'd been studying abroad, and he'd rarely had any money beyond his immediate needs. It had kept him soberer – and freer of venereal infections – than many of his fellow students.

Stepping out of the tent into the glaring sunshine, Imbaso pulled the edge of his shema (part of his desert dress, basically a scarf held in place on his head by a sort of headband – and infinitely adjustable) down a little further to shade his eyes. As he made his way toward the gates, he was once again scanning for any signs of Suleiman.

There! A flash of ruddy color as a tall chestnut horse came cantering toward the tent he had just left. The color was very common among Gaspari horses, much less so in the desert; and no Hisan had ever stood so tall. But who was that diminutive figure on the horse's back?

He stood transfixed as the horse flew toward him. It certainly appeared to be Wapesi! As horse and rider came closer, Imbaso began running toward them, hand held up. The rider appeared to be a young girl, a member of his own Amhari race. She was small and clad in a white cotton tunic split at the sides, baggy white cotton trousers gathered at the bottom, and black riding boots. She wore a white shema on her head.

That *had* to be Wapesi! So where was Suleiman? "You there, stop!" Imbaso commanded in Kiswa. The horse and his rider pulled up as if they were one flesh. The Amhari had to take second place to the Daregs as horsemen, but this girl looked as if she'd been born in the saddle. She flashed him a white smile, black eyes sparkling.

"Yes, Bwana?" she asked.

Imbaso stepped forward and grasped the horse by his headstall. He certainly *looked* like Suleiman's horse. "Wapesi?" he asked, looking into the horse's eyes. The gelding nickered in recognition and nudged him affectionately on the shoulder. The young man had been down in the hold with Suleiman on more than one occasion, visiting with the animal. He was one of the sweetest-natured of his breed Imbaso had ever met.

The young man glared up at the girl in the saddle. "This is Suleiman Abaza's horse!" he said accusingly. "How did you come by him?" The girl's eyes widened slightly, then a huge grin came over her face.

"You must be Imbaso!" she crowed, throwing him into confusion.

In seconds the rider had leapt down off of the horse's back and was digging in an inner pocket of her tunic for a folded piece of paper. "I bought Wapesi from Suleiman not an hour ago!" she declared. "Here, you must read this!" She thrust the paper into Imbaso's hands.

"My dear Imbaso," it read. "With this letter I introduce you to Usiku, who tells me that she is traveling to Namei to live with her uncle and his family. I regret to inform you that when I went to pick up my messages I learned that my employer, whom I have worked with for nearly thirty years, has been stricken ill. His son, who will take over the business, is desperate that I return to Miradil and assist him. So, my leisurely trip along the Pana has been cancelled, and I am leaving immediately on the coaster *Pepo* for Iskand. From there I will take a fast ship for Miradil. But the *Pepo* has no room for horses, so I have reluctantly sold Wapesi to Usiku. I am hoping that you might take her under your wing, so to speak, as she is very young and all alone now until she reaches the shelter of her relatives' home in Namei. I have greatly enjoyed our friendship, and regret that it has been cut so short. May the Eight smile upon you." It was signed, in a bold and masculine hand, "Suleiman Abaza."

What an astonishing turn of events! Though not so surprising, Imbaso realized, if you considered that Suleiman was a grandfather twice over and that his employer was still older. More surprising, really, that the old trader had not retired and handed the business completely over to his son long since. But Imbaso had some experience with the older generation, and he knew that they could find it hard to let things go.

Imbaso looked down at the girl, Usiku. "I apologize for my rudeness," he said. "I feared that my friend had been set upon by thieves, but I realize now how foolish that was." She was such a little thing, scarcely more than five feet high, and looked to be barely past sixteen. Hardly a likely horse thief! Usiku was grinning up at him now, radiating feelings that he found hard to track. Pleasure at his discomfiture? Attraction? As he looked down into that little face, he realized that she was lovely. Heart-stoppingly lovely.

Chapter 12

Usiku was not charged any less for her caravan fare, though she was bringing her own horse. The horse's fodder, it seemed, was costly. Leila supposed that the stuff was bulky to haul along, and likely there would be no grazing available as they crossed the desert. But she was beginning to wish she'd brought more money with her.

During her second day in Halath, she went out into the city cloaked in shadows to see what opportunities it might offer to enrich her coffers. Compared with a city of comparable size in the Dominion Halath was primitive and shabby-seeming. In a climate where it seldom rained, most of the goods available were sold at outdoor venues. There were four major market squares with permanent stands, scattered around the city; and roaming vendors might throw down a blanket on which to display their wares wherever space permitted.

This meant that there were no cash boxes, no safes. The merchants kept the coin on their persons, and Leila wasn't prepared to commit strong-arm robbery or risk harming anyone in the process of stealing their cash. She turned to bank robbery instead.

There was a branch of the Bank of Palambo on Halath's foremost commercial street – one of the few in town broad enough to allow two wagons to pass side by side. Unlike so many aspects of modern life that had originated in the realms of the Hando, banking was a Gaspari invention. Worldwide traders had found it so useful you could now find banking institutions nearly everywhere.

Wrapped in her shadows, Leila stood inside the bank observing as a very respectable-looking Palamban, clad in rich robes, came inside and presented a bank note to one of the young men who acted as clerks. After studying the note, the clerk unlocked a strong box below the counter and counted out stacks of coins, before stamping and sealing the note and tucking it away as he locked the box once more.

She waited until there was a lull in the bank's business, then ducked out the door and came back in again immediately, appearing to be a middle-aged Palamban dressed in finery similar to what the previous customer had worn. She stepped to the counter and presented an identical bank note, requesting two hundred Palamban asand – a gold coin similar in weight and value to Gaspari florins.

The paper was real, its appearance illusory – and requiring Leila to maintain physical contact with it. This was the most complicated thing she had yet attempted with her new power, keeping a finger on the "bank note" while the "Palamban merchant" stood at the counter with his hands at his sides and the clerk took the note for inspection. When he held it up to check the watermark on the back she had to scramble to avoid having his fingers brush hers. For a split second the illusion vanished, but the clerk didn't appear to have noticed.

He brought out the coins and handed them over to the merchant, swiping the paper off the counter and failing to notice its change of appearance as he tossed it into the strong box and locked it again. "Thank you, young man," the Palamban merchant said quietly in his deep voice and took his leave. Outside the door, as soon as no one was looking, he vanished into shadows.

Gleefully pleased with herself, but sparing a few seconds to pity the young clerk when the "bank note" he'd paid out on was discovered to be a blank sheet of paper, Leila returned to her cell at the women's hostel. Imbaso had insisted on calling for her here later today, to treat her to supper at a restaurant he liked. Usiku admitted that she had never been in Halath before, though she had lived most of her life within a day's ride of the city.

Wow, she thought, my days of needing to primp for an outing are over. I can make myself look exactly the way I want to with just a thought. That ought to save some money on face paints, at least! The young man called for her in late afternoon, after the day's heat had begun to ebb. Rather than have him deal with the matron, Usiku awaited him in the hostel's common room and they went out into the city streets together.

A couple of years before Leila had played Rosa Estares as a young woman three years older than herself, but innocent of the world and its ways. Usiku, she thought, should be a little bit younger. She wanted to reinforce the notion implanted by Suleiman's letter that Imbaso should look at her as a younger sister, somebody to take care of, rather than a prospect for romance. Though it was clear he was attracted to her, so far he'd been completely gentlemanly.

"So, Usiku, have you had much chance to explore the city as yet?" Imbaso asked as he escorted her along.

"Just some of the market squares, is all," she replied. "And the harbor, of course. I had just gotten into town and was walking along the waterfront trying to figure out what to do next when I came upon Sayyid Abaza. He had just gotten the ship's mate to agree to carry him to Iskand, and was wondering what to do with Wapesi, and there I was! I think it was fate."

Imbaso smiled. If he knew Suleiman Abaza, and he thought he did, he would have given the girl an amazing bargain on the horse. "Did you have to pay much?" he asked, taking her arm and leading her around a corner onto one of Halath's broader streets.

She smiled up at him. "He practically gave him to me for free!" she exclaimed. "A good thing, too, after old Jammal got through with me. Who knew it would be so expensive to take a caravan across the desert?"

"If your funds are tight, I can lend you some until we get to Namei," Imbaso assured her gallantly. Usiku gave him a sisterly smile.

"Thank you, Imbaso, you are most kind." They took a meandering path through the city, Usiku's young guide pointing out buildings of architectural interest, the street of dyers where the space between the buildings above their heads was hung with myriad swaths of cloth in a hundred different colors, and other Halath high points. Being on the flat coastal plain and quite a few miles from the low Rabiyat mountain range to the south, the city didn't offer the interesting views to be found in cities along the Center Sea's rocky northern coast.

And after all that wandering, Leila was not surprised to see, they fetched up at the exact same café where Imbaso had lunched with Suleiman yesterday. "Oh, this is delightful!" Usiku said, admiring the tree-shaded patio area and the cool interior. "Is the food good?"

"Not the best I've had, but not bad," Imbaso admitted. "I think my tastes have been warped by spending the past three years living abroad."

That, of course, launched a discussion of Imbaso's time spent in the Gaspari Dominion. Wide-eyed, Usiku hung on his every word and had a hundred questions about the strange people and sights of that far-off northern land. They dined on marinated lamb chunks, skewered and grilled over charcoal, and served with a grain pilaf and seasonal vegetables that had been sautéed in olive oil. As they drank kaf after the meal and waited for their dessert (little bite-size pastries with honey and nuts), Imbaso realized they'd been talking about him and his travels the entire evening.

"So tell me about yourself, Usiku," he asked belatedly. In fact he was burning with curiosity to learn where this pretty little creature had sprung from.

"There's not much to tell," she said shyly, taking another sip of the bitter kaf and wishing for some cream and sugar. "I've never been anywhere or done much of anything."

"Are you from these parts originally?" he asked. After the Palamban conquest had added the desert region to the kingdom many Amhari people had emigrated here from other areas. But the Daregs were still the predominant ethnic group outside of the cities.

"I was born in Zambei," Usiku said, "but my family moved here when I was around three. I don't remember anyplace except the area around the shores of the Thabban, about fifty miles north of here."

"Your family are farmers, then?" Imbaso asked, just as the little tray of pastries arrived. "Try these, they are really good," he assured his companion, offering her the tray so she could select one. Usiku grinned and took two, delicately holding a sticky little square between thumb and forefinger and popping it into her mouth. Then she licked the digits.

"Mmm, that *is* good," she said, and downed the other one before washing away the cloying sweetness with some of the bitter kaf.

After a moment she realized that Imbaso was still waiting for an answer to his question, and her face clouded over. "My family *were* farmers," Usiku said quietly. "I'd rather not talk about it, if you don't mind..." By Betsalel, the girl looked like she might be getting ready to cry! And she'd been so gay and cheerful the rest of the evening. Imbaso guessed that the story of her family, and the mystery of why she, a young girl, was traveling on her own to stay with relatives in Namei, would have to wait until they'd known each other longer. Maybe after they'd become closer friends, she would open up to him.

Imbaso escorted Usiku back to the women's hostel before it got dark, and she left him with thanks and a sweet kiss on the cheek that sent a little thrill through him. All the way back to his inn, he was in turmoil. She was so beautiful, so desirable! And such a child, he felt ashamed to be having those thoughts about her.

She had admitted to being sixteen – almost. More than five years his junior, which was a significant gap at their age. In another five years, it would be nothing. Hell, if he were a member of the royal family, he'd be bedding sixteen-year-olds when he was in his sixties – assuming he could still get it up. But Suleiman had asked him to watch over Usiku, and he had taken on the task as a sacred pledge. It would be wrong to violate that duty by trying to lure her into his bed.

Meanwhile in her cell at the women's hostel, Leila was busy finishing the job of sewing gold coins into hems, hidden pockets, and various other hiding places in her pack and garments. She'd decided to leave some of her less-suitable clothing behind to save weight. As she worked, she sighed. She missed Tevo so, and longed for his touch. But creeping into her thoughts when she considered making love was the dark, handsome face of Imbaso.

She liked him a lot, and he was a very attractive young man. Plus, she hadn't had any loving in weeks and it was starting to affect her judgment. But Imbaso was the son of the arch-priest of Betsalel in Namei, and that meant that his family, if not he himself, were up to their necks in the evil practices that had spawned the dark djinn. Was it possible that the father could be steeped in evil while the adult son remained innocent as a babe? It didn't seem likely, but time would tell.

Chapter 13

Almost before dawn light began shining over Halath, bathing its whitewashed buildings in a rosy glow, Usiku had gathered her possessions and retrieved her horse. Few people were stirring yet, and she was able to canter along the stone-paved streets until she came to the outskirts. Then she gave Wapesi his head, and he joyfully burst into a gallop that had her approaching the caravan gathering ground within another minute or two.

All tents in the fenced area had already been taken down and stowed, final items of freight added to wagons, horses and camels watered in preparation for a long, hot walk. Further to the east were some miserable stretches of desert where one did not even attempt to travel in the daytime; but the climate in this area of Palambo was mild enough to permit it even now as summer approached.

Imbaso had arisen early as well and jogged here from his lodgings in town while it was still dark. He knew Hassan intended to get as much traveling in as possible during the daylight hours, shortening the trip. The fewer days spent on the road, the less would come out of his pocket for food and fodder.

He was talking with the caravan's hostler, picking out a mount for this day's journey, when they both looked up at the sound of galloping hooves to see Usiku racing in atop her oversized chestnut mount. She flashed them both a white-toothed grin as she pulled up near the remount herd and hopped nimbly to the ground.

Imbaso caught himself staring at her in open-mouthed admiration. She had owned Wapesi less than two days, yet already it seemed as though horse and rider were one. And what a magnificent mount the gelding was proving to be – he appeared to be not the least bit winded after galloping here from the heart of Halath. Imbaso wondered how he would do in a race – those tall Gaspari horses might not win in a sprint, but they had a stride far longer than that of the Hisan breed.

Usiku hurried up to Imbaso, eyes sparkling with excitement, and threw her arms around him in a sisterly hug. "Are you picking out your horse, Imbaso?" she asked. He smiled down at her, nearly a foot shorter than he was. "Apparently, since I'm just using horses provided by the caravan, I have to take what's available on any given day. Do any of these look good to you?" He gestured around at the tethered mounts, nibbling from a small pile of hay that had been strewn on the ground.

Imbaso doubted Usiku was a better judge of horseflesh than he was. While his family were city people and only dabbled in horse breeding for fun and profit, a knowledge of the equine species' finer points had been drummed into him from a young age.

Usiku wandered among the dozen horses that were as yet unsaddled, inspecting them. Leila was certainly no expert, but she had picked up many pointers while traveling with the Nima. And years of owning Nimble had taught her a lot about what qualities to look for. He was the finest beast she had ever known, made finer now by the god's gift of tirelessness.

The caravan's horse herd were all of the desert Hisan breed, between fourteen and fifteen hands high with relatively short, sturdy legs, compact torsos, and finely shaped heads. They ranged in color from nearly white to a deep glossy brown that looked nearly black. Leila suspected that any of them could outrun Wapesi in a short race, but none of them would be able to match his endurance in a longer one – especially with his new abilities!

After some time, while both Imbaso and the caravan's hostler watched her with bemusement, Usiku pointed out a dappled gray mare. She looked to be no more than six, close in age to Wapesi. "This one," she said. "What's her name?" The hostler took a closer look. Though these animals were his daily charge, many of them looked similar to one another.

"Ah," he said with a grin that exposed teeth turned brown from chewing keto. "That's Lateefa. Good choice! A very nice horse, but she'll go fast when you need her to." The mare was secured by a rope tied to her headstall, on the other end of which was a stake pounded into the hard desert soil. Usiku untied the rope from the stake, and walked Lateefa over to where Imbaso stood, smiling.

"Here you go," she said, as if selecting horses for other people were her daily work. "If she does well for you, maybe you can keep her for the duration of our trip. I don't think the others here are as good."

"Your family bred horses on their farm?" Imbaso asked, curious. The girl seemed awfully sure of her judgment for someone who'd just come in from the country.

Usiku smiled, remembering happier times; but then her face darkened as those memories were overtaken by more recent ones and she said only, "Yes. Once." Imbaso got Lateefa tacked up with saddle and reins supplied by the caravan. As was the case with the Nima, the Dareg people trained their horses so well that bits were not needed. The rope was removed from her headstall, and he was ready to ride. The caravan, however, was not yet ready to leave.

"Come ride with me, Imbaso!" Usiku urged. "I know it's foolish since we'll be seeing it all as soon as the caravan leaves, but I'm eager to explore the road ahead!" The air was cool and pleasant, and it seemed like a fine idea to go for a little ride before the caravan got underway. He was startled at the resemblance between Lateefa and his own Kizuri, back home. It was if Usiku has somehow known, but he had not described the mare in any detail during their conversation last night.

The two of them went at a gentle canter three miles down the road. The terrain sloped gently up toward the far-off Rabiyats, but the grade was so slight that it was scarcely noticeable. "Usiku, I think we should turn back," Imbaso finally said. The horses (and their riders' backsides, in contact with the saddles) had many miles yet to go today. Not much point in wearing them out prematurely!

"All right," Usiku said with a flash of white teeth, turning her horse. "Come on, I'll race you!" She kicked Wapesi's flanks with her boot-clad heels, throwing her weight forward, and he burst from a standstill into a full-blown gallop.

"Wait! This is crazy!" Imbaso protested as the tall chestnut gelding surged away from him. They'd been riding, not on the stone-paved road, but on the hard-packed dirt to the east of it. This provided a better surface for a running horse, and Wapesi was already a hundred feet away when Imbaso realized Usiku didn't plan to stop and urged Lateefa after him.

She needed no urging. Catching up with a horse in front of you was a natural instinct for the breed, and the little mare's legs were soon a blur as she hastened to draw even with her ruddy companion. She really had a turn of speed, Imbaso realized, and she was game enough; but the long-legged gelding's head start was not going to be easy to overcome.

Lateefa gave it everything she had, and she briefly overtook the larger horse before they had gone a mile. But then she began to flag, and by the time Wapesi and Usiku had returned to the caravan Imbaso and his mount were nearly a quarter of a mile behind.

He dismounted and began walking the mare to cool her down, as Usiku grinned up at him mischievously. Then, as if realizing something, she too began walking her horse – though the chestnut wasn't even breathing hard. "I'm sorry," she said false-contritely, her triumph plain. "It wasn't really a fair contest, and I got a big head start. It seems like these Gaspari horses are good for something after all, though – eh?"

"I hope you and he are still able to walk by this afternoon," Imbaso reprimanded her. "That was foolishness, at the start of a long journey." Usiku hung her head.

"You're right," she said, this time with genuine regret. "I won't do it again." Then she blew it by adding "...Father."

Imbaso fumed. He felt like taking the girl over his knee, but then followed that thought to its conclusion and felt a surge of sexual desire that mortified him. He said nothing. By the time both horses were cooled down, it was time to mount up again. The caravan was under way.

Chapter 14

As Leila and Nimble had found in the short time they'd spent traveling with the caravan in Oester the year before, the pace was frustratingly slow. They needed to stay all together, not letting the slower members of the caravan fall behind. And that meant that no one could move faster than the slowest oxen pulling the heaviest wagon. She and Imbaso soon became accustomed to the plodding pace.

This was the first time Leila had ever seen camels close up. And once again she found herself in a position of being fascinated by a new thing and unable to reveal her interest, because the person she was supposed to be would have regarded it as commonplace. Usiku had lived thirteen of her sixteen years on a farm, in the green strip along the banks of the Thabban river. She would certainly have come into contact with camels many times before.

They were enormous, so ungainly-looking with their curious humps, knobby knees, and odd, flat feet. Yet their long eyelashes over the huge, liquid brown eyes gave them a sweet look – at odds with their frequently cranky dispositions.

They traveled most of that first day with only a brief stop in early afternoon, to allow all of the animals to drink from the caravan's casks of water. The people nibbled on trail food and drank from water skins as they rode. Then as the day's heat was approaching its greatest, they came to the first oasis. The royal Palamban government, following the example of the Gaspari Dominion, had decreed that good roads should be built linking the kingdom's principle cities. These facilitated trade and also helped the royal guard, which maintained civil order when they were not fighting wars, rein in bandits.

The guard ran patrols along this road as well as others in the kingdom, anywhere that offered remote stretches where bandits might prey on travelers. But the road was long and the patrols came infrequently enough that it was only by joining a guarded caravan that you could assure yourself of a safe passage.

Usiku assisted some of the women of the caravan, including Hassan's wife Zahra, in erecting a large communal tent on a broad, level area away from the watering hole. It was in frequent use by caravans along this route, and kept clear of the scrubby brush that sprouted elsewhere in the dry expanse.

After unsaddling Wapesi and rubbing him down, Usiku saw to it that he was fed and watered. The road here, some forty miles south of Halath, was still relatively close to the Thabban and the watering hole was a long and narrow pond ringed by date palms. As the horse drank, the girl gazed longingly at the cool water. She just wanted to strip off all her clothes and wade in, but settled for splashing some water on her head and arms. Ugh! The heat today was worse than anything Leila had ever experienced before. But she'd better get used to it. Likely it would be much worse after they crossed the Rabiyats, and humidity was added to the heat.

Usiku napped on her bedroll in the women's tent once Wapesi had been seen to, sleeping until she was awakened for supper. The food supplied by the caravan was simple, reminiscent of meals Leila had cooked herself many times while traveling in the wilderness. Many of their supplies were dried. But a small herd of goats had been brought along, and one was slaughtered every couple of days to provide fresh meat. Usiku ate whatever was available, and was thankful for it. Leila was thankful, too, that her current disguise was very much like herself. It would have been awkward to have an apparent large man eating no more than you'd expect for a small teenage girl.

After the meal had been consumed there were a couple of hours just to enjoy the cool darkness – sitting around the remnants of the cookfires and talking, singing, and telling tales. Usiku began to make friends with some of her fellow travelers besides Imbaso, but it was the young man who was her main target of interest. She intended that by journey's end they would be the best of friends, as he would provide her entrée into the church of Betsalel in Namei.

Leila found herself regretting that she had not asked the dark god to supply her with the Dareg language as well. Kiswa had become a *lingua franca* throughout the continent south of the

Center Sea, and there were few people within the kingdom who could not speak or understand it. But the Daregs had preserved their own language along with their culture after being absorbed into the kingdom of Palambo, and among themselves it was the harsh, guttural Dareg tongue that they spoke.

What secrets were being revealed? Leila could only assume that whatever was being said was of no consequence to her. She didn't know these people and they didn't know her – and when the caravan reached Namei, they would never see each other again.

And so the days went by, as the caravan crawled slowly on its way south. Leila would have liked to call Betsalel, if only to spend some time with someone she wasn't trying to deceive; but there was absolutely no privacy day or night. As the road veered further to the west many of the oases were nothing but a camping ground and a well. There was groundwater aplenty under the desert, so there was no problem getting it if you had the ability to dig deep enough and draw it to the surface.

After nine days the road began to climb into the foothills of the Rabiyats, more vegetation beginning to appear around them and the daytime temperatures less hellish though still hot. In the desert they had seen occasional herds of antelope, and the caravan guards had been on the alert against incursions by jackals and hyenas. Once Usiku had seen a caracal, supposedly also descended from the ancestors of Nima pards like Kathal. They were roughly the same size and color, but the caracal had long tufts of hair on its enormous ears, and a shorter tail.

Now larger predators were afoot, including leopards, and the guards tightened their vigilance. The caravan's dwindling herd of livestock was penned in the center of the camping ground at each stop, surrounded by armed guards and the travelers' tents.

Imbaso had come this way thrice before in his life, and was able to tell Usiku what to expect at the next stop as they set off each morning. She encouraged him to talk freely about his life and family, his studies in the Dominion, and whatever he could tell her about Betsalel worship in Namei. As to her own life, she remained reticent; but gradually details came out.

Prior to her arrival in Halath, Usiku said, she had not left her family's farm except to go to neighboring farms for local social events. In addition to horses they had raised dates and numerous food crops. Her father and elder brother had hauled these to market a few times a year with the family's wagon, or occasionally sold the harvest directly to river traders.

They had had small shrines to Mulia and Andros, the two deities of most import to people's ordinary lives, in their home. But Usiku could not recall having ever been inside a temple until she had come to the temple of Mulia in Halath. Hence, her curiosity about the worship of Betsalel. But what had become of her family? What had sent her fleeing to Halath? And how had she gotten there, if she had needed to buy a horse when she arrived? On these subjects, Usiku remained silent. The mystery only deepened her allure, and Imbaso was coming to believe he was falling in love with her.

Chapter 15

The road was winding ever higher, and the morning air was positively chilly. Usiku was in high spirits. "Will we reach the pass today?" she asked Imbaso as he rode beside her.

"I think so," he said with a smile. He was really beginning to look forward to getting home, after not having seen any of his loved ones in more than three years.

"The pass through the Rabiyats is one of the most dangerous places on the route, though," he warned her before her anticipation could get too joyful.

"Oh?" she asked, looking at him with those huge black eyes.

"It's a natural ambush point," he explained. "Sometimes bandits will get up on the cliffs on either side of the road and roll rocks down on travelers. Then while they're thrown into confusion, mounted forces can come on them from in front and behind. But don't worry, I'm sure our guards are old hands at getting through safely. They'll be checking those cliffs, and they're well-armed. And I'm not too bad with a scimitar, myself," he said with a self-deprecating grin to show he didn't mean to boast.

"I know how to use weapons too, you know," Usiku said with a hint of defensiveness. The image of this tiny girl swinging a sword was so ludicrous it made Imbaso smile.

"Bows?" he asked, guessing that life on a farm might give one occasion to become good at shooting marauding wildlife.

She nodded with a grim smile. "Yes, bows. I don't have one with me, though I suppose the caravan could lend me one… But daggers, too."

Imbaso reined Lateefa up and turned in the saddle to gaze at her in surprise. "Daggers? Really?" For answer she reached casually into the sleeve of her tunic and in another second an unusual-looking knife stood quivering, buried point-first to the depth of around an inch in the wooden cantle of his Dareg saddle. What the?

Imbaso grasped the slender knife by its handle and pulled it out of the saddle with some effort. They continued sitting their horses as the caravan crawled past beside them. After examining the dagger for a few moments he handed it carefully back to its owner. "Remind me not to anger or surprise you!" he said, eyebrows raised. "Where on earth did you learn how to do that?" A less-likely skill for a farm girl he could hardly imagine.

Usiku flashed him a white-toothed grin, but there was something a little hard about her eyes as if using the knife had triggered bad memories. "It was all boys around our place, except for me and my mother. My brother and some of his friends got interested in knife throwing, and I was kind of a tomboy so I was determined to become better at it than them. I used to practice every chance I got, and eventually I was. Not that it did all that much good…" Her face fell, and she lapsed into silence. What dark secrets was this lovely girl hiding, Imbaso wondered for the hundredth time?

The sun was well down toward the western horizon by the time the caravan's forward riders reached the pass. Using spyglasses and scouts, they made sure there were no lurkers on either side of the road, or a party waiting down the hill on the far side. When they'd determined it was safe Jammal hurried them along, anxious to get the entire caravan through the pass and to the stopping point on the far side before dark.

They made it safe and sound, though setting up camp was trickier this high in the mountains. There were no real level spots big enough for the entire caravan to encamp, as there had been on the nearly level plains to the north. And there was much more vegetation on this side of the pass, tall broadleaf trees that were unfamiliar to Usiku. The air was warmer and more humid than it had been just a few miles back, and heavy clouds filled the sky.

"Looks like we might get some rain tonight," Imbaso told Usiku with a grin as they dismounted. This campground's water was supplied by a small spring-fed stream, running south out of the mountains. They watered the animals from their casks, and would refill those casks at the stream in the morning. From here on to Namei the going would be easier, with no worries about water or food supplies and mostly downhill.

The girl grinned back at him. "Oh, I love when it rains!" she said. There'd been water aplenty from the nearby river on their farm, but the rain that produced it had mostly fallen hundreds of miles away in the mountains.

Imbaso shook his head. "You will most likely find that the novelty has worn off, by the time we get to Namei. This is the season of the monsoon."

"If you say so," she said with a smile, and they joined the rest of the caravan as one and all rushed to set up camp. This had been their longest day of travel on the trip so far, and people were scrambling to get settled. The wood they'd carried with them for cookfires was nearly used up. Now they were surrounded by wood – but all of it was wet, and soon to be getting wetter.

The women's communal tent had barely been erected, on a cleared spot not far from the stream, when there was enormous crack of thunder and the heavens opened. Shrieking, Usiku and the other occupants of the tent rushed inside with their belongings. The tent had stood them well on the way from Halath. It was sturdy and well-made, but it was also old. And not completely waterproof. As the downpour commenced, half a dozen leaks soon made themselves known.

Wafia, a Dareg woman in her fifties who had mentioned that Jammal was her brother, immediately began ordering the women in the tent to deal with the situation. Cooking pots were laid out under the leaks to catch the water pouring in, and people's usual sleeping positions were rearranged to take advantage of dry spots.

No cookfires would be lit tonight, and whatever camaraderie was to be had would take place as the women in the tent gathered around the largest dry area and supped on dates, crisp flatbread, and goat cheese. Despite the conditions, all the women were in high spirits. The deluge was so unusual, so unexpected for most of them that there was an air almost of festival. After their cold meal had been consumed, they sat in their circle singing familiar songs of the Dareg, and playing a women's circle game of the Amhari.

Leila climbed into her bedroll with a warm feeling. She suspected that the combination of heat and humidity would soon become unpleasant, but she had enjoyed everything about the evening: the startling rain, thunder and lightning, the all-girls gathering. Soon they would be in Namei, and her grim work would begin. But for now she was content.

Chapter 16

Leila awoke to shouts and screaming, and the whinnying of horses. The white fabric of the tent, through which rainwater was still streaming in several spots, had a spot of light shining on it from a little to the left side of its front flap. Oh shit, it has to be bandits, she thought, and was on her feet in a moment. She had stripped down to her underwear before crawling into the bedroll, and now hastened to get into her thieves' garb and gather her weapons. Then she went to shadows, and opened the flap to peer out into the night.

The rain was still pouring down as it had done since before night had fallen, and she wondered what time it might be. Surely, not much past midnight? The bandits, familiar with the caravan master's tricks, must have waited in hiding for everyone to be asleep before launching their raid on the south side of the pass.

The campsite was arranged as a flat-sided circle beside the road, with a series of smaller leveled sites carved into the jungle around it like spokes on a wheel. The stream ran down at the bottom of this, now swollen to more than twice the size it had been when they'd pitched the tent. And up the slope, near the central area where the livestock was penned for the night, there was a bright white globe floating in midair. The rain seemed to pass right through it. The bandits must have a mage with them!

Leila went visible again long enough to turn to the other women in the tent, all of whom had been awakened by the clamor and were looking around in confusion. "Bandits have attacked the caravan, and I think they must have a mage with them!" she cried. "Gather your weapons, or flee!" With that she slipped out past the tent flap and went invisible again, moving up the short trail to the campground's central area.

Panic and confusion reigned there, as the mysterious globe of mage light illuminated the scene. The caravan had of course set guards overnight, as they did every night. But somehow the bandits had slipped past them, and there was now a pitched battle taking place. Invisible, Leila hesitated at the edge of the circle while she tried to make sense of what was going on.

81

In a few moments the scene resolved itself. The remaining caravan guards, augmented by Jammal Hassan himself and others who were not necessarily paid to defend the caravan but could be called on to pick up a weapon at need, were fighting man to man against what looked to be at least two dozen armed bandits. The rain was still pouring down steadily, with no sign of letup, and everyone (herself included) was soaked to the skin and rapidly becoming covered in mud. Soon, it would be impossible to tell the attackers from the defenders.

But who was providing the lighting for this exercise? Leila, long-time sneak thief that she was, wondered why the bandits didn't just slip in quietly in the darkness and make off with the valuables without alerting anyone. Unless maybe they were hoping to take prisoners. Slavery had been banished since ancient times in the areas now controlled by the Dominion. But the practice was still alive and well in many areas of the kingdom of Palambo and was also in force in some if not all of the Hando realms, according to what Leila had read.

There, on the opposite side of the central circle and standing on the road, she spotted a man who must surely be the bandits' mage. He appeared to be a Dareg, dressed in robes that seemed inappropriate for this conflict. He was hanging back, watching, and occasionally his lips were moving in a way that suggested an incantation. Or, according to Leila's new understanding of the way in which magic worked, a plea to his angel or djinn for assistance.

Should she call on Betsalel? Leila would be willing to bet that the Shadow God could outdo any supernatural being manufactured by man. But the timing didn't seem right – and anyway, hadn't he furnished her with a power that should enable her to defeat almost anything?

Leila carefully made her way around the perimeter of the circle, avoiding contact with any of the combatants, until she too was standing on the road. The mage had cast his illuminating globe of light at a height of around fifteen feet above the center of the circle, so the road itself was not very well lit. The rain pouring down made visibility difficult despite the light.

As the bandits' mage stood watching the conflict and occasionally requesting a service from his djinn, he suddenly found himself confronting an enormous warrior who sprang up out of the gloom a few yards down the road to the south. Belantos forfend, the man must be nearly seven feet tall! And he was wielding an enormous blade, which was even now traveling in the direction of the mage's neck.

Iblis leapt back out of range, and focused a spell of weakness on his attacker. He seemed to falter for a moment, then stood straight and continued his attack. The mage pulled his own blade, swinging it wildly to block the sweep of the sword that was homing in on his neck. He had half expected that the much-larger blade would cut through his as if it were not there, continuing on to cleave him from shoulder to hip. But it rebounded harmlessly, and he swept his scimitar forward across his attacker's neck.

The mage stared in amazement as the blade passed through the gigantic warrior's neck and the head did not topple to the ground. The eyes of his attacker looked as startled, then filled with anger. With his unoccupied left hand, Iblis' adversary grasped his head by the hair and removed it from the neck where it had been severed. Blood cascaded down, but the warrior paid it no mind. The severed head, now held in the warrior's left hand, glared at him and said "Now you have *really* made me angry! You will die!"

As the decapitated warrior readied another swing of his sword, Iblis turned and fled. He had not quite reached the far side of the road when he fell, a dagger buried to the hilt just to the left of his spine. The globe of light went out, and the melee in the campground's central circle went dark. There was much shouting and confusion, as the bandits realized that their secret weapon had been nullified and tried to disengage. No torches or candles could be lit in this torrent, but eventually storm lanterns were found.

Imbaso, who had been among the first to draw a weapon when the alarm had been raised, was carrying a lantern around the outer perimeter of the circle. Any bandits who were still able to appeared to have fled. The man he thought was their mage was lying face down in the road, the hilt of a dagger protruding from his back. Then he stumbled over Usiku, lying a few feet away on her side.

Usiku, no! His heart in his throat, he put a hand down and felt for a pulse. There was one, strong and steady – yet she appeared to be unconscious. There were no signs of injury, as much as he could tell in the lantern light and driving rain. He scooped her up off the streaming pavement and hurried to the tent where he'd been sleeping.

This was another large tent belonging to the caravan, occupied by caravan guards and other male personnel who were not on duty. It was somewhat less leaky than the women's communal tent. Imbaso laid Usiku down on his bedroll, oblivious to the fact that both he and she were soaked to the skin and running with water. He set the lantern on the tent floor beside her, and dug a spare tunic out of his pack. Using it to blot the water from her face, he anxiously scanned her for signs of life.

When it seemed that the time was right, Usiku's eyelids fluttered. Then she gasped as though emerging from watery depths, and struggled into a sitting position. Imbaso, kneeling beside her, enfolded her in an embrace. "You're all right?" he murmured, unwilling to let her go.

"Imbaso?" she choked, "Where am I?"

"You're in the men's communal tent," he replied, releasing her from his arms so he could study her face in the lantern light.

"Oh!" she said, pulling her legs up as if she meant to rise to her feet. "What about the bandits?"

"They've run away," he told her, putting his hands on her shoulders, "those that aren't lying out there dead."

Usiku sank back in relief, clinging to Imbaso as if she no longer had the strength to stay upright. After a moment she asked, "Did I kill him?"

"The mage, you mean?" Imbaso asked. He'd thought that dagger hilt looked familiar.

"Yes!" she said fervently. "When I heard the commotion I sneaked out, and I knew he must be a mage from the way he was acting. I threw my dagger and he turned, then as I was trying to run away he threw some kind of spell on me. I couldn't move, just fell to the ground!"

Imbaso, still kneeling, drew her to him in a firm embrace. "You stopped him, Usiku, and you saved us all. Without his help the rest of the bandits just gave up and ran away!"

"Oh," she said weakly, snuggling into the shelter of his arms. "Good."

Chapter 17

The rain eased off, and by morning it had stopped. Imbaso spent the rest of the night sleeping beside the fully-clothed Usiku where she lay on his bedroll, with a protective arm thrown over her. As dawn lit the campground, the bedraggled members of the caravan began trying to assess the damage.

The four guards who had been on night duty had all been killed, presumably stunned by a spell from the mage before having their throats slit by other members of the bandit gang. Perhaps they had sensibly intended to visit the camp silently after all, Leila realized. But their attempts to get at the horses had raised the alarm. She'd be willing to bet it was Wapesi. She'd trained him well, and he wouldn't have liked any strangers sneaking around him – let alone trying to lead him off.

Once alerted, the rest of the caravan's defenders – both employees of Hassan's and armed paying customers – had taken their own toll of the bandits. In addition to the mage, six of them were left behind. Four of those were already dead, and the other two wounded. They were soon enough dead as well, summarily executed by Jammal Hassan. In Palambo, being caught in the commission of a crime was enough to condemn you on the spot and any citizen could carry out the sentence.

An additional two caravan guards had been killed, and there were many with the caravan who had suffered small wounds. Imbaso was among them, having taken a shallow cut to his hand. Usiku, grateful for his bravery and kindness, made sure that the wound was thoroughly cleaned and treated. Leila knew that the warmer an area was, the likelier a wound was to fester if not kept clean, and she didn't want anything happening to her boy.

The caravan got on the road again, but far later than they should have. No one was willing to stay here another night, though – suppose the bandits came back seeking revenge? They spent the rest of the morning and on into the afternoon winding down the road as it left the mountains behind and cut through the foothills to the south and west.

They camped at an unofficial spot where there was enough level land on either side of the road for them to pitch their tents. There was no water nearby, but they had filled their casks before getting underway. The cloudy sky looked threatening, and they could see flashes of lightning far away over the plains; but the rain held off long enough for them to make cookfires.

Hassan slaughtered the last two of the goats he'd brought along, and the caravan's surviving members had a feast. Their dead had been buried near to where they had fallen, for in this climate you could not wait long before a body would begin to rot. They all drank palm wine, toasting their departed friends, and Hassan produced a couple of bottles of wasagi.

Usiku was offered a pull from one of those bottles, and took one out of solidarity. The attack had forged a bond among them that had not been there earlier. The bottle was of dark brown glass, hard to say what its contents were, and Leila had never heard of wasagi. She took a slug, then burst into a coughing fit. Betsalel, how that burned! Then, to the amusement of everyone around her, she took a second swig and grinned broadly before passing the bottle along.

It was clearly some kind of distilled spirit, reminding Leila of gin but without the smooth taste one could usually expect from the spirits of the Dominion. Imbaso, at Usiku's side, squeezed her elbow and asked, "Are you all right?" She smiled sweetly at him.

"I've never tasted anything stronger than the beer we brewed on our farm before," she admitted. "I hope it won't make me drunk!"

The party was rained out before it would otherwise have run down, and everyone made a dash for the tents. The next day they came down out of the heavily wooded foothills and the road ran through a broad expanse of savannah. Leila was pleased that Usiku's back story made the farm girl from the Thabban River area as unfamiliar with this part of Palambo as she herself was. She could gawk all she wanted to, without blowing her cover.

These vast, gently rolling grasslands stretched as far as the eye could see. Dotted here and there with trees and brush, they supported herds of grazing animals beyond anything Leila had ever dreamed possible. Thousands, tens of thousands of gazelles, antelope, creatures like horses but covered in black and white stripes, spent their days in constant motion, eating their way through the constantly renewed grass.

Usiku was fascinated, and Imbaso was happy to tell her about the creatures they were seeing. It tickled him that this girl who'd been born not that far from Namei had no memory of the sights of her homeland, and it made him feel important as she hung on his every word.

It was not all grazers on those plains. Lions, leopards, cheetahs, several kinds of hyena, jackals, wild dogs, foxes, and even brown bears that looked similar to those of the Dominion made a living preying on the grass eaters. And lurking in the small rivers they came to, each of them crossed via a stone bridge, were enormous, lazy crocodiles.

They dined nightly on fresh meat, the caravan guards proving to be adept with their bows. And once a large herd of enormous gray beasts with legs like tree trunks, ears like palm leaves, and prehensile noses as long as Leila was tall forced the entire caravan to halt and wait while they crossed the road. This must have been a regular crossing spot for the huge creatures, as the stones of the road were cracked and nearly pulverized in the vicinity.

"You've never seen tembo, Usiku?" Imbaso asked as she sat her horse transfixed with amazement. Leila's god-given language ability translated the Kiswa name to the Gasparto "oliphant." Her friend Oliphant from the Night Guild in Marsine had been aptly named, but these creatures would have made ten of him.

"We didn't have any in the desert," she said, barely paying attention to what he'd said.

"In my studies in Wena I learned that these are only one kind of tembo," he went on. "They have another species in the western Hando realms that can be tamed and trained to do work."

Usiku turned to him, her eyes sparkling with interest. "I would so like to ride one! She exclaimed. "Imagine what it must be like to be so high up – you could see everything! And no enemy would dare to attack you!" He smiled at her. For a girl who'd led what seemed to him to have been a sheltered life, she could certainly be fierce on occasion. Her dagger throw to end the life of the bandits' mage had earned her widespread praise, and she'd been awarded the mage's belongings. He wondered what she planned to do with them, though perhaps she just hoped to sell them to get money.

On their seventh day since leaving the mountains the road ended at a broad river. It had been raining for at least a few hours every day during their journey, and the mighty Pana was in spate. The water was roiling, the color of kaf with a lot of milk added, charging fiercely westward on its way to the far-off Western Ocean. It served as a conduit for many of the goods of central Palambo.

Here on the north side a road as broad and well-paved as the one they'd been traveling on these weeks ran east and west at a goodly distance from the river's edge. It had a four-foot wall running along the side nearest the water, as a discouragement to crocodiles. What with bandits, rebel raiders, and wildlife, traveling the roads in Palambo could be a hazardous enterprise.

They turned right here. Had they turned left they would have been in Zambei in less than a full day's travel. Now Namei beckoned, only a day to the west. It was time for Leila to make her move. They stopped for the evening at an official camping ground a short distance north of the road, and after supper had been eaten Usiku approached Imbaso with an uncharacteristically serious expression on her face.

"Can we talk?" she asked, gesturing him to come with her. It was not safe to be walking around in the darkness outside of camp, so she led him to the women's communal tent. It was unoccupied now, as all the rest of the women were enjoying the nightly socializing.

"What is it, Usiku?" Imbaso asked concernedly. She was usually so full of light and life, and it bothered him to see her looking as if she bore some great burden. They each sat cross-legged on a bedroll, facing each other. A little light from the cookfires kept it from being pitch dark in here, but barely.

"We have become friends, have we not?" the girl asked him. He leaned forward to take her hands and squeeze them.

"The best of friends!" Imbaso assured her, though platonic friendship between young men and women was not a common thing in Palambo – and truthfully, his feelings for her had never been entirely platonic.

She squeezed his hands back, then said hesitantly, "I have something to confess to you…"

Imbaso was immediately on edge. Was the girl he had come to love about to admit to some hideous crime – or to being, perhaps, already wed to another? The suspense was killing him, and when she didn't continue he urged, "Go on…"

"You recall I said I was going to Namei to live with my uncle and his family?" Usiku asked. The topic had not come up in weeks.

"Yes, I remember," he replied solemnly.

Usiku took a deep breath, and sighed. "I lied. There is no uncle, no family. I am all alone in the world."

"But… what will you do in Namei, then? Why this long perilous journey?" There was a moment's silence before she spoke again.

"Let me explain something to you first, so you can understand," she said at last, and let loose another deep sigh before continuing.

"My family had a happy life on our farm along the Thabban. I lived there with my father, my mother, my older brother and my two younger brothers, and it was the only life I had ever known. The Ran whose jurisdiction included the Thabban from thirty miles south of Halath to the mountains was a corrupt pig. He charged everyone in the region taxes that were far higher than those required by the crown, Father said, so that he could live like a king himself."

She paused, and Imbaso squeezed her hands again. "That's far from unusual," he admitted with a sigh. Usiku continued.

"It was hard, but we put up with it because what else could we do? We were just farmers and the Ran had a private army and a fortified castle. If we refused to pay, he would just send his soldiers to take whatever he wanted. So we paid, and paid. He took the best of our horses as his army's mounts, took the lion's share of what we made from selling our crops. Then one day, he and a large troop of his soldiers came to visit our farm in person, assessing how much more we might be able to pay."

Imbaso sat nearly quivering with tension, wondering what was going to be revealed. Usiku's eyes flashed in the dim light, glistening with moisture, and she continued in a quavering voice. "He saw me riding, training one of our colts, and he liked what he saw. He demanded that my father give me to him, to take as a bride."

"He was a member of the royal family?" Imbaso asked. In all of Palambo, only members of that lineage were permitted to have multiple wives.

"Not in the least!" she laughed bitterly. "He had been married for many years to a woman little younger than he was, and had grown children far older than me. I think he meant to bring shame on our family by taking me as a concubine, and thought to still my father's wrath by pretending that we would be married. Such an alliance would be more than a humble farmer could hope for, or so he thought."

"Your father turned him down?" Imbaso asked, beginning to feel a creeping horror as he realized where the story had to end. It was a wonder Usiku was here to tell it.

"Father had hated the Ran for years, of course, and that was the last straw. He told him that his daughter would never be a whore for the likes of him, and demanded that the Ran and his soldiers leave our property or there would be hell to pay."

Imbaso came across the gap between the bedrolls and sat beside Usiku, throwing a comforting arm around her shoulders. He could feel them quivering, hear the tears in her voice as she continued her tale. "The Ran killed my father first, then his men killed my older brother when he tried to come to Father's aid. The younger boys fled when they seized Mother and me, but two of the Ran's soldiers chased them down and killed them."

A sob escaped Usiku's lips, and she could not continue. Imbaso held her close, murmuring "There, there…"

With a shuddering sob and an angry swipe of her forearm across her face, Usiku sat erect and took up where she had left off. "My mother was too old to appeal to the Ran, but she was comely enough for a woman of her age. He gave her to his soldiers, and they took turns with her until they tired of the sport. Then they left her dead in the dust of the farmyard. He dragged me off to the house, and… took me, in my parents' bed. Over and over again. I had been a maiden, and the pain was great – but not as great as that of knowing what they had done to my family."

Usiku's tears seemed now to have dried up. Turning to her left, looking up into Imbaso's eyes, she went on. "He thought me unconscious, defeated, I believe. For when he had satisfied himself he left me lying. I am sure he intended to drag me off and install me in quarters in his castle, where he might enjoy me whenever he wished until it was time to cast me aside. But by now it was dark out, and as soon as he left the room I was out the window."

Imbaso stroked her cheek, his eyes filled with sorrow and sympathy at her tale. No wonder she had been reluctant to discuss it! "I would have taken one of the horses, but the Ran's men had rounded them up and were guarding them. I ran across the fields and up into some nearby hills. There was a cave there, little more than a small crevice in the rocks, where we had played as children. I hid there, I'm not sure how long. Two days maybe. Until finally hunger and thirst drove me out again."

Usiku turned to Imbaso again, staring him in the eyes. "Do you know, I had thought that our farm was a valuable thing. A living for us, and a source of revenue for the Ran. But it seems that he considered it worthless. He slaughtered my family, and when he found that I had escaped his clutches he burned the house and the outbuildings, set fire to the crops in the fields, and killed all of the livestock except for the horses. Those, I guess, he and his men stole and took back to the castle with them. We had some fine breeding stock."

"So you came to Halath, then?" Imbaso asked, still holding her tenderly.

"I found some food stores that had not been destroyed," Usiku replied. "The house was a ruin, but there was a root cellar under the barn. And they had not poisoned the well, so there was water to drink. After I had recovered my strength I buried the bodies of my family. They had not destroyed the skiff we kept at our river dock, and I used it to float downstream to Halath. Then I met Suleiman, and soon thereafter I met you."

Imbaso held her tight, but he was casting his mind back to the first time he had met Usiku. She had seemed light, joyful, a will-o-the-wisp. Not a young girl devastated by having her maidenhead taken by force, as an accompaniment to the murder of her entire family and destruction of her home. How had this transformation been wrought?

Leila sensed Imbaso's failure to completely buy her story. She had let too much of herself through on their first meeting, joy at finding the perfect person to help her slip into the temple of Betsalel at Namei bubbling up to the surface. "I had not shed any tears for my family," Usiku said, "until today. When I fled for the cave I knew that everyone I loved was dead, and the life I had known before was lost forever. Over the time in the cave, and during the days it took to float downriver to Halath, my grief was turned into resolve. And then, my resolve became turned into joy."

Imbaso turned to look Usiku in the eyes. A few teardrops were still sparkling on her dark cheeks. "Joy?" he asked. "I don't understand."

"It's well known," she said, "that the temple of Betsalel in Namei hides a secret cult of assassins – pledged to the dark god, and deriving special powers from him."

"The Makucha Nyeusi, the Black Claw?" he asked in disbelief. "That's just a fable!"

Pulling away from his comforting arm, Usiku confronted him with a glare. "You, whose family for many generations has been a part of the priesthood of Betsalel, you would try to tell me this? I thought we were friends!"

"I, uh…" Imbaso sputtered. He didn't know what to tell her. Sure, there'd been rumors for years. And sure, Father was involved in some stuff with the temple that was very hush-hush secret. But he was twenty-one years old and his family had sent him away at the age of eighteen to study in the Gaspari Dominion – not inducted him into some black cult. The idea was ludicrous!

The girl he was convinced he was in love with was still glaring at him. Imbaso held his hands up in a gesture of surrender. "I swear by Betsalel and all the Eight, the Makucha Nyeusi is as much an old wives' tale to me as it is to anyone. My family didn't really try to push my involvement with the temple, which is odd considering I'm their only surviving child. But if it's real, I know nothing about it."

"The Makucha Nyeusi is real," Usiku declared. "I am going to join it, and I will become the most lethal assassin the world has ever seen. When the Ran and his men captured me I tried to use my daggers on them and they *laughed*! They took them away from me and threw them aside, but I was able to get them again when I returned to my burned-out home. They'd just left them lying in the dirt of the farmyard like they were garbage! The same as they did for my family…"

With that, the girl burst into full-blown, racking sobs. She guarded herself from her anguish by telling herself a fairy tale about the Black Claw and revenge, Imbaso realized. And I just punched a gigantic hole in that by knowing nothing about it. I've ripped out the false framework that was allowing her to rise above the abyss of despair to the joy that is her natural state. He felt like he'd just kicked a puppy.

Usiku clung to Imbaso, sobbing her heart out, for a long time. For Leila, the sadness that fueled this exhibition of grief was remorse over her need to play this sweet, kind young man for a fool. Finally she got a grip on herself. The evening was wearing on, and there was probably little time left before others would be seeking this tent.

She peered up into the face of her comforter. "You see, don't you Imbaso? I *must* be accepted as an apprentice by the Makucha

Nyeusi. I must become the perfect assassin. Then I can kill the Ran, and all of his men who raped my mother. And perhaps, all of his children as well. His castle is built of stone, and burning it to the ground might be difficult. But I'll think of something."

Imbaso's face assumed a pained smile. He gently brushed the tightly curled hair from her brow, and kissed her on the forehead. It reminded Leila of similar kisses delivered by Betsalel. "Usiku," he said gently. "I do not know whether the Makucha Nyeusi is anything more than a tale. But if it is, we'll join it together. I will fight at your side, and together we will seek your vengeance."

Chapter 18

Namei was not what Leila had expected. Though it was a major port on the Pana river, and had once been the capital of Palambo, the city itself was situated more than a mile away from the river docks. The ancients who had first built here must have seen the rocky rise around which the mighty river flowed as an ideal stronghold, standing nearly a thousand feet above the surrounding land. And strong it remained.

It was not as big as Parat, certainly, the river port with which she was most familiar. But it was impressive nonetheless – and completely enclosed within thick walls of stone. A single broad road wound its way up from the main highway to the city's only gate. As Usiku gaped at it in astonishment, Imbaso said "Two hundred thousand people inside those walls, at the last census. And probably another fifty thousand in the surrounding area. It's been more than a generation since a battle was last fought here, though. I shudder to think what it would be like if everybody outside the walls wanted to shelter inside."

"It's amazing," Usiku replied. She and Imbaso were at the head of the caravan, which was stretched out for half a mile behind them as they approached the turnoff to Namei proper. The caravan itself would be camping in the ground set aside for such activities, another mile to the west. But Usiku didn't want to wait for it to get there.

"I'm going to get my baggage," she announced, "and go up there. I'm sure Wapesi can carry us both." Imbaso eyed the gelding uncertainly. Usiku had not had much to take with her when she fled the ruins of her home, of course. She was fortunate that there'd been a cache of gold under the floorboards, enough to get her on the way to Namei. But after receiving Father's summons he'd packed everything he owned – everything accumulated in three years of living abroad.

"Tell you what," he suggested, "Why don't we just go up there together on Wapesi now. I can get my own horse from home, and we can come back down for our baggage later after the caravan is settled."

"Good idea," she replied. "I'll just let Hassan know what we plan." The caravan master and his wife were riding in the lead wagon, so she didn't have to ride far. Meanwhile Imbaso dismounted from the caravan horse he'd been riding and tied its reins to the rear of Hassan's wagon.

Usiku rode in back of Imbaso, on Wapesi's generous rump, holding to him with her arms tight around his waist. Imbaso was glad she was not riding in front of him, as she surely would have noticed the hardness between his legs. Just being in proximity to her made his pulse quicken, which was insane – she was far too young, and they were close friends not lovers.

No doubt it had just been too long since he had had a woman. He and his classmates at the university had often visited the whorehouses together – though on his tight budget, he had not been able to do it as often as he might have liked. The chances for a young man of limited means, and with his complexion, being able to find a paramour in Wena were essentially nil. His right hand had stood in for a woman on many occasions over the years.

Imbaso's mind was in turmoil as they climbed the road, picking their way through slower traffic as they approached the gates of Namei. The ominously mysterious way in which he'd been summoned back from Wena was one thing, but his anxiety about that had faded over the weeks it had taken to get here. Then it had all come rushing back again last night, when Usiku had revealed her personal tragedy and her quest for revenge. Why in all the hells had he said he would help her achieve it?

At this hour the gates stood wide open, but there were guard towers on either side and a complement of half a dozen armed guards monitoring traffic. Each entrant was required to declare their name, point of origin, and business before being allowed into the city. Though of course the guards had no way of knowing if they had been lied to.

As they approached the gates one of the guards, a tall and muscular young man with beautiful features, called "Imbaso? Is it you?" Pulling the horse to a halt, Imbaso jumped down and seized the young guard in a bear hug.

"Nuzuri! You became a city guard? I thought you'd have been off to Iskand seeking your fortune by now!"

Nuzuri looked his childhood friend up and down, grinning ruefully. "That was the idea, the last time you were here," he admitted. "But you remember Meneema?" Imbaso eyed him disbelievingly.

"Meneema? I thought she couldn't stand you. Or me, for that matter." Nuzuri shook his head.

"Things change, don't they? Anyhow, she's expecting our second child in a few months' time. Our boy is almost two now."

"Mulia smile on you, then," Imbaso grinned. While he'd been off leading the cosmopolitan high life in the Dominion, his buddy had fallen into the clutches of a designing woman. As he recalled how Meneema had looked the last time he'd seen her, he had to admit it wasn't a complete surprise.

"Are you home to stay, then?" Nuzuri asked, recalling he was on duty.

Imbaso shrugged. "Father called me home, but his letter didn't say why. Has anything earthshaking happened in the last couple of months?" Nuzuri looked thoughtful.

"Nothing I've heard about that would make him call you home, I don't think. There have been a few mysterious happenings around the area, but things have mostly been quiet. I suppose you'll have to ask *him*, then. I'll just put down that you've returned home from abroad."

After making a notation on his board, Nuzuri looked up at Usiku where she still sat on the tall gelding's rump. Then he turned a speculative glance on his friend, a slow smile forming. "Am I perhaps not the only one to have been captured by a beautiful woman since last we met, Imbaso? Who's the lady?"

Imbaso's dark complexion turned darker still, and he said stiffly, "This is Usiku, from Halath. She's... just a friend. We came here together on the same caravan, that's all."

The guard raised an eyebrow. "If you say so, old friend." He looked up, addressing Usiku directly for the first time. "Reason for visiting Namei?" he asked officially.

Usiku looked down at him solemnly. "I am here to pray at the temple of Betsalel for the death of my enemies," she said flatly.

Nuzuri gaped at her, his stylus hesitating above the board. "Uh... I'll just put down 'religious pilgrimage,' all right?" She pierced him with an eagle's gaze from her night-black eyes.

"That will be fine," she said. "May we go in?"

Up on Wapesi once again, Imbaso said to his companion behind his back, "That was a little unsettling."

"It's the truth, isn't it?" Usiku replied. Clearly there was no point in his raising any further objections.

"I'm taking us to my family's home first, all right?" he asked her. "I need to find out why my father sent for me, and I need to get Kizuri so we can go back to the caravan and collect our belongings." She didn't reply, but squeezed him tightly around the waist. It sent a flood of warmth surging through him. This girl, this woman, was driving him insane!

The city of Namei had been built on a broad hilltop, and the street they had entered on encircled the entire city immediately inside its wall. No structures had been built against that wall, a sign that war in this region was at least a recent memory if not a constant threat. Imbaso guided Wapesi up one of the streets that acted like spokes in the wheel, and they climbed the hill before taking a left and continuing on a road that formed a concentric circle with the first one.

"What's at the very top?" Usiki asked, speaking into Imbaso's back.

"It used to be the royal palace," he explained, taking on the role of tour guide for the young first-time visitor. "This was the capital of all Palambo hundreds of years ago, before the kingdom really began its expansion. But after the Palamban forces captured Iskand, the capital was moved and the palace here became a center for the government offices. Ruling over a kingdom the size of this one takes a lot of clerks and administrators – it's not all soldiers!"

Leila knew all this, of course. But Usiku, growing up on a farm in the desert, would have had few opportunities for education.

"And where is the temple of Betsalel?" Usiku asked.

"Not too far from the palace," Imbaso replied. "All eight of the deities had their temples distributed around the circle immediately below the level occupied by the king. And of course, there are temples to many of the lesser deities scattered throughout the city."

Lesser deities? This was something Leila had *not* known. Nor had Betsalel mentioned to her that other beings (presumably the daemons of which he had spoken) were being worshiped openly and quasi-officially in Palambo. She was still having trouble understanding how ignorant the Eight could be, given their otherwise nearly limitless powers. Apparently the plane in which they resided did not offer windows into the physical plane where she and the rest of the world lived. They could learn about events here only as any mortal did.

"Oh, which ones?" Usiku asked casually. As she thought on it, it stood to reason that any daemon created by a melding of human belief and a human soul could gain much by being adopted as a god or goddess. They might well achieve equal power with any of the Eight, if their worship spread far enough. And presumably, the way to do that was by providing the customers with what they wanted. Leila shuddered to consider what the worshipers of the djinn masquerading as Betsalel were likely to want.

Imbaso laughed. "I'm sorry," he said deprecatingly, "I truly am not a religious man. I couldn't begin to tell you any of their names."

Usiku was silent for a while, as Wapesi continued his winding way higher and higher toward the summit of Namei. Then she remarked, "I'm puzzled, Imbaso. You said that your father was only the latest of many in your lineage to be a priest of Betsalel, and you are his only son. Why did he send you go off to study in the Gaspari Dominion, instead of insisting you join the priesthood?"

Now it was Imbaso's turn to be silent, as he guided the horse through the turnings, climbing ever upward. "You know," he said at last. "I'm not entirely sure. I suspect that he may have had a crisis of faith, somehow. He didn't ever really discuss it with me, but when I was much younger I was guided in the worship of Betsalel just as I would have been if the priesthood would be my final destination. But when I was around twelve, it seemed as if Father had turned aside. As if the god had failed him in some way. He stopped trying to push me in that direction, and there was a whole world of other things to capture my attention. I was ecstatic when he arranged for me to go to university in the Dominion. Even if I haven't managed to obtain my degree, I am sure that what I've learned will make me an asset to Palambo."

Though Usiku had constantly encouraged Imbaso to talk about himself, he had never revealed such detail before. Leila pondered his story, and understood what must have happened. For nearly two centuries, successive generations of Betsalel priests had been turning away from their god without realizing it. They had gone deeper and deeper into perverted rituals, until the Shadow God himself had lost the ability to communicate with them. But the god they thought they worshiped had been only an imaginary construct. Until now. What horrid plans had Imbaso's father conceived, now that his god was real again?

Chapter 19

They came at last to the third ring down from Namei's summit, inhabited by the city's elite. Here the houses were set further apart, with land around them. Most were built surrounding a courtyard, similar to the ruined temple where Leila had first encountered Betsalel. Imbaso guided Wapesi in through a gap in a stone wall and then took him down through lush gardens around the side to the rear.

The house formed a square-edged U, two stories high and open at the back. At the very rear of the property were the stables, and Imbaso dismounted then offered a hand to Usiku as she hopped down. He tied Wapesi's reins to a nearby post. "We'll just stay long enough to let everyone know we've arrived, I think. No need to unsaddle him." He seemed to have become less easy-going, more commanding now that he was on his home turf.

Usiku's eyes were wide. She had known that Imbaso's family must be wealthy, but this place made Josef Sampson's miniature palace in Marsine look like a hovel! Maybe it was just the different climate… Since they'd come down out of the mountains the air had been hot and sticky, and Leila had not gotten used to it yet.

Several open stalls stood in a row along the front of the stables, and a pretty-faced dapple gray Hisan whinnied at them. "Kizuri!" Imbaso said, and hurried over to pat the mare on the neck and make much of her. In the next-door stall was a well-grown colt, a dark bay. "And this must be the boy I've heard about!" he crowed, giving the young horse a little attention.

Turning to Usiku, Imbaso said "This is my mare, Kizuri. I've had her for years. And the bay colt is hers by some local stallion Father fancied. I think he made a good choice!" Leila was charmed by his enthusiasm. Here they had all of these dark, serious undertakings and he was driven to delight by the sight of a nice-looking horse. Once again she felt a pang as she considered how much more she would have liked to relate to Imbaso with complete honesty.

Taking Usiku's hand, he led her toward the rear of the house. There were formal gardens, and a large stone-lined pool set in a central location on this side of the bottom part of the "U." The water looked cool and inviting. "Do you swim?" Imbaso asked.

The girl shook her head shyly. "I've never learned," she admitted. "The waters of the Thabban are turbulent, and the current is strong. Mother wouldn't let us kids anywhere near it."

"Maybe I'll teach you!" he suggested. Leila could see that returning to the home where he'd been born and raised had filled Imbaso with a jubilation beyond anything she'd yet seen in him. She stifled a sigh, wishing that she had had such a home – and fearful that his joy would be short-lived. It seemed likely that his father was about to reclaim him for the dark god. Or, the dark god's understudy.

They let themselves in through a set of double doors that were made up of many panes of glass. Usiku had never seen anything like them, and Leila had not seen their like in Palambo. As they stepped through into the relative coolness of the house's entryway, Imbaso led her to the left and called, "Mother? Aunt Uzuri? I'm home!"

From the room ahead of them, there was a startled exclamation and a tall, dark woman dressed in one of the colorful robes the Palambans called a dashiki appeared. "Imbaso, my boy!" she cried, and rushed to embrace him. She completely ignored his companion. This had to be his mother, Leila guessed. She stood back, not wanting to intrude on their tender reunion. Seeing how much Imbaso's mother loved him filled her with a hollow longing for her own mother, dead these nine years.

The young man broke away after a few moments and said, "Mama, this is my friend Usiku. We traveled together on the caravan from Halath. Usiku, this is my mother Faradhi." Usiku bowed her head and made the usual Palamban *salaam*, a gesture of respect. As an impoverished teenage orphan greeting a wealthy matron, it was on her to be submissive.

Faradhi greeted her politely, but with no warmth. "Is Father here?" Imbaso asked his mother. She shook her head.

"Since the… incident, he is often away on business during the afternoon. But I know that he is anxious for your arrival. Where are your bags?"

"Still with the caravan," her son replied. "Usiku gave me a ride up here on her horse so I could collect Kizuri and use her to bring my belongings up the hill. But… what 'incident'?"

Faradhi's face fell, and a look of sadness came into her liquid brown eyes. "Since you went away to school, son… Well, it was your Aunt Uzuri. She was lonely, I think, but she did a very foolish thing. She had an affair with someone, and she had a baby. Your father was very angry that his sister had shamed our family so, but what could he do? When the boy was a few months old, as has been the tradition, he took him to dedicate to Betsalel."

Imbaso nodded, a similar look of pain on his own features. He had always loved his Aunt Uzuri, and had felt a little sad for her being forced to live as little more than an unpaid servant in their house. But for her, a woman in her forties, to have had a baby out of wedlock – it was unthinkable! "So I'm told was done with me, at that age," he remarked to his mother.

"Yes, as was also done with your father and every member of his line back through the generations, so his mother told me when we were wed. But this time, something different happened." Usiku was standing a bit apart, somewhat surprised that Imbaso's mother would broach this subject in the presence of a stranger. But she was also listening hard.

"What happened, Mama?" Imbaso asked, bracing himself for the worst. Faradhi gave an involuntary little shudder.

"The god took him," she said flatly. "Manifested in his idol and took the boy away. Uzuri has been disconsolate since."

Chapter 20

That has to have been it, Leila realized. *The moment when the djinn stole my master's idol!* But if every male member of Imbaso's family had been similarly dedicated to the Palamban cult's imaginary dark god, why had it not happened decades ago? Unless perhaps Imbaso's father was a shaman of unusually strong spiritual power, able to empower the belief construct in a way others had not?

Shocked by what his mother had reported, but still not seeing why it should have resulted in his being called back from the university a year short of graduation, Imbaso embraced his mother. Aunt Uzuri was not here, he learned, spending all of her days praying at the temple of Betsalel for her son's release.

Imbaso saddled Kizuri, and he and Usiku took the horses back out the gates and turned right along the main road near the river. By now the caravan had reached the camping ground, and was a hive of activity as goods were unloaded and travelers departed. They collected their respective baggage, bid farewell to the people they'd become acquainted with on the journey, and returned to the city.

"What do you make of your mother's tale, Imbaso?" Usiku asked as they rode side by side.

"I don't understand it," he admitted. "So far as I know, Betsalel has not manifested at the temple in Namei in many generations. Some people theorized that he would not come because the capital had been moved to Iskand, but I have not heard of him manifesting there either. Truth to tell, I haven't been paying much attention to the gods – even if I was dedicated to the Shadow God as a baby."

"You didn't go to the temples in the Gaspari Dominion?" she asked.

He hung his head sheepishly. "Not once in three years, not even after the big news last year that worship of Betsalel was once more being allowed. Of course, they haven't gotten around to putting an idol of Betsalel back in the Temple of the Eight at Wena, in any case."

Truly, Leila thought, Tevo and I have our work cut out for us. The number of Betsalel worshipers was growing exponentially – but the Shadow God was not everyone's idea of the number one deity to devote oneself to. It would probably be years before he had been restored to every temple of the Eight throughout the Dominion.

Her next question was one Imbaso had been wrestling with for weeks. "Why do you suppose your father called you back?" Usiku asked. "Does the incident with the baby mean he wants you active in the church now?"

"I suppose it's possible," he mused. "And I've promised you I will join the Makucha Nyeusi with you, if such a thing truly exists. I guess that would count as getting more involved with the church, since the Black Claw is supposedly based in Betsalel worship. It's likely I'll find out later today, after Father gets home."

Now it was Imbaso's turn to ask questions. "Where are you going to stay, Usiku? Have you given that any thought?"

"I don't suppose Namei's temple of Mulia has a women's hostel, like at Halath?"

"No, none of the temples offer those kinds of services," he replied. "I suppose you could stay at a regular inn, but they cost money."

"I have enough for a few nights' lodging, at least," Usiku admitted. That she probably had enough asand sewn into her clothing and luggage to purchase a small house in the lower city was not something she could admit to without awkward explanations. "I think I will go to the temple of Betsalel and pray to the dark god. If he has manifested here recently, perhaps he will hear my prayers and provide me with what I need."

Waving to Nuzuri as they came in through the gates again, Imbaso turned Kizuri's head to the left and they began retracing their journey toward the top of the hill. "I admire your faith," he said to his companion. "I really feel like a fish out of water in my family, all those generations of priests and I have no interest at all in bothering the gods. Why not just let them do whatever it is they do, while we deal with our own lives? To me it seems as though seeking divine favors is like being a perpetual child, looking to one's parents to do things we should do for ourselves."

Usiku smiled solemnly at Imbaso as they walked their horses side by side through the twists and turns of the city streets. Wapesi was three hands taller than Kizuri, so she was looking down at him. "I have to believe in the gods, because I know they can do things I cannot. If Betsalel can grant me the death of the Ran, I will worship him for the rest of my life." Imbaso just shook his head.

They parted at Imbaso's home. "I wish you could stay here," he said sadly. "The house is huge, and there are a dozen rooms we don't use now. The expectation is that after I marry and have a family, we will all live here together. But there haven't been any efforts to find me a bride, yet. Thank the Eight!" Usiku gave him an uneasy look at that remark, and a flicker of hope sparked in Imbaso's breast. Might she be wishing, as he did, that she could become that bride?

After getting directions to the temple Usiku squeezed Imbaso's hands without dismounting. "I'll see you at the temple before long," she promised, and rode off. He watched her go with a pang. The Black Claw! What had he gotten himself into?

Imbaso's directions had been accurate, and Leila soon found herself on a broad circular road looking at the temple of Betsalel. In Palambo, she'd learned from her conversations with Imbaso, only Iskand had anything similar to the Temple of the Eight in Parat. For the most part, even larger cities had individual temples rather than one honoring all eight of the deities. The widespread belief in daemons as minor gods probably meant that for many people, a temple to the eight true gods and goddesses that omitted their favorite daemon would be seen as an insult.

The architecture was quite different from any of the temples Leila had seen in the Dominion: both more massive and more ornate, with towering stone pillars. She'd passed the temples to Belantos and Deline on her way here, and all that she'd seen so far were similar in overall construction. But the stone facades were each carved with symbols and images specific to the deity being honored.

There were only temples on this level, one for each of the Eight original deities. Each had a good-sized patch of ground around it, maintained as gardens. Leila tied Wapesi to a hitching post at the front, patted him on the neck, then walked through the gate and into the grounds. In keeping with the dark god, the gardens had been planted with dark plants. Most of them had foliage of deep purple or dark green, and there were some surprising black lilies in bloom.

Leila looked around her, then seeing no one else she quickly faded into the shadows and became invisible. She moved silently around to the front of the temple and went in through the front doors, which stood open. Since the worship of Betsalel was often carried out at night, she guessed these must stand open twenty-four hours a day – except maybe when there was a storm. Though she had gotten rained on every day since arriving at the mountain pass to the north, today had been dry so far.

There was an anteroom with a black-robed priest in it, and beyond that more doors opened to the main sanctuary. I'll bet this place has a basement level like the temple in Parat, Leila thought as she looked around. There was another door off to one side at the back of the room, shut tight. Benches were arranged on either side of a center aisle leading to a rectangular altar at the center of the back wall. And above that altar was a painting of the dark god – no idol!

Had this recently-spawned djinn *literally* stolen the idol? That made no sense… or did it? Certainly when Betsalel had manifested in his enormous idol in Parat, he had then run more than two miles down the hill from the Imperial Treasure House where it had been hidden to the Temple of the Eight. So if this djinn had manifested in Betsalel's idol here, claiming it for himself, why couldn't he just walk off and leave it anywhere he pleased? What a thought.

There were few worshipers of the God of Night to be found in the temple at this hour. One, an old man who appeared gnarled and bent by arthritis, was praying silently from his seat on a pew far to the left of the first row. Praying for the surcease of death, perhaps, Leila thought. The only other worshiper was a handsome middle-aged woman, dressed all in black, who was kneeling before the altar on the hard stone floor with tears in her eyes.

Invisible and silent, Leila stepped closer so she could hear what the woman was praying. "Please Dark One, I beg you Betsalel, return my Usafi to me." She was repeating it over and over again, tirelessly, as the tears ran slowly down her cheeks. Tears filled Leila's own eyes at the woman's piteous display. This had to be Imbaso's Aunt Uzuri. Her name in Kiswa meant "beautiful one," and she probably had been a beauty in her youth. Now she was ravaged by grief and despair, and it had left marks that would probably never fade.

Leila was sure this could be none other than the mother of the baby who was "taken" by the dark god. Killed? But no, if the baby had merely died during the rite of consecration (the details of which Leila could only speculate about) the mother would have had her son's corpse. Betsalel had mentioned that he could somehow transport her through his non-material plane from one place to another on this plane – provided he had an idol, a conduit for his physical form, at either end of the journey. Might the djinn, in awakening, have carried the infant away to some other location?

Too many questions, and not enough answers! Uzuri's appeals almost suggested that she'd heard about Betsalel's "new power" of resurrection. It had been nearly a year since the incident in Parat, after all. But if worshipers in Palambo, or at least here in Namei, were to try to call on Betsalel as he was – and not as the demonic figure he'd been painted by centuries of perverted worship – they would have no idol available. And without an idol, a true scion of the idol in Parat, the Shadow God could not manifest to perform miracles in this plane of existence.

Leila had the pouch with the tiny idol of Betsalel in her pocket, where she'd been carrying it for all the months since he had given it to her. She was tempted to whip it out and set it on the altar, and see if the true Shadow God would come to Uzuri's pleas. Might the woman become for Palambo what Leila had become for the Dominion, the seed to reestablish Betsalel's church?

But she was unsure what would happen if she called Betsalel to what she had to assume was the djinn's principal nexus of power. Here at least, if nowhere else that she knew of, he had a cadre of loyal worshippers who had been fueling his existence with human sacrifice and who knows what abominations over many generations. Better to wait until she knew more.

Standing at the rear of the sanctuary near the doors from the anteroom, Leila became visible once again. She assumed the appearance of the old man, and hobbled out of the doors without drawing so much as a second glance from the priest on duty. It was time to find a place to live.

Chapter 21

Before unhitching Wapesi and riding off, the "old man" took a turn through the gardens. A minute or two later a young man in his early thirties, of medium height and a build that suggested he had enjoyed many delicious meals, climbed onto the chestnut gelding and made his way down the hill toward the city's outermost ring road. His garb was respectable and of fine quality, if not opulent.

During their first trip to Imbaso's family's house earlier today, Leila had spotted a sign identifying the Palamban equivalent of an estate agent's place of business. Another Dominion idea that had seemingly taken hold in this southern kingdom, and a useful one for her purposes.

Tying the tall gelding to a hitching post outside, Tajiri walked with a somewhat rolling gait in through the open door of the shop. Having no actual merchandise to display, the shop was scarcely eight feet in width and no more than fifteen feet long. There was a desk at the rear, and the wall down the left side had been covered with a layer of cork. Pinned to that wall in a haphazard fashion were sheets of paper, or in some cases parchment or papyrus, on which descriptions of housing available had been written.

The man behind the desk might have been a brother, or at least a first cousin, to Suleiman Abaza. "Good day, Bwana," he said politely, rising to his feet and performing a *salaam*.

"Good day to you too, my good fellow," Tajiri boomed cheerfully. He was not Amhari, like most of the people of the original kingdom of Palambo. The housing agent thought this potential customer looked more like a Hutu, with his nearly black skin, broad blunt features, and wooly hair.

"Sayyid Dawud, is it?" the chubby visitor asked, reading Abbas' name from a plate on the desk.

"Abbas Dawud, at your service," he said, offering a hand. Tajiri touched fingertips with him, the Palamban equivalent of a firm handclasp in the Dominion.

"I am Tajiri of Dikka," he said. "I have just arrived in Namei to set up a branch office of the trading firm belonging to my father, Muanaume of Dikka. I will eventually of course need to acquire warehouse facilities, and a large enough house for my wife and four children. But for now I need someplace small where I can live and work while I am building trade contacts."

Dawud's eyes widened slightly. The commission due to him should he broker the sale of all this real estate would be great indeed. The large sign out front seemed to have paid off. As a Dareg, he had not always found it easy doing business in Namei where nearly everyone was Amhari. If he was able to please this Tajiri by swiftly finding him a temporary home, perhaps the rest of that business might fall to him as well.

"Would an apartment do for you?" Dawud asked, coming out from behind the desk and gesturing toward the wall of real estate listings. "There are several buildings offering vacancies, especially in the outermost ring of Namei, and they are conveniently located near the port facilities." Tajiri squinted at some of the notices on the wall. Most apartments had only two rooms, and of course toilet facilities would be in the back yard – maybe down several flights of stairs. Flush toilets had not, for the most part, yet come to Palambo.

"I'd really prefer a small house or cottage," he said. "Something with a bit of a yard where I could stable my horse. I'll be needing to ride him frequently on my business calls, as we intend to do business all the way from here to Zambei. And it should have at least three rooms and some cooking facilities. I plan to hire a girl to… look after me while I'm here." He grinned at the Dareg in a way that left little doubt that the "girl" would be expected to do more than cook and clean. After all, he was a healthy young man a long way away from his wife.

Abbas did not particularly approve. He was a widower, his children all grown up and far away, and he had led a celibate life for years. But on the other hand, who was he to pass judgment on another? He scanned the wall, then saw the notice he was looking for. The cottage had belonged to a widow, and it was too small for any of her children to live in with their families. Now that she had died, they wanted the place sold so that they could divide up their little inheritance.

"There's this place on the fourth circle," he said, handing the notice over to his would-be client. "It's not the best neighborhood, of course, but not a bad one. I'm afraid the garden's not much. A bit overgrown, and the buildings on either side shade it. I doubt you could grow food there, for instance, but your horse could have a cool place to rest when you're not riding it. What do you think?"

It sounded to Leila a lot like the property she, Kathal, and Nimble had shared while she was living as Rosa Estares and working as an employee of the Count of Oester's collections curator. It had better not be as ruinous and overgrown as *that* place, or he could forget about it. "Is that the only thing you have?" Tajiri asked with a slight tone of disappointment.

"I'm afraid so," Abbas replied. "Have you been out and about in the city much yet?"

The trader shook his head. "Just got here, and you were my first stop. I've never been to this city before."

"You'll find, I'm afraid," the housing agent said, "that houses with gardens around them much below the top two or three levels are very hard to come by. And they are usually very grand, and very expensive. Land within the protection of Namei's walls is at a premium."

"Hmm," Tajiri said. "And that price of two hundred-fifty asand is firm?"

Anxious to preserve his commission, Abbas nodded. "The widow paid more than that for it when she bought it after her husband died. As she had only daughters and no other male relatives, the laws permitted her to keep the proceeds of his estate and live on her own. Now the daughters are eager to realize what remains of their mother's estate."

"Very well, beggars can't be choosers I suppose," Tajiri said with a wry grin. "But I must see the place first before I'll buy it."

"No problem," Abbas said, "I'll just lock the office and we can go up there." This was the first client he'd had all day, and it was now well into the afternoon.

"You have a horse?" Tajiri asked, concerned. The fourth circle would be quite a hike, uphill all the way.

"I'll just hail a *ritzha*," the housing agent said as he locked up his shop, after hanging a sign in the window stating that he would shortly return. Since arriving in town Leila had noticed a few conveyances that looked sort of like sulkies, little two-wheeled carts with a single seat in them. In the Dominion they'd have been pulled by horses, but here in Palambo they were pulled by young men. Strong ones, to tow that weight up and down the hills of Namei. The word was not Kiswa, and she suspected it had its origins east of the Killtops.

"Very well," Tajiri said. He stood patiently until Abbas had attracted the attention of an unoccupied *ritzha* operator, then mounted his horse. "Lead the way," he said with smile, and they set off. The boy pulling Abbas along was moving at a trot, but Wapesi was forced to go at a walk to follow him without overtaking him.

They wound their way around and up the tiers of the city, and at the fourth tier (with the outermost ring being the first) they turned right instead of left as Usiku and Imbaso had gone when climbing to his family's home. The buildings of this ring were mostly three to four storeys, packed tight side by side. Some of them might have a little bit of yard in the back, but nothing reachable by a horse. What Abbas had said was true.

Suddenly Abbas directed the *ritzha* driver to halt, and they were there. Sandwiched in between two three-storey buildings of stone or whitewashed brick was an expanse of ground no more than 25 feet wide. It had a low masonry wall across the front with a gap in the center, and a walk of crushed stone leading to a single-story cottage built of timbers cut from some rot-resistant tropical hardwood – possibly even bloodwood. From the degree of weathering, the house was far older than the places on either side. Leila wondered why some enterprising developer had not just bought the place and torn it down, to erect an apartment building on the site.

The roof was made of shakes of the same wood, and looked to have been replaced within the last few years. They were a much darker color than the rest of the house, which didn't appear ever to have been painted. The house was longer than it was wide, allowing a three-foot pathway down either side to the back yard.

There was a sort of lean-to shed in the back yard, butted up against the building behind it at the rear and partially open at the front. That would certainly provide Wapesi with some shelter from the torrential rains they got here, Leila thought. The garden was full of lush tropical vegetation, palms and ferns and orchids all over the place, so that there was scarcely room for Tajiri and Abbas to move about in it. A covered porch around six feet deep ran across the rear of the cottage, a nice feature as it looked out on the garden.

Abbas let them in through the back door with his key. "This is a very unusual house for Namei, you must have realized by now," he said. "Probably one of the oldest houses still standing in this part of the city. When Namei was founded more than a thousand years ago they built the outer walls first, of course. Then they began building from the top down, or so I've read. The space in between has been filled in gradually over the centuries."

Leila had been camping out for most of the time that she'd spent in Palambo, and had not had much opportunity to learn what constituted standard Palamban housing. She suspected there were many villages in the country where people were still living in mud huts thatched with palm fronds and cooking over an open fire in the center of the living area; but Namei clearly qualified as high civilization.

Just inside the back door, with wide windows giving out onto the porch, was a kitchen of sorts. It had a counter with a large sink set in it and a water pump that let you bring up reasonably cold water from a well. There was also a small cast iron wood stove, a supply of wood, and a cabinet with some dishes, brass utensils, and a couple of cast iron pots. All of it looked ancient and well-worn, so it was not surprising the heirs had left it behind.

A door in the kitchen led to a hallway with a small bedroom on one side, while an even smaller bedroom shared the space on the other side with a tiny bathroom. There was a small bathtub one could fill using buckets from the kitchen, and a privy stool. Leila had never seen one like this before, and wasn't sure whether Tajiri would have been likely to have seen one in Dikka, either. There were some things it was hard to learn from books!

Abbas spotted Tajiri's glance, and said "The night soil collectors will come and empty your cesspit every fortnight. They sell the products, of course, big demand for such things in the manufacturing that goes on further down the river. They also charge for their services, but it's only a few coppers."

"Excellent," was all Tajiri said in reply. Leila wondered how bad the smell was going to get, in this climate, toward the end of that fortnight. At least the bathroom had a door, and the toilet had a tight lid. And there was a bucket of ashes set on the floor nearby.

Well, if things went as she planned, she would not be living here that much in any case. The entire front of the house was given over to an airy living room, like the kitchen with large, glassless windows that could be covered by heavy wooden shutters. By opening the kitchen door and the windows front and rear, one might even get a breeze coming through that would make it bearable. After spending the winter in Parat Leila had thought she would enjoy a trip to warmer climes; but this was pushing it a bit too far.

Tajiri pulled out Leila's pocket watch, which caused the housing agent's eyebrows to go up. The enormous horse, clearly one of the Gaspari breed, had already impressed him. He was now nearly ready to expect this visitor from Dikka (the seaport on the Western Ocean near the Pana's mouth) to pull the two hundred-fifty asand out of a back pocket.

"The Bank of Palambo branch here should still be open, I think?" Tajiri asked.

"Yes, for another hour I believe," Abbas replied.

"Please tell me where it is, and I will go there and cash a bank draft while you return to your office and prepare the paperwork," the customer said – suddenly all business.

Abbas considered for a moment. "I have another idea. Directions to the bank branch would be complicated. Why don't you tie up your horse in the back yard here, safe from any who might see him, and have the *ritzha* boy take you to the bank, then back to my office. After we sign the paperwork, he can carry you back here."

"But what about you?" Tajiri asked, solicitous of the older man's health.

"Ah, it's all downhill!" Abbas declared. "I ordinarily walk two miles every day between home and work, in any case. It's what keeps me young and vigorous!"

The trader grinned at him. "Very well then," he said. "You go ahead and start walking and I will take the *ritzha* in just a moment and return to your office with the gold."

After tipping the *ritzha* boy with a few coppers to assure that he would wait, Tajiri led Wapesi to the rear garden and left him there. He removed Leila's pack, which contained everything she owned on this part of the continent, and tucked it into a tool shed that was incorporated into the lean-to. Briefly, Leila considered digging the gold out of her existing stash. She had more than the two hundred-fifty asand needed. But that would take time she didn't have to spare right now. Better to "cash a bank draft" as she had done in Halath, then remove the gold she was currently carrying at her leisure and use it to pay for daily living expenses.

Shortly Tajiri returned to the *ritzha* and the boy received an additional tip as he waited outside the Namei branch of the Bank of Palambo. A richly dressed, middle-aged Amhari who matched the description of a hundred men Leila had seen in the streets of Namei today successfully cashed a bank draft in the amount of two hundred-fifty asand, and thereafter the trader Tajiri transferred those funds to Abbas and was given the keys to the fourth-circle house along with paperwork declaring that he was now the owner of said property with all rights and responsibilities thereto. An official deed would eventually be prepared, and Tajiri should be able to pick it up at Abbas' office in around four weeks' time.

Tajiri had asked the *ritzha* boy to wait yet again, and they now ran several errands in town before returning to the house. The conveyance had a rack at the back for luggage or parcels, and by the time the boy had been paid off (handsomely, with two full gold asand in addition to the coppers that had come his way during the course of the afternoon) that rack was full – and Leila felt he had earned every copper. It was common usage to refer to the people who pulled the *ritzhas* as "boys," but this one was a burly young man who looked to be at least six years older than she was.

She got him to carry the bale of hay around to the back of the house, where Wapesi was standing patiently on guard. Also several sacks of sorghum, the grain that was commonly fed to working horses in Palambo. Aside from that there was a collection of non-perishable groceries for the kitchen, which Tajiri carried inside himself after sending the *ritzha* away.

There was no icebox in the kitchen, nor were ice deliveries possible in this tropical land where the nearest snowy mountains might be hundreds of miles away. Leila set her sacks on the counter, then hurried out to minister to poor, long-suffering Wapesi.

She got him unsaddled and unclipped the reins from his halter, curried him and made sure that there was clean water in the wooden trough. Clearly other occupants of this home in times past, if not necessarily the late widow, had kept a horse or two on the property. With daily rain showers (and another now looked to be on the way) at this season, the trough was brimming.

Patting him affectionately after breaking open the bale of hay, Leila returned to the house. She'd assumed the appearance of Usiku, in case anyone should spy her. She planned to become the "girl" that Tajiri had hired to "do" for him in his temporary home. Anyone inquiring would learn that her master was out at this or that business meeting. She just hoped they wouldn't wonder why he didn't take his horse on these trips.

Ugh, it was so unbearably hot and sticky! The shutters in the kitchen closed, Leila stripped to her underwear and pumped some water into the kitchen sink. A pity they couldn't have put a pump in the bathroom as well, but the sink was nearly big enough for a person her size to climb into. She gave herself a sponge bath and pumped water over her head, soaking her hair and providing at least temporary relief.

During Tajiri's expeditions after buying the cottage one of his stops had been at a food stand, where he'd devoured a plate of mixed vegetables and cooked grains with little bits of some unidentifiable meat in it. He'd bought a little extra for the *ritzha* boy, while he was at it. Now Leila was fed and reasonably clean, it was time at last for her to confer with her god.

Chapter 22

The house had come furnished, to some extent. The furnishings were sparse, and probably there might once have been some family heirloom pieces that had gone to one or another of the widow's daughters. But there was a more-or-less intact rattan settee in the living room and in front of it, a low table consisting of a heavy slab of dark hardwood sitting on two squared-off stone pedestals.

In the larger bedroom a bed had been left behind, a framework of what looked like bamboo supporting a sturdy woven mat with a thin quilt laid across it. Leila had emptied her pack out onto it, pawing through her mismatched collection of clothing for something more comfortable to wear. She'd decided on a long, flowing skirt she'd acquired in Halath and the undershirt she'd had with her when she began her journey in Parat. She opened up the shutters in the kitchen and closed the ones in the living room, anxious that no prying eyes might see what happened next.

Leila set the idol of Betsalel on the table, a surge of love flowing up in her as she beheld it. If you had casually asked her whether she loved Tevo or her god more, she would have chosen Tevo in a heartbeat; but the dark god had a powerful hold on her. It was almost as if he were the father she had never known.

"Betsalel, come to me!" she said, leaning forward on the rattan (which could really have used some cushions). "We need to talk!" There was no immediate response, but in less than a full minute Leila saw the tiny figure move and begin to grow. In moments the dark god stood before her, as yet only a few feet tall. He smiled at her, all three red, glowing eyes open, and stepped down off the table. Then he grew to the six-foot height they both found comfortable.

Leila rose to meet him, and they embraced. Then the dark god stepped back a little and looked around at the small, shuttered, room. "I thought you were going to call me more often," he said with a slight suggestion of reproach, then added "Where are we?"

The lack of omniscience that seemed to be a basic feature of her world's gods still struck Leila as strange. What little religious

120

training she'd had as a child had led her to expect them to be all-knowing and all-powerful, not magical but flawed beings whose divinity was only as potent as their worshipers could provide. But she had never actually met any gods before Betsalel had claimed her as his own.

"We're in Namei!" she said with a grin. "I guess this is Shadow Manor South, now. I just bought it!"

His red eyes sparkled in the dim light. "With money you got through donations to my reborn church in Palambo, I suppose?"

"Something like that," she replied casually. Betsalel knew full well that Leila was an inveterate thief, and he seemed to consider it part of her charm.

Leila flopped back down on the rattan settee. Even this late in the afternoon, with evening coming on, the heat was enervating. Betsalel looked around at the otherwise unfurnished room and materialized a small throne, so that he could also sit while they talked. It appeared to be carved out of bloodwood, in the Palamban style.

"Tell me of your journey," he said.

"I had been going to travel here as an elderly trader's agent," she replied. "But I discovered that one of my fellow travelers, a young man I met on the ship coming over from Jena, was the son of the arch-priest at your temple here in Namei. I figured that his father must be at the heart of whatever it was that brought the djinn into being, and that I could get closer to him if I were more like who I really am. So I became Usiku, an Amhari girl whose family had migrated to the desert near Halath."

Betsalel looked troubled. "You seduced this young man, then?" he asked with a hint of asperity. As a god he was nowhere near as familiar with human sexuality as his brother Dionos was; but he had interacted with human beings for thousands of years. He knew what sex was. Leila immediately understood. He loved Tevo, as he loved her, and he knew that Tevo would be greatly saddened to learn of such a thing.

"Not at all," she assured him. "Usiku is young, barely sixteen, and Imbaso is twenty-one. Five years makes a difference at that age, and I have been encouraging him to think of her as a younger sister in need of protection." She did not mention that she knew Imbaso longed for her in a way that was anything but brotherly. Nor did she say that she had been having some similar thoughts toward him. It had been a long time, and Tevo was so far away!

It was no use. As Betsalel was a part of her, so he knew her innermost heart as she did his. "I hope you will not abuse this relationship," he said softly. "He is a good man?" Leila dropped her gaze, ashamed of her feelings.

"Very sweet, very kind," she said. "I do not believe that he has any part in his father's wickedness, but he is surely about to be caught up in it. And I am partly to blame for that."

The god just looked at her, waiting for her to explain. Their bond was complex and hard to explain, but it was nothing like telepathy. "In order that Usiku might be able to penetrate the mysteries of the cult that has spawned the daemon, she needed a compelling reason to come to Namei seeking the dark god. When I told Imbaso of my plan to join the Black Claw in order to wreak revenge on Usiku's imaginary enemies, he vowed to join with me and fight at my side." She looked down again, tormented by her own perfidy.

"He is this arch-priest's only son?" Betsalel asked, and she looked up.

"Yes, and he had been raised when he was younger with the intention that he too would join the priesthood. I think that maybe the arch-priest had become discouraged, about to give up on the god he had imagined. But then something happened. Imbaso was called back from studying in the Dominion, and the message didn't say why."

"Leila, you need not take all the blame," the dark god said. "I am sure this Imbaso's father has called him home so that he can become immersed in the cult of the newly-awakened djinn. Had you not been there to encourage it, he would have been brought in all the same." She sat up straight, no longer slumping, and smiled at him.

"You're right," she said. "I just wish I didn't have to be so deceptive… Usiku is close to me in appearance" – at that, she assumed the younger girl's guise – "But her back story is complete and utter bullshit. I think Imbaso only bought it because he's in love with her, even though he knows he shouldn't feel that way. It's a mess," she sighed, and sank back down.

Betsalel gazed at her. He didn't know what to tell her. Lies and deception were Leila's strong suit, the qualities that had enabled her to rescue him from oblivion. And he treasured that characteristic of hers, that she felt remorse for deceiving kind people who only meant her well – rather than despising them as brainless marks, the way many grifters and con artists came to feel about those they tricked. But he knew that same compassion caused her pain. Pain she was undergoing on his behalf. Had the situation with the djinn not been so dire, he had better never have called on her aid.

Leila perked up again. Her saving grace was that she could shake off whatever was bothering her and knuckle down to the task at hand, when needed. "So anyhow, I visited the temple today. I saw Imbaso's aunt there, praying to an empty altar for you to give back her child. I think if you could manage to do that, she might be the kernel of a new church for you here."

"What became of the child, and when?" the god asked.

"According to Imbaso's mother, the baby was taken by his uncle – that would be Imbaso's father, the arch-priest – to be consecrated to the dark god. Is that something you ever required or requested?"

He shook his head. "I never asked for worship from any until they had reached the age of reason," he said. "This is part of the new rituals established by the Palamban church after Lucia's coup had weakened me, I fear."

"Supposedly the dark god 'took' the baby during the ritual," Leila said. "It wasn't explained if the boy was killed, or taken away, but Imbaso's mother said there was no body, nothing for the child's mother to bury. The poor woman spends every day at the temple just praying for his return, and it's been two months. But I thought it odd that there was no idol in the sanctuary. It seems as if the dark cult, the ones who have perverted your worship until you could no longer communicate with them, have moved the idols – or at least the one here in Namei – to some secret location."

"That sounds likely," Betsalel said thoughtfully. "So you will find out where they have taken it?"

"That's my plan for this evening," Leila said as casually as if she were planning a night out on the town. "I hope to meet Imbaso and his father at the temple and convince them to let me join the secret ceremonies. I'm guessing they're in the basement. Should I bring your idol with me? I could call you up and you and this djinn could have it out..."

The god stiffened. "I don't think the time is right for that, Leila. Overall, thanks to your efforts and Tevo's in the Dominion, I am probably stronger than this djinn. But in the heart of his sanctuary, surrounded by an unknown number of his worshipers and with only you on my side, I fear he might defeat me. And it would surely bring ruin on you. We must wait until a new core of my true worshipers can arise in Palambo, before we can make our move against the djinn."

Leila sighed. She was hot and sticky and uncomfortable, she felt like a faithless whore manipulating Imbaso, and she missed Tevo terribly. But it looked like she was going to be in this for the long run. "Is there anything you can do," she asked casually, "to make this place a bit less of a hell-hole?" She gestured around at the hot, thick air and the flying insects swarming around in it. A lot of them had come in through the kitchen windows when she'd had the shutters open earlier.

Betsalel smiled and rose to his feet. The carved bloodwood throne vanished as he stood. He went throughout the house from window to window, gesturing with his arms. The sacred signs of the dark god appeared, tiny and nearly invisible, around the frame of each one. And the insects flying around fell dead. "No insect or other intruder will come into the house now," he promised her. None may pass the doors either, save by your leave."

Leila stood and clapped her hands in joy. "*Thank* you, master!" she cried. "Can you do anything about the heat?"

He looked around. "This is not comfortable for you?" he asked, as in puzzlement. When he saw the look she gave him he explained, "I appear to be more or less human, and my soul is in many ways as human as yours; but this body in which I take shape is not constructed as are mortal human bodies. I do not sense heat and cold as you do."

She smiled at him. "All right. Could you make it cooler, please? I'll tell you when it's comfortable." The Shadow God spread his arms wide, and the temperature of the interior of the cottage began to fall. "And take some of the moisture out of the air, too?" Leila suggested. When the air inside the cottage (all of its rooms at once) had reached the temperature and humidity one might expect to find in Parat on a morning in spring, she declared "Perfect! Will it stay like that?"

"The house has become an envelope of protection for you," Betsalel assured her. "You can open the windows and doors if you like, but nothing you do not wish inside can come in. And the air in here will remain at this temperature and humidity. Can I do anything else for you?" Leila looked around. The place was certainly sparsely furnished. And there was that issue of the plumbing…

Chapter 23

Imbaso had unpacked his bags, moving back into the room he'd last lived in at the age of eighteen. He felt he was no longer the same person he'd been then. But was he ready to become a minion of the Shadow God? He'd never really understood religion or the people for whom it was important, his own father included. And Usiku's naïve belief that Betsalel would grant her revenge on her enemies left him wondering. If she was right, the world was a very different place from what he'd imagined it to be these past few years.

Though their house could have accommodated twenty residents with ease, it was now occupied only by his parents, himself, and his aunt Uzuri. They had a cook and housekeeper who came in days, and after she had served them supper this evening and cleaned up after it, she would return to her own home far down in the city's third circle.

The place felt cavernous to him, not the childhood home he recalled. Though in truth, there had been few more people living there then than there were now. The family had dwindled over the generations. This evening Aunt Uzuri had returned from the temple only to retreat to her rooms, the marks of grief plain on her face.

Imbaso and his mother were sitting together in the house's main living area talking quietly when his father Mauaji returned. He was dressed in ordinary clothing, rich and respectable-looking, not the black robes of a priest of Betsalel. His face lit up with joy at the sight of his son, returned at last after three years away, and he embraced him.

"I am so glad that you are safely returned!" Mauaji exclaimed, then held his son at arm's length. The boy had become a man, nearly two inches taller than his father though not yet so robust. He took after his mother, that way. "It's good to be home, Bapa," Imbaso said – using the term of affection by which he'd called his father when he was a child.

Mauaji had always been reserved, not the kind of father who rolled around on the floor or played silly games with his children. There had been a younger sister, but she had died before reaching the age of five. Deadly fevers were a fact of life in Namei, and Mauaji's prayers to the Shadow God to spare his daughter had gone unanswered.

The little family gathered together, sitting around the room on enormous cushions, until the housekeeper announced that supper was served. "Memsahib Uzuri is not feeling well and is taking her meal in her rooms," the woman explained as the rest of them were seated. Uzuri had not eaten with them since her child had vanished.

The meal was simple but delicious, familiar comfort food that Imbaso had missed more than he'd realized during his years in the Dominion. The cold climate there, especially in Wena (high up in the Antels) led to a preponderance of heavy, rich foods smothered in gravy and lacking in spice. He'd gotten used to it, but this was so much better!

After the meal they rose, and Mauaji took his son by the arm. "Excuse us, wife," he said coolly. "Imbaso and I have things to discuss." They went down the hall to the room that the head of the house had designated his private study. It was there that he kept his personal mementoes, entertained his male friends, and sometimes conducted church business outside of the usual hours.

Mauaji closed the heavy bloodwood door behind them, and took a seat. Imbaso felt tension rise as he sat opposite his father, studying his face in the dim lamplight as he tried to guess what was coming. "Imbaso," the man began, his voice warm and deep and serious, "you are probably wondering why I have called you back home before you had completed your schooling. I know that you were intending to graduate."

"Yes," Imbaso replied with a nod, "but I'm glad to be home! I hadn't realized how much I truly missed this place."

Mauaji smiled slightly, then continued. "I regret that your education has been cut short, but a new opportunity has been opened for us. I have been remiss in providing you with an education of another sort, and now I must make up for lost time."

"Betsalel?" Imbaso asked, half hoping he was wrong.

His father gave a brief nod, then shook his head and said, "Betsalel... has abandoned us. Or perhaps, he has been transformed and taken a new name. We of the temple's secret congregation now worship Kivuli, as he has been revealed to us by manifesting in his true form within the inner sanctum."

"Kivuli? I…"

"Never heard of him? Nor had I, or any of the priests and acolytes within the temple's inner mysteries. You, son, were never inducted as an initiate. After my prayers to save the life of your sister went unanswered I lost faith, and I decided to break the chain. You would become a man of the world, a man who could rise high in the kingdom, with the finest education I could buy for you. But the temple was my life. Though I was halfway convinced we were praying to empty air, I went on with the secret rites, the obeisances, the supplications."

"Secret rites, Father?"

"Only those inducted as initiates and taking the oath were permitted to learn of what we did in the inner sanctum," Mauaji explained. "I never took you into the secret, because I did not intend for you to become a priest. Have you never thought it odd that there is no idol in the main sanctuary at the Temple of Betsalel?"

Imbaso pondered for a moment. As he had told Usiku, he was truly not a religious man. "It never occurred to me to wonder," he admitted. "All that church stuff I did as a kid, it was just a game to me. Like make-believe. I didn't expect the gods to be real. I went into a couple of the other temples, Belantos' once when I was learning to fight with swords and to Andros' temple a few times after I discovered girls. But even though I prayed, I didn't entirely believe."

"Many years ago," Mauaji explained, "perhaps in the time of my great-grandfather's great-grandfather, a change came over the church of Betsalel as it existed in Palambo. I believe this was in the time when Betsalel's worship was outlawed in the Gaspari Dominion, and all of his worshipers slaughtered or forced to recant their beliefs. A great prophet arose in the desert, who called himself Rasulbiyi. Some say he was of the Daregs, others that he was Amhari like the people of Palambo. Still others say he was a tall white man with a long red beard. But he was a worshiper of Betsalel, and the Shadow God had granted him a vision."

Imbaso just stared. For generations his family had been involved in the worship of Betsalel, and all this time the temple was just a façade, a lie? The concept was staggering.

"Rasulbiyi came out of the desert with sacred clay tablets, on which were inscribed the Secret Scriptures that had been dictated to him by the god. Betsalel had given him the power to sway men's minds, and he began to change the church from within. Gradually, in temple after temple, the idols were removed to hidden locations where they were guarded by the inner circle, following the forms of worship as laid out in the Secret Scriptures."

"And the Makucha Nyeusi?" Imbaso asked, horrified realization dawning. "Not just a myth to scare children with?"

"Quite real," his father answered calmly. "I was never a member, as I lacked the physical aptitude. But a chapter exists within our own temple here. You have met Kifozi, I believe?" His son nodded. "Our Black Claw master. It is he who trains the new recruits."

The man had been among the friends Imbaso's father entertained at their home on some occasions. He was lean and capable-looking, but far from grim enough to be a master assassin. If anything, he'd seemed amiable. "And what of the Secret Scriptures?" Imbaso asked.

"Those you will read after you have taken the oath and become a novice. You are old for it, but we must make up for lost time. With the power of Kivuli, you are destined for great things."

Imbaso remained silent for a time, pondering what Father had told him. He'd always known that his family expected a lot of him – that was why he had been sent to the university in Wena at fabulous expense. But was his path to greatness to be delineated in blood?

"I met a girl on the way here from Halath," he said at last.

"Your mother mentioned her. A religious pilgrim?"

"Her family were slaughtered by the Ran of her district," Imbaso explained. "She has pledged herself whole-heartedly to

Betsalel, and wants to join the Makucha Nyeusi so that she can become an assassin and seek her vengeance. Are we going to the temple tonight?"

Mauaji nodded. "I was planning to bring you tonight for the ceremony inducting you as a novice," he said. No question of whether this was what his son wanted in life. "The god demanded that we call him by his true name of Kivuli, and this has caused some controversy among the priesthood. They question why this information was not made known to Rasulbiyi. But the reality of the god who has come to us cannot be denied. Since that night two months ago when he appeared at last, he has come to our call each time. And he tells us that he has begun manifesting in the other idols hidden within temples of Betsalel around the kingdom. Yet this information cannot yet be made known to the public. For now, you will refer to the god as Betsalel in public. But do not speak that name in the inner sanctum!"

Feeling as if he were stepping off a cliff into a bottomless black abyss, Imbaso said "Very well. I will go with you to the temple and take the vows, provided that you will also bring Usiku into the fold. She is already quite skilled with blades, and I think she will make a good assassin. And I want to train for the Makucha Nyeusi, too. I have told her that I will make her fight mine, and help her to kill her enemies."

His son's involvement with a girl Mauaji knew nothing about did not please him. But Imbaso's willingness, yea apparent eagerness to become a part of the dark god's reborn worship, and all the power that embraced, filled him with pleasure and he brushed the other concern aside. If the girl proved worthy, let her join in the slaughter to come.

Chapter 24

As darkness fell outside, Usiku was kneeling in the sanctuary of the temple of Betsalel. She had walked there, a considerable uphill hike from her new house on the city's fourth circle. But she was young and fit, and the air had cooled enough to make exercise bearable. After the improvements her god had made to Shadow Manor South, Leila had felt most reluctant to leave home. The place was an oasis of comfort in a sea of humid, insect-infested, unbearable heat.

She was dressed in something that was close to her burglar garb from her years in the Night Guild, loose-fitting lightweight garments gathered tight at wrist and ankle. These had no secret pockets though, nor a hood. And rather than dark gray, they were jet black. They were all part of her illusion, of course. Leila hadn't thought to ask Betsalel whether she need fear that the djinn could penetrate the powers he had granted her. He had warned her once that the priests of Lucia had that ability, but as the djinn was only a corrupted offshoot of Betsalel she hoped she would be safe. If she was proved wrong, she had her daggers and her feet.

Getting up again after a couple of minutes spent murmuring nonsense to the empty altar, Leila took a seat on a bench in the front row. Other worshipers were coming in, though not many. Likely none except those involved in the inner mysteries truly believed in the Shadow God as anything beyond an idea, here in Palambo where he had been unable to manifest in generations.

There was a bit of a stir at the back, and Usiku turned to see Imbaso coming in, also dressed in black, accompanied by a gray-haired, imposing man wearing a black priest robe. That must be his father! The resemblance was clear, though the arch-priest was shorter and broader than his son. She rose to her feet in a swift motion, and came to meet them.

Mauaji was somewhat taken aback as the girl materialized in front of them. Such ferocity in the glittering black eyes, and such an odd costume for a young Amhari woman. She looked more like a Dareg bandit, except they generally wore white. She dropped to one knee and bowed her head to him, and he turned to his son.

"Father, this is the girl of whom I spoke," Imbaso said. "Usiku, my father Mauaji – arch-priest of Betsalel's temple in Namei."

"Rise, girl," Mauaji said, discomfited. She was a tiny thing, scarcely above five feet in height. But she fairly quivered with suppressed energy. "You wish to become an initiate of Betsalel, is that right?" he asked sternly.

"That is my heartfelt desire," she replied. Her dark eyes bored into his own. "I wish to devote myself completely to the dark god, and become one of his servants." Her sincerity was unmistakable. The dark one's worship tended to draw men disproportionately to women, but what priestesses there were often surpassed their male counterparts in bloodthirstiness.

"Very well," Mauaji said solemnly. "Come with us." He led the way to the back of the sanctuary, and opened the door Leila had seen there earlier with his key.

The door led to a small anteroom, and was flanked by two figures clad all in black. Their garb was not that dissimilar from what Leila's imagination had conjured up, except that these two were also hooded – and were armed with scimitars. They nodded to the arch-priest, unspeaking, and he led his two charges down a flight of stairs to the lower level Leila had guessed must exist below the temple proper.

They came into a room decorated with the signs of Betsalel, though not the same signs Leila and Tevo had used to guard their home in Parat from intrusion. "We are here to swear in two new novices," Mauaji told his subordinates. "My son Imbaso you know. This girl is Usiku of Halath. Please prepare the chamber."

A number of smaller rooms led off of the one they were standing in, and two of the acolytes on duty hastened to bring vestments from where they were stored and light holy candles in the one that was designated for the initiation of newcomers. The nature of their worship required the utmost secrecy, and those who would join the cult must swear blindly never to reveal anything that was seen or done here, or anything they learned in the course of their indoctrination into the mysteries.

Another corridor led away to where double doors closed off the inner sanctum; but these two would not be allowed there until they'd taken their final vows. Before long Imbaso and Usiku were ushered into the room. Mauaji now stood within, in front of a table on which black candles burned with a red flame, and several grisly objects sat. He was still in his black arch-priest's robes, but was now also wearing a sort of crown that appeared to have been made from the skull of a leopard. Around his neck, hanging down from his shoulders on either side, was a necklace of what looked very much like the skulls of human babies.

Leila schooled Usiku's illusionary appearance to maintain an expression of impassiveness, tempered with a hint of eagerness for the ritual to come. Inside that façade, she was writhing with revulsion. Every made-up tale of terror Lucia had spread through her pawn the emperor Fernand had, it seemed, been eagerly taken up and put into practice by Betsalel's former worshipers in Palambo.

"Remove your clothing," Mauaji said coldly, gesturing to chairs on either side of the room that had been placed there to receive the cast-off garments. Leila had to think carefully, to appear to strip off her illusory clothes without actually removing her real garments. Considering the temperature outside, she had opted to go out wearing her underwear and real boots "beneath" Usiku's black costume.

Usiku was revealed to be a burnished dark brown all over, slim and muscular of build but with dark-tipped breasts a little larger than you might expect for a girl her size – essentially she was Leila with a good tan. Both Mauaji and Imbaso were careful to let their eyes slide past her without any apparent reaction, though this was a tough task for the younger man. He had been dreaming of that body for weeks, and there it was, every bit as luscious and desirable as in his imagination, at scarcely arm's length! He could reach out and... Stop it!

For her part, Usiku remained standing stiffly looking straight ahead while Leila ogled the young man at her left side. Considerably taller than Tevo, Imbaso's build was similarly slim.

His smooth, glistening skin the color of dark-roasted kaf overlaid firm, rippling muscles. Mmm, and his manhood was of a considerable size and growing larger... Stop it!

Imbaso's embarrassment was so acute that he was spared standing at attention before his father in this solemn religious ceremony with his penis standing similarly at attention. Now, Mauaji spoke. "Imbaso and Usiku, you are here to make the most important decision of your lives. If you agree to take this vow, you can never break it. The penalty for doing so is death. Do you acknowledge this?"

"I do," both said in unison.

The arch-priest turned to the table behind him and picked up a bowl of a red substance, in which a paint brush had been dipped. First with his son, then with the girl, he painted the signs of Betsalel on their bodies. Leila detected no mystic frisson, and guessed that this ritual did not actually have any supernatural support. As she understood it, the gods and daemons and wandering souls that inhabited the plane of the spiritual could not affect things on the material plane unless they took material form. But then, their powers were far beyond human.

Replacing the bowl on the table, Mauaji took up another bowl containing an off-white powder, and sprinkled it onto the two naked inductees. It clung to the paint (Leila had decided it was paint, and not blood, from its consistency) where it was still wet. Then he set that bowl back into its place, and addressed them both.

"Our dark god, whose true name is Kivuli, the Death Who Comes in the Night, requires our service in all things. This name and only this name will be spoken while you are in his presence, and you will do his bidding always. In return for your loyal and correct worship, he may grant you certain favors. But requests for favors from the god will be relayed only through his priesthood, according to our hierarchy. You will not speak his name elsewhere, except in converse with one who is an initiate of our mysteries. Do you so vow?"

Father already broke that one, Imbaso thought, but he murmured "I so vow," as Usiku did the same.

134

The arch-priest went on, "The correct forms of Kivuli's worship have been revealed to us by the Secret Scriptures delivered by the prophet Rasulbiyi, and by Kivuli now that he has made himself known to us. Each of you will study these, and you will be tested on them. When you have mastered these, you will be inducted as acolytes in our order, and will be permitted to participate in our rituals – in which the god will come among us. You will not reveal any of this to anyone outside our mysteries, or the Death Who Comes in the Night will surely come to you, as it will to any who displease our master. Do you so vow?"

"I so vow," both of them said again. The paint was drying on Leila's bare skin where it was exposed, itching, and her underwear would probably have to be thrown away after this. It was good to know, though, that it would be awhile before she would be called upon to participate in any of this Kivuli's grisly "rituals." Maybe she could be so intentionally obtuse when quizzed on her catechism that she could flunk that part of the procedure until after she'd figured out a way to accomplish her mission.

Finally, Mauaji took up a wickedly sharp-looking ceremonial dagger. "Hold out your left hand," he commanded Imbaso and his son held it up, palm down, without flinching. The arch-priest gripped the hand in his own left and turned it palm up, muttering words in a language that was not Kiswa, and brought the point of the knife down to cut the flesh – just enough to draw blood, not enough to damage ligaments or tendons. He made one cut around an inch long side to side, then a much shorter cut crosswise in the exact center of the line. Blood welled up, and he commanded, "Press that hand to your forehead, and give me the other."

The arch-priest repeated the ritual on his son's right palm, and told him to press that one to his heart. As Usiku continued to stand straight staring ahead, Leila was watching in horrified fascination. Poor Imbaso, to have been born to such monstrous wrongness! She did note that Mauaji himself had fresh-looking scars from similar cuts in both of his own palms. This ritual had probably only been added since the djinn had come on the scene, and he'd required it of all his worshipers. Either that or the arch-priest had dreamed it up on his own and insisted on setting an example. It was certainly a way for members of the cult to recognize one another.

As Imbaso stood there with his bloody left palm pressed to his forehead and the bloody right one over his heart, Mauaji said "Repeat after me: 'I, Imbaso, do swear to serve Kivuli in all things, and to reveal nothing that is Kivuli's to anyone who has not also made this vow." The young man repeated it, word for word, and his father said "Hold out your hands, now." He lifted a third bowl from the table and sprinkled some powder onto the blood-smeared palms. The bleeding immediately stopped.

Leila braced herself as it became her turn, tuning her illusion so that Usiku's palms appeared to be cut, and to bleed, while her own hands remained undamaged. No way was she going to do anything like that! Particularly, she did not want to place a hand marred by the dark djinn's blasphemous ritual over the heart wherein a piece of Betsalel, the true Shadow God, rested.

As for the vow, she spoke it fervently while denying it in her heart. If the djinn was manifest in this plane and had the power to strike her down, or to give his servant Mauaji the ability to discern her true nature and intentions, then the game was up. But nothing happened. Mauaji told them to gather their clothing and directed them to leave by a side door. No one had noticed that, during the ritual, Leila's clothing had temporarily vanished from the chair on which she had appeared to set it.

They found themselves in a chamber slightly larger than the last one, where masked and robed acolytes with cloths and ewers of water washed all signs of the ritual from their bodies before they were given towels to dry themselves off and told to get back into their clothing.

Imbaso was dumfounded to discover that the ritual cuts in his palms had already healed, leaving only scars such as those his father bore. Leila was equally surprised, and had to act fast to adjust the "bleeding cut" illusion to match those scars. She was now standing there in wet underwear, thankful that after maintaining the Usiku illusion for weeks she had gotten so adept at it.

The two young novices reported back to the central chamber, and were shown to the scriptorium. There they were welcome to come, at any time of the day or night, to study the Secret Scriptures. When they felt they had mastered them, they would arrange for a testing. And if they passed it, they could join in the worship of Kivuli in the inner sanctum. Oh, joy.

"What about the Makucha Nyeusi? Did Imbaso tell you I wish to apprentice as an assassin?" Usiku asked the arch-priest quietly. She had the feeling that even among the secret cult of Kivuli some practices were more secret than others.

Mauaji seemed a little annoyed, but resigned. "Yes, he did. And that he intends to join it with you." That earned Imbaso a glowing smile from Usiku that made his heart skip a beat.

"Apprentices are selected only from among our cult, of course," the arch-priest explained. "As you now both bear the scars, you are eligible to be considered for training. But you will have to impress our master, Kifozi, with your abilities before he will agree to accept you. It may surprise you to know that the training of Black Claw assassins takes place in broad daylight, at our gymnasium on the third circle, near the corner of Weaver Street. The sign on the door says only, 'Private Athletic Association,' and anyone arriving there without the signs of our cult is politely turned away. Report to Kifozi tomorrow morning no later than nine."

Chapter 25

In the morning Leila as Usiku donned similar garb to what she'd had on yesterday evening, after a marvelously comfortable night spent sleeping in her cool, dry, bedroom on its thick featherbed. Religious devotion had its perks, no doubt about it.

Last night she'd had to leave hurriedly before she started dripping unexplained water all over the floors in the temple of Betsalel's secret underground complex. Imbaso was expected to stay there and return home with his father, some hours hence; so he planned to spend the time studying the Secret Scriptures while he waited.

To the best of her recollection, Leila had never given Imbaso any reason to believe that Usiku was literate. In Palambo, many people were not – especially those in rural areas. So she had hesitantly and shame-facedly confessed that she could not read the scriptures. She would have to be tutored, or better yet first taught to read and write so that she could be of more use to Great Kivuli.

"Where are you staying?" Imbaso had asked, concern writ large on his beautiful dark features. He hadn't had time to broach the subject earlier, and for all he knew she was wandering the streets with her horse, homeless – though he hadn't seen Wapesi when they arrived.

"I had the most amazing luck!" the girl said with a smile. "I might not know the Secret Scriptures yet, but I know the dark god is smiling on me. I went to an agency, and I was able to get a job house-sitting for a trader who is away on business. He will be gone for two months, going all the way to Iskand and back, and he was most anxious to have somebody living there to keep the place up and make sure that it was not damaged or robbed while he was gone. There's not much pay, but it's enough for food and some hay for Wapesi. And at least I have a place to sleep."

Imbaso stepped forward and gave her a slight hug, kissing her gently on the top of the head. "Have a good rest, then. I'll see you tomorrow morning at the 'athletic club'!" She smiled and waved at him, and made her way up the stairs and back out past the two men she was sure were Black Claw guards.

Now, Leila's actual garb was quite close to what Usiku was wearing. She needed her daggers at hand, and hoped that though she had not often practiced the tricks drilled into her through her four years of intensive training with the Night Guild in recent times, she was still fit and active enough to be able to impress the Black Claw's master.

She made sure Wapesi was comfortable and well-supplied before going off. She didn't know how long she might be required to stay at the "athletic club" today, and thought it would be better to leave him at home. Besides, apparently she needed the exercise!

Usiku loped around the fourth circle, on which her house stood, until she came to Weaver Street. Each of the circles was nearly level, the connecting streets fairly steep. When she got to the next circle, the third, she began examining the buildings on the corners. Ah, there it was, an imposing four-storey stone structure second from the corner on the left, outer side of the circle.

As she was approaching it she heard a clatter of hooves and spotted Imbaso mounted on Kizuri coming down Weaver Street behind her. What a pretty horse she was, Leila mused. She half wished Wapesi was a stallion and not a gelding so she could breed him to the lovely mare. It was a silly, whimsical thought, of course. His disposition would not be half so sweet had he not been cut as a colt, and in any case she doubted if any owner of a Hisan mare would have wished a half-Gaspari foal.

Imbaso dismounted and tied the mare to a hitching post nearby. Like the Nima, Palambans generally trained their horses so that stealing one would not be easy or lightly undertaken. "All ready to knock him dead, Usiku?" he asked with a mischievous grin. Damn, the boy was so *cute*. And why did she want to think of him as a boy, when he was four years her senior?

"You seem to be taking it pretty lightly, Imbaso," Usiku said seriously. "Did not the ritual last night frighten you a little?"

He squeezed her arm. "Yes," he admitted, "a little. But the arch-priest is my own father, and I am his only son. How bad could it get? I know he has only my best interests at heart."

"I suppose you're right," she said. "Shall we go in?"

Imbaso tried the latch and they found the heavy door unlocked. He pushed it inward, and they stepped inside a tiled entryway with a closed door at the rear of it and a desk along one side. At the desk sat a rather ordinary-looking young man, a clerk evidently. Leila guessed that any casual visitors were turned away without forming any suspicions of secret goings-on. But all she and Imbaso had to do was present their palm scars (his real, hers illusory) and he pulled a lever beneath the desk. The door at the rear swung open, and they walked on through.

They were ushered past a succession of young people, mostly male, all dressed similarly to what they'd seen on the hooded guards yesterday evening in the temple. Then they came into an enormous room, the ceiling high enough to take up most of the building's second storey. Leila wondered what else was up there, on the third storey and beyond. It was a pretty sure bet the church of Betsalel-cum-Kivuli owned the entire building.

Students were engaged in a number of activities around the room – sparring barehanded, fighting with knives or other weapons, throwing or shooting at targets. A slim young man in black seemed to be overseeing their activities and calling out to this or that one if he saw anything that needed correcting. And standing over to one side, a much older man in black stood with legs slightly apart, in a balanced stance, arms crossed as his eyes missed nothing that went on in the room.

"That's Kifozi," Imbaso murmured to Usiku as they came into the room and approached him. "He's an old friend of my father's, so I'm hoping I'll be a shoe-in."

"Don't count on it," Leila replied softly through Usiku's mouth. She had the idea Mauaji's plans for his son would not include putting him into a secret society where his life might be on the line every day.

The old (relatively; the man appeared to be in his early fifties, but was strong and straight) man spotted them immediately and let his arms fall to his sides, watching at their approach. He could tell much about a candidate just by observing how they moved, and he thought the girl showed as much promise as Mauaji had said.

The two stopped before Kifozi and inclined their heads slightly in a gesture of respect. He nodded to them as well, then got right to the point. "So, two nestlings who believe they might become the instruments of death," he said sardonically. Then addressing Usiku, he said "What skills do you have, girl, that make you think you might have aptitude for our... line of work?"

Barely sixteen and barely above five feet in height, Usiku drew herself up as tall as she could manage and looked the master assassin in the eyes. Her own black eyes sparkled with defiance and determination. "I have some small skill with daggers, Master Kifozi," she said with humble deference that belied her ferocity.

Kifozi clapped his hands, addressing the room at large. "Attention, everyone. Halt while we examine the skills of this new applicant for our order." The various activities around the room stopped as the students broke off what they'd been doing and gathered on the side of the room where the master stood, curious to see what these newcomers might have to offer. Imbaso dimly recognized a couple of the students, young men who'd been kids involved in the temple back before Father had had his crisis of faith.

There were three targets set across the rear of the room. The walls of the gymnasium were paneled with wood, though the building itself was of stone. Probably the acoustics of the cavernous space would have been deafening without this amelioration. They were bad enough as it was.

Kifozi gestured to the targets, and Usiku stalked toward them with the grace of a panther. The fact that she was already dressed as one of them helped to reinforce the idea that she was meant to be here. When she reached what anyone would think a comfortable distance for throwing daggers, standing in the center of the room, she turned to look at the master.

"Go ahead," he said with a wave. Thok! Thok! Thok! Three targets were pierced by daggers in the space of a heartbeat. Oh good, she hadn't lost her touch. She threw the fourth dagger into the wooden wall above the center target, at a calculated height well above her head. Her audience was wondering whether it was a bad throw, or what. Then she dashed forward, leapt over the center target (retrieving the dagger from it as she did so), ran up the wall a couple of paces and retrieved the dagger there before executing a somersault and landing on the floor, knees bent to absorb the shock as she came down. It was *mostly* not an illusion.

Panting a little, Leila threw the two daggers she'd retrieved over the heads of the students and their master, to land in the wall a foot above the height of the tallest of them, together in a six-inch circle. Then she took a bow. The group of students went wild, breaking into a cacophony of excited comment. Kifozi remained standing silent, but a slow grin was spreading across his face.

Usiku returned to the group, breathless. Kifozi, eyes glinting, said "Very impressive. Have you killed before?"

"Only twice," she answered truthfully. "But I am eager to learn all of the ways in which I may do so. I will kill as Kivuli commands, but I have my own scores to settle."

Kifozi nodded, and looked speculatively at Imbaso. "Where did you find this girl?" he asked.

Imbaso shrugged. "We met on the caravan from Halath," he said without further comment.

"You are in," Kifozi said to Usiku. "Now you, Imbaso. Show us what you can do." Imbaso had a sinking feeling. He'd been happy for Usiku, dazzled at her display of skill with the daggers and surprised that the Ran and his soldiers were still left alive to need killing. But now he realized, he had nothing remotely as impressive to show. He was tall and strong, lithe and athletic, but his weapons training had all been with swords and scimitars – the sort of fighting where you generally expected your opponent to be similarly armed. Of what use was fencing for an assassin?

He gave it his best shot, anyway. He'd come armed with a saber and a couple of scimitars, and he'd become fairly adept with the latter weapon at the kind of showy maneuvering that was intended to impress and intimidate one's opponents and didn't make a hill of beans' difference to the final outcome of the contest. He had never killed anyone in his life, though he'd wounded a couple of those bandits during the attack at the mountain pass.

Imbaso juggled and flashed his scimitars, sending the glistening sharp blades spinning in circles, sheathing and unsheathing them and making cuts at the heads of imaginary enemies. And with his saber, he attacked a pell that was set up in one corner of the room. His moves were sure and swift, and there was a lot of power behind them. Leila was sure that if he'd had a live opponent, he would have made a good showing. But she already knew what the outcome would be.

Imbaso sheathed his weapons and returned to the master, bowing slightly as he had when they'd first approached him. Kifozi, inches shorter, put his hand up on the tall young man's shoulder. "I'm sorry, Imbaso," he said, "I do not believe that the Makucha Nyeusi is right for you. You are too tall, for one thing. Better you should study the Secret Scriptures and join your father in the priesthood. I regret that I cannot accept you as an apprentice."

Eyes filled with shame and disappointment, Imbaso turned away from Kifozi and cast a helpless look at Usiku. She stepped closer and raised a hand to his cheek. Looking deep into his eyes, she murmured softly "It's all right, Imbaso. Some things were not meant to be, and I release you from your promise. But say you will be my friend. Could you not become my tutor in the Secret Scriptures?"

Imbaso's sense of failure turned to joy, and he embraced Usiku without caring who was watching. He still intended to help her win her revenge, even if it would not be as a highly-trained member of the Makucha Nyeusi. He did possess some skill at arms. And perhaps on his own, he could train more – even if not with the Black Claw's legendary master. "I'll do anything you ask, Usiku," he murmured back. "Anything at all."

Chapter 26

Usiku's training began immediately that day, as Imbaso returned to the black temple and went back to his religious studies. The Night Guild had made sure that its members were able to get themselves out of tight situations, but while assassination had been an occasional item on their list of services it had never been a specialty. There were many, many techniques that Leila had never even heard of, let alone been trained in.

The Makucha Nyeusi had apparently been a very early offshoot of the schismatic Palamban church of Betsalel, starting after the prophet Rasulbiyi's entirely made-up "revelation" had taken over the church completely but probably before the prophet's death. Had he himself been an assassin? The lore was unclear, and Leila (as the illiterate Usiku) was unable to do much studying on the subject.

But it was clear that by the time of the prophet's death, circa 875 m.e. by the Dominion's reckoning of dates, the cult of assassins had been well established throughout Palambo. In every case it was operated as a secret cult within the cult of those who followed the prophet's Secret Scriptures. The majority of its killings were carried out on the orders of the church's arch-priests, usually for the purpose of furthering their personal or religious goals.

In the absence of an active god to beg favors of, the priests had turned to their own ingenious methods to achieve the same aims. The Black Claw could not rescue one's loved ones from the plague or assure the prosperity of one's trade ventures, but it could surely eliminate any enemies standing between one and one's ultimate objectives.

And, the church leaders soon discovered, there were many outside the church who would be happy to pay – and pay big – for the services of those highly skilled assassins. A church needed money to thrive, and as more and more of Betsalel's ordinary worshipers found their idols gone and their god no longer responsive, the prophet's followers had discovered another revenue source.

Usiku learned how to move utterly silently. She had thought she had mastered that skill before, and it had been useful coupled with her god-given ability to become one with the shadows. But she now realized she had been as noisy as a herd of oliphants by comparison with the skill she had now acquired.

She learned to remain motionless for hours, as she waited in hiding for the moment when she might spring on her prey. She became adept at unarmed combat, and at using other weapons besides the daggers with which she had won her place as an apprentice.

Skill in archery was a large part of a Black Claw assassin's training, Usiku found, and she was pleased that she already had some ability there. But what she had learned before was just the beginning. The classes often went out into the countryside in the dead of night, invisible in their dark clothing, and practiced their skills in the outdoors away from the gymnasium – in conditions where rain or wind could affect the outcome of a shot.

But the assassin's art was subtle, and it was not enough merely to see the target dead. In the majority of cases where the Makucha Nyeusi was hired by a client outside the church, what was wanted was a death that appeared to be natural, or only an accident. This was far more difficult to achieve.

Two months passed, and Usiku informed Imbaso that the owner of the house she was caring for had sent word asking that she remain on duty for a further half year. He had encountered an unexpected business opportunity in Iskand, and was required to stay on site while it was put into operation. But he was still anxious to preserve his base in Namei, as he would someday return.

Imbaso had not yet seen the house. Leila longed to invite him there, but explaining its constantly cool interior and lack of insect infestation would have been difficult. And there was that other issue. She had been away from Tevo for more than four months, and she didn't think she could trust herself alone in the house with Imbaso.

Betsalel passed along messages from Tevo, and she sent messages on; but on the occasion when he had offered to physically carry her lover to her here in the house, she had declined. Her emotions were in turmoil, and she didn't want to face the conflicts between the love they had shared and the life they had lived together, and what was going on now.

Usiku and Imbaso saw each other a few times per week at the temple, where he was studying the Scriptures and then trying to tutor her in them after he had absorbed the information. The "two clay tablets" Rasulbiyi had come with when he returned from his desert visit with the dark god had grown over the generations into a medium-thick book, and a great deal was being added to it now that their death god had begun speaking to them.

Usiku had always seemed bright before, but she seemed to have some kind of problem when it came to learning her Scriptures. Imbaso would read them to her, and she would smilingly repeat... But she always got confused, seeming unable even to grasp the general intent. Three months now, and she could not recite even the first two chapters without making so many mistakes that she became hopelessly bogged down.

Having flunked out of assassin school before he even started, Imbaso was eager to excel in some way. Why had he come here, if not to become a part of the church? His desire to please his father seemed to have overrun his common sense, and Leila was horrified at some of the requirements of worship that he read to her – without so much as a quiver of concern for their content.

Usiku had thought that she already knew much about poisons and the psychoactive substances that could be derived from plants. But seemingly the tropics offered a thousand times the botanical opportunities for murder and mayhem than anything the Night Guild had been able to teach her. While she continued her physical training, she spent hours every day in the laboratories upstairs (those floors of the Makucha Nyeusi's facility she'd wondered about on day one) learning to identify the plants as they grew, as they were prepared, and as they could be introduced into one's target's environment – food, drink, bathwater, clothing – so as to produce a death that any doctor on earth would conclude was natural.

This concentrated program of study had taken Usiku away from her seemingly futile studies with Imbaso, and it was more than two weeks later that he came seeking her at the "athletic club" with the big news: he was confident that he now had the entirety of the Secret Scriptures down pat (including the two pages that had been added to them since his studies had begun), and he had applied to be tested. Soon, he was confident, he would be a fully accepted acolyte – privileged to participate in the rituals with which Kivuli was worshiped.

Usiku couldn't stand it. "Imbaso, are you sure you want to do this?" she asked, after taking him into a room where they could be alone. He looked at her questioningly. Her rapid progress in her studies as an assassin, especially the parts of the training that required memorization, seemed inexplicable in the face of her inability to absorb even a small part of the Scriptures. Now, she was questioning whether the Scriptures were even something he should heed?

"Usiku, how could you say that?" he asked. "Everything that we're doing hinges on the worship of Kivuli, and father says that he is far more responsive than Betsalel ever was. How could we not want to move forward, to achieve a deeper relationship with our god?" Leila lowered her head. She wanted to shout it to the rooftops: "Kivuli is not a god, he is an evil djinn created by the wickedness of man!" But she could not. "Go forward, then," she said softly, throwing her arms around him and holding him close. "But come and tell me how it went, will you?"

Chapter 27

Two nights later, tired from another hard day of training at the cult's gymnasium, Leila had just barely dropped off to sleep when she heard a pounding at her front door. Her feet were on the floor in an instant, and she faded into invisibility. Then she crept silently down the hall. The door was solid, the shutters closed, but a voice was calling "Usiku! Please come!" And it was a voice she knew.

Still invisible, Leila hurried to the kitchen and lit a candle. Then she became Usiku, clad in a light robe, and went to open the door. Imbaso stood there, wearing a black acolyte's robe. His dark face looked ashen even in the yellow candlelight, and his cheeks were streaked with tears.

"Imbaso!" Usiku cried. "How did you find me?" He stepped into the room and looked around in the dim light, disoriented. What kind of bizarre house was this in which Usiku had found lodging? And why was it so cold in here?

"I.." he gasped, nearly choking on the words, "I followed you one day. I just wanted to see where you lived, to know that you were safe…"

Or didn't trust the story I made up, Leila thought… "What's wrong, Imbaso? Why are you here?" A considerably more ornate table now stood before a comfortable upholstered sofa in the Gaspari style, and Usiku set the candle on it, then urged Imbaso to sit down. He was trembling, in the grip of some strong emotion.

"I passed my test, Usiku," he said, fresh tears welling from his eyes as he looked into hers. "I passed yesterday, and became an initiate. Tonight was my first ritual, in the inner sanctum, I…" He gasped for breath, swiping an arm angrily across his eyes as he struggled to continue.

"I was at the back of the room, with the other acolytes," he said more calmly after a moment. "The idol – it was nothing like the painting in the temple's main sanctuary. Kivuli is *not* Betsalel, not even close!"

Usiku put a comforting hand on his arm, stroking it gently. "I know," she murmured, and he went on.

"M-my father came in, after everybody was in their places for the ritual, and we all began chanting – calling the god. He had a bundle in his arms, and he went to the altar. Black flames flared up, just like in the Scriptures!" Usiku looked at him owl-eyed. Leila knew, or at least guessed, that the cult of Kivuli was following the Secret Scriptures to the letter – and probably had been for centuries. But seemingly Imbaso, sweet cheerful Imbaso, had believed it was some kind of mummery, a charade.

"As the chanting went on, I heard a wail above the sound of our voices. That was when I realized that what Father had in his arms was a baby. He unwrapped it and held it up to the idol, and the little boy was screaming his head off. I don't think he was a year old, yet." Gasping for breath, still clearly in shock, Imbaso continued. "The idol looks like a cross between a man and an enormous black panther, with clawed hands and feet and a long tail. As Father held the child up the idol began to stir, its eyes glowing golden and its mouth opening in a snarl. Then, Father..."

Her face a mask of concern, Usiku stroked his arm again as he sobbed before continuing his tale. "He laid the baby on the altar and killed it with a ritual knife, like the one he used on us when we took our vows!" He said. "Then Kivuli awakened fully and crouched on the altar, devouring the corpse!"

Usiku drew him into an embrace, hugging him hard. When Imbaso had calmed down, he added "That was when I threw up all over the inner sanctum floor and fled. The other acolytes were grinning and laughing at me, like it was something that happens a lot the first time an acolyte participates in a ritual."

"Did Kivuli pay any attention to you when you fled?" Usiku asked sharply. Attracting unfavorable attention from a bloodthirsty djinn seemed like a really bad idea.

"No," Imbaso said, after considering the question. "The god seemed to have eyes only for the sacrifice – and I think maybe he was paying attention to Father, too. But the rest of us might not have been there for all he cared. He seemed more like an animal, or a greedy uncaring child, than a god."

Usiku hugged him again, and Imbaso hugged her back as if his grip on her was the only thing keeping him from being swept away on a sea of madness. She murmured into his chest, "Imbaso, surely you realized that the cult worships their god according to the Scriptures? What did you expect?"

He sat up and put his hands on her shoulders, looking into her eyes. Was she blaming him? She had said something a couple of days ago about questioning the wisdom of becoming an acolyte. "No! I thought… I thought it was just a grisly game, I guess." He hung his head. "Usiku, this is my family we're talking about, what my people have been doing for generations. Are you saying that my grandfather, my great-grandfather, were all slaughtering babies on the altar of Betsalel?"

She looked back at him sadly. "I'm afraid that's what I'm saying, Imbaso." She was trembling on the cusp of a decision, but she had to know one thing before she went any further. "Do you reject Kivuli? Or will you follow in your father's footsteps and someday be the one holding that knife?"

Imbaso looked stricken, but resolve was flickering in his tear-reddened dark eyes. "Father said that Kivuli would bring death to me, to us, if we broke our vows. But I don't care. I can *not* worship such a monster."

Usiku, Leila really, threw herself into his arms and kissed him soundly on the mouth, throwing the young man into confusion. While he was still trying to make sense of that, she smiled at him and said, "Imbaso, I have a confession to make. I hope that you will still be my friend after I tell you that I have lied to you about some things…"

He didn't reply, just stared at her, waiting to learn the worst. He'd already had the shock of his life tonight, and he thought he knew that there was worse to come. Would Father really have killed his own nephew? That was the only explanation he could think of for the disappearance of Aunt Uzuri's baby.

"First," Usiku said, "You must understand that I am a priestess and an agent of the god Betsalel. The *true* Betsalel, not the monster that misguided men in Palambo have been trying to worship since the prophet took over the church. Kivuli, the being that the cult is calling a god, is actually a djinn – a concept of the minds of men, built up by the power of belief and brought to life by a human soul."

Imbaso goggled at her. It felt as if his world was dissolving under his feet. "You... You didn't come here to join the cult so you could take revenge for the deaths of your family?" She shook her head. This was so painful, but it must be done. She needed an ally, someone who could work from inside the cult in the way that a young girl could not. Male supremacy was as alive and well in Palambo as it was in the Dominion.

"The part about my family, that was just a story. I'm sorry I had to lie to you, but I couldn't very well say 'hey ho, I'm off to Namei to find out what happened in the temple of Betsalel and do something about it,' could I?"

He shook his head and mumbled "I guess not..." but his face was a mask of misery.

In a moment he added, "If Betsalel sent you to do something about his church in Palambo, why wait hundreds of years? Why didn't he send someone as soon as the prophet had started his takeover?" Good, Leila thought, he was using his mind. That meant he was recovering from the shocks he'd received tonight.

"The prophet struck at about the same time that Betsalel's sister, the goddess Lucia, used her influence over the emperor of the Gaspari Dominion to get Betsalel's worship banned, his followers slaughtered, his idols destroyed," Usiku explained. "The power of the gods comes from us, from the worship we give them, and without it there is little they can do. By the time Betsalel realized that he was no longer receiving power from worshipers in Palambo, I believe that all of his true idols had been removed to secret locations like the inner sanctum here in Namei – and the people worshiping there were worshiping a creature of evil, a destroyer of life who hungered for the blood of innocents. He could not get through. And his church in the Dominion had been destroyed, as well. He lacked the power to find a champion."

Imbaso's eyes were wide. Though Usiku had proven to be a liar, he now believed her utterly. That he had believed her before as well might have shown him that his instincts were not to be trusted, but he paid it no heed. "The god told you all this?" he asked, and she nodded. "So last year, when Betsalel came back and was restored to the pantheon in Parat, was the first time since the prophet that he had the power to start doing anything about the way he was being worshiped?"

"That's right," Usiku confirmed. "And just five months ago, the false version of Betsalel that was being worshiped in Palambo suddenly acquired a soul – here in his temple at Namei – and became a real being, a djinn. That was when Betsalel called on me to come here and learn what was going on. He feared the worst, and I believe he was right."

The wheels were turning behind Imbaso's dark eyes. He might be innocent for a man of his age, but he was not an idiot. "But if Betsalel had no true worshipers in Palambo, how was he able to contact you?" Leila flushed. She had been hoping to reveal only part of the story to Imbaso, to maintain the persona of Usiku to some extent. But it was not going to work. If she was going to have him on her side, fighting her battles, he needed to know *all* the truth.

"When you were studying in Wena, Imbaso, and got the news about the dark god's reappearance in the temple in Parat, what story did you hear?"

"Betsalel's main idol from the big temple had not been destroyed, but hidden away," Imbaso recalled. "There were a couple of young kids, a boy and a girl, who found it and freed it from its imprisonment. Then after the god manifested in his idol, half the city gathered around the temple for the confrontation. Everyone thought Lucia would blast him to smithereens, or something. But the girl had gotten all the other gods, the six beside the deities of light and darkness, to say they supported him. And Lucia got chased away. There was something else, the boy had gotten killed during the fight and the dark god brought him back to life. Even in Wena, they're saying now that you can pray to Betsalel to bring back your loved ones…"

He tailed off, looking wide-eyed at Usiku. "You?" he breathed in wonder. Leila dropped the illusion of Usiku and sat beside him as she was. Much the same, but lighter of skin and with green eyes, less kink to her hair. And, she suddenly realized, stark naked. She caught a hint of something besides amazement in Imbaso's gaze and, blushing, quickly reestablished the illusory robe.

"Betsalel gave me the power to appear however I wish to," Leila explained. "My real name is Leila, and my father is Palamban. I expect he looks very much like an older version of you, if he still lives. But my mother is truly dead, and I have lived as an orphan, fending for myself in the Dominion, since I was eight."

Imbaso reached out gently and took the hem of her robe between thumb and forefinger, feeling it. It felt as real as anything, yet he had just seen it vanish and rematerialize. He gazed at Leila, marking how like Usiku she was. Her mixed heritage gave her an exotic look, somehow even more appealing than Usiku – who had looked as if she might be his own first cousin.

"Last year," Leila said, still trying to help Imbaso understand, "I stumbled on the last remaining true idol of Betsalel in the Dominion – besides the one hidden in Parat – in a ruined temple in the Blackwald." He nodded. Wena was not all that far away from Oester, after all. She went on, "I… I was running from the law, and I thought that the dark one was just a boogeyman, an old tale with no power any more. I was sort of right about that, though he had power enough right there in that one spot at least. I stole the third-eye gem from the idol, and with it Betsalel was able to embed a part of himself within my being. It lies beneath my heart."

"So he forced you to do his bidding?" Imbaso asked. Leila nodded slightly. "It was like that in the beginning, and he scared the crap out of me when he manifested, I can tell you. But the thing is, because of the bond between us, I know his soul as he knows mine. So when he told me that the evils attributed to him were lies,

I knew he spoke the truth. I went voluntarily to Parat to free him, and I am now his high priestess there."

"But what can you do here, to drive out the djinn and restore worship of the true dark god?" Imbaso asked.

"To start with, just get close to the cult and learn exactly what happened," Leila replied. A thought occurred to her, a horrifying one, and she looked up at Imbaso with the eyes of a frightened child. "Five months ago… Wasn't that when your aunt's baby…"

"Yes," he gritted, and held her in his arms again. For the first time, as herself.

"Then Kivuli's soul must be the soul of a baby, unless the baby had been occupied by an older soul flown there from a dying body," she said. "Betsalel told me that the majority of souls, when their body dies, immediately seek a new one. But some wander bodiless, some go to join a sort of big cosmic well of spirit called The One, and some – like your poor little cousin – enter a belief construct and become djinns, or demons, or angels."

"Is there a difference among the three?" Imbaso asked, curious.

"I think djinns and demons are just two different words for the same thing. Angels are called that if they are beneficent instead of evil. Those would usually be given souls through a conscious act of self-sacrifice, or maybe just by having someone who'd contributed to the belief structure themselves going into it when they died naturally. It's pretty confusing."

"But Uzuri's baby didn't know anything about the beliefs or worship of the false Betsalel," Imbaso mused, "He didn't know anything at all, except the love of his mother. He couldn't even talk yet! Why would he inhabit, and become, something so evil!"

"It was probably the nearest place his soul could flee to, when your father cut out his heart," Leila said with an edge of coldness to her voice. She didn't want Imbaso to forget that his father was an evil man.

Imbaso sighed, and sat beside Leila with his hands in his lap. He had gotten over his shock, and his grief had become manageable. Now he was beginning to notice his surroundings.

"Why is it so cool and pleasant in here?" he asked. "And what's with this furniture?"

Leila smiled impishly at him. She really *was* Usiku, minus that girl's tragic history and burning desire for revenge on her imaginary enemies. "I think maybe it's time for you to meet the real Betsalel," she said, patting his hand and rising from her seat.

Chapter 28

As Leila padded off barefooted (over some very thick, nice-looking Hando carpets) toward the bedroom, Imbaso tensed. "Wait, what? Is there going to be some kind of ritual? I'm wearing the robes of Kivuli! Can't we do this some other time?"

She reappeared almost immediately, smiling sweetly and cupping a cloth bag in her hands. She flopped back down on the cushiony sofa and removed what Imbaso realized was a tiny idol of Betsalel from the bag, setting it on the table. It looked exactly as the dark god was pictured in the painting in the temple.

Terror surged through Imbaso. He had just participated in a human sacrifice in the dark god's temple, before the idol that had once belonged to Betsalel! Would the god of darkness, dreams, and death strike him down for blasphemy? Leila picked up his reaction and clasped his right hand in her left. "Don't worry," she said reassuringly. "The real Betsalel is nothing like what you've been led to believe."

She called to the idol, her right hand over her heart, "Betsalel, come to me! I have a new recruit for you!" Imbaso found that Leila's light-hearted confidence buoyed him, but he still clutched her hand tighter as he saw the tiny figure writhe and begin to grow. In a second or two the dark god stood before them on the floor behind the table, six feet tall. The ceilings in this house weren't all that high. All three of his eyes were open, glowing red, and there was a beatific smile on his face. Imbaso sagged in relief.

"Leila!" he cried in a deep, warm voice redolent with affection. He turned his gaze on Imbaso and raised an eyebrow. "A new recruit?" he asked. "Are you sure that's wise?" No booming, no fangs, no death threats. *Not* what Imbaso had expected. But he thought he had better speak for himself.

"I am Imbaso, uh, sir," he stammered. "For many generations, the males of my family, and occasionally some of the women as well, have been priests of Betsalel. Or so I had always thought. My father, who is the arch-priest of the temple here in Namei, called me back from my studies in the Gaspari Dominion and more or less commanded me to become a part of the hidden church, the secret cult that operates beneath the ordinary temples throughout the kingdom of Palambo."

"So not everyone in Palambo knows of this cult and their evil rituals?" Betsalel asked.

"I certainly didn't, until around three months ago when I returned to Palambo," Imbaso replied. "I would guess, given the cult's secrecy, that very few people actually know of it. It should be possible to tell who, by looking for these signs" He held up his palms, and dark god's eyes narrowed as he saw the marks.

"Then why have I been unable to reach any ordinary worshipers in Palambo for centuries?" Betsalel asked. "After I had recovered somewhat from the blow dealt me by my sister, I tried. But there was nothing."

"It was the idols," Imbaso replied. "Is it correct, that you can only manifest in this plane through the nexus of a true idol?" The god nodded. "The prophet Rasulbiyi spent years traveling around Palambo, establishing worship based on his Secret Scriptures. In every temple, the true idols were removed and replaced with false ones or mere paintings – while in hidden sanctuaries below, the cult members practiced their grisly rituals."

"Yet you joined this cult?" Betsalel asked pointedly.

Imbaso squirmed. "I have always been an obedient son, and my father is a very commanding man. He gives no outward appearance of the evil that lurks in his soul, and I assumed that the dark rituals and foul practices described in the Secret Scriptures, which I had to memorize to be admitted as an initiate, were just frightening silliness. It was very hard to believe that these upright, ordinary citizens whom I had known all my life would ever actually *do* what the Scriptures described."

"And tonight you learned differently," the god said. I was not a question.

"I am still having trouble believing that what I saw was real," Imbaso admitted shame-facedly. "Could that possibly have been an illusion, such as Leila employed in convincing me she was Usiku?"

"I'm sorry," Betsalel said quietly. "It was not. I felt it when your Kivuli took over my idol here in Namei five months ago, and I have felt it again and again in the months since. Now that the djinn has become a living spiritual entity, shaped by the foul worship laid out by your prophet, he has become able to manifest in any of my idols in Palambo where men are worshiping the dark being they created in their minds, forcing those idols that were once mine into the shape of Kivuli. I will never be able to manifest in any of them again."

"Imbaso has been accepted by the cult, master," Leila said, "and his lapse this evening in vomiting and fleeing the inner sanctum when his father made the sacrifice will not be looked at askance, I believe. He has said that he renounces Kivuli. Is there a way you can protect him from the djinn, so that he might be able to work with us to destroy the cult from the inside without being caught out? What powers does Kivuli really have?"

"You were inducted into the cult recently?" Betsalel asked Imbaso.

"Leila – Usiku as I thought her then – and I took our vows on the same day around three months ago. Never to speak of Kivuli, the cult, or its secrets to anyone who had not taken similar vows." He glanced down at Leila's palm, and realized it was unblemished. "The cuts were part of your illusion?" he asked her wonderingly.

She nodded. "I could not permit such a thing on this flesh which encapsulates a part of the true dark god," she said quietly.

"At the time," Imbaso went on, "my father warned that if we broke our vows the dark one, Kivuli, would come to us as Death in the Night. That's apparently his... sobriquet, you might say. Evidently it was what he called himself on the night he first appeared, five months ago."

"You have broken that vow," the Shadow God pointed out. "Do you now fear for your life?" Imbaso shook his head.

"That was part of what convinced me that the cult's scriptures were so much fiction," he explained. "My father had already broken that same vow, which I'm sure he must have taken decades ago, explaining to me what had happened recently before we went to the temple that night. When you think about it, how would they ever recruit any new members if they weren't allowed to talk about it to the uninitiated?"

Betsalel nodded solemnly. "Good point," he said. "But tonight was the first time that you were allowed to participate in the actual worship of Kivuli. Is that right?" Imbaso shuddered. He was feeling a lot better now, but mental images of what he'd seen in the inner sanctum this evening would haunt him for the rest of his life.

"Yesterday I requested testing on the Secret Scriptures, and I passed the test. My father was most pleased, and he performed the Ritual of Initiation himself. It was similar to the one Leila and I went through, with more fearsome oaths, and I was given this." He pulled out from inside his tunic a leather cord, on which was hung what appeared to be the canine tooth of a large cat.

Both Leila and Imbaso were dismayed to see the Shadow God recoil from the sight of it. Then he recovered himself, his red eyes glinting momentarily brighter. "It is a part of Kivuli," he said in an awful voice. "Something your father probably requested as a token of the god's favor, a little bit of himself to accompany each initiate of his cult. But it is also a nexus, like a true idol. With this, the djinn might sense what is going on around any person wearing one."

"Master," Leila put in, "I do not believe that Kivuli is so devious as that. Imbaso and I believe that his soul is that of a sacrificial victim, a baby not a year old, that Imbaso's father killed some five months ago. He said that the djinn appeared to be more like a wild animal or a greedy child than a god."

"The soul of an innocent baby!" Betsalel said, sadness in his voice. "That makes a difference. We can destroy this thing, but he will sense it just as I sensed his usurpation of my idol. He probably lacks the sophistication to pinpoint the exact location, to know which of these teeth he supplied was destroyed. But to make sure you are sheltered, Imbaso, I will take this with me. It can be destroyed in the temple in Parat, beyond Kivuli's reach."

The god somehow removed the pendant tooth, which was capped in gold topped by a ring for its attachment to the cord, without breaking either the ring or the cord. The tooth vanished. Then he reached up to his forehead. There was no change to his red-glowing third eye, but a small, sparkling red gem now glittered in his palm. He closed his palm, and when he opened it again the gem had become a tooth identical to the one he had removed. With a gesture, he hung it on the cord around Imbaso's neck.

"Imbaso," Betsalel said, "This is a nexus for me just as the tooth was a nexus for Kivuli. While you might reject him, your fear of him and your understanding that he is real might have been enough to let him manifest through it. It would not have been a pleasant experience. Wearing this, you will be invisible to him and have my protection. Mind you, don't stand in front of any crossbows or jump off any cliffs! My protection is mostly spiritual, unless I am manifest in the physical plane. But if you need me, place the tooth on a suitable surface and call me. I will come to your aid."

Imbaso held out the tooth on its cord and studied it with awe. Never a religious man, he was now having the religious experience of his young life, and he was having a hard time coming to terms with it. Kivuli was not a god, he was a monster – a sad blending of his little cousin's soul and centuries of human perversion. But Betsalel was a god he felt he could truly devote himself to.

He fell to his knees, tears coming to his eyes. "Master, I pledge my service to you! Together we will rid Palambo of this misbegotten djinn, and restore your true worship to the temples!" He clutched the claw as he spoke. Betsalel looked a little disconcerted. Well, new converts were usually the most fervent. He had seen nearly every variation on human worship in his millennia of existence, but the recent centuries-long hiatus had given him the capacity to be surprised all over again.

"Rise, Imbaso!" he commanded, and the young man scrambled to his feet. The look of adoration in his eyes was almost embarrassing. "Leila will be your guide as we continue our campaign to defeat Kivuli, dismantle the cult founded by Rasulbiyi, and restore my normal worship to Palambo. Is there any other boon you would ask of me?" he asked.

Imbaso looked around. "Leila's illusion ability, this house, those were all your work?" he asked. "I have granted Leila the ability to take any appearance, or to disappear entirely." Betsalel replied with a hint of amusement in his tone. "The conditions present in this house, what your friend calls 'Shadow Manor South,' are not illusions. With the strength granted me by the return of my worship to the Gaspari Dominion, and in the presence of such a worshiper as my high priestess there, I have not yet tested the limits of my powers."

Make her love me, Imbaso thought, and then cringed as it seemed the Shadow God might have heard him. "I thank you for your offer, Master," he said. "With this protection, and with Leila's help, I hope I will have all that I need. But I can call you through the tooth if anything comes up, right?" The Shadow God's red eyes glinted and he smiled. Then he stepped up onto the table and shrank in an instant to the tiny idol Leila had first placed there.

Chapter 29

As soon as the tiny idol had stopped moving, Leila scooped it up and returned it to its protective sack. She suspected that the power of indestructibility that the willing self-sacrifice of Betsalel's priesthood centuries ago had laid on his main idol at Parat meant that all scions of that idol since then – all that had been budded off in the modern age – were similarly indestructible. But she preferred to take no chances.

That done, she turned to Imbaso – her face glowing with joy – and threw herself into his arms. He locked his mouth on hers, kissing her deeply. He loved her, he wanted her, *so much*! Still locked in the embrace, he broke from the kiss and looked her in the eyes. "Leila?" he asked tentatively, "You... weren't actually raped by the Ran, right?"

She smiled up at him beatifically, squeezing him tight. "Nope," she replied breezily. "I was *almost* raped once when I was thirteen, but I knifed him before he got there." That gave him pause, but not much. He kissed her again, savoring the taste of her mouth, the feel of her body beneath the thin (and apparently illusory, still more exciting!) robe. She definitely seemed to be cooperating.

Imbaso suspected that Leila was not *quite* so young as Usiku had claimed to be... but she couldn't be a hell of a lot older. "Are you virgin?" he had to ask. She looked up at him, her expression halfway between annoyance and affection. *"That's* a rather personal question," she said. And kissed him again, long and hard. He came up for air, gasping "Was that a 'no'?"

For answer, Leila moved her left hand from his right shoulder and groped for the section of his priest's robe a little south of the waistline. She got a firm grip on him and squeezed hard, then went back to kissing him. Imbaso's mind exploded in delight. Had the dark god truly granted his unspoken wish? Or had Leila, masquerading as Usiku, loved him all along?

Some considerable time later, Leila stirred in Imbaso's arms. They were snuggled together in the house's master bed, so soft and luxurious it was hard to get out of it. He had not truly been sleeping, or else had awakened as soon as she moved. He kissed her, and a flood of emotions ran through her like a torrent of cold water. Love, fulfillment, happiness… guilt.

She truly had come to love Imbaso, and making love with him had been a joy long-delayed. The months of living under another name, always in hiding, had worn her resistance away until only the raw need for intimacy – physical and emotional – remained. But what of Tevo?

He was her first love, her first lover – and they had now been separated for nearly half a year. He was in Parat, presumably alone, carrying the entire burden of running the church of Betsalel in the Dominion – and here she was, giving in to her desires in Palambo without so much as a thought for him… until now, after the deed had been done. Her mother, so well educated, had chosen whoring over more respectable occupations when she'd been cast out on the street. Was it because she was, at heart, a whore – and her daughter the same?

Leila slipped quietly out of the bed, leaving Imbaso drifting into sleep behind. He was so different from Tevo – tall where Tevo was short, skilled in love beyond what she had experienced before. He had known other women, that was certain. Yet Imbaso was also somehow more innocent – Tevo had been raised as a thief, after all, while Imbaso had been the prized only son of a wealthy and powerful family.

Betsalel had contributed some surprising ideas of his own when Leila had importuned him for improvements in Shadow Manor South's plumbing facilities. In addition to a Parat-style flush toilet, the contents of which vanished to some unspecified dimension, the bathroom now offered an enormous tub, which would at a touch of a button be filled with hot water. When drained the water went to the same place as the contents of the toilet.

But that was not all. In a corner, a square enclosure flanked by tile along the sides enclosed by the room's walls and glass on the other two had a panel with a glowing red light on one side and a glowing blue light on the other. Above the panel was a curious fixture such as Leila had never seen until Betsalel had created it for her.

It consisted of a single narrow pipe, perhaps three-quarters of an inch in diameter, protruding from one of the enclosure's tiled walls. Mounted on its nether end was a gleaming metal circle four inches in diameter, pierced with innumerable tiny holes. The cold showers she'd enjoyed while apprenticing with the Night Guild in Marsine had issued from a simple pipe – a gush, not a rainstorm.

Leila pressed her index finger against the panel only a slight distance from the blue end. Water immediately began gushing from the holes in the circle, pouring out at a pressure just short of painful as it pounded against her naked flesh. The temperature was just warm enough to keep her from shivering. She stood there, the cool water rushing down, for a long time.

Chapter 30

In the morning the two woke together, and made love again. Leila felt a twinge of guilt. But Tevo was far away in both time and distance; and Imbaso was here, and beautiful. Her hunger had been deep. When the afterglow had faded they rose, and she had the fun of watching his amazement when she showed him the bathroom. Not even in Wena had he seen anything like it – who could say what amenities they might have east of the Killtops, but possibly there was not another bathroom like it on earth.

Leila donned her assassin garb and resumed the illusion of Usiku. Betsalel had furnished the kitchen with a cold chest, so it was possible for her to keep food here and cook for herself; but she hadn't been shopping lately so they went out for breakfast. Before leaving though, she brewed herself a cup of herbal tea.

This tropical plant, one Leila had learned about in her studies here, would prevent a man's seed from lodging in a woman's belly if drunk the day after intercourse. She had been celibate and traveling for months, and had long since stopped her daily drinks of the contraceptive herb she'd been drinking regularly in Parat since last summer.

There was another herb she now knew of, also from Palambo, that need be drunk only once during a woman's monthly cycle to prevent conception throughout the month. Assassins did not always kill – sometimes what the client wanted was only to assure that their enemies had no heirs. Leila had stolen small quantities of all of the substances she thought useful, and now had a potent pharmacopeia here in her home.

The two of them went out and breakfasted in a nearby café, griddle cakes sweetened with honey and plenty of dark, bitter kaf to wash them down. Then they parted ways, Imbaso to return to his home and face the music there while Usiku went to her classes at the gymnasium.

"What will you tell your father?" Leila asked him as they stood on the street outside the café. Imbaso put on a faint, determined smile. "I'll apologize for getting sick and running out," he said. "I'm sure he'll understand I never saw anything like that before. I'll tell him I went out and got a woman, which he'll likely believe. I think he was surprised I haven't been visiting the whorehouses since I returned home."

Usiku grinned, eyes sparkling. "Why Imbaso, were you saving yourself for *me*?" she asked sweetly.

"Yes," he answered seriously, "I was. A man has his needs, but one of those needs is for love. And I love you. Well, the real you. Uh…" He had the good sense to shut up before digging himself any deeper. Leila squeezed his hand. Public displays of affection were considered to be in bad taste, in Palamban society.

"I love you, too," she murmured. "See if you can find out what Kivuli has been doing in exchange for the sacrifices, will you?" Imbaso nodded, and bade her farewell.

When Usiku arrived at the Makucha Nyeusi's secret training facility on Namei's third circle, she nodded to Master Kifozi and made her way to the floor. She was still working with poisons and other substances upstairs, but needed to maintain her physical condition and weapons skills. She usually worked out in the gymnasium for two hours at the start of every day, while it was still relatively cool. Then after a rest and a good drink of water, she would spend the rest of the day studying with Master Sumundi, the Black Claw's poisons instructor, on the upper floors. The apprentices were provided with a Spartan meal at midday.

But today, Usiku had barely begun her warm-up exercises when Kifozi called out and beckoned her over to speak with him. "Usiku, you have learned well in the short time you have been with us," he said. The girl bowed her head in acknowledgment of the compliment.

"Thank you, master," she said softly.

"I have discussed it with Master Sumundi, and we are in agreement. The Makucha Nyeusi has need of your skills, and it is time for you to receive your final testing and become a full-fledged member of the cult."

A thrill of panic ran up Leila's spine. Now that she knew initiates of the cult were given a piece of the djinn to wear around their necks, she was less eager than ever to become one. "But I have been unable to learn the Secret Scriptures," Usiku protested. "I cannot pass the test."

Kifozi eyed her thoughtfully. It seemed odd that so apt a pupil would have any trouble memorizing the Scriptures, even if she was an illiterate girl from a remote farm in the desert. But that was of no concern. "You need not become an initiate of Kivuli to join the Makucha Nyeusi," he explained. "Of course you are expected to continue your study of the Scriptures and work toward achieving full status as a member of our religion. But you are much more valuable to us as an assassin, doing the god's work, than you could ever be as a mere acolyte of the temple."

Leila let relief shine in Usiku's eyes, hoping that Kifozi would interpret her objections as fear that failure to master the Scriptures would have barred her from her goal of becoming an assassin. The master assassin went on, "The Black Claw's test is a physical one. Complete your assignment, and you will become a full member and no longer required to take instruction."

"And the assignment?" Usiku asked seriously.

"You will be given a target for assassination," Kifozi explained. "Someone local. You will have one week in which to study your target and plan the killing, but no longer. It must be carried out within seven days of the time you are given the task, and in accordance with our instructions. If everything is done correctly, you will pass."

"What if I should fail?" Leila asked in Usiku's voice. Becoming an assassin had seemed like the best way for her to infiltrate the church without having to become involved in actually worshiping the djinn, but now it was crunch time. Was she prepared to slaughter some random, possibly blameless citizen just to maintain her cover?

"Fear not, Usiku," the master assassin assured her. "If you fail to complete the assignment correctly within the time limit, it will be back to training until you are ready to try again. But I feel confident that you are ready. And we will soon have need of your skills for a special project in Iskand. Once that is complete, I can give you leave to return to Halath for however long it takes to wreak your revenge on those who destroyed your family. Would you not like that?"

Usiku's expression became one of fierce determination. Now that Leila no longer needed to fool Imbaso with that melodramatic tale, she was growing eager to discard it altogether. But she needed to keep up the pretense for the sake of the Makucha Nyeusi. Usiku's tragic past and her burning desire for revenge were her primary motivating factors in joining the cult, after all.

"I think, I hope, that I can justify your belief in me," Usiku said with conviction. "Do you have an assignment for me?"

"Indeed I do," Kifozi smiled. "His name is Mkuuzo, and he is a man aged fifty-three who lives on the sixth circle with his wife, as well as his two grown sons and their wives and children. He is employed as an overseer in the Royal Taxation Office, and travels to work in the royal offices at the top of the city daily."

"May I know the reason for his death?" Usiku asked, and Kifozi grimaced.

"An assassin is to kill on command, not because he or she has decided that the target deserves to die. But as this is your first assignment, I will make an exception this one time."

Kifozi went on, "Mkuuzo is also a member of the Namei City Council of Elders, which controls most of the local government, and he has been speaking up in their meetings against the worship of Betsalel. While we no longer worship the dark one, at least not under that name, we need to preserve the temples above in order to facilitate our activities below. We do not want to see the same thing happen here that occurred in the Gaspari Dominion at around the time of the prophet – witch hunts, our people chased down and slaughtered. But we want Mkuuzo to be killed publically, in a way that will remind people it is not wise to speak out against the dark god. You of course will not be seen or suspected. Is that clear?"

Usiku nodded. "I will immediately begin studying this Mkuuzo and decide how best to bring him down," she said forthrightly. "I assume that the details of his demise, other than that it should be public and clearly not a result of accident or natural causes, are up to me?"

"Absolutely," Kifozi assured her. "Report back to me when the deed has been done, no later than seven days from now."

Chapter 31

Leila was in a quandary. If anything, she and Betsalel would welcome a public outcry against the practices of the Kivuli cult. It would be easy enough to make it known that the cult and the djinn, not the Shadow God, were to blame for the atrocities that were being committed, the babies that disappeared. But it was too soon to try that, now. And if she failed to kill Mkuuzo, the Black Claw would just send someone else to do the job.

She decided she must follow her target, and learn what sort of man he was. If he were worthy, kind to children and small animals, a pillar of the community, she might be able to use her powers to shelter him from the cult. But that would undoubtedly require that he and his family flee the country, and even that might not be good enough.

Donning the appearance of one of Namei's solid citizens and mounted on Wapesi, Leila rode the long and winding way from her home on the fourth circle to the very top, past the circle where Imbaso's family lived, past the circle on which the eight temples had been built.

The royal palace had been converted more than two centuries ago into government offices. While the Palambans had not developed bureaucracy to the level achieved in the Dominion, the running of their sprawling kingdom required many full-time functionaries and mountains of paperwork – in addition to legions of soldiers.

Entrance to the city's top level was via four roads up from the temple level, and each of those was blocked by a gate tended by royal guards. The entire royal compound was a city within a city, not unlike the Imperial compound in Parat. But here it was completely surrounded by a high stone wall. In a pinch, Leila guessed, this area might serve as a citadel within the walled city of Namei, a last strongpoint should the lower city be overrun.

But no enemies had overrun Namei, or even come against it in force, within living memory. The soldiers guarding the gate passed the richly dressed middle-aged man on his impressive-looking horse through without any request for official documents. They even gave him directions to the Royal Taxation Office, located in an area that had once been a royal ballroom.

The former royal palace had been a large, sprawling building constructed in stages over the course of centuries. Surrounding it were lushly landscaped grounds, and a number of subsidiary buildings had sprung up around it: the royal stables, the royal menagerie, the servants' quarters, the guard barracks, and more. Some of these retained their original uses, but most had been repurposed after the royal family had relocated to their much-grander palace in Iskand.

Hmm, Leila mused, as she tied up Wapesi near a watering trough in the royal stableyard and tossed the stableboy a coin to look after him while the local businessman in search of a consultation with the Taxation Office was gone. Kifozi had mentioned a special project in Iskand. Surely Betsalel's temple in Iskand must have been taken over by Kivuli just as had the one in Namei. What project there could not be carried out by Iskand's local chapter? With the djinn able to appear here and discuss things with Mauaji, then relay instructions to the arch-priest's counterpart a thousand miles away in a matter of moments, why would they need to send a party of assassins on that long journey?

Perhaps she would understand it better after Imbaso was able to learn exactly what favors the "god" was doing for his worshipers in exchange for their sacrifices. The Namei businessman ducked in among the foliage on the palace grounds, and became invisible. Then, moving as silently as she had been trained to these past few months, Leila slipped in through the palace's main entrance unnoticed and made her way to the Royal Taxation Office.

She had thought herself the mistress of sneakiness when she'd completed her similar, if less grisly, final examination to become a journeyman thief with the Night Guild four years before. But her training with the Black Claw had truly completed that education. Though the office had a dozen workers and many people coming in and out, Leila slipped inside without anyone being aware of her and took up station near the counter in front.

People owing taxes, usually landowners and those who operated businesses within the kingdom, were encouraged to come here and pay their taxes in person. If you did not, the Taxation Office kept records on everyone and they would send the Royal Guards out to collect directly from you on your premises. Part of that encouragement was the knowledge that bad things could happen to you when they came.

Many people, for whatever reason, might find that their tax assessment was more than they could pay. Then they would come to the Taxation Office to request an extension or a reduction based on hardship. The large space, where in times past Palambo's nobility had emulated the nobility of the Dominion at lavish balls, had been left mostly open. Desks and furniture designed to hold files occupied it. But three large private offices had been carved out of the space against the far wall.

Nobody here had a name plate, though surely everyone involved with the bureaucracy must be literate. The literacy rate in the kingdom was high, at least in the cities and among the wealthier classes. Out among the cattle-herders and jungle gardeners, there was probably one man in a hundred – and no women – who could read.

Kifozi had implied that Usiku's target was the head man in this office, definitely a prominent citizen. But other than the mention of his age Leila had no idea what he looked like. So she couldn't just assume that the largest of the three offices was his. She lurked invisible near the front counter, ears pricked to hear the conversations of those who came in, for more than an hour. Finally an obviously wealthy man, finely dressed and looking to be of a similar age with Mkuuzo, came in and spoke to the clerk at the counter. "Jumandi," he said with the air of a refined person forced by circumstance to interact with underlings. "I have an appointment with Mkuuzo."

Leila drew closer, and as the gentleman was respectfully ushered in past the counter and delivered to the largest of those offices, she was right on his heels. As the two of them slipped inside she darted silently for the room's far corner. It was far enough away from the massive bloodwood desk that neither of the room's other occupants was likely to bump into her, but close enough she should be able to hear and observe everything.

The man behind the desk looked as if he might be Tajiri's father, or much older brother. Clearly a Hutu, but doing quite well in this area dominated by the Amhari. The extra fat beneath his skin had kept his face from becoming lined, and except for the creeping gray in his wooly hair he looked far younger than his actual age. Life had been good for Mkuuzo, it seemed.

He rose from his comfortable chair when the visitor entered and threw out his arms, greeting Jumandi as a brother while the clerk was dismissed. "Take a seat, old friend," he said with a gesture as he closed the office's door. Hmm, Leila thought. Not only were the two close in age, they seemed to have known each other for a long time. Might they have been boyhood friends?

Mkuuzo seated himself in his chair again, and looked across the desktop at Jumandi. "So," he said, "how can I help you today?" No pleasantries, no beating around the bush. Jumandi, a thin and aristocratic-looking Amhari, opened a finely-tooled leather satchel he'd brought with him and removed a piece of paper.

Palambo had no shortage of trees, and the art of paper-making had flowed from the Hando to the Gasparis and now here – though it was said that in ancient times, the ancestors of the Dareg who had first inhabited the valley of the Azraq had developed papyrus, very similar – a millennium at least before the Hando had discovered how to make true paper. While the civilization that flourished at that time was keeping careful written records, the ancestors of today's Dominion citizens had still been living in mud huts.

Wherever it came from, paper and the marks men made on it were the new rulers of the modern world. Swords and crossbows and spears might open the way, but it was with words – indelible, transferrable words – that conquerors ultimately controlled their kingdoms and what went on in them.

Mkuuzo took the tax bill from his friend and looked it over. "Quite high, my friend!" he said. "It seems that you are doing well since last we met."

Jumandi grimaced. "So the royal assessors would seem to believe," he replied mournfully. "But the truth is otherwise. There have been disasters manifold in the past year – my lands ravaged by floods, plantations destroyed by herds of rampaging tembo, two of my trading caravans wiped out by bandits in the passes to the north. It has been an absolutely devastating year!"

The plump tax official leaned across the desk – his face a mask of sympathy, his hands in a posture of prayer. "I am so distressed to hear of these calamities, Jumandi," he said. "I am sure that with a little work we can arrange for a hardship exemption. Shall we say, fifty percent of the total due?"

"I was hoping for sixty," Jumandi admitted, "but I realize that this will certainly entail expenses for your department. Someone will have to be sent to verify my losses since the assessors' last visit. Do you suppose that forty asand will be enough to cover the costs?"

Mkuuzo's face fell. "I fear it will be more, friend Jumandi. More likely fifty or even sixty, as some of your properties are remote and will require days of travel." Jumandi eyed him with a look that was anything but friendly. "But!" the tax man added hastily, "You are a member of the City Council of Namei, as am I. I know you share my concern that the worship of Betsalel has become a menace to our society, with the increasing incidence of unexplained disappearances and deaths. We should annex the property on which the temple stands and raze it to the ground, as was done in the Gaspari Dominion centuries ago, do you not agree?"

Jumandi's expression had changed from one of hostility to one of speculation. "I believe you may have the right of it, friend Mkuuzo. Shall we say a sixty percent hardship deduction from my tax bill, I will reimburse you forty..." – he caught his "friend's" expression and corrected himself – "I meant to say, fifty asand for the expenses of verifying the hardship, and I will support you in the Council as regards the church of Betsalel. Fair enough?"

Mkuuzo smiled and waited while Jumandi handed over the requested bribe. No "team" would ever be sent to verify the hardship, Leila knew. The fifty asand would go into the tax man's personal fortune, and the kingdom would be out more than half of whatever it had hoped to obtain from Jumandi. Mkuuzo's future existence was beginning to look less certain.

Remaining invisible for most of the day, Leila wandered out of the Taxation Office near noon. She lunched at a nearby café that served the royal office workers, relieved herself at the toilet facilities, then returned to Mkuuzo's office and stayed until closing time. She had to be certain that the exchange she had witnessed was not just a sweetheart deal extended to a lifelong friend. But Mkuuzo interviewed five other applicants for extensions or tax relief during the day and extracted bribes from four of them. The fifth ignored the tax officer's blatant suggestions, and had his application denied. Clearly, Bwana Mkuuzo was as bent as they come.

The day had not been taxing, physically. Leila had spent most of it with her butt parked on the tile floor of Mkuuzo's relatively-cool office, while a parade of supplicants passed through and were relieved of their spare gold. He had gathered in almost as much in bribes during the course of the day's work as she had made, in five minutes, presenting an illusory bank note to a hapless teller at the Bank of Palambo a few months ago. And he did this six days a week? The man must be rich beyond even *her* dreams of avarice!

As Mkuuzo locked up his desk and prepared to leave for the day, Leila rose to her feet (stifling a moan) and slipped out before him. She exited the palace and waited near the front entrance for her quarry to emerge, so she could follow him home.

He soon came out behind her, and hailed a *ritzha* from a line of them that had appeared in the road outside. Most government workers who could afford to must go back and forth to work this way every day. The cleaning and maintenance staff and the guards were quartered here on the palace compound, but everyone else lived in one of the circles below. Mkuuzo had the look of a man who never walked if he could avoid it.

Leila was annoyed, wishing now she had not brought Wapesi with her today. But the poor animal got out so seldom – and he'd be all right at the stables, even if she had to leave him overnight. As Mkuuzo was boarding his *ritzha* Leila hastily dashed into some nearby foliage. Then, adopting the appearance of a workman returning home on foot, she reappeared and trotted after the tax man as he was carried toward home.

Chapter 32

As Mkuuzo was a married man, head of a large extended family all living together in his home, Leila had expected him to return straight there after work. After all, he was packing a considerable amount of gold in that valise he carried with him. But no.

The sixth circle, where Kifozi had said Mkuuzo lived, seemed ridiculously downscale for a man taking in as much in bribes as she had seen today. But the *ritzha,* an unremarkable-looking workman loping amid the crowds fifty yards behind it, went down past the sixth circle. It passed the fifth, then the fourth where Leila herself lived, and came to rest finally in the third circle – a long, curving street mostly inhabited by domestic servants and similarly low-paid laborers.

It wasn't exactly a slum, but… Leila squeezed into a nearby recessed doorway and went invisible again. She was beginning to get tired and hungry again, not to mention thirsty and in need of a toilet break; but without trailing Mkuuzo to his home, how could she case it? The man's venality and his apparent desire to raise opposition against the church of Betsalel solely so temple property could be confiscated by the city already had him nearly in his coffin; but she needed to see him with his family before she made her final decision. Would they be devastated by his loss?

After paying off the *ritzha* boy, Mkuuzo let himself in at the front door of a four-storey apartment building with a key. Before it had swung shut, the modern latch locking automatically behind him, Leila had wriggled in behind him. There were yet hours of daylight, but little of it came in through the building lobby's filthy windows and she blended into the shadows with ease.

Mkuuzo knocked twice at the door of an apartment on the first floor up from the lobby, and a woman soon came to let him in. She was a beauty in her early twenties, a tall and graceful Amhari with large, liquid eyes. She appeared to be wearing lacy lingerie imported from the Gaspari Dominion, and she greeted the squat and rotund tax official with expressions of the deepest affection.

Leila barely managed to squeeze in behind him, nearly brushing Mkuuzo's rear. But he had other things on his mind. Great Betsalel, Leila thought, it's the Namei version of Musette! At the age of fourteen Leila had masqueraded as the cast-aside mistress of a wealthy man in order to sell an emerald necklace she'd stolen for its full market value. Civilization in the part of the continent south of the Center Sea was ancient, far pre-dating the Dominion; but it seemed that wealthy Palambans had taken to emulating Dominion culture when it came to the sins they committed.

Leila seated herself in "Musette's" comfortable parlor, furnished as the young woman was in a Gaspari style, while she assured herself that nothing here was more than it seemed. Mkuuzo was not plotting treason, nor seeking to undermine the church of Betsalel. He was getting his rocks off, preening at his mistress's declarations of passion and love for him, and demonstrating to society at large that he was a man of substance, a man who could take what others wanted and could not have.

While the middle-aged fat man was heaving himself slowly to orgasm amid his mistress' cries of ecstasy, Leila helped herself to some food and a cool drink of Palamban palm wine from the kitchen, and relieved herself in the apartment's toilet. Then she silently let herself out of the apartment and sat down on the floor in the hallway, waiting for Mkuuzo to emerge.

When he came out, Leila suspected from the way he moved, the valise was considerably lighter. The tax official's mistress had worked out how to be a whore in a way that paid far, far better than anything Leila's mother had ever managed. Miriam had not lacked for intelligence, but her daughter felt she had definitely made the wrong choice. But then her mother had been far more sheltered, at this same age, than Leila was. She'd lacked the information necessary to make an informed choice, and both of them had suffered for it.

That was all ancient history, now. Mkuuzo had remained in his mistress' apartment for well over an hour, but it was still short of the time at which most families – in the Dominion or here in

Palambo – usually sat down for the evening meal. *Now*, surely, he would go home?

He did, by another *ritzha*. And Leila was forced, remaining invisible now that pedestrian traffic along Namei's roads had eased, to trot behind him up three circles. It was a good thing her assassin training had left her in such fit condition, nor did it hurt that the day's heat had now eased considerably. They were coming into the middle of autumn, and the rains had become occasional instead of a daily fact of life. This close to the equator, though, there was little difference in the length of the day.

Silently sucking in deep breaths as the sun fell toward the western horizon, Leila watched as Mkuuzo paid off the boy and walked in, self-satisfaction apparent in every limb, through the front entrance of a fairly substantial three-storey compound on the sixth circle near Gold Street. The place was large, probably as large in square footage as the house of Imbaso's family three circles closer to the summit. It lacked the spacious grounds, though she suspected there was at least a little land contained in its inner courtyard. Not palatial – but very, very nice.

Leila heaved a sigh of relief. Now that she knew where the tax official lived, she could come here tomorrow morning and observe him in his home environment. At this point she was disgusted with him but not hostile to him. Left to her own devices, she would never in a million years have murdered this weak and pathetic man just for being a corrupt piece of shit who cheated his employer out of tax revenue and spent the money keeping a fancy woman. But under the circumstances she had little compunction about doing him in as a requirement of maintaining her cover with the Makucha Nyeusi. He would be no great loss – unless something she saw tomorrow convinced her otherwise.

Chapter 33

Leila, invisible in the nearly deserted streets, trotted quietly down two levels to circle four and her own home. What a day! Having eaten enough to satisfy her at the mistress' apartment, she was looking forward to a hot bath followed by a cold shower, and bed. She found Imbaso lurking in the darkness near the front door, hiding behind a small palm tree.

"Oh!" they both exclaimed, as she went visible and he emerged from hiding at nearly the same moment. In her eagerness to reach home, she had stopped trying to move silently – and he had heard her coming. He seized her in a hug, grinning in the darkness. The memory of their time together the previous night and morning occupied his thoughts, and he was eager for them to be together again. Not just for the sex, mind, though at his age there were few human motivations more compelling. He had news to impart!

"Betsalel save us both, Imbaso, you would not *believe* the day I've had," Leila said with an edge of crossness as she let them both in. Once the door had closed, he pulled her into his arms and just held her, radiating his love. It was plenty cool enough for physical closeness, in here. After a moment or two Leila relented and hugged him back.

"Have you eaten?" she asked, breaking away from the embrace and looking for the box of Lucifer matches she kept near the door. Betsalel could just as easily have provided her with room lights that would come on at her command, but her imagination had stopped short of requesting such a thing.

Leila lit a lamp on the wall near the door, and the dark room glowed with warm light. They gazed at each other, looking for signs of changes. There were none. Now, he stepped forward and pulled her into his arms, kissing her with a nice mix of tenderness and passion. A minute later, she drew away panting.

"Imbaso, stop!" she begged. "You drive me crazy, and I really want to take a bath. You didn't say, have you eaten yet?"

He smiled down at her. "Yes, I ate with the family before coming down here. Have you?" He seemed improbably cheerful, considering the state he'd been in less than twenty-four hours previously.

"I had something to eat earlier," she said dismissively. "Just let me get into the tub and I'll tell you all about it later."

"I'll join you!" he declared with a grin. He'd taken the first shower of his life this morning and loved it, but that tub looked wonderful as well. And it was plenty big enough for two.

She glared at him, but his enthusiasm was irresistible. Sighing, she said "Come on then," and led him toward the bedroom. A couple of minutes and some hanky-panky later, the two of them – naked – crossed the hall and stepped into the bathroom. Leila had placed Lucifer matches in every room, and it was soon lit with a golden glow. Then she pressed the button, and in an instant the tub was full of steaming, clear water.

Imbaso was so fascinated his erection began to subside. "Won't it overflow when we get in?" he asked.

"See this hole?" Leila pointed. "Excess water runs down it and vanishes, like the way the toilet works." After considering the size of the hole and the mass of herself and her companion, she added "Better let me get in first."

Eventually both of them were able to enter the tub without spilling any of its contents on the bathroom's tiled floor. They sank down face to face, she at the drain end and he at the other, and let the hot water come up to their chins. His knees were bent, protruding slightly from the water; but it was truly an enormous tub.

"Ah, this is wonderful!" Imbaso declared. "Our god is good!"

"You're preaching to the high priestess," she murmured, slowly sinking lower until her head was submerged. She blew some bubbles, then came back up. When she blinked the water out of her eyes, she found him gazing at her, eyes dilated with desire. The erection was back in full force.

"Come over here, lovely," Imbaso murmured, and held out his arms. Leila leaned forward onto the surface of the water, and floated into his embrace. She slipped down over him. Quite a lot of the tub's water eventually found its way to the floor, and they had to blot it up with towels after they got out. Then they showered together, a cozy experience, before getting dressed again.

Clean and dry, they sat snuggled up together on the front room sofa and talked. "How did it go with your father?" Leila asked. Imbaso squeezed her close.

"It's funny," he said. "Last night I didn't think I would ever be able to look him in the eye again without my revulsion showing through. But he is my father, the man I've known – or thought I knew – all my life. And this has been going on in my family for generations. I don't think he's truly evil, just inured to something that has been presented to him as normal, as expected."

"That may be," she replied, "but what he does is evil. He has lost his sense of right and wrong, and he and the cult must be stopped. Did you ask him what Kivuli is giving back to his worshipers?"

Imbaso nodded, then spoke. "After I'd apologized for my behavior last night he was very kind about it, said he'd done the same his first time. But he'd known for sure that the Secret Scriptures were not make-believe. It was just the reality of the blood. Plus back then, the 'god' was just an inanimate idol that did not come when called."

"Anyhow," Imbaso went on, "we had an intimate talk during the afternoon, a long one. He confessed to me that though Kivuli comes willingly enough, he has not been as forthcoming with favors as Father and the rest of the cult hierarchy had expected he would be once they finally got him to manifest."

Leila turned in her seat and looked up at him. He was nearly a foot taller than she was. "So?..." she prompted.

"The first thing Father wanted from Kivuli was that he should manifest in the other idols when called, and tell the worshipers there that the temple in Namei was responsible for bringing back their god in his new form. He also wanted the teeth, and Kivuli didn't seem to understand why but he didn't mind. It causes him no pain, and as soon as a tooth was taken another appeared in its place. That was no trouble. But other things Father wanted, the god did not want – or did not know how – to do."

"The djinn is limited by the form he was given by men's minds," Leila said. "The Scriptures seemed only to focus on Betsalel's aspect as the God of Death. I would guess that Kivuli would have the ability to kill anyone within range of a supporting group of worshipers, but he would lack the subtlety the Makucha Nyeusi could bring to the job. Am I right?"

"Father is... frustrated, I think," Imbaso said. "He had expected that by succeeding in getting the god to manifest where others had failed for generations he would become... like, ultimate high priest of Palambo or something. There would be honors – and whatever he wished, the god would grant him. He intimated that he has great plans for me, as well, plans he expected Kivuli would fulfill. But the god has been less than fully cooperative."

"Of course!" Leila exclaimed with some relief. Having a powerful god-like being under the complete control of a malign priest was a frightening thought. Not that having such a being under no control at all was a lot better... "Kivuli is an infant! Babies are cute, and we love them instinctively, but consider how it would be if they were, say, twice our size and had long, sharp fangs. They are greedy, selfish, and completely unreasonable – and their only skill is in getting us to give them what they want, or at least what they need."

Imbaso's eyes were wide as they looked into Leila's. "I believe you're right! Father said that he has to beg, and plead, and instruct, to get Kivuli to do anything at all. And sometimes his requests are just ignored, and the god flees from his idol leaving Father haranguing a lifeless statue."

"I hope this is a good thing," she said thoughtfully. "Certainly, I think we had better figure out how to drive the djinn away or disable him before he becomes a teenager!" Imbaso leaned down and kissed her, and Leila sensed that he was already thinking about going another round. He was a few years older than Tevo, but just as insatiable.

Then a thought occurred to him, and he pulled away to say, "I almost forgot! You are so irresistible, I can't seem to hold any information in my mind when you are near." She poked him in the ribs.

"Flattery will get you nowhere. You were probably all agog to find out about *my* day?"

Imbaso slapped his forehead. "Yes! *That* was it! What happened, that you were so tired and cross when you came home?"

"You're not the only one rising in the cult, it seems," Leila said with a touch of bitterness. "Kifozi believes I am far enough advanced in my assassin training that it's time for me to graduate, so he assigned me a target. I have a week to kill him, publicly, or go back to studying – and I don't think he would be too happy about that outcome."

"But, Leila! Just murder some random citizen? How could you?" Imbaso, though older and with far more years of training in arms than his little lover, had never killed anyone.

"I'm not crazy about the idea myself," she said quietly. "But if I don't do it, they'll just assign somebody else to the task and he'll be dead anyway. It's not like I haven't killed anyone before."

He hugged her close. "But nobody who didn't deserve it, right? Does this guy deserve to die?"

"I haven't made my decision yet. If Mkuuzo is truly a worthy man, it will take a great effort on my part to save him. But what I saw today didn't help his cause any."

"You watched him?" Imbaso asked, and Leila nodded.

"I got the assignment right after I got to the gymnasium this morning, so I went right up to the palace complex to see him at work. I sat invisible in his office most of the day, listening to him extort bribes from nearly everyone he spoke to. He's high up in the Taxation Office, and it's his decision whether people are given relief from tax bills they can't pay."

"I've heard of him," Imbaso said. "Isn't he on the Namei city council?"

"Yes," Leila replied, "that's why the cult wants him dead. Evidently he's been speaking out against the worship of Betsalel in the council, trying to build up support for the kind of anti-dark god program that Emperor Fernand put into effect a couple of hundred years ago."

"That might seriously inconvenience the cult," Imbaso mused. "But it wouldn't be very good for our master either, would it?"

"I don't know about that," she responded. "The idols in those temples have all become corrupted by Kivuli, and Betsalel is convinced they cannot be reclaimed. But if we could drive out the djinn, and destroy those idols, Betsalel could place new ones in those temples. Most people don't know anything about the evil practices of the cult, and normal worship could resume. But having them believe he was actively evil, as everyone thought in the Dominion until last year, would *really* not help our cause."

"That sounds like another mark against Mkuuzo," Imbaso said, "one case where we and the cult are on the same side. But only because we're 'roommates'!"

"I'll go and see him at home with his family tomorrow," Leila said, "and make my decision then. And I need to go up to the palace complex and get Wapesi back. I had to leave him in the stables there today, so I could follow Mkuuzo from work and find out where his house is. But instead, he went to his mistress' place."

"That fat old toad has a mistress?" Imbaso laughed. "The dog!"

"Just wait until *you're* old and fat," Leila said.

"And will you be old and fat then, too?" he asked, his expression saying he would love her even so. She looked at him strangely. Did Imbaso believe they would be growing old together? Their lovemaking was sweet, but she could not remain here in Palambo forever. It was not her home, and her work was in the Dominion, restoring her god to the worship he deserved. Which thought immediately brought her back to Tevo. When she returned, they would have to have a long talk. Could it ever be the same between them again?

Leila pushed those thoughts away with a will. At this moment it was Imbaso by her side, and if she felt inner conflicts there was no denying that she loved – and wanted – him. "Let's go to bed," she said. "I need to be up way early tomorrow so I can get to

Mkuuzo's house before he leaves for work." Grinning wickedly, Imbaso pounced and scooped her off the sofa in one swift motion. Then he carried her away to the bedroom.

Chapter 34

Imbaso still lay abed when, before the sky had begun to get light, Leila kissed him on the cheek and put her feet on the floor. "I'll be back later this morning," she murmured. "Will you wait for me?" His eyes opened, but saw barely a shadow in the darkness.

"Is there anything here to eat?" he asked sleepily.

"Sorry," she admitted, "I haven't had a chance to go shopping yet."

"I could get some food for us," he suggested, "but…"

"There's a spare key on top of the dresser," Leila told him. "It's yours. But remember, the protections of our master will exclude anyone with ill intentions from entering. Don't bring anybody home with you, in case they might trigger the wards. It would be hard to explain, eh?"

She was getting into her clothing as they spoke, and at the door she added "Bring us something good! I'm going to be starving when I get back!" With that she was gone. Imbaso heaved a deep sigh and lay there thinking about things for a few moments. Damn, she'd gotten away from him! Soon he drifted back off to sleep.

Cloaked in shadows, Leila jogged quickly around the fourth circle and up a radius road to the fifth. She turned right then, and had only a short distance to go before another road led her up a fairly steep hill to the sixth. The air was still reasonably cool at this hour, and she wasn't perspiring too heavily by the time she arrived at the enormous house where Mkuuzo lived with his extended family.

There was faint light showing in the ground floor windows of golden-colored bottle glass that flanked the front door. It appeared that all of the house's windows had glass in them, a luxury here in Palambo. All on the upper floors remained dark, and Leila guessed that the household must support a large servant staff. They were probably up making breakfast while the family slumbered on.

Perfect! She thought, and bent to the keyhole on the front door. Unlikely, she hoped, that the door would be barred overnight. Leila's skills with lockpicks had recently been reinforced – another example of dazzling her instructors with her "aptitude" for the new subject. She was probably now as good at picking locks as she had ever been, and the old lock opened to her in less than a minute.

Still invisible, Leila pushed the heavy bloodwood door open a crack, and peered into the entryway. Similarly to the layout at Imbaso's family home, the front door gave on a good-sized sitting room with double doors beyond it leading to the courtyard. There were lamps lit there, and off to the left she could smell food cooking.

Sliding inside and silently pushing the door closed behind her, Leila took a look to see what was to the right, first. A long hall led to a stairway going up, and was lined with small rooms that were probably for storage or the housing of servants. As she watched, she was astonished to see Mkuuzo himself emerge from one of those rooms. He was wearing a nightshirt, and yawning. Had the missus kicked him out of their marriage bed for showing up late to dinner? That didn't seem likely, somehow.

The middle-aged wives of middle-aged, wealthy men like Mkuuzo did not usually have the option of objecting to their husbands' peccadilloes. If they did, they might find themselves summarily divorced and sent back to live with their parents, or a brother if the parents were no longer living. The concept of women's rights had not penetrated very far into Palamban law, as yet.

The lord of the manor hastened up the nearby flight of steps, presumably returning to his own bedroom or perhaps going to take a bath. As Leila continued to watch the corridor in bemusement, a very young, very pretty maidservant clad in a dull-colored shift, presumably the household servants' uniform, peered cautiously out of that same door and looked anxiously up the stairs to make sure her master was no longer in sight. Then, an expression of distaste and resignation on her face, she hurried toward Leila.

The invisible intruder stepped silently and hastily aside and let her pass, as she went through the entry area toward the kitchen wing. The rat! It wasn't enough that he was taking bribes and keeping a mistress, he was forcing himself on the female staff as well – disgusting!

Mkuuzo's life was hanging by a thread as Leila made her way in the direction the maid had gone. The smells wafting from the kitchen down the hall were driving her crazy! She ought to have had a little fruit to eat, or something, before leaving the house.

There was a large formal dining room with two good-sized tables and an extensive sideboard in it, looking out through screened doors to the courtyard. The outdoor area had a formal pool in the center of it with a fountain at the far end, and was nicely landscaped – lush and pretty at this time of day, as the sun was just rising.

Beyond the dining room was one of the larger kitchens Leila had ever seen. There were six adults in the household, and an unspecified number of children; but the four women working frantically in there looked as if they were turning out enough food for a small army. Perhaps Mkuuzo's build, and lusty appetites, ran in the family? It occurred to her that the staff probably got to eat the leftovers, so maybe that accounted for what looked like a generous surplus.

Leila was tempted to sneak into the kitchen and lift some of the food that was now being served up on platters, but there were too many people moving too fast in there. Invisible as she was, somebody would be sure to walk right into her. Instead, she hovered in the dining room where she imagined family members would soon be arriving – and was rewarded when the maids began laying platters of food out on the sideboard near at hand. Evidently breakfast, at least, was served buffet style.

Silently thanking Betsalel for this piece of good fortune, Leila helped herself to some bits of food as soon as the maids had left the room again. There was a sort of sticky grain porridge with dried fruits in it, too hard to eat by hand; but there were also thin slices of cooked meat, fried plantains, and an assortment of cold fresh tropical fruits. They were all delicious, and she had managed to assuage the rumbling in her stomach without disturbing the arrangements too much before the maids returned with more platters.

After that, Leila just leaned up against the wall in the rear corner of the room and waited for the family to arrive. First into the room were a family group Leila took to be one of the sons, with his wife and children. There were a boy of around six, a girl of four, and a baby held tight to its mother's body by a carrying sling.

Ah yes, little children were always up with the dawn and demanding that their parents do the same. The father of the little family bore an unmistakable resemblance to Mkuuzo, but he was taller and not nearly as stout. On the other hand he looked to be still on the sunny side of thirty, so perhaps he hadn't had time yet to grow into his heritage.

Leila had expected them to serve themselves from the buffet and sit down to eat – or perhaps to seat the children while the parents prepared plates for them. But the entire group came in and walked in single file to four chairs along the side of the table nearest the side of the room where she was standing. Then they took their seats and sat upright, staring out at the lush vegetation of the courtyard, with their hands in their laps.

Next to arrive were the older son and his family. He and his wife, a lovely Amhari woman in her early thirties, had two boys – the elder perhaps eleven or twelve, the younger maybe nine. They repeated the performance, greeting their family members formally and then taking their apparent assigned seats. For a few moments there was silence in the room, then the little girl whined, "Mama, I'm hungry. Can I have some fruit while we're waiting, please?"

"Hush," her mother reprimanded firmly. "You know that no one eats until Bwana Mkuuzo is here."

What? Leila couldn't believe her ears. He made his entire family, including his little grandchildren, wait until he bothered to show up for breakfast after shagging the help, or perhaps his mistress, all night? And he made his children and grandchildren call him *Bwana*? Her sense of outrage was beginning to overcome her reluctance.

At long last, Mkuuzo himself appeared with his wife (whom Leila was now ready to nominate for sainthood, on the grounds that she had not killed the man herself a decade ago). She was looking sober, though dressed in a colorful dashiki, and walking two paces behind him. His sons and their families immediately stood up and chorused, "Good morning to you, Bwana Mkuuzo!" He went to the buffet and grabbed a plate. "Good morning all! Please, come and eat!" he said expansively, as if they were guests he'd just invited in off the street.

As they filed past him to the end of the buffet line, he reached out and patted his daughter-in-law, the prettier one, on her rounded bottom. She shrank away from his touch, a look of helpless loathing on her face that Leila was well-positioned to see from the corner where she lurked. The thread snapped.

Leila, as Usiku, returned to Shadow Manor South riding on the back of Wapesi at around eleven in the morning. He'd quite enjoyed his stay at the palace compound's stables, getting the chance to socialize with others of his kind for a change. It had been a lonely time these past months, all by himself in the shady but far from spacious back yard. Leila seldom had time for him, and he had been ridden hardly at all while she was going every day to the gymnasium.

Little did he know, that was about to change. After they arrived home he was soon ensconced in the house's little rear yard once again, and Leila went in through the back door to the kitchen. She found Imbaso, wearing a bath towel as an apron, cooking lunch for them on the house's little wood stove.

Her hasty and improvised breakfast had long since slid down, and the smells were tantalizing though it was not yet midday. "Imbaso!" Leila said in astonishment, "You... you..."

"Cook?" he asked, with a broad smile. She nodded vigorously, trying to get past him so she could lift the lid and see what was on the stove.

"Ah-ah," he said, blocking her move and enfolding her in a hug. "It'll be ready in another half hour. No peeking until then!"

"Imbaso!" she said in exasperation, then gave it up and hugged him back – lifting her face for a kiss. He kissed her until her toes curled.

After releasing her, he asked cheerfully, "Well? What's the verdict?"

Leila rummaged in the cold chest and came up with a bottled beer, something that had not been in there this morning. She pulled the cork and took a seat at the kitchen table. After taking a long swig, she said "The pig dies. Violently, publicly, and soon. His wife and family will celebrate, mark my words."

Imbaso lifted the lid on the pot and stirred it, inspecting the contents. Just a little while longer, he thought, and moved the pot a little off the hottest part of the stove. Then he helped himself to another of the beers in the cold chest, and joined her at the table. "That bad, eh?" he asked.

"The man is utterly vile," Leila affirmed. "He abuses the public trust, causes harm to everyone he meets, and is utterly without shame. I half expected him to be fucking the cook on the dining table after breakfast, while the family looked on." Imbaso's eyebrows raised.

"Remind me," he remarked casually, "Not to get on your bad side."

"Damn right," his beloved replied shortly, and took another swallow of beer.

The meal proved to be simple enough, a savory goat stew with vegetables and a grain that added body, served with fresh flatbread perfect for soaking up the gravy. "This is amazing, Imbaso!" Leila declared, hunger increasing the meal's savor. "Where did you ever learn how to cook?"

He preened, delighted with her reaction. "When I was little," he said, "before my sister died and before Aunt Uzuri came to live with us, Mother was often away from home. I wonder now if she had some suspicions of what Father and his friends were getting up to down at the temple. But she was frequently visiting with her people to the south, taking my sister along. I think Father wouldn't let her take me with her – maybe he was afraid that she would just take both their children and vanish. But anyhow, I was left for hours each day in the care of our housekeeper. She lived with us, and cooked and cleaned."

"So she taught you how to cook?" Leila asked, surprised. Having *been* the servant as often as not during her own childhood, what Imbaso described seemed a fairy tale.

"She swore me to secrecy!" he said with a fond smile. Clearly the woman had been someone special to him. "Young men of my station were not supposed to possess any domestic skills. But she said that every human being on earth needed to eat, and everyone should be able to rely on themselves in case there was no one around to help them – therefore every person should learn to prepare food. It made a lot of sense."

"She sounds like a very wise person," Leila said. "What became of her?" A shadow crossed Imbaso's face. "The same fever that took my baby sister took her, I'm afraid. Things were very bleak there for a while. But Aunt Uzuri's husband was another who died, and she came to live with us. It was all right after that."

Her plate cleaned, Leila reached across the table and squeezed Imbaso's hand. "I can cook a little, too," she said. "Mostly Dominion dishes, of course, and mostly just my personal favorites. I only taught myself a couple of years ago. Maybe you could give me some tips on Palamban cuisine?"

The look of love he threw her way send a shiver down through her core. What was she getting into, here? For dessert there was more fresh fruit, chilled in the cold chest. They moved to the front room and called Betsalel, reporting to him what was going on.

"Would you like me to kill this Mkuuzo for you, Leila?" the Shadow God asked. "He could have a heart attack at his desk even as we speak, and you would be spared having his blood on your hands."

"Thank you, Master," she replied. "But that would not meet the requirements. The master of assassins indicated that we are to travel to Iskand soon for what he called a 'special project.' I suspect that it is something Mauaji would not entrust to his fellow cult members there. So I think it best that I kill Mkuuzo as requested and join the Makucha Nyeusi on this project, whatever it might be."

Betsalel nodded solemnly. "Very well," he said, with a hint of sadness. His beloved priestess was a thief through and through, but he did not believe her to be a callous murderer.

"Master," Leila said, broaching a subject that had been turning in the back of her mind since learning of Mkuuzo's attempts to have worship of the dark god banned.

"Yes, my beloved?" he asked.

"The true idol through which you come to me is quite small," she said. "What would be the smallest size it could be and still be a true idol, a nexus through which you could manifest?" The dark god pondered. All of these thousands of years he had been in existence, interacting with the endlessly fascinating creatures who worshiped him – yet they still kept coming up with new questions!

"I would guess," he said finally, "about the size of a grain of rice. Any smaller and a worshiper would not be able to discern the nature of the idol."

"Oh, I don't think that would matter!" Leila cried, excited. "In every one of your temples in Palambo, your true idols were taken away and have now been corrupted into idols of Kivuli. But your true worshipers still exist here! They have been futilely praying to paintings and carvings and man-made statues, placed in the temples to keep the general public from understanding what was going on. Your worship has declined here because none who prays to you here has ever had a response, nor is there a priesthood urging them to ignore that fact!"

The Shadow God stood motionless for a while, considering. Despite their millennia of sentience the Eight appeared to be not particularly brighter than their average human worshiper; but it seemed to Leila that her master was wiser than some. "A minute speck of a true idol," he said, following her thought, "could be placed on the altar in the temple's public sanctuary. Or even, perhaps, on the floor behind it. It would go unnoticed by the cult members, would appear to be nothing but a bit of detritus. But if it were in range of a true worshiper calling me, I could hear them. And I would be able to sense if Kivuli were near. If he were not, I could manifest. And by granting what my worshipers seek, I could gradually restore my church!"

Leila rose to her feet, smiling brilliantly. Imbaso was right behind her. This could work! Of course, it would not deal with the issue of the cult or the djinn they worshiped, but it would give the true Shadow God a foothold in every temple they were able to place a true idol in.

"Try it!" Leila urged, "See how small a pinch will work!" Betsalel, who as usual was standing on the floor behind the table, bent down and picked up a Lucifer match. It was the one Leila had used to light the lamp that sat on the table before they'd called the god.

Carefully, Betsalel extended his left hand and used the end of the matchstick, held in his right, to gouge out a tiny chunk of his flesh. It was no bigger than a millet seed, and the eyes of his two young worshipers were able to detect a change but they could not resolve the details of the tiny idol that had formed. "Does the second generation make a difference?" Leila asked, curious. The dark god shook his head.

"This flesh is all the same with the flesh of my idol in Parat," he explained. "Each is a nexus, enabling me to come to those who would worship me."

He dropped the tiny black mote into her palm, then shrank to around four feet in height before stepping up onto the table and shrinking the rest of the way to the miniature idol that Leila had originally set there. Then it went still. The god had left them, and she carefully set the nearly-microscopic bead of Betsalel's substance on the table before scooping up the other idol and returning it to its pouch. Was this going to work? If so, how?

Imbaso was utterly fascinated. Was Leila's idea going to be the breakthrough that would allow the true worship of Betsalel to be restored to his homeland? He fervently hoped so. Across the four-foot distance between the sofa back and the dark bloodwood table top in front of it the two, even with their young eyes, could barely make out the minute black idol. They both leaned forward, staring at it avidly.

"Betsalel, return to me!" Leila intoned, and the little blob twitched. It had been lying on its side, and as it grew they saw it was clearly Betsalel. It grew still larger, got up onto its feet, hopped down off the table onto the floor and in moments the dark god stood before them again – exactly as he had before. It worked!

Betsalel grinned at them, his teeth a glistening white. "Leila," he said, "you are a treasure beyond price. How many do you think you will need?"

"Do you have any idea how many of your temples lie between here and the Azraq?" she asked. "I would assume this 'project' we're undertaking will have us traveling on the main road beside the Pana, then taking ship downriver to Iskand."

She half expected him not to know the answer, after being cut off from his temples in Palambo for half a dozen human generations. But he knew exactly. "Unless the cult has built more, there should be eight of my temples in towns and cities along the Pana east of Namei," Betsalel answered. "You had better have twice that many, in case any other opportunities come your way."

While they watched, the Shadow God dug an additional twenty miniscule true idols from his flesh, each excavation site healing immediately. The little grains were gathered on a saucer, and when he'd finished Leila carefully emptied them into a small bottle of the type employed in the herbarium on the Makucha Nyeusi training facility's upper floors. "Take one of these, and expect big things!" she said with a grin. Betsalel smiled on the pair of them, then repeated his shrinking act after climbing up onto the table. This time, as he left them, another of the miniscule idols was left behind. Leila tucked it carefully into the bottle with the rest, then put the cork firmly into the bottle and the bottle into another soft cloth drawstring bag.

"Divinity in a sack!" Leila said, gesturing jubilantly with the little bag. "Just add prayer!" Imbaso grinned back at her. This was genius!

"I suppose I had better get going," he said shortly. "Even though I've passed my initiation and there are no rituals planned for a couple of nights, Father expects me to be at the temple every evening. I'm supposed to be doing what acolytes do, whatever that is."

"Scut work, would be my guess," she replied. "Sometimes I think the whole point of organizations is to make sure that those at the top never have to bother with anything dirty or boring. Just so they're not asking you to kill babies, you should be all right. Do you want to take one of these (she indicated the bag) along with you and start the ball rolling?"

Imbaso pondered. He didn't want anything to interfere with the project Leila had mentioned, as that would give her the opportunity to seed the temples between here and the Azraq River with Betsalel's true idols. But he trusted the Shadow God to remain discreet. There was a good possibility that he would only manifest when it was safe to do so, without anyone in the cult seeing anything.

"All right," he said, swallowing his anxiety. "Give me one." Leila fetched another little glass bottle with a tight stopper. She'd lifted quite a few of those along with a goodly selection of pharmaceutical herbs. "Be careful, sweetie," she said, handing the bottle with its tiny occupant over to him. "Don't get caught!"

Chapter 35

After Leila had seen Imbaso off with a kiss and a hug, she turned her attention to planning the demise of Mkuuzo. Presumably Betsalel knew her innermost heart, but she wondered if he had truly understood that she not only wanted Mkuuzo's blood on her hands, she was eager for it to stain her arms up past the elbows. If ever a human being needed to climb on the wheel and try it again from the beginning, it was this man.

He was to be killed in public, in a way that made it clear his demise was the result of his outspoken opposition to the worship of Betsalel – but without casting suspicion on any human agents of the dark god's temple. Which she, of course, was.

The Makucha Nyeusi had been in existence since the early years of Rasulbiyi, and most people had heard of it. Imbaso had thought it nothing but a tale – as Leila had once thought Betsalel himself to be. But the association in the minds of most people between the Black Claw and the Dark God was not strong. Betsalel was the god of death, among many other attributes. The Black Claw were assassins, and brought death. But that didn't necessarily mean they had anything to do with Betsalel.

Therefore, it was reasonable to think that the manner of Mkuuzo's death might raise suspicions of Black Claw involvement without people immediately assuming that those within the temple hierarchy had called for his death. So how was she to get the point across? It must seem to be the action of the god himself, not his human followers. People witnessing the event must fear that any show of opposition to Betsalel could result in a similar demise for themselves.

Those considerations aside, there was the issue of choosing the time and place. The main road of the sixth circle was not all that busy at the time when the tax official usually hailed his ride to work in the morning. And during that ride, anything that happened to him would likely be blamed on his hapless and impoverished *ritzha* boy. No, it must be in the afternoon after Mkuuzo left work, as he stood outside the palace complex seeking his ride home – or to the apartment of his mistress – that he was struck down in front of a throng of fellow government workers leaving for the day.

Leila had decided that the assignment would be carried out. She had decided how, where, and what time of day it would happen. No point in putting it off any longer, then. She relieved herself in the bathroom, and donned appropriate clothing. Then, in the guise of a porter carrying a load of bananas, she began walking at a comfortable pace up the eight levels to Namei's summit. It was the hottest part of the day, and she was in no great hurry.

Imbaso walked in the main doors of the temple of Betsalel, and nodded to his colleague who stood in the foyer. There was a locked and guarded entrance to the cult's underground chambers at the back of the building, but most of the cult members – especially the lower-placed ones like Imbaso – usually came in through the front. He let himself into the main sanctuary and closed the door. Unsurprisingly, it was empty at this hour. Even Aunt Uzuri had slacked off in her appeals to the dark god to return her son, after months of futile effort.

Silently, Imbaso approached the altar. It was not the original that had sat here when the idol was also a fixture of this part of the temple, but just a stone platform some four feet wide, three feet deep, and a bit more than three feet high. On the wall behind it was the painting showing the god as he was intended to look. How he *would* look, when he manifested in the tiny grain his newest convert held in a pocket of his robe.

Imbaso carefully considered the surroundings. The tiny true idol need only be in close proximity to a sincere worshiper, to permit Betsalel to manifest within it. Atop the altar seemed more appropriate, but behind it seemed safer. In case someone was performing routine housecleaning here in the temple, he didn't want the god's true idol swept up and carried away with the trash.

Ducking behind the altar, he carefully set the tiny object on the floor no more than a quarter inch from the back edge. From the looks of the floor back here, nobody had bothered to sweep in ages. That ought to do it! With a silent prayer that what he had done would work, Imbaso glanced around again to be sure he was unobserved, then walked over to the door at the rear and requested admission.

Though the banana porter had taken his time climbing to the palace level, Leila was perspiring fiercely by the time she arrived and beginning to feel dehydrated. The afternoon was young, with probably two hours to go before Mkuuzo would be leaving work. In case he altered his schedule she didn't want to miss him, but it seemed reasonable that she could take a break first.

After the porter had carried his burden in among the shrubbery of the gardens a finely-dressed middle-aged matron emerged, strolling as if she were killing time admiring the scenery while she waited to meet a friend for an early supper. She entered one of the cafés that served the government workers, and ordered a tall glass of cold (well, cooler than ambient temperature) herbal tea and a small pastry.

Less than an hour later, much refreshed, the matron sauntered out of the café again and once again slipped in among the palms and other vegetation. Then Leila, invisible, made her way carefully inside the main palace entrance and to the Taxation Office. Yes, she quickly saw, Mkuuzo was still in his office. She sat down outside the entrance to the former ballroom to wait.

Huddled in a swath of black fabric, Uzuri made her way into the public sanctuary at the temple of Betsalel. She was the only worshiper today, in fact had been the only one most of the many, many days she had spent here pleading for the return of her son. The months had taken their toll. She looked a decade older than her forty-five years, her hair had turned white, and she had lost much weight. Her face was deeply lined with sorrow, and with a growing despair.

She had faltered from her pattern of daily visits, sometimes not leaving her rooms for days at a time. But today she had made a decision. She had risen from her bed, bathed, and donned a clean mourning wrap. Today, she would pray to the dark god until sunset. And if he did not answer, she would return home and draw another bath. Then she would lie down in it and open her veins. Without Usafi, life held no joy for her.

She knelt painfully on the floor before the altar, the cold stone hurting her old knees. But the physical pain was as nothing to her psychic pain, and she ignored it as being of no consequence. "Betsalel," she cried softly, "Dark one, come to me. Return my son!"

Betsalel heard, and Kivuli was not manifest anywhere near Namei, this afternoon. He arose in the tiny idol, stepping back from the altar as he grew in size. He kept growing until he was eight feet tall, towering above the surface of the altar. Uzuri looked up and nearly fainted.

Her eyes filled with tears as she gazed in disbelief at the black god towering above her. He was real! He was here! The Shadow God knew her, knew what was in her mind as he placed a gentle hand on her shoulder. He stepped around from behind the altar, and shrank to a less-intimidating size.

"I am here, Uzuri," he said softly. "I have come to your call. I am sorry I was not able to come before, but those who claim to be my priests in Palambo now worship another." She didn't understand.

"My son, my baby," she said. "You took him."

He shook his head sadly. "It was not I who took your Usafi," he said. "Your brother took him, not to consecrate him to me, but to sacrifice him to a false god." Uzuri's eyes widened, her mouth twisted in grief. But in her heart she had known. She had been fooling herself for months, unwilling to believe that her brother would do such a thing, praying that the dark one would return the boy if she just asked fervently enough.

"They said you could restore life!" she told the god, grasping at straws, "You brought back some young man in Parat!"

"I would if I could, Uzuri," he said, "but the child's body is gone. And his soul has gone to where I cannot reach it." She rose to her feet, grief being replaced by anger.

"If my son is gone forever, then bring death on he who took him – kill Mauaji!" she demanded.

The Shadow God reached out with his mind. With Leila and Imbaso here in Namei, and this worshiper before him, he had enough power to seek out the arch-priest. He was not here at the temple, nor was he at home. Out somewhere in the city, then, probably working his political contacts and trading favors. Had such a man been truly the arch-priest of Betsalel, the dark god would surely have prospered.

Betsalel found him at last, saw him, saw his heart beating within his body. He reached out his hand, closing it around the organ – and met adamant resistance. Kivuli had warded the man who had awakened him against supernatural harm!

Uzuri stood silently watching him try, watching him fail – watching him hang his head. "Something protects him," she said flatly. The Shadow God nodded.

"His false god has erected protection I can't get past. I cannot do even that for you, Uzuri. I am sorry."

"There is one thing, then," she said with resignation, "that you can do. It is a small thing, easily accomplished. End my pain, and bring me death." Betsalel could do no more, it seemed. He could hardly do less.

"Please, Uzuri, lie down," he said, and gestured her to a bench in the first row. She lay down on it and an expression of joy, of relief, came over her features. All of her burdens would soon be gone! She closed her eyes, and let out a breath as the dark god gently kissed her brow. She did not take another.

The Shadow God felt miserable. His first interaction with an ordinary Palamban believer in centuries, and it ended with that believer's death. Now he was alone in the sanctuary, and vulnerable should the forces of Kivuli be marshaled. He quickly stepped back behind the altar and shrank once more to the size of a flea before leaving his tiny idol untenanted.

Leila looked up each time a person exited the Taxation Office, and had done so three times when Mkuuzo finally emerged. He was once again carrying a heavy valise, and she guessed he was probably hauling off another day's take of bribes. She rose to her feet silently and trailed close behind him, knowing she would need to strike fast once they got outside of the palace and he began looking for a *ritzha*. At this hour the street would be full of them, all the "boys" eager to take a fare downhill all the way.

Mkuuzo stepped out of the main entrance and stood on the verge of the road, scanning to left and right for a *ritzha* to carry him and his valise full of ill-gotten gains to his mistress' apartment. Suddenly he heard a low snarl behind him, a sound that somehow awakened an ancestral memory of cowering in caves while outside fanged death was on the prowl. He spun to see an impossible figure, a man nearly seven feet high, naked, covered in short black fur. The head was that of a black leopard, glowing yellow eyes and white fangs in a red mouth.

Mkuuzo's scream was cut short as the creature raked him across the face and throat and down the center of his torso with one of its clawed hands. People all around ran screaming, then turned to watch in fascinated horror. The black monster savaged the tax official, tearing his clothes asunder and putting a line of claw marks from collarbone to crotch as the hapless man lay in a widening pool of blood on the pavement. The long series of parallel cuts was then crossed by a shorter set running at right angles to them across his belly, partially disemboweling him; but by then he was already dead.

The guards on the palace main entrance had come running, but had been paralyzed with fear at the sight and were just standing there in the crowd staring in disbelief. Then suddenly the monster vanished into thin air, only a trace of shadow remaining behind. Nobody noticed that the dead tax official's valise, which had been flung to the ground when he was attacked, had also vanished.

Chapter 36

Leila came back down the hill from the palace complex as the banana porter once again, this time without his bananas. The valise had been hidden as part of the illusion. Then she'd cleaned her tools and put her clothing into the sink to wash the blood out with cold water, before climbing into a cool shower herself. Her anger at Mkuuzo had been strong enough to overcome her reluctance to killing him – but in the end, it turned out, not enough to erase her revulsion and remorse after the deed had been done.

She decided that she would cook a Dominion dish for Imbaso tonight, as repayment for the delicious lunch and to give her something to take her mind off her grisly afternoon's work. She didn't have all the ingredients she needed – many were simply not available in Palambo. But she could make substitutions. It was heavy fare, more suited to the climate of Parat than that of Namei; but it was cool enough for it inside the house.

When Imbaso returned from the temple, well after night had fallen, there were tears in his eyes. "What is it?" Leila asked, hugging him to her.

"I placed the tiny idol of Betsalel in the public sanctuary this afternoon," he said. "I killed her, Leila! As surely as if I had held a pillow to her face and smothered her!"

"Killed whom?" she asked, mystified.

"Aunt Uzuri!" he replied, fresh tears falling from reddened eyes. "Another worshiper went into the sanctuary this evening and found her lying dead on one of the benches, peaceful as could be. And it's all my fault!"

"Mightn't her heart have just given out?" Leila suggested, "She was pretty old, wasn't she?"

"Not that old, mid-forties maybe," Imbaso objected. "She hasn't been going to the temple every day like she was a few months ago, but she went today. Mother said she left in early afternoon, and she was looking determined. Then she got to the temple, and I have to assume Betsalel came to her call and granted her the only thing she wanted that was within his power to give."

Leila looked stricken. What had happened to Uzuri and her baby was a tragedy, but there really hadn't been any way to make it right again. "Don't you see, Imbaso?" she said urgently. "Uzuri has been crazed with grief since your father took her baby. She was probably going to kill herself anyway, if our master hadn't granted her wish. Your placing the idol there so Betsalel could come to her probably only cut her life shorter by a couple of hours. And the death he granted was peaceful, not painful."

Imbaso saw the wisdom of her words and stopped blaming himself, though his grief was still raw. Aunt Uzuri had been like a second mother to him during a period in his adolescence. Later, as they were eating the meal Leila had prepared, he remarked "I saw Kifozi at the temple tonight. He was very concerned about what happened to Mkuuzo, and wanted to consult with Father about it. Father told me later that he wanted to know if Kivuli had been requested to kill the target, as from what the witnesses said they saw that certainly appeared to be what had happened. But Father hadn't known anything about it, of course."

"I'm hoping the claws and the valise will be enough to convince Kifozi it was me doing my assignment," Leila said. "I was going for a 'supernatural retribution' effect, but I might have overdone it. It would be too ironic if I ended up not getting credit and they sent me out to kill someone else."

"But if you do get the credit, you'll have passed your exam and you'll be an assassin of the Black Claw. Of *course* they're going to ask you to kill someone else. Lots of someone elses, probably," Imbaso pointed out. Now that he knew Leila for who she was, now that they were together, he was unhappy about her career path – though he'd have been willing to join her in it, earlier.

"Kifozi said that once I had passed my test the next thing was to be this 'project' in Iskand," Leila said. "That's probably going to take weeks for us just to get there, and I'll be able to take on the project of seeding all of the public sanctuaries of Betsalel between here and the Azraq with the god's true idols. And I'll be going as part of a team, so maybe once we get there they'll have other jobs for me to do besides killing people."

Imbaso wiped his mouth on a napkin and pushed his plate away, then rested his head in his hands. It had been a momentous and exhausting day. "I hope you're right," he said. "But what am I going to do while you're gone, Leila? I can't stand the thought of being parted from you for weeks."

Leila sighed as she thought of the parallel between his words and Tevo's five months before. She had blithely packed up and left her first lover, and now she was about to do the same to the second. Would she just skate through life loving them and leaving them, one after the other?

"Maybe you could engage in a project of your own, Imbaso," she said thoughtfully. "Tell your father you want to make a pilgrimage of the other temples of Betsalel to see whether they're engaged in the proper worship of Kivuli and if they need any advice. I could give you some of my 'seed idols' to take with you. And you could always have Betsalel come and make more for you, if you run out. You're one of his priests now, too, you know. He will always come to your call."

"That would be one hell of a trip," Imbaso replied. The areas around the country's great highways were civilized, but some of the temples of Betsalel were miles out along narrow byways surrounded by wilderness. Would the dark god be able to protect him from lions, hyenas, and black mambas? "And I'd still be missing you," he pointed out.

"That's the thing," Leila said. "Betsalel told me that he could transport me between two places where he is able to manifest. So he ought to be able to bring you to Iskand, after I arrive and can place a true idol in the Temple of the Eight there. There's just a fake statue of him there now, right?"

What an idea, Imbaso thought. Once again, his head was aswirl with ideas Leila had planted there. But her presence sparked other ideas, as well, less confusing ones. "Let's sleep on it," he suggested. "You can report to Kifozi in the morning, and get the details about the trip to Iskand. Then we can decide what we're going to do."

They cleared the dinner dishes and Imbaso washed while Leila dried. A few more ideas for home improvements had come to her, but she was hesitant to barrage her deity with demands for conveniences when deadly events were afoot. The chore done, they embraced and kissed.

"Are you living here, now?" Leila asked. She'd given him a key this morning, but he still had no spare clothing or other belongings in the house. He grinned at her, the first such expression she'd seen on his usually cheerful face since he came back this evening.

"I told Father I'd acquired a paramour, and had been spending nights at her house," he explained. "He was suitably impressed. But he made me swear it was not that orphan girl Usiku!" Leila grinned back.

"Which, of course, I am not. I am some completely different orphan girl."

"Exactly right," he said. "I suppose I should bring some of my things over here, it would be a lot more convenient. But I probably should wait until we find out about the trip. No point in doing that if you're going to be gone in two days." She squeezed him tight, then they made their way to the bedroom.

Chapter 37

On her arrival at the gymnasium in the morning Usiku showed the assembled masters of the Makucha Nyeusi Mkuuzo's satchel, laden with bribe money, and her clawed knuckle dusters as proof of her kill. "But the witnesses spoke clearly of seeing him felled by an enormous black panther that walked as a man!" Kifozi objected. "Mauaji swears that our lord was not present in his idol yesterday afternoon, but the whole city is saying that the killing was done by a manifestation of Betsalel!"

Goes to show how much those idiots know, Leila thought sourly. The Shadow God, when he granted death, did so by simply stopping the heart and letting the soul fly free. There was never a mark on the bodies of his "victims." "That *was* the point, was it not?" Usiku said with a shrug.

"But how did you do it? There was nothing in your training to allow such a feat!"

Leila sighed internally. She was reluctant to do this, but she needed some more leeway. And she was very anxious to make that pilgrimage of the temples along the road to the river Azraq. For just a second, she assumed the image of Kivuli, based on the description of the idol Imbaso had given her. The men surrounding her started back in fright.

A second later the small, dark girl stood before them again. She lifted out a curious-looking necklace from inside her tunic, on which some strange symbols were graven. It was not the claw necklace of Kivuli. In fact, it was a necklace she'd taken a fancy to during the long caravan trip from Halath and had bought from one of the traders on that journey.

"This necklace belonged to my dead mother," Usiku explained. "It is the only thing I have left of her. After I got to Namei and was permitted to take my vows and begin training for the Makucha Nyeusi, I prayed nightly to Kivuli that I would succeed in my studies and be able to wreak my revenge on the evil Ran. And two nights ago, after master Kifozi had given me my assignment, the dark god answered my prayers."

They were all staring at her in awe. They were not superstitious men, but the being they worshiped was, after all, very real. Who knew what he might accomplish, if he chose? Perhaps little Usiku's hunger for revenge had called to the black one's bloodthirsty nature.

The girl continued her tale. "In a dream, Kivuli came to me and said, 'You will kill in my name, and take my form when you wish that all may know you for one of mine.' He held up a necklace, and I realized that it was this one you see here." She gestured with it. "Then he told me, 'Touch the necklace and think of me, and you will appear as I do. Touch it again to return to your true semblance.' And when I woke up, the necklace was around my neck though I had placed it on the dresser before lying down in bed. I jumped up immediately and tried it, as the god had commanded. And it worked!"

They gathered around her, anxious to examine the mystical necklace. It looked perfectly ordinary, but was it perhaps unnaturally warmer than it should be? "It's just an illusion," Usiku assured them. "I am not really seven feet tall with long white fangs and I don't really have a tail. But I *do* have claws!" She gestured to the knuckle dusters, which she'd explained she had bought from a mysterious Dareg trader in the markets at Halath.

"So you see," the pretty and petite young woman said with a sweet smile, "with the power granted to me by our lord Kivuli I can strike terror into the hearts of our enemies. And with the skills taught to me by master Kifozi and the rest of you, I can bring death to them – day *or* night."

An excited discussion ensued, while Usiku stood there waiting for them to calm down. She was pretty sure they'd bought her explanation. The gods surely did work in mysterious ways. Even the ones who weren't really gods… Finally Kifozi acted as the group's spokesman to say, "Usiku, you have proven yourself. The Makucha Nyeusi does not have quite so many arcane rituals as they perform down at the temple, but there is a small ceremony. And a token, which you will bear with you always. Please follow us."

Usiku was led into a small room, and requested to kneel while Kifozi intoned, "Usiku, now and forever you are part of the Makucha Nyeusi. You will execute your orders faithfully, and never reveal anything about the Makucha Nyeusi, about your fellow members of the cult, or about your orders to anyone outside the cult. Tell me that you accept these strictures."

"I accept these strictures," Usiku said firmly. Accept that they exist, not that I intend to obey them, Leila thought. Kifozi tapped her lightly on the shoulder with an elegant-looking dagger, seemingly of steel but gleaming jet black.

Then he commanded her "Rise," and when she had gotten to her feet he handed it to her hilt first. "This dagger is a badge of your membership in our cult," he said solemnly. "Never part with it."

Usiku took the beautiful knife in her hands and turned it, trying to examine the details. The handle seemed to be incised with mysterious runes, and the blade was curved and razor sharp on one side only. Clearly it was not intended to be thrown. "Thank you, Master," she said and tucked it away with a deep nod of her head.

"Master Sumundi will apply your tattoo now," Kifozi said. "Please pull down your pants and expose your right hip." It made sense, Leila thought. Such a location could remain hidden most of the time, but you could show it to someone who needed to see it without disrobing. Not that she intended she herself would bear this tattoo, any more than she truly bore Kivuli's scars on her palms. But wait, how could this work? Leila herself had skin light enough, barely, to show tattoos if they were done in the blackest of ink. But Usiku's skin, like that of most Amhari, was the color of the darkest kaf – nearly black.

As she bared her hip, Usiku asked "How will my tattoo be visible, master Kifozi?"

Sumundi replied, "It is a special ink produced not by a plant, or by a mineral, but by a fungus that lives in hidden caves. It glows in the dark." Like a glowstone, Leila realized. She still had the ones she'd gotten while working with the Night Guild all those years ago, but they had been lying within a bag at the bottom of her dresser for more than a year now. They would have to be recharged by exposure to daylight before they would glow again.

"Do I need to expose it to light?" Usiku asked, as the poisons master came forth with a virulent-looking yellow-green substance and a long, sharp needle.

"Not at all," he assured her, as he dipped a narrow reed in the ink and drew a small figure, less than an inch across, on the exposed, deep brown flesh of her hip. "The ink reacts chemically with your body's own fluids to produce the glow."

"And it won't poison me?" Usiku asked a little nervously. "I've had mine for more than forty years and it hasn't poisoned me yet," the old man chuckled. "I've even fathered four children in that time, and all of them were quite healthy." She grinned at him, and let him get on with it. Leila needed to concentrate hard to create the illusion of the tattoo being applied so that Sumundi, who must have done this many times, saw nothing amiss.

As a child roaming the docks in Marsine, she had seen many regular tattoos applied. She hoped this special ink was not supposed to give a remarkably different appearance as it went in! Master Sumundi showed no surprise at what he saw, and Usiku hastily covered up her tattoo with her pants once he had finished. Intriguingly, the Makucha Nyeusi's identification mark was one of the traditional symbols of Betsalel, not one of the new ones being used by the worshipers of Kivuli.

"Keep that clean," the old poisons master admonished Usiku when he had finished. "And don't pick at it. It should heal up in a week or two. Come to me if it shows any signs of infection, all right?"

"Thank you master, I will," she said with a smile. Then added, "Master? Might you show me your own tattoo? I am curious to know what it might look like in forty years."

Sumundi's dark face split in a white smile, and he gestured her over to where the door of a supply closet stood open. They stepped inside and shut the door, and he pulled down the waist of his pants to show her the same design on his own hip. The once-thin lines had spread over the years, but it was still glowing a pale green color. Good, now Leila knew what illusion to create if anyone asked to see her tattoo.

After the ceremony was completed it was back to business. "So, master Kifozi, what of this special project you mentioned? Will we be leaving for Iskand soon? I have always wanted to see the capital." That was not a lie.

"Ah yes," he said, pleased at her enthusiasm. "We will be setting forth in one week's time. It will be me, master Sumundi, and four full assassins of our order, in addition to you. We will be accompanying arch-priest Mauaji and his son, your friend Imbaso."

"We will be traveling by road, then taking a riverboat northward on the Azraq?" Usiku asked, hiding her excitement that Imbaso was to be included on the journey.

"That is right," Kifozi said. "You still have your horse?" Leila was somewhat surprised he was aware of Wapesi's existence, but then the Black Claw were experts at observation – among other skills.

"Yes," she replied. "I have obtained a post house-sitting for a trader who is away a lot on business, and he lets me keep Wapesi in the back yard."

"Good," Kifozi replied. "You will be riding him on this trip, and our horses will ride with us on our river transport to Iskand. We may need them later. You will need to contact the agency and arrange for someone else to take over your duties so that your trader doesn't return to find a family of monkeys living in his house, I'm afraid. You will be out of the city for at least two months, longer depending on how long it takes you to exact your revenge on the Ran who killed your family."

Usiku bowed her head in acknowledgement, excitement plain on her face. "I will need to come in each day and do my workout, keep myself fit," she said.

"Yes," master Sumundi put in. "And it were well if you could find some more time to study with me, Usiku. There is yet much I can teach you." She nodded again.

Kifozi reached into an inner pocket of his tunic and came out with a handful of gold asand. He passed them to Usiku, who took them with a look of questioning. "In addition to maintaining your fitness and continuing your studies with master Sumundi, and making arrangements for your trader's house to be looked after, you should spend some time in the coming week shopping for clothing."

Usiku looked at him blankly. "Our cover, the supposed reason for our journey," he explained, "is a religious pilgrimage. Arch-priest Mauaji, and the senior members of Makucha Nyeusi accompanying him, will be going as priests and acolytes visiting the temples of Betsalel as we travel to the great Temple of the Eight in Iskand for a conference with others of our church. Although both you and young Imbaso have taken our vows, and he is now an acolyte, you two will not be traveling as church members but as Mauaji's children. Imbaso is Mauaji's son, coming along on the pilgrimage as he considers whether he wishes to take up orders. And you are Imbaso's daughter Zurina, who is traveling with her father to Iskand in hopes that he can find a marriage alliance for her. You need to dress the part."

Chapter 38

Imbaso and Leila were in bed, though it was the middle of the day. When she'd returned from the Makucha Nyeusi's gymnasium with the signs of her new status in that organization and the news that the two of them would be traveling to Iskand together, joy had reigned.

Leila saw absolutely no reason why she should waste perfectly good gold buying clothing that would be overly warm, uncomfortable and impractical, and only good for the purposes of deception. Since the entire persona of the Black Claw assassin Usiku was an illusion, why should she not dress in garb that was comfortable and easy to move in, make the clothes part of the illusion, and tuck the gold into her pockets instead?

So Usiku (and occasionally, other characters) had staged a private fashion show for Imbaso. He had moved in the upper echelons of Namei society (though more three years ago than recently, admittedly) and had some idea what sort of garments a sister of his would be likely to wear if she were out to snag a wealthy and well-connected husband.

Leila had been glad to learn that the little girl who had died all those years ago had been named Sadhima, not Zurina. It would have been pitiful, had they selected the name of the actual sister. But the girl had been dead for more than a decade. It was unlikely that anyone out there in the vast expanses east of Namei would know that Mauaji's only daughter, who would now have been almost fifteen had she lived, had died ages ago and had a different name.

In between the "outfits" that Zurina (identical in appearance to Usiku, of course) modeled for Imbaso, developing her illusory wardrobe, Leila appeared in a succession of costumes that would have made a harem dancer blush. It wasn't long before her audience leapt up off the bed and ravished her. Then they'd gone back to the project, and less than an hour later he'd done it again. At the back of their minds, they both knew that while they would be able to keep company with each other daily on the forthcoming journey, there would likely be very few opportunities for the supposed siblings to get intimate.

Later, ravenous, they ate some leftover flatbread rolled up with slices of cold meat. Though many Palambans raised cattle and drank both their milk and their blood, cheese making was not advanced in the kingdom. Maybe the temperature and humidity were too high? Leila had no idea, but she made a mental note to add some Dominion cheese to her next Betsalel wish list.

"Your father hasn't mentioned this trip to you at all?" Leila asked around a meaty mouthful. Imbaso shook his head and took a drink of cold bottled beer. They would soon be out.

"I've scarcely spoken half a dozen words with him in the past two days, other than when Aunt Uzuri was discovered," he said.

"Was he upset?" she asked, a thought crossing her mind.

Presumably Mauaji had not been overly fond of his only sister, if he'd decided the baby she clearly adored was an appropriate sacrifice for his "god." Likely he'd been terminally ticked off with her for the shame she'd brought on him, bearing that child out of wedlock. But that she was known to come to the temple daily, begging the dark god for the return of her child, made the fact of her body being found there, lying peacefully on a bench, somewhat indicative of the dark god's intervention.

Did Mauaji even know that Betsalel, the god he had supposedly been worshiping all his life, still existed and had power? Or was he convinced that the appearance of Kivuli in response to his sacrifice only indicated that the god formerly known as Betsalel had changed his shape and his name, there no longer being a deity by the name of "Betsalel"?

A trip to the Dominion would certainly straighten him out on that issue, Leila thought. Or if they could just sit the man down in a room with the real Shadow God… Perhaps such a thing could be arranged, on this trip they would all be taking together…

The week flew by, and early on a Belanday morning the party gathered at the temple to begin their journey. This had required that everyone in it climb at least one if not several levels to meet there, then return all the way down from the temple level out the city gates and thence to the road east; but no one minded much.

Leila and Imbaso had been making love morning, noon, and night as they anticipated weeks of celibacy, and she was hoping fervently that the contraceptive herbs the Makucha Nyeusi had introduced her to worked as well as was claimed.

"Usiku, it's so good to see you!" Imbaso said, as if he had not just spent much of the previous day in her arms. His father had insisted that he spend last night at home, so that he could complete his preparations for the trip. The six men traveling as priests of Betsalel had only black robes to pack, but the arch-priest's son had an elaborate wardrobe for every occasion they might encounter. After all, once they reached the capital, they would be hobnobbing with the kingdom's elite.

"You too, Imbaso," the girl replied. "You're a vision of sartorial splendor!" He grinned shyly at her. Father and Mother had collaborated on the purchase of an entire new wardrobe for him, two orders of magnitude more elegant than anything he'd worn before.

"You're looking lovely as well, sister Zurina," Imbaso said – getting into character.

"Thank you brother," she simpered. She had ended up buying half a dozen outfits with some of the Black Claw's spending money, with which to fill out her traveling bags. She'd forgotten to consider that it would look extremely odd if Zurina had on a different magnificent outfit each day – all from a small valise. And the chance existed that some member of the party, at least, might happen to look into those bags. They needed to contain what everyone expected them to. As to what she was wearing at the moment, that was as much an illusion as Zurina's deep brown skin and black eyes.

In addition to the two masters, there were four Makucha Nyeusi assassins disguised as acolytes or priests. They were all male, all at least a decade or two older than Usiku. She had never met any of them before, not surprising as presumably they would no longer be spending much time at the training facility with the apprentices.

"Usiku," Kifozi said, "This is Zhendibi." He gestured to a small, alert-looking young man, an Amhari, who was probably the youngest of the lot. Moving on he introduced Mbando, the tallest of the group; Bdejiyi, nearly as tall as Mbando but slimmer-looking; and Nindao. He looked like he might be in his mid to late thirties, the eldest of the group; but he was even smaller than Zhendibi. Men so compact were rare among the Amhari.

Usiku smiled and nodded at each of them in turn, saying "Pleased to meet you. Please call me Zurina." They grinned back. Turning to Kifozi, Usiku asked, "Am I the only woman in the order, then?"

He smiled ruefully. "No, dear, there are others. But our line of work is not something that draws very many women. We have two others, both of them now in their forties. We needed someone much younger for this assignment."

Interesting, Leila mused. Other than the cover story for their expedition, she had been told nothing about what they were to do when they got to Iskand. It looked as though Zurina would just be on vacation for the next few weeks, so she might as well relax and enjoy it.

Each of them had a horse to ride, and there were four pack horses as well for their baggage; but there were no remounts. The plan was for them to take the main highway from Namei to Aswa, a river port on the upper Azraq, in easy stages with at least a night's stop in every town with a temple of Betsalel. A perfectly pleasant trip, now in mid-autumn with the summer rains behind them. Leila was looking forward to it, except for the regrettable detail of no sex with Imbaso for an indeterminate period of time.

Chapter 39

Zambei, the purported birthplace of Usiku, was the first stop on their journey. Imbaso now knew Usiku's entire story to be fictitious, and none of the other people in the group had ever heard that detail; so there were no comments or explanations required.

They arrived in late afternoon, and took lodgings at an inn. Few of the temples in the kingdom, whether for Betsalel or others of the Eight, had any residences associated with them. It was one of the major differences between the structure of the churches in Palambo and those in the Dominion. As Zurina was the only female, she got a room to herself. But the eight men bunked together in two large rooms, Imbaso with Mauaji and the two elder assassins.

The men, Imbaso included, would be going out to the temple after supper. Had Zurina been the nubile daughter of a well-placed cleric in the Dominion, it would never have been considered for her to travel more than a thousand miles without a female companion – an aunt, perhaps, or at least a lady's maid. But here in Palambo, it seemed, shutting her up in her inn room alone for hours every evening was considered acceptable. Not that Leila had any intention of remaining so for long.

There was still some daylight before the inn would serve dinner, so the siblings were allowed to tour the small city's markets. Imbaso had been here before, a few times, and he showed Zurina around as they talked quietly. Zambei was a low town without a wall, spread out into the hills north of the Pana for more than a mile. But the markets, and most of the older structures in town including the temple, were in the riverfront area.

"Mmm," he murmured, taking her by the arm as they examined the colorful profusion of booths. "You look so delicious in that dress I want to eat you up."

"Hush!" Leila replied. "You ate me up already less than twenty-four hours ago, and that's going to have to hold you for a while." They examined the colorful bolts of cloth displayed at one of the booths, then moved on.

"You said you could make us both become invisible, as long as you were touching me. Right?" Leila glanced sideways at him. The man was incorrigible!

"Are you proposing we just go invisible and start humping here in the middle of the marketplace?" she asked sweetly. "I'm afraid someone might trip over us, and besides there would be a certain amount of noise…"

He squeezed her elbow, and directed her to a stand where the seller, a middle aged man whose few remaining teeth were stained brown from chewing keto, offered live creatures from the nearby jungles for sale as pets. There were colorful birds, lizards, and a screeching monkey in a cage. Leila looked down at the pathetic little creature, and formulated some plans for later.

As they made their way to the next booth Imbaso continued the conversation. "I was thinking of someplace more private and romantic," he confided. "Like maybe the altar in the temple of Betsalel."

"Too hard!" Leila declared, as if that were her only objection to the suggestion. She smiled secretly. Love with Imbaso had proven to be so much fun!

They toured the rest of the marketplace and Imbaso bought his sister a little packet of roasted nuts to snack on as they strolled back toward the inn. "I think I'll go to bed right after we eat dinner," Zurina said. Leila added, "I'll be right behind you guys when you go to the temple, and I'll seed the public sanctuary with a true idol. Maybe check out the layout a bit. Then I'll go back to my room and have a conference with our master before I go to sleep."

Having abandoned his half-joking efforts to get into Leila's pants this evening, Imbaso nodded and kissed his sister on the cheek. Though her courage, her audacity, and her skills were part of what made him love her, it bothered him a little that she was taking decisive, important action on this trip while he was apparently along as nothing but window dressing. When was *he* going to get to do something bold?

As they left the market square and walked up the street toward their inn, which was in a fairly respectable area a few blocks from the riverfront, Leila suddenly seized Imbaso by the hand and pulled him into a narrow alleyway. Before he could speak she went to shadows, saying "Wait here for a minute. I'm just going to do something."

He stood there obediently in the alley, wondering what was going on. Back at the animal-seller's stand, as the stall keeper was busy getting a bird out of a cage for a customer, she slipped the lock on the monkey's cage. The little creature cowered, not understanding what was happening. But when she reached in and drew it forth with an invisible hand it got the idea. It was off across the plaza like a shot, vanishing into some nearby trees, before its owner even realized what was happening. Leila latched the cage again, then eased away silently and returned to Imbaso.

"What was all that about?" he asked, as she reappeared beside him.

"Just a little jailbreak," Leila replied. She declined to explain further, but there was a satisfied smile on her face as they returned to the inn. They found the other seven members of their party occupying a couple of tables in the inn's common room, enjoying some bottled beer and waiting for dinner to be served. It was early for it, but they had things to do this evening.

The meal was simple but filling, and they all washed it down with bottled beer. Safe drinking water was always a dubious proposition in towns and cities both here and in the Dominion, and nobody wanted to spend the next few weeks traveling on horseback with a case of the runs.

As they were finishing the meal Mauaji said, "Zurina, your brother and I and our church members must go to the temple this evening to pray and confer with our Zambei counterparts. As it appears that our host's wife is on duty here in the common room, I will permit you to stay here while we are gone – if you wish. You will of course not speak with any strange men, but otherwise you are free to enjoy the evening in company."

Zurina bowed her head. "Thank you Father, I greatly appreciate your consideration. But in truth I am sore and tired from our journey today. It's been far too long since I have spent so long riding. I think that I will retire now, if you you don't mind."

"Very well, my dear," the arch-priest said, kissing her on the cheek. Considering Mauaji's disapproval of Usiku and Leila's loathing of the baby-killer masquerading as her father, it was a convincing sham.

After Zurina had mounted the stairs heading for her room, key in hand, the rest of them went to wash up before going out. As soon as she was inside the room Leila set wedges in place, went invisible, and was out the window. She left it closed, the casement held shut with a small and nearly invisible sliver of wood.

The men were soon finished with their ablutions and walking along in the gathering gloom, Mauaji carrying a torch to light their way. Here and there in the downtown area lanterns had been lit, but clearly there was no municipal effort to keep the streets safe at night. Considering the group was a large party, they didn't fear being set upon.

The temple of Betsalel here had taken the "dark god" theme to the next level. It was smaller by quite a bit than the one in Namei, but had been constructed of a black jungle hardwood. Lanterns were lit on either side of the front door and above the lintel, all three of them glowing red. This, Leila now knew, was due a certain chemical substance that had been mixed with the lamp oil. It was also used in church rituals, to create a red-flaming sacrificial knife.

From a distance the building almost looked like the head of the true Betsalel, as if it were an enormous idol buried up past its shoulders in the soil of Zambei. Imbaso and the party of priests and acolytes stopped off at the front door and talked to the acolyte on duty. As he directed them around the back to the Kivuli cult's secret entrance, Leila slipped silently past them and into the sanctuary.

As at the temple in Namei, there was an anteroom inside the front door and a public sanctuary beyond it with benches for worshipers arrayed before the altar. Here, though, there was a small idol atop the altar – perhaps three feet high. There were no other worshipers in the sanctuary. Leila placed an invisible hand on the idol and knew at once that it was not a true one.

The workmanship was superb, though. It was almost as though a mold had been made from a true idol and this likeness poured in some substance like a black version of cement. If most of Betsalel's true worshipers saw these, they would surely have been fooled into thinking the dark god had simply abandoned them. An idea came to Leila, and she decided to put it into practice before really thinking it through. Pulling out one of her tiny seed idols, she set it on the altar between its nearer edge and the cunningly wrought statue. Then she slipped back out of the sanctuary.

The anteroom attendant was down at the far end, sitting in a chair and reading a book by the light of another red lantern. He'd be going blind before he hit thirty, if he kept that up. He didn't notice as she slipped silently from the sanctuary, then out the open front door. It would stand open all night, this acolyte or another ready to greet worshipers, answer questions, or guide cult initiates around to the back.

Moments after Leila had left, a tall and stout woman of perhaps thirty-five came in. She was wearing a black shawl over a colorful dashiki, apparently as some token of respect to the dark one. Planting her feet in the dimly lit anteroom, she peered left and right. "Hello? Anyone here?" she called."

The acolyte hurried up, scanning her palms quickly though he had not expected to find any marks on them. The vast majority of the cult membership was male. "Good evening, memsahib, can I help you?" he asked.

"Well, aren't you a cutie!" she said, peering down at him. "Are you here often?" She looked as if she might be considering having him for a late-night snack.

"I'm just here to do Betsalel's bidding," he said nervously. "Do you wish to pray before the god?"

"That's what I usually do at the temple," the woman leered. "Unless you can think of something else?"

"Um, no!" he said, flustered. Here he was a member of a powerful death cult, and she was treating him like some fluffy little boy-toy!

Drawing himself up and struggling for dignity, the acolyte said coolly. "You may enter the sanctuary and pray to Betsalel, memsahib. Beyond that I can't help you." She gave him a regretful look.

"All right," she said resignedly. "But I want some privacy in there. I don't want nobody else barging in while I'm communing with the god, understand?"

It was hardly a problem, the acolyte knew. Most of the evening shifts he'd worked, there had been nobody at all. But he was anxious to get rid of this particular customer. "Tell you what," he suggested. "You go in and close the doors," and if anybody else comes while you're in there I'll tell them they have to wait, all right?"

She grinned broadly at him. "That'll be fine. And don't you be listenin' at the door either, mind! Me 'n' Betsalel got some *personal* things to discuss, if you know what I mean…" He felt like pointing out there was a temple to Dionos up in Namei. That sounded like it would be more up her alley. Still smiling, she sauntered into the sanctuary and closed the door firmly behind her.

The woman walked to the back of the room and stood before the altar. Then she murmured, "Betsalel, come to me." For all Leila knew, the men downstairs were barbecuing up a baby as a special treat for Kivuli and the Namei visitors – in which case the true Shadow God would probably not risk putting in an appearance, and all of this would have been a waste of time.

But in moments the tiny grain on the altar began to grow, and soon Betsalel – little taller than the statue behind him – stood there looking at her with what Leila took to be a hint of amusement. "That's an interesting look," he said softly, "What's the occasion?"

"Can you ward us from being overheard, and assure that the door will not be opened?" Leila asked. He nodded, and instantly the sanctuary had become a bubble of protection. Should Kivuli manifest below, he would be unable to penetrate here. And no eavesdroppers would hear what took place behind the sealed door.

Leila immediately dropped her illusion. She was wearing a camisole and matching drawers, into which she'd sewn pockets. Noting the god's raised eyebrow, she said "It's the Palambo version of my burglar garb. It's awfully damn warm here." She still had her usual well-fitted, soft-soled boots suitable for sneaking down corridors or scaling the walls of buildings.

"We are in Zambei," he said. "Good. My idol here, too, has been corrupted by Kivuli." He turned and looked at the statue behind him. "This is good work," he mused.

"I thought so," Leila replied. "Can you make it vanish?"

Betsalel considered the request. "You think to replace this statue with the true idol in which I'm now manifested?"

"Why not?" she asked. "Nobody will notice anything different if it's exactly the same size and pose. Then you can start manifesting when true worshipers call you. But the cult downstairs will know they're the ones with what they believe is the only true idol, so they won't suspect what's happening. I hope."

"It could work," the dark god said thoughtfully. "And if something goes wrong, another can always be made. Guide me, please, as I adjust my size." He stood beside the false idol and assumed the classic pose, then began to shrink very slowly.

"Almost there, a little more… stop, perfect!" Leila said. Betsalel broke his pose to smile at her. Then he gestured at the statue and it began to shrink, until it was no more than a quarter of an inch in size. The details, black on black, could barely be discerned.

"Damn," Leila said, "I should have pried that ruby out before we shrank it so small." She was grinning.

"I'll give you all the rubies you could desire, beloved," the god replied. "You have only to ask."

"Just kidding," she replied, scooping up the minute statue and tucking it into a pocket. "Move over a little more to the right. No, my right. More, all right, good."

Used to speaking to Betsalel at a height of six feet, Leila found it odd talking to him at the size of a toddler. It was as if, instead of his being like a father to her, she had become his mother. Her, as a mother! Now there was an absurd thought. She hoped. Should she find herself pregnant there were of course other herbs that would make the problem go away – but would she find it so easy to dismiss a baby fathered by Imbaso?

"You're perfect," Leila told her god. "And you can probably use that 'circle of protection' trick whenever you're manifested. Can you look into your worshipers' souls when you're in communion with them?"

"Other than you, whom I know always," Betsalel said, "I can reach only as deeply as they allow. Some are completely open to me, others erect walls to hold me out."

"Well then," the high priestess said, "maybe just the open ones, you could try revealing the whole situation. Swear them to secrecy and all that, or give them permission to tell only those closest to them that the Shadow God is once again answering calls. We need to get a sort of wave going, more and more of your true believers able to contact you and supply you with the power you need to defeat you-know-who." Circle of protection or not, Leila was not about to name the djinn this close to his nexus of power.

"You are wise beyond your years, beloved," Betsalel said softly. "I will release the circle now." With that he resumed the standard pose, looking exactly like the statue that had sat here earlier (and for centuries before), and was no longer there.

Leila quickly resumed the semblance of the dark god's plump and lusty petitioner. "Thank you, lord!" she bellowed, as she made for the door and pulled it open. "And thank *you* acolyte!" she added, as she stepped out into the anteroom. He'd returned to his chair, but had found it hard to concentrate on his book. "My dreams will be sweet tonight!" she declared, cocking a generously-padded hip and rolling her eyes at the young man. "I think maybe *you* will be starring in them, too! Would you like that, sweetie?"

"Uh!" he started violently. Was this woman insane? Of the few visitors the public sanctuary got, none had emerged in his lifetime claiming to have had a successful session with the "god." Getting a grip on himself, the acolyte began ushering her toward the front door. "Betsalel answered your prayers, then?" he asked casually. She turned to him before stepping out into the night.

"Not so much *answered* them, per se," she admitted. Then she grinned and pointed a slim black finger at her head. "But I can feel it inside. I just *know* he's looking out for me. Right?"

Chapter 40

Leila was burning to discuss some things with Imbaso after she had climbed back up to her room at the inn. But it was to be many hours before she had the opportunity. She had tossed the tiny, powerless statue of Betsalel away into a flower bed near the rear of the building before beginning her climb. Then, still invisible, she let herself out of her room and went down the hall to listen at the door of the room where Mauaji, Imbaso, and the two Black Claw masters were staying. As she'd expected, they had not yet returned. So, she climbed into bed and went to sleep.

In the morning Leila gave herself a cool sponge bath using the basin and hand towel provided with the room. She was already sorely missing the comforts of home, as well as her lover's body in her bed. They breakfasted in the inn's common room while staff hurried to get their baggage repacked and their horses saddled and ready to leave. Master Kifozi, who appeared to be the co-leader of this expedition with Mauaji, had the inn staff pack them lunch in a large sack, which would be taken along and eaten on the road.

This trip was very different from, yet somehow reminiscent of, Wolfgang's journey from Parat to Jena nearly half a year ago. Leila only wished that the weather now were as cool and pleasant as it had been then – or that the journey were as short. Wapesi was still perfectly capable, even in this heat, of going at a comfortable hand gallop for eight or ten hours a day without tiring – thanks to Betsalel's gift. But their other animals had not been so equipped, and though the journeys were similar in length it would take their party more than twice as long to reach its destination.

They trotted along the highway, which was thronged with traffic, through the morning and on into the afternoon at a steady pace. Clouds filled the sky, and there were occasional raindrops falling; but it was only enough to increase the humidity while cutting the temperature somewhat. Leila was thankful that she was actually wearing a pair of loose-fitting, lightweight pants with gathered ankles below and nothing but a thin camisole top above, instead of the elaborate head-to-toe wrappings of brightly-colored, block-printed cloth that everyone saw. She would happily have ridden naked, but saddles required some protection for the inner thighs.

Shortly past midday they pulled off the road into a campsite, one that had been set up for the convenience of caravans and other travelers, to rest and eat their lunch. A well had been dug, not needing to be sunk very deep so near the river, and there was a broad stone basin with a hand pump. Imbaso pumped the basin full of water for the animals to drink, and Zurina washed her face and hands before they began.

They seated themselves on the large flat rocks and logs that had been pulled in to define the boundaries of the campsite, feasting on soft flatbread rolled around chickpea paste, pickled vegetables, and fresh tropical fruits – all washed down with more of the mild bottled beer. At ambient temperature it was far from refreshing, but at least it was wet.

As the meal was finished Usiku stood up. She caught Imbaso's eye as she said, "Excuse me gentlemen, I have need of some privacy." She headed off into the brush behind them. She was a trained assassin, a member in full of the Makucha Nyeusi. Nobody was worried that she was going to run into trouble with hyenas or driver ants out there in the bush while she was doing whatever it was that ladies needed privacy for.

"Ulp!" Imbaso said as soon as she'd gone. "That chickpea paste was a little oily. I think I could use some 'private time' myself. Excuse me!" With that he dashed off into the scrub in the opposite direction and was soon lost to view behind some tall bushes. He urinated while he was there, then began furtively moving through the brush in an attempt to get around to where Leila had disappeared. Fortunately he hadn't been at it long when an unseen presence suddenly pushed up against him and murmured, "Where do you think *you're* going?"

As Leila materialized less than six inches away Imbaso seized her in his arms and engulfed her mouth in his, kissing her greedily. Clearly, she realized, her missing him in her bed had been a pale shadow of his reciprocal feelings. Ah, the irrepressible libido of the young human male!

"Quick! Get your pants off!" he murmured, running his hands over her body. "Hold it!" Leila hissed. "That's *not* why we're here!"

"No?" he said softly, looking like a whipped puppy.

"Sorry," she said, and gave him a squeeze in the crotch by way of sympathy. It didn't necessarily help.

"We'll get our chance soon, I promise," Leila murmured as close to his ear as she could given the difference in their heights. "Come on," she said, going invisible again before taking him by the hand and leading him over a few feet to where a cluster of bushes created a shady little glen in the midst of the savannah. It was home to a colony of meerkats, as evidenced by the burrows everywhere among the roots; but the little creatures were mostly away from their dens at the moment and those remaining ceded the central area to the invisible humans without much complaint.

They sat on the soft earth among the bushes, Leila holding Imbaso's hand to maintain their invisibility. Here, the bushes provided some screen for their words and it was unlikely they would be heard. "We've only got a few minutes before the rest will be wondering what happened to us. You'd damn well better be able to budget at least half an hour the next time you plan to make love to me!"

Leila could not see Imbaso any more than he could see her, but she sensed he was abashed. She filled him in on the results of the trip to the temple last night, Betsalel's ability to create a circle of protection for himself and any worshipers while he was manifested in one of the idols they had smuggled in, and her intent to replace any false idols she found with identical real ones. Within five minutes they'd hugged and kissed and parted ways, and Leila was coming back out of the bush from the direction she'd gone in earlier, while Imbaso came in from the opposite direction wondering aloud whether there'd been something wrong with the beer.

Their stop that night was at a town too small to boast any temples at all other than small shrines to Mulia and Andros – the two deities of the Eight most important to the lives of common everyday people. Mauaji had apparently put considerable effort into their travel plans, though, and they had lodgings for the night at an estate owned by an old friend of his.

The place was magnificent, similar in size to Imbaso's own family home in Namei but with much more extensive grounds. As was the case in Imbaso's family there were far fewer people living here now than the house had been designed to hold. Each member of the nine-person party had their own private bedroom, and within an hour after they had all gone to bed Imbaso's room was invaded by a silent presence.

He'd been awaiting her since turning in, lying on the bed wearing only a pair of lounging pants. After closing the door behind her Leila turned visible and then gleefully threw herself onto the bed, entwining herself with his body. Passion surged, and there was no discussion for, more or less, half an hour.

After they had recuperated a bit and tidied up, Leila murmured, "Sound is an issue that's been bothering me a lot. If our master can create a circle or bubble of protection, I wonder if he can grant me the power to do so."

"Let's ask him," Imbaso suggested cheerfully. It had been a few days, after all, since he had spoken with the living god to whom he'd pledged his service.

Once again respectfully dressed, Leila brought out the small idol Betsalel had given her months ago. She carried it with her everywhere, even setting it on a nearby shelf when she took a bath. She had no worries about the Shadow God seeing her naked – he wasn't that kind of god. She'd never in a million years willingly stand naked before Dionos, now…

When the god came Leila made a circular gesture. He nodded and instantly they were enclosed in a bubble of protection. No listener at the door would hear anything, nor could anyone break in. Betsalel knew Leila's heart, and he knew that she and Imbaso had become lovers. It saddened him for his priest Tevo, who loved her as well; but he understood human nature. Only time would tell how this triangle might play out.

"Have you learned anything yet of your mission in Iskand?" the Shadow God asked his high priestess, though the question was directed at both of them.

"Kifozi has promised me that my role in the project will be revealed to me after we arrive in Iskand," Leila said. "Until then, I am just to maintain my cover as the daughter of Mauaji and keep a low profile. It's my intention to see your true idols placed at every temple we encounter, though."

"And I thank you for it," Betsalel said. "Already I have begun interacting with worshipers in Namei and Zambei. I am even now feeling stronger."

"Excellent, master," Imbaso said, eager to be included. Leila's dominance still bothered him, and he wanted a more active role. "My father and I went with the assassins masquerading as your priests to the temple in Zambei last night. We spoke with the arch-priest of the temple there and inspected the inner sanctum, affirming that Kivuli had been in contact with the cult there."

Betsalel nodded. "I knew he had taken that idol like the rest," he said simply.

Imbaso went on, "Father told me that one of his first requests of the 'god,' as he believes it to be, was to manifest in the other idols around Palambo and inform the cult worshiping the dark god in accordance with the Secret Scriptures of his new name and appearance. I think that most of those people believe that they still worship you, but that you have chosen a new name to suit your new aspect. Part of what we're doing on this trip seems to be checking up on Kivuli's work."

The dark god lowered his head in sadness. To have such wrongness done in his name! But it had been going on for centuries, and now for the first time there was a chance to do something about it. "And why did Mauaji bring *you* with him on this trip?" he asked.

Imbaso shook his head. "I've been trying to figure it out ever since Leila learned I was to be included," he said. "But Father refuses to tell me everything."

"But he definitely has plans?" Leila asked.

Imbaso nodded. "He's been hinting at 'big plans' for me almost since I got home," he said with annoyance. "It's like he'd bought me the world's biggest birthday present, and couldn't resist giving me hints even though he didn't want to spoil the surprise. But there's more to it than that. Even though I'm all he's got in the way of a son to shower benefits on, I don't think he entirely trusts me. Maybe that incident in the inner sanctum has him convinced I'm weak."

Imbaso sighed deeply and threw himself back on the bed, on which both he and Leila were sitting. Then he sat upright again. "Maybe I *am* weak. I'm certainly not made of whatever stuff was required to keep the men of my family cheerfully slaughtering babies for the benefit an imaginary god all these years." The bitterness in his tone was sharp.

Leila turned to him, throwing her arms tight around him. "You're the first in generations of your family who is truly a man!" she declared. Appreciating her support and feeling better for it, Imbaso hugged her back. Then they broke apart, and she rose to her feet. "Your father loves you, Imbaso, in his own twisted way," she said, her eyes burning into his. "He wants the best for you, or what he imagines to be the best, but I also think he knows you are not the man he is. He probably expects that he will be at your shoulder for years yet to come, guiding your footsteps – even though you are already an adult."

Imbaso shuddered. He would rather throw himself into the Pana and let the crocodiles have him, than let his life be guided by his father. The knife that had spilled the blood of that infant sacrifice more than a week ago had also severed Imbaso's last thread of filial devotion.

He went on, "Father entered the cult's secret installation below the temple at Zambei as if he were a visiting dignitary on an inspection tour. It may be that this trip is intended to reinforce his position as the foremost priest of Kivuli in Palambo. Maybe he's hoping to become something like the High Archon in the Dominion."

"You may be right, Imbaso," Betsalel said thoughtfully. "But the nature of the Kivuli cult is that those who are drawn to it are usually ambitious men who seek personal power. They care not what harm may be done to others, as long as they achieve their goals. Your father will not find it easy to subjugate other arch-priests in the cult."

"You don't know my father!" Imbaso replied. "At least, the guy at the Zambei chapter rolled right over and did him obeisance. And then, consider that our party consists of Father, me, and seven assassins counting Leila. I think he's prepared to remove any obstacles that stand in his way."

Leila shuddered at the thought. But wouldn't being assigned to kill high officials of the Kivuli cult just be like getting paid to do what she was hoping to do in the first place? "Well," the dark god said after considering his acolyte's words. "Call me if you learn anything more. Do you need any assistance?"

"I was wondering, master, if you could grant me the ability to cast a bubble of protection around myself and those close to me as you have done just now," Leila asked.

The dark god considered. "The protection prevents anyone or anything from entering, and prevents sounds from coming through to the outside of it. It is only in effect while I am manifested in my idol, and I don't think I can transfer such a power to you, Leila. But I could give you the power to cast a ward against eavesdropping, at least. It would form in a sphere ten feet in diameter, with you at the center of it. Would that help?" he asked.

"That would at least allow Imbaso and me to confer privately," she replied. "It's been very hard for us to get away from the other members of our party long enough to exchange information. And, could you give the power to Imbaso as well?" Betsalel smiled. Imbaso was open to him, and he knew the young man craved the "special status" Leila had.

"Very well," the Shadow God said, and stood with his arms wide beckoning them inside. The two stood before him as if they were his children, and he squeezed them tight for a moment. Then he released them and stepped back, saying "It is done."

Imbaso didn't feel any different. He'd been expecting some kind of little ceremony, perhaps, as Leila had reported had accompanied the two special powers Betsalel had granted her. "How does it work?" he asked.

"The ability is within you as if you had been born with it," the dark god explained. "Just form the thought that you wish the sound barrier to be in effect, and it will be. Cancel it with the thought that you wish it gone."

Of course they had to try it. The room was large and magnificent for a spare bedroom, fifteen by twenty feet. Imbaso sat on the bed near the rear wall and wished the ward into existence while Leila stood over near the door. Betsalel's protection still encompassed the entire room, but they discovered that the bubble of silence could be created within it. He shouted his head off and Leila could see his mouth moving, but heard nothing.

"It works," she confirmed, then realized that the barrier worked both ways – he had not heard her speak. She went over and joined him on the bed, stepping inside the bubble, and told him "Works fine, love." He kissed her, then released the protection. This was awesome!

They bid their god farewell and Leila gathered up the little idol and restored it to its pouch. She made sure the door was latched, then returned to the bed and threw a bubble of silence around it. They made love again, without fear of being overheard. Lying there with her in his arms afterward, Imbaso nuzzled Leila's neck and murmured, "Oh, sister! It is so good to be with you again."

"Pervert!" she responded, and slapped him on the shoulder.

Chapter 41

And so the journey went on, as the party of nine slowly crawled their way across the breadth of eastern Palambo. At each town or city with a temple of Betsalel, Leila went into the public sanctuary as a worshiper, placing a true idol on or near the altar. Crude pictorial representations of the Shadow God, usually painted on the walls behind the altars, stood in for the stolen idols in perhaps a third of them while the rest had man-made statues.

With each idol seeded Leila called Betsalel, helping him to keep up with her progress. In each case, he created a bubble of protection within the sanctuary so that none could enter while he conferred with his high priestess. And with each idol established, more and more of the faithful, the ordinary worshipers who wanted to petition the god for restful sleep, sweet dreams, or a painless death found their prayers answered. Some of them told their loved ones, and a trickle of believers began to return to the temples. The first stirrings of uneasiness began to arise within the cult.

Two days after Zambei Leila's period began, an inconvenience but also an occasion for rejoicing – the herbs worked as advertised! The hunger that had built up in her over the long months after leaving Tevo and before succumbing to her desire for Imbaso had taken her by surprise. For a further five days, the hours spent in the saddle daily were a penance.

At their fifth stop after Zambei, staying in a block of inn rooms, the party were forced to stay another night when the arch-priest of Kivuli at the local temple of Betsalel unexpectedly died of an apparent heart attack. "Nindao killed him, I think", Imbaso confided to Leila within the bubble of silence he'd erected. The rest of the party were at the temple, participating in the ritual that raised a new arch-priest in the old one's place. The god Kivuli was to be invoked at this ceremony by Mauaji, demonstrating his special favored status.

"Yesterday evening while you were placing Betsalel where he belonged, we were downstairs conferring with the arch-priest. And he didn't seem to think that Father deserved any special honors. He said they were all equal in Kivuli's worship, and here within his own city's temple Father could bow to him, not the other way around. I was sharing a room with Father, Bdejiyi, and Nindao, and when I woke in the middle of the night to the moonlight streaming in I saw Nindao was not in his bed."

"From his build, Nindao is a second-story man," Leila concurred. "He probably went up the wall to your arch-priest's bedroom and pricked him on the scalp with a needle dipped in oualit. A little of the concentrated extract will stop your heart in minutes."

"Oualit? The pretty shrubs growing in our garden at home?" Imbaso asked, astonished. She nodded with resignation.

At each stop where there was a temple, Zurina was expected to remain shut up in her room for the evening as the men would usually be at the temple until late. But Leila had no such intentions. After reestablishing a true idol of Betsalel in the public sanctuary, she could roam the town invisibly or still in disguise as the worshiper who had been praying. If the weather was foul, or it was too dark out to make sight-seeing a possibility, she would return to the inn – generally in the guise of a large, ugly workman – and spend the evening enjoying snacks and drinks while listening to the conversations around her if not participating in them. It made the evenings less lonely.

Imbaso was deeply frustrated. Now that he and Leila could converse without fear of being overheard, they could keep each other updated about what each of them was doing and thinking. But there were so few opportunities to be alone together in the way he wished.

Imbaso had bedded many women, in the past. But Leila was his first real lover. He too had been long without sex when they'd at last gotten together, and the double hit of their new love and his new relationship with Betsalel had nearly knocked him off his feet. He thought about her day and night, ached for her – and she was just right there in front of him. Yet completely out of reach.

Then one evening, eleven days after their departure from Namei, Leila was enjoying a cool bottle of beer at their inn, appearing to be a pot-bellied old man, when Imbaso and the six assassins dressed as priests came in. She'd expected them to be gone for another hour or two, at least. Mauaji must have needed to have a private conference with this temple's arch-priest, and had given his companions the rest of the night off.

The old man upturned his bottle and downed the rest of the beer, making an "ah" of appreciation and wiping his mouth on the sleeve of his dashiki before tottering to his feet and leaving by the front door. Moments later a tall, sloe-eyed woman of perhaps thirty came in, dressed as a lady of negotiable virtue. The inn discouraged blatant prostitutes from frequenting its common room, but if an attractively-dressed woman wished to come inside for a little refreshment and conversation, and that conversation were to lead to a sexual liaison later on, who were they to turn away that woman's business?

She paused in the doorway, looking around the warmly lit room. Then her eyes lit on Imbaso, and she made her way to his side. He was, without a doubt, the youngest and handsomest man there. And his rich clothing left little doubt that he would be able to buy a girl a drink.

The entire table was occupied by Imbaso and his companions, and they were all grinning and nudging each other as the strange woman invited herself to sit down with them. The four younger assassins were all feeling the discomfort of days of travel without any female companionship, and the arch-priest's son was far younger than they were.

Embarrassed at the erection that had popped up like an uninvited guest the moment he set eyes on her, Imbaso offered the lady a drink. She murmured her thanks and stroked his arm, gazing into his eyes with blatant promise and plunging Imbaso into an agony of desire. Prostitutes had been his only available sexual outlet while he was studying in Wena, and all of his friends had frequented them as well. But he had no wish to hop into bed with some strange woman. He loved Leila, only Leila – and what if this woman was carrying some vile disease?

He was about to suggest she try her wiles on one of his companions – Bdejiyi was relatively tall and not bad-looking, and closer to this woman's apparent age – when she leaned close and murmured into his ear, "It's *me*, you dolt. Please tell me you would not really take strange women to bed?" He hoped she was teasing him.

Imbaso put his arm around the woman and murmured to her, but loudly enough for those sitting nearest him to hear: "Why yes, I do have a room here. Um, how much?" The younger men at the table burst into raucous commentary, while masters Kifozi and Sumundi glanced at them and each other and shook their heads. They remembered what it had been like to be young.

Leila leaned in and whispered into Imbaso's ear, too softly to be heard by anyone else, "I'll get you for that..." This inn had no larger rooms, and Imbaso's was shared only with master Sumundi.

"Bwana Sumundi," he said respectfully, "I think that I would like some private time in our room for a while. Will you be enjoying the common room here much longer?"

"The evening is young," the old poisons master said in tones of affection. He had known Imbaso since babyhood.

Imbaso jumped to his feet nervously, taking the lady by the arm. "I'll be back soon," he promised, and got a chorus of "Take your time!" in response.

As he and the lady of the night made their way up the stairs, Leila murmured to him, "Yes, please do take your time."

Tevo had reacted uneasily to Leila's shape-changing ability, but then he had never made love with another woman besides Leila. Imbaso had vastly more experience, and he was hugely intrigued by the idea that he could enjoy dozens of different women without being untrue to the one he loved. And now it was Leila who was unhappy with the idea.

"You just want to fuck Fatima because she's got bigger breasts than me, don't you?" she demanded in mock anger after seeing his disappointed reaction. She had transformed back into herself as soon as they had closed the door behind them, while he'd been secretly hoping to continue enjoying the fantasy.

But Imbaso was not an idiot. "I'm a man, I can't help but be intrigued by every beautiful woman I see," he pointed out. "But it's you I want, Leila. Only you. Before you revealed yourself I was going to tell Fatima to take a hike." She took him into her arms, satisfied with his answer. They threw a dual globe of silence around themselves and fell into bed.

Thereafter, whenever circumstances favored it, Imbaso's companions witnessed his amazing success with Fatima after Fatima. Some were tall, some short, some light, some dark. Most were lean but a couple were plump, and one had the most preposterously enormous breasts any of them had ever seen. One and all they were beautiful and enticing, yet each of them had eyes only for young Imbaso. It didn't seem fair!

They had been moving on the highway alongside the Pana for weeks, through terrain that was mostly savannah interspersed with patches of jungle. The wildlife mostly stayed away from the road, but occasionally they had to wait or go around as herds of grazers or tembo decided to visit the river instead of going to one of the local water holes. Then after Tsimbei, the last river port on the Pana, the now much-narrowed river dived off toward the south and its sources in the distant Talj Jabal. The highway became narrower and continued nearly due east while climbing into the arid hills.

Now they had to carry more food and water with them, because the towns were fewer and farther between. Only traffic on the highway between Tsimbei and Aswa, the southernmost port on the mighty Azraq, gave reason for there to be any towns at all in the hilly wasteland. After their trip through the desert a few months ago, Imbaso and Usiku were well prepared. But the rest of the group, Mauaji especially, found it rough going.

The temple of Betsalel in Tsimbei had been the eighth they visited, the eighth to be seeded with a true idol of the dispossessed dark god. There would be no more until Aswa, and after that they would board a riverboat and not set foot on land, probably, until they docked near the mouth of the river at Iskand.

Alas, even Imbaso's magic touch with the ladies could not avail him here. For a week they rode hard every day, stopping to pick up water and supplies wherever they could. Some nights they camped rough outdoors, watchful for leopards and lions who might see them or their horses as a welcome source of food; others they were able to rent an entire small house for the night and sleep all together, bedrolls laid out on the hard stone floor.

While Imbaso rode in silence, visions of a delectably nude Leila dancing in his head, she was dreaming of her cool and pleasant house in Namei – and the hot baths or cool showers she could take there whenever she liked. When they crested the last rise in the seemingly endless desert hills and caught their first sight of Aswa gleaming below them, it seemed to everyone in the party that they had reached paradise.

Chapter 42

They arrived as the last light of the sun was shining on the city's towers and minarets, and hastened to book rooms at an inn not far from the riverfront. As Tsimbei was the port furthest upstream on the Pana, beyond which the river was too narrow and shallow for commercial traffic, so Aswa was as far up the Azraq as most boats of any size could come.

Even this far upstream the fabled river, which drained all the northern reach of the Talj Jabal, was so wide one could scarcely see from one side to the other. Aswa was a walled city built of stone, gleaming a pale golden color in the afternoon sunlight.

As soon as they had arrived at their inn Usiku insisted on a bath. The inn did not have its own bathing facilities, but the public baths were only a couple of blocks away. All of the travelers were grimy, and their entire party went down together. Usiku entered the women's side alone while the eight men went in at the other.

Leila had never experienced anything like it. After she'd stripped down to her skin (both in reality and in the illusion that presented her as Usiku) a girl of perhaps ten, wearing a damp shift, poured an urn of warm water over her. Then she was lathered up all over and scrubbed, before more urns of water rinsed the dirt and soap away. And finally, she was permitted to soak to her heart's content in the large, deep communal bathing pool. Fires in a tunnel beneath the pools, on both sides of the divider, kept the water at a temperature a little warmer than human blood.

The men had been toweled off and had their limbs oiled before dressing in their last clean clothing. Then they had waited outside the baths for a further half hour before Zurina emerged, glowing. Leila had run out of clean clothing days ago, and was in truth wearing nothing but her underwear. Zurina was more modestly dressed.

"Don't you think we had better get some laundry done?" Usiku remarked as the men escorted her back to the inn. "I wouldn't like to arrive at the royal palace looking bedraggled." They were all in agreement with that, and fortunately the inn was happy to gather their dirty clothing in sacks and have it washed and dried for them. It would be ready before they checked out in the morning.

Leila was fascinated by this ancient city, and eager for the chance to explore it. There was still another hour of daylight left by the time they'd returned to the inn and dealt with the laundry issue. "Imbaso, brother, do you think you could escort me around so I can see something of Aswa before it gets dark?" Zurina asked sweetly.

"Be sure you get back by dark," Mauaji warned sternly. "The temple here is an important one, and our last before Iskand. I'll want you with us, Imbaso." Stifling a sigh, he replied dutifully, "Yes, Father. As you will." Aswa was not as large as Namei, and while it stood on a slight rise it was not nearly as hilly. It didn't take the siblings long, this close to the riverfront area, to find one of the city's teeming marketplaces.

Everything about this city seemed ancient, as if some long-forgotten race had carved the entire place out of stone millennia before and nobody had seen fit to build anything here since. The majority of its inhabitants seemed to be Daregs or their relatives, people several shades lighter than Imbaso and Zurina and with black hair that was often nearly straight.

Instead of the colorful, loose-fitting dashikis popular further to the west, many people here were dressed in smooth robes – djelabas and caftans. The former had capacious hoods, which could be employed to carry things in when you weren't using them to keep the sun off your head. The latter, women's garb, covered the wearer from shoulder to ankle and were often decorated with beads and embroidery. Leila stored mental impressions, so she could "wear" such garments in the future.

Even this close to sunset the air was quite warm, and they stopped at a stand to purchase freshly-squeezed fruit juice. To Leila's astonishment it was cold, with little bits of ice floating in the glass. The vendor grinned. "It's the work of the angel Aeshma," he said. "My master obtains many boons from her, and this ice is one of them."

After draining the glass between them and returning it to the vendor, Imbaso and his sister strolled out of the marketplace and into a shaded alley. Leila put a bubble of silence around them. "Have you ever heard of such a thing, Imbaso?" she asked. Had not Betsalel told her that mages obtained their powers from daemons, she would never have learned it. Did the "mages" in Palambo not wish the source of their powers to be kept secret?

He was holding her hands and gazing into her eyes, his thoughts plain. But he responded to her question. "I have heard some of the lesser gods or goddesses in Namei referred to by the name of angel, Leila. Usually it is the benign deities called so, but Palamban folklore is full of tales of angels who were creatures to be feared. They usually handed out retribution to wrongdoers."

She pondered that. Perhaps the vendor's supernaturally-produced ice was not such an oddity as all that. Even after months of living in Palambo, the country could often take her by surprise. Imbaso squeezed her hands, and said, "Leila, this is our chance! I'll probably be at the temple all night after dinner, and tomorrow we'll be on a boat and there won't be any opportunities at all. Turn us invisible, and we can do it right here!"

His urgency struck a chord in her, but Leila looked around and saw only a narrow alleyway flanked on both sides by multi-story stone buildings. The stone-paved street beneath their feet was dusty and strewn with litter. "Here?" she asked, "Where are we supposed to lie down?"

Checking to make sure they were unobserved, Imbaso clutched her tightly to him and murmured into her ear, "Who says we have to lie down? We have a perfectly good wall right here, and I'm guessing that all you have on is some underwear?" He knew her too well. An electric thrill of desire shot through Leila, and in another instant the two of them had vanished from sight.

In the morning, the party milled around on one of the wharves jutting out into the broad river while their horses were loaded aboard one of the biggest river boats Leila had ever seen. This climbing onto watercraft was becoming old hat for Wapesi, not that he liked it any better for the familiarity; but the rest of their mounts had never been on the water before and the loading process was taking a long time. The pack horses they had sold, having no further need of them until they were ready to leave Iskand – whenever that was. Neither Leila nor Imbaso had any idea.

"Your Wapesi is remarkably calm," Mbando remarked as they stood idly watching the proceedings. "I've seldom seen his like. Might I ask how you acquired him?"

"Father bought him from a Gaspari in Halath," Usiku told him. This was not the story Imbaso had originally heard, but it would do. "He was trained by the Nima that roam that land, so Father told me. Certainly he is a very biddable beast. I was very glad that he broke free and escaped the Ran and his soldiers when they killed my family and destroyed our farm."

Mbando looked down, a little embarrassed to have triggered bad memories for his young colleague with his thoughtless question. Everyone in the Namei chapter of the Makucha Nyeusi knew of Usiku and her quest for vengeance, even those who had not yet met her. She was the youngest apprentice to have graduated to full assassin status within that group in living memory, let alone the youngest girl; and they all expected great things of her. The masters who had examined her had not revealed her secret, Kivuli-granted power to the rest of the membership.

Finally the horses and the rest of the passengers and cargo had been loaded onto the *Khanzira*, and the enormous tub was pulled from her moorings by capstans attached to anchors cast well out from the piers, before reorienting herself with oars and heading downstream.

The ship was like nothing Leila had seen before. Growing up in a port on the north shore of the Center Sea she was used to seagoing vessels. This one, whose name in the old Dareg language meant "pig," would never have survived a sea crossing. She was broad of beam and shallow of draft, able to negotiate river shoals even when fully loaded. She carried sail, enough to give her steerage way as she floated down the Azraq toward Iskand.

Once there, she would take on a crew of oarsmen and begin the long, arduous journey upstream. Zurina learned from chatting with one of the ship's officers, who was happy to answer questions from the lovely young daughter of the impressive-looking arch-priest, that they made a slim profit on the upstream run and a good one going the other direction. Walking around the deck and chatting with people, or visiting with Wapesi and the rest of the horses in their below-decks stalls, were about the only sources of entertainment on the slow, stately voyage.

As Imbaso had feared, the accommodations on the *Khanzira* allowed them no opportunities for fun. Mauaji had gone for the more economical option – he and the rest of the men in their party slept in a sort of floating dormitory with a dozen bunks, while Zurina was similarly housed in a room with ten other women. They met on deck and amused themselves discussing ways in which they might get together, all to no avail.

"We could go over the side with a rope, and make love in the water as the ship tows us along," Imbaso suggested as he and Zurina stood gazing out over the ship's wake within a bubble of silence.

"I can't swim!" Leila protested. Imbaso sighed, recalling Usiku had mentioned it before. It bothered her more than she was willing to admit, to lack a skill that others possessed.

"I will teach you in our pool at Namei, when we return," he said softly. Leila squeezed his hand. She was beginning to get the feeling that if she and Imbaso ever returned to Namei it was going to be a long, long, time from now. Whatever plans Mauaji had in mind would soon be coming to a head, and she didn't think that she was included in them.

Above the ship's main deck stood a long and broad pilot house, providing some protection from the weather for the steersman. On its roof a lookout was stationed, calling down through the pilot house's unglazed windows as he spotted obstacles in the stream ahead.

Leila had not realized how hazardous river travel was, her previous experience with this mode of transportation having been only a few hours along the river of which Parat was a major port. But unlike the sea, rivers were constantly changing.

A storm in the mountains far to the east could wash down snags that would rip the bottom from the ship. Or sand could drift to form a bar on which they might be stranded. It was far too dangerous for a ship the size of the *Khanzira* to travel at night, so each day as the sun sank behind the hills to the west they would either tie up at a dock or move closer to shore and put out anchors.

Which gave both the young lovers some ideas. But how could each of them sneak out from a room full of fellow travelers, then meet without being seen? They only managed it once during the week-long voyage. Imbaso claimed that, as the night was clear, he wished to go out and study the stars. Astronomy had been among his studies at the university in Wena, after all, and he had brought a spyglass with him.

"Study the mosquitoes, don't you mean?" Bdejiyi asked. The insects were thick along the river, especially near the banks.

"I hope it won't be too bad, but I'll come back inside if I have to," Imbaso said. At this point he was willing to sacrifice as much blood as the little biters cared to suck, and risk the fevers they might bring, for a chance to hold Leila in his arms. Besides, they had not been able to speak with Betsalel in days.

"Ugh, this rocking is making me feel ill," Zurina said to her female companions as they were making ready to go to bed. The river current was strong enough that even tied up as they were, the *Khanzira* was bobbing up and down. "I think I will go out and see if the fresh air over the water will make me feel better."

"Watch out for crocodiles, Zurina!" Jamila said. The young Dareg girl, perhaps fourteen, was traveling with her family to Iskand and had befriended Zurina – the only person on the voyage close to her in age and circumstances.

The two made their separate ways on deck, and were dazzled by the brilliance of the stars gleaming overhead. In most of the Dominion's larger cities, streetlamps and other man-made illumination had already made it impossible to see half of the celestial bodies that surrounded their little planet.

Though they were not underway, the *Khanzira* kept a night watch fore and aft. River pirates were a possibility not to be ignored, especially for a large and unwieldy merchant vessel resting at anchor. Leila and Imbaso carefully avoided them, and met at the center of the ship along the rail, looking out at the river.

They surrounded themselves in silence, and Leila quickly made them invisible. The moon was not yet up, but the starlight was enough to see by. She didn't want the watchmen speculating on who the lovebirds were, leaning on the rail amidships. Imbaso pulled his lover tight beneath his arm and they gazed up at the brilliance of the sky, in awe of its magnificence.

Leila murmured, "Betsalel told me that many of those stars are suns like ours, with planets orbiting around them and sentient life forms on those planets – worshiping their own gods created by The One."

"Different gods?" Imbaso murmured back, his mind expanding as he tried to picture them. Leila turned her head and stood on tiptoe to kiss him.

"The universe is a remarkable place," was all she said.

He enfolded her in a tight embrace, kissing her passionately. Their uncertain future only made him want to cling to her harder, to hold her and never let her go. In some ways, it seemed as if they were the only two "normal" people in a world gone insane. Probably, he reasoned, that was just what you got if you hung around with his father for too long.

Imbaso glanced up to his left. The darkened pilot house loomed against the background of stars, while at either end of the ship little circles of light marked the lanterns of the men on watch. "The roof of the pilot house is only about seven feet above the deck," he pointed out. They moved toward it, their bubbles of silence preventing their footfalls from being heard.

Imbaso boosted Leila up, then climbed up himself. The roof was slightly curved and made of wooden planking. Not what you would call a soft surface on which to make love. "Let's call Betsalel first," he suggested. In moments she had her small idol out and the dark god was manifesting on the rooftop. Sensing his environment, he had grown to less than three feet in height before stopping and looking around.

"On a boat?" he asked, surprised.

"We have a silence bubble on us," Leila said quietly, "But there are watchmen ahead and behind." She gestured at the lamps on prow and stern. The god shrank slightly, until he was no more than a slight black protrusion from the roof.

"Leila, come forward and surround us with shadows," he said. "Then we can converse without fear of discovery."

Pulling Imbaso by the hand, Leila leaned forward and tucked the little Shadow God into her lap. All three of them vanished from view. Oh, this was so strange. Even more than before Leila felt displaced, mother to a child who was in actuality her father. She had a bizarre urge to cuddle Betsalel as if he were a baby, or one of Kathal's kittens.

"We are on the Azraq, a couple of days south of Iskand," Leila told her child-sized god. "I have still been given no hint of what my assignment is to be once we have landed. But it can't be long now before they are forced to tell me something."

"Earlier today Father let slip something I found odd," Imbaso contributed. "He apologized that there'd been no opportunity for me to enjoy the company of women lately, but promised that soon after we got to Iskand I would be picking what he called 'the first of my wives.' As if I were a member of the royal family."

"Are you sure you're not?" Leila asked. With kings taking dozens of wives, and all of their sons entitled to do the same, might not half the population of Palambo be related to the royal family?

"My mother's mother was a daughter of King Simbanji, who was king before Faraj. Faraj was King Omali's older brother. But the privileges of the royal line, including being eligible to be chosen king by the Council of Eight, only go through males," Imbaso explained.

Leila's recent readings had touched briefly on the Council of Eight, which had been selecting the kings of Palambo for centuries – though she had first learned of it when she was only a child. Her father was a prince, but his poor chances for ever becoming king had led to him traveling with his uncle to Marsine on a trading voyage, and that had led to Leila herself being born.

It seemed like a good system to Leila, better than simply making whichever royal son happened to be born first the sole heir. At least people with brains and common sense were able to choose the best from among the crop of eligible men. You'd expect it to cause less fratricide among the royal offspring, too, since a conniving scion determined to succeed his father would have to slaughter *all* of his brothers, not just the ones older than him. Plus all of his father's brothers as well, it appeared – as the current king was the brother, not the son, of the previous one.

All this passed through Leila's mind in a couple of moments after Imbaso had spoken, and then suddenly an uneasy thought occurred to her. "The Council of Eight chooses the kings, but who chooses the Council?" Leila asked. Betsalel's knowledge of Palamban politics was centuries out of date, and it was Imbaso who answered.

"In Iskand, and nowhere else in Palambo, there is a Temple of the Eight like the one in Parat," he said. "Is there anything particularly holy about Iskand?" he asked in an aside to the diminutive god perched on his lover's lap.

"Parat is the holiest of the holy sites on our world," Betsalel explained, "But the site in Iskand is holy as well. The idols in the temple there are scions of the originals in Parat, and the pedestals on which they stand grew up naturally from the earth before the temple was built around them. My siblings and I believe that all such sites, and there are several of them, are a sign of the hand of The One, and they form a strong nexus for us. While manifested there, our powers are increased."

Huh, even the gods have a god, Imbaso thought, and continued his interrupted explanation. "It has been the custom for at least the past three hundred years for the Council to be made up of the arch-priests of the Eight at that temple. The office of arch-priest for whichever god or goddess it is goes hand in hand with the seat on the Council, and when one of the members dies the remaining Council members will elect the new arch-priest from among the members of that deity's Iskand church."

"I suppose being on the Council is just sort of an honorary thing?" Leila asked. "They couldn't have much to keep busy with, if they're only called on to elect kings and arch-priests."

"No," Imbaso replied, "the Council involves itself with other affairs as well. They have become sort of a high court for all matters pertaining to the gods within Palambo – a little like the powers of the High Archon in the Dominion."

"Except the High Archon is chosen by the gods themselves, and the Council by their fellow men," Leila mused. "Betsalel, how is it that your sisters and brothers permit mere mortals to select who will head their church?"

"The structure of our churches mostly has to do with human politics," the god explained. "Human worship is vital to us, but we care little how you choose to organize yourselves as long as that worship is forthcoming. I chose you myself mostly to keep you out of the hands of the thief takers, and raised Tevo to the office of priest as well because after more than two centuries there was no human church hierarchy left. But I expect you two will eventually develop some. I don't plan to be hand-picking my church officials forever."

None of them could see the others, sitting as they were in the darkness cloaked in shadows. Imbaso could not see Leila's guilty start at the mention of her former lover, nor could she see his look of speculation. Who was this Tevo, and why did Betsalel expect that he would be working with Leila on an ongoing basis?

They wound up their discussions with the dark god, and before he departed Imbaso asked, "Master, could you add a little something to the power of the silence bubble?"

"What would that be?" Betsalel asked. The strength of an ability he granted to one of his worshipers, which could be activated without him present to feed it with divine power, was limited. Both Leila's shadow power and her transformation ability were linked to shadows and illusions, solidly in Betsalel's purview. But the silence bubble was no part of the Shadow God's traditional powers.

"Do you think that the bubble could repel insects, too? I'm getting eaten alive here." The god laughed, a short bark. Then he grew slightly, putting an arm around each of them, and concentrated.

"Henceforth your bubble will protect you from small creatures as well as from being overheard," he told them. "Any already within the circle will flee, as well. But I wouldn't try it on anything bigger than a mouse, if I were you. Fare you well until next time." With that, he shrank and became once again an inanimate, toy-sized idol.

The flying biters had already beaten a hasty retreat, and Imbaso put his arm around Leila. They were both still invisible. "My love," he murmured softly, though of course no one could hear them, "this may well be our last chance to get together for quite some time. I have no idea what our accommodations will be like when we reach Iskand. I know this rooftop is not very soft, but…" Leila fumbled to locate his lips and pressed two fingertips against them.

"Hush," she said as quietly. "It will do."

Chapter 43

They half-drifted, half sailed into Iskand in mid-morning three days later. The brackish estuary of the Azraq had been excavated and reconfigured into one of the Center Sea's foremost harbors in ancient times, a magnificent lighthouse standing tall at its entrance. River craft like the *Khanzira* docked fairly far inland, miles from the point, while sea-going vessels moored in the deeper part of the artificial bay to the north.

Once again the party from Namei had a long wait while the crew dealt with their gear and horses. The animals were skittish and sour after their days of being cooped up, but they soon began to work out the kinks as they were temporarily loaded down with all of their riders' gear as well as the riders themselves and began the long walk through the sprawling royal city's stone-paved streets to the place where they would stay during their visit.

"Are we going to an inn, master?" Usiku asked Kifozi. Mauaji answered her question.

"You will be pleased to learn, daughter," he said – lest she forget that their cover story must be kept in place, for addressing Kifozi as "master" was an oversight – "that we are being hosted during our stay at the royal palace itself. It is one of the marvels of the world, and it is a huge honor to be invited to stay there. But after all, king Omali is your grand-uncle. Your grandmother and he shared a father, if not a mother."

"Thank you for the reminder, Father," Zurina said, bowing her head slightly. Huh, Leila thought. Royalty. Her father had been a prince, supposedly one of the sons of the late Faraj. If Omali was Faraj's brother, then Leila herself could lay claim to being the king's grand-niece just as Zurina could – had she actually been Imbaso's sister. Then a horrible thought came to her. Did that make Imbaso her third cousin or something like that? Incest! But the connection seemed tenuous. Keeping the wealth in the family, it was not uncommon for families in the Dominion to marry their children to their first cousins – a much closer relationship.

Iskand was quite spread out, sprawling to the west from the near bank of the Azraq and bounded by desert on the other side.

The delta was rife with agriculture, the river's seasonal flooding providing some of the richest soil in the world. But get very away from the river, and everything was as dead and dry as those hills they'd passed through coming from Tsimbei.

Like Aswa, much of Iskand was built of the pale golden local stone. But there were lots of whitewashed adobe structures, too – many of them little more than huts – as they made their way toward the city center from the river docks. The palace complex, similar in concept to the one in Namei but far grander and far older, sat surrounded by its own wall on a low promontory with a view of both the Center Sea and the river.

Moving along at the best pace the horses could manage in Iskand's crowded streets, it took them nearly two hours to travel the seven miles from the river docks to the nearest of the palace complex gates. They had passed through some of the most squalid slums Leila had ever seen, districts that made Namei's first and second circles seem like luxury housing.

Leila allowed Zurina to goggle like any back-country girl on her first trip to the big city as they arrived at the broad gates blocking the road that led up through the palace complex wall. Up close the wall was enormous, twenty feet high at least, and faced with smooth stone that would have made scaling it almost impossible.

It was more than six feet thick too, she realized, as they came inside. The gates were standing open at this hour, but were guarded by a squad of royal guards in red-and-blue uniforms with ostrich plumes on their hats. The number of plumes seemed to correspond to the guardsman's rank, and one of their officers looked like he was sprouting a bouquet on his head.

Mauaji assumed the leadership of their little band, and presented some paperwork to the guard who questioned them as to their business. Then after comparing the information the black-robed arch-priest had given him with a ledger book kept in the guard house, he passed them through. Already half a dozen parties behind them were waiting for admittance.

This place must have hundreds of deliveries a day, Leila realized. All these guards, and everyone else who lived here, would need a lot of food and other supplies. Why bother scaling the wall when you could simply come in with a load of grain sacks and then slip away once you were inside? There was something about coming upon large accretions of wealth – especially in close proximity to poverty as severe as what they'd seen earlier today – that set Leila's inner thief to scheming.

Get a grip, girl, you're not here to steal the crown jewels. Just murder a few people, that's all… They dropped their horses off at the royal stables, which made the ones at Namei look like a country cottage. Young stable hands rushed to relieve them of their mounts, giving each of them a numbered tag. A matching tag was tied into each horse's mane. Seemingly there were so many horses kept here that this was the only way to keep track of them all!

A swarm of liveried palace servants (their garb a deep sea-blue color, matching the blue of the guards' uniforms, but not including any feathers) arrived to carry their baggage to the suite of rooms that had been set aside for them. It felt to Leila as though they might have walked more than a mile, through mazes of corridors and occasionally across little garden courtyards, to reach the area where they were to live during their stay.

As Leila was already undercover as Usiku, who in turn was undercover as Zurina, she found it required a certain amount of concentration to move as she should. Usiku was not that far off from her true self, a little younger and driven by a fire for revenge. But both she and Leila moved with a pantherine grace that was inappropriate for the gently-raised, ornamental Zurina. Zurina minced along with small strides, stopping often to gaze with wonder on the palace furnishings or admire the flowers in the gardens. And she complained a tiny bit about what a long walk it was, too.

Their troop was being guided by a small, middle-aged woman who Leila took to be the chatelaine. Or perhaps *a* chatelaine. After getting a look at the size of this place on their walk from the stables, she was convinced you would need a staff the size of a large village just to keep it in some kind of order. And while it might, as Mauaji had said, be a big honor to be guested here, they had already seen dozens of other people who appeared to be fellow guests.

Still, they had been given an entire apartment to themselves. There was a broad and comfortable sitting room, a private bath with running water, even a small kitchen supplied with fruit, snacks, and bottled beverages. The eight men would sleep two to a room, and Zurina – as usual – had a room to herself.

"You do not have a lady's maid with you?" the chatelaine asked. Leila thought it best to ingratiate herself with the help, as soon as possible.

"No, … um, may I know your name?" Zurina asked prettily.

"Malanda, mwali Zurina," the woman replied with a very slight bow.

"Thank you, memsahib Malanda. Our journey was so very long, I didn't wish to put my maid at home through such an ordeal."

"Very well, we will provide one for you. She will report here shortly. You have come after the midday meal, so I will have that sent to your rooms as well. Expect it within half an hour."

The woman definitely seemed to know her job. "Thank you, Malanda," Zurina said, returning the bow. "You are very efficient. Have you served his Majesty Omali for long?" Malanda's mouth quirked in an expression that was almost but not quite a smile.

"You might say that," she replied. "He's my younger brother." With that she left the room, while Zurina stood there in the sitting room with her cheeks burning.

Two servants with trays of food arrived at the door to their apartment at the same time as a plump and pretty girl of around Zurina's age. She was clad in the same palace livery, and immediately picked out her new assignment. After all, they were the only two females in the vicinity. Bowing, she said "Mwali Zurina, I am Mbina. I will be acting as your personal maid during your stay, and will also be keeping the apartment clean and tidy." Everything Leila had seen here was spotless, so the staff must take their jobs seriously. It was probably some of the better employment available locally. She wondered how many of the servants scurrying around were of the royal blood.

After eating, Leila was thinking that perhaps she might take a bath and a nap. Presumably they would be invited to dine in the palace's grand dining room this evening, but there would be a few hours before then in which to explore – unseen, of course. But Kifozi had other ideas. "Everyone please gather your dirty laundry," he said. It had been more than a week since everything had been washed in Aswa, and among the nine of them there was quite an accumulation. When it had all been piled in the center of the sitting room's handsome carpet Kifozi told Mbina to take it all away. She was to see to its washing and drying, and return it to the apartment folded and clean.

The girl looked like she wanted to argue, but Kifozi was a middle-aged man and a commanding figure in his priest robes. She just bundled it all up into an enormous sack and carried it off. After she'd left, he said "Good. That ought to occupy her for a few hours. I hadn't considered that of course the palace would saddle us with a maidservant. Usiku, Sumundi, and you four" – gesturing to the four young assassins – "come with me to my chamber. We have things to discuss."

Here it was, Leila realized. She was finally going to find out what the group was doing here. It certainly wasn't to find a royal husband for young Zurina! And whatever it was, it seemed they didn't want Imbaso party to the tale. He would be anyway, she thought, just as soon as he and she could get a moment alone.

Closing the door behind him, Kifozi stood side by side with master Sumundi and addressed the five young assassins gathered around the bed. "You have no doubt wondered why we have come to Iskand," he said as a preamble. "Now you will be given your assignments. Our target is none other than King Omali, but we have other targets as well. These will be taken out as quickly as possible, and in the meantime we will gather intelligence to assure that our termination of the primary target will be carried out flawlessly. His predecessor, his own brother Faraj, also died at the hands of an assassin and it is said that he is very well protected. The fact that he has ruled for more than fifteen years is proof of it."

Fifteen years didn't seem like all that long a time to Leila, though it was a significant percentage of her lifetime. Evidently the kingdom of Palambo was hard on its rulers, probably one of the reasons it had failed to subdue all the rebel groups within its borders – and had not yet tried to attack the Dominion in force.

Kifozi produced folded pieces of paper, each with the seal of the cult of Kivuli stamped into it, and handed one each to Mbando, Bdejiyi, Zhendibi, and Nindao. "You will each handle one target, according to the instructions enclosed. Memorize these, then destroy them. You may take them to your rooms for now," he said with a hint of dismissal. The four trooped out of the room, each with his lethal instructions, and closed the door behind them.

"Usiku, remind me after you get back from wreaking your revenge to have you tutored in reading and writing," the master assassin said mildly. "It's an important skill, one we have only been able to overlook because time was short."

"Yes, master," the girl said respectfully, looking a little discomfited.

"What we need from you now, Usiku," Kifozi went on, "is for you to insinuate yourself into the royal household and observe as much as you can about King Omali and those closest to him. As Zurina, you are here in the hopes that your youth and beauty will catch the eye of someone well-placed in the royal family. I understand that King Omali recently wed a girl little older than you are, the old dog, so perhaps he might be interested himself. Or if not him, he has two sons of marriageable age. One of them hasn't even married yet – you would be his first wife."

"But the king is Zurina's grand-uncle, is he not?" Usiku asked, appalled.

"True," Kifozi said. "I suppose that would make you an unsuitable match, though he still might want to bed you. And his sons are just your cousins."

"I'm not actually going to have to marry any of them, am I?" she asked in alarm.

"Would that be a problem?" Kifozi asked, puzzled. "Whoever it was, you would soon enough be a widow."

"The thing is," she said, "I am not a maiden. I was raped repeatedly by the Ran while his men were slaughtering my family."

"Ah, I see," Kifozi said – not seeing at all. "If you married one of the princes he would certainly expect to be taking your maidenhead. But there are ways of faking that sort of thing. If the occasion arises, master Sumundi can help you with it." I just told him I was brutally raped, and he thinks I'm worried about the lack of a hymen? Leila thought in disbelief. Men!

"In any case, this is going to take some while. Once the men have completed their assignments we will have to wait and see if any further removals are required. Meanwhile, you will get to know everyone with whom the king usually associates – men and women both. Learn what guards surround him, how he takes his meals, what his usual habits are as regards his harem, everything. Do you understand?"

"I understand, sir," Usiku said coolly. "I assume that this work will not begin until formal introductions have been made?"

"That is correct," Kifozi said. "We are all invited to a small gathering this evening at six, then at eight we will be dining in the royal dining hall with most of the adult members of the royal family and a few dozen other guests. Dinners here at the palace are definitely mob scenes."

"I had better bathe, then," Usiku said, "and as I'm feeling a bit tired from our trip and it might be a long evening, I think I'll take a nap afterward."

"Good idea," the master assassin said, and they all left the room together. Usiku went to her room, which she noticed had a second, much smaller bed in it. Evidently Mbina was intended to sleep here in the room with her. That might be awkward...

Some of the palace complex's buildings rose as high as three storeys, but the residential wing they were in was all on the ground floor. Zurina's room had a nice big window looking out on the little courtyard, which featured lush plantings and a tinkling central fountain. There was even glass in the window, something Leila had not seen often in Palambo. Currently the window stood open, allowing a slightly cool breeze from the shady courtyard into the room. It would still not be as comfortable as her bedroom in Namei, she thought with a sigh.

Throwing on a robe, Zurina took a quick bath. Then, asking everyone not to disturb her until five (which was still more than two hours away), she closed her door. Quickly, Leila dressed in her abbreviated burglar's outfit and loaded it with her daggers and pocket watch. She artfully arranged some pillows under the covers, just in case someone should look into the room through the window while Zurina slept, wedged the room's door shut, and climbed silently and invisibly out the window. She pushed it shut behind her.

As Leila entered the little garden she spotted Imbaso sitting on a bench in the shade, admiring the brightly-colored little fish that were swimming around in the fountain. He appeared lost in thought. She stepped close but was careful not to touch him, lest he suddenly vanish while someone inside the apartment was watching. Throwing up a bubble of silence (which immediately drove the fish and several dragonflies away), Leila said "Imbaso, we need to talk. Pretend you heard something in the bushes over there and go investigate."

She hurried to the spot she'd indicated, and Imbaso did a studied impression of someone who'd just noticed an unexpected sound. He started up, craned around to look behind him, then got up from the bench and walked off into the miniature jungle that surrounded the courtyard. As soon as he got there, he disappeared.

"Did your father tell you anything while we were gone?" Leila asked.

Imbaso shook his head, and then realized the foolishness of that maneuver and said, "Small talk. Then he excused himself, said he had some reading to do, and I wandered out to the garden. It's pretty out here," he added.

Leila sighed. "I have a bad feeling about this, and I think that you're being kept in the dark because you're supposed to be the beneficiary of it all. The good news is I don't have to rush right out and kill anyone – I'm still sweet, innocent Zurina as far as anyone here is concerned."

"And the bad news?" Imbaso asked, dreading the answer.

"Our four young assassins were each handed sealed instructions and a target. They're killing four people, and I have no idea whom. But Kifozi admitted that our ultimate target here is King Omali."

"Shit, the king?!" Imbaso exclaimed. It wasn't the enormity of a plot to kill the king that bothered him. That sort of thing happened at least two or three times per generation. It was the thought of the penalties that would fall on everyone connected with the plot, even those who had not been given details about it, should they fail.

"What do you know about this Omali?" Leila asked. "Is he a particularly awful king?"

Imbaso considered, then replied, "No, not really. He's been king since I was a little kid, and I can barely remember the guy before him. But he was assassinated, too. It happens a lot."

"Is being king here such a big deal then, that people will kill for it?" Leila asked.

"People in the kingdom of Palambo, at least educated and well-off people, admire and try to emulate the Gaspari Dominion," Imbaso explained. He'd been one of those well-educated, well-off people his whole life, and had reason to know. "But our government is very different. There is no constitution, no Grand Assembly. The law of the land is basically whatever the king says it is, and when he – whoever he is – makes new decrees, the royal guard stands ready to enforce them."

"Seriously?" Leila asked, scarcely believing a country the size of Palambo could be run on such a primitive basis in this modern age.

"Well obviously," Imbaso replied, "communication is an issue. And there are some parts of this country so remote and hard to get to that it might take two years between the issuing of a decree and its enforcement in the hinterland. Small villages scattered around out there are effectively ruled by groups of village elders. But with control of the army, the king definitely has power – far more power than the Gaspari emperor does."

"So…" she said, working it out. "If Omali has stayed king for most of your lifetime and nobody has killed him yet, either he's got super-good security or he must only issue decrees that are pretty popular, huh?"

"There hasn't been anything really awful that I can think of. And, it wasn't him that had the previous king assassinated, either," Imbaso replied.

"Really? You mean the people who killed the old king weren't able to get their own candidate voted in?" Leila was starting to wish she'd spent more time studying recent Palamban history before coming on this trip.

"They expected to, but it didn't work out," Imbaso explained. "Faraj was Omali's older brother, though there was a pretty big age gap between them. From what I heard Omali figured the throne was never going to come his way, and had become a trader. When Faraj was killed he was away on business, and then the people who had arranged Faraj's death kidnaped him, intending to keep him away from Palambo long enough that the voting would already be over. But he escaped, and got back to Iskand in time to present himself for the voting."

"Wow, it sounds like a fairy tale," Leila said.

"I think the Council of Eight might have been counting the kidnaping in Omali's favor," her tutor went on. "They are usually a bunch of elderly clerics, and I don't think they're much fond of regime change delivered by assassin. Omali's story was proof, sort of, that he had not been involved in his brother's death."

"Why did they pick Faraj's brother, instead of one of his sons?" Leila wondered.

"Elderly clerics, again," Imbaso said. "Faraj's sons were all pretty young, the eldest only in his middle twenties. He already had a dozen of them, but most of them were just children. Whereas Omali was a man in his prime, and a solid citizen with some understanding of the virtues of hard work. The Council really does think of the country as a whole when they make their choices. It's a sacred trust."

Leila remained silent for a few moments, digesting all this, and without being able to see her face Imbaso wondered what was going on. Finally she said, thoughtfully, "The people who killed Faraj could just have easily killed Omali instead of kidnaping him, if they thought he was a threat to their plans."

"They were the friends and supporters of another of Faraj's brothers," Imbaso explained. "He had twenty-three of them, I believe, and a similar number of sisters. My grandmother was one of those. So probably that brother liked Omali and thought he'd be fine to keep as a family member, just so he didn't interfere with their bid for the throne."

"And it bit them on the ass..." Leila mused. "So I guess the conclusion is that assisting in the demise of Omali is not going to leave me with a feeling of satisfaction for a job well done. Next question: what would happen to all of us here if the plot were discovered?" Imbaso shuddered, which Leila felt through the contact that was keeping him invisible.

"There would be no trial," he said. "The justice system here is part and parcel with our government by decree. One would need little more than some reasonably reliable witness standing up and saying 'those guys are plotting to kill the king,' plus maybe one single piece of physical evidence, and we would all – you, me, Father, the six Makucha Nyeusi assassins, and probably your little maidservant – be thrown into the dungeons to die of starvation. Unless maybe they decided to torture us to death instead."

Oh shit, Leila thought. So much for blowing the plot and Revealing All. Mauaji could go hang, but she was fond of masters Kifozi and Sumundi. They might be professional killers, but they had been kind to the young Usiku. The four younger assassins who'd come on this trip were all personable as well, nice young men in a questionable line of work. And the thought that anything like that might happen to Imbaso, who had been truly ignorant of the plot right up until she'd just brought it to his attention... No, she realized, she would not be alerting Omali of the threat to his person. But maybe she could foil it quietly.

Chapter 44

Too much time had gone by. In only a little more than an hour, Zurina would need to be rising from her nap and getting ready for the pre-dinner gathering at which she was to meet (and wow) prospective suitors. "I need to go exploring a little," she told Imbaso.

"Take me with you!" he urged.

"No," she replied, "It's too much trouble to hang onto you so you'd stay invisible. Besides, somebody inside the apartment may be wondering why you vanished for so long. Go on back to the pool. I'll be back soon!"

Leila released both Imbaso's shoulder and the bubble of silence, moving away from him with a slight rustling of shrubbery. The several apartments in this part of the residential wing had their courtyards linked, though screened by vegetation. With a sigh, Imbaso returned to his contemplation of the fountain. At least Leila wasn't planning on bringing the wrath of the royal guards down on them. But why in all the hells did Father want to assassinate the king? It wasn't as if he had a personal stake in who might occupy the throne.

Concerned about too much rustling shrubbery, Leila came out into the courtyard of an adjacent apartment. It was occupied, but the guests all appeared to be napping away the hottest part of the day. She slipped in through the open doors to their sitting room, and out the front door to the corridor beyond.

Now if only I can manage to find my way around without getting lost! Leila thought, as she turned left and headed up the hallway in the direction from which Malanda (grand-aunt Malanda, she realized) had led them a couple of hours before. Part of her training, with the Night Guild and again with the Makucha Nyeusi, had given her a superior ability to pay attention to her surroundings, always being aware of her exit routes.

Leila threaded her way out to one of the palace's main corridors, and began drifting – invisible and silent – along it while keeping her eyes and ears on full alert. As in Parat, the palace itself was only one building in a small walled city that included numerous others devoted to the workings of the government. The Palambans might have a rather more direct approach, but they still needed an army of bureaucrats to keep the wheels turning.

Iskand's palace compound also included the famous Library of Iskand, founded in antiquity and the repository of some of the most important works, and historical records, of the western part of the continent. Leila hoped she might get a chance to spend some hours there during their visit, but right now her mind was on other things. Where did the king spend his days, anyhow?

Being invisible rather reduced one's opportunities for asking passing strangers for directions, Leila realized. But she was out of her area of expertise here. She didn't know enough about who might belong and who didn't to chance taking a disguise. Suppose she guessed wrong? Instead she gravitated down the corridor to an area where a lot of people seemed to be going out, then pressed herself into a corner and just stood observing.

After half an hour Leila had worked out that the expected personnel within the palace included two groups: palace staff, who might all be classed as servants (by longstanding tradition, the palace did not keep slaves), and guards. The staff were there to do everything that needed to be done, and the guards to make sure that everyone was where they belonged. There were of course also myriads of official palace residents, most of them probably members of the royal family, and dozens at least of temporary guests like herself and her party. How could the guards keep track of them all?

Leila checked her watch and realized with a start that she needed to get moving back to her room. She glided hurriedly down the corridor and then wound her way back to the wing where their apartment was. She found the door of their own apartment unlocked and, peering inside, saw no one in the sitting room. The rest of the party must be making their ablutions and preparing for the party, she realized. She scooted through the open doors to the courtyard and was soon through the window and inside her room.

Redistributing the cushions in the bed so that it looked like an ordinary bed in which someone had recently taken a two-hour nap,

Leila removed the wedges from the door and unlatched it. She was just considering the clothing that was available to her when Mbina burst in through the door, a pile of folded laundry under one arm.

Leila was dumfounded. She had expected it to take until late tonight, at least, for the girl to accomplish the task of washing, drying, and folding all of their dirty clothes. Yet here she was only a little more than three hours later! Fortunately she had assumed Usiku/Zurina's appearance before unlocking the door, just as a precaution.

"Sorry I am late!" Mbina panted. "The palace laundry was very busy today, lots of extra customers!"

Zurina gathered herself and asked, "How did you get this all done so quickly? I had expected you would not return until after dinner." The girl eyed her as if she'd said something peculiar.

"But I must dress mwali for the party!" she exclaimed. "Of course I must be here now."

As Mbina poked and prodded Zurina into one of the outfits that had returned with the wash, combing her hair and putting it up into a sort of topknot, the story of the Iskand palace laundry came out. Seemingly there was an area of the palace where enormous vats of water were kept hot at all times, where armies of laundresses worked, where brass cages six feet in diameter were filled with damp wash and then tumbled above roaring furnaces by the efforts of dozens of spit boys. Good grief!

Leila was exceedingly glad that she had brought along some real fine clothing, and some real jewelry as well, on this expedition. Having never experienced life with a lady's maid, she had confidently expected to dazzle the upper classes with finery that was completely illusory. Now it appeared she was going to have to go shopping.

The male members of the household were left to fend for themselves, of course. Considering that seven of the eight were supposedly priests of Betsalel, who wore simple black robes for every occasion, there was little effort expended. But Imbaso emerged from the room he was sharing with his father looking... Looking like a prince!

Since Leila had first met Imbaso, the words her mother had spoken more than ten years before, regarding her father, kept coming back to her: "He was a very beautiful man." She had been struck by Imbaso's beauty while he and Suleiman were conversing aboard the ship that had carried them both to Halath. And since Leila had come to love him, she realized it even more. Seeing Imbaso garbed as a member of the royal family made her wonder if she was looking at the same image her mother had seen, eighteen years ago.

They stood gaping at each other across the breadth of the sitting room. "Sister!" Imbaso cried, quickly covering the moment of embarrassment, "Mbina has done wonders with you!"

"Ah," Zurina replied, "because without her assistance my naturally wretched appearance would be appalling."

"Sad, but true," he came back. She walked daintily over and socked him on the arm. True sisterly affection.

Soon the group was ready to leave for the party, the whereabouts of which none of them knew. "I will escort you to the gathering," Mbina said, "then return here and be about my duties until you return."

"Have you had anything to eat, Mbina?" Zurina asked solicitously.

"Oh yes, mwali, we servants are all fed early so that we will be free for our evening duties."

Well, at least they were getting something to eat. All this business of servants deserving so much less than their masters was part of the reason Leila had never felt guilty about stealing from the rich – and keeping it for herself. Hey, she was a member in good standing of the poor…

Imbaso took Zurina's arm as they followed Mbina down the corridors, enjoying the touch even if they could not converse properly. The bubble's ten-foot diameter would have included most of the group. Agh, she looked so good he wanted to throw her to the floor and ravish her on the spot! But instead, he'd be escorting his "sister" to a party where she would be introduced to other men whom his father hoped would also like to throw her to the floor and ravish her. He was not feeling very happy.

Mbina left them at the door of the smallish ballroom where the party was being held, hurrying back to their apartment to resume her duties. They were right on time, but it appeared that here in the Palamban palace the concept of being "fashionably late" had not yet caught on. The room was already packed with people drinking, nibbling on appetizers, and talking as a small group of musicians tucked away in a corner provided soothing music.

Now Imbaso was at her side but it was her father Mauaji who took Zurina's elbow to guide her into the room. Leila gave it her best shot, tweaking up the girl's beauty a bit beyond what nature had given her. She was younger and prettier than Leila, and far more innocent than Leila had been since before her tenth birthday.

The person who had arranged for them to have invitations to this relatively exclusive gathering (and, for all Leila knew, also arranged for them to guest at the palace) proved to be one Farendhi, a tall and good-looking Amhari in his mid-to-late forties. Leila later learned that he was another of Omali's twenty-two surviving brothers, one of the younger ones – and an agent of the cult of Kivuli. But at the moment he was just their beaming, jovial host.

Smiling broadly, Mauaji approached and Farendhi turned from addressing one of the servants to welcome them with open arms. He embraced Mauaji and kissed him on both cheeks, then gazed at Zurina with a flickering of lust in his dark brown eyes. "My son, Imbaso, my daughter, Zurina. I would like to introduce you to Prince Farendhi. It is he who has so kindly extended us the hospitality of the palace during our visit here."

The prince gave Imbaso a similar embrace to the one he'd given Mauaji, but settled for squeezing Zurina's extended hand between his two, while smiling into her face. My, Leila thought, the Palamban royal family certainly bred for beauty. But considering that the wives of the kings and princes would be chosen for precisely that quality, was it any surprise?

Mauaji had moved on to introduce Farendhi to his six colleagues from the temple of Betsalel in Namei, and Imbaso swooped to Zurina's side and took her arm again. He felt like he was leading a fat calf through a pack of hyenas. But of course, he realized, just because Leila happened to look at the moment like a beautiful ingénue didn't mean she couldn't take care of herself. Some drunken party guest who tried to squeeze her butt might find himself missing a hand.

Mauaji, Farendhi, and the rest of their party soon joined them and their host led them like a flock of ducklings toward the far side of the room. "Come," he said suavely, "I am sure you are most eager to meet my brother." The king! Well, Leila had already met the emperor of the Gaspari Dominion on a couple of occasions since the dramatic events in Parat last year. What was another ruler? Although the fact she was expected to help kill this one did increase her anxiety.

They approached the tall man standing near the dais where the musicians were playing. He had a beautiful young woman on his arm – it was Linda Cervantes! Marriage to the king had suited her well enough, so far. She fairly sparkled as she clung to his arm, engaging in repartee in heavily accented Kiswa. A slight bulge in her midsection suggested that the king might already have planted a prince or princess in her belly – probably the last child he would ever sire, unless Leila could think of a way to stop the assassination that wouldn't result in her and her companions being killed in nasty ways.

Omali himself shared the good looks that seemed a hallmark of his family, but his face was lined and he had put on a few pounds. He'd been living the high life in the palace for most of Leila's lifetime, so perhaps it was to his credit that he was not as fat as a pig. His curly, once-black hair had now gone mostly silver and he wore it cut short by contemporary standards.

On the opposite side from Linda another man stood, clearly a member of the same family line. He looked to be in his mid-thirties, with only a few silver strands among the black, and he remained clean-limbed and straight without a trace of fat on his body. He was too old to be one of Omali's sons, from what Kifozi had told her, so perhaps he was a still-younger brother?

Farendhi drew up in front of the king and his party with his entourage close behind him, and waited deferentially for their conversation to cease. Then he said, "Brother, these are the people I mentioned, the visitors from Namei. May I present arch-priest Mauaji of the temple of Betsalel in Namei, his fellow priests Kifozi and Sumundi, and their acolytes Zhendibi, Nindao, Mbando, and Bdejiyi." The king and his party nodded briefly.

Farendhi went on, "Arch-priest Mauaji has been on a tour of the temples of Betsalel between here and Namei, and he has brought along his son Imbaso and daughter Zurina so that they might see something of the world and possibly find suitable marriage alliances. They are, as Your Majesty may know, our grand-nephew and grand-niece through our sister Faranha. I would like to introduce you all to my brother, His Majesty King Omali of Palambo, his lovely wife Linda, and our nephew Vandao, the king's right-hand man."

Zurina's pretty face smiled graciously at them all, not quite empty-headed but innocent of any emotion except excited pleasure at being introduced to such exalted and powerful people. Beneath it, Leila's expression was one of shock. Dear Betsalel, she thought. I am finally going to get the chance to kill my father!

Chapter 45

Zurina hung on everyone's words, encouraging all she spoke with to talk about themselves and thus building the impression that she was a great conversationalist. The two-hour party was her group's main opportunity to insinuate themselves into the palace social scene, and all of them made the most of it.

Leila was surprised to learn that Vandao, whom she found pleasant enough if a little stiff, was unmarried. She knew he was heterosexual, so how had he managed to escape having at least a small harem by now? She was burning to get him alone, imagining the satisfaction of explaining in gruesome detail how he had ruined her mother's life and her own with his callous actions half a lifetime ago – right before she cut out his heart.

But the opportunity didn't arise. She met the king's two marriageable sons, Omaso and Samindhi. Omaso, the elder at twenty-four, already had two wives – and had broken with custom somewhat by bringing both of them along to this party. Samindhi was a year older than Imbaso and looked enough like him to be a first cousin, though Leila figured they were actually second or third cousins at best.

Samindhi was very interested in Zurina. He'd been under pressure for years already to select his first bride, and he wouldn't have minded wedding (or at least bedding) the powerful arch-priest's beautiful daughter. Before they were all called in to dinner in the palace's enormous dining hall he'd secured her promise to come riding with him tomorrow morning. Imbaso fumed.

Kifozi had not been jesting about the mob scene in the dining hall. The room was bigger than any ballroom Leila had ever seen, with tables and chairs everywhere. An enormous table that sat fifty was at the rear end of the room on a raised platform, and it was here that the king and those he wished to honor sat to eat. Linda, Vandao, several of the king's children including Omaso and Samindhi, and a lot of people the visitors from Namei had not yet met, made the cut; but they, along with Farendhi and some of his own wives and children, were seated at one of the tables below. It seemed every person living or visiting within the palace was eating with them, except for servants and guards of course.

But there were quite a few of both in the room – dozens of servants brought dishes, took away others, poured beverages, passed out damp towels for the cleaning of hands, and saw to everyone's needs whatever they might be. Should you desire some other dish, you had only to flag a passing servant and some would be fetched for you. Wow!

And a squadron of finely-bedecked royal guards, whom Leila took to be King Omali's personal bodyguard, stood at attention on the dais behind the royal table. More guards were at the doors and all around the room, ready to quell any violence that might erupt; or, perhaps, repel an armed invasion.

Linda sat at the king's elbow, but on his other side was not Vandao, but a man Leila had noticed at the party earlier but had not been introduced to. He appeared to be in his middle fifties, close in age to Omali. And she noticed that before the king was served from any of the dishes on the table, the man beside him would eat some. Perhaps it was this necessary caution that had kept Omali relatively slim over the years. Or perhaps it was his familial heritage. To a man, all of the royal family members Leila had met were tall, slim, and dark-skinned with black or deep brown eyes and tightly curling glossy black hair that went silver as they aged.

"Who is the man that is so honored as to sit beside our king at table?" Zurina asked Farendhi. He smiled indulgently at her.

"Ah," he said, "that is Dasembi, one of my brother's oldest and dearest friends. They were partners together in the trading venture Omali engaged in when our brother Faraj was king. He took it over completely after Omali became king, of course, but has remained a true friend. You might say he puts his life on the line for his old friend at every meal, for it is he who first eats and drinks anything that the king will touch."

Zurina's eyes went wide, at the thought of a life where any bite of food or sip of a drink might bring your death. "Oh!" she exclaimed. "He must be very brave!" Farendhi smiled again.

"Well, he has performed this function for our king for more than five years now, since the last royal taster died. So far it has done him no harm, though his waistline has expanded somewhat."

"The last taster died?" Zurina asked, a look of delighted horror on her sweet face. "Was he poisoned?" Farendhi chuckled, and those around him joined in the laughter.

"Oh no dear, not at all. He was beheaded when it was learned that he had been seen consulting with a group of people suspected of plotting against the crown. He, and all of them as well."

With a little "Eep" Zurina subsided, and sat staring down at her plate as she idly poked at the food remaining there with her fork. Betsalel, Imbaso knew what he was talking about earlier, it seemed! No whisper of suspicion must fall on them, or they were all as good as dead.

The dinner, which had more than a dozen courses and was accompanied by every kind of beverage imaginable, went on for two full hours. Only when the king and his party got up and left the room did others begin to go. One did not walk out on one's monarch, it seemed, not when he was standing you to a feast literally fit for a king.

Zurina covered a yawn and thanked Farendhi for his kind hospitality. It had been a very long day, and the yawn had not been illusion; but Leila was determined it would not end just yet. Young Samindhi came over from the dais to remind Zurina that he would see her at the stables tomorrow morning after breakfast, and she thanked him again for the invitation. Then they all went back to their apartment. All of them were familiar enough with the route by now, and should they get lost they would only need to ask one of the guards. There were dozens of them stationed within the palace twenty-four hours a day.

When they entered the apartment they found Mbina dozing on the settee in the sitting room; but she awakened the moment they came in and jumped to her feet, anxious to return to her duties. Nothing would do but that mwali Zurina should submit to being undressed by her maid, her clothing and jewelry carefully put away, her hair taken down and combed out before she could lie down. It was past eleven by the time Zurina lay down in bed. Then Mbina blew out the lamps and went to her own small bed, tucked away in the far corner of the room.

The girl must have been exhausted, because it was not ten minutes after the room went dark that Leila heard her begin snoring gently. Enclosing herself in a bubble of silence and becoming invisible, she was on her feet immediately. She arranged the pillows beneath the thin sheet again, then put on her abbreviated burglar gear and tucked her daggers into their sheaths. Another moment and she had slipped out the window into the courtyard.

She was relieved not to see Imbaso there. They had had no opportunities to talk privately since this afternoon, but also there had been no opportunities for making love in days and she didn't doubt the thought had crossed his mind that the two of them could rendezvous in the garden and knock it out in the shrubbery. After all, it had crossed *her* mind…

But her discovery of her father Vandao here, alive and enjoying life as the "right hand man" of the king all these years while her mother rotted in her grave – if she'd ever even *had* a grave, which was not certain – drove thoughts of love right out of Leila's mind. Sexual satisfaction could wait until she'd had the satisfaction of long-delayed revenge.

Leila let herself back into the apartment through the doors to the deserted sitting room, then out into the corridor. She crept along invisibly toward the palace kitchens, the location of which she'd pinpointed during the evening. Unsurprisingly, they were situated near at hand to the enormous dining hall.

It was not that late, and there were still many people moving in the hallways. Leila stayed close to the walls, avoiding running into anyone while observing the scene. The guard presence seemed heightened now, at least as a percentage of those still afoot. She slipped into the main kitchen, a room larger than her entire house in Namei, and watched with interest as a male evening-shift cook directed a staff of scullions and serving girls.

The palace would be feeding all the people who'd been at dinner tonight three times tomorrow, and the kitchens never slept. Even now, a short while before midnight, dozens of people were at work. She watched as a teenage girl in servant blue came in and picked up a tray on which were two wine bottles and a pair of glasses.

The evening shift supervisor, if that was what he was, appeared to have a female lieutenant issuing orders to the servants, and it was she who said, "Take the tray to Memsahib Suduri's room, then return here immediately. No dawdling!"

"Yes, Memsahib Mnamene," the girl replied, snatching the tray without looking up and then scooting from the room as quickly as she could – shoulders hunched as if expecting a blow.

A minute later a small, frightened-looking girl of perhaps twelve, dressed in servant blue and carrying a tray on which a bottle of wine, a glass, and a bowl of roasted nuts rested came scurrying down the corridor away from the kitchens and tentatively approached the palace guard who stood watch at the intersection.

"Please, Bwana?" she said hesitantly, looking up at him with enormous brown eyes. The guard looked down at her curiously.

"What do you want?" he asked, with a little less kindness than Leila had hoped.

"Oh please… I am so very sorry to bother you, but I must take this tray to the quarters of Prince Vandao and come back quickly, or Memsahib Mnamene will beat me!"

She looked ready to burst into tears, and the guard took pity. He was well-acquainted with the old rhinoceros who ruled the kitchen during the evening shift. "New, are you?" he asked, and she nodded shyly. "Don't know how the find the Prince's quarters?" She nodded again, this time hope shining in those eyes.

The guard crouched, bringing him down to her height, and gestured on the floor. It was spotless, no dust in which to write, but with a series of finger gestures he showed the terrified serving girl how to reach her destination. "Oh thank you, Bwana, you have been most kind!" she said, and moved off as quickly as she could without spilling the tray.

As soon as no one was looking in her direction Leila was invisible again, moving silently along the path laid out for her by the helpful guard. As one might expect, Vandao's quarters were in the section of the palace reserved for the royal family – a group that could have filled up an entire good-sized village all by themselves. But his were rather closer to King Omali's than some, in keeping with his favored status.

It was the first door down from the crossing corridor where two of the royal bodyguard stood, barring access to all comers now that the king had retired for the evening. They were not above thirty feet away, standing on either side of the tee intersection.

Invisible and moving in complete silence within the bubble she had once again erected around herself, Leila tried the door. It was locked. Probably Vandao had already gone to bed – but she would wake him and give him all the grisly facts, enjoy his reaction, before she killed him. Oh, what if he was not sleeping alone? Just because the man had never married, didn't mean he wouldn't have a bedmate. Well, the girl could be rendered unconscious. Maybe Leila could even drag her out into the corridor, cloaked in invisibility, so that she would not be blamed for the prince's death.

The lock was nothing, and Leila had it open in seconds. But there were two guards standing down at the end of the corridor, leaning up against the wall of the cross-corridor. They had their backs to the wall and were looking right down the corridor where she was standing, though turning occasionally to look around them and sometimes speaking to one another.

She stood there for nearly two minutes, trying to think of a way to distract them so she could enter the room she had just unlocked. Then she realized she had a couple of gold asand tucked down in one of the hidden pockets of her outfit. Well worth the price!

Leila moved silently toward the crossing corridor, off to one side, and then flung the coins as hard as she could – far down toward the end of the corridor in which the guards stood, near a door that was probably the door to the royal apartments. Instantly they went on the alert, questing down the corridor after the source of the sound; and in another few seconds Leila had let herself in the front door of Vandao's suite of rooms.

He was alone, and he was not in bed. The prince sat at a writing desk, pouring over a sheaf of papers by lamplight. To be doing so at this hour, he must be the hardest-working man in Omali's government. Or perhaps, he just could not sleep?

Her silence bubble in effect, Leila quickly closed the distance between them so that he would be contained within it. Then she donned the semblance of her mother, the same image of her she had taken on for Tevo's benefit all those months ago in Parat, right after obtaining her new power.

This time the blonde teenager was not nude. She was wearing an outfit similar to what Leila recalled wealthy women in Marsine wearing, during her early childhood. Then she became visible, standing five feet from the man working away at his desk, and murmured "Vandao…"

He glanced up from his paperwork, startled. Who would be here, calling his name, at this hour? Then his eyes fell on the vision Leila had prepared for him and a remarkable transformation took place. It was if he had been a statue molded of sand and painted to look like a man, and now the tide was coming in.

His dark eyes went wide, his dark skin ashen, lips trembling as he began to crumble. "Miriam," he breathed, "Miriam, my love!" Then he seemed to realize that what he imagined to be true was insane. "No," he moaned, tears starting from his eyes, "it can't be you! You would be past thirty, you would not be… this…"

Leila was astonished. He'd casually dumped Miriam nearly eighteen years before, yet the apparent sight of her spurred such reactions? She stepped back a pace involuntarily as he rose from his chair and lurched toward her. He probably thought she was a hallucination, and that his hand would pass right through if he reached out to touch her.

The semblance of the teenaged Miriam melted away and was replaced with Leila. Herself, but clad in her richest vestments as the high priestess of Betsalel in Parat. She was only a teenage girl, and not much above five feet tall; but she still managed to look somewhat impressive.

Leila threw out a hand to prevent Vandao from stepping closer. "You are right, Vandao," she said in her closest approximation of a Voice of Dread. "Miriam would not look like that today. She has been dead for nearly ten years, and it was you who killed her – you who destroyed her life."

Vandao wove on his feet as if drunk, then sank back down into his desk chair with a thump. He put his head in his hands, and sobbed. "Mad, I have gone mad!" he wailed, and Leila was glad that he stood within her bubble of silence. So far, this was not quite going as she'd planned.

After a moment he looked up again through red-rimmed eyes and found the apparition still standing there. He'd half expected her to vanish. "Who…" he rasped, then cleared his throat. "Who are you?" For just a second the vision of Miriam wavered before Vandao's eyes and then resolved again in the regal-looking dark girl standing on the carpet before his desk.

"I am Miriam's daughter," Leila said proudly. And then, less forcefully, added "and yours." She had expected terror or rejection to follow that pronouncement, and was surprised when Vandao's ravaged features turned to joy.

"Our daughter?" he asked, as if that were the most wonderful news in the world. "Miriam bore my child?"

Good grief. Hello, you left her hanging, her entire life was ruined because of you and now all you have to say is how great it is that she had your baby? All of this passed through Leila's mind in an instant, and to her great surprise she spoke none of it. Instead she said, "Why did you leave, Vandao? Did you not know that Miriam would be ruined?"

His face fell again, so woeful she almost wanted to go up and pat him on the shoulder and say, "there, there." "I did not leave by choice, uh…"

"Leila," Leila replied, feeling annoyed. "She named me Leila."

"Dark beauty! Yes, she named you well!" he exclaimed, then continued. "My father was killed, murdered by an assassin," Vandao said. "Uncle Omali and I had been in Marsine for a few weeks, negotiating the purchase of trade goods and setting up contacts, and Miriam and I had become lovers. She was everything to me, the most beautiful girl I had ever known and the brightest as well. I didn't understand her father's objections to me as a suitor – after all, I was a prince and he was just a merchant. He should have been delighted for me to wed his daughter!"

"The old man is a dried-up husk without a shred of human warmth in him, if he still lives," Leila remarked. "But he had a virulent prejudice against people with dark skin. He thought us all devil-worshipers, yet I believe that his primary objection to me personally was my lack of a penis."

Vandao eyed her wildly, confused by her words; then continued his tale. "Uncle Omali and I had not yet heard the news about Father when we were set upon one night as we made our way along the waterfront in Marsine," he said. "We were knocked out, and when we awoke we found ourselves bound and apparently confined in the hold of a ship somewhere on the Center Sea."

"So you escaped when Omali did, and returned to Iskand?" Leila asked. Vandao nodded.

"We barely made it in time, traveling overland along the shore between the sea and the desert. We had killed some of Rajari's men when we escaped, but there were others and they pursued us."

"Rajari?" Leila asked.

"My eldest brother," he explained. "He was eight years older than me, and I had always looked up to him. Everyone thought he would be the next king, and I guess he did too. But he didn't want to wait." The sadness in his eyes was unmistakable.

"But he didn't kill you, or your uncle," Leila said. A truly ruthless politician wouldn't have hesitated to eliminate his enemies permanently.

"Once Rajari was chosen king," Vandao said, "whatever evil he had done to get there would have been washed away. It is probably a fault in our system of government, but the king is above the law. As is anyone he chooses to join him in that status. I think he hoped we would come over to his side, once his star had risen."

Leila stood, arms crossed, trying to think it through. Vandao's reaction to the sight of his lost love had taken the momentum out of her rush to revenge, but she still had a bone to pick with the father she had never met before today. "Omali became king, and had all power in Palambo. Why did you not just go back and claim your bride? Mother had only just realized she was pregnant when you vanished from her life."

Vandao hung his head. "I should have," he said softly. "I wanted to. But things were in turmoil in Iskand. Though I was not yet twenty I was the only person in the royal family whom Uncle Omali truly trusted in those times, and he needed my help to secure his throne. We had to track down Rajari, and all those who had joined with him in his conspiracy to become king. By the time things had settled down it had been more than a year since we had been forced to leave Marsine."

Now it was Leila's turn to tear up. "Miriam loved you until the day she died!" she declared, glaring fiercely at Vandao as the tears ran down her cheeks. "You could have returned even then, could have rescued her from the degradation into which she had sunk. We could have been a family!" She threw an arm across her face, angrily wiping away the moisture. She was here to be an avenging angel – not a weepy child, damn it!

"Degradation?" Vandao asked. "But she was the daughter of one of the wealthiest families in Marsine! I mourned the loss of the love we had, but I assumed that a woman as beautiful as she was would have been married off to some rich merchant or the son of a count by that time. Her suitors would have been legion, and her father hated me. Surely she would not have waited for me?"

Her tears dried, Leila curled her lip. "Oh yes, her suitors were legion. After I was born and her father realized that no male heir was to be had, he threw the two of us out onto the streets of Marsine. Up until then, my mother had no understanding of what it was to be poor. She took shelter in the only place she could find that would accept her, with her dark bastard babe."

Vandao was staring at her, not comprehending what she was saying. "Miriam's suitors were legion," Leila went on with grim satisfaction, "and sometimes she bedded as many as five or six of them a night! She was a *whore*, Vandao, and it was all because of you!"

He put his head in his hands, sobbing now. "No, no, it can't be true! Miriam was an angel, my only love!" Leila had intended to wound him, and now that she had she felt like she had struck a child. She stepped closer and put a hand on his shoulder, and he looked up at her in wonder. Until now, she realized, he had thought her only an apparition.

"You have never married, Vandao," Leila said quietly. "Is that because of Miriam?" He rose to his feet again and looked down at her.

"You are so like her," he said in hushed tones. "Yet so like me..." When he realized she was waiting for an answer he said, "Miriam was the only woman I have ever loved. There are dozens of my family living here in the palace, and hundreds more scattered around the country. What need was there for me to marry, to produce children? So I have remained alone."

Suddenly Leila felt pity welling up in her. Damn, what a completely crap assassin I make, she thought ruefully. All the target has to do is evince the slightest redeeming grace and I'm on his side. Vandao was still gazing at her, seeing his lost love in the angle of her jaw, the curve of her breast.

Leila heaved a deep sigh, her mind working fast. If she was not going to leave Vandao in a pool of his own blood, she needed to come up with plan B. While she was still working out the details, he spoke again. "How is it that you are here, Leila? I don't understand."

"Have you heard of the events regarding the Shadow God in the Gaspari Dominion?" she asked, with what she hoped was appropriate hauteur.

"Yes, yes, of course," he replied. "One of my primary functions within Uncle Omali's government is in intelligence. All reports on whatever is happening in the world, whether in Palambo or outside it, come through me."

"The young woman who freed Betsalel's principle idol from its imprisonment and restored the dark god to his place in the Temple of the Eight in Parat was me," Leila said simply. This evening had been an unexpected emotional journey for Vandao, and he was now entering a new phase of it.

"You?" he asked, staring at her as if expecting her to sprout horns.

"Me," she replied, stepping closer and reaching out a hand to touch him on the chest. Like Imbaso, he was nearly a foot taller than she was. "My god has revealed to me that his worship within Palambo has become corrupted," she said. "And now a djinn, little more than a savage beast, has come into existence and taken over the idols of Betsalel in every temple throughout Palambo."

Vandao was having trouble grasping what Leila was saying. She had gone from a deeply personal attack on him for abandoning her mother to what sounded like a folk tale. Evil djinns? Educated people didn't believe in such nonsense.

Leila was watching these thoughts pass through her father's mind, and she sighed again. While her seemingly magical appearance in his rooms had stunned him, what she had to say was not something he was prepared to hear. How could she get through to him? "My lord Betsalel is trying desperately to free Palambo from the ravages of this false god who has usurped his temples, but it is difficult," she said.

Vandao eyed her with some suspicion. "Can't the Eight do whatever they want, with a thought?" Like her, like Imbaso, Vandao's religious education had been less than complete. And this was not the time for Leila to enroll him in the crash course.

"The power of the gods in any part of the world is largely dependent on the worship and belief they receive from the people in that area," she summed up. "They are not nearly as omnipotent as most people think."

Leila longed to tell Vandao that the cult of Kivuli was involved in a plot to kill the king, but she dared not speak the djinn's name or tell her father anything that might lead to the exposure of her and Imbaso's unintentional involvement in that plot. Vandao might not be the monster that she had thought him for all of the years since she first learned of his existence; but he showed a keen intelligence, and she feared that even a hint might lead him to ferret out the plotters. Even having mentioned Betsalel, and revealed that the church had been corrupted throughout the kingdom, might be enough to condemn all of them to the dungeons or the headsman's block.

That keen intelligence was already at work, Leila realized. She had always attributed her own intelligence to her mother, but perhaps her ability to cast emotion aside and react analytically to unforeseen events had come from Vandao, instead? Miriam had run straight to a whorehouse and a life in virtual bondage, where her father had ended up as one of the most important people in his uncle's government.

No longer frightened, or ravaged with guilt, or in despair, Vandao looked his daughter in the eyes. "Leila," he said calmly, "I accept what you have told me, and my sorrow and regret for what became of Miriam will never end. Yet I am delighted to learn that I have a daughter, and proud that you have accomplished great things. But tell me, how is it that you have appeared in my rooms? Is this the action of your god?"

Leila took a step backward. It was time for her to depart. "Vandao," she said as calmly, "You were little more to me than a tale I heard as a child. But when Betsalel called on me to address the djinn's threat in Palambo I learned that the man I had been told about still existed. I had to see you for myself, and my lord Betsalel made that possible for me. I understand now that the hurt to my mother and me was nothing you intended, and I no longer seek your death. I am glad we had the chance to meet."

Leila stepped forward and stood on tiptoe, kissing her father on his cheek. Why the hell couldn't you have been there for me when I was two, she thought, though she knew the answer. The vision of her life as the daughter of a prince (and in that vision, he would of course never have taken any other wives) passed before her eyes as she closed them. Paradise, lost. But had that life path opened for her, experiences she treasured with people she loved would never have happened.

Vandao drew her into his arms for a gentle hug and kissed Leila on the forehead, an action reminiscent of the times Betsalel had done the same. She felt a surge of longing, and deflected it with anger. You are in the middle of a life-or-death struggle, she told herself harshly. This is no time to get all sentimental!

"Leila," he said softly, releasing her and looking down into her deep green eyes. "There is one thing I would ask of you, before you go." She took a step back, planning her escape.

"What is that?" she asked, firmly keeping the quaver out of her voice.

"I never knew you existed," he said, voice freighted with regret. "And I have no right to claim it from you. But would you, just once, call me 'Father'?"

"Very well," Leila said quietly. "I feel that you are worthy of the name. Goodbye, Father." With that she vanished, then hastily made her way over to the alcove between two of the room's pieces of furniture and crouched there. The notion that she was nowhere near the royal palace in Iskand was one she was anxious to foster. It would not do for Vandao to be combing the complex searching for her. She hoped he believed she was still in the Dominion, visiting him through supernatural powers.

Vandao stood there for a long moment staring at the spot where Leila had been standing when she had disappeared. Then he shook himself, walked to the door of the apartment and peered out. One of the nearby guards asked, "Everything all right, Your Highness?"

"No problem," he responded. "Thought I heard something, that's all."

"Nothing stirring out here," the guard assured him, and he stepped back inside. Then he set about getting ready for bed. It was late, and he no longer had any thought for the affairs of the kingdom.

Chapter 46

Leila had had to wait, sitting on the floor of her father's apartment, for nearly half an hour before she'd dared stir from her hiding place. Vandao seemed to have gone to bed, and stepping out the doors in his sitting room she found herself standing in yet another courtyard with a garden. She felt close to collapse.

Still invisible and in a bubble of silence, she pulled the tiny idol from a pocket in her clothing and called her god. "You met your father," he said softly when he had grown to around her own height. He was black all over save for his glowing red eyes, and at this dark hour it was likely that no one would see him in the midst of the garden's vegetation.

"Can you completely read my mind?" Leila asked, her curiosity piqued despite her exhaustion.

"This close I can, to some extent," Betsalel replied. "He was not the ogre you had hated for most of your life."

"He's just a man," she replied with a deflated air. She felt robbed, somehow, of the hatred that had given her drive. Or maybe it was just that she was tired. Had she killed Vandao, she might probably be feeling the same thing. At least this way, she had an actual father. And maybe someday, she might have a relationship with him.

"And he was just a kid not much older than I am when he and my mother were together," Leila added. "He was dragged away by circumstances beyond his control – basically the same reason I left Tevo. Except he didn't find anybody else, it seems. I love Imbaso, and I love Tevo, and I don't know what to do about it. But Imbaso is here with me now..."

Betsalel let her follow her thoughts, saying nothing for another minute. Then he said "You are tired. Shall I restore you?"

"Yes," she said, hoping it wouldn't leave her unable to sleep. She needed to be up and going riding with one of her "suitors" in the morning. With a touch of the god's hand Leila felt her fatigue wash away – and with it, some of her discouragement.

After telling him of the plot the Makucha Nyeusi was involved in, or as much of it as she knew, Leila added "I'm kind of lost here.

I can't go back out the way I came in or the guards may wonder why Vandao's door opened and closed on its own."

"Am I not the god of sleep?" Betsalel asked, surprised it wasn't obvious to her. "The guards in the corridor on the far side of your father's apartment are sleeping now. They will awaken in fifteen minutes, or sooner if anyone disturbs them. I suggest you go now."

With that he shrank back to the tiny idol and Leila scooped it up, hurrying back through Vandao's apartment silently and invisibly. The guards were dozing on their feet, and no one else was nearby as she re-threaded her route and returned to the apartment where she and her party were staying.

She found Imbaso in the sitting room, sitting quietly in the dark. He rose as she came in, still invisible, and she dropped her shadows while maintaining her bubble of silence. She was still only slightly visible, in the moonlight coming in through the doors to the courtyard. But he found her anyhow.

"Where have you been?" he asked worriedly, after embracing and kissing her.

"I went to see my father," she replied.

"Your...?"

"I mentioned that my father was Palamban, and probably looked like an older version of you, did I not?" Leila asked.

"A lot of Palambans, especially Amhari descended from the royal line, look like me," he protested. "Why didn't you say anything?"

She pulled him down to sit beside her on the settee. "My father is Vandao, the king's nephew and right-hand man," she explained. "And I promised myself half my life ago that if I ever found him I would kill him, for what he did to my mother and me."

Though the two of them had been intimate for weeks, she had not given him the full gruesome details of her earlier life. Would still prefer not to, in fact, but how could she hide such things from him if they truly loved each other? "Did you kill him, then?" Imbaso asked with a hint of dread.

Leila squeezed his hand in the darkness and sighed. "No," she said resignedly. "I did not, and I won't. I realize now that he was not truly to blame for what happened to us."

"I don't understand," Imbaso said. If Vandao had "done something" so bad he deserved death, how was he not to blame?

"He didn't actually *do* anything to us, Imbaso," she tried to explain. "He didn't even know I existed, never learned that my mother was pregnant or what happened to her after he vanished. He was kidnaped with his uncle, by the supporters of the prince who had Faraj killed. He was physically unable to return, and he just thought that my mother would have moved on so he never tried to contact her again."

"But she didn't move on…"

"Right," Leila answered a little snappishly. It had always bothered her that Miriam had chosen whoring over some more respectable work she might have gotten, with her gentle upbringing and good education. "When she had me and my grandfather saw I was a girl, he just turned her and her bastard child out on the street. She was sixteen."

"So if Vandao had not been kidnaped, if King Faraj had not been assassinated just at that time, there would have been a hasty wedding and your life would have been totally different," Imbaso mused.

"Exactly," Leila replied. "I was an orphaned street urchin at age eight and a professional thief by age thirteen. Then I had to go on the run, and for years I had no true friends, nobody who knew me for who I really was. I blamed Vandao for all of that."

"But you've become the arch-priestess of Betsalel, the head of his church in the Dominion, and you're not even eighteen yet! You would never have achieved that if you'd grown up safe and warm with mummy and daddy," Imbaso pointed out. Leila threw back her head and laughed.

"And just look at the perks that position offers!" she crowed. "A five-month, all-expenses-stolen tour of the gods-forsaken desert, free membership in an insane bloodthirsty cult, and now I've added 'professional assassin' to my résumé! What's next, mass murderer? At this rate, I'll need to figure out how to destroy the earth and all living creatures on it, just to keep up my progress past age twenty-five."

Imbaso squeezed her hand, and kissed her on the cheek. "But at least now you have a true friend," he said softly. She melted into his arms, and they kissed for a long time. She could feel his eagerness. It had been a long time since they'd last made love.

"Aren't you tired?" she asked, breathing faster.

"I had a couple of hours sleep, but then I woke up and decided to see whether you'd left your window open. You had, but you weren't in your bed. So I've been waiting."

"Betsalel restored me when I called him this evening to tell him about recent events," Leila said, "so I'm no longer tired *or* sleepy. But I feel a little uneasy about doing it right here in the sitting room. What if somebody gets up to use the privy? Your father and the two Black Claw masters are up there in age…"

There was a small but very fine throw rug on the floor in front of the settee. "Why don't we go out into the garden?" Imbaso suggested. "We can lay this rug down on the ground in among those bushes, and later we can shake off the leaves and bring it back. We'll be invisible and silent, so who's to notice?" For answer Leila jumped to her feet and picked up one end of the rug.

"Grab an end," she said jauntily.

Chapter 47

Later Leila slipped back into her room, latching the window and crawling into her bed without disturbing Mbina. The girl worked hard all day, she was sure, and deserved as much rest as she could get. But for Leila, sleep would not come. Her mind was abuzz with a thousand concerns.

Would Vandao take what she'd said about the Palamban church of Betsalel to heart, and send the guards after Mauaji and their party? Who had the four journeyman assassins been told to kill, and how soon would that happen? She and Imbaso might not have been the only occupants of the apartment who were not in their beds, this night.

And assuming they were not caught and thrown into the dungeons or summarily executed, if they succeeded in killing King Omali what then? Would a purge of the key people in his administration see her father executed or exiled? What was Mauaji's ultimate goal in this plot? Perhaps he meant to see a Kivuli cultist on the throne. She didn't know for sure that Farendhi was one such, but it seemed likely he was if he'd arranged for them to come here and stay at the palace. And he was as eligible to be chosen king as any of his brothers – or any of their myriad sons, including Vandao.

As dawn light began shining through the lush tropical growth outside the window Leila slipped out of bed. Lying there in the dark and silence was giving her mind too much free rein to chew over problems that as yet had no solutions. She needed to go riding with Samindhi, and then she needed to arrange an expedition (maybe with her "brother," that would be nice) to Iskand's world-famous Temple of the Eight. Soon, she hoped, that temple would once again house a true idol of Betsalel.

Mbina had started up from her small bed just as Leila's feet had hit the floor, and in moments she had become a blur of motion. Throwing on her servant's shift, she said "You will of course want to bathe before going riding with prince Samindhi." It was not a question. If Mbina was this bossy at seventeen, Leila shuddered to think of the terror she would strike in her fellow servants (and some of her clients, as well) by the time she was in her forties.

"And after as well, no doubt!" Zurina said with a smile.

"I will draw a bath," Mbina said. "Please put on a robe, and you may wish to take some kaf or tea while the water is being readied."

"Yes, mwali," Zurina responded mischievously, and received a questioning look from her maidservant. Was she being made fun of?

Clad in a light robe that covered her from shoulder to ankle Leila stepped out and saw that trays of breakfast had already been brought and arrayed on a counter in the apartment's kitchen area. There were mountains of fruit, pitchers of kaf and tea, warm breads hot from the oven and some sticky pastries heavy with honey and nuts. Mmm!

None of the other apartment residents had as yet put in an appearance, and Leila couldn't resist taking one of the sweet pastries. She washed it down with some bitter kaf, then rinsed her fingers off in the kitchen sink. Mbina arrived to say the bath was ready, and Zurina obediently followed her down the hall.

The sunken bathtub was in a separate room from the privy, a good thing with 10 people resident here at this time. Others began stirring, and by the time Zurina emerged scrubbed, shampooed, oiled, and glowing all eight of her companions were gathered in the sitting room nibbling from plates of food and drinking either kaf or tea.

Again, Leila was thankful that she had bought some real clothes to go with her illusory wardrobe. Allowing Mbina to bathe her while maintaining the illusion of Zurina's darker skin and curlier hair had been tough enough – she did not think she was up to the task of convincing the canny maidservant that she was assisting her mistress into garments that did not exist.

For riding, Zurina's costume was a sort of tropical-weight version of a ladies' riding habit from the Dominion. A great many of the styles and habits of Palambo's upper classes had been adapted from those of the same classes to their north. A thousand years ago, throughout much of what was now the kingdom of Palambo, the top social echelons had been inhabited by tribal chieftains whose distinctions principally involved a larger, fancier mud hut and a bigger headdress. The nobility of the Gaspari Dominion had stepped in and shown them how it was done.

Leila was somewhat surprised that Mbina was also expected to accompany her on this ride, as sort of a chaperone. "You know how to ride, Mbina?" she asked. Women riding horses was fairly common among the Daregs, but rare in the regions south of the Rabiyats.

"Of course I do," she replied shortly. "I will need to go to my quarters and get my riding clothes, though. We will stop there on our way to the stables."

Zurina and Mbina took on some breakfast before leaving, but there was little conversation among the group. If anything much had been going on since they all went to bed last night, nobody was talking about it – at least not in front of Mbina.

As they walked the corridors of the palace heading for the servants' wing, Zurina asked "How is it, Mbina, that you have learned to ride?"

"Oh, we all learn," the girl assured her. "All of us who grow up in the harem." That set Leila back a bit. Was this "servant girl" actually a princess?

"You grew up in the harem, Mbina? Who is your father?"

"Was," she said, chin up and eyes proud. "He was Prince Rajari, nephew to King Omali." The prince who had plotted to kill his father Faraj, Leila recalled from her conversation with Vandao the night before. Perhaps royal "justice" didn't extend to exterminating the condemned's line, then.

"They forced you, a princess, to become a servant because your father plotted against the old king?" Zurina asked, and Mbina looked surprised. She had not expected this apparent twit of a girl from far-off Namei to know anything about royal politics.

"I am not a princess," she said. "My mother was not one of my father's wives, but one of his concubines." Oh. Leila knew about concubines. They were a lot like mistresses, but their relationship was more formalized. In a way, they were nothing but pampered slaves. Yet history was full of powerful men who had loved their concubines more than they had loved their official wives.

"You work hard," Zurina replied, "but I suppose there are worse things. In the Gaspari Dominion, I have read, some fatherless children beg in the street and live like animals."

"As you say, mwali," Mbina replied shortly. They arrived at the servants' quarters and Zurina waited outside. It took no more than three minutes before the maidservant returned, dressed in an outfit that was nearly identical to Zurina's own but lacking in ornamentation and of the same blue color as her household garb.

They hurried along the corridors and out by a familiar route to the stables, where Zurina's party had left their horses just yesterday afternoon. They found Samindhi and several other young people milling around outside it, as their horses were saddled and bridled and brought out of the stables by a small horde of stable boys. Leila realized they were not all boys, which surprised her. In the Dominion women rode horses, but none she'd ever heard of had taken a job caring for them.

Samindhi flashed a brilliant white smile at the sight of her. "Zurina!" he exclaimed, taking both her hands in his and then bringing one to his lips in Dominion fashion. He was dashingly attired and astonishingly handsome, and had not Leila's heart already been firmly held by both Tevo and Imbaso, she might have swooned. As it was, she appreciated him from an aesthetic viewpoint. Zurina, on the other hand, was deeply impressed.

"Mbina," he added, nodding politely. They were not that far apart in age, and had probably known each other since childhood. What a strange experience it must have been, Leila thought, to grow up surrounded by hordes of people who were all your relations! In her whole life she had known her mother, long dead, her grandfather – whom she merely *hoped* was dead – and now her father. A complete stranger, until just last night.

Samindhi introduced Zurina to his friends, two other young men of around his age whom he said were his cousins, and two young women – astonishingly, no relation whatsoever. Evidently the royal family had to work hard to prevent inbreeding – even Zurina, from a city a thousand miles away, was a cousin to all three of the young men.

When the boy brought out Wapesi heads turned. Almost without exception, the horses in the royal stables were Hisan. The young gelding had enjoyed a long rest on their boat ride from Aswa, followed by a long enough walk yesterday to work out the kinks – and he was excited to be going out.

Zurina came up and clucked to him, stroking his neck, before getting into the saddle. He wore no bit and bridle, but was guided by reins clipped to his halter. Samindhi's black eyes lit at the sight of him. "This is yours, Zurina?" he asked in awe. "He's magnificent."

"Thank you," she simpered. "When I was fourteen some Gaspari traders came through Namei and were selling off their horses before taking ship west to Dikka. I told Father I simply must have him, and he's been my baby ever since."

The party of seven set off along one of the thoroughfares through the royal compound, then turned off down a dirt path. More than fifty acres of the hilltop had been left as parkland, far less manicured than the Count of Oester's royal preserve near Chanton in the Dominion but perfect for letting your horse get a little exercise. The weather was fine, scarcely a cloud in the sky, and it would probably be hot later. But right now it was lovely, and Leila felt her heart lift a little.

Samindhi soon burst her bubble, however. Riding beside her he asked, "Did you hear the news?"

"What news?" Zurina responded cheerfully. "We all went to bed not long after dinner last night, and when I got up this morning our breakfast had already been delivered. Did something happen?"

"Two members of the Council of Eight, Khaziq Samiri of Belantos and Selinde of Lucia, both died in their sleep last night!" Samindhi exclaimed with the glee of someone relating juicy gossip.

So much of that tone was in his voice that Zurina had to ask, "Were they sleeping together?"

Her young companion gave a bark of laughter at the thought. "Eight preserve us, no!" he exclaimed. "They were both in their seventies at least, maybe older. From what I heard they were found in their beds, both of them being accustomed to sleep alone, and both had passed away gently overnight. Probably heart failure. But what a weird coincidence!"

Some coincidence, Leila thought, dread seeping into her heart. Zurina said "I certainly I hope I go that way when it's my time. A long time from now, of course!"

"You could try praying to Betsalel for such a death, I suppose," Samindhi said thoughtfully, "though nobody I've ever heard of has had a response from the Shadow God. He's not like the rest of the Eight."

"Maybe he's supposed to come to you in your dreams instead of in person," Zurina replied. "You know my father's a priest of Betsalel, don't you?"

"Sorry," he responded. "No offense meant." They urged their horses forward as the track opened up into what almost looked like a miniature patch of savannah dotted here and there with trees and bushes. A small herd of impala was grazing some distance away.

The horses moved from a walk to a trot, and Zurina looked around. "There are wild animals here!" she exclaimed. "No lions or leopards, I hope?"

Samindhi grinned at her. "Father has a pair of tame cheetahs, and sometimes he brings them out to hunt the impala we keep here. But there are no predators out there waiting to pounce on our horses, rest assured."

"Let's run, then!" Zurina cried, an infectious grin on her face as she leaned low over Wapesi's neck. The big chestnut gathered his hindquarters and leapt forward, Samindhi on his dark bay Hisan stallion in close pursuit. The smaller horse quickly took the lead, but as he began to flag Wapesi was just getting going. His god-given endurance, a completely unfair advantage, enabled him to win any race if it went on long enough.

They reached the compound wall on the far side of the parkland, and pulled up whooping and laughing. This girl is a lot more fun than I expected, Samindhi thought. I *like* her! He'd been digging in his heels, trying to prolong his bachelorhood for a few more years. The peculiar nature of his royal family meant that not every member of it necessarily had to marry and produce children. Look at Cousin Vandao, thirty-six and never wed!

But on the other hand, maybe *one* little wife wouldn't hurt. He could always get more later. But he didn't want to let Zurina slip out of his grasp. As they cantered gently back, rejoining the group (Mbina, chaperone or not, had made no effort to catch them on the horse lent to her by the stables), Samindhi asked her, "Would you and Mbina care to join us for lunch after we get back from our ride?"

"I'll need to return to our apartment for a bath first, of course," Zurina replied. And have a little talk with Kifozi, Leila thought. "And I am very anxious to visit the Temple of the Eight here. Father has told me there is nothing like it in the kingdom. But I really would like the opportunity to meet more of your family."

Samindhi considered. If she were to marry him she would of course want to visit the harem and meet some of the other women who would become her in-laws. Some of the princes, his older brother Omaso, for instance, lived in their own quarters with their wives and children but kept concubines – and *their* children – in the harem.

Father had only nine wives and three concubines, and his latest one, that count's daughter from Catal in the Dominion, had been sharing his bed every night since the wedding a few months ago. The others all now lived in the harem. "Perhaps your father should be the one to go with you to the temple," Samindhi suggested. Religion was not something he cared much about. Why beseech the deities for favors when you could make your own luck? Praying was for the poor and downtrodden masses, as far as he was concerned.

Zurina looked a little disappointed, but Leila had never wanted Samindhi's company on that errand. "Do you think I could come by the women's quarters this afternoon, and meet some of the people who live there? I'd love to meet your mother, if she yet lives."

"Oh, she's alive and well," he replied. And long-since resigned to being relegated to the harem. She had been the second of Omali's wives, long before he had become king. Omaso's mother was the first, and the two women had remained fast friends over the years and their startling change of fortune.

"I can arrange that," Samindhi assured her cheerfully. "Why don't you and Mbina come for tea at three this afternoon? She can certainly guide you there." The young people rode for another hour and then cantered back to the stables, leaving it to the personnel there to unsaddle the horses, walk them until they were cool, and rub them down.

Wapesi seemed to be in a remarkably good mood, as if this was the most fun he'd had in ages. Poor fellow, Leila thought. Ever since she had begun her plot to steal Count Wilhelm's treasures, the horse had been getting the short end of the stick – dyed, bleached, forced to pull farm carts, and stabled in tiny urban back yards for months at a time. It would have made much more sense for her to have sold him to someplace in the Gaspari countryside where he'd have room to roam – but he was a friend, and she didn't want to part with him. The two of them had been together for nearly four years, now.

Zurina squeezed Samindhi's hands and thanked him for the fun time, saying she'd see him at three. Then she and Mbina made their way back through the palace corridors to their apartment. The maidservant was moving a little stiffly. "Has it been awhile since you rode, Mbina?" her mistress asked, and got a rueful smile in response.

"I guess you're in good shape for it, riding all the way from Namei?"

"Especially those last few days through the hills west of Aswa," Zurina replied. Mbina seemed to be warming up to her, a little. Good.

Leila endured her second bath of the morning. It would not be proper to arrive for tea at the harem smelling of horse. Mauaji was out somewhere, no doubt conspiring with somebody or other, and Mbando, Nindao, and Sumundi had gone with him. But the other two young assassins and master Kifozi were relaxing around the apartment, and Imbaso had slept late. He was only now getting dressed. Considering what he'd been up to in the middle of the night while others were sleeping, that was not a surprise.

After Zurina was clean and dressed again, she said to Mbina, "It scarcely seems fair for you to be on duty all day and all night. Would you like some time to yourself today?"

"I wouldn't mind," the girl admitted. "But I must be back here by 2:30 to escort you to tea at the harem."

"All right," Zurina replied. "I'm going to get my brother to take me to the temple, then have some lunch. See you later this afternoon."

With a word of thanks the girl had vanished out the apartment door, and Leila heaved a sigh of relief. Mbina was a nice enough person, and quite competent as a maid, but she did *not* need someone at her elbow at every hour. It added an entire extra layer of effort to all of her clandestine activities.

Imbaso was perched on the settee, sipping a cup of kaf and eating a piece of fruit. "I feel like I didn't get enough rest yesterday, so I think I'll lie down for an hour," Usiku told him and Kifozi. The master assassin was reading a book, and nodded to her. The other two were in their room, perhaps catching up on their own sleep.

As soon as she was inside the room Leila threw the latch and silently inserted her wedges. Then she went to the window and unlatched it before lying down on the bed and closing her eyes. It didn't take long before Imbaso, who'd decided to go for a stroll in the gardens, was climbing in her window within a bubble of silence.

He lay down on the bed beside her and drew her into his arms, kissing her passionately. "This is a lot more comfortable than a rug in the bushes," he remarked thoughtfully.

"No time for that," Leila said – kissing him sweetly. "Did you hear anything about two old arch-priests dropping dead overnight while I was gone?"

"Not a word," Imbaso replied. "I only got up a short time before you and Mbina came back from your ride. Are you dumping me for Samindhi?"

"Thinking about it," she said, looking at him sideways. "Not right away, though. But he told me something that I thought was very interesting. Apparently two elderly members of the Council of Eight, the arch-priest of Belantos and the arch-priestess of Lucia, went to bed last night and never woke up."

"Oh, shit," Imbaso said. He had an agile enough mind, and he was already working out the implications. "You said each of our four assassin friends received a sealed commission?" She nodded. "So two of them were successful," he mused, "and probably the other two will complete their missions in the next day or so."

"Which will, unless my guess is completely wrong, leave exactly four members of the Council of Eight to select replacements for the four who all suddenly dropped dead of natural causes," Leila followed the thought. "Or perhaps, divine intervention. And at least one of those members is certainly a Kivuli cultist. Could it be that the others are *all* in your father's pocket?"

"He would only need three of the four, or two besides the Kivuli man, to select the first replacement," Imbaso mused.

"And then whomever the survivors selected would become part of the group that selected the next one, and so on?" Leila asked.

"I don't think there's ever been a situation like that since the Council of Eight was first formed," he replied. "But that's probably how it would work. And each time a replacement was selected, that man or woman would be somebody hand-picked to favor the cult."

"Shit!" Leila hissed. "I'm not ready for this!" She lay flat on her back, gazing up at the ceiling and thinking as Imbaso lay on his side next to her, leaning on one elbow. After another moment she turned to him and asked, "How long will it take to refill the Council? Is there some kind of time limit?"

"Usually a new member is selected right after funerary rites have been performed for the deceased one," Imbaso explained. "Rarely, an arch-priest or priestess has resigned from the Council on the grounds of age or infirmity, and in those cases a new member was selected to take over before the old one left. And then there's the issue of ties. If one candidate can't get a majority of the Council's votes, there could be days of arguments and campaigning, and repeated votes until a majority was achieved."

"So fastest would be immediate, slowest would be maybe a couple of weeks," Leila summarized.

"That's about right," he replied.

"And where do they get the list of candidates?" she asked next. "Are they submitted by the church?"

"The pool of candidates is every member of that deity's Iskand church, both at the Temple of the Eight and at the gods' individual temples around town, who holds the rank of full priest. Almost always the Council has selected the elder, more senior priests for the honor. They don't want to rock the boat and piss off the temple hierarchy."

"In Iskand each of the Eight is represented at the big temple, plus each of them has another temple devoted to that god or goddess alone?" Leila asked.

"I think there are actually two stand-alone temples to Mulia and another two to Andros," Imbaso replied. "Iskand is a big city, maybe as big as Parat, and those two have a lot of worshipers to handle."

Leila sat up. She had only been "lying down" for around twenty minutes of the hour she'd requested, but her anxiety would not let her rest. "I think we need to get out there without any delay," she told her cohort. "We'll visit the Temple of the Eight and see what's going on there, maybe plant an idol if we can. And we need to visit the stand-alone temple of Betsalel too, same routine. We need to know where the Kivuli idols are. So go on out, then knock on my door and remind me I'd asked you to take me to the temple today."

Imbaso looked disappointed. What she said was true. If his father succeeded in putting a Kivuli cultist on the throne of Palambo, the king's almost limitless power could result in citizens being required to deliver up babies to the temple for slaughter, the savage Kivuli idols displayed publically in temples throughout the kingdom, and who-knows-what atrocities being committed as the bloodthirsty djinn's power exploded. But that didn't mean he wouldn't like a little nooky…

Sitting up beside Leila, Imbaso squeezed her tight. "Couldn't that wait… say, half an hour?" he murmured in her ear, nibbling on the earlobe. A thrill shot through her core and Leila locked her mouth on his, her tongue sliding into his mouth. She gave him a firm squeeze in the crotch. And then she put her feet on the floor and pointed at the window.

"Later, lover," she said with a touch of regret. "Get moving!"

Chapter 48

They had a lot of ground to cover, so the "siblings" from Namei went back to the stables and got their horses. Crap, Leila thought. My skin's going to wear off, at this rate. Will I need a third bath before teatime? The Temple of the Eight was located on another low rise to the south and west of the palace compound, overlooking the western outskirts of Iskand and the desert beyond it.

From what Betsalel had said, people had probably been worshiping here since before the city itself arose – thousands of years ago. It took them half an hour to get there from the stables, going out the palace compound's west gate and then just zigzagging their way through the city streets as they navigated by line of sight. The great temple was visible from almost anywhere in the city, except possibly from the Center Sea docks north of the palace.

It had appeared to be nearer than it was, which Leila realized as they finally came up the main road leading to it was due to the oversized architecture. Enormous columns of stone, not the pale gold of most local buildings but gleaming white, rose sixty feet in the air holding up a circular tiled roof. There were, of course, eight of them.

Not nearly as much weather came to Iskand as did to Parat, and the temple seemed open to the elements. "Spells, or I guess you'd call them divine boons like your shadow power or the protections on your house in Namei, keep wind, sand, and the rare rainstorm from coming inside the temple," Imbaso explained. "This is one of the oldest buildings on earth, I think. It dates from at least the founding of Iskand by the ancestors of the Daregs."

Yet it was not in any way ruinous. The Eight looked after their own, it seemed. Betsalel had certainly made every effort to look after Leila. They walked in through one of the massive portals and gazed around in awe. The eight idols here, each standing on what looked like a natural column of stone that had been flattened at the top, were nearly identical to the ones at the Temple of the Eight in Parat. Yet these were slightly smaller, maybe only fifteen feet in height. They still towered so far above the worshipers that many might be intimidated and never try to get a deity's attention.

But some clearly did. As Leila and Imbaso stood near the center of the room, watching, a young woman well short of thirty approached with her four children – aged six, four, three, and perhaps one – gathered around her. She cast some small coins into the offering bowl before the idol of Mulia, and fell to her knees.

"Please, Mother Mulia," she prayed aloud, "hear my prayer. Your bounty has been rich, and I love my children dearly. But my husband and I are poor, and we are having trouble feeding them. Please, send me no more babies – let them go to others who want them and have none."

Mulia manifested in her idol, and quickly shrank to only a little more than five feet in height. That still left her a few feet above the supplicant. Her warm, motherly features were filled with compassion as the woman and her children gazed up at her in awe.

Bending down, the goddess touched the woman on the shoulder. "Saretse, I will grant what you ask. May you and your family prosper. No more babies will come to you. But if you change your mind, visit me again." Saretse looked up, her face a mask of joy, tears of happiness running down her cheeks.

"Thank you, mistress, thank you! My children and I will honor you every day of our lives!"

Swiftly Mulia grew and the idol returned to its dormant state. The goddess-blessed Saretse led her overly large family away, having gotten good value for her money. The gods of this world were dependent on their worshipers for power and life, and responsive to their needs. How much more true religious dedication it must take to worship an unresponsive belief construct such as Kivuli, or any other daemon, had been before receiving a soul!

A couple of priests seemed to be on duty in the sanctuary, not doing much at the moment but Leila supposed they were there to assist people, answer questions, perhaps mediate with the gods if people felt their prayers were being ignored. Though she was an arch-priestess herself, the finer details of organized religion were not something she'd studied much.

As was the case in every temple Leila had ever visited, there was a door at the rear leading to another section of the temple that was not open to the public. "Does this temple have residences attached?" she asked Imbaso quietly. He threw up a bubble of silence, so their conversation would not be overheard.

"I understand that it is one of the few in Palambo where the priests live and work on site. There are administrative offices through the door there at the back, and stairs down to a level with simple quarters for the priests and acolytes."

"Are we silent?" Leila asked in an undertone, and Imbaso nodded. "Since this place is dedicated to all the Eight, I can't see how they could have a secret inner sanctum down below. Especially since the idol would be fifteen feet tall and wouldn't fit down there, during all those decades when it was just an idol."

"You're right!" Imbaso said. He had not considered that. How had the prophet and his followers ever managed to take over here, in this one temple where Betsalel was included but was not the only god? "Could this one be real, but damaged somehow so that our master could not manifest in it?"

This was a question Leila really wanted to ask Betsalel himself. As she understood it, his idol in the Temple of the Eight in Parat had been the original source of all his other true idols throughout the world. But that idol, and all that had sprung from it, had been vulnerable to damage from the hand of man up until a couple of centuries ago.

During Emperor Fernand's pogrom two centuries ago, all of Betsalel's true idols within the Dominion had been destroyed except two: the one in the ruined monastery in the Blackwald, which the marauding soldiers had been unable to reach; and the original in Parat. That one, he had said, had been rendered indestructible by a spell many of her master's true believers had died to empower.

It was Leila's theory, as yet untested, that all of the idols that had been seeded from the original *after* the spell had been applied, would also share the spell and be indestructible. She hoped! But how much damage need be done to an idol before the god would be unable to manifest through it – did it need to be perfect?

"Let's take a little stroll around the grounds, shall we?" Leila suggested, and the pair walked back out and into the lush gardens that surrounded the temple. The administrative wing, off to the south of the circular sanctuary, was a low one-storey edifice of the same white stone, and not all that large. She wondered how deeply the underground parts of the temple had been dug. Maybe the followers of the prophet had excavated a secret sub-basement?

It was getting close to midday, and most people who would usually be coming to the temple were elsewhere, going about their business. The gardens were nearly deserted, and it was easy for Leila and Imbaso to find a shady nook where they could call their god for advice.

They sat down on a curved stone bench overlooking a small pool, surrounded by what appeared to be banana trees. Leila set the small idol on the bench beside her and called, "Betsalel, come to me. But stay small, please." The idol animated, but grew to no more than six inches in height. "Is this small enough?" the god's voice spoke in her mind.

Imbaso had maintained his bubble of silence, and Leila turned to him. "Can you hear him as well?" she asked, and he nodded. It gave her a little frisson, as if she and Imbaso had been brought closer together by this gift they shared. "We are here at the Temple of the Eight in Iskand," Leila said – in case the god could not figure that out for himself. She still did not truly understand the scope of his powers, which seemed to change situation by situation.

"Yes," he said, "I see."

"Your idol is there with the rest," she went on. "And it's fifteen feet high and probably weighs a few tons. I can't see how the followers of the Secret Scriptures could have created a duplicate and spirited away the original. Are you sure you can't manifest in it?"

The little god froze for a moment, then spoke again. "It's as it has been for centuries," Betsalel said. "I do not have a nexus there."

"Yet there are priests of the Eight present in the sanctuary, and presumably they believe in you as much as any modern Palambans do," Leila said. "Would physical damage to a true idol make it unusable to you?"

Betsalel considered. "Nearly all of my idols in the Dominion were smashed, and I was no longer able to manifest in them," he said. "My siblings and I automatically protect our true idols, at least those that remain within range of living believers, from the kinds of incidental harm that would befall a stone statue – deterioration from wind and weather, cracking in an earth tremor, and so forth. But I don't know how much intentional damage would be needed to make an idol useless."

"Can we go take a look?" Imbaso suggested. "You could get a little smaller, and Leila could bring you inside."

"Good idea," Betsalel replied and shrank to only an inch in height. Leila picked him up and cupped him in her right hand, as gently as if he was a baby bird though theoretically he could not be physically harmed.

The two, in their bubble of silence, strolled back inside the temple. No more worshipers had come in, and the two priests on duty seemed to be taking a lunch break. They were over at a small table near the side of the circle on which the administrative wing was attached, eating bread and fruit.

Leila and Imbaso stood before the idol of Betsalel. It looked perfectly intact from this angle, two eyes closed while the unsleeping third eye, an enormous red gem, stood open. The column on which it stood was more than three feet high and four across, and Leila laid her hand down on it and let the tiny god scramble down from her palm.

Remaining the size of a Palamban cockroach, Betsalel scampered across the top of the column and touched the stone foot of what had once been a true idol, a nexus that permitted him to enter the material plane of existence. "Ahhh," he breathed, after exploring the idol with his mind for a few moments. "I don't know how they did it," he said in his worshipers' minds, "but the idol is hollow. I suspect that the prophet's followers raised themselves up on ladders and drilled down through the top of the head, all the way down to the level of the heart. It would be completely invisible from below, of course. The shaft is nearly three inches across, and it has been filled with some black substance that is not stone."

This was beyond incredible, Leila thought. That the prophet should have come up with a very wrong idea and somehow promulgated it to the point that every idol of the dark god in the kingdom of Palambo had been stolen away from its true worshipers to become the object of a perverted and essentially futile worship, was amazing enough.

But this intentional vandalism of Betsalel's principal idol within the kingdom suggested more – that the prophet had *known* that what he was doing was cutting the true Shadow God off from his worshipers. Had he been deep enough in the mysteries to understand that the creation of a daemon was possible? Had he perhaps intended that his own soul should go to give that daemon life? If so, he had failed.

"What is the nature of the black substance, master?" Leila asked. She and Imbaso waited for more than a minute as Betsalel employed his powers (not too shabby, standing as he was on a holy column in near proximity to at least two loyal believers). Finally he released his grip on the big toe of what had once been his true idol.

He said simply, "It is dried blood."

Chapter 49

Leila and Imbaso left the Temple of the Eight. Before departing they deposited one of the tiny seed idols atop the column on which the desecrated idol stood. It would go unnoticed, tucked slightly behind the curve of the idol's left foot. If a true Betsalel worshiper came here before Leila could return, the Shadow God would simply arise – cloaking the old idol in shadows. Otherwise, she would come here to call him later on and they would remove the old idol in much the same way they'd disposed of the statue in Zambei.

It was already past noon, and they had much to do before Leila had to be back at the apartment, *not* smelling of horse, and ready to go have tea with Samindhi and the ladies of the royal Palamban harem. Busy, busy. Betsalel himself was at the moment still manifested in Leila's personal idol, and no larger than a grasshopper.

"Turn left at the next intersection," the Shadow God spoke in their minds, and they hurried along. Betsalel's stand-alone temple had been at the same location in Iskand for more than a thousand years, and the entire city was so ancient that he had no trouble directing them.

But as that edifice loomed up before them he said, "I sense Kivuli's presence there, while I did not at the Temple of the Eight. I should not be manifest when you go in." It bothered both of them, that the god they had devoted themselves to should seem so… cowardly, in the face of opposition. But Imbaso had the right of it.

"Betsalel is an immortal god," he said as they approached the temple. "He can be harmed, can be weakened, but he cannot be killed. That more than two-thirds of his power as a god was wiped out a couple of centuries ago yet he is still with us is proof of that. But if he is manifest within the nexus of the djinn's power, it will trigger a conflict between them. A conflict he would be unable to win. And it's a pretty sure bet you and I would be the big losers."

Leila guided Wapesi over to the left with her knees and reached out her left hand to him. They squeezed hands, then rode on. The temple of Betsalel in Iskand was no larger than the one in Namei. Surrounded by other buildings, its grounds were less expansive. The usual golden stone of the region had here been faced with a shiny black marble, cunningly fitted. But it was showing some signs of deterioration. There might not be snow or even much rain here, but two centuries of hot sun had left their mark. Here, there had been no god resident to hold off the elements.

They tied the horses to a hitching post after climbing down, and went inside. Both of them guessed that this was where Mauaji and the three missing assassins had gone, and feared running into them. A pilgrimage here might be a little hard to explain.

At every temple of Betsalel along their route here from Namei they'd encountered an acolyte on duty in the anteroom, and here was no exception. There was no one else around, and before they stepped inside the front door Leila, arm-in-arm with Imbaso, cast an illusion over both of them.

They held no bubble of silence over themselves, and she murmured "hobble a bit" near his ear as they stepped inside. The acolyte, who'd been pacing the antechamber as if he had too much physical energy to simply sit and wait for customers (who were as scarce here as anywhere else in Palambo, two hundred years after the Shadow God had stopped answering his calls) saw a tiny, wizened old couple come inside. They looked as if they had been married since before his grandfather was a gleam in great-grandpa's eye. He gave them a grim smile. Kivuli had no use for the old and infirm, preferring the vital life energy of the newly born.

The old folks murmured something he didn't hear, bobbing their heads at him, and continued on into the unoccupied sanctuary. There was a good-sized idol on the altar, nearly eight feet tall. Another excellent fake. Maintaining the illusion and throwing up a bubble of silence, Leila deposited a tiny seed idol beneath the arch of the statue's right foot. Betsalel should have no trouble manifesting there, and growing to an appropriate size.

"Betsalel, come to me if you can," Leila said. Both she and
Imbaso, appearing to any who saw them as shrunken ancients,
waited for a full minute. And the god did not come. "Damn, that
has to mean that Kivuli is manifest here," Leila said. "I think we
should get the hell out, *now!*"

The two old folks tottered out of the anteroom and down the
stone path toward the street. On the way, they became two much
younger people who immediately untied their horses and set off at
as fast a pace as was possible in the crowded streets, in the
direction of the palace complex on the hilltop to their north.

"Shit, that's two seeds planted and we weren't able to activate
either of them," Leila said within their bubble of silence as they
rode. "Do you think your father's really in there doing something
awful?"

"Maybe scaring the pants off of somebody he wants to come
over to his side," Imbaso replied thoughtfully. Consciously at least,
Mauaji had gone from being the man Imbaso had loved
unquestioningly as a child to The Enemy, someone he must
pretend to get along with as he worked secretly to defeat him. But
were he and Leila, with Betsalel's aid, *strong* enough to defeat
him?

Betsalel had left Leila's personal idol at the still-smaller size,
easy to cup in her hand. As they rode, she called him to it again.
Knowing her mind, he remained small but wriggled in her palm to
let her know he had manifested. "Kivuli was there!" he said in
their minds. "I guessed as much," Leila said. "I left the seed idol
there, under the false idol's right foot arch. You might need to
duck a bit if you manifest there."

"The first chance I get to manifest there," the god assured
them, "I will absorb the essence of the false idol as I grow. No one
will notice the difference."

"We've done what we could at the temples, then," Leila said.
"But we're running late. Can you guide us by the quickest way to
the palace complex?"

They left their horses at the stables and nearly ran through the
corridors, hurrying back to their apartment. It was past two, and

they had not yet had anything to eat since breakfast – which in Leila's case, was many hours ago. On the other hand, she was about to go have "tea" with the women of the harem, and presumably there would be food served.

No one was in the sitting room when they came in and Leila, in a bubble of silence, said to Imbaso "Smell me." He gave her a wicked smile and drew her into his arms, pressing his nose to her neck. Did the man never stop wanting to throw her down on the nearest horizontal surface and ravish her? Not that she totally minded, of course…

"Do I reek of horse?" Leila asked, and for answer Imbaso inhaled deeply.

"You reek of love, of desire," he breathed. Oh, good grief.

"Imbaso!" she said sharply, stepping back out of his embrace, "Get a grip! Mbina's going to show up any minute and I need to know if I smell bad. She will notice!"

Leila had maintained the appearance of Usiku/Zurina throughout their trip around the city. Imbaso was almost as in love with the fictional Usiku as he was with Leila, and had positively incestuous feelings toward the even more fictional Zurina. "Can't you just include your smell in the illusion?" he asked, crushed at her rejection.

"I never tried," she said, surprised at the idea. She had considered the power of illusion to be a visual-only thing, but she had fooled people into thinking her voice was that of a much-larger man. And that bandit mage in the mountain pass before Namei had been convinced that his scimitar had removed the head of the enormously tall man he thought he was confronting.

Leila imagined herself drenched in the scent of lavender, a familiar herb that grew most places in the Dominion and was often used in soaps and perfumes. "Whoa!" Imbaso cried, backing away. "That is a bit too much!" Even Leila, from whose imagination the smell had come, could detect it. Well, *that* was pretty cool…

Before Mbina arrived to collect Zurina for her visit to the royal harem she had modified her scent to a clean one with just the hint of a pleasant fragrance. Her clothes were all clean and fresh, and appropriate for the planned visit. Imbaso remained reading in the sitting room, wondering when somebody else was going to return to the apartment – and wishing that he could shrink to the size of the idol in Leila's pocket, riding along with her and keeping her safe from harm. And from the machinations of that obvious lecher Samadhi.

It troubled Imbaso that Leila, in her role as Usiku, might be expected to actually marry and bed one of the royal princes. He didn't doubt she'd be able to request a swift widowhood from her Makucha Nyeusi handlers, but the thought of his girl, his love, in the arms of another filled him with sorrow. Yet he would be expected to take it without so much as a whisper of complaint. Father and the rest of the cult did not even know that Imbaso and Usiku were anything but friends.

Mbina arrived, looking more cheerful than they had yet seen her, and scooped Zurina up for the walk to the quarters of the royal household. They went right past the door to Vandao's rooms, but didn't see him. The harem was down and around several more turnings, beyond where Leila had thrown the coins to distract the guards. Was that only last night?

They found two more guards flanking the entrance to the harem chambers, an enormous wing that included its own bathing facilities, many large airy bedrooms, private gardens, and a great many servants seeing to the needs of the woman and children who lived here.

"Here it is," Mbina said, gesturing around. "The place where I was born and grew up."

"It's very nice!" Zurina assured her. "Do you still live here?"

"Oh no," the maidservant assured her. "Boys aged twelve and girls aged fourteen leave here and go elsewhere. As I was to become a servant, being only the daughter of a concubine, I went to live in the servants' quarters."

"Oh," Zurina said, looking down. She seemed to have a positive gift for putting her foot in her mouth. Mbina patted her on the shoulder.

"It's all right," she said. "If I'd been the first daughter of the king's first wife instead of the offspring of a concubine and a prince who went to the headsman's block for plotting the death of his king, I'd have been married off by now to some man I'd never met before the wedding, probably. At least as a servant I have a chance to order some parts of my own life. I'm engaged to one of my fellow servants, in fact."

"Oh, how wonderful for you Mbina," the rich girl squealed. "Is he also of the royal line?"

"No, thank the Eight," the maidservant replied. "His family did a service for one of the princes and in thanks my Ganibo was given a position here at the palace when he was thirteen. We're waiting for one of the married servants' apartments to become available, before we wed."

"Well, I wish you every happiness," Zurina said, sincerity shining in her dark eyes. "Might as well leave marrying your cousins for the royals. Did you know Samindhi and I are second cousins?" Mbina's eyebrows rose.

"Are you marrying him, then?" she asked.

"Maybe," the girl said thoughtfully. "I like him, and I suppose I have to marry somebody. But there are a lot of cute princes around, aren't there? Anyhow, it will probably be between Father and the king."

Just then Samindhi, whose ears might perhaps have been burning, came in and saw them there. "Oh, you're early!" he said, taking Zurina's arm. "Come, let me introduce you to Mother." He led them through the large central room, where women and children were relaxing, playing games, or reading books, into a good-sized parlor with double doors that gave on a small garden area similar to the one attached to the apartment where Zurina and her party were staying.

There was a large, low round table in one corner of the room with eight chairs around it, and six of those chairs were occupied by women. They all rose as Samindhi approached, female deference to an adult male being automatic.

He approached one of the older women, who must have been past forty but was still very handsome, and kissed her on the cheek. "Mother," he said, "I would like you to meet Zurina. She is the daughter of the arch-priest of Betsalel in Namei, and a cousin of ours as well. Zurina, my mother Dulesa."

The woman smiled at her and took her hands, squeezing them ever so slightly. "Welcome to Iskand, Zurina. I trust you are enjoying your stay?"

"Indeed, it is a most wondrous place, memsahib," Zurina said. Then dropped her gaze and put her hand to her mouth. "Or it is Your Highness?" Clearly the poor thing was a provincial.

"Memsahib will do nicely, dear," Dulesa said sympathetically. "Most of us are technically princesses, of course, but the title means little and we have no need to stand on ceremony here within our haven."

Haven, Leila thought. An interesting term. She had certainly seen (and lived in) worse places, but the guards on the door gave it just the tiniest feel of being a prison as much as a sanctuary. Zurina was next introduced to Chitra, Omaso's mother (older still by a couple of years than Dulesa), and to Sarinda – mother of Mbina. She looked to have been a rare beauty in her youth, but had expanded over the years in a way that suggested some Hutu blood. Amhari usually just got leaner and stringier with age.

The other three ladies, ranging in age from late twenties to mid-thirties, were also wives or concubines of King Omali. After the introductions had been made Samindhi kissed Leila's hand and made a deep bow, then said cheerfully, "I'll leave you ladies to your hen party, then. It would be rude of me to hang around and make it impossible for you to talk about me behind my back!" And he left.

Ouch, Leila thought, he hit the nail on the head. But it's not him so much as the king I need to work into the discussion here. There was a pot of tea on the table and fine porcelain cups and saucers, presumably imported from the Dominion, were set at each place.

"Now that we're all here," Chitra said, "Shall we have some refreshments?" As the senior of the king's wives, it seemed she was playing hostess for this little gathering. Ooh, and there was food on a nearby sideboard. Blue-liveried servants, some of Mbina's colleagues, passed around plates and everyone served themselves with little flatbread rolls, small pastries, fresh grapes and various tropical fruits. It was all quite light fare, and Leila was hard put not to devour everything that was put in front of her. She'd eaten nothing since breakfast, and her stomach was growling fiercely.

She looked up, licking her fingers, and realized she was getting covert glances from several of the ladies around the table. "Oh, please excuse me!" Zurina said prettily. "My brother and I thought to visit the temples today, and we didn't realize what a long trip it was going to be. I missed lunch!"

Dulesa smiled at her. "Ah, of course as your father is an arch-priest you would have wished to see our Temple of the Eight. I have not visited the Gaspari Dominion, but it is said only their Temple of the Eight in Parat surpasses ours here in Iskand."

"I certainly found it very impressive," Zurina said. "Imbaso and I were privileged to witness Holy Mulia manifesting in her idol and granting a blessing to a petitioner. It was a very moving experience. Do the ladies of the harem worship there?"

"We have a shrine to Mulia here within the harem itself, with a small true idol of the goddess," Chitra explained. "But when one of us wishes to approach others of the Eight, we can get a guard escort and travel to the Temple of the Eight or to one of the gods and goddesses' individual temples for worship."

Interesting, Leila thought. How many other "unofficial" temples were there scattered around Palambo, ones with true idols? And were any of them once dedicated to Betsalel? It might be far harder to root out the Kivuli cult than she'd hoped.

After they'd finished their refreshments Zurina looked around. The harem wing seemed to stretch on and on, yet there were few people to be seen. "These quarters are quite lovely and extensive," she said. "But there don't seem to be all that many people living here."

Another faux pas for Zurina, but that was part of her charm. And it made it a lot easier for Leila/Usiku to extract the answers she was looking for. Chitra smiled indulgently. "This part of the palace was built centuries ago," the king's First Wife said. "In modern times, the kings and princes of Palambo do not go in for quite so many wives. And as for the children of course, there is that shrine to Mulia…if you know what I mean."

Maybe this place *was* truly a haven. It was unlikely any male would intrude on the women's inner sanctum or interfere with their relationship with the goddess whose purview was all things connected to women. Mulia would be happy to grant a faithful worshiper a child, or a safe childbirth, or a future with no more childbirths in it as she had the woman in the temple today.

"I hope you won't think me rude," Zurina said hesitantly, "but I'm very curious about life in the palace. As you probably know, my father expects that I will find a husband from among the princes here. I would know what that entails. For instance, how many wives are usual for a prince to have?"

Dulesa smiled at her, empathizing. She had been through the same questions herself, at that age – though she'd not truly had a choice in the matter, and probably neither did Zurina. "Most of the princes have no more than two or three," she explained. "The king is expected to have more of course – many more. Chitra and I were already wed to our husband Omali and both of us had given him sons, back when we expected to be the wives of a prosperous merchant. After he was chosen for the throne, of course, it was incumbent on him to marry again and again. But even now, after wedding little Linda from the Dominion (Leila detected a hint of disdain there, or was it just envy?), he has only nine."

"And three concubines, don't forget," the plump and cheerful Sarinda chimed in with a smile that revealed dimples. A dozen official women for a man who ruled a nation every bit as vast as the Gaspari Dominion? Given the Palamban culture, Leila supposed that almost made Omali an ascetic.

"So if I were a prince's first wife," Zurina said shyly, "there's a pretty good chance I would live with him in his own house, or his quarters in the palace, and have one or two sister wives under me?"

"That's right," Chitra replied. "As the first wife you have status, but of course that usually means you are the oldest and eventually their interests wander to younger women. But I think it is no different with commoners, is it? Do not all middle-aged men wish to bed women young enough to be their daughters, to make them feel young again?"

Thanks to the power of Leila's illusion, Zurina flushed beneath her darkly pigmented skin. "I wouldn't know about such things," she said in a small voice. "My mother is only a little younger than my father, yet he still cleaves to her." A moment later she added, "So far as I know…" The older women laughed quietly, and she shrank into herself.

The conversation flowed around the table, and at close to five Chitra had a servant bring wine and more appetizers. Then it flowed even more freely, with frequent gales of laughter. Zurina had a little bit too much to drink, though Leila remained clear-headed enough. Along the way she learned far more than anyone noticed about the king's daily habits, the situation within his private chambers, and the security arrangements he surrounded himself with. Any king of Palambo who did not keep tight precautions was very soon a late king of Palambo, given all the competition for the job.

The party from Namei had no pre-dinner party to go to this evening, but they would be dining in the great hall at eight. After six Mbina, who'd truly been enjoying herself this afternoon, took her young charge by the elbow. "We need to return to the apartment, mwali."

"Oh please, Mbina, call me Zurina!" the girl said gaily. "You're as close to being descended from the royal line as I am!" Mbina and her mother embraced, and they thanked the ladies of the harem for hosting them. Then the two threaded their way out through guarded doors and returned to the guest wing.

"Ooh!" Zurina declared, as they zigzagged their way through the corridors, "That was fun! And your mother is so beautiful, and so nice! It's too bad old Rajari couldn't have married her, then you'd be a princess like my grandma!" Mbina sighed. She rather liked the young girl from Namei, but Zurina certainly could stand a little more self-discipline. She supposed it was only to be expected from somebody raised in the boondocks.

"You will need to bathe again before going to dinner," Mbina said firmly.

"But I've already bathed twice today!" Zurina wailed. "Can't I just use some perfume, or maybe have a little sponge bath?"

"I suppose a sponge bath will do," the maidservant said reluctantly. "And I think maybe it would be a good idea if you lie down for a while before getting ready to go out. Are you not feeling tired?"

"You know," Zurina said thoughtfully, "I b'lieve you're right. A nap sounds like a good idea." She sagged slightly against her companion, hoping not to oversell it.

"I'll tuck you into bed when we get back then," Mbina said firmly. "I have neglected my duties for most of the day, and there will be work to do while you are napping."

Excellent, Leila thought. They returned to the apartment to find everyone gathered in the sitting room. "Did you enjoy your visit to the harem, daughter?" Mauaji asked. The man certainly knew how to apply gravity to a simple question.

"It was great, Father! I met Samindhi's mother, and Omaso's too, and even Mbina's! And I learned ever so much about what life is like in the royal family!" Zurina wavered slightly and added, "But I'm feeling pretty tired. Mbina suggested I should take a nap before dinner, and I think that's a good idea."

Chapter 50

After tucking her charge into the bed, Mbina returned to the sitting room and began getting to work. It was her duty not only to chaperone the young mwali but also to maintain the apartment in a suitable condition of order and cleanliness.

She dealt with the kitchen area, and then Mauaji directed her, "Please see to the bathroom. And after that I would like the bedding changed in the other bedrooms." Mbina bowed her head to him, then scurried down the hall to the bathroom. Though the eight men in this party bathed nowhere near as often as the young lady, a cleaning was still overdue. She ought to have been dealing with it instead of taking time off through the middle of the day, she knew. She should not to have let young Zurina's kindness interfere with her duties.

While Mbina was hard at work housecleaning, master Kifozi rapped lightly on the door of Zurina's room. "Enter," he heard, and stepped inside. "What do you have to report?" he asked, and Usiku, who had already risen from the bed and put on a robe over the underwear Mbina had left her in, said, "I grilled the first and second wives, and I believe also the sixth and seventh wives and two of the concubines."

"Excellent," Kifozi said, then waited for Usiku to continue.

"King Omali is currently very enamored of his most recently-acquired wife," she said. "She is not ensconced in the harem, but has been living in his personal quarters and sharing his bed since the wedding."

Leila felt as if she were standing on a shore, watching an enormous wave come in from the sea. It stood above her, vibrating with potential energy, and there was nothing she could do to prevent it crashing down – carrying her and everything she had known away in its path. Nothing she could do was going to prevent the six members of the Makucha Nyeusi from completing their mission here in Iskand. And any obvious hesitation on her part might only see her status changed from "operative" to "target."

So, she told all. The fact that no food or drink, not even a glass of water in the middle of the night, ever passed King Omali's lips without first having been tested for poison. The fact that five of the "party guests" at last night's gathering had been guards in disguise. The fact that the king's bedchamber was a windowless room with only one door, which was guarded by half a dozen guards overnight in the room on the other side of that door – and another dozen in the room beyond that. Short of a major frontal assault by an army, there would be no getting to the king while he slept.

"You have done well, Usiku," master Kifozi said. Leila saw the wheels turning behind his eyes. She was a highly-trained assassin with more resources than the old man knew; but he had been doing this job since long before her mother had been born. She saw him rejecting plans and putting others into place.

"We are not yet ready to approach our final target," Kifozi said, "but you have given us enough to go forward with. You should continue to ingratiate yourself with the royal family."

"Master," Usiku replied, "Things are progressing too quickly with Prince Samindhi. I believe he wishes Zurina for his bride. It would be good if another suitor could appear, one to give him some competition – and motivation."

Kifozi nodded, decisively. As far as he was concerned, Usiku was just a cunningly wrought tool that had fallen into his hand, one he was pleased with. "Good idea," he said. "I will arrange for you to meet another eligible prince or two this evening. "Are you really in need of any rest?" Usiku sighed.

"I wouldn't mind a quick nap," she admitted. "It's been a long day, and I suppose it will be a long night?"

"It's possible," the master assassin admitted. "Catch an hour, if you can." We will be going to dinner a little before eight." He left her room, and Leila darted silently to the door and latched it behind him. Then she inserted the wedges, and unlatched the window before lying down on the bed again. She wasn't at all sure if Imbaso would be able to get away from the rest of the group. His suddenly deciding he needed to hang out alone in the garden within minutes of her retiring for a nap would soon begin to look very suspicious.

It was more than fifteen minutes before Imbaso, shrouded in silence, came in through the window. Leila had nearly, in truth, almost nodded off. She started up as he stepped inside, and waited for him to join her on the bed. She wasn't sure what the result of overlapping silence bubbles would be.

He drew her to him and kissed her, then sat beside her on the bed with his back against the headboard. "You took your time," Leila said. "I was about to fall asleep." He kissed her again.

"We can't have that!" he exclaimed, then added, "While you were gone today I did some exploring. I figured out how to get out of the guest wing and into the gardens. All of these little courtyard gardens are connected, and if you wriggle through the bushes you can go from one to the other all the way down. The guys outside" – he gestured to the room's door – "think I went to rendezvous with a serving girl I chatted up earlier today."

"You dog!" Leila said, slapping Imbaso on the chest but smiling. "I've got a girl in every port, and all of them are you," he smiled back. "So," he went on, "what did you tell Kifozi?" She leaned back against the headboard and her face fell.

"Everything," she admitted. "I can't see any way that we can prevent the Black Claw from assassinating the king, without getting all our heads chopped off."

Leila's knowledge of the Makucha Nyeusi was greater than his own, Imbaso knew. And he was in awe of their powers. If she believed they could not be stopped, there was no point in fighting it. "They surely plan to put a Kivuli cultist on the throne," he said. "And whenever they move to kill the king, that will be at a point where Father believes he has the Council of Eight on his side."

"That's my take on it," Leila concurred.

"What if we were to eliminate his candidate?" Imbaso asked. "Preempt his move, by leaving him without the man he'd intended to fill the position. Would that stop the plan?"

"You mean Farendhi," Leila said.

"He's the obvious candidate," Imbaso replied. "But maybe before we think about bumping him off you should do a visual check of the palms of every other prince on the palace scene."

Leila sighed. "Do you have any idea how many princes there are in this place? Between Omali's generation and their sons, there must be dozens! I checked Farendhi and he definitely has the scars – but what if there's another half dozen princely Kivuli cultists who don't live at the palace? Your father might have any number of backup choices, and presumably once he has the Council in his pocket they'll elect whomever he tells them to."

Imbaso looked unhappy. It had seemed like such a great idea! "Even if you're right, Leila, I still think eliminating Farendhi would be a good idea," he said. "At the very least it will slow Father down. And we can get a better idea from his reaction what his plans are."

"Well," Leila said reluctantly, "I *am* a trained assassin… But it would need to be done in such a way that no suspicion falls on us. If Farendhi is obviously killed by assassination, your father will know that somebody opposed to the cult is involved. And what if he can ask Kivuli to tell him who?"

"I thought the djinn had the mind of a bloodthirsty baby?" Imbaso asked.

"The soul, not the mind," Leila explained. "The structure of the djinn's essential persona was built up over two centuries of fruitless worship using the Secret Scriptures. He's only been a real entity since capturing the soul of your infant nephew, and that informed his motivations and interactions. But even babies learn. With guidance from the priesthood, who understand what the powers of a god should be, they could well be training him."

Fear gripped Imbaso's heart at that thought. Then he had another thought. "Maybe Betsalel could help? He might just be able to kill Farendhi in his sleep, or from an apparent heart attack while he's going about his daily business."

"We're getting short on time, here, Imbaso," Leila said. "Let's do it now."

In moments the tiny idol Leila kept close to her always had grown to around the size of a baby and was balancing on the mattress, standing between his two principle adherents within Iskand. "I have manifested to a worshiper in the Temple of the

Eight!" he announced proudly. "The desecrated idol I absorbed as planned."

"Good!" Leila declared. "That's a ray of hope, at least. But things are getting worrisome here. We're convinced that Mauaji means to place a Kivuli cultist on the throne of Palambo, probably Farendhi. Would it be possible for you to grant him a peaceful death?" Taking the image of Farendhi from Leila's mind, the dark god stood in concentration for a while, his powers seeking the man. Then he spoke.

"I am sorry, but Farendhi has been shielded by Kivuli from supernatural harm. Much as I have shielded you, Imbaso. He should be vulnerable to more mundane means of dispatch, though."

"Can you search throughout the palace compound for others so shielded?" Leila asked, and the god complied. This took far longer, as he needed to scan hundreds of people. Leila and Imbaso sat holding hands, watching him apprehensively. How widespread was the cult within the circles of power in the kingdom's capital?

The answer surprised them both. "I sense three more individuals within the walls of the palace compound with a similar protection from the djinn," Betsalel said at last. "In addition to Prince Farendhi, the princes Caradhros and Utruri, and the servant Mdaleye all bear the marks of Kivuli's protection."

That wasn't nearly as bad as Leila had feared. Perhaps this relative power vacuum at court had been the motivating factor for Mauaji to make a journey of a thousand miles to put his plot in motion. Not enough local talent to do the job? "Caradhros and Utruri are both sons of Faraj as is your father, Leila. Does it concern you to plot the death of your uncles?"

Just a little while ago Leila had been musing about how she had so few family members. It had somehow escaped her notice that all of Vandao's relatives were *her* relatives too. She wasn't an orphan – she had enough uncles, aunts, and cousins to pack a good-sized amphitheater! "I went to Vandao's quarters last night perfectly prepared to kill *him*," she replied. "If any of my myriad recently-discovered relations are sunk in evil, I have no problem doing away with them."

"Very well," the Shadow God said. "Do you know of Mdaleye?" Both Imbaso and Leila shook their heads. Betsalel sat on the bed between them then grew to a normal human size, before suddenly becoming a middle-aged Amhari with a hooked nose, short-cropped hair gone gray at the temples, and what looked like an old knife scar running through his right eyebrow. The power the god had given to Leila, he of course could employ himself. His fellow god Dionos had also demonstrated shape-shifting abilities.

"I've seen him in the company of Prince Farendhi," Imbaso said. I got the idea he was a household servant of the prince's, like a valet or a major-domo.

"Or a bodyguard, or perhaps an agent!" Leila said. "It would make sense he's more than he seems, if his master urged him to join the cult."

"Thank you master," she added, and Betsalel resumed his true shape. He and his fellow deities had been molded over millennia by human belief, and it was uncomfortable for them to remain in any other form for long while manifested in their idols. "I fear our time will soon be up," Leila said. "You two had both better go." The Shadow God shrank to his toy-sized idol and Imbaso, after another hug and kiss and a sigh of frustration that there could not be more, crawled back out the window.

Chapter 51

Imbaso had taken his bubble of silence with him. Leila removed the wedges and unlocked the door then lay down on the bed and waited. It wasn't long before Mbina knocked briefly, then came inside. "Are you feeling better, Zurina?" she asked, a sign that her attitude toward her young charge had softened. From a servant's point of view, the pretty young thing from Namei must be nothing but a pain in the butt.

Zurina sat up, rubbing her eyes. "Lots better, thank you. I suppose it must be time to get ready to go to dinner?"

"That's right," the maidservant said, bringing in a bowl of warm water and a sponge. She set it on the chest of drawers in the room, then closed the door. "Come on, let's get you cleaned up," she said briskly.

They left Mbina behind, still with housework to do, as they made their way to the palace's great dining hall. Leila wondered what conferences had gone on among the assassins and Mauaji while she and Imbaso had been consulting with the Shadow God earlier. The fact that no further arch-priest deaths had been announced, and that all four of the young assassins were joining them for dinner, suggested that the other two targets would be attempted tonight – probably after everyone else was in bed.

Another thought came to Leila – might Mbina be having secret liaisons in their apartment with her betrothed Ganibo, while they were all out? If so, that might be a piece of leverage she could use to get a little more freedom. Having an overnight guest in her room was putting a crimp in any number of her activities.

They all knew where they were going, and the men seemed to be in something of a hurry. Imbaso escorted his sister, and they gradually fell behind until a big enough gap had appeared for them to use a bubble of silence. "I've been thinking about it," Leila murmured, "and I think we need to get the princes away from the palace. Do you think you could ask Farendhi to take you to a good local tavern, or something?"

"Or maybe he'd accompany me to the Temple of Betsalel," Imbaso replied as quietly.

"Or perhaps a whorehouse, even," she mused in response. He raised an eyebrow. His beloved had told him she'd lived in a whorehouse until the age of eight, but he had not found her all that sophisticated a lover. She was picking up more tricks the longer they were together, however.

"I'll see if I can get seated next to Farendhi and buddy up with him," Imbaso suggested. "He's my cousin, so maybe he'd like to show the kid some manly fun." Leila elbowed him with a smirk, and they dropped their bubble and closed up the gap.

In the dining hall they were seated at the same table as before, but Zurina now found herself flanked by two men she had not met before. She recalled she'd asked Kifozi to ring in a couple of extra princes to keep Samindhi interested – though her intention was to keep him at a distance. She liked the boy, and saw no reason why she should be faced with a choice between staying married to him for life or having him killed.

These two were older, late twenties, and resembled Vandao somewhat. But one of them had lighter skin, around the same hue as Leila's own, light green eyes, and curly hair that was dark brown with streaks of blond in it. Clearly Omali was not the only king to have sought a bride from the Dominion. Very intriguing! Farendhi made the introductions, and Leila's initial attraction vanished.

"Zurina, I would like you to meet my nephews Caradhros and Utruri. They are sons of the late king Faraj." Oh, shit. "Caradhros" had seemed an unusual name for a Palamban, and Leila would be willing to bet the blonde Gaspari woman who had borne him had something to do with that. Dozens of princes, and Kifozi just happened to saddle her with the two in the entire palace who were also Kivuli cultists? That didn't look good. But maybe she could make something of it.

As first Caradhros, and then Utruri, took her hand to kiss in the Dominion style, Leila examined their palms. Sure enough, both had the scars. She was seated between them, and was pleased to find that Imbaso had found a berth beside Farendhi. The man was remarkably jovial for being the adherent of a bloodthirsty black demon.

After the first course, which included candied fruits and cold pickled vegetables, Zurina excused herself from the table and went to the women's privy. Time to start building her story – she did not intend to stay here for the full two hours the meal would be expected to stretch on.

On her way back to her seat she leaned close to Kifozi and murmured in his ear, "Do they know I'm not Zurina?" He shook his head slightly. "They were just convenient, that's all," he said as quietly. She smiled and said "Thanks," slightly louder. As she sat back down Caradhros eyed her questioningly. "Everything all right, dear?" he asked solicitously.

Zurina gave an embarrassed nod. "I'm so sorry, but I am feeling a little ill. Kifozi has said that we have some medicines in the apartment, so if I'm not feeling better soon I may return there for a time." The light-skinned Amhari patted her hand.

"I would be devastated if you could not spend the evening with us," he said gallantly. "We have only just met!"

Of the two, Caradhros definitely seemed more interested in her. Dinner service continued, and Zurina managed to choke down enough food to tide Leila over for what she thought might be a very long night. Soon, though, the girl excused herself again. "Please forgive me, but I must go to our apartment for something," she told the men on either side of her. As she passed Kifozi she bent low again and murmured, "Starting my period, dammit! I'll be back in a while."

There was nothing quite like the mention of women's blood to send strong men and hardened killers running for the nearest exit. That was an advantage female assassins had over their male counterparts, Leila thought, as she made her way to the door and headed for the apartment. One of many.

She hurried along, just the young girl from Namei going back to her apartment for some absorbent pads. As she approached the door, however, she threw up a bubble of silence until she was standing immediately in front of it. Then she dropped the bubble and put her ear to the door.

Aha! She heard the sounds of two people talking, well moaning anyhow. Excellent. First she made just enough noise to give them a second or two to get disentangled. She didn't actually want to catch them *in flagrante*. Then she pushed through the door and found Mbina, scantily clad but not naked, sitting beside a very surprised and anxious-looking young man on the settee. He appeared to be wearing a towel and nothing else.

"Oh!" Zurina squealed in surprise. Then a big conspiratorial grin came over her face. "You must be Ganibo," she said, holding out a hand to the stricken youth.

"Uh, um, pleased to meet you," he mumbled, touching her hand with his. "Uh..."

"Oh, that's alright," Zurina said. "Mbina told me you're betrothed, and with both of you living in the servants' quarters I suppose there would not be many chances for you to be together. I won't tell Father or Imbaso, not that I think *he* would mind either. You wouldn't believe the things that boy gets up to!"

Relief washed over both their faces. Positions at the palace were hard to come by, and getting fired from theirs might spell ruination to their chances of ever having a home together. "Thank you, Zurina!" Mbina said warmly, meanwhile thinking "Hmm, Little Miss Innocent isn't as innocent as I thought..."

"Excuse me," Zurina went on, "I had to leave dinner to get some things from my room, uh, personal things..." She rolled her eyes, managing to convey what was meant. "As soon as I've cleaned up a little I'll be going right back, so you'll have your privacy again for about an hour."

The caught couple sat transfixed on the settee for around five minutes while Mbina's mistress was busy behind the bedroom door. "What was that about?" Ganibo whispered to his fiancée.

"Girl stuff," she whispered back. "Just be glad it was Zurina and not Mauaji that caught us. She's really kind of all right."

Zurina emerged wearing a slightly different outfit than she'd had on earlier, and bid them a hasty goodbye. It was some time before they returned to their previous activity. Beneath Zurina's semblance of an evening gown Leila was dressed in her full assassin gear, pockets laden with every lethal item she could think of bringing to the party.

The two princes looked up as she rejoined them, Caradhros with a big smile on his face. "I do apologize for having to leave," Zurina told them, "but I'm feeling much better now." The meal proceeded, and Zurina learned that Caradhros had just one wife and two children, whereas Utruri, a couple of years older, had twice that many of each. No wonder he was less enthusiastic about the prospect of another one!

Seeing Utruri as a lost cause for the moment, Leila began pouring all of her attention into Caradhros. He was eating it up with a spoon, brushing against her thigh as they sat close together at the table and, when that didn't provoke any rebuffs, taking more liberties. Leila wondered whether he wanted to add Zurina to his harem, or just pop her into bed.

Zurina glanced up and noticed that Samindhi had excused himself from the king's table and was coming their way. Hmm, a complication. She had intended to insert another prince or two between him and his apparent goal of marrying her, but that was before she'd known the princes would be people she needed to kill.

They were now on the dessert course, and Leila had eaten plenty. Any more and she might not be nimble enough for the rest of the evening's activities. "Oh, I see someone I must speak with!" Zurina said, rising quickly to her feet and intercepting Samindhi before he should get any closer.

His expression was not all that friendly as she approached. "I see you've met Caradhros," he said. He must have been watching their interaction from his perch on the dais, and was now feeling betrayed. And as Caradhros' mother would have been a standout in King Faraj's harem, so her son was a standout among the nearly identical (if all quite handsome) princes. The rest of them probably all hated him.

Zurina dipped her head and gave him an appealing glance through her lashes. "I'm sorry, I had no idea Father had other candidates for my hand. He just appeared at my elbow when I sat down to eat."

"But he's already married and has two children!" Samindhi objected. "If you were to wed me, you would be my First Wife!"

"Chitra told me that's a big deal, and I do appreciate it," Zurina assured him. "But I'm not sure that my own preferences will decide the issue. I think Father is seeking a good bride price, or political considerations." His anger was defused. He had grown up in this milieu, and he knew better than she did that courting was not a simple matter of love – or even of attraction. Too bad his status as the son of the king was of so little worth. Should his father die, he'd be no more likely to become king than any of his dozens of uncles, cousins, and brothers.

"Zurina," Samindhi said, taking her hands, "say that you will join me at the king's table tomorrow for dinner." At least being the son of the current king had *some* perks. Her eyes lit with excitement.

"Really?" she squealed. Ah, so young. "Could you arrange it with Father?"

"I'm sure I can," he said confidently. She stood on tiptoe and kissed him on the cheek, and a little shot of lust swept through him but he kept it tightly under control. There was something so appealing about all that innocence.

"See you tomorrow!" Zurina said, and returned to the table. She discovered that in her absence Utruri had apparently departed. "Oh, what happened to your brother?" she asked Caradhros.

"He and I had a little discussion, and he decided to cede the field to me," the young man said with a hint of bravado. "Truly, I'm not sure he wants another wife."

Zurina looked down at her lap, seemingly embarrassed by this frankness. She was, in some respects, meat on the marriage block; but that didn't mean she wanted to be reminded of the fact. Sensing he'd committed a faux pas, Caradhros patted her on the shoulder. "There there, I was just joking!" he said. "My older brother rises quite early, that is all. I think it's already past his bedtime."

The girl looked up again, black eyes sparkling and a hint of a wicked smile playing around her lips. "And for you," she said, "when's *your* bedtime?" Caradhros caught a shadow of a double entendre in her words, but decided he must be imagining it. What was this girl, fifteen or sixteen?

"I like to stay up late, myself," he assured her. "Iskand is a city of many pleasures, and some of the finest of them only get started after dinner!"

Zurina gave him a look as if she'd suddenly realized she was out of her depth. This man was far more experienced than she was, more than ten years older. Whatever did he mean by "pleasures"?

"Sorry, joking again," Caradhros declared. "But there really are some fine sights to be had after the sun goes down. From the citadel, over atop the palace guard quarters, you can see for miles on a clear night. When the moon is up it glistens on the Azraq to the east, and sparkles on the waters of the Center Sea to the north. And all the lights of the city are spread out around you. It is a sight to take your breath away."

Why in all the hells would a fantastically good-looking guy like Caradhros – with a wife and kids, and a silver tongue to match his looks – decide to dedicate himself to the worship of a god that demands to be fed on freshly killed babies, Leila thought? It was beyond comprehension. Was everything she saw in this prince as much an illusion as what he thought he saw in Zurina?

"It sounds wonderful!" Zurina breathed, an expression of awe on her face. "Is the moon up tonight?"

"Not for another two hours," Caradhros said. The girl dropped her gaze, then looked around to see if her father or any of the priests in his party were watching. "I could sneak out later and meet you there," she murmured. Caradhros' cock went half stiff at the thought. This was too easy, like fishing in a barrel! The girl would part with her maidenhead, and no bride price would be forthcoming. He had no use for another wife.

"The entrance to the stairs leading up to the citadel is within the compound of the guard's headquarters," Caradhros said softly, handing her what appeared to be a small metal brooch. "Show my token, and they will let you in." Zurina would have had to be an idiot not to realize that she wasn't the first girl the prince had lured to this "romantic" rendezvous. But then, idiocy was one of Zurina's specialties.

The gathering broke up, the black-robed priests forming up into a cadre. Caradhros approached Mauaji and said, "Thank you for allowing me to meet your charming daughter. I am looking forward to spending more time with her in the near future." Then he was on his way.

Kifozi informed Usiku, "We are off across town to the Temple of Betsalel now, and will be involved in worship and temple business until late. You may return to the apartment and get some rest. I think tomorrow will be a busy day." Usiku nodded, then Imbaso spoke up, "Cousin Farendhi has said he'll take me to see some of the night life in Iskand this evening. I'm just going to stop by the apartment for a change of clothes and then I'll be meeting him at the stables so we can ride into town."

"Good, brother, you can escort me back," Zurina said. She'd gone there and back earlier this evening unaccompanied, but at this hour it might be considered improper for a young girl to be wandering the corridors by herself. The parties split up and as soon as there was some distance between them Leila threw up a bubble of silence.

"Things are getting complicated," she said. "I've got an appointment with Caradhros in a couple of hours to 'admire the moonlight' up on the citadel above the guards' compound. How long do you think you and Farendhi will be carousing?" "Could be most of the night," Imbaso said, stifling his annoyance at the thought of Leila having a tete-a-tete with the good-looking prince. The fact that the outcome of that meeting would probably be Caradhros' death helped to take the sting out of it.

"If Mdaleye is Farendhi's body servant, possibly body *guard*, there's a good chance he'll be along for the ride," Leila pointed out. "And there's no guarantee that you could take Farendhi one-on-one." Imbaso seemed crestfallen.

"If only Kifozi had accepted me for assassin training, I might now be as deadly as you are!" he moaned.

Leila manipulated her Zurina illusion so that the girl continued to walk down the corridor beside her brother while she reached out and squeezed Imbaso's butt. "Sweet love," she murmured, "you are *never* going to be as deadly as I am. Unless maybe Betsalel grants you extra powers as he has done me. But I've been trained in this stuff since before my tenth birthday – don't feel bad."

Imbaso was not particularly mollified. But he had to admit, "I need you there, Leila. Our party needs to be set upon by thieves, Farendhi and his manservant killed, their money stolen. I think I might get off with a few bruises and maybe a knife wound that will produce a romantic scar."

"That's exactly the stuff!" Leila declared. "But how will I find you after I've disposed of Caradhros?"

"You have your watch?" he asked, pulling his own from an inner pocket. The things were even less common in Palambo than in the Dominion, but his family was rich. "It's 10:15," she said. They were approaching the apartment. "I've got 10:12, let me adjust mine to yours," Imbaso said.

Leila assumed that Ganibo would have long since departed, but likely Mbina would still be awake. Instead of going right into the apartment she pulled Imbaso aside. There was no one in sight within the corridor, and she drew them both into shadows. "I'll go a little early to the citadel," she said. "Get there maybe by 11:30 and see what the situation is. If it looks good I'll wait for Caradhros and dispatch him. If not, I'll leave. Did Farendhi say where exactly he was taking you?"

A little shudder ran through Imbaso. This was not just an exciting game anymore. They were plotting to kill people, people who had not done them any personal harm. "He only said he would take me to a few of his favorite spots. There are some drinking establishments with musical entertainment, a gambling hall, and a high-class whorehouse. These princes are hip-deep in women, but they still want a little on the side."

Leila embraced him and stuck her tongue in his mouth. "Don't *you* be getting 'a little on the side,' if you know what's good for you," she said.

"Well I *am* getting awfully horny," he replied. "How many days has it been?" Ooh, too long, Leila thought. "Do you remember the marketplace in Aswa?" she asked, drawing him closer.

Far less than half an hour later they resumed their discussion. "Why don't you just have Betsalel guide you, as he did when we were returning from the temple?" Imbaso asked. "If he can pick out Kivuli cultists, I'm sure he can locate me." Leila felt like slapping her forehead, but refrained. After a lifetime relying only on her own resources, she was always forgetting that she had the powers of an immortal god at hand.

"All right, then," Leila said. "Sometime around 12:30 or later you might expect to find me masquerading as a gang of footpads somewhere in your vicinity. Try to encourage them to wander the streets on foot. If I spot Kizuri where Betsalel tells me to find you, I'll cut her loose and drive her off. I assume she'd let me do that?" Imbaso considered. "You, probably. She's known you for weeks now. But she's not likely to go far."

"Don't worry, we'll work it out," Leila said. "Do you really need anything from the apartment?" "I thought it might be good to arm myself a bit," he said, and she suddenly realized how vulnerable her lover might be. It was going to be Farendhi and Mdaleye both, almost certainly – and while she had no idea what the prince's blade skills were, it was a sure bet that Mdaleye was as skilled as any assassin. On the other hand, she had some advantages neither of them knew about.

Brother and sister entered the apartment well before 11 and found it deserted. Mbina, it seemed, had already gone to bed. She had left some lamps burning, and Imbaso soon returned from his room after collecting his scimitar and a dagger Leila had given him. He kissed her deeply, then went out the door saying "See you later, sister!"

Leila had been toying with the idea of learning where Utruri's quarters were located, slipping in and administering the same death Nindao had given to that recalcitrant high priest early in their journey from Namei. But there was no time for that now.

She considered going into her bedroom as Zurina and leveraging her knowledge of Mbina's misbehavior to extract her complicity with her own, but decided against it. Even though Betsalel had told her that a person's rectitude or lack thereof had nothing to do with the destination of their soul after death, Leila still felt as though every deed that she knew was both wrong and unnecessary weighed against her.

Her personal sense of right and wrong might have been a bit skewed from that of the average person in the Dominion; but it still counted. Mbina was now asleep and blameless. Let her stay that way. Leila went out the apartment's front door invisible, heading for the citadel.

Chapter 52

The guards' quarters were in a stand-alone building not far from the sprawling palace complex. There were guard substations within the palace building itself, as a large number of the guard force had their duties inside. But guards were stationed all over the city, and the majority of them came here to sleep, and eat, and receive their orders. It even had its own little wall.

The gate was open and well-guarded, an opening twenty feet across. Leila didn't bother showing Caradhros' token, drifting silently and invisibly through the exact center of the space. No one noticed. No doubt the sly, lecherous prince had expected Zurina to ask directions to the steps leading up to the top of the citadel, but Leila had to find them for herself. It wasn't hard.

The main guardhouse was a broad, blocky-looking stone building three storeys high. Probably a lot of administrative functions went on in there during the daytime, but at this hour the place was dark. There was a sentry standing near the foot of a stone staircase going up the side of the building, and Leila slipped past him.

The steps wound around the building with landings at the second and third floors, then began spiraling around a circular tower that sprouted from the roof of the rectangular building and rose straight up, like the erection of all erections, for what must have been another six storeys in height. There were another two guards on the roof of the main building, but none of them close to where the stairs mounted the tower.

Leila crept past them silently, using the skills taught her by the Black Claw. They were too close to be excluded by the bubble of silence she wore. Once she'd gotten some distance she dug in and began trotting up the interminable staircase with a will. There'd been far too many hours on horseback, and little opportunity for working out on the journey here; but she was not yet eighteen years of age and had been fit for most of her life.

Puffing, Leila came up at last onto the roof of the citadel. As she'd hoped, no sentries were posted here. The roof of the three-storey main building, some sixty feet below, offered as much of a view of the compound's surroundings as was likely to be needed in the middle of the night, during peacetime.

The staircase up here had been narrow, less than four feet wide, and had no railing. Clearly it was intended to be highly defensible. The tower top was perhaps forty feet across, and was surrounded by a crenelated stone wall between three and four feet high. A small force of archers and swordsmen up here could hold out for as long as their food and water remained. And there was a trap door in the center – presumably leading to the top floor of the tower below.

Still invisible, Leila walked over to the edge and looked out on the city. This elevation added to the low rise on which the entire palace compound sat and offered a superb view of the great city of Iskand spread out below. The Temple of the Eight, on its own little promontory, was lit up and easily visible to the southwest. Ooh, how Leila would love to come up here with Imbaso and a bedroll or two, watching the full moon come up beyond the Azraq to the east and making love for hours as it gradually rose above them. At the moment, however, there was no Imbaso. And no moon. Sighing, Leila hunkered down with her back against the wall to the south, and prepared to wait.

Another fifteen minutes had passed, and a faint glow in the east suggested that the third-quarter moon would soon be appearing over the horizon. Leila was sitting in a sort of meditative state, motionless and scarcely breathing but intensely aware of everything around her. She heard footsteps on the stairs on the far side of the roof, and instantly rose to her feet.

Caradhros had of course checked with the guards on his way here, and had learned that no young woman had been seen. He trotted up the last few steps and appeared on the roof, a shadow against the stars. He seemed full of energy, striding toward the wall on the south side of the tower top where Leila had been standing earlier, and gazing out at the view. Clearly, he could not wait to relieve Zurina of her virginity.

Silently, Leila checked down the stairs to make sure no guards had decided to follow the prince up here. The temptation to do so, spying on his defloration of the girl he expected would soon arrive, would likely not strike until after the guards had gotten a look at her. At the moment, there were at least half a dozen witnesses to the fact that Prince Caradhros was alone here, atop the citadel.

The prince continued gazing out at the view to the south, anxiously waiting for his prey, when a guttural sound made him turn. The light was faint, but a reddish glow seemed to emanate from the tall figure standing ten feet away. "Caradhros," it said again, the voice half a panther's growl.

Leila had no idea what Kivuli's voice actually sounded like, but then Imbaso – who had actually witnessed the djinn's arrival within the inner sanctum – had reported that the djinn had not spoken. At least, not before Imbaso had fled the scene. But something between human speech and a bestial growl seemed like a good bet.

The eyes glowed golden in the dark, and Caradhros cried out, "Lord Kivuli!" Proof enough, right there. Obviously terrified, the prince babbled "What do you need from me, lord? Was not the child of my body enough?" The "nice, handsome" prince had sacrificed a baby of his own to the djinn? Leila was rapidly losing any regrets she might have had.

"You hunt, tonight?" the apparition growled.

"Yes! Fresh young meat!" Caradhros replied. "A virgin, recently arrived from the hinterlands. Do you want her? I had meant only to take her maidenhead and cast her aside, but if you desire her blood she is yours!" He seemed to be on the verge of soiling his fine garments. Clearly, Kivuli inspired terror more than love and devotion in his followers. And clearly, it was time for Caradhros to die.

The dark figure confronting the prince seemed to loom even larger somehow, though it had not moved. "I tire of unwilling sacrifices," it said. "I demand true faith, true devotion!" Caradhros cowered still more. His relatively pale complexion grew ashy in the dim light.

"Whatever you wish, master!" he promised. "Ask and I shall give it to you."

"Jump from the tower," the figure the prince took to be Kivuli growled.

"B-but I will die," Caradhros protested.

"AM I NOT THE GOD OF DEATH?!" the apparition demanded, growing another foot. "I will protect you, you will not die! But you must show your faith by jumping willingly. Will you jump, or will I have *your* blood, in place of this girl you thought to offer me?"

The prince raised his hands in supplication. "I understand, and I will obey, lord," he said. No need to tear me limb from limb, here I go, no worries, right? Leila thought as Caradhros climbed up onto a crenel. The young man was not entirely without courage. "Hold me to your breast, lord!" he called, and leaped out into space.

Chapter 53

Invisible once again, Leila went to the wall and watched. Caradhros was visible only as a rapidly-dwindling dark shape against the torchlight in the compound. He screamed briefly as he realized that his god had lied about saving him, then she heard a faint "thump" followed by a big commotion as the startled guards rushed to the motionless corpse. There was a slight chance of surviving a fall like that, but it appeared this had not been Caradhros' lucky day.

Leila went to the opposite side of the clock face that was the circular tower top and crouched, invisible, as she waited for guards to come up. Two that had been stationed on the rectangular roof below the tower hurried up with torches, checking to see if there were any intruders or signs of a struggle. They found nothing. Seemingly the handsome and charming Prince Caradhros, who had often used the tower top as a site for romantic assignations, had gone mad and thrown himself off.

There would be no further reason for guards to come up here now those two had left, and this seemed as good a place as any for Leila to call Betsalel. The god manifested at close to seven feet high, seeming to welcome the wide open space. She'd been keeping him the size of a small child a lot, lately.

"Caradhros is no more," the god said. He had erected a bubble of protection encompassing the tower top, so no one could interrupt their conference.

"His god appeared to him and demanded a test of his faith," Leila said sardonically. "His faith was strong, it proved, but as it happens also unjustified." She remained invisible, so her expression of grim satisfaction went unseen.

"Imbaso has asked Farendhi to take him out on the town tonight," Leila informed her god. "We intend that he, and probably Mdaleye as well, should die at the hands of footpads. Could you tell me where Imbaso is, now?"

"I can guide you to him," Betsalel replied, "but he is a long way from here. How will you get there?"

Going to the stables for her horse would be a lot of trouble at this hour, and take time she didn't want to waste. "I suppose you can't transport me?" she asked.

"I could become very much larger and carry you," he said thoughtfully. "And cloaked in shadows none would see us. But the risk to passersby and property would be great, and damage hard to explain."

"Can you do for me what you did for Nimble?" Leila asked next, reverting to the name she'd given the horse when she'd first acquired him. He'd been Wapesi for months now.

"Certainly," the Shadow God replied, putting a hand on her shoulder. When he was manifested in this plane he could affect things from a distance, but he always seemed to want physical contact for conferring blessings. Leila felt a little surge run through her, all fatigue melting away.

"Will it hurt you if I carry you in my pocket?" she asked.

"Not at all," Betsalel replied. He shrank to around six inches in height and she picked him up, then he shrank still smaller until he was no more than an inch tall. She tucked him carefully into an upper pocket of her tunic.

She and the god in her pocket were now invisible. "Release your sphere of protection, so I don't push people aside as I move," Leila requested. Then she erected her own sphere of silence and began going down the long spiral staircase. The guards who had come up earlier were back on their station, but noticed nothing as she crept silently past.

Caradhros had leapt with such enthusiasm that he had cleared not only the staircase but also the rectangular building at the tower's base, landing on the stones of the courtyard a few feet in front of the building. That area was ablaze with light as a dozen or more torches had been brought out. Officers, medical personnel, and investigators had been called in and while some had turned the prince over and straightened out his limbs others were interviewing the guards who had passed him through this evening.

All would have the same tale to tell: the prince had arrived a few minutes before moonrise, happy and confident and asking whether a young girl had yet arrived. When told that one had not, he smilingly told them to expect one soon, showing his token, and to send her up to the tower top. No, the girl had not come, they would all say, not even to the outermost gates. If she had arrived after the prince had taken his dive, perhaps the commotion had frightened her off.

Leila moved carefully, silent and invisible, across the crowded courtyard and out through the main gates. "Which way shall I go?" she asked the god.

He spoke now in her mind, saying "Turn left at the main road and go out through the south gate." Outside the guard compound almost no one was stirring at this hour, and she launched herself into a run.

The pounding of her boots on the pavement was hidden away by her bubble of silence, and she herself was nothing but a passing shadow. Leila's short stride didn't help her speed, but she was young and athletic and could move her legs fast. And now, with the god's gift, she could keep doing so for as long as she wanted to without tiring.

As she moved out of the south gate, the same way they'd come in by two days previously, Leila formed a thought in her mind. "Can we speak mind to mind, master, without my opening my mouth?"

"Of course we can," came the silent answer.

"Good! Where next?"

The god in her pocket directed the speeding Leila turn by turn through quiet residential streets and onto a thoroughfare lined with lights. It was not all that far from the palace, and she guessed this district must largely be supported by the wealthy royal family and their hangers-on. There were restaurants, taverns, and at least three establishments that were clearly whorehouses – judging from the scantily-clad women hanging out the upper story windows and calling cheerfully to passersby on the street below.

This brightly-lit business district was not what Leila had expected or hoped for. There was no need here to pass along expanses of quiet, night-dark streets to get from one establishment to another. One would not even need to get on one's horse, but could visit a dozen businesses just by walking along this one street. And no gang of footpads, however bold, would try to ply their trade here.

Even this late there was quite a bit of foot-traffic – much of it at least slightly inebriated. Near the end of the street connecting to the quiet boulevard they'd come down, there was a long hitching rail with horses tied to it. A boy of around twelve had been set to watch them.

"Where is Imbaso?" Leila asked silently.

"In the second tavern on the left there, where the music is coming from," Betsalel replied in her mind. She carefully looked over the horses along the rail. The third horse down from the far end was Imbaso's Kizuri, the pretty little Hisan mare. She had spent much time with this animal over the past month, and recognized a little bald patch on her chest – a minute scar from a mishap with a thorn bush when she'd been a filly.

But Leila had no idea which of the other horses belonged to Farendhi and, presumably, his man Mdaleye. Nothing for it but to scatter them all. The boy was leaning up against the wall, looking bored. A kid that age should have been in bed hours ago, no doubt, but when you were poor you did whatever you could to make a living.

Invisible, Leila went down the rail loosening the reins of each horse in the line. She radiated a slight scent of hay, which seemed to calm them. None reacted unduly to her ghostly presence. Keeping a tight grip on Kizuri's reins, Leila changed her illusory scent to an overpowering musk, the smell of a large cat on the prowl.

In an instant the line of horses dissolved into shrieking, whinnying panic. Tugging at their reins in an effort to get away from the odor that meant mortal danger to any four-footed grazer, the horses all came loose at once and began running in all directions. All except Kizuri, who reared in panic – unable to run because of Leila's grip on the reins.

Leila had already canceled the wave of lion scent, but enough of it lingered to keep the horses on the move. She vaulted into Kizuri's saddle, rendering the horse invisible, and rode her off fast down the street – looking for a nice dark alley. She soon found one. The bright lights of the entertainment district were all very well, but some seekers of entertainment required darkness for their transactions. In the confusion, no one noticed.

The alley ended at a crossing alley far enough away from the well-lit street that little of that light reached its end. "Can you hold her while I go get Imbaso and his companions?" Leila asked.

"I'll put her to sleep on her feet," Betsalel replied. "She'll waken at a touch." They left the sleeping mare standing with her head halfway down, hipshot, and returned to the main street. The boy whose job it was to watch the horses was frantically trying to round them up, and many of them had settled down now that the cause of their panic had vanished. Too soon!

Leila sent out another, still more powerful wave of musk and once again the horses began milling, rearing, squealing, and running off. Most of them had been trained to stop when their reins were hanging down, but their mortal fear of lions (creatures that had surely been a major predator on their ancestors) had them too panicked to obey their training.

Going visible in the semblance of the horse boy (who was now running down the street half a block away trying to catch some of his charges), Leila ran to the door of the tavern where Imbaso and his companions were drinking and enjoying the music. Ooh, there was a dancer, too – the kind of harem dancer she'd envisioned before she'd ever visited Palambo. Actually there had been nothing of the sort to be found in the palace's actual harem.

"Anybody here have horses outside?" the boy bellowed. "They're all loose and running around! Come help!" With that he darted back outside the tavern and immediately vanished. Moments later half a dozen men came out through that door, looking around anxiously for their mounts. Confusion still reigned.

Ah, there was Imbaso – and with him were Farendhi, and Mdaleye... and Utruri! Shit. The man had *not* gone home to his wives and children as his late, lying brother had suggested. How the hell was one small girl, however lethal an assassin, supposed to masquerade as a large enough group of footpads to take down four armed men?

But he *was* on her list. The three had split off from Imbaso, who was looking around trying to make sense of what was going on. Leila slipped up beside him and murmured, "Imbaso, it's me! I scattered the horses to get you out of there. Kizuri's waiting for us down the alley over there on the right, but I don't see how we're going to handle this many people."

The chaotic scene was such that nobody was paying any attention to Imbaso, but a bubble of silence ten feet across wouldn't be much use. Instead he just murmured back, "I had no idea Utruri would be joining us. Did you take care of Caradhros?"

"Oh yes," Leila replied. "It turns out he was suicidal. Very sad." Imbaso grinned. He hadn't much liked the interplay that had been going on between Zurina and the striking-looking prince at the dinner table.

"Utruri's pretty drunk, though," Imbaso added. "And I'm not sure he's even armed. At least he's not wearing a scimitar. But Mdaleye is. And I'd bet he has other weapons on his person, too."

"Betsalel, can you help?" Leila asked silently. The god answered in both their minds. "Get them to tie their horses up again, and help you look for yours. When they have entered the alley, I will neutralize them"

"I thought they were protected from supernatural harm?" she asked, aloud but quietly this time.

"When I am manifested in the physical plane," the Shadow God explained, "I have some powers that are more physical than supernatural."

Within another couple of minutes all of the loose horses had been rounded up and tied to the rail again, amid much cursing. Utruri, who seemed to be a mean drunk, had had to be restrained by his companions from beating the hapless horse boy half to death, settling for a cuff that sent the lad flying. Leila came up in the guise of a nameless reveler a moment later and dropped a couple of gold asand into the boy's hand as she helped him up, saying "I know it was not your fault."

"Where the hell is my horse?" Imbaso was saying, as the four companions gathered in the road. Now that the excitement was over, the street was rapidly becoming deserted as patrons returned to the taverns and whorehouses. Farendhi was still trying to calm down his drunken nephew.

"There's no harm done, Utruri, relax! Your horse is back safe and sound, just forget about it."

"I'm half thinking somebody scattered all the horses just so he could steal mine," Imbaso said worriedly. "Kizuri was a gift from Father, and he'll kill me if I've lost her while out carousing!" Mdaleye held himself like a professional, his cold eyes assessing everything to be seen on the streets, but Farendhi was his usual calm, obliging self.

"You don't want to be searching down alleys in this district by yourself, Imbaso," he said, putting a hand on the younger man's arm. "Come on, we'll all go look for her together."

They formed up, Imbaso slightly in the lead, and went down the street to the first dark alley on the left. It was a short one, and dead-ended only a block or so away – more like an air shaft between buildings than a road of any kind. "Kizuri!" Imbaso called plaintively. "I know she'll come if she can hear me," he assured his companions, then added "If she's not halfway to the river by now being ridden by some horse thief…"

There were rats and garbage in the alley, but no horses. And no horse thieves. Across the road on the far side of the alley where Kizuri slept, Leila briefly became visible as she removed the tiny Shadow God from her pocket and set him on the sidewalk, where he grew to seven feet in height. Then both of them vanished again, as they waited for their quarry to emerge.

The alley they waited beside was the next one in the direction Imbaso and his party were searching, and he led his three companions into it with a certain amount of trepidation. "Kizuri!" he called, but it would require a touch to wake the mare and she made no response. "How far down does this go?" he asked, and

Farendhi replied "There's another alley at the end of this one. If your mare has gotten lost in the maze of streets here it may take a while for us to find her. But keep your eyes peeled. This can be a dangerous neighborhood."

Imbaso looked a little scared, and drew his scimitar. It was common enough for young men of high rank, all of whom had been trained in edged weapons since boyhood, to go around armed all the time as a sign of their status and wealth. Farendhi thought the boy was overreacting. He had a dagger on him, but had not brought a sword.

Imbaso was slightly ahead, the other three in a tight group behind him. Mdaleye had also drawn his scimitar, and was walking on the right side. Farendhi was in the middle, Utruri stumbling along on his left. And behind them, two menacing figures suddenly appeared. The one on the left was enormous, nearly seven feet tall, and appeared to be worst sort of armed robber. He held twin cudgels. His companion, a large man equally ill-favored, held a glittering dagger.

They came up silently behind the three men, and struck simultaneously. Leila judged Mdaleye to be the only serious danger, especially with his weapon out, and she made sure of him. Her assassin training had included hours of anatomy lessons – with books and with corpses – and she knew exactly where to place the razor-sharp dagger to sever the cultist's spine between the fifth and sixth cervical vertebrae. Fortunately he was not a very tall man.

As the scimitar clattered from Mdaleye's lifeless hand and the man himself slumped to the filthy paving stones of the alley, Farendhi and Utruri also collapsed, unconscious, from blows to the back of the head. Then Betsalel grew slightly and scooped up all three men like a shepherd gathering up lambs, carrying them further down the alley.

Imbaso turned at the groan that had issued from Mdaleye as he was struck, and goggled at the sight of the Shadow God, appearing to be an absurdly oversized street thug, picking up their three assassination targets. The smaller thug spoke to him in Leila's voice, warning him "Don't touch Kizuri yet, or you'll wake her. It'd be better if she were asleep while we finish this."

Betsalel dropped the three Kivuli cultists in the crossing alley a little way up to the left, then stood back (shrunken once more to human size, but still maintaining the illusion in case anyone should chance to see them), cudgels at the ready, as Leila began working their victims over. "Go sit against the building over there, Imbaso," she commanded. "In case there are any unseen witnesses, I want your story to match theirs."

Imbaso was fine with leaving it to her, and he sank to the filthy stones and sat there, thinking "What in all the hells ever made me think I was cut out to be an assassin?" The Kivuli cultists were evil, they were plotting darkest treason, and they eminently deserved to die. Yet he was pathetically grateful that it was not actually *him* doing the killing. What kind of a man left such things to his girlfriend?

As he sat there half-dazed and miserable, Leila quickly stripped the unconscious men of everything they had on them that was of any value. This included their fine embroidered tunics and silk trousers, their weapons (in addition to the scimitar, Mdaleye had also carried four daggers and a garrote), jewelry (including their Kivuli cult pendants, which she gave to Betsalel to destroy), and of course cash. Then she slit the throats of Farendhi and Utruri. It was what any self-respecting robber would do, to assure no witnesses were alive to testify against him.

Farendhi's personal assassin was already dead from the dagger cut through his spine, by the time she'd finished robbing his companions. She didn't bother with his plain clothing, but took his weapons and money. There had been little blood from the wound. Now it was time to deal with the fourth member of the party.

"Imbaso," Leila said, as the disguised god continued to stand guard, "You and your companions were searching for your horse, and saw her disappearing down this alley. You were set upon by two enormous thugs, who killed Mdaleye immediately with a knife from behind and knocked the other two out, then went after you. You had your scimitar out and managed to wound the gigantic one slightly, but then he caught you a glancing blow on the temple and you were knocked cold. They turned their attention to robbing your companions, and when you awoke to see them at their work you crept away into the darkness and fled after your horse."

He was back on his feet, shaking slightly with adrenaline. "Swell," he said. "Then what do I do?"

"I think you run Kizuri as fast as you can back up to the palace, and tell the first guards you see what happened. Can you find your way back?" Imbaso was shaken but had been drinking far less than he had appeared to during the evening.

"I'm all right," he said with determination – willing it so.

"Give me your scimitar," Leila said. She could see he was very upset by what had happened and longed to give him a hug and a kiss – but she wasn't ready to release her illusion yet and she doubted a show of affection from a six-foot street thug would be all that comforting.

Imbaso realized he was still holding the sword, white-knuckled, and he handed it over. She carefully applied a little blood to the blade, not too much, and then set it down near one side of the alley in among a pile of trash. "That's where it fell when you were knocked out," Leila said, "and the thieves were busy with your companions. Before they had a chance to go looking for it, they got scared because you'd escaped so they beat a hasty retreat and didn't add it to their loot."

Imbaso managed a weak smile. "Good," he said, "I'm kind of fond of that blade. And it's worth a lot of money."

"Always thinking of you, love," Leila assured him. This was all going on within a bubble of silence, in near complete darkness. She didn't fear anyone would see them… yet.

"So, I guess you're going to have to sock me on the head?" Imbaso asked, not liking the idea much.

"No need for that, beloved," Betsalel spoke up. He had been a silent, hulking presence in the darkness for so long they had nearly forgotten he was there. He put a hand to Imbaso's forehead and a lump appeared on it, a small oozing cut in the center of it. A few spatters of blood appeared on his clothing, and he became grimed with alley dirt.

Imbaso raised his hand to his head. "Hey," he said, startled, "it actually hurts a little bit."

"That's to remind you it's there," the Shadow God assured him. "It would be unseemly for a man with your injuries to be going around as if he felt perfectly fine."

"Right," Imbaso said.

"Go on and wake Kizuri," Leila told him. "It might be best to lead her down the alley so the smell of blood doesn't make her run off again. Then ride her out of the alley and gallop off for the palace. We'll be along later."

Imbaso did as instructed, and the two thugs turned to examine their handiwork. The larger now had a sackful of loot taken from the three corpses. After surveying the "crime scene" and making sure nothing looked out of place, they moved back into the alley they'd come in on earlier. At the spot where Leila had knifed Mdaleye she said, "Can I have a little bit of light, master?"

"Use your imagination," the god suggested. The illusion of the smaller thug sprouted a lit candle in his hand, and it *cast a glow on the alley's floor!* Amazing, Leila thought, as she stooped and checked hastily to see if any blood had spilled. Such evidence would not have been in keeping with Imbaso's story; but there was none.

The candle vanished, and the two dashed out of the mouth of the alley and turned right, running down the lit street before vanishing into another alley mouth on the left side. Probably a few of the people still out and about on their revels would remember seeing two such large and scary-looking individuals.

As soon as they had gone a little way down the last alley Betsalel resumed his customary shape. "Thank you for going in disguise for me," Leila said. She knew it was uncomfortable for any of the gods to diverge from the forms they'd been given by their worshipers. She dropped her illusion and went invisible, while the god shrank again to a size small enough to fit into her pocket. He remained manifested, though, lest she encounter more obstacles.

After all this excitement and physical activity, Leila was beginning to feel sleepy and psychically tired. But physically, she was fresh and ready to run. Yet she was in no danger of catching Kizuri. They had heard the horse galloping down the road off to their left when they'd come out of the alley a couple of minutes before.

It was now around one in the morning, Leila thought as she ran through the darkened streets of Iskand moving up the hill toward the palace's north gate. Fairly early, and depending on what Mauaji and his fellow Kivuli cultists had had on their agenda for tonight they might still be busy at the temple – or riding back from it. She was anxious that Usiku should be all tucked up in bed and long since asleep by the time they returned, and she increased her speed.

Leila did catch up with Kizuri, in a way. As she approached the south gate she spotted the mare standing with her reins down just inside it. A throng of guards, far more than the number who'd been on watch here when she came down an hour ago, were milling around near the east side of the gate, torches ablaze, and two of them were supporting Imbaso as he sagged between them. Tears were running down his face, as he gasped out the story of the terrible end to the evening's tavern-hopping.

My Imbaso is a pretty good actor, Leila thought with pleasure. Quarters were too tight for her bubble of silence to be effective, so she dropped it and moved silently around near the west side of the gate, where only one sentry stood guard. As she moved past she heard Imbaso sob, "He was the biggest man I have ever seen! As big as a house!"

Chapter 54

It had been a night of carnage, but not all of it had been caused by Leila and her cohorts. Breakfast in the Namei party's apartment was a somber occasion, delivered with stunning news by a gossipy serving maid. "The world is coming to an end!" she declared, half-terrified and half-delighted to be living in such interesting times. "His highness Prince Caradhros went mad and threw himself from the top of the citadel in the guards' compound. Some are saying he killed himself in despair because some woman had rejected him."

Eyes in the apartment turned to Zurina. Mbina was there in the apartment, or the reactions might have been a bit more pointed. The girl's face was a mask of shock. "I declined his invitation to meet him there, of course," Zurina said. "For a maiden to meet a man under such circumstances would be most improper! But he didn't seem all that unhappy about it. He was smiling, the last time I saw him. Maybe he had some *other* girl in mind."

"But that's not all!" the serving girl said as she laid out the trays and began serving breakfast. "Arch-priest Balzamo, who was not even that old, died last night in his sleep. And so did D'zenge, the arch-priest of Deline! That's four members of the Council of Eight dead in two days! They are saying that Betsalel is moving against the arch-priests of the other seven because he is angry at the decline in his worship. He can kill you with a thought, they say!" She shuddered dramatically.

She had been going to crow about the news of two princes and a servant from the palace having been murdered by footpads as well, the crowning piece of awfulness. But then she recalled that Imbaso, the young man sitting on one of the chairs in the kitchen with a bandage on his head, had been involved in that particular calamity. Better to keep her mouth shut while she was ahead.

Mauaji was burning to have a discussion with his team, and Mbina's presence was becoming an annoyance. "Mbina," he said, "my son was also involved in an unfortunate occurrence last night and I am not eager to have it become palace gossip. Will you please leave us for an hour, so that we may discuss this privately?"

"Yes, Bwana," the maidservant said. She whisked herself out the apartment door in an instant. She considered lingering in the hall with an ear pressed to the door, her curiosity piqued. But she was a sensible person, and soon decided against it. She had wakened in the wee hours of the morning when Zurina had crept in through the bedroom window, and knew that something was going on here. But the girl held a secret of Mbina's own, and she was bound to hold her peace.

All were present and accounted for but they had not all been up for more than ten minutes when the arrival of breakfast had put paid to any discussions. "Imbaso, are you hurt?" Usiku asked with the concern of a good friend.

"A little battered, but I'll live," he said.

"What happened?" she asked. Mauaji and his cohorts had apparently not returned until after Leila had come in, and seemingly they had not yet heard the full story.

"As you know, Cousin Farendhi invited me to come out with him and some companions to sample the Iskand night life," he said. He looked washed out, tired. Probably he had not had as much as four hours' sleep. Imbaso took a gulp of kaf and nibbled on a pastry, then had another drink. He looked grief-stricken.

"Everything was fine, we were having a blast," he went on mournfully. "He'd brought along his manservant Mdaleye and Cousin Utruri, your other dinner companion last night." He directed that last statement to Usiku.

"He didn't seem much interested in a third wife," she remarked coolly. "But his brother was hot to trot."

"We were enjoying the music and dancers at a tavern on the strip nearest the palace," Imbaso went on, "when suddenly the boy who was looking after everyone's horses along the block poked his head in and announced that all the horses were loose. We'd all left our horses hitched, so we ran out and found them running all over the place."

"Any idea what caused this?" Mauaji asked. There had been way too many coincidences last night, but rack his brain as he might he could not make sense of it.

"Utruri was convinced that the horse boy had done it on purpose, perhaps as a screen so that an accomplice could make off with one or more horses," Imbaso offered. The reason for the horse stampede was a weak spot in their story.

"Anyhow," he went on, "Farendhi and the others recovered their horses and hitched them again but my Kizuri was still missing. We went searching for her, looking down the dark alleys on either side of the main road. I was calling for her, but there was no response. Then as we went down another alley, I saw her and hurried toward her but she ran away! I think something must really have frightened her. There was a hint of the smell of big cat. Do lions or leopards ever come into the city?" he asked the room at large.

The three older men had all been here before. The eldest of them, Sumundi, said "Sometimes in very severe drought years, leopards have been known to come into the city seeking prey. There are no lions near enough, and leopards are more likely to take a man than a horse. But a horse would certainly be frightened of a leopard." None of them said what they were thinking, that their god took the form of a black leopard nearly the size of a lion.

"The animal that most often preys on man is man," Imbaso said ruefully. "We turned down an alley crossing the one we had entered on, and were taken from behind by two footpads. I was ahead of the others, Kizuri in my sights, and noticed nothing until I heard Mdaleye groan. When I turned, all three of my companions were down and the largest of the footpads was nearly upon me."

"A very large man?" Mauaji asked.

"Huge, Father! I would guess he was nearly seven feet tall! Surely there cannot be that many known felons of such outlandish size operating in Iskand. I hope the guards will soon find him and his companion, and bring them to justice!"

The group were working on their breakfast, while riveted by Imbaso's tale. He continued, "I had my scimitar drawn, and I attacked the cutthroat though he towered above me. I managed to cut him on the arm, but his reach was enormous and he struck me with his cudgel." He very lightly patted the bandage on his brow.

"This robber was armed with a cudgel, not a sword?" Mauaji asked, "So your companions had been knocked out and not killed?" Imbaso lowered his head, shoulders slumped. He had had the chance to save them, however small, but had failed to do so.

"I imagine they didn't want to get blood all over the fine clothing of their victims, thus lessening its resale value," he said bitterly. "I awoke from unconsciousness after the cudgel blow to find that my scimitar had fallen from my hand was lost in the litter of the alleyway. The thieves were dim shapes in the darkness, bent over my companions and apparently robbing them of their valuables. Weaponless and dazed, I got to my feet and ran on down the alley as quietly as I could. I spotted Kizuri standing near its exit and called to her, and this time she came to me. Then I just mounted her and dashed for the palace."

"Then you reported the crime to the guards?" Mauaji asked. His son nodded feebly.

"They sent a squad to the location I'd described to investigate," he said, "but before they had returned the medic they had brought for me decided that I should be escorted back here. No one had yet returned from the temple, and I was just tucked into bed and then left. My head was aching abominably, but somehow as soon as I lay down I just fell into unconsciousness."

So, Leila thought, Imbaso got more sleep than I thought he had. He was probably in bed not long after I got in. Mauaji rose to his feet. "We must find out what happened!" he cried. He and his party had come in, also by the south gate, but more than an hour after the excitement had died down. No one had even mentioned to him that his son had been injured.

Maybe we were too quick to dismiss that gossipy maid, Mauaji thought as he stepped outside the door. He walked down to the junction of this hall with the corridor crossing it, and found a guard. "What do you know of the events last night in town involving Prince Farendhi?" he demanded sharply.

The young guard had come on duty only an hour before, but there'd been plenty of news circulating. The twin occurrences of Caradhros' fall from the citadel and Farendhi's demise at the hands of footpads had been the talk of the barracks. Then he realized who he was talking to. "You are Mauaji, father of Imbaso?" he asked, and the older man nodded curtly. "I think you had better speak with my commanding officer," the guard said crisply. He stopped a passing servant and ordered him, "You will go immediately to the guard headquarters and request that Commander Lmambela accompany you back here. He is to speak with arch-priest Mauaji regarding last night's incident in Iskand."

The servant ran off immediately, and Mauaji found that his fangs had been pulled. There was nothing he could do to obtain information any faster. "Thank you, guardsman," he said stiffly, and went back to the apartment. The rest of the occupants eyed him questioningly. "They are sending an officer to inform us of the outcome. Meanwhile, we may as well finish breakfast."

They all dug in, Imbaso eating more than you might expect for someone who seemed so weak and shaken. Leila was a little short on sleep, but felt absolutely marvelous. Betsalel's gift of tirelessness was like a permanent health tonic. Was this how Wapesi had been feeling, all these months?

The food had been consumed and the trays and plates stacked for the servants to carry away, before a knock came at the door. Mauaji opened it to find a guard officer on the other side, wearing a headdress covered with ostrich feathers. "Arch-priest Mauaji?" he asked, and was admitted.

The nine of them were spread around the sitting room, all of them looking intently at the officer who had come to tell them what they wanted to know. "I apologize that I was not here sooner," Lmambela said, "but I wished to give you time to breakfast before bringing you distressing news." He nodded toward Imbaso, still managing to look bruised and vulnerable even after consuming a hearty meal.

"I was not on duty last night when the incident occurred," the commander said, "But I have received a full report from the team who investigated it. I am sorry to tell you that all three of your companions, princes Farendhi and Utruri and the servant Mdaleye, were killed and their valuables taken."

There was a shocked gasp from Usiku and murmurs of regret from the rest of the party; save Imbaso, who hung his head in shame. "I was unable to save them," he murmured.

"You did what you could," the guard commander assured him. "There is no shame in being unable to defeat two such assailants, especially when you had lost your weapon."

Lmambela produced Imbaso's scimitar from a bag at his side, now cleaned of blood. "We found this amid a pile of rubbish in the alleyway," he said, "and your assailant's blood was on it. I hope that the wound on his arm will help us to identify him, if he can be found."

"If only I'd run him through the heart!" Imbaso declared. Ease up on the drama, dear, Leila thought. But she was smiling inside.

The guard commander handed over the weapon to Imbaso, who reclaimed it eagerly. "The two thieves were seen running away from the scene of the crime at some point around the time that you managed your escape," he said. "They must have nearly finished robbing your companions and were about to start on you when they realized you had fled and would raise the alarm."

Imbaso looked a little pained, and Lmambela was eager to assure him there was no shame in it. "Had you not fled, your stripped corpse would have been lying in that alleyway beside those of your companions. Is it not better that you were able to bring the tale to the guards? At least we now know who we are looking for."

Imbaso nodded reluctantly. He might have done all right, but it was going to take a long time before the sting of his failure had faded. Mauaji thanked the guard commander, and ushered him out the door. Then the nine of them sat around looking glum. Finally Mauaji spoke. "Farendhi was our host, the man who invited us here in the first place. And his nephews were among our supporters and will be missed." No mention was made of the manservant/assassin, which left Leila wondering.

Mauaji went on. "But they are not about to kick us out of the palace, at least not yet. Things are very unsettled now, with the recent deaths of four Council members. The Council will soon be meeting to elect not just one new member but four of them, and until that has been completed the rest of you are more or less at your leisure. Enjoy your visit here in Iskand while you may. I will be busy."

Chapter 55

After the hectic, blood-soaked pace of the party's first two days in Iskand, the days that followed were like a pleasant vacation on a desert island. Though Mauaji had his suspicions, he lacked the information to know for certain that agents opposed to his plans were responsible for the death of all four of the Kivuli cultists within the walls of the palace compound – let alone that two of those agents were sharing an apartment with him.

Zurina dined beside Samindhi at the royal table that night, and was suitably impressed. But the next morning Usiku begged Mauaji to come up with some excuses for why he could not simply enter into a marriage contract with the earnest young man, as she had absolutely no intention of being married off. To anyone.

Kifozi had explained to him that the girl was anti-sex, having had a bad experience earlier in life. So to keep the household running smoothly he arranged for a succession of other princes to attend her. The chance to woo a beautiful young maiden only remotely related to them was something few princes would pass up, and Zurina's time was fully booked most afternoons.

Prince Samindhi, balked in his desires, became ever more adamant that the lovely Zurina would be his and his alone. He wooed her extravagantly every chance he got, pressing lavish gifts on her as well as on her father. Yet he could not seem to get a commitment from either of them. Zurina assured him that he was her favorite, but that the decision was up to Mauaji. And the arch-priest of Betsalel was often… unavailable.

The hour was late, and Mauaji was meeting with Couadin – Council of Eight member and arch-priest of Dionos in Iskand. They were in the priest's private quarters, and the young lady who had been sharing them with him had fled in a hurry when the black-clad stranger appeared. Couadin, more than a little drunk, couldn't figure out how Mauaji had gotten in. But he was sobering up fast.

This was the last of them. Mauaji and his Makucha Nyeusi team had not bothered to kill the Council members they considered to be soft targets. Kizhalo, the arch-priest of Betsalel here, was already in their hands. Astramba and Mbala, the arch-priestesses of Mira and Mulia, were just a couple of weak old women and it had required only the most veiled of threats from Mauaji to convince them to pledge their votes. He had given each of them the list of candidates to be elected to the Council, and they would vote for them.

Couadin was another story. A tall young man of Dareg ancestry but raised within the political hothouse of Iskand, he had decided to devote himself to the god of debauchery. But that did not make him a fool or a coward. "What the hell do you mean, Mauaji, coming here in the middle of the night and chasing off my mistress?"

"I mean," the tall priest of Betsalel said menacingly, "to discuss with you the forthcoming election in the Council."

The funerary rites for the second two arch-priests to die mysteriously in their sleep had taken place earlier today, and tomorrow the Council would meet. They planned to consider the candidates from among the priests of Belantos, Lucia, Andros, and Deline one god at a time, hoping to select a candidate at the end of each day's deliberations so that on the following day the newly elected Council member could join them.

"We start deciding on the new arch-priest of Belantos tomorrow," Couadin told him. "And will then proceed to the other three. We expect to have the Council back to full strength within four days. But what concern is it of yours? Kizhalo of Betsalel is still alive and well. Or is he feeling ill?" The young arch-priest glared at the man in black.

"Are you?" Mauaji said, glaring back, and Couadin recoiled slightly. It was well-known that among the Shadow God's powers was the granting of a quiet, painless death. This was usually prayed for by a person suffering pain or unbearable loss, or by the relatives caring for them – when a cure was out of the question.

Recently there had been a rash of people reporting that Betsalel had come to them, manifesting in his enormous idol within the sanctuary at the Temple of the Eight. Could it be that, buoyed by his resurgence in the Dominion, he had now decided to take a more active role in the lives of his worshipers in Palambo? And could that role include killing people randomly at the request of his arch-priest?

"What do you want?" Couadin demanded, voice trying to sound forceful but his fear beginning to show.

"Nothing much," Mauaji said soothingly. "Your colleagues have already agreed to aid me in this matter. I will give you a list of names, and you – and your fellow Council members – will vote these people into the offices so recently vacated by those who would not heed my instructions."

Well, *that* didn't sound so bad. It wasn't as if political maneuvering hadn't played a part in the Council's choices in the past. "Let me see the list," Couadin said, and Mauaji removed a sheet of paper from a pocket and handed it over. The four were all men, but Lucia had had men at the head of her religious hierarchy before. He knew them all, from his time on the Council – and they were all no older than he was. Some of them were younger! But other than their youth, about which he himself was in a bad position to object, he could see nothing about any of them that would make it a crime to select them.

"All right," Couadin said, "I'll do it. Trying to fill the Council up with young blood, are you?"

"Younger people are so much less likely to just pass away in their sleep, don't you think?" Mauaji remarked. "Though of course you can never tell…"

"I said I'd do it, all right?" the young arch-priest burst out. "Just… get out of my rooms, will you?"

"One more thing," Mauaji added. "I think it best that the Council's deliberations on each new member should still take a full day. We don't want anyone to think your decision was rushed."

With that, the black clad man turned and departed. Couadin, hands shaking, went over to the table and poured himself a stiff drink.

After a brief period of recovery from his injuries on the night of the robbery Imbaso had bounced back, once again out cutting a swath through the young, attractive, and female members of the palace staff. The four young assassins, already impressed with his prowess during the trip here from Namei, were relieved to see that the youngster had gotten over his injuries so quickly. He had become something of a hero to them.

Leila and Imbaso finally had time for love, more than they'd been able to enjoy since those few nights in Namei before the start of their journey to Iskand. One night, invisible, she led him up onto the roof of the citadel. She had no remorse over the fate of Caradhros, only regret that so well-favored a young man should have proved such a waste of a human life. The experience had not poisoned her enjoyment of this spot as the site for a romantic tryst. There was no moon at all until close to dawn, but they made love under the stars for hours.

Mauaji took his son aside, during one of the rare times when the two of them were together in the apartment. "Imbaso, I am pleased that you are having such success with the serving girls. But I really think it is time for you to turn your attentions to the princesses and more respectable young women here. You need to be considering a candidate for your first wife."

Imbaso's heart sank at that. They had eliminated all the princely Kivuli cultists within the palace, and for days he had hoped that had put a stop to the plot against King Omali's life. But here was Father talking about "first wives" again.

"Don't you mean 'wife' period, father?" Imbaso asked. "Or have you forgotten I'm not a prince?" Mauaji grinned slyly at his son.

"You're more of a prince than you think," he said. What, was his father about to reveal that it was not him, but some member of the royal family who had actually sired Imbaso? That was absurd. He decided not to press the issue.

Leila lay with her head pillowed on Imbaso's shoulder. Mauaji and his fellow Kivuli cultists were absent, and Zurina had told Mbina to take all the time she liked doing their laundry. Perhaps she would like the chance to steal away and spend some time with Ganibo? A couple of gold asand had been pressed into her palm, a tip for good service and a suggestion that maybe they could leave the palace grounds entirely and have dinner in a café. Imbaso was out tomcatting around again, and Zurina welcomed the chance for some quiet time to herself. She was thinking about sitting down and composing some poetry about Prince Samindhi.

The maidservant may have rolled her eyes a bit at that last statement. But the prince was young and handsome, and had been showering the girl with attention and gifts. It was only natural for her to respond – though their visit to the harem had suggested that Zurina had a bit more sense than that.

The rare opportunity to make love in a large and comfortable bed, with nobody else around, had spurred them to new passions. But now the glow was fading, and Imbaso had to broach the subject that had been bothering him. "Leila," he said, stroking her head as she nestled into him, "Father started talking about picking my 'first wife' again a couple of days ago. And when I made a joke about not being a prince, he said maybe I actually was one. What do you suppose he was getting at?"

"You look like a younger, much cuter version of him," she mused lazily, leaning over to kiss his left nipple. "So probably he's not trying to hint that you were secretly fathered by King Faraj during a state visit to Namei." She lay there resting peacefully, but her mind had been kicked into gear and she suddenly sat bolt upright. "Oh, shit!" she muttered, as Imbaso heaved himself up on his elbows and looked at her in concern. "What if your Father means to get the Council to put *him* on the throne of Palambo?"

Four days passed, and on each day the surviving members of the Council of Eight met and deliberated. At the end of each of those days, the number of Council members increased by one, and each new member had received the same instructions from Mauaji. On the fifth day, Mauaji told Kifozi "It is time."

Chapter 56

For a change all of the party from Namei spent the day in their apartment. Kifozi was closeted in his bedroom with one or another of the four young assassins during the afternoon, but he had no specific instructions for Usiku. She was to continue to dangle her lovely self as bait for the young princes around the palace, acting the innocent; but he had evidently decided not to give her any targets for assassination on this trip.

Leila had begun to suspect that, while the masters had clearly been impressed with Usiku's skills and the dramatic way in which she'd dispatched her "final exam" target, she had risen from apprentice to full member of the Makucha Nyeusi so quickly not because of her astounding prowess but because she was young and female and good-looking, and they had had no one else available with those particular skills.

She wondered what they would think if they'd known she had taken out four Kivuli cultists by herself. Well, with some divine assistance, it was true. Without any of the gifts she had received from Betsalel, Leila was a talented thief and a dangerous person to meet in a dark corridor – but that was about it.

Imbaso and Zurina hung around the apartment, he reading books to her. Both of them would probably have preferred to be elsewhere, wrapped in each other's arms – but they wanted to keep an eye on the Kivuli cultists and see what they were up to. There were so many questions: Why, since this trip began, had Mauaji involved Imbaso so little with cult activities, having him hide the fact that he was an acolyte of Betsalel (Kivuli)? How could Mauaji possibly hope to have the newly-packed Council elect him king, when none of his ancestors for more than a century had held royal blood?

They got no answers, and finally evening had come. Zurina had been invited to dine at the king's table with Samindhi again this evening, a signal honor, and she was wearing her best. The prince himself, accompanied by a manservant, stopped by the apartment to collect her and escort her to the dining hall.

The manservant walked two paces behind, there for propriety and protection but not wanting to intrude on his master's privacy. Samindhi took her arm, squeezing it slightly through the silken fabric of her dress. "You look beautiful, tonight, Zurina, absolutely stunning!" he said, gazing into her sparkling dark eyes.

Leila believed he meant it. The young man (a year older than Imbaso, it was true, but lacking the worldliness that his years of study abroad had given her lover) had, under the influence of her teasing and the obstacles Mauaji had obligingly thrown in the way of his courtship, convinced himself that he was completely in love with the young, lovely, but shallow and immature Zurina.

Perhaps he sensed her underlying shrewdness, and knew she'd make a good wife? Nah, he was just desperate to get into her pants, and since she wasn't putting out that desperation had risen to a fever pitch. Leila suspected that had the liaison with Caradhros gone the way the late prince had expected it to, he would simply have overpowered the hapless teenager by main force and left her bleeding and crying on the tower top to find her way home – ruined. Samindhi, by comparison, was a paragon among men. She rather liked him.

"Is the Council of Eight all patched up now?" Zurina asked innocently as they made their way along the corridors to the dining hall. They were a few minutes early for dinner.

"They announced the final appointment yesterday evening," the prince assured her. "The kingdom is now safe again, guarded by a Council ready to weigh in on complex religious matters or provide us with a new monarch should, the Eight forbid, anything happen to the old one."

Since the "old" monarch was Samindhi's own father, he could hardly say otherwise. "That's a relief," Zurina said. "It was very upsetting when all those people died in their sleep in just a few days' time. I certainly hope the same thing doesn't happen to your father!" Hint, hint.

"My father is extremely well guarded and watched day and night," the prince replied – showing himself not a complete fool. "Those poor priests slept alone, and three of them were quite old.

If there had been someone with them they could probably have been revived."

"So, when the Council has to choose a new king does it happen fast, like the new Council members?" The girl seemed unwilling to drop the subject. "I read that King Omali and Prince Vandao were kidnaped by the forces supporting Prince Rajari after he had old King Faraj assassinated. But your father and cousin were able to escape their captors and make their way to the capital before the Council had finished its voting. That must have taken a long time?"

Every time he believed Zurina was lacking in intellect, Samindhi thought, she demonstrated that lurking somewhere below that pretty exterior was a mind with the potential to be as sharp as his own. What a wife, what a partner, she could make! He must have her! "The voting has usually taken less time than that," the prince explained. The entire history of the Palamban royal dynasty had been required reading for the myriad young princes, and he'd paid perhaps more attention to it than most.

"So what delayed it that time?" Zurina asked. "It's almost as if the Eight wanted your father on the throne!" Divine intervention in human affairs was a reality in their world, and always suspected whenever an outcome was a surprise.

"I believe that it was partly the fact that King Faraj had been clearly murdered," Samindhi replied, speaking to her as an equal. Leila liked that!

"After the deceased king has been put to rest with the usual pomp," the prince went on, "usually no more than three days later, the Council is convened and anyone who wishes to propose a candidate for king may submit an application to them. Only candidates qualified by virtue of their royal blood through the male line can be considered of course, but that can also include some sons of concubines."

"Really?" Zurina asked, surprised. "I thought the children of concubines were considered to be commoners."

"Only the daughters," he replied, and went on. "Some princes apply on their own behalf, but that's a fools' move. You need a lot of political support to be a serious candidate for king, and it's expected that a highly placed supporter or group of supporters will submit the application on your behalf."

"So Omali already had an application submitted?" Zurina asked, connecting the dots.

"That's right," Samindhi replied. "Father was always well-respected among his generation of princes, the more so because he hadn't been sitting around on a velvet cushion but had gone out and worked for a living. But the candidate must actually be present on the date when the final selection is made, and no one knew what had become of Father. A fast ship had been dispatched to Marsine, but he and Vandao had vanished."

"Do you remember that time, Samindhi?" Zurina asked with a touch of the awe the very young can reserve for those just a few years older.

"I wasn't much above three," he replied. "Omaso says he remembers it, but he was only five so I doubt he truly remembers much. It's all in the history books, now." They were approaching the dining hall.

"So how does the Council decide on the applications?" Zurina asked. "Is there a deadline for submitting them?"

"All applications must be delivered to the Council by the end of the day after the late king's funeral rites," Samindhi replied. "But how long they take to decide on them depends entirely on the Council. They had no obligation to delay their decision until Father had returned, and if he'd been another few days later they probably would have moved on without him."

They had arrived, and Samindhi dismissed his servant and escorted Leila up onto the dais. The room was beginning to fill up, but the royal table was less than half full and the king and his wife had not yet arrived – nor had the Royal Taster. The prince pulled out a chair for Zurina and seated her. They were on the opposite side of the table and down a couple of seats from the king's place, on the side where Dasembi would sit. But it was still a great honor for the young arch-priest's daughter from Namei to be seated so close to her king.

"Thank you for the history lesson, Samindhi," Zurina murmured to her companion as he sat beside her. "Things here in the capital are a great deal more interesting than they were in Namei. I'm glad I came!"

"So am I," he replied, squeezing her hand.

The hall filled up with people. With her back to the tables below, it was hard for Leila to see whether all of the party from Namei were in their usual seats without craning around. Beneath Zurina's calm cheerfulness her anxiety was rising. Now that the Council was complete, could it be long before the Makucha made its move? She had done her best to present Omali's security precautions as nearly undefeatable; but even she, novice assassin that she was, could think of half a dozen ways in which he might be dispatched. A lot of it depended on whether they cared about creating the illusion that the king had died of natural causes, or from an accident.

Presumably the way for Mauaji's candidate, even if it were himself, would be smoothed if Omali – a man in his middle fifties, after all, the age when many men drank or ate themselves into an early grave – were seen to have expired without help. Perhaps he would die of a heart attack while servicing his insatiable teenage bride?

Leila's appetite was impacted by her worries but the food was absolutely superb and she couldn't help enjoying it. Wines were poured with each course, first a light, pale, and delicate vintage from the central Dominion. It had been kept cool in cellars carved out of the bedrock of the hilltop on which the palace sat, and was so delicious she let herself have two glasses.

Everyone seated near enough to the king to be sharing the same bottle waited for Dasembi to have some, though. This little fact was so very out of keeping with the relaxed, festive atmosphere. The Royal Taster took a hearty swig from the king's golden goblet, then washed it down with a swig from his own. Everyone laughed and smiled, and joined in. Hooray, we're not all about to die a horrible death!

The king's guards were prominent around the perimeters of
the room, with the largest group of them standing along the wall
that backed the dais. Their eyes were alert, constantly watching for
any signs of threat as their monarch wined and dined with his
subjects.

But servants were still more numerous. It took an enormous
cadre of serving maids and men to keep that hall full of palace
residents constantly supplied with food and drink. They were
nearly invisible – all subservient, anonymous, clad in their blue
livery. Leila glanced up from a particularly succulent bite of lamb,
marinated in herbs and oil and grilled on skewers, and was stunned
to recognize the face of Zhendibi beneath a mop of black curls and
a blue kerchief.

He was the youngest and prettiest of the four Black Claw
assassins master Kifozi had brought with him on this trip, and not a
tall man. He looked quite comely in his maid's outfit, padded out
on top to give him a generous bosom. He did not make eye contact
with her as he poured the wine, a light red for this course.

Usiku's relationship with her fellow assassins had not
deepened much during the more than a month they'd spent
together, and Leila suspected that master Kifozi had warned them
off of her. He didn't want his tasty tidbit's attention distracted by
romantic entanglements, and her declaration of being a rape
survivor must have had some effect.

Dasembi drank from the king's cup, and then from his own.
He was of an age with the king, a lifelong friend, and his capacity
for alcohol must be stupendous. He remained jovial and showed no
signs of growing incapacitation despite who-knows-how-many
cups of wine during the evening so far.

By drinking the wine directly from the king's own drinking
vessel, and eating samples of the food from the king's own plate
using the king's fork, Dasembi warded his monarch against the
possibility that the poison was in the cup or on the plate or
silverware.

Leila relaxed fractionally after Dasembi drank from the cup
Zhendibi had just filled. He showed not the slightest signs of

distress, and she finished her lamb. These massive feasts left her feeling bloated. How was it that everyone in the palace was not as big as a house? Most of them did no exercise that you could notice. Perhaps it was some magic of the royal blood, a natural tendency to remain slim despite overindulgence and inactivity.

Zurina rested, letting the next course and its accompanying wine pass her by. Samindhi was happily digging in beside her. "Zurina, you should try this dish!" he urged. "It is amazingly delicious!"

"Oof, I'm getting full," she replied prettily. "Can I have a bite of yours?" she asked, and he presented a mouthful of it on his fork. Ooh, it *was* good! It seemed to be yams that had been baked with a thick, sweet sorghum syrup.

"It *is* delicious," Zurina assured her companion, "but I am just too full to eat anything for a while. I need to let it all slide down."

"Don't worry about it," Samindhi assured her, as he continued eating. She was such a little thing, it was no wonder she could not keep up with him. And all to the good – she would not be getting fat as she began bearing his children.

If Zhendibi was not here to poison the wine, what was the plan? Leila wondered. Had he been laid out as a necessary sacrifice to achieve Mauaji's goal, driving a dagger into the king from behind before being killed himself by the guards that surrounded him? She felt an absurd touch of sorrow at that thought. Her fellow assassins were ordinary, personable young men – but they were also cold, merciless killers. Just like me, she forced herself to add. It almost made her want to break down and cry.

The "serving maid" was there again, pouring a new vintage of deep red wine as another meat course was served. This was a beef dish, almost worthy of inclusion in Dominion cuisine. The meat had been simmered for hours in a broth of red wine, mushrooms, and other vegetables until it was reduced to a heavy, rich, meat porridge. It smelled wonderful!

Raised in the Dominion as she was Leila had developed a taste for the darker, richer red wines that often accompanied beef. She decided she was ready to have another glass, and nodded to

Zhendibi as he beckoned with the bottle. Samindhi took some as well. They waited while the seemingly illimitable Dasembi took a deep quaff from the king's goblet.

He smiled, enjoying the rich flavor, then took a generous forkful of the beef stew. "Delicious!" he exclaimed, and dug into the serving on his own plate. Omali smiled, his fondness for his friend plain on his dark face, and began eating his own serving of the stew. Then he washed it down with a deep swig of the rich, delicious red wine.

Everyone dug in, enjoying the course after the vegetable dish that had preceded it. Even Leila, already nearly bursting at the seams, had a few bites just because it was so good. When she considered her year on the streets of Marsine running with Tomas' gang of street urchins, she felt as if she had died and gone to Lucia's imaginary heaven.

But five minutes later, well before everyone was finished with the course, the king suddenly went ashen and a grimace of pain crossed his face as he dropped his fork and clutched at his left arm with his right. "Ungh!" he said, sagging in his chair as his young bride turned to him anxiously. "My heart!" he groaned, and collapsed.

Linda was on her feet in an instant, calling to the guards that lined the wall behind them. "His majesty is having a heart attack!" she cried. "Take him to his quarters immediately, and call the royal physician!" Everyone at the table went into a panic, Zurina in particular as she clutched her companion's arm and burst into tears. Beneath the mask Leila was thinking, nyoka venom. It had to be.

When the nyoka, a small and inconspicuous snake native to the savannah regions of Palambo, bit you, you died in violent convulsions. But if the snake was captured and its venom milked from it, that venom mixed with a stabilizing chemical extracted from certain mined minerals, it became a poison that if ingested, soon entered the bloodstream through the stomach and produced heart palpitations which would accelerate until the victim collapsed and died.

This, and much more, had been part of the lessons Usiku had learned from master Sumundi. The poison had an antidote, best ingested almost immediately after the venom had been swallowed. Or, it could be taken up to half an hour in advance. Dasembi had been dosed with the antidote in his own cup, while the king's cup had held the poison.

Chapter 57

The unconscious king was carried to his quarters, his young wife following anxiously behind as the king's personal healer was sent for. The lavish dinner ended in an instant, never reaching the dessert courses, as people rose to their feet in shock and began milling around anxiously.

Samindhi was disappointed that Zurina, the object of his affection, ran not to him for comfort in this moment of consternation but down off the dais and into the arms of her brother. Imbaso was standing there, dark eyes wide and glistening, with a look of extreme consternation on his face as his sister threw herself into his embrace and sobbed on his shoulder. "There, there," he said impotently, patting her on the back and looking at Samindhi with an expression that said "what can I do?"

The prince decided that he had better join his stepmother at the king's quarters, and told Imbaso "You all should return to your apartment. I'll come by later to see if Zurina is all right, and bring you news if there is any." Imbaso nodded, and with an arm around Zurina began leading her toward the exit. There was a flood of other diners doing the same. The door guards had remained on station, but they weren't trying to stop anyone from leaving. So far as anyone knew, the middle-aged king had been stricken with a heart attack.

When Imbaso and Zurina got back to the apartment, closely followed by Mauaji and five of the six Black Claw assassins masquerading as priests, they found Zhendibi already there. "I sent Mbina away," he said. "Told her the king had been taken ill and she should return to the servants' quarters and see if she was needed there."

"Good," Mauaji said shortly. The nine of them were milling around in the sitting room, energized and on edge. "Sumundi," the arch-priest asked, is there any chance the king may survive?" The old man shook his head.

"Unlikely. His healer is most probably a mage, and if he had been standing at Omali's side at the moment the king was stricken his angel might have effected a cure. But by the time the guards are able to carry him from the dining hall to his quarters, he will be dead."

Leila had a sudden wild impulse to dash to the king's quarters and call Betsalel to perform a resurrection. But that was too risky. She would reveal herself to the Kivuli cultists – and suppose Omali's soul had gone to join the One? There surely could not be many unsouled life forms near at hand for it to inhabit. She just had to accept the fact that Mauaji and his cohorts had succeeded in packing the Council of Eight with their supporters and killing the king, and start planning her next move.

An hour later Samindhi came calling at the apartment door, tears in his eyes, to inform the group that King Omali had died of a heart attack. Zurina cried again, this time hugging the prince instead of her brother. "When will the funeral rites be held?" she asked. "I will need to get some mourning clothes."

"Three days hence," Samindhi replied, "At the Temple of the Eight, ten o'clock in the morning. I fear I will be busy until then, but might you accompany me to the ceremony?" Zurina turned to look at Mauaji. Girls her age had no say in where they went or with whom.

"That will be all right," he told the prince. "Will you ride there?"

"I will come here to collect her," the prince said. "My mother and Omaso's, as well as Omaso and his First Wife, will be riding in the state coach. There will be room for Zurina as well." So, Samindhi was according Zurina status as if she were a member of the family! That spoke volumes about his intentions. But surely, they would all be here no more than another week. Then Kifozi was supposed to grant Usiku leave to go carry out her revenge near Halath. Alas, poor Samindhi – his hopes were doomed.

The Makucha Nyeusi crew, Usiku included, had now completed their main mission and were free to relax and enjoy their time in Iskand. The city was full of wonders, after all. Mauaji was not spending much time at the temple of Betsalel, but instead was out and about for hours during the middle of the day. That left Imbaso and Leila with the apartment to themselves for long stretches at a time, as Mbina had gotten quite used to being asked to take herself elsewhere and raised no objections.

Relaxing after lunch in the sitting room with his arm around Leila, Imbaso asked "What do you suppose Father is up to?"

"At a guess," she replied thoughtfully, "he's out either drumming up support for his bid to become king or using intimidation to prepare the Council members for passing a resolution to change the rules of eligibility. Or grant him special status, maybe."

"They can do it, if they want to," Imbaso said. "Until they name a new king Palambo essentially has no government. The royal army guards stationed all over the country are all pledged to defend the kingdom and obey its existing laws during these times of transition, but a strong enough leader might be able to get the guards here in Iskand to back him for a takeover of the throne, royal lineage or not."

"Really?" she asked, turning to look up at him. Imbaso's education in matters like history far surpassed her own. He probably knew more Dominion history than she did, even though she was the native there.

"It's how the current dynasty came to power," Imbaso smiled. "A little over three hundred years ago it was a different royal lineage running things. But Selisi, a powerful general of the royal army and commander of the Iskand garrison, stormed the palace and executed the king for crimes against the people of Palambo. Then he offered the Council of Eight a choice between approving him or receiving the same fate."

"Crimes against the people?" Leila asked. "Was the old king that bad?"

"Something of a monster, the history books say. But of course the history books were written by the victors in King Selisi's little war. It was claimed that he forced people to deliver young boys to him for his pleasure, after which the children would be... disposed of."

"Ugh," his lover replied. "Probably he did deserve to die. But is that any worse than slaughtering babies for the appeasement of a bloodthirsty djinn?"

Imbaso bent over on the settee and rested his head on his arms for a moment, rubbing his eyes. Then he sat up again. "No," he said with a sigh, "it's not. If Father succeeds in coercing the Council of Eight to put aside the rules and elect him king, we will have no choice."

"You mean...?" Leila asked, a worried look on her face.

"Yes," Imbaso replied resolutely. "Mauaji must die."

Chapter 58

A layer of thick clouds rolled in off the Center Sea overnight, and the day of King Omali's funeral dawned under an appropriate gray pall. He had reigned for more than eighteen years, longer than many of his predecessors, and had not been an unkindly man.

The mood of Iskand was somber, and anxious. The events of the past week had been tumultuous and filled with unexplained and frightening events. And now the country was leaderless, at the mercy of a Council of Eight in which four of the members were under thirty and had been in their jobs for only a few days. Whom would they choose?

Zurina, cloaked and veiled all in mourning black, rode with Samindhi and his family in the royal coach and arrived at the Temple of the Eight an hour before the ceremony. Already the streets around the temple were filling with people, most on foot, coming to witness King Omali's final farewell.

The elaborately carved and ornamented bloodwood bier, atop which Omali rested, had been set on a specially-constructed stone platform in the center of the sanctuary – equidistant from the idols of the eight deities whose place this was. The arch-priest here had begged a boon from Andros and been granted it, preserving the dead king's flesh so that it would not begin to rot and smell in Iskand's warm climate.

Samindhi and the rest of his family, along with many other members of the royal family, were arrayed in a circle a respectful distance from the platform. It would not do to stand too close, for what was to come. Leila spotted Vandao nearby, and he looked racked with grief. She suspected Omali had been more of a father to him than Faraj had been. She wished she could approach him as herself again, but it was not yet time to let him know she was here.

So many members of the royal family thronged the sanctuary that no one not intimately connected by birth or marriage with the late king could even squeeze inside the building. The outer area and the slopes of the rise on which the temple stood were completely covered in people come to pay their respects. They would not be able to witness much of the ceremony.

Samindhi had not told Zurina anything about these rites beforehand (though she'd pumped him often for information about Palambo and its history and government), and they had not spoken since the evening of the king's death. As one of Omali's two eldest sons, the only two who were adults, he had been very busy with family matters over the past three days.

Zurina's artless and incessant questioning hadn't seemed appropriate during the coach ride here from the palace, and now no one was speaking at all. There was slight murmuring as people took their places, but for the most part they were required to stand there, neither moving nor talking, for nearly an hour.

At last the arch-priest, garbed in a robe of the eight official colors plus a black mantle indicating his role today as the conductor of funerary rites, stepped forward and stood near the center of the room beside the platform. He raised his arms, and from somewhere near where the circular part of the building joined the administrative offices at the back eerie music sprang up. There must be musicians hidden back there in the shadows behind the idols, Leila realized.

The music went on for two full minutes while the arch-priest continued to stand there with arms raised. Are his hands growing numb? Leila wondered. She had not attended any funerals since arriving in Palambo and didn't have any idea whether this music was a traditional part of death rites or something especially laid on for the king.

The arch-priest's arms fell, and the music chopped off abruptly after one final note. Then he spoke, his voice seemingly enhanced. Considering all the "enhancements" Leila had been granted as gifts of her god, it didn't seem unreasonable that this man who conversed daily with the Eight (or at least seven of them, up until recently) might have received the ability to make his voice heard over long distances.

"Citizens of Palambo!" he cried, and what little murmuring had been heard within the sanctuary died away. "We are gathered here to bid goodbye to King Omali, son of Simbanji, our good monarch who has ruled us happily for eighteen years."

The priest then launched into a biography of the late king, from his birth to one of Simbanji's innumerable wives, to his boyhood, his launching of his trading enterprise, and onward. All the events and accomplishments of his reign were enumerated, and Leila was beginning to sag on her feet. Samindhi, sensing her distress, put an arm around her and whispered into her ear, "Hang in there. Almost done."

Indeed, only a couple of minutes later the arch-priest had completed his recitation. And now something much more interesting occurred. Beginning with Andros and going around the circle, he called to each of the gods to appear. "Great Andros, I beg you to come to us and honor our fallen king!" With a shimmering, the god of all things masculine manifested in his idol and stood there looking down from the height of fifteen feet (plus the height of the column) on the dead king where he lay atop the bier.

"I come at your call, Entabi," he said in his deep voice. "I will do honor to Omali." Leila wondered whether Lucia would put in an appearance. She had not laid eyes on the Goddess of Light since she'd routed her so effectively last year in Parat's Temple of the Eight. From what Betsalel had told Leila of the nature of the shadow and illusion powers he'd granted her, Lucia would be able to see right through them. Just in case, she pulled her veil over her face and bowed her head, seemingly in respect and awe.

One by one the deities came, manifesting in their idols and remaining at the full height of fifteen feet. Most, Leila knew, would shrink to a more manageable size while talking with worshipers. But this was a ceremonial occasion, and they were here not to answer prayers but to perform a ritual.

Lucia did come. Seeing the ambient light brighten Leila risked a quick glance up and saw the goddess glowing white. She had adopted a veil of her own, it seemed, though that was not yet reflected in her idol. Rumor had it that Lucia was now starting to be cast as the goddess of purity, perhaps in a campaign to make people forget the lies she had told and the harm they had caused, centuries ago.

Seven of the eight now stood on their columns. Dionos had even arrived sober, for this was a sober occasion. Leila was still looking resolutely down at her feet, and was astonished to see an orange rose appear there. She glanced up at the God of Debauchery, and he winked at her before resuming his expression of seriousness. She gasped involuntarily.

Now at last the arch-priest Entabi came to the towering idol of Betsalel. He was an old man, and had performed this rite for King Faraj eighteen years previously. At that time, the Shadow God had not come. The denial of the arch-priest's call was considered to be sign of divine disfavor, a reproach to the deceased. But of all the Eight, Betsalel's favor was probably the least sought.

He had the feeling, from things he had heard from his fellow priests here, that this time would be different. And he was not wrong. "I come at your call, Entabi," the dark god said as he opened his sleeping eyes to reveal them glowing red. There was a gasp from the crowd filling the sanctuary. Betsalel had come! In that instant the process of restoring the Shadow God's religion within Palambo took its biggest leap forward since the campaign had begun.

Mauaji, Imbaso, and the six "priests" from Namei had not made it anywhere near the sanctuary. They had hired a coach to come here and pay their respects to the man they had conspired to murder, but had arrived too late to be more than halfway up the slopes surrounding the temple. Murmurs and rumors spread down the hill, "Betsalel has come!"

I thought that idol was dead, Mauaji mused when the word had reached them. He knew nothing of course, of the way in which the prophet and his followers had desecrated the idol that was too big to be removed from its column, only that it had never been the focus of worship using the Secret Scriptures – far too public. It remained in the shape of the old Betsalel, and that meant Kivuli had never manifested in it. Had the god reverted back to his old form for the sake of this solemn occasion? The Kivuli he knew would not have the cunning to undertake such a deception.

When all Eight of the deities had gathered, the arch-priest spoke one last time. "Our gods and goddesses have gathered to do honor to King Omali," he declaimed. "Let them shepherd him into the next world." With that he stepped out to the rear of the sanctuary, and the eight deities bent their gazes on the corpse of Omali. It began to glow white and black, green and red, yellow and brown, purple and orange. Then the nimbus of light became flames, consuming the wooden bier and the man upon it. Billows of similarly-colored smoke arose toward the sanctuary's high ceiling, entwined like a rainbow. Then each color split off in a separate column, and was inhaled by the god or goddess whose smoke it was.

Leila was fascinated, and forgot to hide her face as she looked up in wonder at what was happening. Omali's soul would have long since fled, unless maybe it had decided to wander the palace as a ghost, moaning of poison and perfidy; but the appearance here was that the king's essence was being taken into the realm of the gods by the gods themselves. Quite a show, and probably a huge belief boost for the deities, too. They would emerge from this ceremony overflowing with power.

The smoke and flames died away in under two minutes, leaving only a small quantity of powdery gray ash on the stone platform. There were no scorch marks on it. The flames had burned hot and clean, yet the heat had somehow been contained by the gods so that none of it reached the onlookers.

One by one, the gods and goddesses once again froze in their traditional positions and became lifeless idols once again. Betsalel lingered though, looking down at Leila in her guise of Zurina. "Shall I tell them?" his voice asked in her head.

"No, please don't," she replied silently. "It could bring ruin on us all." He shook his head sadly, then closed his eyes and was gone.

Chapter 59

Zurina returned to the palace with the royal party in their coach, and Samindhi invited her to lunch with them. Omali's two original wives from the time before his coronation, and the children they had borne him, had all truly loved the man it seemed. Leila felt miserable in their presence, glad only that Betsalel had not announced to everyone that the king had been murdered.

Zurina begged to be escorted back to her apartment as soon as the meal was over, complaining of tiredness and a headache. Samindhi and his manservant delivered her there, and finding none of her family or companions yet returned from the city he kissed her thoroughly before leaving her to return to his family. Leila shed a genuine tear at the pain she had caused – and the additional pain she would be causing in the near future.

Mauaji led his party to a café a few blocks away from the temple. There was little said during their meal. Then he told them he would be back in the evening, and was gone. The rest of them were left to their own devices, and Imbaso walked back to the palace with the older men while the four young assassins went off for some fun in the city.

They found Mbina straightening up the apartment and scrubbing the kitchen area. She told them quietly that Zurina was lying down. Both Kifozi and Sumundi indicated that seemed like a good idea after their long walk up the hill, so Imbaso announced he was going to go visit a friend and left again by the front door.

Fifteen minutes later he was climbing in through Zurina's window, which Leila had evidently left unlatched for him. He was surprised to see a girl who looked like Zurina asleep on the bed. Moving in a bubble of silence across the room, Imbaso stood at her bedside, reaching out to stroke her shoulder. "Leila?" he said.

She rolled over and sat up, transforming before his eyes into the woman he loved. Not that he didn't love her when she was being Zurina, but he enjoyed it most when it was just the two of them and she was nobody but herself. The fact that he was the only person in this part of the continent who knew her thus made him feel as if she had given him a rare and priceless gift.

Leila made room for him on the bed and Imbaso joined her, drawing her into a tight embrace. She hugged him back with ferocity. "What's the matter?" he asked, though he knew.

"Oh Imbaso," she said forlornly. "We should have tried harder, should have found a way to save Omali!" She felt the sting of her own cowardice in the face of the grief that had come to others because she had been unwilling to risk her own life and Imbaso's to save the life of the king.

"Our mission for Betsalel is more important than the life of a king, any king," Imbaso replied – trying to make her feel better. Though he, too, was haunted by regrets. What if Leila had gotten into Omali's bedchamber after hours and brought the god to speak with him? Might he have used his nearly limitless royal powers in the cause of rooting out the Kivuli cult? It was no use speculating. That opportunity, if it had ever been one, had been lost long since. Now they had to face what the next few days would bring. Would he be forced to help assassinate his own father, the man who had loved him for as long as he could remember?

Leila hugged him tightly again. "You're right," she said, as if willing herself to believe it. As he squeezed her tight, Imbaso thought "Leila has all the skills to make a perfect assassin except one: she cares about human life. And for that I love her."

They sat on the bed taking comfort from each other's closeness and not speaking for a while. Then Leila seemed to shake herself out of her funk. Her life had been full of setbacks, and every time she had risen to the top. "The Council of Eight will convene tomorrow?" she asked, and Imbaso nodded.

"I checked," he said, "and they have their own special chambers in a building elsewhere on the palace grounds – it's not part of the palace itself."

"I would have thought they'd convene at the Temple of the Eight," Leila mused. "They're all arch-priests, after all."

"Hundreds of years ago they did," Imbaso replied. "But there are no really suitable spaces in the administrative and residential wing there. As the Council's powers expanded, they requested rooms more in keeping with their perceived importance and the king at that time – grateful to them for giving him his job, I would assume – had a special building put up. Some of the other rooms are used by the government bureaucracy, but there are offices for the individual Council members and a grand chamber where they meet formally."

"So, the public can come in and watch them at their work?" Leila asked, surprised. Such openness might work against the kind of schemes Mauaji was involved with.

"Oh no," Imbaso said. "The chamber is closed to the public when they are voting on new Council members or a new king. But it is opened to members of the various gods and goddesses' clergy when they're weighing on religious matters, and tomorrow it will be open between the hours of eight and five for the filing of applications for the office of king."

How bizarre, Leila thought. They treated the job of king as if it were no more important than that of, say, city mayor or town councilman – and then, once someone had attained the office, granted him the power of life and death over every man, woman, and child in the country. This place could *really* use a constitution!

"I think we need to be there tomorrow, to see whether your father proposes himself for king or has one of his agents do so," Leila said. "Perhaps if Mauaji shows up there in person with such an application, I can just quietly knife him when he leaves." Imbaso stared at her, feeling a stab of pain at the callous way she had made that remark. She looked back at him, and her face fell.

"I'm sorry, love!" she cried. "I didn't mean to be so insensitive. But we agreed he has to die, if he's going to try to put himself on the throne, didn't we?" Imbaso squeezed her tight.

"Yes," he said miserably. "But actually talking about killing him makes me feel... I don't know, like I'm four years old again and Bapa is the center of my universe, and something is threatening him. It's ridiculous, but it's how I feel."

Now it was Leila's turn to hold Imbaso tight. She had heard of having such feelings toward a father, but having grown up without one she couldn't truly empathize. And Imbaso's father had forfeited his right to filial love, at the moment when he put his infant nephew under the sacrificial knife – if not sooner. She didn't think that was the first bloody victim he had offered up to his twisted idea of a god.

"You stay here, tomorrow," Leila said, "and wait. Zurina is feeling unwell and will remain shut up in her bedroom for the day, and you'll stay here in case she needs anything – freeing Mbina to go on about her personal business. I have a suspicion that our black-clad buddies will all be out about their *own* personal business. And I'll be there invisibly, watching, to see what that business is."

"Better bring a bottle to pee in!" Imbaso said, breaking the tension. They both dissolved in gales of laughter, which progressed to tickling and hysteria, which progressed to a fierce and impassioned session of lovemaking. And at the end of it, peace.

Chapter 60

Well before eight Leila, invisible, was standing watch outside the main entrance to the building in which the Council of Eight had its chambers. She watched silently as the Council members made their way inside, as if they were ordinary office workers going to a job.

Entry was barred by a pair of royal guards, who admitted the arch-priests but allowed no one else inside until the stroke of eight. Leila was content to wait, eager to see who would be anxious enough to arrive with an application before opening time. She was disappointed. Seemingly anyone involved with the process that would produce Palambo's next king was *way* too politically savvy to show up early. As long as you made it in before the deadline at five, that was good enough. And apparently entries would be judged on style.

Leila remained at her post until nearly nine, before she finally spotted someone coming toward the building's front entrance. It was a small party of richly-dressed men she thought she recognized from the palace's dining hall, and she slipped past the guards and into the Council's grand hall ahead of them. Time to take up a position closer to the action.

The room reminded Leila of a description she had read in a book, of a courtroom in the Dominion. There were rows of seating on either side of a center aisle, and beyond that near the rear of the room was a long dais with a slightly curving bench like a desk on it. There were eight chairs behind it and in each of those sat a Council member. Two of them were elderly women, the priestesses of Mulia and Mira she assumed. And the rest were... not callow, certainly, but far younger than you might expect for such significant rank.

They were each clad in robes of their deity's color, which created a rainbow appearance across the length of the bench and also made it easy to name the participants. The black-clad arch-priest of Betsalel, surely a Kivuli cultist like the dark god's entire religious hierarchy now, was the eldest of them besides the two old women. And he was no more than forty.

The three men, probably princes Zurina had somehow managed not to meet, approached the dais and were directed to a desk on the right – where the Council's official clerk presided. The standard application form was available at some obscure government office at all times, and applicants were expected to have it filled out in full when they arrived on this day of days. Most in the room had not yet been adults the last time such an event had occurred. Leila had not even been born.

The clerk rose to his feet and cleared his throat. "I hereby receive your application on behalf of Prince Sendhal for the office of king of Palambo," he said in a loud and clear voice as if his audience consisted of more than the Council members, the petitioners, and one royal guard who was stationed inside to preserve order. The invisible girl in the corner didn't count.

The clerk went on, clearly enjoying his moment, his day, of prominence. "Your application will be considered to determine if your candidate is eligible for the office of king, and if so it will be included in those the Council will vote on tomorrow," he said. "I am advised to inform you that due to a special resolution of the Council passed yesterday, eligibility for the office of king of Palambo has been amended. It now embraces any and all males who are descended from a former holder of that office at a remove of three generations or less. This includes those who are so descended through the female line."

What?! The rules had just been rewritten, and there had been no public announcement? Growing up her whole life in an empire that was really a constitutional monarchy had ill-prepared Leila for understanding Palamban politics. How could a nation run by such insane rules (or lack of rules, entirely) have managed to dominate nearly a third of the continent?

Hadn't Imbaso said something about more than three generations removed from the royal line for Mauaji? Leila struggled to remember, but it had been only a brief remark and she hadn't been paying full attention. Three generations back meant that your great-grandfather, one of four that most people had, must have been king. Or one of your two grandfathers, or your father, obviously.

Omaso and Samindhi, and any of their half-brothers, would be eligible. But some princes who'd descended from old King Simbanji's brothers would lose their eligibility. The new resolution simultaneously expanded and contracted the applicant pool; and as Leila thought about it, it seemed more fair that way. They still weren't opening the office to women, and it would be a frosty day in Namei during Sunheight when that happened; but at least the male descendants of royal women now had a chance to be included.

One of the princes who'd brought forth the application for Prince Sendhal was at pains to mention, "Prince Sendhal is the son of King Faraj, and is eligible for consideration under the rules you have stated." The clerk thanked him for his time and set the day's first application on his desk. Then they all – clerk, Council, guard, and invisible witness – sat waiting for another.

It was half an hour before another arrived, and after that there was a steady procession of applicants until the clerk announced, "The Council will take an hour recess for lunch. Any wishing to submit an application may do so after one." Leila dashed out of the Council chamber, and began looking around for a privy. She should have taken Imbaso's suggestion more seriously, or perhaps not had that second cup of kaf.

After Leila had relieved herself she returned to her corner of the Council chamber and pulled the food she'd brought out of her pack. The room was deserted except for the guard, and as she was surrounded by a bubble of silence he remained unaware of her presence.

All that had taken but a fraction of the hour the Council had given themselves for the midday meal, and Leila moved silently over to the clerk's unattended desk to have a look at the applications that had come in. All of them had been neatly and carefully filled out, and all but one of them would be eligible for the office under the new rules.

The change – which Leila had to assume had been instigated by Mauaji, using whatever leverage he held over the reconstituted Council – had been so subtle one might hardly even notice it. She doubted there would be any repercussions, and marveled at the arch-priest's political skill. Her own skills in that area were those of a neophyte, and at this point she was wondering if they would get good fast enough to save them all from what was coming.

The Council of Eight re-convened at precisely one, and Leila refocused her attention. The eight men and women might almost not have been there, for all they had to do today; but she guessed it was required for form's sake. Suppose somebody had challenged their resolution? But no one did.

Finally at three in the afternoon, after the flow of applicants had begun to ebb, Mauaji himself appeared in the Council chamber. He was not dressed in the black robes of an arch-priest of Betsalel, which he had worn nearly every day since before they had departed Namei. Instead he was clad in rich robes like you might see on any of the princes who had appeared here today. Leila tensed.

If the clerk announced that Mauaji had proposed himself – which certainly seemed at odds with what she'd seen today – then Leila planned to follow him silently out of the chambers and prick him with a dart dipped in oualit. He would die of heart failure within another minute, as the poison found its way into his bloodstream and paralyzed his autonomic nervous system.

She felt sorrow for Imbaso, but neither he nor she was willing to see the Kivuli cult obtain ultimate power in Palambo. If Mauaji was here to propose someone else as a candidate – as seemed likelier considering that not a single application today had been filed by the person named – Leila would seek that person out and administer the same quick, painless death.

Mauaji stalked grandly up to the clerk's desk and handed over his application. After studying it for a moment, the clerk rose to his feet to begin his announcement. "I hereby receive your application on behalf of Imbaso of Namei, great-grandson of King Simbanji through his daughter Faranha, for the office of king of Palambo.

Your application will be considered to determine if your candidate is eligible for the office of king, and if so it will be included in those the Council will vote on tomorrow."

Chapter 61

"He *what*?!" Imbaso exclaimed, after Leila had once again gotten him alone and inside a bubble of silence within Zurina's room.

"Put in an application for *you*," she assured him. "All this time we've been imagining the darkest plots to place a Kivuli cultist on the throne, and it was *you* he wanted as king all along!"

Imbaso didn't know what to feel. That Leila had not arrived to tell him that his once-beloved father was dead was a relief. But he was having a hard time wrapping his mind around her news. "But I *am* a Kivuli cultist," he said at last in a small voice.

"It's perfect, don't you see?" Leila crowed. The evil Mauaji had exerted all of his dark powers for the goal of placing his son on the throne – a son who had been actively working against him for weeks.

"He must still believe me weak and malleable," Imbaso mused. "He thought it would be easier to put me on the throne and rule from behind the scenes, than to deal with all that would be entailed in becoming king himself."

"He's kind of old for a first-time king anyway, isn't he?" Leila asked.

"That's true," her lover replied. "He's past fifty. He and Mother tried for years before they were finally able to have children, and then they only managed me and Sadhima – and Sadhima died in the great fever. He must have figured that he could rule through me for a decade or two, accomplish all the sick goals of the Kivuli cult, and then die with a legacy he could be proud of." He put his head in his hands.

"What are the chances that the Council is going to elect someone else?" Leila asked. There had been some perfectly reasonable choices among the candidates for whom applications had been submitted – including her own father Vandao, a man with years of experience in the higher echelons of Palamban government.

"Shit," Imbaso said, still struggling with the enormity of Leila's revelation, "probably somewhere between nil and zero. He has the Council in his pocket. He planted four of them himself, and a fifth is his own Betsalel priest and therefore also a Kivuli cultist. They'll probably be announcing 'King Imbaso' before lunchtime tomorrow. The world has gone mad!"

In fact the Council waited until closing time on the following day to announce that they had made their choice: Imbaso of Namei would become King of Palambo at his coronation three days hence. The country was without a head of state in the meantime, but the pomp associated with such things took time – and it could not be brushed aside.

Those who knew Imbaso personally were mostly stunned with disbelief. He was a nice enough kid – but when, in all the history of the kingdom, had the Council ever elected a wet-behind-the-ears 21-year-old who had not yet taken his first wife? It was absurd! Others assumed that what they fervently hoped to be the case was fact – the Council knew what they were doing, they had chosen the best man for the job, and everything was going to be all right. All was moving according to tradition and plan.

Imbaso knew himself, and he was in the former camp. "Leila, how can I do this?" he demanded.

"Did you not live in Palambo all of your life until after your eighteenth birthday?" she asked in reply.

"Yes, of course! But I was never trained to rule, I have no idea how to do things!" he protested.

"As I understand it," she said, "You give orders, and people obey. Is that so hard to do?"

"But *what* orders?"

"Imbaso," Leila pleaded, "please calm down. You have a fine mind, it is part of what I love about you. Think about Palambo, think about what its people need. You will be a good ruler, the best this country has seen in generations!" She hugged him close, and he believed.

Another thought occurred to him. As soon as he had become king, people would be expecting him to marry and begin producing heirs. The fact that the king's sons were not necessarily any more likely to become king after he was gone made no difference. It was an aspect of manliness, an essential part of what Palambans expected in their king.

"Leila," Imbaso said, "marry me!" She gaped at him. It was supposed to be the fulfillment of every girl's dream of love. Had Tevo said that to her a year ago, she would probably have jumped on it and they'd have been wed by this past spring – right before Betsalel demanded her help with the problem in Palambo.

Now, her lover's impassioned plea filled Leila with an irreconcilable mix of longing, fear, and rejection. "Imbaso, I love you!" she declared. "But I was born and raised in the Dominion, and I am Betsalel's high priestess there. I cannot marry the king of Palambo and become the first of many women to fill his harem – isolated and without power."

As she hugged him tight, Imbaso thought it through. It was time for him to be bold, to throw off his fears and the chains of tradition. He was about to be handed more power than any other single individual in the world was able to wield. What would they do in the Dominion?

"Then," Imbaso said at last, "be my queen. I will take no other wives, and only our children will be eligible for the succession. We will rule jointly – I will make it happen!" He seized her hands in his, looking into her eyes. They still had a deeply-entrenched Kivuli cult and a thousand enemies to get past, Leila thought. What were the odds that the two of them would live long enough to see Imbaso's vision become reality? Hells, once Mauaji learned of his son's marriage plans, Imbaso might not live to see his coronation. "I'll do it," she said, and he seized her in an embrace he never meant to end.

Chapter 62

Though Imbaso was not technically king until after his coronation, he was the man the Council had elected to hold the job – and when he talked, people were willing to listen. At Leila's suggestion, he turned to her father Vandao for support. He was probably the most able man in the palace, after his years spent in his uncle's administration.

Timing was a problem. Leila insisted that she would marry Imbaso, and rule beside him, as herself – Leila, the half-Palamban high priestess of Betsalel born and raised in the Gaspari Dominion. But until Imbaso was king and could command the palace guards, Mauaji and his Makucha Nyeusi cohorts could not know Usiku's identity.

Having Usiku suddenly vanish, and Leila mysteriously appear – a girl exactly Usiku's size who looked just like her except for her coloring – would quickly reveal that she (and therefore likely, Imbaso as well) were working undercover against them. Mauaji was not a stupid man, nor were the master assassins under his command.

So Usiku, still masquerading as Zurina for the benefit of others in the palace – including her persistent suitor Samindhi – continued to stay near the apartment most days and apparently slept there at night. But appearances could be deceiving.

Mbandele, an expansive man in his late fifties, was chief of the palace's servant corps and had been, for many years, responsible for organizing all of its most important occasions: balls, weddings, formal betrothals, and the coronation of the late King Omali to name but a few. He liked that last assignment the least, as by law coronations must be planned and put into motion within three days – no time for the careful, consummate artistry he demanded in all his productions.

When Imbaso took him aside, sworn to secrecy, and told him that the coronation in three days' time was to be a double one, immediately preceded by a marriage ceremony, he nearly fainted. "But Your Highness, this is impossible!" Mbandele protested. "You are to be the king of all Palambo – you can't have a wedding without any of the necessary trimmings! It will take *weeks* to plan!"

"I'm sorry, Mbandele," Imbaso said patiently. He had met the man's type before and knew their egos were delicate and easily bruised. "I would never ask you to do such a thing under ordinary circumstances. But the kingdom is at a critical point in its history now, and time is of the essence. I will need my queen beside me, from the first, if we are to weather the storms to come."

The royal event planner looked at him anxiously. The affairs of state he was most comfortable with involved music, refreshments, and colorful décor. Imbaso gauged his mood and said "Don't worry, Mbandele. Everything will be fine. I'll let you throw a grand ball to celebrate the wedding and the coronation in a few months' time, all right? But for Mulday we will need to have the guards arrayed in their best uniforms, priests and priestesses of Andros and Mulia – and *not* the arch-priests who are on the Council, please – it must be some other senior members of those temples. My bride and I will be writing our own vows, and Entabi must be instructed that he will be crowning both of us – my wife will be ruling beside me as queen."

Surprisingly this news didn't send Mbandele off the deep end – or at least, not in the way one might expect. There had not been a ruling queen in the region that now constituted the kingdom of Palambo since ancient times, since before the original builders of Iskand had controlled this part of the continent. But the event planner expressed only one concern: "Crowned? Where on earth will you get a crown in time for that? There has been one and only one royal crown in Palambo for as long as it has been a kingdom!"

The happy couple sought divine guidance. Everything they had done so far, including falling in with Mauaji's murderous plan to put his son on the throne, had been in aid of restoring Betsalel's true worship in Palambo while trying to destroy the evil djinn and his bloodthirsty cult. He owed them, and as his strength grew he was happy to help.

Imbaso asked Lmambela for assistance. "I am in need of a secure storage room where I may keep some items I'm accumulating in preparation for my coronation," he told the day shift guard commander. Shortly a room in the guest wing was found for him: fifteen by twenty feet in size, with a stout locking door and no windows. The linens and cleaning supplies that had been stored in it were relocated elsewhere, and Lmambela handed over the key. "Don't lose that, Your highness," he warned the newly minted prince. "That's the only one we've got, and that lock would not be easy to pick."

"Thank you, Commander," Imbaso said off-handedly. Not much later he and Leila, hidden in shadows, opened the door and locked themselves inside. And shortly after that, the Shadow God had joined them there. "A storage closet?" he asked, puzzled. While his closest worshipers could communicate with him mind to mind, he preferred not to pick details from their thoughts without asking.

"It really is for storage," Imbaso said. "For some things we'll need that I want to keep hidden until the day. But I want this also as a safe haven, a bolt-hole for Leila and me in case my father and his Black Claw buddies get the wind up. I have to assume that if he concludes I'm not the puppet he was expecting, they'd have little enough trouble assassinating *me* and finding some other Kivuli cultist to take the job."

"That is troubling," Betsalel said. "I cannot afford to lose you, either of you. Let me see your tooth necklace." The leopard's fang on a cord Imbaso wore as a badge of his having been initiated into the mysteries of Kivuli was not the original. It was one Betsalel had made as an exact duplicate, and instead of offering a pathway for the djinn it guarded Imbaso from spiritual attack.

"I cannot defend you physically when I am not manifested in this plane," the god explained. "But my symbols placed on the door and within the room will provide a powerful psychological barrier. No one with ill intentions will be able to enter, will even want to touch the door. And I can give this necklace the power to warn you of danger. Within a distance of around ten feet, if a person means to harm you or there is poison in your cup, a nyoka under your bed, or anything like that, you will be warned."

Thanking him, Imbaso took the necklace back and placed it around his neck. "Will it tell me what specifically the danger is?" he asked, and Betsalel nodded. "It won't tell you which man in the nearby crowd has a dagger aimed at your heart, or which of the foods on your plate contains the poison; but you will know what kind of danger is present." Turning to Leila, the Shadow God said "You had better have the same protection, beloved."

Leila removed the old necklace she'd bought during the caravan trip from Halath and handed it to him. "The Black Claw masters believe this necklace gives me the power to appear as Kivuli," she said. "They expect me to wear it all the time, so they won't be surprised to see it. I suppose it might as well have some *actual* supernatural powers."

Moments later the necklace was placed around Leila's neck once again. She and Imbaso now had a much better chance of surviving the next week, she thought. Though she still wondered what was going to happen once she came out of the closet. Oh, speaking of closets…

"Master," Leila said, "If this room is to be a safe hiding place for us it will need some improvements. There is no ventilation, and no furniture. Could you give it a similar treatment to what you did for me at the house in Namei?" A short while later the room had hot and cold running water, a couple of comfortable chairs, a marvelous bed, and even a cold chest full of fruit and bottled beer.

Both Leila and Imbaso were well pleased. Having the dark god for a partner was full of amazing delights as well as deep peril. Betsalel smiled to see their joy. The two of them, Leila especially, had done so much for him. And it seemed that he was changing, little by little – he felt much less the dark figure of mystery and menace he had been throughout his immortal life.

"There are a couple of other items we'll need before Mulday," Imbaso said, "and I don't believe that there's time to acquire them by mortal means – especially not when we need to preserve secrecy." "Anything within my power, I will happily provide," Betsalel assured him. By helping these two human agents of his, he was helping himself.

"First," Imbaso said, "We need a pair of matching crowns of Palambo – one each for me and Leila. You know what the official crown looks like?" The dark god nodded. He had been an active part of the religious life of the kingdom from its inception, up until a couple of centuries ago. "Do you wish any changes?" he asked, and the king-elect replied, "I was thinking that at the front of each crown we should add a Rosette of the Eight in cut stones."

The Rosette of the Eight was a circle studded with eight smaller circles, a symbol of the Eight gods and goddesses who made up the pantheon. It was often employed as an architectural device, and the ceremonial scepter of the Emperor of the Dominion had one as a head. It was not used on any royal crowns that Leila knew about, though the realms of the Hando were myriad. Who knew what *they* might be using? "How did you come up with that?" she asked, curious.

"I saw it in a book I read at university," Imbaso replied. "Saint Jorgas, the priest-king of Gaspar in 350 b.m.e., had the Rosette on his crown as a sign of divine approval for his reign. The crown was buried with him, though, and the device was added to the scepter but never to the crown after the Dominion was united."

"I like the symbolism," Leila said. "With the Eight on your scepter you are saying the strength of the gods is lent to your arm. But when it's on your crown, it says that the wisdom of the gods is guiding your mind. That's got to be a better approach for a ruler. Maybe after we kick Kivuli's ass, we can institute some reforms around this place."

Imbaso could see that marrying a foreigner and making her his co-ruler was going to result in some interesting times down the line. For now, though, he looked expectantly at Betsalel. The god held his hands out palms up, and on each of them appeared a golden crown. They were the same design, but of different sizes. The traditional crown of Palambo was open at the top and ringed with spikes. These had an open circle replacing the top of the spike at the front, studded with equally sized, round-cut gems: white diamond, onyx, emerald, ruby, brown diamond, citrine, amethyst, and carnelian.

Imbaso's eyes lit up, and Leila looked equally entranced. She was, down beneath the deadly assassin and priestess of dark powers, a teenage girl. "Those are perfect!" he declared, and Betsalel smiled. He could look into his worshipers' minds if they opened them to him. In another instant the crowns, which had only been illusion, became solid and real. He handed them to Imbaso, who took them gingerly and set them down on the room's small table.

"Something else?" the Shadow God asked. "My wedding dress!" Leila beamed. Betsalel had known, but he felt conflicting emotions about her decision. It was he who had pried her out of the arms of her first love, the man back in Parat who loved her still. But time would heal all wounds.

"You know what you want?" he asked her. "I have a couple of ideas," Leila said, and instantly became attired in a Dominion-style floor-length confection of satin and lace, in a medium green color that complimented her eyes. "What do you think?" she asked, spinning around. Imbaso was speechless, gazing at her with his heart in his mouth. She was so beautiful, and she was to be his – forever.

"Why do you not simply use your power of illusion to create whatever gown you desire?" Betsalel asked. "The gift you granted me has been of great use," Leila said. "But sometimes when I'm living in an illusion for months at a time I lose track of who I really am. I intend to pledge my vows to Imbaso in front of everyone at the palace as me – just myself, without illusions."

"Very well," the god replied. "Decide what gown you want, and I will make it reality. You can hide it here until the day of the wedding." Leila, after some consultation with Imbaso, settled on a dress in a more traditional Palamban style, multi-colored and ornamented with thousands of tiny beads. It included a lacy veil, which would delay the moment at which everyone saw who she was.

Betsalel created a wardrobe space up against one of their hideaway's walls so the dress could be hung. Then, after receiving their profuse thanks, he shrank to toy size and departed his idol. He was now receiving many calls from worshipers all over the Dominion and Palambo as well, and while it was possible to manifest in two idols at the same time he thought it cheated the worshiper who had called him, not to have his full attention.

When they were alone again Imbaso and Leila just stood looking around at their "supply closet." Other than a window with a view, which of course would have been a security risk, it lacked nothing. "It's perfect!" Imbaso crowed. He was getting used to the idea of becoming king, and starting to think that with Leila, Vandao, and the Shadow God on his side it might not be so bad. "What do you say," he added quietly, "we try out the new bed?"

Chapter 63

Imbaso had been spending as much time as possible away from the apartment, even being gone overnight sometimes, but Mauaji managed to corner him at lunchtime on the following day. The day before the coronation, when all of Mauaji's plans would finally come to fruition.

"You're looking well, son," he said by way of preamble. "Getting any sleep?"

"Some," Imbaso admitted bashfully. Mauaji shook his head. What habits the boy had picked up during his years in the Dominion! Of course he was young and good-looking, and if the women were willing why should not a man help himself to what was offered? But the time was coming when he needed to settle down.

"I've been wanting to talk to you about some of the programs we will implement once you're king," the arch-priest said seriously.

"Oh no, Father! The day after the coronation will be time enough to discuss such things. I'm far too busy to even think about them now, but I promise I will give you my full attention first thing on Andday morning. Good enough?"

Imbaso's cheerful tone gave nothing to suggest that he was not going to be as malleable as Mauaji expected. "Good enough," he chuckled, fondness for his son showing in his face and tone. It gave Imbaso a pang, but he'd become good at hiding his feelings.

"There is that other matter, son," the arch-priest began. "You've been having a lot of fun with the serving girls in the palace…"

"Not just serving girls, Father! Some of them are bona-fide ladies. But they all seem to like what I have to give them. I know you are anxious for me to marry, and believe me I have been thinking about it since you first mentioned it."

Mauaji looked somewhat mollified. What he wanted from his son, first and foremost, was obedience. "Do you need me to enter into negotiations for you?" he asked. "I have a great deal of influence now at court…" I'll just bet you do, Imbaso thought bitterly. All backed up by death threats…

"That won't be necessary, Father," he announced smilingly. "I have selected my bride and the arrangements have been finalized. She and I will wed in a ceremony immediately before the coronation tomorrow."

The arch-priest sank back in his chair and stared at his son in disbelief. Finally he said, "Before the coronation? Isn't that a little irregular?"

"Oh perhaps," Imbaso replied airily. "But am I not a rule-breaker? An outsider, made eligible by a brand new resolution, and elected after only one day's deliberations as the youngest king of Palambo since the system was first instituted? One more little matter of protocol won't make any difference."

Mauaji eyed Imbaso with suspicion. Was there a hint of irony there, a suggestion that his election had not been on the up and up? Which of course, it had not. But the king-elect's cheerfulness gave the lie to his tone. He was just a young man full of his new power, and had decided to exercise that power to claim his first bride without going through channels.

"Do I know this young woman?" Mauaji asked.

"I don't believe so," Imbaso replied without providing any more details.

Feeling irritated, the arch-priest asked "You have spoken with her father?"

"Indeed I have," his son said, "at great length, in fact. We are of an accord." About what, was left to Mauaji to assume.

Mauaji waited, hoping silence would elicit more information. But Imbaso remained cheerfully silent as well. Finally the arch-priest said, "Will you not introduce her to me as a matter of courtesy, or at least tell me who she is?"

"And spoil the surprise? Of course not! You and everyone else in the palace will just have to wait until tomorrow morning to see her when she removes her veil!"

Vandao was at work in his office within the part of the palace dedicated to government functions. As Omali's chief executive officer he had devoted far more of his life to the actual running of the kingdom's government than the old king ever had. A king's job, first and foremost, was to be there at the head of the government, a visible symbol of the kingdom and its power. Some kings left it at that, others wanted to set policy, and a few went completely berserk with power and had to be put out of their misery before they inflicted too much of it on the people of the kingdom.

Omali had mostly been one of the first type, content to maintain the status quo and only apply the occasional tweak to the land's fluid laws if a problem arose that needed reacting to. It had been his nephew bearing the lion's share of the work of ruling – making sure every task was delegated, every rule obeyed. In a time when instantaneous communication could only be achieved through divine intervention, running a country the size of this one was a nearly-impossible task.

But Vandao had done well at it, and he was now finding that throwing himself into the piles of work that always awaited him helped to keep his grief for the loss of his uncle at bay. He held no great illusions about Omali's fitness to rule the country; but he had been a decent man, and his nephew had loved him as he had never truly loved his own father.

The mysterious and presumably god-driven apparition in his rooms the other week was something he had shoved firmly into the back of his mind. He was sad beyond measure to learn of the fate of his one true love, yet thrilled to have met the child they had made between them – a woman now, though she would not yet have reached her eighteenth birthday. The mix of emotions Leila's visit had inspired in him had been so upsetting, so perplexing, that he didn't even want to think about it. There was just too much work to be done!

Vandao finished with a piece of paper and placed it in the "done" pile. A clerk would be by later today to carry it and the others away, and distribute them to their next destinations. As he reached for another from the top of the "to do" pile on his desk, he glanced up and saw a young woman – appearing out of nowhere on the carpet in front of his desk. He did not remembering hearing the office door open.

"Leila!" he said, paperwork forgotten. "Are you truly here?" She smiled beatifically at him, Miriam's smile that tore at his heart to behold it. She was so unlike her mother in coloring, but the shape of their faces, of their eyes and mouths, was nearly identical.

She seemed to have gotten over wanting to kill him, which was a relief. She walked right over and put a hand on his arm, assuring him of her solidity. "I have been in Palambo for months, Father," she said. Another little thrill ran through him. He scarcely deserved the name of "Father," yet she gave it to him freely!"

"My lord Betsalel called me last spring from the temple at Parat, and bid me journey here to learn what had happened at the temple in Namei. Are you familiar with the concept of daemons?"

"Mythical creatures," he replied. "Angels, djinns, and demons, said to grant their human familiars magical powers. Some claim that they are the same thing as the lesser gods worshiped throughout Palambo."

"They are not mythical," Leila said. "The gods themselves rely on human belief and worship for both their powers and the forms they have taken. But sometimes human belief and worship focus on an idea, on an imaginary being that does not truly exist."

"Right," Vandao said. "I think that's what mythical means…"

Leila eyed him. Had she acquired some of her own tendency to be a smart-ass from her father? Miriam had certainly never shown any signs of it… "These imaginary beings, if enough people believe in them and feed them with psychic energy, can become something called a 'belief construct.' And that construct is capable of being entered by a human soul, and becoming a real supernatural being similar to a god – inhabiting the spirit realm but able to manifest in this one with all the powers a god might have – if enough people will worship it and give it energy."

Vandao was stunned. What she said explained a lot about the way religion in Palambo worked. He'd seen little of that during his short time spent in the Dominion. He realized he was sitting while she was standing, and he gestured her to the guest chair sitting beside his desk. "The Shadow God told you this?" he asked, and after taking her seat she nodded.

"In the Dominion," Leila explained, "daemons are usually the creation of mages who cultivate them and then ensoul them themselves when they die, infusing their creation with powers their successors can use to perform magic. If the magic is beneficial, the daemon is called an angel – or a demon, if otherwise. These creatures possess a human soul and have their own needs and desires – but they are dependent on those who worship them to supply them with the energy they need to use supernatural powers."

"All right," Vandao said. What his new-found daughter had imparted was vital information, something that he as the kingdom's chief government official (an office confirmed by Omali's young successor) needed to know. "A djinn, a daemon with malign powers and intent, was created by a secret cult within the church of Betsalel?"

"That's right," Leila said. "After I came to Palambo I infiltrated the temple of Betsalel in Namei, where the daemon became ensouled. I learned that more than two hundred years ago a man the cult calls 'the prophet' came out of the desert bearing something he called 'Secret Scriptures,' new rules for worshiping Betsalel which he claimed had been dictated to him by the god himself. Betsalel did no such thing, so either the man was a lunatic or he was using his tale to obtain power for himself."

"These so-called Secret Scriptures, you have seen them?" Vandao wanted to know. Leila sighed.

"Yes," she said. "As a new inductee into the cult I was supposed to memorize them, before I could become a full initiate and participate in the worship of what they believed to be the true

Shadow God. They are vile beyond description. It is a sad testament to human nature that the prophet was not only able to avoid being locked up as insane or executed for his views, but instead succeeded in spreading his schismatic notions of worship throughout Betsalel's entire church within Palambo."

"But the temples of Betsalel, at least the ones I have seen, appeared perfectly normal!" Vandao protested. He must truly believe what his daughter had to say, yet he kept hoping she was wrong somehow.

"In each case," Leila said, "when the prophet's followers took over a temple they removed the true idol. You know that the gods and goddesses can manifest only through the focal point of a true idol, one grown from the originals in the Temple of the Eight in Parat?"

He had not. Like so many men of wealth and education in Palambo, Vandao had regarded worship of the gods as a culturally important, but personally insignificant, relic of a bygone era. Leila could see this was the case from his expression. Imbaso had not been much different – even *she* had thought the gods a sham, until she had met one personally and her life had been changed forever.

"Take my word for it, that's the case," Leila said, moving along. She needed to relay this information to Vandao, as it was about to become very important to the kingdom in the next couple of days. But that was not the reason she had come. "The prophet's followers excavated secret temples beneath the existing temples, and took away the real idols to these hidden locations where they could perform their unspeakable rituals before them. The prophet had promised them that thus they could obtain power beyond anything Betsalel had granted before; but it was all a lie. They placed false idols in the temples above, or merely paintings; and for two hundred years my lord Betsalel was unable to manifest to any of his worshipers within Palambo. He could not reach the true worshipers through the false idols, and he could not reach the cultists because the god they were worshiping in his name was not him."

Vandao was flabbergasted. His whole life, the other gods had been real and Betsalel had been nothing but an idea? "Recently," he said, "People have begun reaching out to Betsalel and he has come to them – as at Omali's funeral a few days ago. Your doing?" Leila nodded.

"On the trip here from Namei, and after we arrived in Iskand, I visited each temple of Betsalel and placed a tiny true idol where the false one had been laid."

She put a hand into her pocket and then held it out to him across the desk. Three tiny black objects, roughly cylindrical and smaller than a grain of rice, lay in her palm. "Betsalel made these for us from his flesh," Leila explained, "when he manifested to us in Namei. The original idols in Parat can be duplicated over and over again, but only by the volition of the god whose idol it is. And once the god has used the idol as a conduit into our plane of existence he or she can become whatever size is desired."

Was his daughter approaching eighteen, or eighty? Leila's seemingly limitless knowledge of things divine (at least by comparison with Vandao's own) seemed far more than a girl her age should possess. But then, she was supposed to be an arch-priestess in the Dominion.

"You came here from Namei? And what do you mean by 'us'?" Vandao asked. He had thought Leila temporarily transported to his rooms from Parat, when he had first seen her. "Imbaso and I," she explained. "I won him to my cause in Namei, and he has also become a priest of Betsalel."

"I never saw you at the palace," Vandao said, "except that time when you came to my rooms. Imbaso came here with his father and sister, and a band of Betsalel priests."

"All of them the djinn's adherents," Leila replied. "And the six 'priests and acolytes' are all full members of the Makucha Nyeusi."

So far, this visit had been a non-stop series of shocks. "The Makucha Nyeusi exists?" Vandao asked in disbelief.

"Oh yes, Father, sadly it does," Leila said. She was dressed in loose-fitting trousers and a short tunic, and pulled down the waistband of the pants to expose a glowing tattoo on her hip. It was illusory, but a true representation. "I'm a full member of it myself."

The kingdom's chief servant recoiled in shock. Had all this really been a prelude to Leila's killing him after all? A second later he got a grip. It was ridiculous – had she truly wanted him dead he would never have survived their first encounter. Now his mind was taking paths it would rather not. And in another second he asked, "The four Council members?" She nodded. "King Omali?" Leila hung her head, and there were tears glistening in her eyes. She nodded again.

"Tell anyone and you bring my death," she said.

"I would never!" Vandao declared, though the news had devastated him.

"It was not my doing," she assured him. "I was undercover with them, trying to stop their plans, but in the end there was nothing I could do without bringing us all to ruin. And I love Imbaso."

Vandao put his head in his hands. There had been too much information, much of it emotionally charged, and he was having a hard time absorbing it all. Then he looked up, and said, "Leila? How have you been here all along when I have never seen you except that one time in my rooms?"

She smiled at him, a sweet expression with pain around the edges. "It is a gift my master Betsalel gave to me, to help me complete this mission he assigned me," she said. And became Zurina. Vandao had witnessed her taking the appearance of her mother on their first meeting. It had nearly destroyed him. Now that he understood more, he was intrigued.

"Poor Prince Samindhi!" Vandao said, understanding at last. Leila smiled at his appreciation of her problem.

"He is sweet," she said, "but it is Imbaso I love. Here is Usiku, the true Makucha Nyeusi assassin – the girl Mauaji and his cohorts believe me to be. My role was just to impersonate Imbaso's nonexistent sister and try to get in good with the royal family, so at least I was not required to kill anyone."

The two girls were physically identical, but somehow Usiku had a hard edge while Zurina was sweet, innocent. Remarkable! Leila became herself again, and sat gazing at her father – assessing his reaction. Taking the plunge, trusting him with her secrets, had been hard for her to do. But her longing to reach out to him had overcome her reluctance. And if she and Imbaso were going to be able to rely on him to help them with what must be accomplished during their reign, she had needed to know his true heart.

"Your god has given you a very good gift indeed," Vandao said seriously. "Aside from having read their scriptures, what proof do you have that the djinn's cult is engaged in wrong practices?"

"Imbaso himself went through their initiation and witnessed a ritual at which Mauaji sacrificed a baby on the altar hidden below the temple in Namei. The djinn, Kivuli as he decided he was to be known, manifested in the idol that once belonged to Betsalel and devoured the corpse."

Vandao's expression was one of revulsion. "That's what put Imbaso on my side," Leila continued. "And we're almost certain that the event that ensouled the daemon in the first place was Mauaji's sacrifice of his own sister's infant son. The slaughtered baby's soul fled to the nearest available receptacle, which was the belief construct worshiped there. After that happened, the djinn began manifesting in the former idols of Betsalel at temples all over Palambo, corrupting them into his own image."

Her father shuddered, then asked "What does this Kivuli look like?" Leila demonstrated, and Vandao flinched back. "But you haven't seen him yourself?"

"As I was pledged to Betsalel, I feared bad things if I attempted to infiltrate the inner sanctum and stand in the djinn's presence," Leila explained. "I based this illusion on Imbaso's description, and I know that it is accurate."

"Um, you can stop now," Vandao suggested and Leila became herself again.

"You recall the late Prince Caradhros?" she asked.

"Yes, that was very odd," Vandao said. "There are certain plant substances people sometimes ingest for amusement, and I have wondered whether he might have been taking them."

"It was worse than that," Leila said. "Betsalel identified to us four men within the palace who were Kivuli cultists. At that time, a couple of weeks ago, Imbaso and I were convinced that Mauaji intended to put one of these, probably Prince Farendhi, on the throne so that the cult could come out in the open. He might have ordered families to provide infants for their sacrifices."

Vandao's eyes widened. "And Caradhros was one of them?" he asked. Leila nodded.

"As Zurina, I was assigned him and his brother Utruri as dinner companions. The fact that they were both cultists was beside the point. Caradhros believed he had lured an innocent young girl from Namei into an ill-considered rendezvous with him atop the citadel tower. He planned to seduce or rape Zurina, then cast her aside."

"You threw him off?" Vandao gasped. He was finding out some things about his beautiful daughter he would just as soon not have known.

"Not at all," she replied with a half-smile. "He threw himself off, willingly." In response to her father's blank look, she continued. "I appeared to him as you just saw me, and he immediately recognized the image of the beast he worshiped as a god. He asked if I were not satisfied with the 'child of his own body' he had sacrificed, and offered Kivuli the blood of the 'young virgin' he expected would soon be arriving for their tryst. Instead, his god demanded he prove his faith by jumping off the tower. I must admit, he *was* faithful."

Vandao slumped in his chair at this tale. Then a thought occurred to him. "But the guards all swore no one had gone up onto the tower top but Caradhros! How did you get past them?"

"Watch," Leila replied, and faded from view. In the chair was nothing but a hint of shadow. Now her father leaned forward, intrigued, and put out a hand. He managed to touch hers, gently.

"Another gift from Betsalel?" he asked.

She reappeared and said, "This was the first gift he gave me, when I agreed to champion his cause and rescue his last true idol from its hiding place in Parat. Not that I really had much of a choice at the time."

Vandao sat digesting all she'd told and shown to him for another few moments. Then he smiled. His face still bore a cast of seriousness bordering on melancholy, an expression it had probably held since he'd been torn from the arms of his lover more than eighteen years before. But it lightened somewhat, and Leila saw love and admiration in those dark eyes.

"Leila," Vandao said, "thank you for revealing yourself to me. It means more than I can tell you, after my seeming abandonment of you and your mother to an unkind fate, that you are willing to come to me freely with this information. I pledge to you that I will tell no one of any of this, unless it is your wish that I do so. And as soon as Imbaso is crowned, our work will begin to root out this pernicious cult. I will serve him with my life."

She smiled mischievously at him. "He has not told you, then?"

"About any of this?" Vandao asked. "I assumed he had asked you to tell me of the cult, since its destruction was your mission from the beginning. Was that not why you came?"

"Partly," Leila admitted. "But my real reason was to ask you to walk me down the aisle tomorrow at my wedding."

Chapter 64

Imbaso rose early on Mulday, claiming the bathroom ahead of the rush. Mbandele had arranged for him to be fitted in magnificent clothing for the twin occasions ahead, and in turn he had entrusted the palace event planner with passing along the new crowns of Palambo to Entabi. As the arch-priest at the Temple of the Eight in Iskand, he was the closest thing Palambo had to a High Archon – and the rulers of the kingdom had been using his services at coronations and funerals for generations.

He would preside at the wedding as well, though a priest of Andros and priestess of Mulia would play their own parts. Imbaso and Leila had closeted themselves in their hideaway during the evening, writing their vows. A copy of these had been delivered to Entabi early this morning. Both the marriage ceremony and the coronation ceremony had been changed for this unique occasion in the history of Palambo.

Mauaji had expected to be asked to accompany his son to the vast formal audience chambers where both ceremonies would be held. But Imbaso told him cheerfully to go there in company with the rest of the priests and take their seats in the first row. He had arranged for an escort, who would be meeting him shortly. "Zurina is going to be a part of the wedding party too," he said, as Mbina was in the kitchen cleaning. "She and I will be meeting our escort and going to the hall as soon as she's finished bathing, so we'll see you there before too long."

The arch-priest was deeply offended at his son's lack of respect for the proprieties. Marrying a girl none of his family had ever met? Refusing to include his own father in the wedding party, yet bringing along a little gutter-rat girl assassin? But he wanted to keep Imbaso sweet – he was going to need his cooperation for some very important endeavors in the coming weeks. So he swallowed his bile, clapped his son on the shoulder, and said "Very well. We will see you there."

The hall would begin filling up with guests, all of whom must show invitations (and arranging for *those* to be delivered in time had been one of Mbandele's triumphs), an hour before the ceremonies that were supposed to begin at ten. It was anticipated that the whole show would be over by noon, at which point everyone would troop over to the great dining hall for a celebratory luncheon. Considering how quickly Mbandele had had to work, it was a miracle guests had not been asked to bring a box lunch from home.

As soon as Mauaji and his black-clad crew had disappeared around the bend of the corridor, Imbaso ducked out and went to the storage room. He retrieved Leila's magnificent dress, wrapped in a clean sheet, and returned to the apartment. Zurina had emerged from her bath, having managed to convince Mbina over the past weeks that she was perfectly capable of washing herself without help.

Imbaso came in as she sat on the settee in a robe, and their eyes lit as they saw each other. It's about time, Leila said to herself, and rose to her feet. "Mbina," she said, and the serving girl turned to face her. "I have a confession to make," Leila went on. Mbina had a look of speculation on her face. How much had she already figured out?

"I am not Imbaso's sister Zurina," she said, and Mbina's expression didn't change. "I am also not Usiku, the girl who was hired to portray Zurina. There is no such person as Zurina." With that, Leila became herself. "My name is Leila, and I am the arch-priestess of Betsalel in Parat, in the Gaspari Dominion to the north. And in a little while, I'll be marrying Imbaso and will become your queen."

Leila wasn't sure what she'd expected in the way of a reaction. Shock, denial, fear? A lot of people reacted badly to manifestations of the supernatural, and Betsalel in particular had a dark reputation. Mbina stood flat-footed, eyes widened slightly, full lips pursed, as she digested what Leila had told her. Then a wide smile slowly washed across her face, and she said "*That* explains it! I'm so glad to know that Imbaso is not your brother!"

She turned to the man in question, who was standing there looking resplendent and holding something wrapped in white cloth. Mbina looked from Leila to the object, then back again. "Is that your dress?" she asked, and Leila nodded. "Well hurry up," she said commandingly, shooing her charge toward the bedroom. "There's no time to lose!"

Some minutes later there was a knock at the door, and Imbaso opened it to Vandao. The man looked rather resplendent himself. He grinned warmly at his soon-to-be monarch and gave him a quick, manly embrace. "She's still primping," Imbaso told his future father-in-law. Vandao pulled out a gold pocket watch, imported from the Dominion, and looked at it anxiously.

"We'd better…" he started, but just then the door to Zurina's room opened and Leila emerged, trailed by Mbina.

Both men gaped at her in open-mouthed admiration. Imbaso had already, sort of, seen his bride in this dress. But Mbina had taken it to a new level by dressing Leila's glossy black curls into a pile on top of her head, delicately applying kohl to make her deep green eyes look enormous, and was there a hint of extra pink on those cheeks? Possibly not. From the way Leila's eyes were glowing, she was feeling as excited as he was.

Vandao stepped close and, very carefully, kissed his daughter on the cheek. "You are a vision of loveliness, my dear," he said softly. In his heart he felt a pang as he imagined what her mother would have looked like dressed for their wedding. She smiled brilliantly at him, and kissed him back. Then she got a worried look.

"What time is it?"

"Time to get going," Imbaso said. "We need to have a brief consultation with the clergy before it's time for the ceremony to start." He pulled a slip of paper out of his pocket and handed it to Mbina. "I'm sorry it's such short notice," he said, "but I'm sure you can see there were reasons why we couldn't tell you sooner. If you can, we would love to have you be there."

Mbina's eyes went wide. "Dressed like *this*?" she said in horror.

"Do you have something in your quarters you could wear?" Leila asked, and the maidservant nodded. "Run, quickly, and get changed, then get to the hall. We'll tell the guards to make sure you have a decent seat. And Mbina – after the wedding and coronation, don't come back here. The men who have been staying here are not the kind of men you want to cross, and if they suspect you've been helping us it would not be good." The girl's eyes widened still more. Then, clutching her invitation, she dashed to the door and ran down the hall.

With help from Imbaso Leila got the veil positioned on her head, hiding her face. Then the wedding party – all three of them – picked up the guard escort Vandao had brought with him at the main corridor and hurried across to the section of the palace where the audience room was located. They arrived at the front doors, where guards were checking invitations and assigning ushers to take the guests to their seats. "A maidservant named Mbina will be coming here, probably a little bit late," Imbaso told the senior officer. "Please admit her along with anyone she might have brought with her, and see that they are positioned near the front."

The guard looked surprised at this instruction, but nodded and saluted. "Yes, Your Highness," he said. "I'll see it done."

"Thank you," Imbaso said. Then they hurried around to a side corridor to go up to the private anteroom connected to the audience chamber. If the ruler were holding formal audiences, it was here where he could go to relax for a few minutes, have a meal, or use the chamber pot.

They found a mix of guards, clerics, and servants in the room. Entabi looked very nervous. Never in his long life had he ever imagined such an affair as this, let alone been ordered to participate in one. Imbaso seemed more like the king he was about to become than a nervous bridegroom, and Leila shone with pride. He would make a wonderful king, she was sure of it! There must truly be some cosmic justice in the world, that Mauaji had dug his own grave with his plans to put his son on the throne.

"Are the two thrones positioned on the dais?" Imbaso asked, and got an anxious confirmation from the old arch-priest. The king-elect removed a small statuette from his pocket, a miniature of Betsalel from the look of it, and handed it over. "Please place this between the thrones and behind them," Imbaso told him.

"We'll be needing it for the ceremonies." This drew a blank look, but Entabi took the little statue and passed it along to a servant boy to carry out the request.

A small orchestra, with both traditional Palamban instruments and the Dominion ones that were so popular at formal balls for Palambo's elite, struck up a Palamban wedding tune. Finished discussing details, the wedding party went back to the front of the hall while the priests and priestess went in through a door leading to the rear of it near the dais. Soon they would meet again.

While Leila had not really been the kind of little Dominion girl who devotes hours to dreaming of her "perfect wedding," the fact that she was marrying a prince and was about to become a queen had gone to her head just a bit. So she'd requested that elements of both Palamban and Dominion wedding customs be included. After all she was wearing a Palamban dress. It was only fair that the land of her birth get some recognition as well.

Thus, when she and her escorts reached the front doors again, all guests now inside and seated, a small servant girl handed her a bouquet of colorful flowers to hold. The orchestra struck up the traditional wedding march of the Dominion, a piece by a famous composer who had died only a few decades before. And with Imbaso on her left and Vandao on her right to help her keep a straight line (the veil didn't give her a very good view), Leila set off at a stately pace down the center aisle between the rows of benches. For this occasion, a thick carpet the color of the Palamban royal livery had been laid down it.

The wedding was to take place in the space between the rows of benches and the dais, the coronation on the dais itself. No advance announcement of the unusual nature of today's ceremonies had been made, and the audience had been abuzz for more than an hour with speculation about the twin thrones. And what was it the servant boy had deposited on the floor of the dais behind them?

Mauaji in particular was worried about it. What did all this mean? That his son meant to elevate his bride as a queen to rule beside him was so far from sense that it didn't even occur to him.

As the wedding party at last reached the area where the three clerics stood, the priest of Andros and priestess of Mulia flanking the arch-priest of the Eight, both Leila and Imbaso were pleased to receive no warnings of danger from the necklaces Betsalel had enchanted for them. So far, so good.

Vandao took his daughter's hands and squeezed them. Then he took a seat in the front row on the opposite side of the aisle from where Mauaji and his group were seated. Entabi, dressed in his multi-colored formal robes of office, was about to start the ceremony when Imbaso leaned forward and murmured something to him. He looked taken aback, but nodded.

Then he turned his back on the wedding couple and their guests, and spoke toward the rear of the room, toward the dais. "Betsalel," he intoned in the ringing voice that had been a gift from the gods, "I, Entabi, call you to come forth and bear witness to the joining of two who are dear to you."

For the second time in the past few days, the long-absent Shadow God came to Entabi's call. He arose seemingly out of nowhere at the rear of the dais behind the thrones, growing quickly to a height of only six feet – less than half the size he had appeared at during Omali's funeral. A collective gasp arose from nearly everyone in the room.

"My heart is filled with joy to see these two wed," he said – in a voice every bit as ringing as Entabi's. Then he stepped forward and down off of the dais to stand a few feet to one side. Any physical attacks against the couple, from whatever distance, would be impossible while he remained here in the flesh.

"Entabi, please continue," Betsalel said, and the old arch-priest – perspiring a little – went on. He nodded to Imbaso, and the groom lifted the elaborate veiled headdress from Leila's head and handed it to the priest. He set it aside. There was a murmur of many voices as people realized that the bride was not familiar to anyone here. And what connection did she have with Vandao? Everyone knew he had never wed, never had children.

"We are gathered here to join Imbaso of Namei, son of Mauaji of Namei and Faradhi of Namei, with Leila of Marsine, daughter of Vandao of Iskand and Miriam Sampson of Marsine, in marriage." More gasps. Had Vandao secretly married in the Dominion, but never returned here with his wife? Or was the king-elect marrying a bastard?

Now the priest of Andros stepped closer, standing facing Vandao, and said "Marriage was ordained of the gods, as a way that the human race might endure, growing greater in love and faith. Our lord Andros teaches us that a man must be strong yet kind, providing for his wife and children and doing nothing that might harm them."

He went on in that vein for some time, enumerating the virtues of a man. Then the priestess of Mulia stepped forward to speak with Leila of the corresponding virtues of a woman. All of this was not dissimilar to such ceremonies in the Dominion, at least among the wealthy and powerful. But the Palambans set much store by individuals adhering to gender-specific roles, and this priestess might well have fainted had she known some of things this bride was capable of.

The spokespersons for male and female returned to their original places, and Entabi stepped forward again to address them both. "In lieu of the usual vows, Imbaso and Leila, pledge to each other as you will." The traditional ceremony was all about hubby providing financial support and not beating the little woman too hard unless she deserved it. For her part, she was to keep his house and bear his children cheerfully, cleaving to him only while he basically took any additional wives, concubines, or casual liaisons he cared to – with no obligation to consult her first. Leila thought there were likely indentured servant contracts that were less one-sided, and she had demanded a complete rewrite.

Imbaso went first. "Leila, beloved, I promise to love you always – in youth and in old age, in good times and bad. I take you for my wife and I will take no other, cleaving to you and you alone. I will be your lover, your partner, and your friend, until death parts us."

That was pretty close to as short as the original, though a murmuring had arisen at the part about "taking no other."

Everyone knew the king of Palambo had to have many wives. Then to further confound the audience, Leila's vows proved to be identical. "Imbaso, beloved," she said in a voice so ringing that it was assumed Betsalel had supplied it with extra power for this occasion, "I promise to love you always – in youth and in old age, in good times and bad. I take you for my husband and I will take no other, cleaving to you and you alone. I will be your lover, your partner, and your friend, until death parts us."

There had been nothing whatsoever about obedience, about raising his children, about keeping his house! The audience was scandalized, even though as this was a royal wedding a king's wife would have a large staff of servants to handle all those domestic chores. Mauaji had just witnessed what should have been a moving ceremony, his only son taking a wife for the first (and it seemed, only) time, but he had a frown on his face. He had never seen the girl before. Why was she so naggingly familiar? And where was Usiku? Imbaso had said she was to be part of the wedding party…

"By the authority of the Eight and the laws of the kingdom of Palambo I declare you two to be wed," Entabi intoned. "You may kiss the bride." The orchestra broke out into some triumphal music, and Imbaso bent Leila back to kiss her deeply. Cheers and applause were heard around the hall.

But it was not quite over. The Shadow God stepped forward to embrace each of them gently – kissing first Imbaso, and then Leila on both cheeks. "May you live long in happiness," he blessed them. Then he turned to fix Mauaji, who was gazing at him in wild surmise, with his ruby stare. In the arch-priest's mind, he heard the god speak: "I am not Kivuli, priest of Betsalel. Reconsider your actions before you are lost."

Betsalel climbed back up onto the dais and stood behind the thrones. But he did not shrink back to the toy-sized idol before departing it. Instead he grew, to the full fifteen-foot size of his idol in the Temple of the Eight, before going still again. He would return for the coronation ceremony, which would take place in less than an hour. As he withdrew his presence, he felt a surge of belief flooding him with strength.

Waving to the crowd happily, Imbaso and Leila let Vandao and a party of guards escort them to the royal chambers. They would rest there and take some refreshment before returning to the audience hall. They walked past within a few feet of Mauaji and the Black Claw assassins, and still sensed no danger.

Chapter 65

As they made their way along the corridors Vandao was as cheerful as anyone there had yet seen him. "You had your backs turned," he said jubilantly, "but you should have seen the faces! It's not that often somebody gets the God of Death to show up at their wedding and wish them a long, happy life!"

"Betsalel is not just the god of death," Leila pointed out. "He's also the god of sleep and dreams, of nocturnal creatures. And in his role as the god of death he is mostly there to provide release to tortured souls, not kill those who cling to life."

"I stand corrected," Vandao said, but his good mood seemed unquenchable.

Linda Cervantes had been ensconced in the harem with the other widows and orphans, where she was finding that her sister wives treated her less unkindly than she'd feared. The royal quarters had been cleaned from top to bottom and completely redecorated – mostly by bringing in furniture that had been put in storage by previous generations. The palace was full of exquisite antiques.

They joined Vandao in a large parlor in the king's suite of rooms, having some tea and tidbits to fortify them for the next stage in today's preparations. The guards had been asked to wait outside, as they had things to discuss. "I'm wondering how soon we should begin to move against Kivuli," Imbaso said. He'd erected a bubble of silence around them to be certain there were no eavesdroppers.

"I fear it will be a very slow process, rooting out the cult from beneath every temple of Betsalel in the country," Vandao replied. "It's an issue of communication – it took you, what, a month to get here from Namei?"

"I have some ideas about how we can speed that up," Leila said. "We could probably leave it to the mobs, but I fear they would be more likely to destroy the temples entirely. They would not be able to damage the new true idols we have placed, but I don't want a general feeling to spring up associating Betsalel with the evil practices of the Kivuli cultists. It could damage our master's return here in Palambo."

"At least we can act to root out the cult here in Iskand," Vandao said. "Did you tell me that Betsalel can sense those who have pledged themselves to the djinn?" Imbaso nodded.

"I'm not sure what his range is for that, though. His powers seem to be more or less dependent on how many human worshipers are feeding him energy."

"Should we arrest Mauaji and his party right after the coronation?" Leila asked. "They are not stupid, and they're sure to have figured out from the true Shadow God's presence that we are not supporting Kivuli." Imbaso looked troubled, and she realized that once again she'd trodden on what remained of his feelings for his father.

"I'd prefer that we not slaughter every person who has been initiated into the cult," he said. "Remember, *I* am one of them, and I recanted! Everyone should be given a chance to open themselves to Betsalel, so he can know the truth of their feelings, and be spared if they will renounce their allegiance to the djinn. Many of them are no more than youths, led into the cult by elders they trusted."

"That makes a lot of sense," Leila replied, squeezing his hand. "If anything like a majority of the cultists could be brought to the true worship of Betsalel, our master will have his priesthood as well as his temples and his idols back. He'd be returned to his former power here much more quickly than will be the case in the Dominion, where we're still starting from scratch."

"But as for your father and his assassin friends," she went on, "I think they are too dangerous to be left wandering loose. Maybe after the ceremony they could be taken back to the apartment and put under house arrest? Just station some guards around the place, and nobody goes anywhere until we sort it out with them?"

"I think that's for the best," Imbaso said. "But the Makucha Nyeusi are dangerous men. The guards need to know what they're up against, and remove any weapons they are carrying." It was odd, Leila thought, but in a way she found her fellow assassins to be worthier people than the priests of the cult. Presumably they were all initiates, and had been worshiping according to the scriptures since they joined; but she hadn't gotten any sense that they were particularly devoted to Kivuli.

Nice mindset Leila, she chided herself. Secret murderers are so much nicer people than baby-sacrificing priests. Perhaps it was just that she had worked among them, and that masters Kifozi and Sumundi seemed so much like kindly old men. Clearly, growing up without a father had left her at an emotional disadvantage. Well, she had one now – and she liked him!

The guard captain stepped in to tell them it was nearly time to return to the audience hall for the coronation. Vandao filled him on their plans for Mauaji and the six "priests and acolytes" with him, warning him that the black-clad men were professional assassins and should be thoroughly searched before being taken into custody. The apartment should be searched as well, before they were allowed to remain there under house arrest.

Both Imbaso and Leila went into the royal bedchamber and changed into garments that had been provided for them, the official robes of office for a ruler of Palambo. Compared with the ermine and velvet affected by counts in the Dominion, these were simplicity itself. But a Palamban ruler might well keel over from heat stroke were he to dress as did his counterparts to the north.

The robes were of dazzling white linen, falling in a straight curve from the shoulders to the ankles and fastened at the front with a series of gold clasps. Lucia had never gained the prominence in Palambo that she had held (until recently) in the Dominion, and the white color was symbolic of purity rather than of the Goddess of Light. A shimmering cloth-of-gold shawl collar rose at the back and then curved in a narrow band down the front on either side of the closure, and the robe was usually worn over the top of more conventional dress.

Bareheaded, the future rulers of Palambo strode along the corridors amid their guard escort with Vandao at their side. Without his expertise and administrative skills, the two young people would have helpless to accomplish their task. They had the backing of a god whose power was growing daily – but neither they nor Betsalel had any inkling of how to run a bureaucracy.

Following the wedding ceremony the guests, all of whom had been invited for both events, milled around in the audience hall talking or remained in their seats. Mauaji and his cohorts had stepped over near the wall and were deep in a murmured conversation; but he did not reveal to them everything that was in his mind. Betsalel and Kivuli were not the same, and the latter had not supplanted the former! That was a big enough shock. But the Shadow God as he was traditionally envisioned had been absent from Palambo for generations. Was it because the prophet had been wrong... or had, for unknown reasons of his own, lied?

And then there was the issue of Betsalel manifesting seemingly out of nowhere. Mauaji was the latest in a long line of his family to be in the religion business, and he had always been sure that one fact was clear: the gods could manifest on this plane only through their idols. It was why the prophet and his followers had removed the idols from the temples and hidden them in the secret sanctuaries below: so that only those with the knowledge of the Secret Scriptures could have access to them.

But wait; once the god had appeared he had grown larger and larger, until he was the height of a tall man. And after he had bestowed his blessing on the happy couple (*why* did that woman seem so damned familiar?) he had climbed up on the stage and grown still more, as big as the idol in the Temple of the Eight, before removing his presence. That meant the gods could make their idols whatever size they wanted them to be. So why not small – small enough to carry in your pocket?

A smartly-dressed palace functionary with a megaphone came out in front of the dais at this juncture, interrupting Mauaji's train of thought. "Ladies and Gentlemen," he announced, "Please take your seats. The coronation is about to begin."

There was a flurry of noise and activity as everyone scrambled back into their places. Then the orchestra began a stately march. From a door at the rear of the dais, three people emerged: first Imbaso and Leila, walking side by side to the center of the dais before splitting to left and right to be seated in the thrones; and then Entabi, following and remaining standing in the center between them.

He carried with him the two new crowns, which he placed on a low table that had been set near the front of the dais. The crowd's murmur rose almost to a roar – the rumors were true! People in Iskand would be talking about this for weeks to come, and when the news reached the provinces… !

In his marvelous, gods-given voice, the arch-priest of the Eight addressed the throng. "Imbaso, duly elected to take up the mantle of King of Palambo by the revered Council of Eight, has announced that his reign will begin in a way different from any that our nation has seen. He has commanded that his bride, once Leila of Marsine and now Leila of Iskand, will rule beside him as his queen. Therefore, each of them will take the oaths and each will wear the mantle of ruler of Palambo."

The crowd didn't exactly go wild, but it was definitely another minute or two before it had gotten quiet enough in the high-ceilinged hall for Entabi to continue. Picking up the larger of the two crowns, he stepped to a spot on the floor outside of the throne where Imbaso sat, but facing the audience. Imbaso had wanted Leila to go first, but he had bowed to sense – no point in cramming too much change down people's throats all at once. And it was only his nearly limitless authority as king-elect that even allowed Leila to be named queen in the first place.

"Imbaso," Entabi began, and the murmuring dropped away. This might well be a once-in-a-lifetime event for most people, and no one wanted to miss it. "the office of King of Palambo is marked by both power and responsibility. If you accept it, you will hold the lives of millions of men, women, and children in your hands."

Wow, Leila thought. Considering Palambo's seemingly inferior level of civilization and its lack of anything resembling democratic process, she was surprised to learn that the people of the kingdom were even something the all-powerful king was supposed to acknowledge as a concern. Or was this a change to the standard coronation ritual, something Imbaso had not told her about?

"Do you vow to uphold the honor of the kingdom of Palambo, to protect and defend it, and to keep uppermost in your mind the welfare of its citizens?"

"I so vow," Imbaso swore, and Entabi gently lowered the new crown onto his head.

"I do hereby crown you King of Palambo, and may you reign with wisdom and justice," he said. As he did so, the Rosette of the Eight on the front of the crown suddenly flared to light, dazzling the arch-priest and visible to every person who was watching.

Leila cast a sideways glance up at the quiescent idol of Betsalel, a dark presence at the rear of the dais that was almost lost in shadows except for the glowing third eye. One of the two others winked open for a moment, then closed again. It was true! In the presence of one or more believers, the gods could manifest in their idols without being called.

Next it was Leila's turn. She felt surprisingly calm, considering she wasn't yet eighteen and was being handed enormous temporal power over millions of her fellow human beings. This was a required step in her quest to rid Palambo of the evil djinn, and she had not thought much beyond that goal; but as Entabi settled the crown onto her head (not surprisingly, a perfect fit and quite comfortable as well) plans were beginning to rise in her mind like steam from a kettle reaching the boil. She and Imbaso, working together over the years of their reign (and with Betsalel's backing and their early start, that might well be many decades) could bring a better life for every single Palamban. The future beckoned!

Chapter 66

After the coronation Entabi had stepped aside and Betsalel (shrinking once again to human size, as he had no wish to dominate here) stepped forward and pronounced his blessing on the reign of King Imbaso and Queen Leila. Then he vanished from sight, but Leila knew how that had been accomplished. She looked, and soon spotted the tiny idol sitting on the dais. Applying an illusion of remaining on her throne, she stepped away and collected it, tucking it into a pocket beneath her robe of state. Over the months that she'd had the illusion power, she had gotten so good at it that she herself could be as far away as three or four feet from where the illusory image stood – or sat.

Many courtiers, hoping to curry favor from the new monarchs, had surged forward to the stage and were being held back by the guard corps. Other guards moved to encircle Mauaji and his contingent, but in the confusion Imbaso and Leila were not able to see what was happening.

The newly crowned ruler (or rulers, in this first-ever such case in the kingdom) was expected to remain in the hall to receive the congratulations and well-wishes of the elite members of Palamban society who had been invited to witness the coronation. Thankfully this had a time limit, as they were all supposed to be participating in a celebratory luncheon in the grand dining hall in less than an hour's time.

Leila's earlier elation as she stepped into her new life of power and privilege became muted as she beheld a vision of a future filled with endless, pointless socializing. It was one thing to play Zurina, the pretty little girl hoping for a marriage alliance with an actual prince; and another to endure hours of people swarming around like flies, each of them hoping for personal advantage as a result of sucking up to the queen.

Although the idea of a too-young king deciding to place his even-younger bride on the throne to rule beside him was one the more conservative courtiers regarded with horror, younger people rather liked the idea. It was sort of romantic – the beautiful young couple espousing a new way of doing things. Guards had to step in and hold back the line as it was announced that it was time for everyone to move to the dining hall for the lunchtime banquet.

As Leila and Imbaso were escorted down the hallways, surrounded by guards, Vandao came urgently to their side. "The guards have successfully corralled the six Black Claw assassins," he murmured in Imbaso's ear. "But your father was not found. He somehow slipped away from the hall during the ceremony, we think."

Imbaso was crestfallen. He had nurtured hopes that his father, once he understood the wrongness of the Secret Scriptures he'd attempted to follow his whole life, and the nature of the djinn he had raised, might recant and return to the true worship of Betsalel. But he had committed many crimes, including the murder of his own infant nephew. Perhaps he felt his conscience could never be clean, and he must now flee? At least the rest of them, the most dangerous ones, were now under guard.

Mbandele had risen to the occasion, and outdone himself. Luncheon, normally a light meal in this hot climate, had become a lavish succession of courses – all of them light in themselves, each an exquisite culinary masterpiece – and together, enough food for everyone in the dining hall and everyone else in the city of Iskand, as well.

Leila and Imbaso were dazzled. During their weeks in the capital they'd become accustomed somewhat to royal excess; but now it was them presiding at the king's table – and both of them were very thankful for the god's gift. They had no need of royal tasters, for each of them carried with them an early warning system that should (they hoped!) make it impossible for anyone to deliver to them the fate that had befallen the late King Omali.

By and large, the luncheon was a success. The food was delightful, and toast after toast was raised to the royal couple. This party celebrated not only their accession as Palambo's ruling couple (what would that be, duarchs?) but their wedding as well. Leila had promised herself and Imbaso that she would make her vows free of all illusion, but she saw no need for that situation to persist for the rest of the day.

Holding Imbaso's hand, smiling at him in triumph (though both of them were worried and saddened by the escape of his father) Leila cast the illusion of the pair of them raising glasses, downing cup after cup of every vintage available in the kingdom, it seemed. Had they truly drunk every toast that had been raised to them, they'd have been under the table within an hour.

It was the middle of the afternoon before the party began to wind down. Tonight, for a change, dinner would not be served in the great dining hall. Many of the attendees would probably skip it entirely, having a nap until late and then maybe something light from the kitchens before going to bed.

Vandao and a complement of royal guards accompanied King Imbaso and Queen Leila back to their quarters, where they were met by a frantic guard captain. "The assassins!" he gasped, having only just returned from the visitors' wing and the apartment where Kifozi and his fellow Makucha Nyeusi members had been placed under house arrest.

"You have your idol?" Imbaso asked Leila, and she nodded. They and their guards hastened across the palace to the apartment where they'd lived for the past few weeks. The blood began in the corridor leading to the one on which the apartment opened.

Bodies of royal guards led down it to the apartment's door, which was smashed in. The stone floor was awash with blood, and they had to walk near the walls to avoid stepping in pools of it. The corpses had been rent limb from limb, almost torn to shreds.

Vandao bent and vomited, adding his stomach contents to the pooled body fluids on the floor. Leila was pale, Imbaso tense. Oh Father, what have you done? The Makucha Nyeusi assassins were gone, but the bodies of royal guards littered the apartment's interior and the courtyard outside. Leila thanked the Eight that she had warned Mbina against returning here.

The guard captain who had brought them here had not seen the extent of the carnage until now, having been alerted by some of his underlings. He was shocked, devastated, and disbelieving – an entire company of his finest troops, wiped out without a single enemy casualty?

Surveying the grisly scene, tears in her eyes, Leila asked him "Were guards sent to the temple of Betsalel, as we requested?" He nodded.

"I sent a troop just a short time before I learned of... this..." he trailed off. She realized that the situation was close to pushing the captain over the edge, and she took him by the hand.

"Captain, this was no human enemy who killed your men. It was an evil djinn, called by the man who claimed to be an arch-priest of Betsalel – Mauaji."

Imbaso had managed to keep a grip on his stomach, barely – but he was heartsick. And mindful of his role as the newly-crowned king. "Father has made his choice, it seems," he said bitterly. "He must have figured out that with guidance Kivuli could make his idol small enough for him to carry it off. And he brought it here to free his men. I will not rest until he, and they, have been brought to justice."

Chapter 67

The guards sent to the temple of Betsalel out in the city reported back that it was deserted, the idol of Kivuli gone from the altar in its secret underground sanctuary. As for Mauaji and the six Makucha Nyeusi assassins, they had vanished like the mist that hung most mornings above the surface of the Azraq.

King Imbaso and Queen Leila spent their first night together in the opulent royal bed holding one another tight, wondering what the morrow would bring. But there were no further incursions by Kivuli. In the morning Betsalel, called to his true idol in the temple of Betsalel, identified all of the Kivuli cultists remaining in Iskand and told the guards where to find them. The party from Namei was long gone beyond the range of his sight.

Abandoned by their god, all of the cultists were rounded up and brought to the temple. As a group, Betsalel explained to them the nature of Kivuli. Then each of them was personally questioned as to their loyalties. Would they cleave to the djinn, or be freed from his influence? Most sincerely repented of their mistaken beliefs, and Betsalel destroyed their fang necklaces and removed the scars from their hands. Henceforth, they would worship the true Shadow God.

The few who stood defiant were relieved of their necklaces and given over to the guards for execution. Then Betsalel filled the cult's inner sanctum, and all of the rest of the passages below the temple, with black basalt. It was if the secret spaces beneath had never existed.

Quite a crowd had gathered to witness this drama, and now the dark god addressed them. "Never again will my temple be a home to evil," Betsalel said. "Come to me when you seek the peace of sleep, the joy of dreams, the respite of death from a life no longer sustainable. Do not come to me for power over others, for terror in the night to sway the souls of men, for this I will not grant." The temple at Iskand was cleansed.

Leila, Imbaso, and Vandao were gathered with the Royal Guard Corps' top leadership in their war room, clustered around an enormous table on which was painted the most detailed map of

Palambo Leila had ever seen. Good grief, this kingdom she had agreed to become the co-ruler of was huge! And most of it was not nearly as accessible, as civilized, as was the land of her birth.

"One down, how many left to go?" Lmambela asked. He was still smarting from Kivuli's slaughter of more than a dozen of his guard corps, and had taken a great deal of satisfaction from the Shadow God's actions at the temple earlier today.

Standing near the back wall, Betsalel said "Two hundred seventy-three of them." He gestured, and the locations of the temples under the control of the Kivuli cult glowed in red.

The humans in the room took in the broad swath, glittering with red lights, as if they were the campfires of the enemy. Which, in a way, they were. Leila heaved a sigh, refusing to be daunted. When faced with an enormous task, just start picking at it where you can. "Master," she said, "You can carry a person with you to any temple where you have a true idol and at least one believer at that end?"

"That is correct," the dark god replied. "All of the idols you placed in my temples along the journey from Namei have brought worshipers, Leila. In two of them the Kivuli acolytes on guard above approached me, as they had believed that Kivuli was an altered version of me. When I explained his nature, they recanted and I did for them as I have done for Imbaso – shielded them from supernatural attack by the djinn. They will assist us in cleansing the temples – but we will need more help. In any temple where the Kivuli worshipers outnumber mine, I am at a disadvantage."

"I think what we need to start with is a proclamation," Imbaso said. He had already issued a signed and sealed warrant for the apprehension, dead or alive, of his father and the six Makucha assassins.

"Do people in the provinces even realize that the country has a new king?" Leila asked.

"As soon as King Omali died the word was put out via messengers and all the ships in port at the time," Lmambela explained. "Similar messages were sent announcing King Imbaso as soon as the Council of Eight had made their selection. But there are undoubtedly many people in the kingdom who have not yet heard either piece of news, let alone that we have a reigning queen."

"What about the royal guard garrisons?" Imbaso asked. In every region with a town big enough to support one, the kingdom had troops on permanent station. They helped to keep peace in the region, enforced the kingdom's laws, and supported the local economies.

Lmambela ordered an underling to fetch a list, and they marked the royal garrisons on the big map. More than half of the temple locations also had a garrison, and every garrison had a temple. "I need a clerk," Imbaso said, and one was brought to him. He had soon dictated a proclamation that would be promulgated throughout the kingdom, read in every town and village – in time.

Leila sat beside him and helped him work out the wording. They were supposed to be co-rulers, so it wouldn't do to have official proclamations coming from only one of them. The clerk read back, "By order of Imbaso and Leila, King and Queen of Palambo, to all within the realm: A cult has arisen, pretending to be operating the temple of Betsalel but not connected with it. The cult operates in secret in quarters excavated beneath the temples, worshiping an evil djinn known as Kivuli. In most cases, the true idols of Betsalel have been removed so that worshipers can no longer contact the Shadow God."

He glanced at the king and queen, making sure that what he'd read met with their approval. Then he continued. "The forms of worship employed by this cult, in the worship of the djinn they believe to be a god, involve human sacrifice – including the slaughter of infants. They are both repugnant to us and counter to the laws of our land. The cult of Kivuli is hereby proscribed throughout the kingdom of Palambo. Any initiates of this cult who, now understanding the nature of the being they have been worshiping and wishing to recant, will be forgiven past transgressions and spared if they will cooperate with the authorities in helping to eliminate the cult and its influence."

Leila and Imbaso nodded at him, and he went on. "Of crucial importance in defeating the cult of Kivuli and the restoration of the temples of Betsalel to the worship of the true Shadow God is the destruction of the idols of Kivuli. These will be found within rooms hidden beneath the temples of Betsalel, and will resemble a black being that is half man, half black leopard. These should be smashed whenever found. A reward of one thousand asand will be paid to anyone presenting the smashed pieces of a true Kivuli idol to the Royal Palace in Iskand, or to any garrison of the Royal Guards."

"What do you think, Father?" Leila asked of Vandao. He was twice her age and wise in the ways of the kingdom she had, absurdly, come to rule.

"The reward should help to overcome people's fear of bracing the djinn in his den," he said. Considering what had happened to those guards, it was no small threat. But the idol was only dangerous if there was a chance the djinn might manifest within it. And with the first hammer blow, that would not be possible. Thank fate that all of Betsalel's idols in Palambo had been spawned from the original in Parat *before* the spell that rendered it (and its descendants) impervious to harm.

Vandao went on, "But how will the garrisons recognize the pieces of a true Kivuli idol? Human nature being what it is, many people will arrive with a sackful of black stone rubble, demanding payment." Leila and Imbaso turned to Betsalel to answer that one.

"The pieces of the idols should still possess an ability to resist acid, which no ordinary stone will do. Have the guards test by immersing a small fragment in a jar of strong acid such as is used for the etching of glass or metals. If such a fragment has not dissolved overnight, it has come from one of my true idols – which on this part of the continent, will have been taken over by Kivuli."

The new idols, of course, could not be broken into small pieces in the first place. But this "acid test" should serve to weed out frauds. "Very well," Imbaso said, "Please have this proclamation calligraphed on parchment, and we will sign and seal it. Master, you can produce exact duplicates?" The Shadow God nodded, and the clerk scurried off to do his king's bidding.

While this had been going on the military men had been thinking and planning. By design, each garrison in the country could reach all of the towns in villages in its region – including those with the temples – inside of a full day's march. But each might have more than one temple to cover. What troop strength would be required to overcome the temple's priesthood? How many chapters of the Makucha Nyeusi were there, and where were they located? And what would the troops do, if they stormed a temple's understory and found Kivuli himself awaiting them?

Chapter 68

The proclamation had been read at the Temple of the Eight, and again in the palace's great audience hall before a packed audience. Copies of it had been dispatched by mounted messenger, and on every ship departing Iskand. Within weeks, it should have spread to the entire realm. But that was not fast enough.

The king and queen and a complement of their guards returned to the Temple of the Eight to meet with Entabi. "Arch-priest," Leila told him, "if we are to destroy the cult and put a stop to its depredations, we need to get the word out as quickly as possible. My lord Betsalel's temples were stolen from him, and he is not able to manifest except in fewer than a dozen we were able to partially reclaim. But others of the Eight, with the possible exception of Lucia, might be willing to bring the news to their temples throughout the land. Can you call them, please?"

Last year when Leila had sought to lay the groundwork for Betsalel's return to the pantheon in Parat, she had successfully called six of the gods to their temples scattered around the Dominion's capital. At the time, some of them had agreed to actively support her (and their brother god), and the rest had agreed not to hinder her efforts. But she had no reason to assume that Andros, Mulia, Deline, Belantos and the rest would jump to do her bidding. The arch-priest who had devoted his life to their worship might have better luck.

Entabi was more than willing to assist them. The idea that the temples of one of the Eight might be taken over by bloodthirsty worshipers of an evil daemon was repugnant to him. He called first on Andros, who came almost immediately. "Entabi," the god said calmly. He turned on his column, and picked Leila out of the group. "And Leila," he said warmly. "My brother's little arch-priestess. What brings you here to Iskand?"

Clearly he had not recognized her a few days ago, when she had been here in the temple in the guise of Zurina. Yet, Dionos had. "Had you known, Great Andros, that Betsalel's temples throughout Palambo had been stolen by a daemon?" Leila asked.

"I had no awareness of it, no," Andros replied. His idol had remained at the fifteen-foot height standard in this temple, and he was an extremely imposing figure.

The gods, when not manifested in the physical plane, all inhabited the same spiritual plane of existence. But they did not communicate with each other there. As no adherent of the schismatic church of Betsalel that had grown up under the prophet's Secret Scriptures would be likely to discuss this with, or in the hearing of, any other god or goddess of the Eight, it made sense that they would not have known about it unless Betsalel had told them. But he should have had the opportunity over the past several months to do so within the Temple of the Eight in Parat, if nowhere else. Why had he not?

Leila stepped out into the center of the chamber and faced to the left, where the idol of Betsalel stood. "Betsalel, please join us," she said – in a tone resembling command. Being a queen had turned out to be right up Leila's alley, so far. So much less work when you just gave orders and people obeyed!

The Shadow God manifested in his idol, and greeted his brother. Then he looked inquiringly at Leila and Imbaso. "Master," his arch-priestess said, "we believe that the quickest way to spread the word about the cult and enlist help in destroying the corrupted idols is to get your brothers and sisters to pass along copies of our proclamation to the priesthood at their temples across Palambo. Coming from a god, the news will be treated with the seriousness it deserves. But it seems they have not been informed of the situation?"

Betsalel looked down, but maintained his fifteen-foot height. Usually if there was to be much discussion he would shrink to a less-intimidating size; but here in the grandest temple in Palambo, and in company with his fellow god, he needed to remain large. "I did not want to call for their help at all," he said. "After what happened in the Dominion, it seemed I had become the poor relation, the perpetual supplicant."

Leila kept forgetting just how very human the gods and goddesses of her world were. They had been created male and female, but with no other pronounced characteristics, out of some sort of universal spirit pool – infused into the bones of the earth at a time when the little hairless apes called humans were beginning to reach out and hunger for divinity.

Human belief and worship had shaped them, and they had all of the best and the worst of humans in their makeup – kindness, nobility, intelligence but also pettiness, prevarication, stupidity, and insecurity. Betsalel had failed to ask help from those most able to give it, choosing instead to turn her own life upside down, because he didn't want to pester his relations!

Leila deeply loved Imbaso and was committed to her new life at his side and all the promise that life had to make things better for nearly a third of the world's population. But the life and the love she had lost with Tevo was a wound in her soul that would never heal. And it was her god, another she loved, who had taken her from him.

Anger and sorrow swelled in Leila's soul, and as she carried a part of Betsalel within her the Shadow God was immediately aware of all she felt, and all she thought. He hung his head, and his eyes closed for a moment before opening again. "I am sorry, Leila," he said in her mind. Then aloud, he said "I was wrong. Andros, I need your help. And that of the others, as well. We must spread the word to every corner of the kingdom. Every baby sacrificed on the altar of the djinn is a man who will never grow up to do you honor, a woman who will never pray to Mulia."

He produced an enormous copy of the proclamation and handed it to his brother god. "Duplicate this, please, and give it to whomever has the greatest authority in each of your temples. It must be passed to the commander of the nearest royal garrison, as military force will be needed to penetrate the cult's lairs beneath my temples. There are hundreds of temples wherein I no longer have any true idols, so I cannot go myself. Not yet."

Andros accepted the piece of paper and read it, then nodded. The paper vanished, but could be recalled whenever he wished. "Entabi," he said, "call the others if you will." Six more deities were called, and each of them came. Their brother Betsalel treated with each of them, even his estranged sister Lucia. She was cool, and polite, and accepted a copy of the proclamation. Whether she would do anything with it remained to be seen. But in Palambo, she had never held the exalted position she once had in the Dominion. Her temples were fewer even than Betsalel's, here.

Andros and Mulia far outnumbered the others here in terms of temples and worshipers, and both of them had promised they would spread the word. Mulia had already heard from some worshipers about the mysterious disappearance of their babies, and had found traces of a lingering evil but no hard information. She was furious.

The nightly fabulous dinners in the palace's grand dining hall had been suspended for a few days, but that night the usual participants were once again invited to attend. Leila and Imbaso presided from the head table, with Vandao by their side and the rest of the table occupied by people he had recommended – ones he felt could be trusted, and who could prove useful to them in their reign. So far, no one had been so bold as to express displeasure at the unheard-of installation of a ruling queen, at least not to their faces. But Leila sensed that for most people, her crown was just a bauble bought for her by her husband – her authority an indulgence the king had bestowed. Perhaps they were right.

As the royal couple left the dining hall, accompanied by Vandao and a contingent of guards, Samindhi approached them and asked for a chance to speak with the king. "Come with us to our chambers," Imbaso said. Now that the young man was no longer wooing his love, he could afford to let his liking show. The two of them were close in age, and alike in many ways.

In the sitting room they used as a private conference room, Leila and Imbaso dismissed the guards. "Samindhi," Imbaso said, "do you object if my father-in-law remains with us while we speak?"

"It's all right," the young man said. He had a woeful expression in his deep brown eyes, and looked as if he had not been sleeping lately. After all, he had recently lost his father – and his position in life had changed.

But that was not what was bothering him. "Your Majesty," he said, "I have had no word of your sister Zurina, and she has not been seen in the palace since the night of the coronation. Please tell me that she is all right?" I should have seen this coming, Imbaso realized. He'd had an awful lot of other, seemingly more urgent, things on his mind lately.

The queen spoke up, addressing Samindhi with kindness – and a somewhat deeper tone of voice than usual, with the hint of a Gaspari accent. Nothing like Zurina's speech. "You are the prince who was courting my sister-in-law, are you not?" she asked.

"Yes, Your Majesty," he replied. "I am Samindhi, one of the sons of the late King Omali."

"Ah, I am so sorry," Leila said. She left it up to Samindhi to work out if she was referring to the late king's death or something else. "After it was discovered that my father-in-law and his cohorts were members of the bloodthirsty Kivuli cult," she went on, "Zurina was deeply shamed. And frightened for her life as well. I had just arrived from the Dominion, and I agreed to shelter her. She boarded a ship bound for Atena with a small company of guards early yesterday, and they will escort her to Parat. She plans to take up orders with the Sisters of Deline, there."

Samindhi's face fell and tears came to his eyes. His beloved might as well have been transported to the moon, for all the chance he had of reaching her in Parat. He had a comfortable enough life here in the palace, but at the age of twenty-two he had never worked a day in his life and had no personal resources that would allow him to make a journey half a world away.

The Sisters of Deline did not exist in Palambo, and Leila went on to explain gently, "The Eight do not seek to order the sex lives of their worshipers, Samindhi. But you should know that the Sisters of Deline are an order of celibate nuns. They freely impose on themselves the restriction that they will neither marry nor bear children, instead devoting themselves to scholarship and the worship of the goddess who is their inspiration. They have made many important contributions to knowledge in the Dominion. And they take their vows very seriously. I fear your Zurina will never wed you, or anyone, now."

The prince rose from the chair on which he'd been seated, and bowed to the king and then the queen. "Thank you, Your Majesty," he said, clearly having gotten a grip on his emotions. "I will always remember your sister-in-law as the most beautiful woman I have ever met. Yet you are very like her." With that he turned and left.

Chapter 69

Leila and Imbaso had conferred with Vandao until bedtime, and between themselves after they'd gone to bed. When they had been catching love on the run, in secret and hiding, their passion for each other had burned like an all-consuming flame. Now that they were married and officially sharing a bed, they lay naked in one another's arms – plotting military strategy.

Leila was not happy about this state of affairs, but she knew that their desperate situation required all they could give to it. They were young, and they would have many years in which to love each other and have a happy life together.

They breakfasted alone together in their sitting room, warm late-autumn sunshine streaming in from a courtyard window. All of the doors and windows in this wing of the palace had been marked subtly with the symbols of Betsalel, providing a psychological deterrent to intruders that would be difficult to get past. Even so, guards patrolled the gardens as well as the building's interior.

"I think I have to be the one to go to Namei," Leila said, washing down a bite of pastry with a sip of strong, bitter kaf. Imbaso looked at her and sighed.

"You're right," he said, "but I'm not happy about it."

"Hey, I'm a trained assassin with a god in my pocket and the powers of illusion and invisibility at my command!" she replied. "What could go wrong?"

He squeezed over closer to her on the divan, where they sat eating from a low table, and put an arm around her. "When will you leave?" he asked. "And from where? Here?"

"It will have to be from here this time," Leila replied, "but we should set up a public shrine to Betsalel somewhere in the palace. I could use that as a point from which our master could transport me to places in the future."

After cleaning her teeth, Leila dressed in her assassin's gear – complete with its myriad lethal weapons. Any other outfit she wished to appear in could become part of the illusion she presented to the world, but what she wore beneath that illusion would help her to fulfill her mission.

Still with her small personal idol in her pocket, Leila set one of the seed idols she carried in a small bottle on the floor of the parlor in an alcove. "Do you want to write a personal note to your mother?" she asked, and Imbaso stepped over to the writing desk in the corner.

"Good idea," he said. "She scarcely met Usiku, and has never seen you. Plus there's some chance she has not heard anything about recent events. I'm anxious to see her under protection before Father has a chance to return to Namei."

"It should take him at least a couple of weeks to get there," Leila said. "I assume that he and the assassins will try to get a riverboat and take it all the way downriver?"

"It's the fastest way from the Azraq to Namei," Imbaso replied as he penned the message to his mother. "And Father's power base is there. We can be sure he'll try to go there as soon as he can to marshal his forces for a counter-attack."

"Well, I guess it's time to go," Leila said. Imbaso folded her in a tight embrace, several hard objects poking him through her clothing as he kissed her.

"Don't let anything happen to my mother, and don't let anything happen to yourself," he admonished her sternly.

She kissed him again and promised, "I won't."

Leila knelt before the tiny seed-like idol on the floor and called to it, "Betsalel, come to me. It's time for us to storm the citadel of Namei." The Shadow God grew in an instant, to a height of more than six feet this time. "How stands your idol in Namei, master?" Leila asked.

"The sanctuary there held only a painting, beloved," Betsalel reminded her. "In order for me to prevent the cultists from learning that a true idol had been placed in the temple, I have had to return the idol Imbaso placed there to a tiny grain hidden behind the altar. For me to carry you there, you will need to become smaller than that grain – though I will restore you to your true size once we have arrived."

443

Leila hadn't considered that. But then she only knew Betsalel had said he could carry her through the spirit world between idols – not how it worked. "Will it hurt?" she asked skeptically.

"Not at all," the dark god assured her. "You I would never hurt."

"All right," she said, biting her lip. "Go ahead."

Betsalel bent and picked his arch-priestess up in his arms. He had rarely touched her over the time they had known one another, and it was surprising to feel his cool, yielding flesh as he held her. Then the two of them shrank in unison. Imbaso looked on, heart in his throat, as the god and the woman he held shrank back to the black rice grain that had been there a minute before. He picked it up between thumb and forefinger, peering at it closely. It was the Shadow God's traditional idol, arms at his sides. He held nothing in them.

In Namei, many miles to the west, dawn had not yet broken. A young man in black priest's robes sat in the front row of the sanctuary, his head fallen on his chest. He had been set the night watch, but had dropped off to sleep an hour ago. Two nights before there had been a huge stir among the priesthood. Kivuli had manifested in his idol without a sacrifice being given, warning them that one of their number, the turncoat Imbaso, had been placed on the throne of Palambo and was launching an attack against the cult and all of its members.

The god's warning, the most coherent piece of information any of his priesthood in Namei had ever gotten from him, contained another shocking bit of news: He, Kivuli, was not in fact Betsalel taking a new name after his transformation. The old Shadow God still existed, and had begun trying to take back his temples from the worshipers of Kivuli. They must look for signs of him making incursions here in Namei, and kill any who were found worshiping him. The remaining members of the Namei chapter of the Makucha Nyeusi were to assassinate anyone who spoke out against the cult, or accused Kivuli, the true god of Death, of being nothing but an evil djinn. Anyone espousing such a belief must be put to death.

After that Kivuli had left his idol, and had not manifested to them since. Likely he was busy visiting all of his hundreds of temples throughout Palambo, delivering the same warning. But chapters of the Black Claw were rare. Without the god actually being there to defend them, how were the priests to stop anyone coming in to kill them and smash their idols? As far as Kivuli (and Mauaji, who had sent him on those errands) was concerned, that was their problem.

Leila and Betsalel knew nothing of this, though it was something they had considered as a possibility. Since Mauaji had decided to throw away the chance of redemption and cast his lot with the djinn, he would be taking any steps he could think of to counter Imbaso's efforts to cleanse the temples of Kivuli's followers.

Thus, both the Shadow God and the girl in his arms were cloaked in shadows as they manifested in the tiny idol hidden behind the altar in the public sanctuary in Namei, and grew together until Leila was her normal size. She spoke to him mind to mind, as they stared together at the black-clad youth sleeping in the pew before them.

"Is he a Kivuli cultist?" she asked.

"He is swathed in the djinn's protection, and I cannot see into his mind," the god replied silently.

"He must be here watching for you to manifest, then," Leila mused.

"Kivuli is not here," Betsalel informed her. "In fact there are very few people here now – this young man and another outside, plus two below. All of them wear the same protection. But the inner sanctum is locked up tight."

As Betsalel was the god of night, among his other attributes, midnight had long been a traditional time for his rites. Most of the higher members of the priesthood would probably be in their beds, now. The god let her down onto the floor and she moved silently across to the young priest. Drawing out a small object shaped like a fat disk an inch in diameter, Leila laid it across the back of the sleeping man's neck. The cowl of his robe was down and his hair was cropped short.

As she pressed, the slender needle inside poked out and pierced the flesh, with a sting like that of a biting fly. The young man's eyes flew open, but he saw nothing. No enormous dark god, no small assassin. Biting bugs were a problem in all of the non-desert parts of Palambo, if not usually this early in the morning. He shook himself a little, realizing he had fallen asleep on the job. It was all right, nothing had happened, but he was grateful to whatever had bitten him for bringing him back to alertness. He shuddered to think what his superiors would have done if he'd been caught dozing.

A minute or so later the priest stiffened, and appeared to resume his nap. The oualit on the needle had stopped his heart. After checking to make sure her adversary was dead, Leila spoke silently again to the Shadow God. "I think destroying the idol is the next thing I need to do," she said. "Can you make me a big hammer?"

No one was near, and they both became visible for a moment as Betsalel pulled a large, ornate hammer out of thin air and handed it to her. It was heavy, clearly made of metal but black in color with a slight sheen. One face of the hammer head was pointed, the other flat. "Nice," Leila remarked with a grin. Then she went invisible again. "You probably should stay manifested for a while, on guard until I've finished this part of my mission," she requested.

The Shadow God assented, but remained visible – standing within his sanctuary looking down on the corpse of the man who should have been his worshiper, if the world had not gone wrong. Leila let herself silently out of the sanctuary. There was no one in the anteroom – evidently the man inside here had been considered enough. The "man outside" Betsalel had mentioned must be patrolling the grounds on the alert for anyone trying to get in via the secret rear entrance.

Would the sentry be Makucha Nyeusi? Leila didn't know how many full members the Namei chapter boasted. There had been half a dozen fellow apprentices, none of whom had yet been initiated by the time she and the rest of her company had left for Iskand. Then there were supposedly two middle-aged women, and who knew how many men? Certainly the four they'd brought with them had seemed competent enough, but nothing special. So maybe there hadn't been that many to choose from?

The sky was beginning to lighten, but it would be at least half an hour before the sun began to peep over the eastern horizon. Already there was a racket of birdsong coming from the trees growing around the temple circle. It was not hard for Leila to spot the sentry in the grounds. He was moving silently from cover to cover, keeping himself where he could see both the front and back temple doors.

She carefully set the hammer down in some low shrubbery, shielding the inevitable rustling with a bubble of silence. Then, hands free, she crept up on the man in black. Yes, those were not traditional priest robes. The man was wearing a loose-fitting tunic belted at the waist above baggy trousers gathered at the ankle, and had a hood over his head. Everything was black.

As he turned to move to another location, Leila threw a dagger into his back. The sentry toppled face down, and she was on him in a moment. She pulled the knife from his back and lifted his head to cut his throat, the blood spurting forward and down to soak the turf of the temple gardens. She carefully wiped the dagger on her victim's clothing before putting it away, then rolled the man over. Kifozi had not lied when he'd told Imbaso he was too tall to be an assassin. The most successful ones were little bigger than she was, and this man probably stood not more than five-foot-seven tall.

She pulled off his hood and stepped back to get a good look at him in the growing dawn light. It was master Szendibo, one of the assassin instructors who had participated in her induction into the Black Claw! His specialty had been acrobatics, and Usiku had proved to be already so skilled in that discipline that he hadn't had much occasion to teach her.

Leila dragged the small, middle-aged man deep into the shadow of some dense shrubbery. The flies would soon alert passersby to the corpse, but for now he was out of the way. Which way now, she wondered – front or back? She suspected that the door to the lower level from inside the sanctuary would be barred from the inside. Betsalel might be able to open it for her, unless it had been warded somehow by the power of Kivuli; but she thought there might be a better way to get inside.

Dembale slouched against the wall on the inner side of the back door to the secret worship complex beneath the temple of Betsalel. He had been on duty for only three hours and would continue to be for another nine; but he was already getting bored. Of what possible use was it to stick a full-fledged assassin of the Makucha Nyeusi, a fifteen-year veteran, on guard duty inside a temple complex that was behind two locked, barred doors?

At least master Szendibo, guarding the temple's exterior, got to move around and watch for real threats. But unless Dembale was supposed to guard against misbehavior from the young priest sharing the watch with him, he didn't see the point.

Suddenly there was a loud pounding on that door. What? "Who goes there?" Dembale demanded.

"It's me, you idiot!" The voice of master Szendibo declared – but in hushed tones. Dembale opened the little peephole in the door and saw, in the growing light outside, the eyes of the man who had been one of the Black Claw's masters since Dembale himself was a callow youth. The rest of his face was hidden by his assassin's hood.

"A group of men with weapons is infiltrating the grounds!" Szendibo hissed. "I can't take them all down single-handedly – get out here and give me a hand, now!" The master's tone was urgent, Dembale was itching for some action, and his opinion of the young priest with whom he shared the watch was such that he saw no reason to call him. Hastily unbarring and unlocking the door, he stepped through it. Then he shut it and locked it behind him, and followed silently in Szendibo's wake. The master assassin was already moving away into the bushes, fading from sight.

Dembale, dagger at the ready, crouched low behind a bush as he peered out. Where had Szendibo gone? And where were the intruders? He seriously doubted that any ordinary citizen, however outraged by what they had heard about goings-on at the temple, possessed enough woodcraft to hide from such as he. Suddenly he felt a sharp pain in the back of his neck as a razor-sharp dagger was thrust in between the third and fourth cervical vertebrae, severing his spine. He collapsed to the ground, and felt nothing more.

Leila had not known this member of the cult. She'd known her fellow apprentices and the masters who taught them quite well, but had met almost none of the "rank and file" of the Black Claw chapter beyond the four young men who'd accompanied her to Iskand. How many more were there?

Now taking the appearance of the man she had just killed, Leila returned to the rear of the temple – picking up the hammer on the way. She had taken the key from the corpse, so didn't even need to pick the lock. Lest unexpected Black Claw reinforcements arrive, she locked and barred the door again. Then she went looking for the fourth man Betsalel had said was here.

Leila searched for her god with her mind, but did not reach him. The cult, or its "god," must have surrounded this place with a barrier against supernatural powers. No one was in sight, and she wished she knew that last man's name. Changing tactics, she went invisible and began exploring the rooms in the temple's secret undercroft. She left the hammer leaning against the wall near the entrance to the inner sanctum.

She had been in several of these already, but definitely not in all of them. She tried the doors to the inner sanctum, where the idol was housed, but found them locked. "Here, priestie priestie!" she called in her mind. There was no response.

Leila found the fourth man in one of the rooms she *had* visited before: the scriptorium, where inductees went to study the Secret Scriptures. This was no full priest, just a young acolyte. He looked to be around nineteen, and she'd have been willing to bet he'd been lured into the cult by a father or an uncle, some adult male with enough influence on an impressionable young man to push him into the darkness whether he truly sought it or not.

In an instant Kivuli stood there – seven feet tall, snarling, golden eyes glowing as fresh red blood dripped from fang and claw. The young acolyte very nearly wet his robes. "Master!" he squeaked, terror turning his deep brown skin an ashy color.

"What do you here?" the Death Who Comes in the Night hissed. "Where are my priests?"

"It's – ulp! – early morning, master!" the acolyte stammered. "Everyone has gone to bed except for the four on guard here!"

"Four?" the god asked, and the teenager continued, "Aselme is watching up in the public sanctuary, on guard against any appearances by Betsalel. And the two Makucha Nyeusi are on guard as well, ready to defend your inner sanctum from attacks!"

"As if I could not defend myself," Kivuli growled, insulted. "Why only two? Why not two dozen? Surely if royal guards come, they will come in force?" The boy looked as if he wished the earth would open and swallow him up; but he was on the spot, and must answer. He had seen what his god could do – and would do, on a whim.

"After your warning, master, we have done what we could. But though Namei is fortunate to have a chapter of the Makucha Nyeusi to defend us, six of their best are away – gone these past weeks in Iskand. That leaves only another six, not counting the apprentices."

Wow, Leila thought. A total of eighteen people for all that infrastructure? The assassin business must pay very well indeed. "Then what happens when a large force of royal guards comes here, if I am busy elsewhere?" the god asked. The acolyte smiled in relief. He had a *good* answer for that question.

"But you must surely know that your loyal worshiper Tadelmo is also commander of the Namei garrison?" he asked. "With him in charge, all suggestions of an armed raid on the temple will be deflected. What precautions you see are just in case a party of citizens decides to act on the rumors that have been circulating. It's said that people around the city have had vivid dreams, telling them that they should seek to destroy what lies beneath the temple. We believe that Betsalel may have somehow become able to manifest in the sanctuary above, and be contacting those who prayed to him with dreams. He is sending them to their destruction, if so!"

Betsalel had not mentioned that to Leila and Imbaso. She had to remember that he was an ancient and powerful god, not some guy she was in a dubious relationship with. He was under no obligation to tell her of his every move. She added this commander Tadelmo to her "to do" list and moved on.

Leila paused, considering. She had killed three men today, and her initial take on this acolyte being an innocent had been revised by the depth of his knowledge. Anyone whose loyalties were suspect would not have been given this duty, she realized. Sighing internally, she dropped her illusion. The horrific djinn became a much smaller figure, clad in near-black.

She closed the distance to the acolyte, who stood several inches taller than her, in a silent second. "Who are you?" he breathed, nearly as terrified now as he had been when the figure he took to be Kivuli had appeared out of thin air.

"I am The Death That Comes in the Morning," she said softly, and plunged her dagger into his heart.

Leila was now alone in the echoing confines of the secret temple beneath the one that had stood for millennia. Somewhere in this complex there might be a desk drawer in which was hidden the key to the inner sanctum; but she didn't waste time searching. The lock was robust and relatively new, but it yielded to her lockpicks after a couple of minutes.

Heart pounding, she stepped into the inner sanctum for the first time. She beheld the dark altar, the pit where the black flames would arise, the pathetic bloodstains barely visible against the dark stone. Leila knew quite a lot about gods and supernatural beings from her crash course over the past almost two years, but there was a lot she didn't know. Could the djinn manifest in his idol if there was someone near it who knew he existed but was not a worshiper? Would her fear and repugnance be enough to allow him passage?

With an effort, Leila drove all fear – and all belief – out of her mind as she approached the idol. Kivuli was nothing but the product of twisted human imagination, she told herself, and she was protected by Betsalel. Kivuli could not harm her.

The idol in its new form was crouched over in a pose half-human, half-bestial. There was not that much space between the top of the column that had been stolen from the sanctuary above and the ceiling of the chamber. But Leila stood little above five feet high. She hopped up onto the altar the better to reach the idol.

The hammer was a heavy weapon, nothing she would ever use in combat. Its mass threatened to overcome her own slight mass and throw her off-balance. But it was needful here. The all-black figure with its four clawed limbs, tail, and glowing golden eyes was thinnest in the limbs and tail, of course. But if she snapped one off, would that be enough damage to prevent the djinn from manifesting? The waist, the area between ribcage and haunches, was also relatively thin. Leila decided that her first blow would land there.

She gripped the hammer with both hands, planting her feet. Its handle was well more than half her height. Then, powering forward with all of her wiry strength, Leila swung it around in a half-arc, pointed end forward, and it connected with the idol of Kivuli at a spot in the center of its rightward-facing body, just a little above the groin. The stone shattered, and the top half of the idol fell to the floor.

Chapter 70

After the idol of Kivuli had been reduced to fist-sized particles of black rubble, Leila returned to the sanctuary above via the inside door for a consultation with her god. "You have succeeded, Leila!" Betsalel declared, a rare smile on his stern face.

"You could feel it?" she asked, and he nodded.

"I still find some barrier to my powers here. I am able to see the areas below, and all of the shielded individuals have gone. But I still would not be able to affect anything there. The area itself is under some kind of residual shield."

"If I take you inside that shield, might you be able to use your powers there?" she asked. The sun was up now, and she was not sure how long it might be before the small force here was augmented.

"It is likely," Betsalel said, "depending on the nature of the shield. But at the moment, the believer score here within my temple is one to zero, and I feel strong."

Leila smiled at that. She had the god vanish the corpse of the priest who'd been sleeping on his watch, then reduce the idol here in the public sanctuary to its tiny original size – hidden behind the altar. Downstairs she called him to another tiny idol from her collection. "How does this feel?" she asked. It was a couple of moments before Betsalel spoke.

"Terrible things have taken place here," he said sadly.

"Are you able to reach outside from here?" Leila asked, and after considering for a while Betsalel said,

"I have removed the barriers. Do you wish me to dispose of the rest of the bodies?"

"Yes please," she said. "And even though the shards of Kivuli's idol are worth a thousand asand, could you also cause those to disappear?"

She stood waiting for a couple of minutes. Finally the Shadow God announced that the task she'd set him had been completed. It seemed their work here was done, for the time being. "Master," Leila said, "What shall we do about this place?"

He considered the question. "I believe it best that I fill it in, as I did with the temple in Iskand," Betsalel replied at last. It made sense. The idol was gone, and there was no need to let the remaining Kivuli cultists within Namei have a place in which they could barricade themselves. Likely, most of them would be willing to renounce the evil djinn when faced with no other options. There would be no need to kill every member of the cult.

But the rest of the Makucha Nyeusi would have to die, save the uninitiated apprentices. The cult of assassins had operated for centuries, long before the dark god they worshiped had been anything beyond an idea. They were devoted to killing, theoretically in honor of the god they had believed Betsalel to be; but mostly as a way to make money, Leila suspected. And the guard commander Tadelmo must die as well.

Betsalel shrank slightly and walked out of the temple's secret lower level under his own power, accompanied by Leila. The sun was well up now, but no one was yet to be seen in the area. All of the hollow spaces beneath the temple became solid black stone, and the rear door vanished completely – now a solid part of the stone temple itself. Unless the Namei congregation got word of what was happening, there would be some very surprised worshipers arriving here this evening!

"I am of a mind," the Shadow God said with immense satisfaction, "to complete the reclaiming of this temple. Come with me." The two of them walked, quiet companions, around to the deserted front entrance of the temple and went inside.

The column on which the idol of Kivuli had been sitting before Leila smashed it to bits, evidently the original from this temple and of importance to the god's nexus of power, was now sitting incongruously atop the altar. In another instant the altar had vanished, and column stood on the stone floor as if it had always been there.

Getting the idea, Leila found the tiny seed idol where it lay amid dust near the back of the room, and placed it atop the column. Then Betsalel was momentarily manifested in two places at once – but only separated by the distance of a few feet. "This feels very odd," the one on the column remarked as he grew to the greatest height the space would reasonably allow – too big to be easily carried off. Then the Shadow God left that one, and spoke in Leila's mind as he shrank the other idol to the size of a rice grain. "Put this one back in your collection, beloved. I am sure you'll be needing it."

She scooped it up carefully and put it back in the little bottle where she kept her collection. She still had her toy-sized idol in another pocket. Then she stood a moment, soaking up the feel of the restored temple. It looked, and felt, right. Where to next, she wondered, and decided she would go down to the third circle and visit the Makucha Nyeusi's headquarters. The royal guard commander could wait.

With her new power of tirelessness, it was very nearly a joy for Leila to trot down the streets of Namei in the early morning sunshine. The streets weren't terribly crowded and she ran cloaked in shadows, surrounded by a bubble of silence. Once or twice she was forced to pass others closely enough that they fell within her bubble, startling them as they heard her footfalls. But a moment later the sound had ceased, and each one thought they had only imagined the sound.

Outside the gymnasium Leila hesitated, considering her approach. If the place was not locked up and abandoned, its inhabitants would certainly be on their guard. She could not appear as Usiku, for the djinn's warning might well have included mention of the girl assassin who had vanished.

Another minute had passed, and Leila finally took on the semblance of the late master Szendibo. Of all the remaining members of Namei's Black Claw chapter, he was the one most likely to show up here. It was to be hoped, and she believed it true, that in the three days since Mauaji and his party had vanished from the palace in Iskand they could not have gotten any further than the desert wasteland between Aswa and Tsimbei.

Leila pushed on the door. Always before it had been unlocked, with a clerical-looking assassin in the outer office to turn away casual visitors; but now it was secured. She tried pounding on it.

This door too had a peephole; and as it had before, the face of Szendibo granted her entrance.

Szendibo had a bleeding sword cut on his arm, and a grim expression on his face. The man who had opened the door to him, Yusuf, was very familiar to Leila. He usually manned the desk looking perfectly ordinary. But now he was dressed in the same sort of assassin gear as Szendibo was.

"What happened, master?" he asked in alarm. Szendibo coughed and spat.

"Cursed Tadelmo!" he said.

"Tadelmo, master?"

"As you know, there were but four of us on the late watch," the master assassin said. "Right around dawn, a party of royal guards showed up. Tadelmo must have sold us out – there were at least twenty of them!"

"Dembale?" Yusuf asked. The two were close in age and had gone through their apprenticeships together.

"Dead," Szendibo replied with a snarl. "All dead, save me. I was stationed outside, and was picking them off as chance allowed, but I could scarcely conduct a frontal assault against so many. I killed the guard who gave me this" – he gestured with the bleeding arm – "and then hid to watch. They battered down the door to the temple below. Our master did not come to the aid of those striving to save his temple, I fear."

"The idol!" Yusuf said, "What if they destroy the idol? We will be left on our own!"

"Were we not on our own for centuries before, Yusuf?" the older man asked bitterly. "We of the Makucha Nyeusi need no gods to fight our battles for us. I fear it is too late to save the temple. Let us instead infiltrate the royal guard headquarters and pay our respects to Tadelmo. How many are here?"

"Everyone," Yusuf replied. Leila suddenly had a moment of doubt. She didn't know who "everyone" was, didn't know whether any classes were being held with nearly all of the chapter's masters unavailable to teach. She could sort it out later, of course.

"Tell them all to gather inside the culvert leading out of the top circle as quickly as possible," Szendibo grated. "I will meet you all soon, but I have some things to take care of first. Wait for my arrival."

Chapter 71

The master assassin stepped back out the door before Yusuf could ask any questions. Moments after the door closed he slipped into a narrow space between two buildings and vanished from sight. After locking the door behind him, Yusuf hurried to inform his colleagues of the terrible news, and their planned retribution.

The streets, especially here on one of the lower circles, were becoming too crowded with foot traffic and *ritzhas* to make it possible for Leila to run through them invisibly and silently. Instead she adopted the appearance of a teenage boy, a messenger with the Royal Messenger Service. Many such had gone out carrying copies of the proclamation she and Imbaso had authored, though those had mostly been mounted on horseback. They were also used to run messages up to the top level guard compound from the city gate, though, and those usually went on foot.

Leila was thankful for her tirelessness once again – running uphill in Namei was a different undertaking from coming down it. She wished she had time to stop and visit her little house, of which she had such fond memories. But there was no time now.

During the monsoon, which time it had been when Usiku first came to Namei, several inches of rain in a day was not unheard-of. As the top circle of the tiered city had its own wall, it had been necessary to allow for drainage. A great circular stone conduit, five feet in diameter, ran beneath the wall for more than fifteen feet before taking a right-angle bend and coming up beneath a heavy bronze grate.

Water flowed through the culvert and out another bronze grate, kept locked to prevent unauthorized entrance, down a six-foot fall to a rocky ravine. This ravine soon plunged underground and into a network of storm sewers, carrying rainwater away downslope. But at this season, rains were light and infrequent.

Leila took a footpath leading up from the circular road on the temple level, shedding her messenger illusion and going invisible as she followed a barely visible trail leading up along the ravine. Then she climbed the rocks and examined the padlock holding the grating across the culvert's entrance closed.

Like the grating itself, it was made of bronze. That metal was considerably more weather-resistant than iron or steel, but the lock was showing a heavy coating of verdigris. Leila attacked it with her sturdiest lockpicks, but the mechanism was frozen shut. Shit! Probably nobody had been up here for months or even years, though it was one of the pathways the Makucha Nyeusi used when they needed entrance to the top of Namei without going through the main gate.

She pulled the little idol out of her pocket and called her god. "I can't get this lock open," she said. "Can you free the inside mechanism of all corrosion so that it will turn freely?" "Try it now," Betsalel said, and she found that it opened smoothly. There was still a lot of green crust on the outside, but even a far-less-adept person than Leila was should be able to open it. "Thank you, master," she said softly. "Please stay with me while I go around to the gate."

Moving carefully, Leila went up by the main road to the gate and through it, invisible all the while. She walked back around the side to where the gutters of the top circle merged, dumping their contents into a shallow well with the five-foot-wide upper grate covering it. There was quite a bit of debris scattered across the grating, washed down by the rains of the past monsoon season probably: tree branches, bits of trash, the desiccated corpse of a mongoose.

Ugh, Leila thought. Surely it was some government functionary's job to keep this clean. Any more covered with detritus and the water might just surge up to flood the area, perhaps undermining the wall. "I hate to ask you this, Betsalel," she said in mind talk, "but could you make all this crud vanish?" He chuckled in her mind, and all was gone. He seemed to have the ability to make solid objects dissolve into their component atoms, or create them from thin air.

Maybe that thin air was really awash with some of those same component atoms, Leila mused, as she hopped down atop the grate and checked the lock. Like the other, it was stuck closed. Excellent. She explained her plan to the god in her pocket, then climbed back up and returned out the main gate, back to the lower culvert entrance. Then, still invisible, she hunkered down in some bushes a few feet off the trail to wait.

She didn't have to wait long. She had been sitting there for no more than ten minutes when she spotted two bent old women coming up the trail, carrying bundles of what looked like rags on their backs. As they approached the top they set those burdens down, as if resting from their labors. Then while one kept watch the other, suddenly far younger and more agile than she had seemed a moment before, pulled off her robe to reveal the familiar assassin's gear beneath.

She climbed the rocks and had the newly-freed lock open in a trice. Then her companion tossed the bundles up to her and climbed up herself, before pulling the grating closed and setting the padlock so that from any distance it would appear to be closed and locked. The two women moved back into the culvert, down the center of which a trickle of water was flowing, and crouched in hiding.

So those were the two other female Black Claw members, Leila mused. Usiku might have been well-suited to gathering intelligence under the guise of being an innocent (and beautiful) young woman, but these two could have gone almost anywhere disguised as servants. No one would have given them a second glance, right up until the moment the dagger was inserted between the ribs. She wondered that the cult of assassins didn't actively recruit more women to their membership.

It appeared that "everybody" at the Makucha Nyeusi headquarters had delayed only long enough to make preparations for what they all assumed was going to be a raid in force on royal guard headquarters and the gruesome extermination of the traitor Tadelmo. Not that it was much of a force. The women were swiftly followed by Yusuf, who let himself in without the need to pick the lock, and then a man who looked to be in his later thirties, whom Leila did not recall seeing before. He was smallish, wiry, and very nondescript – perfect qualifications for an assassin.

He, too, closed the padlock almost all the way before retreating away from the grating to hide inside the culvert with the others. Invisible and moving silently, Leila drew close and listened at the grating. "If Tadelmo has betrayed the temple, that means the royal guard will be coming down on all of us soon," one of the women murmured. "We need to get a warning to the membership," the other said as quietly.

"Why don't we visit the mess and slip poison into the pot for today's lunch?" the last man to arrive suggested. "If the entire royal guard garrison is dead, our members can slip away quietly without fear of exposure, and take a boat downriver to Dikka. There's a big chapter there, and one of the largest of our master's temples. We will all be welcomed there, I'm sure."

"That's not a bad idea, but I really want to roast Tadelmo's guts over a slow fire before he dies," Yusuf replied. "Why don't you two do your 'serving woman' bit in the kitchens, and then meet us in Tadelmo's office. He'll just have to forego lunch, today." There was a chorus of soft chuckles and general agreement, and whatever reservations Leila had had about her own cruel plan were discarded.

The group in the culvert were just beyond the range of the silence bubble Leila erected, and they did not hear the "snick" as she snapped the lock closed. Betsalel had remained manifested in the little idol in her pocket, as curious as she was to see what came to their trap. "Return the lock to its original state?" he asked in her mind, and she replied "Yes, please. Then it will be time to begin."

The lock's internal mechanism became a solid lump of corrosion, worse than it had been before. Then as Leila beat a hasty retreat, seeking shelter, a shadow fell across the sun. By the time she was trotting along the circular street serving the eight temples, the sky was full of billowing nimbus clouds and bolts of lightning were beginning to leap among them. She found the temple of Betsalel still deserted, and hurried inside it just as rain began pouring from the sky in an unstoppable torrent.

Chapter 72

The heavens poured out their waters on Namei (and on a surprisingly small area around it) for nearly two hours. Then the rain stopped as suddenly as it had begun, and by noontime the sun was out again – sparkling like diamonds on a billion drops of water.

Leila was getting hungry, and took some dense cake out of her pack to munch on as she and her god made their way back toward the culvert. The ravine was flooded, the trail washed away along with a lot of vegetation around it. The culvert had not filled completely with water, of course, and there was some possibility a person trapped inside it could survive.

But the force of the collected runoff pouring down into the culvert's upper end had been too great to resist. The four plotting assassins had been smashed against the lower grating, bones broken, and then drowned in the torrent that engulfed them. Betsalel confirmed that none yet lived, and did for these bodies as he had done for the others at the temple. No one but he and Leila, and whomever they chose to tell, would ever know what had become of the remnants of Namei's chapter of the Makucha Nyeusi.

Invisibly, Leila made her way through the gates for the second time today and into the guard headquarters. Most of the men were in the mess hall eating lunch, and thanks to her none of them were writhing in agony from poison. The young messenger who had run up from the third circle earlier today reappeared, and approached one of the men who was on duty.

"Message for Commander Tadelmo, sir!" he said, giving a sort-of salute. The Messengers were not a part of the Guard Corps, but they paid them respect. The corps accounted for a lot of their daily business.

"The commander is lunching in the officer's mess," the guard said. "Shall I take the message for him?"

"No sir," the lad replied. "If you can point me to his office, I'll wait for him there."

The guard obligingly showed the messenger around a corner and pointed to the door one down from the end of the corridor. "That's his door," he said. "You'll have to wait outside for him, and I can't say when he'll be back."

"No problem, sir!" the kid said with a cheeky smile. "I'll just sit down for a bit. More than happy to get off my feet!" With that he plopped himself down on the floor, back leaning up against the wall, and the guard smiled back at him and returned to his post.

Leila waited for around five minutes. She was not at all tired from her repeated scurrying back and forth between the eleventh and twelfth circles of the city. But a certain emotional fatigue was beginning to creep over her. She was only killing people who needed to be killed, but that didn't mean they weren't still people. She had rather liked Yusuf.

When she was sure that the guard was going to remain at his post, and that Tadelmo was not cutting short his midday meal, Leila went invisible and set to work on the commander's office door with her lockpicks. The thing was a massive solid slab of bloodwood, with a polished brass plate on it showing the commander's name and rank. She wondered how long the guard commander had been a secret participant in a bloodthirsty cult. While soldiers might kill for a living, and come to enjoy it, there was nothing soldierly about putting infants and other helpless victims under the sacrificial knife.

The lock was a good one, and it was nearly two full minutes before the last of its tumblers yielded and the door opened. Leila stepped inside, then immediately had to spend more time locking it behind her. When the commander returned with his key, he was not to know that anything was amiss.

Now she had some time to kill, and spent it searching through the paperwork in the office to see what she could find out about this Tadelmo. One of the first things she came across was a copy of her and Imbaso's proclamation. It must have been delivered here by one of the Eight, probably Andros or maybe even Belantos, and whomever the god had handed it over to had hastened to put it into the hands of the highest authority in the city: the commander of the royal guards.

A piece of paper had been attached to the proclamation with a small metal clip. It read, "Lembali – I have had this investigated and found no evidence of such a cult here in Namei. Please file with general orders." The note was signed with a squiggle that Leila assumed was Tadelmo's signature, and it was sitting in a wooden tray she guessed was the commander's outbox. With no wars going on locally, the commander's job was an administrative position – similar to the work her father did for the kingdom. Lembali was likely the commander's personal secretary or company clerk.

That evidence was pretty damning right there, Leila mused. This could not have arrived here much before midday yesterday, given the time difference, and had an innocent Tadelmo immediately run out and taken a peek at the temple of Betsalel on the circle below, he could hardly have failed to notice the back door.

Tadelmo's desk was as impressive as his office door, a massive affair of carved bloodwood with insets of ivory and pearl shell. Tastes in the Dominion could be as ornate, but it seemed a strange choice for a soldier. How had he gotten this job in the first place? Was he yet another of the descendants of recent Palamban kings?

The desk was locked, but its locks were primitive and Leila had them open almost faster than she could have done with the key. The top drawer held an assortment of top-quality pens, a few coins, and a small sheaf of letters that proved to be love-notes from Tadelmo's mistress. Leila passed it all by, realizing as she did so that being made queen of a very large country seemed to have (somewhat, at least) cured her of her long-held tendency to steal anything that wasn't nailed down.

Things got more interesting as Leila opened the drawers further down. There were communiqués from Mauaji, an assurance that a Makucha Nyeusi contract Tadelmo had bought had been carried out, and other bits of evidence that had her, finally, convinced that the guard commander was unquestionably working hand-in-glove with the cult of Kivuli. The only thing that remained was how best to dispose of him.

Leila toyed with the idea of using the method she had used to kill Mkuuzo. The idea of appearing as Kivuli and ripping Tadelmo from throat to crotch with the clawed knuckle dusters in her pockets held a certain appeal. She'd be willing to bet the commander had recruited at least a few of his fellow guards to the cult, and the sight of the mutilated body would strike fear in them.

But no. Such a killing was horrendously messy, and a lot of work as well. Plus it would cause a furor in guard quarters, distracting them just when they would be needed for rounding up the remaining cultists in Namei. Betsalel should be able to identify all of the initiates, and a goodly number of guards would be needed to bring them all in so they could be offered absolution – or death.

In the end, the invisible assassin waited for another hour until Commander Tadelmo returned from his long, well-lubricated lunch. He was a man in his fifties, as King Omali had been. Everyone knew that such men, especially those who indulged heavily in the pleasures of food and drink, were wont to drop dead of failing hearts.

Leila waited until he had sunk his bulk into the broad, well-upholstered chair that stood behind the desk. Then she applied the oualit needle to his head – through the mat of thick, tightly curled hair and into the blood-rich scalp. "Ouch!" Tadelmo exclaimed, swatting at his head. There were not supposed to be any biting flies in here!

Leila seized his wrist, bending it backward in a move the Makucha had taught her. Then she went visible, as herself. "What… who are you?" the commander cried. He was already beginning to feel a little woozy.

"The queen of fucking Palambo," Leila snarled low, "that's who. And I am highly displeased with your performance, Commander Tadelmo."

"You're a madwoman!" Tadelmo exclaimed. "Guards! Guards! Help me!" But nothing that had been said between them penetrated beyond Leila's bubble of silence. In another few seconds the oualit hit the commander's heart, and stopped it. He collapsed face down on the desk, and Leila checked his scalp to be sure no blood was welling out. The needle was *very* fine.

Moving around to the other side of the desk, Leila suddenly became the messenger the guard had guided here when she arrived. "Help, help!" he cried, rushing out of the office and around the corner to the guard he'd talked with earlier. "The commander has been taken ill! Call a healer!"

"What, what's all this?" the guard asked. The commander had seemed perfectly fine, if perhaps a little the worse for drink, only moments before.

"What happened?" he demanded, as he moved beside the panic-stricken messenger back to the commander's office. The door was standing wide.

"He let me in when he got back from lunch," the kid said. "He'd just sat down in his chair and was asking me what the message was, when he clutched his chest, like, and then collapsed! It must be a heart attack!"

The guard stepped forward to his fallen commander, lying motionless with his head down on the desktop. He pulled the man's head up, but saw no signs of life. Fingers to the neck confirmed it – the commander was dead. There was a trace of ash in the youth's dark brown complexion, eyes wide.

"Is he…?" The guard put a sympathetic hand on the kid's shoulder.

"I'm sorry, son," he said. "He's gone. No healer's going to help him now."

Tears were threatening to spill out of the messenger's eyes. Nothing like this, clearly, had ever happened to him before. "I need to deliver my message," he said. "It's important!" Such things were beyond the guard's pay grade. But he took the boy by the elbow.

"Come on," he said. "We'll go see the second in command." The guard led the messenger along the corridor, and after they'd turned a corridor they spotted another guard. "Ojinam!" he called.

"The commander's had a heart attack, and he's a goner! I'm going to see Nananji, so get a squad up here will you?" Ojinam gaped, then saluted and rushed to do as he'd been bidden.

They came to another door in another corridor, standing open as a man who could not have been much above thirty-five labored over a desk stacked high with paperwork. If this was the second in command, Leila thought, the commander must have been dumping a lot of his work off on his subordinates.

The man at the desk looked up, surprise in his eyes, as the guard with the messenger in tow came inside. "Nananji, sir!" the guard said, standing at attention and saluting. "At ease, Sergeant," the under-commander said, intelligent eyes taking in the situation and trying to guess what was happening. His guess was way off.

"Commander Tadelmo has just died of a heart attack, sir!" the guard declared. Nananji's eyes went wide. Considering Tadelmo's habits, the news shouldn't have been that shocking. But somehow, he'd been willing to believe that the old reprobate had struck a deal with the devil and would outlive them all – even the raw recruits.

"Have you sent a squad, Sergeant?" Nananji asked in a few seconds, after recovering his calm.

"Yes, sir!" the guard replied.

"As soon as the body has been removed I will need to go to his office and assess what needs to be done," the under-commander (and now, it appeared, acting commander) said. "And I will need to dispatch a message to Central Command immediately," he added. "Have you anticipated that, and brought me a messenger?"

The kid spoke up, still looking half-terrified. "I'll be happy to take your message to Central Command, sir, or at least pass it on – but I'm here because I was about to deliver a message to Commander Tadelmo when he died... sir!" The new acting commander stood up behind his desk and addressed the boy kindly.

"All right then," he said. "I'll be happy to take the message." Giving him a sickly smile, the messenger pulled a document from his bag. It was a copy of Leila and Imbaso's proclamation.

Chapter 73

After receiving Nananji's message, the boy left guard headquarters and then vanished. It would be delivered, but not until Leila had completed her mission here in Namei. She had been working almost nonstop since before dawn, and was feeling in need of a little down time.

Knowing there were many fine cafés here on the city's top level Leila donned the appearance of a wealthy matron and took a late lunch in one of them. Betsalel had departed the idol in her pocket, wanted elsewhere, but she called him again after she had filled her stomach and regained some of her composure.

Strolling around the gardens of the former royal palace, Leila spoke mind to mind with her god. "Nananji seems like a good man, but when he investigates the temple of Betsalel he really *is* going to find no evidence of cult activity. We need to seek out and locate the rest of the cult members, then get him to send his guards out to corral them."

"I was probably too precipitate in reclaiming my temple," the Shadow God said contritely.

"I suppose you could put it back the way it was," his arch-priestess opined, "but then we'd probably have to make a fake Kivuli idol and everything. Why don't we just go over to his office and have a chat with him together?"

So it was that, as acting commander Nananji was trying to make sense of the contents of the late Tadelmo's desk, he had a mysterious visitor. There were guards on either end of the corridor, but somehow she had slipped between them. On stepping inside, she closed the heavy door behind her.

"Greetings, Commander Nananji," she said. An unusual-looking woman, clearly one with Palamban ancestry, but much lighter-skinned than most Amhari and with deep green eyes. Details about the country's new rulers had not yet reached far-off Namei.

"Just acting commander, memsahib," Nananji said, setting his paperwork down. Curse that Tadelmo, dropping dead just when he already had work coming out of his ears!

"Oh, I feel certain that when Central Command receives your message you will definitely be appointed commander," the woman said. Nananji looked at her inquiringly. "I believe you have me at a disadvantage, um...?"

"I am Leila," she said commandingly, "arch-priestess of Betsalel and incidentally now reigning queen of Palambo."

The commander looked at her assessingly. Had a lunatic somehow managed to slip through the guards screening this part of the compound from the public? But she certainly didn't look or act like any lunatic he'd ever seen. "You have read the proclamation, Commander?" Leila asked. "About the cult of the djinn that has taken over the temples of Betsalel throughout Palambo?"

"I dispatched a squad of soldiers to investigate half an hour ago," Nananji assured her. "I'm waiting for their report."

"They will report nothing," Leila replied. "My lord Betsalel and I arrived here this morning, and the temple has already been cleansed. Your men will find nothing but solid rock below, and in the public sanctuary an idol of Betsalel – an idol to which the dark god may be called."

Nananji looked surprised. "But I have been to the temple of Betsalel," he said. "There is nothing there but a painting, from which I got no response."

"You prayed to the Shadow God?" Leila asked, surprised in turn. A god who had not responded to worshipers in generations didn't get a lot of people trying to reach him.

The young commander's face fell. "My mother..." he said. "She had a tumor, some wasting sickness... It was so painful, she screamed for mercy. Begged me to use my sword to put her out of her misery. So I prayed to Betsalel, and I fed her what drugs were available. She was a long time dying." His resentment of the unresponsive God of Death was plain.

"I am sorry, Nananji," Leila said. Her sadness and regret were also plain. "Betsalel has been unable to manifest to any who sought him within Palambo for more than two centuries, because the evil cult had taken over his temples and stolen his true idols. Praying to a painting will never bring a god to your aid."

Nananji believed her. This woman, this girl, really, somehow burrowed into his core with her words and absolutely convinced him that she spoke the truth. "But the temple has now been restored?" he asked, "Betsalel will once again come?"

Leila stooped and deposited her small idol, in which the Shadow God was already manifest, on the office floor beside her. He ballooned in an instant to a height of six feet. Nananji gasped. "Betsalel!" he cried, astonished, "It is truly you?"

"Yes, Nananji," the dark god replied. "I regret I was unable to come to you in your hour of need. Is there anything I can now do for you?"

Nananji gazed at the black figure before him, mind racing. "Have all of the cultists in Namei been destroyed?" he asked at last.

"Those most in need of killing have been dealt with," Betsalel replied. "But I hope that many of the others, especially the youngest among them, were deluded into worship of what they thought was a version of me… at least until recently. I can identify all of those within the city who bear the protection of the evil djinn, and tell your men where to find them."

"Protection?" the acting commander asked. "Will our attempt to arrest them result in the djinn appearing to attack my men?"

"No," the Shadow God explained. "Kivuli's protection is spiritual in nature. I am not able to reach out to those under his protection and stop their hearts, as I might do for those who seek release from a life consigned to pain."

"Then how did 'those most in need of killing' die?" Nananji wanted to know. He was, at this moment, Namei's top law enforcement official.

"I executed them, as is my right as their reigning queen," Leila replied. The acting commander didn't have an answer for that. He had in his possession a proclamation signed by the new king and his reigning queen, though he had no way of knowing whether the woman before him was actually who she said she was. But in a country where all that was required for your legal execution was the king wishing it so, he was not inclined to argue.

"Very well, master," he said, addressing the god. "If you can supply me with a list of names and where the people can be found, I will send squads of men to arrest them. You wish them brought to the temple?" Betsalel caused a piece of parchment to appear, on which the names and locations were written in a dark brown ink. As Nananji examined it, the location of one name faded away and a different one appeared.

"The list tracks them as they move about?" he asked in astonishment, and the god nodded. There were two dozen names on the list, and if these people were to be brought in quickly he'd need to dispatch as many groups of soldiers to collect them. "I'll need a copy for each name," he said, and in another second Betsalel handed him a stack of half-size sheets. Each had one name and one location on it.

Leila had observed this already, during their cleansing of the temple in Iskand. But Nananji was flabbergasted. Like many military men he had been a regular worshiper of Belantos and Andros, but had seldom had up-close-and-personal interactions with any others of the Eight.

Rising from his chair he said, "I'll dispatch teams immediately. Assuming none of them give us any trouble we should be able to gather them at the temple before sundown. Uh, thank you for coming, lord. And your majesty…" Leila extended a hand and squeezed his.

"You will be appointed the new commander of the garrison," she promised him, "as soon as Central Command receives my instructions."

Betsalel shrank again and departed his idol. Leila exited the commander's office and, as soon as she had walked to an unobserved corner, vanished from view. She began making her way back down from the top circle to the fourth, to her little home and its overgrown garden.

The garden was well and truly overgrown again after more than a month without attention. She opened the door with her key and found the house delightfully cool inside. In the kitchen, there were still a few cold bottles of beer and she got herself one, then relaxed in the sitting room with her feet up. What a day it had been, and it was far from over.

Drinking her beer, Leila thought wistfully of how happy she and Imbaso had been here in this little sanctuary, just the two of them with no worries or responsibilities. Then she chided herself mentally, for painting past memories with a golden brush. They had enjoyed those few days spent here together, but in truth there had been no time since she had first met Imbaso when she had not been hip-deep in responsibilities and deadly intrigue.

Still, this little house felt more like home than their digs in the royal palace did. The royal residence offered every comfort imaginable, but it felt more like staying at a posh hotel surrounded by solicitous staff than like living at home. Well, she supposed, she and Imbaso always had their little store-room hideaway to retreat to if they wanted to escape for a while. Leila was probably going to need to sell this place, before months or years of neglect caused it to deteriorate.

Sighing, she lay down on the bed and took a nap for around an hour. Betsalel could manifest in the idol they'd left in the temple and get started sorting out the cult members without her easily enough, but she felt she needed to be there. Locking up the house behind her, she went out into the late afternoon sunshine and trotted, invisible, up to the sixth circle. Then she appeared, swathed in black as a priestess of Betsalel, and hailed a *ritzha* for the trip to the temple level.

A mysterious priestess in black entered the conveyance, but it was the Queen of Palambo, in all her glory, who stepped out of it in front of the temple of Betsalel. The Shadow God had come down from his pedestal, surrounded by new believers, and was examining the captured cult members as they were brought in.

A few of them had turned themselves over to the guards willingly, putting themselves into protective custody, and threw themselves at Betsalel's feet begging for forgiveness as soon as they beheld him. These had been shocked by the djinn's revelation that he was *not* the god they thought they had been worshiping, and had become disgusted by the foul rituals they'd been participating in.

Leila recognized quite a few of them, but others were unfamiliar. And there were some missing: all six of the apprentices with whom she'd trained were not on the list. "You were not able to locate my fellow Makucha apprentices, who had not yet been initiated?" she asked the god mind to mind.

"I found only those with the djinn's protection on them," he replied in kind. "Show me these missing men." Leila pictured them in her mind, each one briefly, and a few moments later the god said "I have found them. They are all together, and they are coming this way from the circle below."

Shit, Leila thought. When none of her fellow uninitiated apprentices had been among the group gathered at the culvert she'd hoped she could discount them. They were all probably as deadly as she was, but she'd hoped that with the cult disbanded and destroyed they would just sink into the general population of Namei.

Commander Nananji and a goodly complement of royal guard soldiers were gathered in the grounds of the temple, as well as some former Kivuli cultists who had truly repented and opened themselves to Betsalel, and a few who had refused to recant and were now under arrest, awaiting execution by the guards.

Surely the six junior assassins could not hope to confront a group of guards three times their number? But maybe they plotted some mischief. "Excuse me, I must go," Leila told Nananji, and hurried inside the temple. It was deserted, and in another moment she was back out, invisible, and on her way down to the next circle looking for the six apprentices.

She soon found them, six teenage men traveling all in a group, and fell in behind them. She was relieved to see they were wearing ordinary street clothing, and were not making any attempts at stealth. The moment they showed signs of splitting up or going into hiding, she would have to start bringing them down – invisibility her only advantage.

And oh, she really didn't want to do that. All of these young men had shown enough aptitude to be accepted by master Kifozi for training, and all of them therefore had shown the desire to become deadly killers in the cause of the god of death they believed they were worshiping. But she had trained with them for months, and they were all decent kids – not cruel, or antisocial, or devoid of human warmth.

They had climbed to the temple circle up one of the connecting streets, and the temple of Betsalel was now visible around the curve of the circle road. They began to pick up the pace, almost jogging now, as the scene outside the temple came in sight. Leila smiled, and gave a heartfelt sigh of relief. The six of them came to where the Shadow God stood, all in a group, and threw themselves onto the ground before him. "Forgive us, master!" they said as one. "We pledge ourselves to you!"

Chapter 74

Dusk was falling as Leila walked down the connecting road to Namei's prestigious ninth circle, heading for Imbaso's family home. Betsalel's large idol was once again on its pillar inside the temple, awaiting the call of any worshipers who might come, and Leila was once again dressed as Palambo's queen. Nananji had told off two spare guards to accompany her, though he rightly suspected this young woman needed no protection.

Leila knocked at the door of the palatial residence, now nearly deserted. She was not even sure whether she would find Faradhi still living here. With Uzuri dead and Mauaji gone from the city more than a month, why would she not have gone to stay with her family in their village ten miles south of the river? Imbaso had mentioned she was often away visiting with them when he'd been younger.

But in due time the woman came to the door. She seemed shrunken, older by years than when Usiku had met her a few months ago. She carried a lantern with her, and stared in amazement at what it revealed: standing on her doorstep was an exotic-looking, unfamiliar young woman dressed in regal garments and wearing a crown – flanked by two of Namei's royal guardsmen.

Before she could think of anything to say Leila spoke. "Faradhi, I am Queen Leila – your son Imbaso's wife. I have brought you a letter from him. May I come in?"

The woman's eyes widened, then she bowed deeply and backed away from the door. "Yes, come in, come in!"

"Thank you, guardsmen," Leila said, dismissing her escort. "I'll need no further assistance now." They bowed to her and left, picking up an animated conversation as soon as they were out of earshot she was sure. It had been a day of surprises for the guard garrison of Namei.

Faradhi led Leila into the front parlor and invited her to sit down. "Would you like some tea, your majesty?" she asked, and Leila politely assented. It was getting time to be thinking about dinner, but there was talking to be done first.

In a couple of minutes Leila's mother-in-law returned with an ornate brass teapot of the style favored in Palambo's desert regions, and a couple of footed glass cups. She must keep a pot of water on the stove all day, the queen realized. The place looked clean and tidy, no signs of dust, and she guessed that Faradhi must continue to have a housekeeper come in daily – even though she was alone here in the house, or perhaps because of it.

"It is true, then," the older woman said, "my Imbaso has become king?" Her eyes shone with pride and delight. A pity there was so little else in the way of good news to tell her.

"Yes," Leila said, "and he took me for his bride just before the coronation ceremony at which he declared me his co-ruler. We have been married for less than a week."

"You are a daughter of the royal house?" Faradhi asked, guessing Leila must have been the offspring of a Gaspari bride.

Leila smiled at her and replied, "In a manner of speaking. My father is Vandao, son of King Faraj and nephew to the late King Omali. But I was born and grew up in the Gaspari Dominion. I am the arch-priestess of Betsalel at his temple in Parat, and now also of the Shadow God's church within Palambo."

Faradhi shuddered faintly, and her eyes went hooded. "As Imbaso will have told you, his father's line have been priests of Betsalel for many generations. I do not much care for such dark doings." Time to start easing into it, Leila thought. But first, the message.

"Do you not wonder how I came here from Iskand in less than a week?" Leila asked, and Faradhi started. She had not truly been focusing on what the queen had said, so astonished had she been by her appearance at the door.

"Even by fast boat it must take nearly three weeks," she admitted. "Were you brought here by your god, then?"

"That's right," Leila nodded. She produced the letter Imbaso had given her. "First, please read what your son has written. Then I have news to give you." Hand shaking slightly, Faradhi took the letter and read it. It looked to have been written in haste, but it was unmistakably her son's writing. She'd had many letters from him over the years when he was studying abroad.

She smiled at first, reading in Imbaso's own words how a change of the rules of succession had made him eligible to become king, and how Leila had captured his heart. But then she read on, and her face took on a look of fear and distress.

"I have not read what my husband wrote," Leila said, "but I'm guessing from your reaction that he told you that your husband Mauaji has become embroiled with a perverted offshoot of the temple of Betsalel, worshiping an evil djinn. Am I right?"

"And more," Faradhi said. "He says Mauaji traveled with a team of Makucha Nyeusi assassins to Iskand for the purpose of assassinating King Omali. And that after they succeeded, they were arrested but my husband called the djinn to free them – slaughtering many palace guards before escaping."

"I'm afraid that is all true," Leila said sadly – carefully gauging Faradhi's reaction. The woman did not look unbelieving, she looked angry.

"I knew it would come to this someday," she said quietly. "When I first met Mauaji, he was young and handsome and swept me off my feet with his family wealth. I was just a village girl from the south – I thought that his being a priest of Betsalel was exciting, a little dangerous."

Faradhi eyed her, wondering how much she shared with this so-very-young woman who had married her son. "I suppose since you married Imbaso perhaps the appeal of bad boys wasn't so strong for you." Leila grinned at her, an expression at odds with her regal garb.

"Oh, your boy may be badder than you think," she said. Her mother-in-law smiled back faintly.

"I had thought we would fill up this cavernous house with laughing babies," she went on. "Mauaji's parents were still alive then, but they died before many years had passed. We finally had a beautiful baby boy, then after years more of trying a little girl. She was the joy of my life!" Leila gave her a sympathetic look. Imbaso, too, had loved his baby sister.

"Then it seemed that Mauaji had become frustrated in his work, and was trying harder at it than he had before. He admitted to me once that he had conceived a great plan for our son, but he never gave me any details about it. He was often gone late into the nights, and I began to wonder if he had taken a mistress. Not that I could have said or done anything about it if so," Samadhi said.

"Imbaso told me something of this," Leila replied. "He said he was often left in the company of the housekeeper, and thus had learned to cook!" The older woman goggled at her for a moment.

"Really?" she breathed in astonishment, then brushed it aside. "If I had been able to, I would have taken my children and gone to live with my brother. You are from the Dominion so may not know this, but our laws permit a woman to seek shelter from her husband with the family from which she came, and he cannot take her back by force."

"But he wouldn't let you take Imbaso, the boy for whom he had such plans," Leila said, and Samadhi nodded.

"Things with Mauaji got better for a while, after the great fever that came," she continued her tale. "We lost our little Sadhima, and Mauaji's sister Uzuri lost her husband and came to live with us. I believe my husband truly loved our daughter, and he had prayed long and hard to Betsalel to spare her. When she died anyway, it was as if he had lost his faith."

"A pity he didn't leave it at that!" Leila remarked.

Samadhi shook her head. "After Imbaso went off to live in the Dominion, studying at the university, Mauaji's desire to make contact with his god grew stronger again. It seemed as though he felt the fault was his, that he had just not performed the rituals in the right way and if only he tried harder what he hoped would happen – whatever that was – would come to pass. I didn't understand it, but I just tried to stay out of his way. Whatever love there was between us had faded away."

"Then Mauaji took Uzuri's baby, Usafi, for a ritual at the temple. And the child did not return," Leila said. Faradhi looked at her in surprise.

"Imbaso told you?" she asked.

"Yes," the younger woman replied. "But it was because of that night that I was called to Palambo in the first place. My lord Betsalel informed me that a djinn had arisen, and that his idol in Namei had been corrupted – stolen from him."

"Djinns are not just creatures of myth?" Samadhi asked, puzzled. The majority of modern, educated Palambans thought such stories to be merely folklore.

Leila gave her Betsalel's capsule rundown on daemons and the way in which they were created, then said "We believe that your husband sacrificed Usafi on the altar in the secret inner sanctum below the temple of Betsalel here in Namei, on that night. The child's soul fled into the centuries-old belief construct the priests had been worshiping, and *became* the god that they envisioned. Before that moment, they had been feeding belief and worship into an idea originally constructed by a twisted man named Rasulbiyi, the so-called 'prophet' whose beliefs swept across Palambo some two centuries ago. And now that idea has come alive."

Samadhi gaped at her in horror. "My husband murdered his nephew, and created a living demon?" she asked, willing Leila to tell her it was all a mistake. Leila nodded her head and reached out to squeeze the older woman's hand.

"I'm sorry," she said, "but that seems to be what has happened."

"Mulia save us!" Samadhi exclaimed. "What is being done about it?"

"Betsalel, Imbaso, and I have been working together," Leila assured her, "and the rest of the Eight are helping too. They have begun distributing copies of our proclamation" – she pulled another copy from her pack, and handed it to the older woman – "and they are already beginning to reach the authorities in towns and cities around the kingdom."

Samadhi studied the paper. It really was true, she was not dreaming. Her son was king of Palambo and this woman sipping tea across the table from her was his wife – and co-ruler. Leila continued, "Mauaji stole the idol of the djinn, Kivuli, from below the temple of Betsalel in Iskand when he freed his six Makucha

Nyeusi assassins from house arrest at the palace. We have rounded up the rest of the Iskand cultists and the temple there has been cleansed. Today, Betsalel and I did the same for the temple in Namei."

The older woman sagged in relief at this good news, but her mind was working and the relief did not last long. "Mauaji and his men are very likely to return here to Namei, are they not?" she asked.

"It would make sense for them to want to do so," Leila replied. "They vanished from the palace three days ago and could be here in a little more than two weeks if they were fortunate enough to find a fast boat."

"Could not their djinn perform for them the same service Betsalel did for you, transporting them instantly?" Samadhi asked, anxiety in her tone.

"I am not sure whether Kivuli knows how to do that," Leila replied thoughtfully. "His mind and his knowledge come only from the humans who created him, and his soul is that of an infant. He lacks the sophistication any of the Eight can command, but he has raw power and ferocity. In any case, I myself smashed the Namei idol today. He could not bring anyone here."

Imbaso was bright, and so was his mother. "There are these idols of Kivuli beneath the temples of Betsalel everywhere in the country except Iskand and Namei?" she asked, and Leila nodded. "Assuming he could be taught to perform this trick of transporting a person, what would prevent him from taking someone to, say, Zambei? That is only a day's journey from here on horseback, probably less by fast boat."

Oh shit, Leila thought for the second or third time that day. She'd been assuming all along that Mauaji and his deadly crew would be heading here, but that they could not possibly arrive for another two or three weeks minimum. Yet if they were able to teach the djinn to perform the transportation trick between one idol and another, Mauaji – or perhaps Kifozi, deadliest of the six assassins – could be here at any time. Though clearly, he had not been here earlier today when Betsalel was seeking out the cultists throughout the city.

Leila felt as if icy fingers were crawling up her spine. This house was not safe! "Samadhi," she said, "I think that we need to get a contingent of royal guards in here to stand watch on the house. And we need to get you out of here. You are far too vulnerable."

"But… this is my home! I have lived here for more than half my life!"

"But what will you do if your husband returns home and announces that this place is now the new temple for the djinn Kivuli? Smile and serve him and his baby-slaughtering coreligionists tea?" Leila was seized with anxiety, as if they must move quickly before something terrible happened.

"No," Samadhi said, hanging her head, "I cannot do that. I wish never to see Mauaji or speak to him again."

"I'm the queen," Leila pointed out. "I can give you a writ of divorce and assign all of Mauaji's assets, including this house, to you."

The older woman stared at her. "Yes!" she said, "Do that! As soon as possible – but where can I go in the meantime? I don't wish to sleep here tonight."

"As it happens," Leila said, "I know just the place."

Chapter 75

In the morning Leila left her mother-in-law with some food and a change of clothing supplied by Betsalel, and trotted up from the fourth to the top level of Namei in the guise of a messenger again. Messengers were always hurrying, and it saved a lot of curious looks as she dashed along at twice the speed of foot traffic.

Her first stop was Commander Nananji's office, where she arranged for a troop of guards to be stationed off-post in the estate home that had until recently belonged to the escaped child murderer and regicide Mauaji, former arch-priest of the temple of Betsalel in Namei. They would keep a low profile and watch for Mauaji or any of the Black Claw assassins, whose names and descriptions they'd been given, to return there.

A much smaller contingent, mounted on the horses belonging to Mauaji's estate, would be escorting Samadhi south of the river via ferry to her home village, where the newly-divorced woman would be taken into the bosom of her brother's family. He had made the offer to her on more than one occasion. After the royal guard was finished using the house for bait, it would be put on the market and the proceeds would go to set her up comfortably for the rest of her life.

Leila's second trip was to the Namei recorder's office, where she registered her writ granting Samadhi her divorce – and awarding all of her former husband's property to her as well. As king of Palambo, Imbaso certainly had no need of any of it. She thought it likely Imbaso would have hoped his mother would join them at the palace; and perhaps she might visit them there sometime. But for now, she needed to be in her childhood home – safe with the family in which she'd grown up.

Leila almost felt like dusting off her hands as she marched jauntily down the hill from the top level of the city, heading for Betsalel's temple. This trip had been a job well done. She now appeared to be herself wearing ordinary garb, no regalia, and the Shadow God spoke in her mind as she walked. After yesterday's activities the number of true Betsalel believers in Namei had hugely increased, and he had more than enough power to reach her from such a distance.

"Ready to go home, little one?" he asked fondly.

"Oh, yes!" she replied in kind. "Have you spoken with Imbaso?"

"Yes," the voice caressed her mind. "He misses you greatly, but was much relieved to hear that all is well and his mother is safe." She missed *him* greatly too, and hurried her steps.

There was no need to shrink this time. Betsalel gathered Leila into his arms, and in an eyeblink she was still held in his arms – but the arms had grown larger, and the view had changed. Where were they? Imbaso stood grinning as she appeared, and in moments the god had set her down and she'd been taken up in her husband's strong arms instead. From the fervency of his embrace, he had been worried for her safety.

Leila kissed him deeply, greedily, then murmured into his ear, "Let me down!" She looked around her. The idol of Betsalel, which it appeared the god had already departed, was more than ten feet tall beneath a fifteen-foot ceiling. Clearly, this was part of the palace. The room was not all that large, maybe twenty by thirty feet, with no windows and a single wide doorway. The idol stood on a short stone pedestal, out perhaps three feet from the rear wall.

"I give up," she said, grinning at Imbaso. "Where are we?"

"Why, the palace's shrine of Betsalel of course," he grinned back. "It's part of the Great Library," he added, relenting. The Great Library of Iskand was a free-standing building within the palace complex, surrounded by gardens. It was said to contain the largest collection of knowledge – plus poetry, written music, folklore, etc. – in the world, at least the part of it west of the Killtops.

"I'd have thought Deline would be the deity for this place," Leila said, walking over to the doorway to peer out. Across a broad corridor floored in polished stone was a row of windows, through which the gardens were visible. The corridor ran far to the left and right, with other rooms and corridors giving off of it.

"No doubt you're right, love. But your idea of having a public place for a shrine to honor our master, not to mention a room where we could keep a large idol for moving from place to place, seemed urgent enough for me to act on it right away. And you have to admit it's an attractive location." She put her arms around his neck, and kissed him again.

Chapter 76

The Black Temple War, they were calling it, though it was really just a series of skirmishes. Over the next week Betsalel reported that he had been able to work with the locals in Zambei and several others of the cities along the Pana where seed idols had been placed. Once the proclamation had been disseminated, outraged mobs had broken into the undercroft secret temples, smashing the Kivuli idols. The reward posted had certainly contributed to their enthusiasm, but when the content of the Secret Scriptures became known the true Shadow God had had a hard time convincing people to let him be the one to pass judgment on the cultists. Those occupying the cult's digs were likely to be beaten to death before any questions were asked.

Leila and Imbaso spent a lot of time conferring with Entabi at the Temple of the Eight, and with at least six of the seven deities who had agreed to deliver the proclamations. In hundreds of temples across the land, the locals had been made aware of the cult presence but without an idol of Betsalel there they were afraid to take action to attack the secret temple – or at least, unable to identify who in their area was a cult member. Not every Kivuli cultist was a supposed member of Betsalel's priesthood, as Mauaji had been. Most were not.

Imbaso applied to Belantos for help. Their fight against a deadly, widespread enemy was something that appealed to him as the god of war. Commander Lmambela called for volunteers, and the War God began transporting teams of two soldiers each to towns and cities in which there temples to both Belantos and Betsalel.

These men, usually dressed in ordinary clothing, would go to the temple of Betsalel to pray for the death of their enemies (a common enough reason for seeking the help of the dark one, though a request he did not often honor), and while one stood guard the other would plant a seed idol. Next they would call Betsalel. If there were cult members in the vicinity they would ring in reinforcements from the nearest royal guard garrison to assist.

Sometimes they would arrive at a town only to learn that local citizens had already raided the temple of Kivuli and destroyed the idol, killing any they found within. In those cases they would usually find that any remaining cult members had fled.

In every case, once the secret under-temple had been emptied and the corrupted idol destroyed, Betsalel would fill the spaces where once the djinn was worshiped with solid stone, restoring the public sanctuary to its original condition. In each, he kept the idol as large as the space would permit to discourage anyone attempting to remove it again.

So, temple by temple, the cult of Kivuli began to fall. Not that the scheme always worked flawlessly. Three teams were dropped off by Belantos and never seen or heard from again. The task force in Iskand, which included Lmambela and his top staff as well as Vandao and the king and queen, were convinced that these locations had probably had chapters of the Makucha Nyeusi. They were marked for invasion by a heavier force later on, after more of the easier targets were dealt with.

For with every temple reclaimed, Betsalel's power grew. The campaign flowed and branched outward from Iskand: south to Aswa, west across the desert. Though the prophet had begun in the desert there were few temples (or towns, for that matter) in that vast stretch of land running between the Center Sea and the Rabiyats, between the Talj Jabal and the Western Ocean. With travel time being cut to nothing thanks to Belantos' (and on a couple of occasions, Andros') help, every desert temple had been cleansed within two months of the reclamation of Namei.

Chapter 77

It was another lavish dinner in the grand dining hall of the palace, a nightly event. Leila had long since learned to ignore all but a few particularly appealing dishes and eat sparingly of them, and Imbaso was following her lead. It was a wonder everyone at court was not spherical, with the capability of eating as much every evening as some of Iskand's poorer families were lucky to get in a week.

Tonight they were hosting some honored guests from the Dominion: a count from the area near Atena, and his retinue. The word had spread to the north that a citizen of the Dominion, in fact Parat's famous arch-priestess of Betsalel, had become queen of Palambo – an actual ruling queen – and feelers from the Dominion were coming in at an ever-increasing rate. Trade concessions were sought, royal princesses considered as brides, dubious offers made. As if they didn't already have enough on their plates!

The fact that the king had also spent time in the Dominion and was fluent in Gasparto made Dominion visitors even more eager to come to Iskand. Leila and Imbaso were willing to extend a dinner invitation to most of these people and give them some time to discuss their concerns, but they didn't go so far as to install them in the guest wing at the palace. Let them rent rooms in town and bring some money to the local economy.

The lighter courses were done, and meat dishes were beginning to make the rounds. The fact that Leila and Imbaso did not use a royal taster was seen by the public as a sign of virtue, two young people so beloved by their countrymen (despite the unconventional nature of their rule) that none would seek to harm them. This was an absurd notion, given that they were engaged in a battle with a deadly, widespread cult; but most people didn't stop to consider that.

At the head table the queen was usually served first, then the king (because Imbaso would have it that way). Lamb simmered in spices was a favorite of hers, and it smelled absolutely wonderful as the dish came hot from the nearby kitchens. Then her necklace radiated a powerful warning – unmistakable, even though this was the first time since Betsalel had given it to her that it had reacted to anything in her environment.

Imbaso's was giving him the same warning, clearly of poison in the food or drink. And as the lamb dish was the only thing on the table that had just arrived, it must be that. Leila inspected the server. It was one of their familiar staff. Since the king's death the new ruling couple had instituted tighter security measures concerning food. The guards who stood watch at mealtime knew all the staff by sight and name, and none were allowed anywhere near the dining hall unless they were both recognized and on the work roster for tonight.

Leila held out a hand, saying "Amdeli, please put the lamb back on the trolley and wait here. I must excuse myself for a time, but you remain here until I return. Do not serve anyone while I'm gone. Is that understood?" The girl nodded, question in her dark eyes. Queen Leila had never been anything but kind, and not stuck-up like some of these royals. Now she'd decided nobody could eat unless she did?

Leila was relieved to see there was no "uh oh, the jig's up!" expression on the girl's face. Clearly, she'd had no idea she was handing out poison. The plate containing the lamb dish went back onto the wheeled cart containing dozens of such plates, and the queen pushed the cart back out through the door behind the royal table, past the guards.

She spoke quietly to the captain of the guards on duty this evening. "There is poison in that top plate of lamb," she murmured. "Have you seen anyone who did not belong here tonight?" Eyes wide with shock, he shook his head. "Roll the cart down the hall to that room on the left, will you?" the queen asked, and he complied.

The room was a storeroom, mostly empty now that dinner had been prepared. Before noon tomorrow it would be filled up again. But at the moment it let her put more than ten feet between herself and the suspect food. "Put the cart there, please, Captain," Leila said, gesturing to the far end of the room. The almost-painful warning sensation ebbed.

Standing as far away as she could get from the cart, the queen next commanded the guard, "Take a dish from the bottom shelf and bring it to me for inspection." He did so, and as soon as he was within the necklace's perimeter she knew it, too, held poison. But she let him bring it all the way toward her, and peered at it as if she needed a visual inspection. She'd prefer that no one suspect the real reason she and Imbaso needed no taster.

Three more plates were brought, and all of them were poisoned. Evidently whoever it was (and surely this must be the work of the Makucha Nyeusi, sent to take vengeance on the king and queen for their campaign against the Kivuli cult) didn't care if every person in the dining hall dropped dead, as long as they got their target. Scum!

Leila put one hand over her heart and the other in her pocket on the tiny idol she kept there, calling the god without speaking aloud. "Please come, Betsalel – but remain small, so that we can confer silently." There was a light squirm under the hand in her pocket, and the god's voice spoke in her mind.

"There is poison nearby," he said. "In the lamb dish across the room there, in every bit of it I believe. The poison was probably added to the pot."

Betsalel's powers probed the stew, and he pronounced "It is sabi. Anyone who ate more than a bite or two of it would be dead within the hour, and even a bite would make you violently ill."

"Whoever dosed the pot must have been in the kitchens, unless they contrived to poison the meat or herbs before it was cooked," Leila mused. Sabi was a desert plant, usually dried and crumbled to a fine powder when used as a poison. It was best put into highly flavored foods, as it was neither tasteless nor invisible.

"There is a man in the kitchen wearing a chef's costume, and he bears Kivuli's protection," the god said. "And there are two more lurking in the corridor beyond the far kitchen door."

"Thank you, master," Leila said. "Please stay with me, while we deal with this."

The guard captain was wondering what the queen was doing, standing motionless with one hand over her heart and the other in a pocket. But he knew she was an arch-priestess, so who could guess what powers she might have? His expectation of her awesomeness was borne out a moment later, when she spoke.

"All of the lamb dish is contaminated with sabi, captain. It needs to be disposed of carefully, but for now I think we'll just lock it up inside this room and post a guard." She moved out of the room, and he followed her and closed the door. The key was undoubtedly on the ring kept by the head of the kitchen staff, but he was busy in the kitchens overseeing preparation of the dinner that was as yet only half over. Speaking silently again, Leila asked "Master, can you lock this door please?" There was a click and it was done.

The guards were milling around in the corridor, anxious but not sure what they were supposed to do as yet. Before Leila could explain the situation, another serving girl came down the corridor from the kitchens pushing a cart with another meat dish: this one tiny quail roasted in honey and stuffed with pine nuts. Before she could take the food into the dining hall Leila halted her.

"Mmm, that smells good," she said, stepping close as if to admire the dish. There were no poison alarms. "Go ahead and take that in to serve everyone," the queen told the girl. "I'll be along just as soon as I deal with a little problem I'm having." The girl smiled and bowed, and wheeled the food on into the dining hall. Leila didn't want anyone poisoned, but she also didn't want a noticeable delay in serving, coupled with her absence, to set off a panic.

Now, with only guards to hear, Leila spoke quietly but firmly. "The man who poisoned the lamb is in the kitchens masquerading as a chef. I can't imagine how he got in there, unless somebody was paid off. But we'll deal with that issue later. He has two cohorts waiting in the corridor outside the far kitchen door, probably there to help him escape after everyone starts dying from the poison. I need all three of them captured alive, if possible – but be very careful. It is almost certain they are Makucha Nyeusi, and extremely dangerous men."

The captain knew his business, and he'd soon dispatched men to either end of the corridor where the two accomplices waited, while others were stationed along this corridor ready to block the exit of anyone trying to come out this way. "Stop any more carts of food coming out and have the servers wait with the dishes here in the corridor," Leila told them.

She hoped the takedown would go smoothly and swiftly, before anyone in the hall besides Imbaso realized something was going on. She would prefer that no word of this ever got out. It would anger whoever had sent these assassins if the mission failed; but it would drive them crazy if they never even learned what had become of their agents. One's imagination can be far more frightening than any known threat, however hideous.

Leila slipped through the door as if returning to her seat in the dining hall, but went invisible as soon as she was through it. Betsalel had said there were only the three Kivuli cultists, and none of them were in the hall; so she could hope that no unfriendly eyes were watching.

She stood behind her chair, careful not to touch Imbaso lest he vanish from sight, and hissed "Imbaso!" He flinched slightly, but then pretended to drink from his goblet while his wife made her report. "There's three Black Claw here, and one of them dumped poison in the lamb pot. The guards are getting ready to take them down, but I want to be there just in case."

His mouth hidden by the cup, Imbaso murmured, "Be safe and hurry back. You're starting to be missed."

"Tell 'em I've got 'female troubles,'" she suggested, and then left the room. It was going to take the guards that had been dispatched to round up the cohorts some time to get into position, as the two groups would have needed to run around the outside of the wing to reach the doors at either end of the corridor. And what would happen when they arrived? Would the assassins flee in through the door to the kitchen, scoop up their comrade, and try to come out through the dining hall? It would be better if that didn't happen.

Leila ducked back into the dining hall long enough to warn Imbaso of that possibility. "If you hear any commotion out in the hall, get on your feet and draw your sword!" Both of them went around the palace and the city well-armed at all times. With her illusion ability the queen could appear to be dressed in the skimpiest of evening gowns while carrying an arsenal, and it was considered normal for gentlemen to carry at least a dagger and often a scimitar as well.

Back in the corridor, Leila slipped invisibly past the guards lining the walls and into the kitchen. The place was a hive of activity, blue-clad servants with white aprons bustling everywhere – making dough, chopping vegetables, stirring pots, darting here and there in a sort of complicated dance that was remarkable to watch. And dangerous to be in the midst of, invisible as she was.

Leila sidled near the wall until she reached one of the pantries, then slipped inside it and emerged a moment later wearing the semblance of Amdeli – the serving maid she'd told to remain on station in the dining room. At least there wouldn't be two of her in the room. But there was a pretty good chance the maid's boss would be unhappy to find her somewhere he or she had not ordered the girl to be, so she kept her head down and scurried along as if she were on an important mission.

Along one wall of the main room was a wall of deep sinks, each with hot water piped from boilers below. Scullery boys were at work cleaning cooking pots and serving plates, readying them to be used for the next course. Leila eyed them carefully, and spotted one rinsing the remnants of the lamb stew from the pot it had been cooked in. He certainly didn't look old enough to be a full-fledged assassin.

"Excuse me," Amdeli asked, and the boy looked up.

"Oh, hi, Amdeli!" he said in a voice that suggested helpless if not necessarily hopeless longings. Undoubtedly the serving girl knew this boy by name, but Leila was just going to have to wing it.

"Her Majesty said the lamb tasted different tonight, and she was wondering if we have a new chef."

He grinned at her and gestured with a thumb at a medium-tall, very portly-looking man in his late twenties or early thirties. He was clad as a chef, with the official hat on his head. "He's Idale's cousin, used to work at a chef at a restaurant up in Aswa. Just started today, in fact."

"Where's Idale?" Amdeli asked. She couldn't have picked Idale out of a crowd, but assumed he was one of the usual chefs. Perhaps the queen should be getting better acquainted with her servants!

"Taken sick," the boy said. "Some kind of pox, he was all over big red pustules and Mnamene said he couldn't work until it clears up. So he said his cousin was here visiting and would fill in for him, and Mnamene said all right."

"Thanks, I'll pass it along to the queen," Amdeli said. "See you later!" He grinned at her and went back to washing the pot.

As she headed in the direction of the "cousin," Leila wondered why Amdeli wouldn't have been expected to know as much about the new chef as anyone. But then she considered that the girl was just a server – not part of the kitchen staff.

"Master, is this the man before me?" she asked silently, and Betsalel replied "It is he. He is a thin man, but he is wearing a false paunch containing weapons and poisons." Shit, she didn't want anyone to die if she could help it. But if somebody had to, she would prefer it were the assassins.

The man had his attention on his work, accepting a bowl of chopped vegetables from a scullery maid and pouring them into the pot – then stirring ferociously as they sizzled with the hot slices of beef that had already been cooking for a while. There was a pre-mixed bowl of dried herbs on the counter beside the stove ready to be added before simmering, but instead his left hand went beneath his apron and came out with a handful of what Leila guessed was the sabi he had used on the lamb. There'd been no sounds suggestive of people in the dining hall collapsing in convulsions, so he'd keep poisoning dishes until something worked – or so he thought.

Using a couple of thick cloth potholders, Leila hefted a medium sized pot of boiling water off the stove and then appeared to trip, splashing a good quantity of the water over the front of the chef's apron and the bare left arm holding the poisonous herbs.

His arm jerked violently, and the handful of sabi flew across the stovetop and onto the floor. He dropped the stirring spoon into the pot and seized his injured arm, cursing. "You stupid cow!" he snarled. "Look what you've done!"

"I'm so sorry, sir!" Amdeli said, bowing and fussing. "Quick, get over to the sink so we can put cold water on it!"

The assassin was still angry and in pain, but he was also in a dangerous position and he didn't want to draw a lot of attention to himself. He'd been waiting only for the sounds of commotion coming from the dining hall to make his getaway. Amdeli had set the pot of water back on the stove immediately, and she led the chef by his right arm over to one of the sinks that was not in use. They had cold water on tap as well, and she soon had a soothing stream of it running over the man's blistered left arm. He was not complaining about the boiling water that had soaked his tunic and apron, because it was not in contact with his skin.

"Does it hurt very badly?" Amdeli asked timidly, crushed that her clumsiness had caused such pain.

"Like bloody hell," the chef gritted. He was in no mood to cut the girl any slack, even if she was trying to atone for her actions. "Would you like some poppy? I have a bottle…"

The poppies that had come from east of the Killtops had spread throughout the world and were grown everywhere the climate would permit. Their resin and its byproducts were a sovereign remedy for pain of any kind, though one must be careful with them as addiction could result from over-use.

Leila pulled out a small bottle, apparently from the pocket of Amdeli's servant's tunic. It had a familiar label, a brand name that was manufactured in the Dominion and exported to the more accessible regions of Palambo. You could buy almost anything from anywhere, here in Iskand.

He looked at the bottle and glared at her, then nodded. Amdeli removed the bottle's tight cork and the injured man snatched the bottle out of her hand and took a good swig before handing it back. That would have been a couple of normal doses of this product – if that were what the bottle had truly contained. It had poppy in it, right enough, but there were some other ingredients as well. After another minute of standing at the sink letting the cold water flow over his burns, the man's eyes rolled up and he sank quickly to the floor.

The scullion she'd been talking to earlier had been watching all this while scrubbing more pots, and he looked at the fallen man in alarm. Amdeli's eyes were wide. "Could it be the same pox Idale has?" she asked in alarm, then said "Please stay with him. I will get some guards to take him to a healer."

Leila became herself again as she vanished from the kitchens. She hadn't noticed any noise from the hallway beyond the other door, and she was beginning to wonder what was going on out there. The guards still lined the corridor that led to the dining hall, on the alert for anyone coming out. They'd already stopped one additional cart, which was waiting down the hall.

The captain had gone with the other parties of men, so the queen addressed his lieutenant. "The man who put poison in the food is lying unconscious on the kitchen floor near the sinks. If anyone asks, you are taking him to the infirmary – but you will take him to a secure cell. Strip him naked, and make sure that he has nothing hidden under his fingernails, in his hair, inside his mouth, or in any of his other body cavities. Am I clear?"

"Yes, Your Majesty," the guard said. He dispatched two of the eight on duty in the hallway to collect the downed assassin, who proved to be surprisingly lighter than they'd expected. They carried him back out through the door and down the corridor to the outside. As the royal guard were Palambo's police force, the lockups were located within the guard compound.

As soon as they'd gone past Leila went over to take a look at the cart. It contained what appeared to be broiled seafood in a lemon sauce, and her necklace had no complaint. "This may be taken in and served," she said – snagging a bite off the platter on top.

Curse the Makucha Nyeusi, she was missing a marvelous dinner – and she'd eaten pretty lightly of the earlier courses. Well, she *was* the queen. She could get them to cook her something just as succulent later, to her special order, after all of this business was over.

Once again appearing to go into the dining hall and then vanishing, Leila moved silently past the remaining guards and into the kitchen again. Someone had come by and taken the stew the assassin had been about to poison off the fire, burning. Leila got a strong twinge of poison warning from her necklace as she slipped past, heading for the far door.

She made it without bumping into anyone, fortunately, and stepped silently out into the corridor beyond. There was no one in sight – no assassins lurking, no guards at either end of the corridor. "Betsalel, where has everyone gone?" she asked, more than a little concerned.

"The two Kivuli cultists who were here have moved off to the north," the god said in her mind. "There are two guards down but not dead outside the door in that direction, and the other guards are giving chase but I think the assassins have escaped them. It's dark out there."

Damn, damn, damn! Leila bolted to the left, north, and nearly stumbled over the three guards who'd been sent to come at the assassins from this end. The two must have realized they were being surrounded and gone, not through the kitchens, but in the direction that seemed least well-guarded. Or perhaps, in the direction where they had horses waiting or a hidey-hole prepared.

She couldn't think of whom she might appear to be that would be of any use, so she just slipped past them invisibly. Two had knife wounds, and the third was applying first aid. At least the assassins had apparently not been using poisoned blades, small comfort. It was indeed quite dark out, no moon yet; but there were many lamps and torches on the palace walls to provide spots of illumination.

As Betsalel had done when Leila was going down into Iskand to murder Farendhi and his fellow cultists, he guided her on her way speaking mind to mind. The other small squad of guards had lost the assassins in the darkness, and had slowed their pace. She soon caught them up, and went visible.

"Having a little trouble, captain?" she asked, and the man cringed. Having his queen catch him in the act of blowing his assignment could not possibly have a good effect on his future career.

"The targets were closer to our end, and I'm afraid they must have heard us arrive," he admitted. We chased them down the corridor, and the other squad tried to stop them but they just mowed them down with thrown daggers."

Leila sighed. "I did warn, you, did I not, that they are Black Claw?"

"Sorry," he muttered. "None of my men have encountered Black Claw before, not counting the ones who were slaughtered by the djinn."

"I'll have to institute a training program, I see," the queen said acerbically. Then she added, "My lord Betsalel is guiding my steps. Stay with me and we will see if we can yet catch them."

The guards eyed her with a mix of fear and admiration, and fell into a formation around her. In their experience, royal wives and daughters lived sheltered in harems, their principal mission in life being to look pretty. They certainly did not go around chasing Black Claw assassins. But with the protection of the dark one, perhaps they could.

The assassins they were pursuing had been moving fast, and during the short discussion had gone far beyond visual contact. "They are doubling back around," Betsalel said in Leila's mind. "They are now moving toward the servants' quarters."

She threw up a hand. "They're heading for the servants' wing," she told her squad of guardsmen.

Leila had now spent more than three months of her life living in the palace compound; but the place was huge, and there were many areas of it she was less familiar with. "Take a left and go through the audience hall building," the captain said. He'd lived in Iskand his entire life and had been a royal guardsman since Leila was still a small child, living at the House of the Golden Fish in Marsine.

This late in the evening the entrance to the wing that housed the audience hall where the king and queen had been married and crowned was closed and locked. But the captain had keys for every area of the complex except the royal family's private quarters.

They ran through the corridors surrounding the great hall and around to a rear exit, a small door that let out on an expanse of landscaping with the building in which most of the palace servants had their living quarters on the far side of it. They saw no sign of any scurrying figures, though. "They have entered the building on the east side," Betsalel said, "and are moving into the wing with private apartments in it."

The kitchens in the royal palace in Iskand were famous throughout Palambo, and the chefs who produced their myriad delicacies were not run-of-the-mill servants. They were accorded a great deal of respect, and even those who were not married were given their own private quarters as part of their compensation. Unmarried, lesser servants were required to live in the sex-separated dormitories or else rent rooms in town at their own expense and commute up the hill to work each day.

"They must be going to Idale's rooms!" Leila exclaimed as they let themselves into the building and began hurrying along the corridors toward the wing in question. It disturbed her a lot to think that one of their own servants, a man with a prestigious and well-paid job in their household, would betray them by getting an assassin placed to kill everyone in the dining hall. He could not be a Kivuli cultist, or Betsalel's frequent scans would have spotted him. Unless maybe he was an uninitiated sympathizer?

As the queen and her escort scrambled around a corner they could hear the faint sound of feet pounding up the stairs at the far end of the next hallway. The entire wing was two stories, with the ground floor apartments offering access to the gardens. "They are on the second floor above you," the god murmured in her mind, and Leila threw up a hand again.

"The assassins are apparently going to hide in the apartment of the palace chef who arranged for them to get into the kitchens," she told the guards quietly. She hoped the men they pursued would believe they were home free. "I don't know Idale personally," Leila went on, "but I can say for certain he is not an initiate of Kivuli. And obviously, he really is a chef. He could have poisoned us himself, or tried to, if he were truly in league with the djinn's people – so perhaps the three Makucha used some kind of coercion on him. If they are holding him hostage, I really want to avoid getting him killed – at least until we can question him. Let's go up there quietly and try to figure out what's going on, before we burst in."

Leila and the guards crept up the staircase at the rear of the quarter and found themselves looking at a deserted hallway with doors on either side of it. "Master, where are they and what are they doing?" she asked silently.

"They are in a small apartment with a sitting room and bedroom to your right eight doors down," the god replied. "There is a man in the bedroom, and he appears to be very ill. His skin is blistered, and he is nearly unconscious. Our two assassins are in the sitting room, and they appear to be waiting for someone but they don't seem to be worried about pursuit."

"Can you speak within the guard captain's mind as you do mine?" Leila asked. "If he will open to me I can," Betsalel replied. "Captain, I want my lord Betsalel to be able to speak with you. Please open your mind to him." The guardsman blinked, but then tried to relax.

"Captain, you have nothing to fear from your queen," a deep voice spoke in his mind, and he nearly jumped out of his skin. Never had he had such an experience, even after half a lifetime of praying to Belantos and Andros.

Leila didn't have to ask him if it had worked. The communication had been personal, too – she had not heard it, and wondered what the Shadow God had said to him. "I believe the

Black Claw men inside think they have escaped pursuit, and are waiting for the man posing as a chef to return. They won't know until he gets back whether their attempt was successful."

So far, only a few people outside of Imbaso and Betsalel himself knew of the illusion power he had given her. And Leila was anxious to keep it that way. But if the four of them just stormed in through that door, someone was going to get hurt. "My god is going to cast an illusion on me," the queen told the captain, "so that I can appear to be the man they're waiting for. The rest of you, go back to the staircase and hide below. After they've shut this door again, you can creep back up. Then Betsalel will let you know when it is time to come in."

The captain was in an agony of indecision. If the Shadow God could cast such an illusion, why not cast it on him or one of his men instead of putting his arch-priestess at risk? But Queen Leila was emphatically not the kind of woman you wanted to argue with, and she seemed to have some secret knowledge of the Makucha Nyeusi that he and the rest of the Iskand guard corps lacked.

"Very well, your majesty," he said softly. "We will be back here, near at hand, as soon as possible." Leila waited until they had vanished below the level of the floor, then transformed into the "chef" who had tried to poison everyone at the royal dinner. She had been close to him, heard him speak. Of course she didn't know his name or those of his companions, but was she not a former gutter rat and con artist? Playing it by ear was her specialty.

The door was locked, and she pounded on it. "Who is it?" a voice came from inside. "It's me! Quick, let me in!" The men on the other side of the door recognized his voice, but the one who came to let him in had a dagger in his hand. He checked to make sure it was his companion, and dragged him inside. Then he peered out, looking up and down the lamp-lit corridor, before closing the door again and locking it.

The erstwhile chef was looking disheveled, and he had a bandage on his left arm. "Did it work?" the taller of the two assassins asked. They were both clad in the same Makucha gear Leila was wearing. It was comfortable garb, had enough pockets for all of her favorite weapons, and with her illusion power she could wear it "under" anything. The assassins' outfits included face-hiding hoods, but they had pulled them off after arriving in the apartment.

"I didn't stick around to see whether everyone died," he admitted. "As soon as I heard the guards in the hall yelling about the king and queen, and calling a healer, I got out of there. Where did you two go?"

"We thought we'd been revealed," the shorter man said. They were both of medium height and wiry build, dark-skinned Amhari with short-cropped, kinky black hair. Typical Makucha.

"We were waiting for the commotion," the shorter man continued. "Then we saw a small party of royal guards creeping up on us. It wasn't like a regular patrol, more like they knew we were there. We beat it for the other exit, and there were three more there but we got past them. These royal guards seem just about competent enough to lace their own sandals – maybe."

The "chef" grinned, a grim expression. "That's useful for us," he said.

"What was all that shouting we heard just before the guards showed up?" the taller man asked. He was eyeing the bandage on his companion's arm.

"Kivuli-cursed idiot of a scullery maid spilled boiling water on me while I was doctoring another pot of stew," came the gritted reply. "It's a good thing the first dish worked."

"You want some poppy?" the shorter man asked.

"What I would really like is a drink," his companion replied. "Is there any wine?" The shorter man looked at him in surprise.

"I thought you never touch the stuff," he said.

"Not while I'm working, I don't. But the job is done. We just need to wait until things die down, another few hours, and then leave. And I want a drink."

"All right, all right," the shorter man said. "No offense meant. The chef's got some bottles over there in the corner." As a chef, Idale no doubt had a greater appreciation of wine (and a greater ability to acquire it) than most palace servants. Leila went over there and looked, finding a bottle of red imported from the region around Jena. It had been uncorked, but there was less than three fingers' worth missing from the bottle.

The injured assassin pulled out the cork with his fingers and took a sniff. "Not bad!" he said. "You guys want some?"

"I dunno," the taller man said. "We need to stay sharp. Those guards that chased us might still track us down somehow."

Leila poured three glasses of wine, emptying the last of her bottle of elixir into two of them. It probably wasn't enough to knock them out, but it would take the edge off the two assassins. She hoped. The injured team member sneered, "Did they have dogs?"

"No," the other replied.

"Then don't worry about it, they're not going to find us. Anyhow, we're not getting drunk. Just a little celebratory glass for a job well done."

It appeared the "chef" had been the dominant member of the team. Certainly he had been the one on the line, while the other two waited as backup for his getaway. He carried two glasses over to his cohorts and handed one to each of them, then stepped back to get his own. "Drink up! To the end of the cursed king and queen!"

The three clinked their glasses together, and drank. Leila took a sip, but the rest of the wine's vanishing was only an illusion. These two must not be the brightest the Makucha had to offer, she thought. Had everyone in the dining hall truly been poisoned, the guards would have quickly learned that a "new chef" for the evening was missing, and that he'd been vouched for by Idale. They would have been knocking on this door by now, no doubt. Yet the assassins seemed to believe they were safe hiding here until it was time to slip away.

Betsalel spoke in Leila's mind: "The captain is becoming anxious. I told him all is going smoothly and to wait for the signal."

"Good," she replied. "They are right outside the door now?"

"Yes."

"Just a few more minutes now, I think," she said to the god in her pocket.

The two assassins had become much less tense, and acceded readily to their companion's suggestion that they break open another bottle of their "host's" excellent wine. Unwittingly they drank it all between them – and then, eyelids drooping, they began to snore. "Tell them they can come in now, and quietly," Leila relayed to Betsalel, "Oh, and please unlock the door for them. Almost forgot!"

The captain and his two squad members came inside, and stared in disbelief at the portly-looking man dressed as a chef and two gently sleeping assassins. They might be muzzy but they could still be dangerous, so each man received a carefully-calculated blow from a truncheon to assure they would not awaken during the process of being searched and bound.

While the guards handled the two prisoners Leila (once again appearing as herself) went into the bedroom. A man she guessed must be Idale lay on the bed wearing nothing but a pair of underdrawers. He was covered from head to foot in weeping blisters, and was moaning slightly as though lost in a fever dream.

"What illness is this?" Leila asked her god, concerned. It would too ironic if they foiled a plot to poison half the nobles in the palace only to have everyone come down with a virulent plague.

"No disease," Betsalel replied. "This man has been given a substance and it has produced an allergic reaction."

Pesis, it must be! This plant, the oil of which could cause blisters and pustules to form on the skin and induce a mild fever, was one she had studied with master Sumundi. But she had not seen anyone to whom it had been administered before now. The effects ranged from painful and annoying to fatal, depending on how much was administered and how one's body reacted to it.

"Can you heal him, please, master?" Leila asked. Without replying Betsalel reached forth his powers and the blisters melted away. Idale's eyes fluttered open and he sat up a little, focusing on the apparition that stood beside his bed.

"The queen!" he cried, and shrank away from her in terror. "I am lost!"

Chapter 78

Leila and Imbaso made love in the morning before getting out of bed. However wide their escape from death the night before, it had still made them realize how precious their time together was. They anticipated a long and happy reign after the successful conclusion of the Black Temple War; but life offered no guarantees.

Betsalel had been able to communicate by mind with Imbaso, all the way from the servants' residential wing to the dining hall, and he had arranged for another contingent of guards to be sent to the apartment of Idale. That unfortunate man, blubbering in terror and swearing that he'd intended to hurt no one, was bound and led off to the cells as the two assassins – stripped and bound and still unconscious – were carried along with them.

The four prisoners had had a night of uncomfortable solitude in which to contemplate their sins, and first thing after breakfast the royal couple, with a contingent of guards, went across to the guards' compound to participate in the interrogations.

Thinking that he at least might be willing to tell them something (Makucha Nyeusi were taught to endure torture, and instructed to kill themselves if caught), Leila suggested they start with the chef. They and the guard corps' chief interrogator waited in a small, windowless stone room as a pair of guardsmen dragged the shackled, still-terrified servant in and chained him to the back wall.

The guard corps had had many generations of experience in extracting information from reluctant suspects, and they had found this technique to be effective. It definitely left the person being interrogated at a psychological disadvantage. In the case of Idale, it looked likely to render him incapable of speech. He took one look at the three people eyeing him from across the room and dissolved in terror, the odor of urine strong in the air as he wet his pants.

"I meant no harm, I meant no harm!" he kept sobbing. Leila and Imbaso exchanged glances, then turned to the guards' interrogator.

"Please unchain him from the wall," the queen commanded. "Have him cleaned up and returned here without the shackles, and bring a chair for him to sit on. And a little tea to drink, I think."

The interrogator looked at her with the air of someone humoring a person in authority who has no idea how to do his job, and saw it done. When Idale was returned a few minutes later, he was considerably calmer. He had truly expected to be tortured to death.

"I think I had better be the one to handle this," Leila told her companions. She tweaked her illusion (she appeared to be dressed in queenly robes, but was actually wearing her comfortable assassins' gear fully loaded with weapons, poisons, and other useful items) so that she appeared a little older, motherly, infinitely patient and loving. Idale gazed at her as if Mulia in her aspect as the Angel of Mercy had just put in an appearance. The queen was not so bad as he'd been led to believe, she had saved him!

"Idale," Leila said sweetly, "I am sorry to have put you through this, but you must understand that we arrested two Makucha Nyeusi assassins in your apartment with you. I need to know how they came to be there, and what you know of the man you told Mnamene was your cousin."

Idale hung his head, tears running down his cheeks. An improvement over piss running down his legs, Leila thought with a trace of impatience. "I met them in a gambling house in the city," he said. As far as residents of the palace compound were concerned, there was only one city in the world worth mentioning: Iskand.

"Oh, you frequent gambling houses?" the queen asked – not in an accusatory tone, but as if it might be a common interest.

"Not often," Idale said. "I enjoy gambling, but while I make a good living cooking for the palace I am not a wealthy man. I've had a lot of success at it, but just lately my luck has been down. And I… I borrowed some money to cover a bet I was sure to win, one that would recoup my losses."

It was a story Leila had heard many times in her life. Gamblers were always convinced that if they just kept at it, that big score would come their way. It had never occurred to her that she'd been a gambler herself for most of her life – gambling with her life, her freedom, as she took deadly risks in pursuit of her goals.

"So you met these three. What did they tell you?" Leila asked, careful not to suggest she was passing judgment on Idale and his ill-considered choices. "They were three brothers from Aswa, recently come into a small inheritance from the passing of their father. They had decided to seek their fortune in Iskand, and the eldest of them – the man I told Mnamene was my cousin – had been a chef in one of Aswa's finest restaurants."

Leila smiled encouragingly and Idale went on. "We had gone to another tavern, one I knew where the drinks were cheap and the women were friendly, and they were buying me drinks. When it came out that J'mendi and I were both professional chefs, it was a wonderful coincidence. We talked about cooking, and I knew that he truly was a chef. I had no reason to doubt his story."

How the hell did a member of the Makucha Nyeusi ever learn to cook that well, Leila wondered? Most assassin apprentices began at around the age of sixteen, and most were not raised to full membership before eighteen. She had been an exception, raised in only a few months partly because of her already impressive skill set and partly just because they needed a pretty young female for a honey trap. Perhaps J'mendi had had an earlier apprenticeship as a cook?

"J'mendi told me that it had been his dream since he was a young boy to one day travel to Iskand and become a chef in the palace," Idale continued. "He was very envious of me and my position, and offered to pay my gambling debts if I would only make it possible for him to get a foot in the door. There were no openings, of course, but he believed that if he could go in as a substitute chef and show what he could do, Mnamene would be impressed and would choose him when another job came up."

Leila didn't speak, just looked at him, and the chef's face fell. "I should have realized that he intended to make his own opening by poisoning me and taking my place!" he cried despairingly. "But he was so friendly, and I knew what it was like to be a young chef trying to get a start in the business. He had a bottle of oil that he said would make it appear I had some sort of pox – something that would make me temporarily unfit for working in the kitchens. Then after the blisters appeared I would report for duty and Mnamene would tell me I could not work. So I would bring in my 'cousin' and he would have a few days in which to impress Mnamene with his skills. The kitchens would be unable to get anyone else at such short notice."

Idale's story was very plausible, and Leila was inclined to believe it. The chef had been guilty of a misdemeanor, nothing more. That and some world-class foolishness. "What happened after that?" she asked, still keeping a friendly tone.

"J'mendi and his brothers moved into my apartment with me," he said. "I told them there was not room, but they had given me the money to settle my gambling debt so how could I turn them away?"

All servants who lived in the housing provided by the crown were strictly forbidden to permit people not also employed by the palace to live with them, other than spouses of course. Another misdemeanor. Idale went on, "Another day went by, and the plan was put into action. J'mendi applied his oil and I soon broke out in convincing pustules. I went home to bed, not feeling very well, and he took my shift for the afternoon and evening preparing the usual royal banquet."

"That was around four in the afternoon," Idale explained. "The brothers had remained at my apartment, and by the time I got back I was feeling really very sick. I told them something had gone wrong and I wanted to go see a healer, but they told me I could not. They said that if I tried to leave the apartment or talk to anyone they would just kill me, because they were Black Claw and had no problem doing such a thing. Then they applied more of the oil to me, and told me to get into bed and stay there."

They didn't want him to be found stabbed to death, Leila guessed. A man found dead of what looked like a hideous infection would do more to sow fear among the Makucha's enemies. But if the other two didn't leave until closer to eight, when dinner service started, Idale would probably have been near comatose by then. She had never heard of anyone receiving an extra dose of pesis.

"Do you remember anything after that, Idale?" the queen asked.

"Nothing, until I awakened and saw you standing by my bed," the chef admitted. "I truly intended no one any harm."

"I believe you are probably telling the truth, Idale," she said. "But I need to make sure. Would you be willing to open your mind and heart to my lord Betsalel?" The Shadow God! Like many Palambans, Idale had a healthy respect coupled with fear as regarded this darkest of the Eight. But if it would clear him of wrongdoing, he would gladly submit.

Leila dipped gracefully toward the floor, doing something Idale did not see, and in another instant the living Betsalel, standing as tall as a tall man, stood before him. His expression was one of serene benignity, as he took a step forward and laid a black hand on Idale's shoulder.

"Let me know your heart, Idale," he commanded, and the chef submitted with a sigh. "He told the truth," the dark god pronounced shortly. "There is no taint of Kivuli on him, and he is by and large a good man – if sometimes foolish. I think that you might release him from his imprisonment, but he will need to pay some kind of penance."

"I have just the thing," Leila replied with a smile. "Idale, for a period of one year you will live in the men's dormitory within the servants' quarters and work as a scullion in the kitchens. Should you perform this work satisfactorily you may be restored to your former position. In addition, each week you will go to the shrine of Betsalel located in the Library building, and pray to him for forgiveness of your transgressions. You will not go into the city, and you will not gamble. And the dark one will know all you do, so do not cheat. Is this satisfactory?"

Idale's face became wreathed in a huge smile of relief and he fell to the floor, prostrating himself before his queen, as Imbaso and the guards' interrogator looked on in amusement. "Yes, your majesty!" he exclaimed, "You have my eternal gratitude for your kindness!"

The interviews with the three Makucha Nyeusi assassins didn't go half so well. One of them, the shortest of the group, was found to have fractured his skull by ramming his head into the stone wall of his cell during the night. He yet lived, but would likely never regain consciousness. The other two were interrogated using the standard techniques, but refused to reveal anything about what chapter they belonged to or who had sent them. After a week of this treatment one of them died under questioning, and the king requested that the other just be executed. Both he and Leila already had a pretty good idea who had sent them.

Chapter 79

The Black Temple War continued, slowly. All of Betsalel's temples in the northern reach of Palambo had now been cleansed, and the apparatus Imbaso and Leila had set in place had reclaimed all of the ones along the Pana from Aswa to Namei. Now the guard teams hopped town by town westward, and south into the kingdom's hot and steamy hinterland.

Leila began a training program for the guards, aimed at helping them to overcome the tricks the Makucha Nyeusi used. She was nowhere near as great an expert as master Kifozi, but she had absorbed much knowledge in her training and she passed it along to the guardsmen. Any among them with some experience in the kind of covert, individual fighting the assassins tended to use was immediately brought in to be trained as an instructor. Every guardsman needed to know these things, and she could not personally train them all.

The weapons and poisons recovered from the three failed assassins were used to demonstrate what the guards might be up against, and it was a lesson that never failed to impress. This must have been what it was like back when Emperor Ostden was in the process of uniting the Dominion, Leila thought. Yet now that nearly all of the remaining southwestern section of the continent had been won, the guards had other problems. Problems she was here to help them understand and ward against. But defeating the Makucha would ultimately be up to the guards themselves.

There were no further attempts to poison food at the nightly royal banquets. All of the kitchen personnel, including the servers, were now required to submit themselves to Betsalel's assessment as a condition of continued employment. Leila felt this was an invasion of their privacy and their individual rights to have a relationship (or not) with the god or gods of their choice; but her god was not cruel – and it was necessary to know that no one with the ability to deal death to the royal couple and dozens of others had any dark secrets.

But there were other Makucha Nyeusi incursions. Men disguised as traders or diplomats, women claiming to be in the employ of local suppliers delivering goods to the palace, came in through the well-guarded gates and then vanished. Imbaso, moving with a guard escort from the royal residence wing to the audience hall, suddenly felt a violent warning from his necklace and dived to the ground as a poisoned arrow shot through the space where he'd been standing and skewered one of the guardsmen instead.

The man died within seconds, and Imbaso was racked with guilt. There had been no time to give warning to others of the speeding missile. After that, he took to carrying his own tiny idol of Betsalel in his pocket. Twice a day, or more often if the royal couple needed to leave the safety of the palace, the Shadow God would extend his awareness across the entire city of Iskand, searching for any who bore Kivuli's protection. With practice he had become better at picking them out, and was able to scan the more-or-less three hundred thousand souls who dwelt there in only a few minutes. In the dark god's awareness, the djinn's spiritual protection shone like a red candle in a dark room.

For a couple of weeks after they began doing this, Betsalel was finding small groups of Kivuli cultists every few days. The squads of guards who'd shown the most aptitude in their anti-assassin training were dispatched under the god's direction to trap them in their lairs – whether hiding within the palace compound or in a basement room in the city's slums, aboard a river craft or within the homes of the wealthy. Not all of Leila and Imbaso's political opponents were members of the Kivuli cult, but were willing to shelter the Black Claw as a means to an end.

A policy decision had been made, after the results of interrogating the initial three assassins, not to bother trying to take Makucha Nyeusi alive. The guards, after being led to where the Kivuli cultists were lurking, would just kick the door open and mow down everyone in the room with a hail of crossbow bolts. And it had proven, so far, that every cultist they found in the environs of Iskand was a member of the Black Claw. Leila had shown the guards how to find the initiates' tattoo on the bodies of the slain.

Then, the incursions by Makucha Nyeusi dried up as suddenly as they had begun. Each morning and evening Betsalel searched, but not a single person within the range of that search showed the mark of the djinn's protection. "Could we have gotten them all?" Imbaso asked one evening as he and Leila were sitting together quietly in their parlor before bed.

"I wish I could believe we have," she replied pensively. "I never had any idea how many chapters there were, or how many assassins each chapter had. It was a great surprise to learn that the Namei chapter had only a dozen fully initiated members in addition to me. And I overheard the assassins Betsalel and I trapped and killed in Namei talking about a big chapter in Dikka. Having them come to us instead of us having to go out and find them has been like a wonderful gift. But it seems like they've grown tired of throwing their best people into the fire."

"We've cleansed more than a hundred temples," her husband replied, "and other than that first time in Namei we've never caught any Makucha. Does that mean that chapters are far rarer than we believed – or does it just mean they were quicker to flee and got out of Betsalel's range before they were found?"

"Well," Leila said with a sigh. "Whether we used them all up or they've just decided to stop trying, I suppose that means we're safe." He hugged her, then kissed her. Then kissed her some more, and before long both of them had forgotten all about what they'd been discussing.

Chapter 80

The next morning after bathing and getting dressed, Leila had Betsalel check for Kivuli initiates. None were found, which was what they'd come to expect. Mbina, who'd been installed with her new husband Ganibo in a small private apartment within the royal residence wing, brought them a tray with their breakfast on it.

There was kaf, tropical fruit, honey-sweetened pastries, and some boiled quails' eggs. They asked the servant to set the tray on the small table in the garden outside their bedroom, as it was a lovely morning. The garden was walled and warded with the symbols of Betsalel. Any who came there with malice in their hearts would find it hard to get past, and the royal couple felt safe enough eating out there without being surrounded by guards.

But as they approached the table both of them felt a sharp warning from their necklaces. They had taken to keeping them on day and night, even sleeping with them. "Poison?" Leila said, a hint of wistfulness in her voice. So far she and Imbaso, with a ton of help from the Shadow God, had done a good job of foiling the djinn's adherents in their attempts to assassinate them. But the feeling of being under constant siege was beginning to wear on her.

Imbaso had called Betsalel to the idol in his pocket, and the god spoke in both their minds: "The honey in the pastries is poisoned. I believe it is nacona." The plant extract was a relatively slow poison, causing first nausea and intestinal cramping, followed by intense fatigue, heart palpitations, and death. Shit!

"Quickly, master! Broadcast to everyone in the palace that they must not eat the pastries!" Leila cried. Not every person in the palace compound was receptive to the Shadow God even now, but most heard his warning. That included the guards stationed in the royal residence wing, and in moments there was a pounding on the apartment door.

"Your Majesties! Is all well?"

"Come in," Imbaso said, and a guard captain accompanied by two underlings came into the suite. "We need to have everything that was made with honey in the palace kitchens over the past few hours gathered up and destroyed," the king commanded. "And the warning not to eat any of it must be broadcast aloud, in case anyone did not receive our lord's words."

Leila had lost her appetite, but after checking to make sure the kaf was not poisoned she poured herself a cup of it and sat in the parlor, sipping occasionally and staring glumly at the table. "I am just so damned *tired* of this!" she wailed. Imbaso gathered her in his strong arms and kissed the top of her forehead.

"I know, love, I know... I'm tired of it too. I had hoped that we would have achieved peace by now, and perhaps have started a family. We've been married for months and you're not pregnant. You're using herbs?"

She was surprised he knew of such things. They were supposed to be secret – known only to women and of course healers and the Makucha Nyeusi. "I'm not about to get pregnant while we're fighting a war," she said, nodding. "I want your baby, Imbaso, I want lots of them. After all, if it's only *our* children who'll be eligible to take the throne after we're gone, we'd better have a selection to choose from!" He chuckled and squeezed her tight.

The king and queen met with Lmambela later in the day, receiving his report – and the news was grim. A fresh shipment of honey had been delivered yesterday afternoon and placed in one of the storerooms adjacent to the palace kitchens. At around four o'clock this morning, after the dough for the pastries had risen and it was time to assemble them on enormous baking pans ready to go into the ovens, the first of several casks of honey from that shipment had been breached.

The kitchen workers had been on shift for hours, and nearly two dozen of them had sampled the honey, the pastries, or both. Ten of them had died, though the others had been saved thanks to intervention by Betsalel. The God of Death had become the God of Life for the royal Palamban palace, and his star was on the rise. Another seven people scattered around the palace compound, including three servants and four members of the royal family, had eaten of the pastries and then collapsed and died before anyone realized they were ill. It had taken hours to locate them all.

Leila's eyes were stinging, though she held an icy calm in the illusion she presented to Lmambela. All those innocent people killed, as the Eight-damned Makucha tried to get to *her*! "Where did the honey come from, Commander?" she asked with no sign of a quaver in her voice.

"Most of it comes from the farms along the east bank of the Azraq, Majesty," he replied.

Beyond the range that Betsalel had employed when he was searching for Kivuli cultists, she realized. "Do the farmers take it to town with them when they come in with their crops?" the queen asked.

"Most of them don't come in at all," the guard commander explained. "There are several firms of jobbers within the city, and they send carts out to collect the produce. It is stored in their warehouses, usually along the river docks, and then distributed to their customers. The jobber who supplied this particular load of honey is a man called Ibrahim Khazir. I have known him for years."

"The poison must have been introduced into the honey while it was on the farms," Imbaso mused. "But I assume there would have been several of them? How could they poison it at farm after farm?"

"I believe the poison was put in during the time the honey was on the jobber's wagon," Lmambela said. "Ibrahim told me that he had hired a new driver a week ago, a man who said he was from the area along the east bank and knew the route. He'd been gathering wheat, cotton, beans, and fruit but yesterday was the first time the farms had had honey to sell. And he did not report for work this morning."

Leila and Imbaso exchanged glances. If this driver was the one who had poisoned the honey, and he'd been based in Iskand, that meant… "The Black Claw is now hiring non-cultists to do their work for them," Leila said. Her heart quailed at the thought.

Chapter 81

After a conference with Betsalel, battle plans were drawn. "I could identify and locate people whose minds are closed to me, and among those some might be plotting you harm. But most would not," the god had told them. Without the beacon of the spiritual protection placed on his initiates by Kivuli, there was no easy way to spot an assassin until it was too late.

But there were other things to try. "If the Makucha is paying non-initiates to kill for them," Imbaso suggested, "we can outbid them. I will offer a reward of ten thousand asand to anyone who turns in a member of the Black Claw, no questions asked provided we make the kill and the identification is proven. Professional assassins are likely to be less afraid of the Makucha than the average person would be, and they do like money." It was an obscene amount of money, enough to let one live like a king for years.

"Good idea," Leila said, taking notes. "And the signs of Betsalel, repelling any who enter with ill intent, should be placed all along the compound walls and at all four of the gates. Plus in other areas of the palace – wherever somebody might try to infiltrate. Those going about their normal business will not even notice them, but they will make it very hard psychologically for those who mean us harm to come inside."

They were alone with Lmambela, and as their lives were to some extent in his hands they decided to reveal their secret to him. "Commander," Leila said, "this necklace I wear, and the one around Imbaso's neck, have been enchanted to provide us with warning of danger. This is why we were able to spot the poison both times it was tried, and why Imbaso was able to escape that arrow."

The guard commander stared at her, impassive. Clearly, he had suspected the king and queen had some kind of divine protection. "We need something like this in the palace kitchens' receiving area," he said. They called Betsalel and he produced three necklaces out of thin air. They were of a plain and simple design, an apparent leather thong with a glass bead strung on it such as might be worn by either a man or a woman.

"Give one of these to whoever is receiving food deliveries, and another to whoever is supervising in the kitchen. I leave it to you, commander, to decide who should wear the third. The warning for poison will come to anyone, but other danger warnings will be specific to the wearer. If a man in the group nearby has a sharpened dagger out but he's intending to stab somebody else with it, the wearer of the necklace will not get a warning," the god explained.

Lmambela took charge of the necklaces, thanking the Shadow God. In addition to his usual devotions to Belantos and Andros, he now regularly worshiped at the shrine of Betsalel within the Great Library. More and more people were using the shrine, even Leila and Imbaso though they could personally commune with their god wherever they wanted to. There was a serene grandeur about the setting.

"Those three cities where the teams disappeared," Imbaso asked, "did you follow up on them yet?" The guard commander nodded.

"We sent a guardsman in the guise of an old woman to the place where the first team vanished. She hobbled over to the black temple to pray for surcease from her pain, and found it guarded by two men in priest robes who did not look like priests – too agile, too alert-seeming."

"What happened?" the king asked. "The 'old woman' dropped the seed idol onto the altar as she stood before it praying to the small statue that was there. Then our man called the god, who shielded the sanctuary while doing away with the statue. He confirmed that the place was full of Kivuli cultists, though of course he could not say for certain which of them were Makucha."

"A few minutes later," Lmambela continued, "The 'old woman' went back out, seemingly having been unsuccessful in contacting the god – as expected. She hobbled off, and went to see the commander of the city guard. This was Esanwe, too small to have a royal guard garrison in the town. But the city government is well-organized, and they were able to mount a dozen guardsmen to attack the temple."

"Was Betsalel able to save any of the cultists?" Leila asked. It bothered her that the first policy she and Imbaso had enacted during their reign was to wage war on their own citizens.

"None from the temple," the guard commander said. "The two on guard outside were Makucha, and though not everyone in the secret temple below was, they were all in league together. The force just had to go in shooting, and check the bodies later. But there were more in town, and most of those were happy to recant after they realized that the Makucha were not enough to protect them."

Leila exhaled slightly. She had had enough of war, but it had not had enough of her. She hoped there'd still be something left when it had. "The same with the other two?" she asked, and Lmambela nodded again. "More or less. We had to fight assassins mixed with armed priests at the temples each time, while the rank-and-file cultists were dispersed around the city in hiding. None of our enemies seem to have figured out yet that the true Shadow God can use the very protection they received from their vile djinn as a way to track them."

They were conferring in the guard headquarters' war room, and bent to examine the huge map. The number of glowing red lights on it had dwindled, with most of those remaining – more than fifty of them – being clustered in the western part of the country south of the Rabiyats, or scattered in remote locations across the far south. Some of those temples were in areas still in rebellion against the crown, and the people there might well consider siding with the djinn before they would obey any writs signed by the king and queen of Palambo.

The queen's eyes fell on a glowing beacon on the far west side of the map: Dikka, at the mouth of the Pana. It was Palambo's foremost seaport on the Western Ocean, a bustling center of trade – and, according to the assassins she'd trapped and killed in Namei, the site of a large chapter of the Makucha Nyeusi as well as "one of the largest" gatherings of Kivuli cultists in the land. "What have we heard from Dikka?" she asked Lmambela.

His brow creased, and he said "Not very much." The proclamation the king and queen had crafted had long since reached every place in the country big enough to have someone who could read it, let alone the sites of the two hundred seventy-three temples of Betsalel.

"Isn't there a large royal guard garrison there?" Leila asked. Wherever there was much trade, the guard was there as enforcers of the tariff laws. And they usually had their hands full, trying to catch those who would evade those laws.

"I had a letter from Commander Osemwe a month ago," Lmambela said. "He indicated that he had sent a squad to investigate the temple of Betsalel there. It is one of the largest in Palambo, I believe, one of the few with residential facilities below the main temple sanctuary. The other gods have similarly large temples in Dikka. But Osemwe's men found no signs of cult activity, and no indication of Makucha Nyeusi guarding the place."

Imbaso looked at her, a flash of pleading crossing his features. But he said nothing. She was not his delicate flower, and were he the mightiest man in the world it would not be enough to protect her if she were. Leila would do what she had to do, and he would support her though it tore his heart to let her go into such danger.

"Commander," the queen said, "This Osemwe is either another covert Kivuli cultist or an incompetent. In either case he must be removed from his post – if not from this life. I must go to Dikka and learn what happens there."

"We have not yet placed an idol of Betsalel there," Lmambela reminded her. "How will you travel? I could certainly get Belantos to carry you there."

"I'm going to our quarters to get ready," Leila replied, "then I'll be going to the harem. I plan to have Mulia deliver me."

Chapter 82

Leila threw her arms tight around Imbaso, and kissed him goodbye. Then she turned to the waiting goddess of all things womanly and was scooped up into her arms. As the patron goddess of such things as family planning and the raising of babies, Mulia in particular had been deeply offended by the Kivuli cult's practice of stealing and sacrificing infants. She'd been more than happy to aid the queen in a way far more active than the tacit support she'd given her in Parat more than a year before.

Leila went invisible, and was pleased to note that while she was in contact with the goddess this contact did not cause the goddess to disappear. That would have been awkward. She knew it was likely (especially considering those three teams who'd disappeared, and might have been interrogated before being killed) that the enemy was aware they'd been infiltrating new territory using the help of Belantos and Andros. But almost all of the cultists and especially the Makucha were men. And no man (other than the rare man born feeling he was truly a woman given the wrong body – caused by the soul of a woman entering a male fetus, she guessed) would have been caught dead hanging around the temple of Mulia.

It had been fairly late in the night when Leila had left Iskand, and was well past dark when she arrived in the goddess' arms in the temple of Mulia in Dikka. The Woman's Goddess got most of her worshipers during daylight hours, except for the odd mistress or lady of the night slipping in to request continued protection from pregnancy. It was a tossup whether Mulia got more women pleading to become mothers, or the other way around.

In any case, no one was in the large circular sanctuary when they arrived, and the enormous twelve-foot goddess set the little five-foot woman on her feet beneath the pedestal on which she stood. "Fare thee well, Leila," Mulia said in her mellifluous voice. She truly embodied everything that was good about womanhood, and had claimed a little part of Leila's heart. What she could spare from Betsalel, at least. "Thank you, Lady," the queen of Palambo replied quietly, and slipped off into the night.

Unfortunately, though the city of Dikka had devoted plenty of space for its temples, it had not thought to create a district for them. Dikka had been built in an area of hills on either side of the Pana, with one enormous bridge (and quite a few ferries) spanning the river some five miles in from the Western Ocean. Deep channels had been dredged in the delta to allow ocean-going ships to sail up to the original docks, and in later centuries the city had sprawled to the north and south with additional harbors being formed. Crossing from one edge of the seaport to the other might require hours, on foot.

Calling her god to the idol in her pocket, Leila walked out of the temple of Mulia and began looking around her. She hadn't realized what she was getting into, and had not thought to consider geography when choosing the goddess as the one who would bear her here. "Where's your temple, dark one?" she asked in her mind as she stepped out onto a cobbled street. Dikka looked to be nearly as well-lit by night as Marsine, and there were streetlamps running down the hill. Mulia's temple had been built on a little hilltop, and commanded a marvelous view. Leila could hardly wait to see what the city looked like in daylight.

"My temple is on this side of the river," Betsalel replied in her mind. "This city is rife with the devotees of Kivuli!" he added. "They are scattered all over the city, but there is a concentration of them…" Leila waited for him to finish the thought, but it took a while. Finally he continued, "Little one, turn to face the river." She did so, the broad stretch of water a dark ribbon between the well-lit shores.

"Now," the Shadow God went on, "turn a little more to your left, upriver. I will create a spark to show you the location." Leila did as told, and her eyes were briefly dazzled by a bright flash that seemed to be relatively close to the river. At least it was on this side of it!

"Master, your temple?" she asked.

"I believe the cultists have taken the idol that was once mine completely away from the temple," he replied. "There is no sign of cultists in the public sanctuary or below it, in the residential quarters of the priesthood."

Well, hooray for Osemwe, Leila thought. The man was apparently neither a Kivuli adherent shielding the cult from the guard, or an idiot. He'd been told to look at the temple, and he'd found nothing. Because there was nothing there to find. She'd have to reserve judgment until she'd actually met the man, though.

It looked like miles, fortunately much of it downhill, for Leila to reach the spot the god had marked. But was she not given the power of tirelessness for just such a situation? Leila set off running, still invisible, through the quiet nighttime streets of Dikka. It was not terribly late, not much beyond nine, but the temple of Mulia was in a mostly residential district and people were all home by now.

Running invisibly within a bubble of silence, Leila pounded down to the bottom of the hill and then up another, lower, rise before heading down again. As she got closer to the river the character of the city changed, with taverns and gambling houses and brothels replacing the homes of the middle class. Eventually she had to drop her speed, as there were too many people on the streets for her to safely run along them.

The neighborhood changed yet again as Leila approached the area Betsalel told her housed the greatest concentration of Kivuli cultists. Public houses serving sailors and dockworkers gave way to warehouses. The streetlights continued, and she saw night watchmen walking their rounds. Breathing lightly, not in the least tired from her run, Leila slowed to a cautious walk as the Shadow God spoke in her mind to direct her steps.

Amid the warehouses – most of them standing three stories tall and lit only with a few lamps for the sake of security – one building glowed with light. Aside from the extra lighting it appeared to be a warehouse like all the others, strongly built of fired brick and maybe three centuries old. From the architectural details, all of the buildings in this block had been put up at the same time, using the same builder. Dikka had been a major port since ancient times, Leila knew from her readings in Palamban history. It rivaled Iskand in its antiquity and importance as a trading center.

A lamp glowed beside the door, and beneath it a sign was mounted on the wall. It read "Private Athletic Club." Well I'll be buggered by a camel, Leila thought – finally, if only silently, getting the chance to try out some of the profanity she'd learned while posing as Usiku during the caravan trip from Halath.

Somehow, for some reason – possibly because unlike all the other temples the one in Dikka already had a lower story – the cult here had instead taken their stolen idol to another part of town. And the Makucha Nyeusi had grown up here, side by side with the worship of the dark god the prophet had insisted could only be properly honored with death in its many forms.

"Betsalel, how many inside?" Leila asked silently. "One hundred and seventeen," the god replied in her mind after a brief interval. Oh, shit. The god was unable to distinguish Makucha from anyone else who had been initiated, and that was a piece of information she really needed to have before planning an assault. Somewhere in this three-story building would be an inner sanctum (presumably a huge one, under the circumstances) with an idol of Kivuli in it. And that idol would absolutely have to be destroyed, before anyone dared come here to challenge the men (and perhaps, women) who worshiped it.

Chapter 83

Leila, still cloaked in shadows, took up station beside the door of the Kivuli cult's center of operations. She lurked just outside the circle of light created by the lamp beside the door, as even her shadows might be detected by someone paying attention. It was early enough that cultists would still be arriving here, coming to join the evening's worship. She suspected that with a "church" this large there was a social element to it, and cultists would be gathering early to press the flesh with their coreligionists before things really got going at midnight.

"Can you fix all the faces you see in your mind, master?" she asked silently. Betsalel had powers far beyond the human, and she needed to tap them if she had any hopes at all of overcoming the obstacle she had discovered. Dikka's cult was like four or five of the worst Leila had yet seen, rolled into one.

"I have already fixed the images of all within the building, little one," he assured her. Two black-clad figures arrived. In a city the size of this one only a relatively small percentage of the "congregation" would include priests, but it seemed black robes were *de riguer* for such affairs. Had she luckily arrived on a special night, or did this go on all the time?

The pair knocked on the door, no special knock, and it was opened to them by a young man also clad in black robes. He greeted them by name, seeming to know them, and they went inside. The young fellow must be fulfilling the role Yusuf had done in Namei, Leila realized. No one would be accidentally wandering in the door of a "private athletic club" in the middle of the night, so he was not garbed as an ordinary clerk. During the day he, or whoever had that shift, would probably simply turn away people thinking they might be admitted to the membership of the "club".

Leila waited until another small party, three men this time, arrived at the door and knocked. It was a risk, she knew, but she needed to get in there and see what was happening. And she felt more than competent to knife them and the doorman as well, should they realize they had an unseen companion.

After identifying the three men as people who should be granted admittance the doorman stepped back and held the door, which opened inward, to allow them to pass. Leila slipped in behind them just before the door was closed again, hugging the wall and letting the men continue on through the entry hall and out of sight before following them. The doorman returned to his desk, where he appeared to be reading a book by lamplight.

A staircase led upward only a few paces from the anteroom, and the three black-clad men trotted up it. Leila was curious, though, and turned left down a darkened corridor. Whatever this section of the former warehouse was, it was not apparently used at night. She found locked doors along the left side, probably offices, and an open one on the right that led into a cavernous space. Aha, the gymnasium!

There were high windows near the ceiling around three of the walls, allowing some of Dikka's nighttime illumination to come in. The place looked like a near-copy of the physical training space at the Makucha's headquarters in Namei, but larger. It was deserted.

Leila returned to the corridor, and headed in the direction of the stairs. "Would you like to plant some bombs, Leila?" Betsalel suggested.

"Bombs?" she asked. People east of the Killtops had discovered the explosive properties of charcoal mixed with saltpeter and sulfur centuries ago, but no one in the Dominion had ever bothered trying to turn this technology into weapons – there had been no wars for a thousand years.

"I can create devices that will explode," the god explained, "destroying everything in a circle perhaps thirty feet in diameter. When I cause them to go off, they would possibly cause this building to collapse or at least set it on fire."

"Killing everyone inside?" Leila asked. She had known the God of Death as a generally kindly and thoughtful individual, but occasionally he seemed to forget himself.

"You're right," he said contritely. "I am over-anxious to see the end of Kivuli."

Leila crept up the stairs. There didn't seem to be any traffic coming down, just the occasional new arrivals climbing up. The second floor looked to be divided into residential rooms, though perhaps there were some labs and classrooms for Makucha apprentices to learn the arts of poisoning and other non-physical skills. The landing gave onto a single hallway guarded by a man she took to be an assassin, and the bottom of the stairway leading to the third floor.

At the top of those stairs there was another doorman, or perhaps gate guard was a better description of his job. He stood beside a locked door, arms crossed. His air of competence gave Leila no doubt that he was Makucha Nyeusi. The landing ran the depth of the building, and she moved silently over to one side. This floor had the same high windows as she'd seen on the ground floor – but here, they appeared to have been covered in black paint.

The party Leila had followed inside had long since passed through that door, and she settled down to wait for another. A lone man came up the stairs, the man beside the door identified him and then knocked in what appeared to be a coded sequence before it was unlocked – and presumably, unbarred – from the other side.

Double security! Leila realized. And that was going to make it hard for her to slip past. The man outside would be alert during the time new arrivals would be passing through the door – not standing back, holding the door open. She could distract him, pull him down to the far end of the entry hall with a noise. Then use the knock pattern she'd heard and memorized – but then what? The man inside would see no one there.

Leila watched two more parties of Kivuli worshipers arrive, the pattern with the doorman repeating, as she tried to decide what to do. She had brought her watch, but could not see it any more than she could see anything else she touched while she was invisible. "What time is it?" she asked, and was told "Ten-thirty, local time" by the god in her pocket.

It suddenly occurred to her what a risk she was running. Behind that door there were more than a hundred Kivuli cultists, waiting for their god to manifest in his idol while she and her god, already manifest, waited outside. Suppose she *did* figure out how to get inside, then what? If Kivuli was manifest in a crowd like that, even Betsalel's superiority throughout the world might not be enough to enable him to prevail. He would have to retreat, and suppose the djinn was able to penetrate her shadows? She would be dead meat.

"I think I know what we'll find behind that door," Leila told the Shadow God silently. "And I think we don't have to get in there and confirm it. At least not now."

"You are wise, my child," Betsalel's smooth dark voice said within her mind. "Let's get out of here."

Chapter 84

Out on the street again, feeling as if she had miraculously escaped with her life, Leila considered what to do next. She had not actually laid eyes on the idol of Kivuli, but she knew as surely as she knew her own name that it must lie somewhere on that third floor. Again she felt the difference between physical tiredness, which did not affect her at all, and the psychic variety. She brushed it off.

"Master, where is the royal guard garrison housed?" she asked, and he directed her to rotate until once again a spark of light marked the spot. Shit, it was on the far side of the river and at least a mile or two to the west. "Any chance you can give me the power to slip between dimensions by myself, or perhaps fly?" Leila asked her god as she set her feet running in that direction.

"Sorry," was his only reply.

By the time she arrived at the guards' compound and had slipped in through a postern door the god had unbarred for her, Leila found that the hour was late and everyone not on overnight guard duty was already in their beds. This seemed like as good a time as any to weed out any Kivuli cultists among them.

"There are only two here," the Shadow God said in her mind. There was a hint of surprised relief about the statement. Of course, any truly loyal Kivuli cultists might still be making their way back from the festivities at the warehouse now. But the fewer she had to deal with at one time, the better.

Betsalel guided her to where the sleeping cultists could be found. One was a captain, sleeping in his own room in the officers' quarters. He and a sergeant, bunking in a small barracks room with other non-commissioned officers, both died without waking as they were pricked on the scalp beneath the hair by a thin needle dipped in oualit.

Feeling pleased that she had only had to kill two people so far, Leila announced she would like to take a nap. Betsalel identified a barracks with an unused cot in it, and she curled up to sleep for a few hours, still invisible, as the god watched over her. It was odd how the tirelessness power worked, she mused as she drifted off. It didn't relieve her of the need to eat or drink, and while it could stave off the need for sleep sooner or later that too would catch up with her.

The sky had not yet begun to get light when Betsalel spoke gently in Leila's mind, rousing her from her sleep. She wanted to be up and away from the barracks before the guardsmen were roused and bustling around. Slipping silently out of the compound, feeling somewhat refreshed from her few hours of rest, Leila adopted the appearance of a businessman up and about early and found a café where she could have a leisurely breakfast and a few cups of kaf.

By the time the day had really begun for most of the inhabitants of the royal guard garrison, their queen was feeling comfortably full, completely alert, and ready for her next move. She appeared as herself, in full regalia, and demanded to be taken to see Commander Osemwe.

The soldiers thought it bizarre that the queen of Palambo should appear out of nowhere more than a thousand miles away from her palace, completely unattended, and request an interview with their commander. But they were used to doing what they were told.

Commander Osemwe proved to be a slightly portly Hutu in his mid-to-late forties, good-looking and charming in a mild-mannered sort of way. He didn't seem much like the sort of hard-bitten soldier you would expect to rise to high office in the guard. But the royal guard's dual purpose as law enforcement and army led to the inclusion of both soldiers and politicians.

He rose as she was ushered into his office. "Your majesty!" he said in astonishment. "Please be seated and tell me what brings you to Dikka." Leila regally took the chair proffered and commanded Osemwe to sit as well. She got right to the point.

"What brings me to Dikka, commander," she said in haughty tones, "is the continued presence of the proscribed cult of Kivuli within the city. It is your responsibility to act upon the proclamation my husband and I sent, arresting all cult members and destroying their idols. Yet I learned that this has not been done, though you have been in possession of the proclamation for months."

His face set in a worried frown, Osemwe said "But Majesty, I sent soldiers to investigate the temple of Betsalel as ordered in the proclamation. We found only a couple of old priests, who are resident in the area beneath the temple. No cultists, no assassins, no demonic idols. I have done as requested, but this cult you say infests our city was not found."

Leila decided that Osemwe's problem was that he lacked imagination, and/or was insufficiently diligent. He had made no attempt to investigate, to learn if any signs of cult activity were present within Dikka. If there was really as big a chapter of the Makucha here as the assassins in Namei had believed, there must be quite a few unexplained deaths.

"Ah, Commander," the queen said. "I have done my own investigation and I have learned that there is indeed no cult activity at my lord Betsalel's temple. But my sources have identified the true headquarters of the cult within Dikka. Your men will find it within an old warehouse along the riverfront on the north bank of the Pana. A sign on the door says 'Private Athletic Club.' It is where the Makucha Nyeusi practices their skills and trains their apprentices."

Osemwe was now registering shock and fear. "Eight preserve us!" he said, "I had no idea! The guard patrols the docks on both sides of the river and also in the ocean harbor areas to the west, but those warehouses are mostly guarded by private security companies hired by the owners. We have never had any complaints."

"I assure you, Commander, that warehouse is inhabited by the cult," Leila told him. "They hold their bloodthirsty rituals on the top floor, train assassins on the ground floor, and house their priests and other personnel on the floor in between. If you send a sufficiently large squad and go during the daytime, you should be able to overcome the door guard and shoot down any members of the Makucha Nyeusi you encounter. The idol should be smashed. Can I count on you to do this immediately, today?"

Still looking terrified, Osemwe stammered "Yes, your majesty! I will send a company just as soon as one can be put together!" At this moment an anxious-looking clerk put his head in the door. He, too, looked terrified.

"Sir!" he cried. "Two of our officers didn't report for duty this morning. They were both found dead in their beds!"

"Murdered?" the commander asked, his concern rising by the minute.

"I don't think so, sir," the clerk said. "There were no marks on them, no blood. They seemed to have died in their sleep, at about the same time in barracks that were half a mile apart." Osemwe looked a little relieved. Dropping dead of a heart attack was something that could happen to any man, especially ones over forty – as many of his officers were. The coincidence was unsettling, though.

"What are the officers' names?" he demanded of the clerk, who had apparently not realized the woman in the commander's office was the queen. "It was Captain Sdembo and Sergeant Mstimbe," he said.

"Thank you Corporal, you may go," Osemwe said. He still looked nearly ready to jump out of his skin.

"It might have been the Kivuli cult, Commander," the queen told him coolly. In a way, it had been.

"I'll look into that as well, Your Majesty. Is there anything else?"

"Thank you, Commander. While I'm here in Dikka I think I will go and pay a visit to the temple of Betsalel. I'll return here later today, after lunch, to find out from you what the company you're sending has found. Until then." The awfully small but still regal-looking woman stood and strutted out of the room, leaving Osemwe gasping. Then he stood and called the corporal back in.

"Please have Sergeant Astambye report to me at once."

Since arriving in Dikka Leila had run miles, and even if it didn't make her tired all that dashing around was beginning to get old. And it would be hours before she could learn what the result of the guards' visit to the Kivuli cult's warehouse had been. She decided to treat herself to a sedan chair ride, and sat in relaxed comfort as the two tall, muscular porters trotted across Dikka's splendid bridge (one of the engineering marvels of Palambo, built in ancient times) and delivered her to the door of the temple of Betsalel on a little hilltop overlooking the Pana's north bank.

Leila tipped the porters generously and sent them on their way. She'd enjoyed the ride, but expected to need more stealth for her other activities today. The temple of Betsalel was on a par with the one in which Mulia reigned, not that far from here; but it had been built all of black stone. Leila found one old priest, eighty if he was a day, sitting in a chair in the anteroom outside the sanctuary. He started up from a doze as she entered, still appearing as the queen.

"Betsalel's blessings on you father," she said. The old fellow got stiffly to his feet and favored her with a toothless grin.

"At my age," he said wryly, "I'd just as soon pass on my lord's blessings for a while yet." Most of the elderly who prayed to the Shadow God asked him for the blessing of a painless death.

She grinned back and held out a hand to him. "I am Leila, arch-priestess of Betsalel in Iskand and also Queen of Palambo. And you are?" The old man was staring at her in awe.

"It is! It's really you!" he said. He tried to get down onto his knees, but she pulled him back to his feet. "I... I am Pandaso, Majesty," he stammered out. "Priest of Betsalel these sixty years, and I have never met my god in the flesh. But I have heard the tales! They say our master has returned to his temples, that he is answering prayers again! That I should live to see it!"

With a smug little smile, Leila took the old priest and led him through the open double doors into the large and cavernous sanctuary. The black idol stood on a square stone platform, not the usual natural-looking pedestal. It was twelve feet tall – an inconveniently large size to have been stolen and replaced with a replica.

"Let's ask Betsalel why he has been unable to come to you for all these years, shall we?" the queen said sweetly. She deposited what looked to the old man's eyes like a small blackened seed, on the stone floor in front of the idol. "Go ahead," Leila told him, "call your god!"

Shrugging his shoulders, the old priest faced the idol – as he had done fruitlessly countless times before – and said "My lord Betsalel, I beg that you would come to me!" Out of nowhere, it seemed, the dark god's image grew up in front of the sanctuary's idol, and came to life.

"Pandaso!" he said, in his deep dark voice, "We meet at last!"

The god had grown to his preferred height of six feet, most appropriate for interacting with humans, and he reached out a hand to steady Pandaso as the old man swayed on his feet. It would have been too ironic if the shock of finally meeting the god he'd worshiped in vain for most of his life had given him a fatal heart attack.

The old priest felt vigor and energy surge through him at Betsalel's touch, as if ten years had been taken from his shoulders in an instant, His vision was blurred, tears running down his cheeks, as he beheld his god for the first time in his life.

"The idol behind me is a true one," the dark god said, "but it has been desecrated as was the one in the Temple of the Eight in Iskand."

"Using the same technique?" Leila asked, and Betsalel nodded.

"The lore of our temple in Dikka says that once there were two idols here," Pandaso said. "We were once second only to your temple in Namei, dark one, and the residential and administrative spaces beneath the sanctuary housed many priests and acolytes. Then a force of men claiming to carry the word of one they said was a prophet, came to us and said that we must begin worshiping you using the new forms that had been revealed to them."

"But you did not?" the Shadow God asked, curious. He had thought every one of his temples had been taken over by the prophet's followers.

"Some said that we should try the new way, as the god had stopped communicating with us. But they were in a minority. The temple leadership turned them out, telling them to go and follow their prophet's teachings if they wanted to. But they would not do it here."

"What happened then?" Leila asked, fascinated at the history lesson.

"The prophet's men, led by those of our number who had joined them, stormed the temple and captured the small idol that was housed below for the private worship of the priesthood," the old priest recounted. "The large idol you see there was captured as well, and the prophet's men occupied the temple for a week. But those of the true priesthood who had not been killed in the attack received aid from the royal garrison. We retook the temple, killing many of those who had occupied it – but others escaped, vanishing with the smaller idol, and were not heard of again. We believed they might have fled north into the desert, where it was said the prophet had arisen."

"All this is recorded in your archives?" Leila asked. Pandaso nodded.

"Those who fled carried the books with them. We had been recording our history for more than a thousand years, and the records were precious to us. The invaders didn't seem to care that we took them, only interested in claiming the idols. After they were gone the books were returned to their place below, and those who had survived the attack recorded all that had taken place, for posterity. Our numbers were greatly reduced, and they have never recovered."

"How many remain here?" Betsalel asked.

"I'm afraid it's just me and my old friend Namende here now. We were acolytes together, and the last the temple ever trained. No one has wanted to go into the priesthood of a god who never answered prayers." He started, and looked ashamed. Here he was, chastising the deity who had come to him at last.

"I do not blame you for losing faith, Pandaso," the Shadow God assured him. "The followers of the prophet captured all of my idols and began worshipping a god that demanded blood sacrifice, especially of innocents, in my name. I could not manifest in them, as there were no true believers calling me. And a few months ago the arch-priest in Namei succeeded in ensouling that imaginary monster – creating a living djinn. Leila had finally restored me to the pantheon within the Gaspari Dominion, and with that power I was at last able to address the situation here in Palambo. I will see to it that you have acolytes again, now there is once again a true idol here."

The old priest dissolved into tears of joy. Betsalel removed the desecrated idol and took its place, though he complained that the prophet's men had stolen his pedestal as well – weakening the connection slightly. Before he departed the idol he commanded "Reach out for me, Pandaso. Tell Namende and any who come here truly seeking me that I have returned to Dikka."

With that the true idol was stone once more, and Pandaso bid Leila goodbye. She strolled out into the mid-morning sunshine, feeling good. It had been so uplifting to grant the old man his lifelong wish! But she had better get on with things. She wanted to be down at the Kivuli cult's warehouse to see what happened when the guards got there, and lend a hand if needed. Glancing around, she saw no one near at hand and went invisible, then burst into a trot and headed down the hill.

A boy of perhaps fifteen, dressed in ordinary clothing, emerged from hiding in the bushes flanking the temple and stared in the direction Leila had gone. Then he walked inside the temple and found the old priest who was always here in the daytime sitting in a front pew, just gazing at the idol in wonder. "Good morning, father," he said politely, taking a seat.

The old man grinned maniacally at him. "Are you here to worship the Shadow God, son?" he asked. The boy looked down as if shy.

"Maybe," he said noncommittally. Few people his age had reason to seek the blessings of Betsalel. "Say," the boy added, as if the thought had just occurred to him, "who was that lady who was just here?"

"That," the smiling priest told him, "was the Queen of Palambo – and Betsalel's arch-priestess as well!" The kid stood bolt upright.

"Excuse me," he said in excitement. "I have to go!" He vanished out the door.

Chapter 85

Betsalel guided Leila's steps along back roads with less traffic on them, enabling her to maintain a full run while surrounded with a bubble of silence. And as the journey was mostly downhill, she made it to the cult's warehouse in record time. In the buildings on either side, warehouse doors were open and freight was being taken in and out. But over the centuries this warehouse had lost the big loading doors and hand-cranked freight elevators its companions still had.

Invisible, Leila tried the front door and found it locked. She rapped on it, prepared to steal away silently if it were opened; but nobody responded. Betsalel unlocked it at her request, saving her the minute or two it would have taken her to pick the lock, and she pushed it open slowly and silently.

Leila closed the door behind her and Betsalel locked it again. Was it possible that a company of guards had been here already and emptied the place of inhabitants? That seemed unlikely. She had hoped that a daylight raid might find the place's nocturnal inhabitants sleeping or elsewhere.

She was about to go check on the gymnasium when she heard people coming down the stairs and backed over into the corner of the room near the wall with the front door in it. The smaller man Leila took for the doorman – not the same one who'd been on duty last night, but from his build and the way he moved he had to be Makucha. The other man was much larger, and dressed in the uniform of a sergeant of the royal guards. What the hell?

As they got down into the entry hall the doorman shook hands with the taller man and said "Thanks, Astambye, for the warning. Tell Osemwe to hold firm, and we'll let him know if we need any more help." The doorman unlocked the door to let the visitor out, then locked it behind him and resumed his post.

The cursed swine! Leila thought in outrage. Here she'd been making all kinds of excuses for the guard commander, and all the while he was in the pay of the cult. She supposed that with death for any who opposed them always an option, the cult members (especially those who were not in the priesthood but held regular jobs) could amass plenty of coin to fund their nefarious schemes. How much had Mauaji spent putting his son on the throne, only to learn he had not crowned a puppet?

Leila considered killing the doorman on the spot, but decided against it. He would surely be missed, and that might launch a search of the building. First, she wanted to go upstairs and see if she could get into that inner sanctum room she'd been afraid to infiltrate last night.

The invisible queen crept silently up the steps, past the second floor residences to the third floor – only to find the door still guarded. But it was open, at least. The place was dimly lit by lamps, there being no daylight admitted by the black-painted windows.

Oozing along noiselessly, Leila slipped through the door as the guard stood with his back against the wall, staring into space. He glanced her way as she went through, as if he'd felt a breath or air or something – but seeing nothing, he continued to keep his vigil.

Inside the door Leila found a broad corridor, which ran for some twenty feet with a couple of doors on either side of it. Offices, probably, she thought. At the end of the corridor, with a set of double doors standing open, was an enormous room that ran the width of the warehouse and continued all the way down to the end of the long building. This was the inner sanctum, and it looked as if it could easily hold two hundred people!

Lamps were lit at intervals along either side of the room, and the usual two rows of bench seating with an aisle in between filled most of the space. In the shadows near the far end, where an enormous altar ran twenty feet across near the back wall, Leila could see three black-robed figures in animated conversation.

They were standing in the open space in front of the altar, some fifteen feet deep and as wide as the building. The idol of Kivuli, as Leila had guessed, was standing on a black stone pedestal that seemed a little oversized for a seven-foot idol, right behind the altar. Old bloodstains marred the altar's surface, and there was a channel at the back of it for the black flames that would arise when the god was called to manifest.

Leila was pretty sure the guy on the door had been Makucha, too. If you knew what you were looking for and they were making no attempt at disguise, the assassins were unmistakable. But these three were not. They were older, high priests probably, clad in black robes. And they seemed to be having some kind of argument.

Leila slipped around them and stood near the altar where she could clearly hear what they were saying. There was a suggestion of their wanting what they said to remain private, as they were speaking so quietly that the door guard would not have been able to hear their conversation.

The shortest of the three, a man who looked to be in his early fifties, seemed near to panic. "They have destroyed more than two hundred of our temples!" he said in low, urgent tones. "We need to take the idol and flee, before they come in force and kill us all!"

The tallest of them, broad and commanding and maybe a decade younger, spoke contemptuously. "Flee to *where*, Bedstamdi?" he asked, in a tone that suggested the phrase "you cowardly idiot" had been omitted only as a professional courtesy. "This is the greatest remaining stronghold of Kivuli in Palambo, and with the Guard in our pocket it is the safest place we could possibly be!"

The older man looked at him fearfully, wanting to be convinced. "With the old Betsalel temple here and clearly free of any 'taint,' what could be more convincing that we are not active in Dikka?" his colleague went on. "And if the money he receives isn't enough to keep Osemwe working on our behalf, there is always the threat of the Makucha to keep him doing what he should. There will not be any raid. The queen will return from her pilgrimage and he'll inform her that nothing was found at the warehouse. Then she'll go home, and that will be the end of it."

"What about the Makucha?" the third man asked, "why don't we just take out the queen while we have her close at hand?" The one who appeared to be the leader didn't like that idea either.

"That is certainly a possibility," he admitted. "The Makucha has been trying for months to kill her and her traitorous husband in Iskand without success. But if we don't get them both at once, you know that Osemwe will be powerless to stop the hammer that will fall on Dikka if she is killed here or was known to be here when she vanished. Royal troops will rip the city down to its foundations searching for her or the ones who killed her. Better to wait until she has definitely gone someplace else."

The other two acknowledged his wisdom. Should anything happen to her, Leila knew, Imbaso would storm the gates of heaven itself – had such a place existed – to bring her back or exact revenge. It seemed the cooler head had prevailed, and the cult would not be packing up and going into hiding. Good. As soon as Leila could get to the guards' headquarters and relieve Osemwe of his command (not to mention his head), she would arrange for the raid to take place. It was a pity, though, that she had not been able to smash the idol first. A lot of guardsmen were likely to get killed or injured if they ended up having to fight Kivuli.

Before Leila could begin creeping around the three, whose discussion had turned to other issues, the door guard suddenly hastened into the room accompanied by a teenage boy. Betsalel, still manifest in her pocket, said "the boy is not a Kivuli initiate." He certainly didn't look like one. They rarely initiated anyone younger than eighteen, from what she'd seen in Namei.

"What is it, Sahibindi?" the man Leila had identified as the leader asked. He stood taller than the Makucha assassin by inches, but she could see that the door guard's deference had nothing to do with physical attributes. Had he chosen to do so, he could have tied the man in knots or left him dead on the floor in seconds.

"You recall Mussi?" the guard said, his hand on the back of the boy at his side.

"The boy hired to keep an eye on the temple of Betsalel?" the leader asked, and Leila immediately got a very bad feeling in the pit of her stomach. How had she been unaware of such surveillance?

Sahibindi nodded, and pushed the boy (who seemed somewhat cowed by his surroundings – especially the gruesome idol near the back wall) forward. "Tell him what you told me, Mussi," the guard commanded.

"Yes, sir... uh, sir, I was on the day watch as usual this morning. There are only two very old men at the temple, and it has been a rare day when I see more than two or three people – usually as old as the priests – coming to pray to Betsalel. But this morning a beautiful lady came, and she went inside the temple with the old priest."

"Yes, the Queen of Palambo. I know," the leader replied. Why must he be surrounded by idiots? The kid blinked in surprise. Nobody had told *him* the queen of the entire frickin' country was likely to put in an appearance. But that was beside the point.

"But that's not the thing, sir," he tried to explain. "I watched her when she left. She walked out the door and looked around, but she didn't see me because I was hiding in the bushes. Then she just sort of... faded from view. Vanished! But I could hear her footsteps as she ran off!"

The leader stood stock still, his mind racing. Reports from the survivors of fallen temples all over Palambo, who had made their way here, had often cited magical powers on the part of the king and queen. The queen, especially, seemed to come and go as she pleased – there one minute and gone the next. Or perhaps not gone, but... merely *unseen*? Shit!

"The Shadow God must have given her the power of shadows to hide herself!" he said, showing more alarm now than he had earlier. His cohort Bedstamdi looked ready to soil his linens, his eyes darting around the room in fear. "Sahibindi, you were on guard at the door," the leader said. "Did you hear or feel anything out of the ordinary, as if an unseen presence may have passed by?" The guard looked uneasy, and he was about to speak.

Leila was inching toward the door, waiting to get far enough away that she could throw up a bubble of silence and run for it. But before she could get there the leader commanded the Makucha guard, "Quick! Lock and bar the doors! She must be here with us now, and has heard everything we said!"

Chapter 86

After the doors had been locked, Sahibindi took up station before them. He was glaring around the room as if somehow the intensity of his desire would cause the hidden queen to be revealed. Betsalel could have those doors unlocked and unbarred in a trice, but could Leila get past an assassin twice her age who was aware of her existence?

And then there was the fact that she very much did not want the secret of her shadow power to become general knowledge among the enemy. She could not just flee this situation. As Leila hesitated, her mind racing, Bedstamdi declared "Kivuli! We must call the god! He will be able to penetrate the witch's shadows!"

For once you are right, Bedstamdi, the leader thought as he approached the altar. Putting all he had into it, he beseeched the creature he believed to be his god, "Kivuli, our need is great! Come to us!" There was no response.

The third priest said, "Our master has never come without a sacrifice, Teramji! He needs blood!"

Without a word, the tall and broad Teramji seized the hapless Mussi by the neck. He ripped the boy's shirt off, revealing a scrawny chest with ribs standing out in it – no wonder the kid had been willing to work for the cult, he probably seldom got enough to eat – and then threw him bodily up onto the blood-stained altar.

As Leila looked on in horror, paralyzed, the lead priest pulled an oddly-decorated curved knife from his belt. Without any ceremony whatsoever he plunged the blade into Mussi's throat just above the breastbone and then ripped it down, sending blood fountaining everywhere. "Kivuli, thy sacrifice is given!" Teramji shouted. "Come to us, or we are lost!"

Black flames burst up out of the gap between the altar and the pedestal on which the idol sat, as the djinn manifested in the idol he had stolen from Betsalel. His glowing golden eyes surveyed the room for a moment and then he crouched, eagerly feeding on the corpse of the hapless boy.

Tears of horror and sympathy were running down Leila's cheeks as she spoke to her god, "Betsalel, shield me! Do not let the djinn have me!" When they were manifest in the physical plane, gods and their bastard kin the daemons had powers both psychic and physical. Leila, and all who opened themselves to Betsalel as worshipers, was already shielded from Kivuli's psychic powers. Just as the djinn's initiates were shielded from his. But in his physical form, here in this room with four of his true believers, Kivuli could rend Leila limb from limb just as if he had truly been the black leopard he resembled.

"I will keep the djinn from touching you," Betsalel promised from inside her pocket, "But it will be up to you to deal with the others. We are greatly outnumbered here." Leila looked down toward the door and saw Sahibindi still standing there barring the way, a look of awe on his face as his god appeared. His attention was distracted, and in an instant one of her daggers was flying toward him. It penetrated the left side of his neck to the hilt, severing the carotid artery on that side, and he collapsed in a spray of blood.

Relief flooding her mind, Leila turned her attention to the three priests. She had taken out the Makucha guard, and the rest she hoped would be easy meat. Teramji was in murmured conference with his god. The blood-smeared muzzle lifted from the ruin of the boy's chest and Kivuli pointed with one clawed finger. "She is there," he said. Though Leila had never seen the djinn in the flesh before, or heard him speak, it turned out she had pretty much nailed him the times she'd impersonated him. The voice was halfway between human speech and the burbling growl of a hungry panther.

The tables have been turned, Leila realized. Just as Betsalel had been able to identify and locate the initiates protected by Kivuli because of the barrier that cloaked them, the djinn knew where Leila was – though he could not see her – by the protection the Shadow God had given her.

All three of the priests had pulled daggers, and had drawn together in a circle back to back. They moved a little closer to their god, whom they hoped would protect them. "Can you not seize and destroy her, master?" Teramji asked, and the djinn replied.

"My father, my enemy, is here in the room with us. I cannot reach her!"

"Your father?" the priest asked. The revelation that Kivuli was a separate entity from Betsalel and not just the Shadow God's newest incarnation had been a surprise to nearly every member of the cult.

"Betsalel!" Kivuli hissed. "He is ancient, and his power is growing!"

Shit, Teramji thought. My god is afraid to take on her god? Just then Kivuli rotated, remaining on his pedestal in order to partake of the maximum power he could obtain, and pointed again. "She has moved!" he declared, "There!" The direction he pointed was the one in which Bedstamdi was facing, and he quailed in terror – holding out his little dagger as if it were a magic wand.

Thunk! Leila's dagger took Bedstamdi in the throat, and he fell to the floor – his dagger skittering away on the floor tiles as it fell from his lifeless fingers. Now Teramji and his companion were all that were left, and the senior priest cried, "Master, defend us!" It was clear the djinn was reluctant to leave the pedestal. The stones on which idols were placed created some kind of bond with the universe and the powers within it, as far as Leila understood. Betsalel had not been able to explain it very well.

Kivuli lifted a hand and threw a firebolt, which sizzled through the air toward Leila and then splashed against the shield her god had erected. For a moment her figure was limned in light, and Teramji left the scant protection afforded by standing back-to-back with his companion, and went after her with his knife.

"Do that again, master!" he urged, and Kivuli obliged him with another blast. The bolts could not harm Leila, but they gave her enemies a chance to see exactly where she was. And this Teramji, if not Makucha, seemed to have some skill with weapons.

As soon as the light from the djinn's attack had vanished, Leila was on the move. Emboldened by the knowledge that Betsalel had truly shielded her from Kivuli's physical attacks, she darted in to where Teramji's companion stood. He might not be as timid as the late Bedstamdi, but he was not bold enough to go chasing after an invisible woman armed with who knew how many throwing knives.

Before Kivuli could speak again or throw another bolt Leila stepped behind him and severed his spine between two of the cervical vertebrae, pulling the dagger back and re-sheathing it as the priest fell to the floor and she darted away again. Now it was just Leila and Teramji battling it out as Betsalel and the djinn held each other at bay.

Kivuli continued to throw bolts at Leila, keeping his priest informed of her location. For a minute they were at an impasse, as he kept a close watch and dodged when she threw a dagger. She had come here with six of them secreted about her person, and now only had two left.

Cursing the two misses, Leila circled around until she had Teramji in between her and Kivuli. The djinn seemed determined not to step down from his stolen pedestal. Now she rushed toward the black priest, as silently as she could. Kivuli could not mark her with a bolt without hitting his own man, she hoped.

But as she came in, dagger at the ready, Teramji sensed her coming and reached for her. As she drove her knife in up under his ribs, hunting for the heart, he stabbed down into her shoulder. With the last of his strength the priest of Kivuli hurled Leila aside, throwing her to the floor in a heap before clutching at the dagger in his chest. She went visible as she landed. Teramji fell to his knees, weaving, then slumped to the floor face down – a pool of blood spreading beneath him.

Chapter 87

"Ow, fucking ow!" Leila snarled, plucking the priest's dagger out of her left shoulder. If Teramji hadn't been a foot taller than her, he'd probably have stuck it somewhere more useful. But though the wound wasn't mortal, it sure as hell hurt – and she was bleeding like a stuck pig.

She had the god in a pocket on her left side, but at the moment her left arm wasn't good for much. Getting back onto her feet, Leila fumbled around until she could dig him out and release him. In moments Betsalel, now eight feet tall, had placed a hand on her shoulder and healed her injuries. The two of them stood confronting the djinn.

"Kivuli, you are an abomination, a creation of evil men, and you should not exist," Betsalel said. It was the first time the Shadow God and the corrupted copy men had made in his name had stood face to face. The djinn had no reply. One moment he was manifested, believer score in the room standing at one to zero in his opponent's favor. And in the next, only a cold idol stood there before the blood-soaked, mangled corpse of poor Mussi.

The two stood watching for a moment, startled by the suddenness with which the fight had ended. Leila supposed there would be no real way for the two supernatural beings to have a decisive battle, at least not while either of them had more than one true idol in existence. But Kivuli's were dwindling.

"I liked that hammer you made for me in Namei," Leila suggested, and in an instant the god was handing it – or its twin – to her. Betsalel's healing had completely restored her physically, and she took to the task of smashing the idol to bits with enthusiasm. Meanwhile the god, at her request, caused the remains of the four cultists and their sad young victim to vanish utterly – along with all bloodstains and other traces of the conflict.

After the idol had been demolished he made that disappear as well, and once she had retrieved her daggers Leila stood there in the dark, grim, room considering her next move. It was probable that the doorman downstairs had been told Mussi's news, but unlikely that he had run around telling anyone else.

Before they left the inner sanctum Leila had Betsalel create a replica of the idol she had just destroyed. It looked identical, but as it was not a true idol the djinn would be unable to manifest in it. It would certainly fool Kivuli's worshipers, though.

The god once again in her pocket, Leila moved silently and invisibly down past the second floor and thence to the entry hall. The doorman had returned to his post, and she slipped up behind him and killed him as she had done to the second of the three priests upstairs. If he had learned what Mussi had to say, he had not taken it seriously enough to be on his guard.

So convenient having a god on hand to clean up your messes, Leila thought as she made her way along the riverfront toward the bridge. Neither the dead doorman nor the blood spilled by her dagger in his neck were to be seen in the entry hall of the cult's "athletic club." She had even left the outside door locked, just to confound the investigation.

When Leila returned at last to the royal garrison headquarters after an hour-long run across town, she appeared as the priest Teramji and demanded to speak with Osemwe immediately. He was ushered into the commander's presence after a wait of less than five minutes.

Osemwe hastened to close his door, going so far as to lock it. Then he returned to his desk, as the commanding priest sat in the same chair where Leila had sat a few hours before – arms crossed and a grim expression on his face. "You should not have come here!" the commander said, keeping his voice down though he was clearly upset.

"And what was I to do, then – send you a letter?" Teramji asked. "Do we not pay you for complete protection? Yet I learn that the queen is here and threatening a raid."

"Threatening, that's all," Osemwe whined. "No troops are being sent. I had Sergeant Astambye notify you merely as a courtesy, in case you were concerned."

Leila didn't know whether Osemwe had informed the cultists of the deaths of the two of their number within the guard, and wasn't sure how to get that information. "Why did you choose Astambye?" Teramji asked.

"Did he not tell you?" the commander asked surprised. "Mstimbe and Sdembo are dead!"

"No," the priest said, "Astambye did not mention that. What happened to them?"

"Apparently they died in their sleep of heart failure sometime during the night," Osemwe said. "Astambye was the only man I had left. If you like, and will provide the funds, I can probably line up a couple of replacements."

Teramji glared at him, a look that told the commander he'd gone too far. "Never mind," he said hurriedly. "Look, the queen has gone over to the temple of Betsalel. Since she's supposed to be his high priestess, she'll probably be there for a while. When she comes back here this afternoon I'll tell her that I sent a squad to the warehouse, and they found no signs of the cult. Problem solved. Or, why don't you send some of those Makucha guys to the temple and intercept her? Problem *really* solved, eh?"

"The idea has merit," the priest said, getting to his feet. "I will give it a try, if she has not already left. But don't forget, Osemwe – if we see any more soldiers at the warehouse, I can easily send some Makucha to visit *you*." The commander got up to let him out, and then sat motionless at his desk. Oh shit, he thought, what have I gotten myself into?

The black-clad priest exited the guards' compound, and moments later vanished. Leila, leaning up against a wall in a well-shaded alley, asked Betsalel, "Master, can you give Osemwe and his sergeant Astambye merciful deaths?"

"I believe I can grant them that blessing," the god replied. A moment later he added, "It is done." Before returning to the compound, the queen visited the same café where she'd breakfasted this morning and ate some lunch.

When Leila arrived at the guards' headquarters the place was in an uproar. Two of the guards had died of apparent heart failure overnight, and now two more – including the garrison commander himself – had just expired as they were going about their daily business! There had been witnesses to the latter two deaths, and there was no question of foul play. Osemwe and Astambye, on opposite sides of the compound, had simply fallen dead on the spot.

The guard who had taken her to the commander's office this morning bowed to her. "Your majesty! I'm sorry to tell you that while you were gone Commander Osemwe passed away."

"Oh dear," the queen replied. "I'm so sorry to hear that. He seemed like a nice man. But it's very important I speak with your acting commander."

He led her to another office within the compound, where a harried-looking man sat behind a desk. Guards were hurrying in and out, receiving orders or bringing paperwork. "Colonel Dashabe, the queen has returned." From the looks of him, the colonel was approaching retirement age – filling in time in a dead-end post. He must have been the most senior officer after Osemwe, but likely he would not be appointed permanent commander. Nor would he wish it.

The guard bowed again and departed, and Leila closed the door behind him. "Please sit down, Colonel," she said, and Dashabe dropped into his chair. He was not looking well.

"You have had four unexplained deaths on the post during the past twenty-four hours," Leila said. It was not a question, and the acting commander nodded bleakly.

"I must inform you," the queen said, "that these deaths were caused by the cult of Kivuli acting within Dikka." She spoke as if she knew what she was talking about, but Dashabe didn't understand.

"But there is no cult activity in this city," he objected. "I went with the troop to the temple of Betsalel myself."

Leila nodded. "In this city, alone of the hundreds that have been cleansed through the crown's efforts, the cult chose to remove themselves from the temple of Betsalel. They have set themselves up in a large warehouse near the north shore river docks, and I informed your Commander Osemwe of this fact this morning. He was to have sent a company of men to inspect the place, but I believe that the cult learned of this through arcane means and arranged his death to stop the raid."

Dashabe's eyes widened in fear. "I have heard of other unexplained deaths in town, and have wondered at them. But your majesty, if the cult can kill from a distance you may also be at risk!"

She smiled at him slightly. "I am protected by my lord Betsalel, the true Shadow God, who is with me always. I would ask you to meet my god, and open your mind to him so I can know you harbor no trace of the cult. If so, he can extend this protection to you as well."

The colonel leapt at the opportunity. Though he was a man who in his younger years had charged into battle against legions of the enemy armed with scimitars and assegais, the thought of death coming for him out of nowhere had him terrified. Leila bent to the floor, and a moment later Betsalel was standing there beside her.

"Dashabe," the god said, "open your mind and heart to me that I may know your worth." The man felt Betsalel's probing like invisible wings pressing on him, and offered no resistance. He was flooded with a sense of warmth, and strength, and patient love – nothing like what he'd imagined the God of Death to be.

"Lord Betsalel!" he declared, "I will serve you!"

"I will accept your service," the Shadow God said. "Please do all that your queen asks of you, and you will be rewarded." Betsalel remained manifested in his idol, shielding the room from intrusion and eavesdropping, and Leila began explaining what the cult's warehouse was like and what needed to be done.

"By this evening I think that the cult will be eager to consult with their god, as they have finally realized their vulnerability," the queen explained. "You should gather as many men as possible, and position them in small groups around the area. A little after midnight they should converge, and come in through the door. There will be a man on the door, and he will be a Makucha Nyeusi assassin. Bring crossbows, and shoot down any who oppose you. I would recommend armor as well, for the Makucha are fond of thrown daggers and poison darts."

Dashabe's eyes were wide again, but he had been bolstered by his contact with the god and had reclaimed some of the fearless young soldier he once had been. "It will be as you say, your majesty," he declared, taking notes.

"You will meet another Makucha guarding the door on the third floor, and inside that door there may be one more," Leila went on. "Shoot them down, and I will make sure that the doors to the inner sanctum will be unlocked and unbarred."

How this little woman could do that, the colonel didn't know. But he assumed Betsalel would be doing the real work. "Will not those in the inner sanctum hear us taking down the guards?" he asked.

"They will be distracted," Leila promised. "When you come inside I intend that all of the Makucha among the congregation will be gathered near the altar, so that you can shoot them down. My master and I hope that others of the congregation can be brought to recant their beliefs, so please arrest them but don't kill them unless they try to attack you."

Colonel Dashabe shook his head slightly at that, wondering what the chances were that a room full of people who worshiped a bloodthirsty djinn would just throw up their hands and surrender. "What about the djinn, Majesty? Will we be forced to fight it?"

Leila smiled again, like a cat thinking of plump young mice. "Kivuli will not be joining us. When your men come in you may see something that looks like the djinn atop the altar, but do not try to shoot at it. It will be an illusion created by Betsalel."

Chapter 88

After leaving the acting commander to put his plans in place the Queen of Palambo left the compound. A block away, down that same dark alley, she became a sailor off of one of the river traders who docked on either shore of the Pana and made her way across the bridge and along the river's north shore. The sailor booked a room in one of the cheap hotels that lined the waterfront, declined the offer of a girl to keep him company, and went up to catch a nap. The Shadow God delivered a merciful death to a goodly number of bedbugs before Leila lay down to sleep.

Once again Betsalel provided her with a wakeup call, and as the sun was going down the sailor arose and had a light supper at a nearby tavern. Then he stepped out into the street and vanished, moving silently riverward to the Kivuli cult's warehouse in the next block.

As she'd hoped, the cult was in an even bigger panic than the guards had been, across town. Many people were going in and out through the front door, and she was able to slip inside behind one of them. The doorman she'd seen last night was on duty, and he was looking worried.

Three of their priests, including the cult's arch-priest, had utterly vanished along with two of the Makucha guards on duty. And this had come on the heels of a visit from the Guard sergeant who was their usual contact with the Royal Guard garrison – collecting payoffs for the commander and taking messages back and forth. But he had not given his message to anyone here now, only to the missing men. What had he told them?

A messenger, another non-initiate in the cult's pay, had been dispatched to the guard compound to find out what the sergeant's message had been – only to be told that both the sergeant and the commander had unexpectedly dropped dead. Was this the work of the missing assassins? The priests had gone, but they had not taken the idol with them. Nor had they taken any of their belongings.

Had they been abducted? Arrested? There was no sign of a struggle, and it was beyond belief to think a force small enough to slip past the Makucha guards could have taken down five men without leaving evidence behind. Unless, maybe, the guards themselves had taken the three priests?

So it was that Leila found the cult headquarters seething with tension. Priests and men she took to be more Makucha guards were milling around, talking quietly in small groups, peering about them suspiciously. Messengers were being sent to notify all initiates that there would be a compulsory meeting tonight. The midnight ritual would provide the answers they needed.

Leila slipped down the hall on the first floor and peered into the gymnasium. It was getting dark in there, and no lamps had been lit. There were several locked offices along the hallway, and Betsalel scanned each of them for her; but all were dark and unoccupied.

So far in her visits to this place Leila had avoided the second floor residences. But now she was anxious to thin the herd of Makucha if she could. Initiate assassins were too dangerous to be left alive. Previously there'd been a man guarding the landing, but it was deserted now and she slipped down the hallway.

Again Betsalel saved her the trouble of opening every door to see what was inside it. At the first door on the left, he said "A man sleeps behind the locked and barred door here. Would you go inside?" Replying mind to mind, Leila said "Can you open the door without sound?" For answer, without so much as a whisper of noise, the door swung open. Good trick!

Moving silently, Leila glanced around the small room. It was not an apartment, rather the kind of room one might find in a boarding-house. Probably there was a bathroom down the hall and some kind of kitchen facilities elsewhere. The room contained a narrow bed, a nightstand, and a small wardrobe. Inside the wardrobe a black robe hung – and beside it, a set of assassin's gear. On the nightstand four daggers had been set.

Leila used the oualit needle on the sleeping man. He twitched but did not wake when the ultra-thin wire pierced his skin, and in another minute he stopped breathing. Betsalel caused the corpse, his working clothes, and his daggers to vanish. Then they moved on, leaving the door locked behind them.

Many of the rooms along the hall were locked but not barred, their occupants elsewhere. Eight more contained sleeping men, six of them identified as assassins by the possessions within their rooms. The arch-priestess and her god moved silently from room to room, eliminating the Makucha as they encountered them. If the cultists had been disturbed by the disappearance of two assassins, what would they think when they discovered a further seven had apparently taken their weapons and left without a word?

Leila noted the bathroom as they passed it, with a second one further down the hall. At the end of the hall was a much larger room, a dormitory containing eight beds. Six of them were occupied by sleeping boys between the ages of fourteen and seventeen – the Makucha apprentices! They had probably been at their practice earlier, but were catching some sleep before the late-night rituals to follow. Or perhaps not. The cultists only allowed initiates to participate in rituals, and these boys were young to have been initiated.

"What of these, master?" she asked silently.

His voice came into her mind, "They are not initiated, and have no protection beyond the skills they have been taught." Those were formidable enough, Leila realized. They were the same skills she had been taught.

"Can you restrain them while I wake them one by one and learn their minds?" she asked, and the god assented.

Leila walked silently to the one in the nearest bed, a compact lad who looked to be close to her own age. She went visible, appearing as the queen in her regalia, and touched the boy on the shoulder. He came instantly awake, only to find himself paralyzed from the neck down. His dark eyes went wide with panic. "Do not fear," the queen said, touching his cheek, "I mean you no harm. What is your name, apprentice?"

Finding he could speak, he croaked out "Sabidi, memsahib."

"Sabidi, I am Queen Leila of Palambo. I am also arch-priestess of the true Shadow God Betsalel. The cult of the evil djinn Kivuli is being destroyed, and the Makucha Nyeusi will be disbanded. Do you believe that all I tell you is true?"

Still looking terrified, the boy stammered "Yes, your majesty."

The other boys were all awake now, finding themselves as unable to move as Sabidi, and listening to what Leila was telling him. "You boys have not taken final vows to Kivuli, and are not as yet under his protection," she went on. "My master Betsalel could kill you with a thought, but he has no wish to do so. Would you instead prefer to repudiate Kivuli and receive Betsalel's protection from the djinn's powers?"

Again the answer was a stammered yes. Becoming an assassin had seemed like a really cool, exciting thing to do. But none of them had killed, and coming up against a reminder of their own mortality had them eager to seize this chance for salvation. One by one, the apprentices opened themselves to Betsalel and were found to be sincere in their conversion.

As each was proven true, he was released from the paralysis. "The cult headquarters are in turmoil now," Leila told the boys. "But later it should be possible for you to slip out and make your escape. I suggest you go to the Temple of Betsalel on the hill northwest of here and apply to become acolytes.

"Oh, we don't have to wait," Sabidi said with a grin. "There's a drainpipe outside the window over there." He gestured to a corner of the room. The windows on this floor were located closer to the floor than on the first and third floors.

I should have known a bunch of bright, agile lads like these would have figured a way to sneak out for some fun, Leila thought. They possessed many of the skills she'd learned as an apprentice thief in Marsine half her life ago. "Go swiftly, then" the queen commanded them. "And do not return here, or ever turn to Kivuli again. If you do, the djinn will likely destroy you for betraying him."

Leila waited until the boys had gone out the window, then looked around the room. They had taken most of their belongings with them, but left behind the tools of the trade they'd been learning. Betsalel caused it all to vanish. Let the cult leaders stew in their own juices, as their forces left like rats from a sinking ship!

Going invisible again, Leila crept silently out into the corridor and locked the dormitory door behind her. There were still a few hours before the congregation would be gathering for the ritual, and she headed for the third floor. A new Makucha guard was on duty beside the outer door, but again it was standing open and there was not a second one inside. That arrangement must only be employed when the cult's rank-and-file membership were gathering.

The double doors at the end of the hall were closed and locked, and Betsalel confirmed that no one was inside the inner sanctum. The offices on either side were occupied, their doors open, as men in priests' robes worked at desks and rifled through boxes of files. Messengers were still coming and going as the word was sent out to gather every member of the flock. The greater the concentration of worshipers in the room with the manifested god, the greater would be his temporal power.

During a lull in corridor traffic Betsalel unlocked the doors to the sanctum, and Leila opened one of them just far enough to slip inside before he locked them again. Now she had some quiet time to herself for a few hours as the evening wore on, and she decided to use it to catch a little more sleep. Betsalel produced a comfortable pad for her to lie down on, and guided her into sleep as he watched over her.

He knew her plans, and awoke her just before the priests came to open the doors and set up for the ritual. The sleeping pad vanished, and in seconds Leila was perched invisible on the broad pedestal where the replica idol sat, feet hanging down. "What did I miss?" she asked cheerfully.

A hint of amusement crept into Betsalel's tone as he said, "When one of the priests went to give a wakeup call to the residents on the floor below, there was another panic. The new arch-priest is becoming convinced that the missing men and boys left under their own accord – perhaps to turn themselves in. They appear still not to have learned of the raid. Evidently they didn't have any other hirelings within the garrison."

"That's a relief," Leila replied. It would have put a big kink in her plans had one of the people Dashabe had detailed to join the raid gone running to report to the cult. But so far, things were going pretty smoothly. She felt refreshed by her nap, glad that she'd eaten some supper earlier, and ready to take on what she feared might be her biggest challenge yet.

As Leila sat watching, the doors opened and men in black robes came inside. First came a couple of higher-ranked priests, judging by their robes. She thought it likely that the three she'd done away with earlier had been the top three in the organization, which left tonight's crucial ritual, and the leadership of this chapter of the cult, in the hands of a man who'd probably never been given such duties before.

The tall, nearly cadaverous-looking man Leila took to be the acting arch-priest came in with his arms full of paraphernalia and laid them out on the broad altar, then knelt and prayed silently. It seemed the cult were aware that their "god," who had been unresponsive for centuries before coming to life, only manifested in response to a human sacrifice. But silent communion with one's god was something humans wanted to do – even when the god couldn't hear them.

As Betsalel had explained it to her, when he was not manifest on the physical plane he could hear all who called to him if they were in proximity to a true idol. The idol could serve as a two-way connection between the spiritual and physical planes. He responded to the loudest or most urgent, or to pleas from humans he had established a bond with. Kivuli was new in the god business, though, and with the soul of an infant he had no idea what he was supposed to do. He came to the call of blood, as a cat might to its owner calling "food!"

Everyone coming into the sanctum and taking seats was wearing the same sort of black robes, with minor differences. There were badges of rank, but these were not standardized from one cult group to another and Leila didn't know what any of them meant. She was pretty sure that some in plain robes were Makucha, from the way they moved.

Her tension heightened as the room filled. By the Eight, there were more than a hundred of them – and more were yet coming! Most who came in sat as close to the front of the room as possible, presumably eager for the gory ritual that brought the presence of their god. But a few others sat near the back. Some of these were younger, acolytes probably. Leila hoped they would surrender and be freed from the djinn's evil spell. As midnight approached the arch-priest nodded to the guard who had stood inside the outer door and he closed the double doors to the inner sanctum, barring them. It was time for the ritual to begin.

Chapter 89

Leila got to her feet as the arch-priest stepped forward carrying a bundle in his arms. A baby! The child at first seemed as if might be drugged, but as it was brought to the altar it stirred and gave a weak, mewling cry. A newborn, probably not two weeks old. Anger rose in her breast. "Ready, Betsalel?" she asked silently, and the god (now manifest in the tiny seed idol Leila had placed behind the altar) replied "Ready."

The priest began to speak aloud, addressing the idol. "Oh Kivuli, Great One, Death Who Comes in the Night, we bring you this sacrifice. Come to us, as we must know what has happened to our vanished brethren!" The congregation repeated the chant. But before the priest could lay the squirming baby on the altar and pick up the knife, the idol appeared to writhe on its pedestal and the stench of big cat filled the area in front of the altar as Kivuli – seven feet tall, red in tooth and claw – stood before them.

"Silence, priest!" the djinn's voice spoke. "Take the child away and do not harm it, for I would have other meat this night!" Despite himself, the arch-priest flinched back a little. Never in his experience, save the one occasion months ago when he'd come to tell them of the peril they were in, had the god ever come before blood had been spilled. Dark flames roared up from the channel behind the altar, and he handed the baby to an acolyte who carried it off to the back of the room. The Makucha guard who'd barred the doors stood before them, and they would not be opened again until this ritual had been concluded.

Kivuli looked around the room, as if tallying everyone who was there. Then he glared down at the arch-priest. "A dozen missing!" he snarled. The arch-priest, whose name was Gambende, had not known until this moment that his god could count. "And you wish to know what has become of them? I will tell you. My assassins, the Makucha Nyeusi who have pledged their lives to me, have betrayed me – and you. They took with them three of my priests and have recanted, gone over to the side of Betsalel. He has removed my marks from them and put them under his protection, so that I cannot touch them!"

561

The congregation gave a collective gasp of horror. Men with the skills of the Makucha were all very well when they were working on your side. Having them join the enemy was another story entirely. When they had settled down a little the panther god continued, "All who are pledged to me as Makucha Nyeusi, step forward and stand before me so that I can look into your souls!"

Sure that their god could strike any of them dead where they stood, the assassins among the group in the room began coming forward to stand in the space in front of the altar, as if they were forming a men's choir about to lead the congregation in a hymn of praise. The guard on the door below and the one standing beside the now-closed door on the third floor were the only assassins who remained at their posts.

Kivuli stood looking them over, each one sure the god was probing one of his fellows as he stood sweating, trying to rein in his thoughts so that no trace of disloyalty could be detected. Finally Betsalel said in Leila's mind, "The soldiers are inside. They sent one in the guise of a night watchman to knock, telling the doorman he had seen an intruder climbing the drainpipe around back. When the man came out to look, a crossbowman took him down."

"I find no further traitors among you," Kivuli growled, "but you have all failed me. Tomorrow you will find the apostates where they have gone, and kill them all. Which of you claims the mantle of leader?" An older man stepped forward, trim and lithe but with white hair at his temples. "I, Talembde, am the master of this chapter of the Makucha Nyeusi."

A brave man, Leila thought. He proved his bravery further by adding, "Several of those who fled were not originally of our chapter. They came to us as refugees from other cities whose churches were destroyed and taken over by Betsalel. It may be they felt our destruction was inevitable."

"It is not!" the djinn roared, so furious that those in the front rows quailed in their seats. "Betsalel is a remnant of a bygone world! Those who come to me seek the ways of true power, and they shall be rewarded. But you, Talembde, have failed me. Your lot is to become my sacrifice, to atone for the sins of those under your command. Give yourself to me willingly, and you will be rewarded after death."

Talembde flinched, but he did not falter. He was a hardened killer, but he knew how to die. His fellow assassins, gathered around him in a group, seemed willing to seize him and put him onto the altar if he did not obey; but he waved them away and began removing his robe. Leila was pleased to see that he wore only a pair of underdrawers beneath it – no assassin's arsenal. If his cohorts were similarly garbed, that would be a big help.

"The troops have taken down the door guard on the landing outside," Betsalel reported. "Again, they used subterfuge. I believe our Dashabe is not without his wiles, or his courage. He leads the way."

"You have unbarred the door?" Leila asked.

"Yes," the god replied. "I caused the bar to vanish, though an illusory one still remains. The doors are unlocked, as well."

"Excellent!" Leila replied, watching as Talembde stepped forward and climbed upon the altar to lie face up on it, closing his eyes. She wasn't going to like this, but it had to be done. "Speak in Dashabe's mind, master. Tell him to bring his men inside and take down the Makucha first, when everyone's attention is on the djinn. Oh, and remind them not to shoot the djinn!"

"I will shield you from stray bolts, Leila," Betsalel promised.

Eyes wide, the arch-priest approached the altar and picked up the sacrificial knife, prepared to offer up his colleague as the god had demanded.

"Go sit down," the djinn growled. "I will take this sacrifice myself." Claws out, Kivuli crouched over the supine assassin and ripped out his throat, raking him from collarbone to pelvis with his claws and appearing to feed on the corpse.

As everyone in the room was riveted by the gory spectacle, attention on the altar, the doors at the back of the room opened and troops poured in with crossbows ready. Some moved around to the right, encircling the seated congregation in the dimly-lit room; but the larger part of the force went left and opened fire on the men standing all together in front of the altar watching in horror as their master, a man they had revered, was torn to bloody shreds by the god they had worshiped.

Not all of the assassins had come to the service unarmed. The guard who had left his post at the door was well-armed, and got off two daggers before he was brought down by a bolt to the eye socket. Nearly everyone had at least one dagger, and they fought like cornered rats. But despite all their skills and training they were small men and dressed only in clothing – while many of the soldiers towered above them and were well-armored.

As soon as the battle had been engaged Kivuli suddenly vanished, apparently having exited his idol as if running away at the first sight of opposition. Many of the panicked congregation noted this, filled with disgust and fear. Kivuli had promised power, yet he devoured his own believers and fled when danger approached?

Few noticed the daggers that were flying from the area on the left side of the altar, taking the embattled assassins in the back as they fought with the soldiers attacking them from the front. Especially after Betsalel, the Shadow God himself, suddenly rose up twelve feet high from the space behind the altar. He knocked the idol off the pedestal and stepped up onto it as the last of the gathered Makucha fell to the assaults of Leila and the soldiers.

"Stop!" he bellowed. "Let there be no more killing! Any who wish to be spared, surrender to the soldiers and await my judgment. None need die if they will forswear the evil djinn and cleave to me instead!" The bulk of the congregation had been unarmed, on their feet and turning anxiously from side to side in a panic. Now they sat down on the benches again and put their hands on their heads. No one noticed as one by one the daggers that had been thrown earlier disappeared. Nor did anyone hear Leila's silent footsteps as she tiptoed out the doors.

Chapter 70

The river sailor woke in his bug-free bed as golden sunlight streamed in through the room's narrow window, and soon went on his way. Ugh, I need a bath! Leila thought, as she went invisible and began trotting toward the river bridge and the guard compound. While the panther god's appearance had been an illusion Talembde's blood, spilled by her clawed knuckle dusters, had been all too real. Her assassins' garb was soaked with it, though she'd sponged herself off in the room's washbasin before going to bed.

She called Betsalel to the little idol in her pocket. "Master, can you cleanse me please?" In a second her clothing was utterly clean, as was her skin and hair. Ah, it felt marvelous! Though not as good as a long soak in hot water would feel. She'd be home soon enough, Imbaso calling to her like a beacon in her mind.

As Leila ran through the city streets she conferred with her god. "How many died last night, master?" she asked. Going back to the hotel soaked in blood had left her awash in remorse for the deaths she'd dealt, though she knew those deaths had been necessary.

"The two Makucha guards on the doors, of course," Betsalel said. "And all twenty-seven of the assassins in the inner sanctum. Several of those were injured but not killed outright, yet all of them requested I grant them death – even though it was necessary for them to renounce Kivuli in order for me to do so. They were much kinder deaths than what their leader received." Leila felt another twinge of remorse. Talembde had been a man worthy of respect, much like master Kifozi, but the cultists had needed to realize the savagery of the being they worshipped. This time the victim had been one of their own, but over the centuries the followers of the Secret Scriptures had slaughtered many innocents.

"And the rest?" Leila asked, feet flying.

"The remaining high priests all refused to recant and are being held for execution by Commander Dashabe's garrison," the Shadow God replied. "Despite your pointed remarks about being granted my protection from Kivuli, they seem to believe that they are committed and cannot turn aside from their fate."

Leila sighed. Likely such men would become martyrs for the cause. Or they would if the cause was not such a perverted one. Humans, while capable of the most hideous cruelties, also had an inborn sense of right and wrong. Standards of right conduct were organic in a way, part of the human fabric that enabled her species to be so successful. Without social cooperation, they'd still be nothing but a few troops of apes digging for grubs on the savannahs of the southern part of the continent.

"The others all recanted, to a man," Betsalel said with a hint of triumph in his voice. "As with the Makucha you killed, some of these were people from other cities who'd fled when their temples had been cleansed. But they were coming to realize that they could not run forever – and that there was nothing, really, to fight for."

"Good!" Leila replied. The fewer people that had to die in the Black Temple War, the better she would like it. Most especially, she was anxious that she and Imbaso should not be among the casualties of that war. There were so many things they could be doing, that would benefit everyone in Palambo.

At the royal guard compound the mysterious queen appeared once again. No one knew where she was staying, or why she had not appeared with at least a personal guard contingent. But the rumors were spreading. She had spent the night sleeping in her bed with the king, but could magically take herself anywhere she wished. She still worked daily as high priestess at the Temple of Betsalel in Parat, commuting home to Iskand at night. She was an illusion cast by Betsalel. She was really the goddess Mulia in disguise. And so forth…

"Would you care to witness the execution of the recalcitrant priests, Majesty?" Dashabe offered politely.

"I think not," the queen said. "I have important business to attend to in Iskand, and must be on my way home. I only stopped to congratulate you on a job well done. The way in which your men infiltrated the warehouse without raising an alarm was masterful."

The old soldier preened. "In my younger days, before the Zulandi finally capitulated, we used many such tricks to get past their sentries. They were a proud people, but not well-skilled in subterfuge."

Leila grinned at him. "If you like, I will put in a request for you to be given permanent command of this garrison."

"Thank you kindly, Majesty," Dashabe said, "but I must decline. I'm nearing retirement age, and I want to serve lord Betsalel during the years remaining to me. I plan to join the old priests at the temple here in Dikka. Compared to them, I'll be just a youngster!"

"You may find yourself in charge of some other youngsters, Colonel," Leila warned him. "Go to the temple and pray to Betsalel if you need to contact me. I'll be leaving now."

The colonel bowed deeply and saw her out, his eyes full of wonder. After decades spent as a soldier, and now behind a desk for many years, life had become stale. But queen Leila had brought magic into his life, and he was looking forward to the future. What new wonders might life bring to him now?

Chapter 91

Betsalel had alerted Imbaso that they were returning, and he was there to meet them when they traveled from the temple in Dikka to the shrine within the palace. Leila had stripped herself of all illusion. When it was just her and Imbaso, she wanted nothing false between them.

"We did it!" she crowed, flinging herself into her husband's arms as he picked her up and spun her around in joy at her return.

"Our master informed me you'd been successful in purging the cult from Dikka," he said, "but he didn't give me any details."

Leila pretended to swoon. "Ugh!" she said, "truthfully I'd rather not discuss it. But Lmambela and Vandao will need to hear about it. I'll tell the story once and once only to everyone who needs to know, and that's going to be all."

"But first, a hot bath and some lunch?" Imbaso suggested. Leila had not eaten breakfast, and had had a long run back and forth across the sprawling city of Dikka twice since getting out of bed this morning. It was several hours later here in the east.

"Lunch first, then the bath!" she declared, and he squeezed her to him as they turned to walk over to where a contingent of guards waited to escort them back to their quarters.

"I'll join you in both," he murmured into her ear.

Some delightful hours later Leila and Imbaso were gathered once again in the war room with their team. The men were jubilant and congratulatory, thrilled at Leila's success. Had they tried to produce the same results by military means, many more lives would have been lost.

They gathered around the map, and as they watched another of the red-lit temples far to the south winked out. When Betsalel had lit the temples he had set the display to be aware of events. Another Kivuli idol had been destroyed, another of his temples reclaimed for the Shadow God.

"Fewer than forty left to go," Lmambela said with satisfaction. "And while Queen Leila was gone we paid out our first reward to a would-be hireling of the cult. He took their money, promised the job, and then ran right to the nearest guardhouse to report the location of those who had hired him. We sent two squads of troops and surrounded them in the farmhouse south of Aswa where they'd taken up residence. They had threatened the family there with death if they did not feed them and put them up while they plotted."

"Did they have an idol?" Leila asked.

"None was found," the guard commander stated. "Two of them were Makucha and three were priests, but they were looking pretty ragged. They had come north from one of the temples we raided a couple of months ago, early in the campaign."

Imbaso had had the arrest reported to him, but hadn't gotten any details. "The Makucha are dead?" he asked, and Lmambela nodded.

"We have found there is little point in trying to question them. These two swallowed poison as we were moving in on them, in any case. But the priests are our guests in the cells, and one of them has proven surprisingly helpful."

Imbaso, Leila, and the guard commander asked the others to get on with planning their campaign while they went to visit the cells. The three priests had been jailed separately, too far apart for any communication among them. Two had remained silent and sullen, refusing to say anything; but the other had talked freely.

They brought Dzibani into an interrogation room. He looked to be no more than thirty and was plump with an open, friendly-looking face. His arms and legs were shackled, but he was not pinned to the wall. Two armed guards were ready to deal with him if he tried anything. They had all been searched, but no weapons had been found beyond the daggers most people carried for cutting meat at table.

"Dzibani," Lmambela said, "This is King Imbaso and Queen Leila. Tell them what you were telling me. They will know if you lie." The young priest looked a bit nervous, but he didn't seem terrified and Leila figured that was probably a good sign.

"My companions and I were priests of Betsalel, as we believed, in the temple at Sidi Imbi," Dzibani began. He named a smallish city some hundred miles south of the Pana. "I was inducted as an acolyte and taught the Secret Scriptures, and eventually I became a full priest and was sometimes called on to perform the sacrifices. We sacrificed and prayed, but the idol remained silent."

Leila nodded, and he went on. "Then one day early last year, while our arch-priest Engdome was sacrificing a young girl we had found, the idol changed before our eyes. It became Kivuli as we now know him, and devoured the sacrifice before telling us of his true name. Engdome was overjoyed, and predicted that this would be the start of the power the Scriptures had promised."

"You had a chapter of the Makucha Nyeusi in Sidi Imbi?" Leila asked. In her experience, it was usually only major cities that could support them. How much money could you make carrying out assassinations in an area with only a few thousand people in it?"

"No, majesty," Dzibani said. "Our two companions, who killed themselves when we were arrested, had fled from a chapter that was destroyed further to the east. They never would tell us exactly where they had come from. But that was quite a bit later, after Kivuli had come and warned us that the king and queen sought our deaths."

"So what did you do when you received that news?" Imbaso asked. "Our cult was small," the priest admitted. Besides us three we had no more than twenty members and a couple of acolytes. And with no Makucha, there were few among us with the skills to defend the temple. But Engdome was convinced that Kivuli would protect us."

"Kivuli cares only for Kivuli," Leila said severely. "He is only a djinn, built from the prophet's bad ideas and given life by the soul of a slaughtered baby. He can do no one any good." Dzibani gazed at her in surprise. Such blasphemy! But the Death Who Comes in the Night was not going to strike her down here at two in the afternoon, it appeared.

Leila removed her small idol from her pocket and set it on the floor. "Dzibani," she said, "We can save you. And your fellow priests as well, if they wish to be saved from the djinn's evil. But you must open yourself to my lord Betsalel. Are you prepared to do that?" He quivered a little inside. Most of his adult life he had thought he *was* worshiping Betsalel, after all. And the god he'd been worshiping had not been a kind one.

"Yes, Majesty, I will do it," he said at last, and Betsalel stood at her side in an instant. He must already have been manifest here in the room, Dzibani realized with a start. It was a good thing he'd told her no lies. "Open yourself to me, Dzibani," the dark god said, putting a gentle hand on his shoulder, "let me know your soul."

The priest was reluctant. But up until less than a year ago, had he not longed his whole life for the chance to commune with the Shadow God? Even though this deity was not whom he'd believed him to be... The god and the man who had professed to worship him communicated privately for some time, as the others in the room watched. Finally Betsalel spoke again.

"I have removed the touch of Kivuli from Dzibani," he said. "He now has my protection. Dzibani, tell the people here all you know." There had been things he had wanted to hold back, not wanting to sell out his companions. But Betsalel had let him understand that they would not be harmed if they, too, would recant. And why should they not want to? The true Shadow God was wonderful, and Kivuli was a bloodthirsty monster.

"We did nothing for a while after Kivuli's warning," he began, "and it seemed that all was as before. But then the two Makucha arrived, and came to our temple. They told us they had met with a party of Makucha accompanied by an arch-priest, one Mauaji, who told them that all followers of Kivuli must seek the death of King Imbaso – his own son, it was said – and the witch queen, I beg your pardon your majesty, this was just what we were told, who had seduced him to the worship of Betsalel."

"What became of Mauaji and the Makucha who were with him?" Imbaso asked eagerly. He still held half a hope that he might reclaim his father and bring him back to the side of right. "After speaking with the men who came to us in Sidi Imbi, they told us, Mauaji and his party went north. They were planning to take a ship east, and go into the realms of the Hando posing as traders. There they would reestablish the church of Kivuli, doing the work the prophet had done in Palambo so many years ago."

That might explain why there had been no word of the fugitives for months, Imbaso thought. Though he doubted what reception the cultists would find among the Hando. Neither Mauaji nor any of his companions spoke the trade tongue they used, and from what he'd read about that mysterious land east of the Killtops the worship of Betsalel had never been prevalent there.

Dzibani continued his tale, the part he had not meant to share. "The two Makucha had not been in Sidi Imbi for a week when an old man came to the public sanctuary to pray for rest. We had an acolyte on guard above, watching for any signs that doom was about to descend on us, but this was just another old man. The temple of Betsalel draws many such. But that evening, a mob came on the temple."

Lmambela knew well who the "old man" had been. He had sent him and his fellow soldier via Belantos, and they had returned to report they'd placed Betsalel's true idol in his temple and roused the local populace against the cult. But when they came in force they had found the cult's secret lair empty – and no idol above the altar in the inner sanctum.

"We had no royal guard garrison, of course," the former Kivuli priest went on, "but apparently agents had been sent to rouse the city against us – just as Kivuli had warned might happen. So had the Makucha assassins, and they whipped us into action as soon as the mob was sighted. There was a young acolyte below with us, and they dragged him to the inner sanctum and threw him onto the altar. 'Kill him, and call the god!' they commanded, and Engdome obeyed."

Dzibani shuddered, eyes wide, as he re-lived that traumatic night. These Kivuli cultists, Leila observed, always seemed a lot more affected by the gruesome aspects of the Secret Scriptures when it was their own people bleeding on the altar. He went on with his tale, his audience rapt.

"Engdome cut the boy's throat with the sacred knife, and called our god. And he came! We were in a panic to leave before the mob arrived, having had very little warning. After Kivuli had fed from the corpse, the senior of the two Makucha told Engdome, 'Request that he shrink the idol to tiny size. We must carry it with us. And quickly!'"

"They had been taught this trick by Mauaji?" Leila asked, and Dzibani nodded wordlessly. Damn, she thought, I knew that must be how he took the Iskand idol away with him. I should never have let him see Betsalel grow.

"Engdome did as he was instructed, and asked Kivuli to shrink to a tiny size so that the idol could be carried to safety," the former priest went on. "The god was very unwilling to do so. He acted like a petulant child being commanded to brush his teeth. But eventually we convinced him that it was necessary lest this idol be destroyed. As soon as he had shrunk to the size of a child's toy, Kivuli departed the idol and we scooped it up and ran."

Lmambela was looking alarmed. They had found no sign of a Kivuli idol anywhere around the farm where the cultists had been captured, but they had not been looking for something as small as Dzibani had described. Suppose river clay had been wrapped around it to give it the appearance of a toy soldier, or a doll?

Having revealed this part of his story, Dzibani was eager to spill the rest. "The mob had reached the temple. Somehow they had awakened Betsalel within the idol that had remained dormant there for centuries, and now they were trying to batter down the door that led to our true temple underground. The Makucha said they were too many to defeat, but we of course knew of another way out. When the prophet's followers had founded our secret church below the old one, they had built a tunnel that led fifty feet away to a grove of trees within the temple grounds. The five of us escaped, and fled."

"What of the rest of your congregation?" Leila asked. "Didn't you say there were twenty people?"

"None of them were there that night," Dzibani explained. "Of our two acolytes one fled after warning us of the approaching mob, and the other became the sacrifice that enabled us to save the idol. I heard later that Betsalel himself helped the townspeople locate all who had worshiped Kivuli, and that they were rounded up and recanted their faith. At the time I thought it a great travesty. But now I understand." He looked at the Shadow God with something approaching adoration.

Almost finished, now. Dzibani felt a compulsion to spill it all out, and continued his tale. "Engdome believed that he was the leader of our group, and said that we would flee to the south and west, away from the wave of attacks emanating from Iskand. But the Makucha demanded that we must go north, and east. Mauaji had claimed supremacy among the priesthood of Kivuli, and while those two were in his presence the god had confirmed that supremacy. And Mauaji demanded that we must gather to attack the king and queen, destroying them and their reign before they could destroy us. So there we went."

"You learned of the many failed attacks when you arrived in the area?" Imbaso asked, and Dzibani nodded.

"After we took over that farm, Engdome posed as an agent of the farmer and took wagon-loads of crops into Aswa. He learned what was happening. We were not in contact with other groups, but there seemed to have been many who had been contacted by Mauaji and his companions. I would have thought they themselves would have taken on the task of killing the king and queen; but I suppose the arch-priest of Kivuli felt he had a more important mission to perform."

There was bitterness in Dzibani's tone. To be ordered to perform a task by leaders who were in the process of hightailing it over the far horizon was something that never went over well with the ground troops. "It seemed to Engdome that Betsalel had taken over the royal palace," he went on, "and that somehow any who were under Kivuli's protection were known to him. So we concluded that we must hire someone outside the church, who could go into the palace grounds and poison the royal food or slip a nyoka into the royal bed or something of that sort."

"I imagine such people are not easy to find, or to hire?" Leila asked. The young former priest almost smiled.

"Not easy, indeed!" he agreed. "Engdome went and stayed in Aswa for days. We were quite safe living on the farm, isolated with no fear of discovery – but there were no resources there for us to call on. Finally he managed to contact someone, a man who said he had cut many throats and would be happy to cut two more in exchange for the relatively small amount of money we were able to offer."

"Ah, and after trailing Engdome back to where you were staying he immediately turned you in to the authorities in exchange for a far greater payment," Leila said. Having learned that they were up against an under-funded grass-roots effort, a feeling of relief had come over her. Dzibani hung his head, but he saw the humor in it. Now that he was saved, he had a whole new outlook on life.

"When one of the Makucha who had been on lookout came back to the farmhouse to report that we were surrounded, it was too late to do anything," Dzibani said. "The only two people we had who might have offered resistance had swallowed poison and collapsed on the floor. Engdome tried to call Kivuli to the idol, but the god would not come."

"No blood sacrifice, right?" Leila asked knowingly.

"That's right," the former priest said. "We had no altar, no sacred knife. Though we had learned on our journey that an ordinary dagger would work as well. There was no time. The soldiers were on us, and we were taken."

"But we found no idol, large or small," Lmambela said. "Did Engdome hide it somewhere?"

"No," Dzibani replied. "He tucked it inside the waistband of his pants." When the party had been captured, two of the priests had been dressed in their black robes. But Engdome, who had been going incognito to Aswa, was wearing ordinary pants and a tunic.

"We searched him!" Lmambela declared. "There was no idol, however small, anywhere on his person." Leila suddenly had an insight, and her stomach tightened.

"You probably did not see it because he would have pushed it through a gap in the stitching into the waistband itself," Dzibani explained. "It was no bigger than a grain of rice."

Chapter 92

The six people in the room exited and ran down the corridor to the cell where Engdome had been imprisoned. This included Dzibani, whom Betsalel had vetted as trustworthy. His shackles had been removed, and he made no attempt to flee. The Shadow God, seventh among them, followed along behind.

They found Engdome in his cell, holding something tiny between his right thumb and forefinger. He looked up at the party with haunted eyes, his face a mask of despair. "No, Engdome!" Dzibani cried, "Don't do it! Kivuli is wrong, and Betsalel is our true lord! Can't you see?"

"Damn you all!" the high priest cursed. He opened his mouth and savaged his left hand with his teeth, ripping away flesh. Blood fell onto the tiny object in his right hand, and in a voice like the wail of a dying animal he cried, "Lord Kivuli, come to me! I offer my own blood – all that I have left!"

The minute idol squirmed in his hands, and Kivuli blossomed to a height of seven feet inside the cell. The djinn seemed to have fixated on that size, the size of the idol in the temple below Betsalel's temple in Namei, as the size he was meant to be. It must have required incredible persuasion on Engdome's part to get him to leave his idol small enough to be hidden from the guards' search.

For the moment the djinn ignored his surroundings, focusing only on the familiar man who had called him. "You offer your blood, Engdome," he purred. "All that you have left. And I will *take* it all!" Clearly Kivuli resented this priest for putting him through the humiliation of becoming tiny, and now he saw his way to revenge.

As the six people and one god gathered outside the cell watched in horror, the djinn attempted to make his high priest fulfill his promise. He didn't get all the man's blood, no – some was spilled on the stones of the cell floor and some splattered around the walls. But when he had drunk his fill, Kivuli looked up and howled.

He had just killed the last man nearby who truly believed in him, and now he confronted his worst enemy in company with half a dozen of that enemy's worshipers. "Father, no!" he screamed, and in an instant there was nothing in the cell but a 7-foot black idol and a few sad, bloody scraps.

The two guards and Dzibani were retching out their guts on the floor outside the cell, while the king and queen, with their guard commander, stood staring in sadness. He could have been saved, but Engdome refused to part with the foulness that had been his religion for all his adult life. Betsalel, without being asked to, erased the remains and all evidence of the carnage.

They got the cell open and the dark god provided the guards, who had now recovered themselves, with hammers. In minutes they had reduced the idol almost to powder, attacking it in a frenzy. "I think that you two should share in the bounty for the destroyed idol," Leila said. They looked at her with eyes that said they would have destroyed it and a hundred more, and asked for no pay.

Still shaken, Dzibani accompanied them to the cell where his last fellow priest sat. The man looked up when the four approached. "Dzibani, you are free?" he asked, astonished.

"Engdome called Kivuli and was devoured for his troubles," his fellow told him. "I have been freed from the djinn's toils by our true god, Arganit. Come and join me!" He got no arguments.

Chapter 93

Leila and Imbaso had made love the night before, and again in the morning. And now they lay abed, plotting the destruction of the Palamban status quo. "It's time for us to reform the Council of Eight," she said, snuggled into Imbaso's muscular shoulder.

The member of the Council representing Betsalel had of course been removed during the purge of Iskand's temple – one of the first acts of the royal couple's reign. He had been replaced by one of his fellow cultists who had recanted – chosen by the remaining members of the Council from among the new roster of Betsalel's priesthood. But the four members who had been voted in under duress from Mauaji still remained.

Though Leila's upbringing and Imbaso's could hardly have been further apart, they were cousins – and they shared an exposure to the Dominion's way of doing things. "We should impeach the members my father brought to power through his murderous methods," Imbaso said. "I doubt whether any of the original members will deny he used coercion on them, now that he's fled the country."

"You're right," Leila said, kissing him on the neck. "But I think the whole notion of the Council electing its own members is wrong. It puts too much power in the hands of the Council itself, and not enough in the membership of the churches."

"What would you have," Imbaso asked – kissing the top of her head – "general elections among the priesthood of each of the Eight?"

"I think so," she said seriously. "We will need to remove the four tainted by Mauaji's machinations, but to be fair we'll need to allow the priesthoods of the other four to vote as well. Possibly the incumbents will be confirmed."

"Let's do that as soon as possible," he said. She snuggled into his side and ran her left hand down his torso. "Like announce it today," he continued.

After another moment, during which Imbaso thought he might be ready to rise again, she said "But that's not all. I think that eight is an inefficient number for a council with the power to make important decisions. I think Palambo needs a High Archon."

Imbaso's nether regions subsided as his mind seized on what his beloved had said. "Like in Parat?" he asked, "elected by the Eight themselves?"

"Why not?" she replied. "He or she could be the tie-breaker for decisions of the Council, whether it's who the next king or queen is or matters of religious policy. And as the choice of the gods and goddesses, that person's influence would be enormous. I know that Lucia got a little carried away a couple of hundred years ago, but she's been put back in her place. The Eight depend on us humans for the worship and belief that gives them their powers. Who could we trust more, to have our best interests at heart?" Imbaso's love for Leila swelled.

"That's a *wonderful* idea, darling!" he said, kissing her firmly on the lips and then rolling out of bed to put his feet on the floor. "Let's get started!"

The king and queen's reforms were met with widespread public approval. Many had felt uneasy since the mysterious deaths, and curiously fast replacements, of half the Council of Eight months ago. Few could argue that there was anything wrong with having the priesthoods themselves elect their own arch-priests. And what person who honored the Eight could object to the gods and goddesses electing their very own tie-breaker? Entabi was elected in a landslide at the Temple of the Eight, Palambo's first High Archon.

There were two more payouts of money to hired killers who preferred adding the ten thousand-asand bounty to whatever the agents of Kivuli had paid them for an assassination attempt; and then the cult's efforts seemed to have dried up. Every morning and every afternoon Betsalel reached out with his growing power, searching for souls with the mark of Kivuli on them, and he found none. Nor were there any more assassination attempts.

Meanwhile, Commander Lmambela's teams continued their march south and west, penetrating to the furthest reaches of the continent as they reclaimed Betsalel's temples one by one. These men were veterans now, at the top of their game, and the dwindling cults had been cut off from outside help when first Namei and then Dikka had fallen.

The last few holdouts were in areas where Palamban troops still fought rebel insurgents. On a paper map, the kingdom of Palambo covered the entire southwestern section of the continent. It was bordered by the Talj Jabal on the east and the Western Ocean on the west, the Center Sea to the north and the Southern Ocean to the south.

But in practice, in half a dozen areas of the continent's hot southern reach, ethnic groups who refused to acknowledge Palamban sovereignty fought on. And though they, too, honored the Eight, there was no way they would obey a proclamation from the Palamban throne.

Lmambela was not to be thwarted. Iskand was a magnet, a place that drew people from all over Palambo seeking opportunity and a better life. And he put out his feelers: if you were from one of those half dozen regions and would like a career in the royal guard – or just a big cash payout – you should apply to guard headquarters for details. No betrayal of your native land would be required – the kingdom was more interested in the eradication of the Kivuli cult than they were in subjugation of the south continent's last resisters.

Recruits came to the call, and the best of them were dispatched via Belantos or Andros to the regions from which they'd originated. They greeted old friends, told them of the atrocities that had been committed in the name of Kivuli, and urged them to join with them in eradicating the djinn's threat from their communities. Seed idols of Betsalel were placed, the inhabitants of the undercroft temples were mostly slaughtered, and the fragments of the Kivuli idols were carried back via the newly triumphant Shadow God to be exchanged for the kingdom's gold. After which, hostilities could resume.

Leila, Imbaso, and the rest of the team (not including Betsalel, who was otherwise engaged) were gathered in the war room at ten o'clock on a morning in midsummer. They all watched expectantly as the last red light, far out near the southwestern coast, glowed its last and winked out. The last of the Kivuli cults had fallen, and the Shadow God was triumphant!

Chapter 94

There had been no more assassination attempts for weeks, and Betsalel (whose awareness now encompassed most of the continent west of the Killtops and their southern reach the Talj Jabal) confirmed that he could find no more people bearing Kivuli's protection. One of his original idols, that had been taken over by the djinn, still existed – and that meant the djinn himself continued to be a threat. But he had gone beyond the Shadow God's reach, presumably beyond the Killtops, to become the Hando people's problem.

Leila and Imbaso dispatched a signed and sealed letter to the Hanshu ambassador in Miradil via Belantos (a true idol of Betsalel had not yet been restored to that easternmost outpost of the Dominion), warning him of their belief that the criminal Mauaji, wanted for multiple counts of murder in Palambo, was believed to be traveling within the Hando realms with a party of six deadly assassins, and carrying the idol of an evil demon that could wreak havoc if invoked. The ambassador was to pass this along to the authorities of the dozens of kingdoms, small and large, that occupied the area east of the Killtops.

"I wish we could do more," Leila told her husband as they sat relaxing over breakfast. They'd continued to wear their necklaces – people with power such as theirs could never count themselves completely safe from the ambitions of others – but they had stopped asking Betsalel to check for Kivuli cultists every day. Apparently there were no more of them to be found within Palambo.

"Let's just count ourselves lucky Father never learned about how true idols are made," Imbaso replied. The idols of the Eight scattered around the world, with the exception of the ones the king and queen had placed over the past year, had been in existence for hundreds or thousands of years. There must have been a time in the remote past when the understanding that the gods themselves made new idols from their own flesh was known to the priesthood; but somewhere along the line that knowledge had died out. It had been an immense surprise to Leila.

"Yes," she mused, taking a sip of kaf to wash down a bite of pastry. "And Kivuli was so limited as a god. I think Mauaji believed he had brought about the dream of his own lifetime and of his ancestors back six generations – but all he got was a bloodthirsty baby monster who needed to be taught everything he was supposed to be able to do."

Imbaso slipped closer to her on the settee where they usually ate their breakfast when the weather in the garden outside was less than ideal. Betsalel had provided the same climate control to the royal suite as he had done for Leila's little house in Namei – now long since sold off to someone who could maintain it. Imbaso's ancestral home on the ninth circle had been sold as well, with the proceeds going to Samadhi and her kin. Mauaji, confounding their original expectations, had not been seen in Namei since he and their party had left for Iskand more than a year ago.

The king put an arm around his queen and nuzzled her neck. "You stopped taking the herbs?" he asked. She smiled at him fondly.

"Yes," she said, "last month. But it may take a while for my body to cleanse itself of them and allow me to conceive." "Couldn't you have Betsalel remove all traces of them immediately?" he asked a little wistfully.

Leila squeezed his hand. "Be patient, will you? We'll have a son or daughter soon enough. We're young, and the assassination threat has been removed, so it's not like we don't have time." She was now eighteen, Imbaso twenty-two – the youngest man to sit the throne since the founding of the kingdom.

"I'm sorry," he said sincerely. "I don't mean to rush you. But I promised that only our children would be eligible for the succession. I can hardly request that to be written into law before we actually have any."

"There are a lot of other things we can work on in the meantime, love," Leila said. "Can we discuss the idea of a Grand Assembly again? And there's also the institution of state schools and universal education."

Leila had been born on the wrong side of the blanket and grew up in the Dominion knowing what it was like for those without the advantages of wealth or high birth. She didn't have any control over what the emperor and the rest of the Dominion's government did, but she was in a prime position to remake Palamban society into her vision of what a fair and just land should be. They had put a stop to the scourge of Kivuli, so how hard could it be to take on the goals of social justice and universal literacy?

The king and queen had taken to worshiping Betsalel publically, in the chapel housed by the Great Library. Though they were both part-time members of the Shadow God's priesthood and could call him to the private idol in their quarters at any time day or night, they liked the ambience of this shrine and felt that it showed their subjects – at least those who lived and worked within the palace compound – that their rulers thought worship was important. They were also seen honoring the Eight (even Lucia!) at the Temple of the Eight across town at least once per month.

The day had been a blazing hot one, typical for Iskand in the summer; but now that sunset was approaching a sea breeze had sprung up and it was pleasant enough to go walking in the gardens. Wanting privacy, Leila had dressed in an abbreviated version of her assassin's costume (hidden beneath the illusion of regal robes, of course) and was carrying a few daggers – allowing them to feel safe enough to send away their usual guard escort.

They found themselves approaching the Library and decided to go inside. Most of the palace servants and guards were eating dinner now, but the nightly feast in the palace's dining hall would not begin for another two hours. There was time for a chat with their god.

They called Betsalel to his idol, which in this place usually stood ten feet high. But he stepped down from the altar, which had been carved from newly quarried stone and possessed no particular magical properties, and shrank to Imbaso's height so that they could converse as friends. There was no one at all stirring in this part of the Library wing. They communed with their god daily, but he had less and less time for them as the number of his worshipers burgeoned across the western part of the continent.

He embraced them both, then they stood talking. "Today a young woman came to me with a sick child," he said.

"To stop its pain?" Leila asked, concern in her voice. Children died every day, but it was not often their parents came to the Shadow God asking for the process to be hurried along.

"No," Betsalel said, a wondering tone in his voice. "There was no congenital problem, just a bad fever. And I healed him. I think that the Dominion's notion of me as a god who can grant life as well as death is spreading to Palambo. My sister will not be happy to learn of it."

As light was associated with life and darkness with death, so Lucia had been the deity traditionally prayed to by those seeking divine help for a life-threatening illness or something that modern medicine (such as it was; as likely to kill you as cure you, some said) could not deal with. She would think Betsalel was poaching on her preserve.

"She'll just have to get over it," Leila said lightly. The dark god who had once terrified her had become someone she loved deeply, and to her he could do no wrong. She, on the other hand, was a thief and a murderer – and he loved her in spite of it.

Suddenly Betsalel froze where he stood, his awareness reaching out. "He is here!" he cried, and stepped past them toward the door. Through that door came Kivuli, seven feet tall and with blood on his muzzle. And behind him came Mauaji – in company with Kifozi, Sumundi, Zhendibi, Mbando, Bdejiyi, and Nindao. Somehow they had masked their coming, and now the Shadow God confronted his bastard offspring – with his believers in the room outnumbered seven to two.

"Their blood is yours, master!" Mauaji cried. "Take your revenge!" As the monstrous djinn came toward Leila and Imbaso she seized him by the hand and the two of them went invisible. Betsalel grew to ten feet tall and blocked Kivuli's path.

"Vile spawn of men's evil!" he thundered. "You shall not have them!"

Leila pulled one of her daggers and led Imbaso quietly to the side as the god and the djinn wrestled in the center of the floor before the altar and Mauaji and his companions spread out around the room to watch the battle. Kivuli had grown larger as well, and leapt upon Betsalel with claws out and fangs glistening. But as the Shadow God's idol here was impervious to harm, the djinn could not penetrate his adversary's skin.

Seeing her chance, Leila threw the dagger. It appeared in the air as it left her hand and flew in under a heartbeat to take Bdejiyi in the throat. As the young man collapsed in a welter of blood Mauaji cried, "They are still here, but invisible! Find them!"

Betsalel seized Kivuli and flung him against the wall, sending the agile assassins skipping out of the way. The impact had done the djinn no harm, however, and he closed with the Shadow God again. Neither could truly hurt the other, it seemed, but as long as Betsalel kept Kivuli occupied he could neither attack the king and queen nor point out their location to his believers.

"Draw daggers and lead with them," Kifozi commanded his remaining four assassins. "We can corner them here!" Careful to avoid the wrestling deities, the five Makucha Nyeusi spread out around the room, daggers out, and began trying to converge on the unseen Leila and Imbaso. Imbaso had a scimitar at his waist, part of standard dress for men of his station, and he drew it with his right hand while keeping his left on Leila's shoulder to maintain his invisibility.

As Mbando drew near, dagger circling in the air in front of him, Imbaso swept the blade across and chopped into his neck. The dagger fell to the floor, and Leila moved back the other way to where Zhendibi was approaching and threw her dagger into his eye. At this range the razor-sharp blade pierced deep, through the eye socket and into his brain.

"This isn't working," Sumundi said. The old man put away his dagger and pulled out a dart gun, stepping back as he scanned the room for any signs of their invisible quarry. Meanwhile the back-

and-forth battle between Betsalel and Kivuli continued unabated. The Shadow God wrenched at the djinn's lashing tail, but could not pull it off. Kivuli tried to scratch out Betsalel's eyes, but they were as impervious as the rest of him.

Leila, still trapped near the back of the room, saw her chance and threw another dagger, bringing down Nindao – last of the four young assassins. Sumundi was old, but his eyes were as sharp as ever. Aiming for the spot a little to the right of where the dagger had appeared, he sent a poison dart flying. It vanished.

"Hey," Imbaso murmured, feeling a pinprick through the cloth of his richly embroidered tunic. Then he slumped. Imbaso, no! Leila thought in a panic, but she dared not speak lest she pinpoint them for Sumundi. The dart would have barely pierced his skin, having to go through a couple of layers of cloth. He might not have received a lethal dose!

Half supporting, half dragging her tall husband, Leila let him down to the floor behind the altar. She would have to leave him visible, but likely any who saw him would think him dead. Pulling her hand away, she spotted the dart and plucked it away from Imbaso's tunic. Then both of them were invisible again as she pulled back the cloth before releasing him again. There was only the tiniest blood spot, and when she put a hand to his neck she felt the pulse racing. She must finish this battle quickly somehow, so Betsalel could heal him before the small poison dose could do its work!

The wrestling gods were making so much noise that Leila could nearly have run across the room in hobnail boots without anyone noticing her footfalls. In the soft, silent boots that were her perennial footwear, Mauaji, Kifozi, and Sumundi could hear nothing. And as long as she didn't release any missiles, they would see nothing. Skirting the corpses that littered the floor, Leila came silently around to stand beside the old poisons master where he hovered near the doorway, eyes scanning the room for signs of his prey.

He sensed something, a breath perhaps or the warmth of her body, and began to turn toward her. With her left hand she seized the blowgun and ripped it out of his hands, and with her right she plunged her last remaining dagger into his heart. Hurry, hurry!

Leila whirled away from the corpse of Sumundi as it collapsed to the floor, searching for Kifozi. He was the strongest, the most cunning of the Makucha and he was already coming in her direction. She could have run out the door, but she needed to stay on the scene. This fight must end before Imbaso breathed his last!

Suddenly the master assassin found himself confronting – himself! Not quite as he had ever seen himself, for this was a duplicate not a mirror image. He still did not know that Usiku and Queen Leila were the same person, but the fighting style he'd seen so far was hauntingly familiar – as was the ability to take another shape.

Leila took advantage of Kifozi's momentary confusion to slash at him with the still-bloody dagger in her hand – which, in her illusion, had become a scimitar. The master assassin flinched back out of her apparent reach, still trying to grapple with the idea of fighting himself. If his knife pierced his adversary, which of them would bleed?

Leila was certain that Kifozi's skill at knife-fighting far exceeded her own, but superstitious fears and imaginative speculations were slowing his movements. And perhaps being past fifty, and having spent most of the past several months on the run or in hiding, had taken their toll as well?

They dodged and feinted, moving out into the hall that fronted the room to stay out of the way of the fighting gods. Mauaji, who appeared not to be armed, was looking sick with fear as he watched the confrontation. He had received sword training in his youth but hadn't picked up a weapon in decades. He had come here in the company of his savage god and six of the most highly-trained assassins he knew. And now five of the six were dead. But at least his traitorous son was down. That left Betsalel with only one believer, while Kivuli still had two.

The blades darted and flashed. Kifozi's belief that his opponent had a longer blade kept him well out of the range of Leila's dagger, and her youth and agility was keeping her from getting sliced as well. But this was going on too long, and it needed to end!

Suddenly Kifozi saw his opponent's guard drop, as if he were wearied, and he leapt to take advantage As he lunged forward, coming in from below with a thrust that would open his opponent's belly, his blade passed through empty air where Leila's torso should have been. Standing off to his left in a crouch, casting the illusion beyond herself, she plunged her dagger into the side of his neck.

Only Mauaji left to go! Becoming herself once more but appearing to be wearing full assassins' garb instead of the glorified underwear she really had on, Leila found the black priest cowering over near the far wall, on his knees beside the corpse of Nindao.

"Mercy, majesty! I plead mercy! I will submit to your dark god, whatever you want, but spare me!" Mauaji begged. His face was twisted in terror, cheeks wet with tears. What a despicable coward! But she could not just slaughter a defenseless man – especially not when that man had once been Imbaso's beloved "Bapa."

She took him in the chin with her booted foot, knocking him over backwards to land crumpled against the rear wall. He lay still, out of commission for the time being. Leila was pretty sure she had not broken his neck, though he richly deserved it.

Stepping around the altar, she bent anxiously to Imbaso. Leila didn't know what poison Sumundi had used on the dart. Might it have been only a paralytic, supposing they wanted the chance to feed her and Imbaso to their bloodthirsty god in an act of symbolic revenge? She could hope so. She checked his pulse and found him still living, then hopped up onto the altar to survey the scene.

Betsalel and Kivuli still struggled, though the pace of their futile battle seemed to have slowed. While manifest in their idols it was possible for even deities to tire. As the Shadow God stood near the center of the room panting, waiting for the djinn's next move, Kivuli stood at bay near the side wall.

"It is useless, Father," he growled, "I am a part of you, and you cannot defeat yourself."

"Give up, Kivuli," Betsalel replied. "Your worshipers are all but gone, your temples destroyed. What you and your followers stole from me has been taken back. Let your soul fly free, and seek another life for yourself – or join with the One, and someday become a true god!"

The djinn hesitated, and Leila suddenly had an idea. She climbed down from the altar to the floor and suddenly Uzuri stood there. Uzuri as she had been before Mauaji had taken her son and destroyed her life. "Usafi," the remembered voice said softly, and the djinn's head turned. He stared at her, riveted, and the fur on his body lay down again. The lashing tail hung quiet.

"Usafi, my baby, come back to me," Uzuri said again, and held out her arms. As Leila and Betsalel looked on in wonder, Kivuli shrank before their eyes until he was the size of a panther cub. The features had become soft, babyish, and he trotted over and leapt up into his mother's waiting arms. "Mama," he murmured softly, and Leila's eyes filled with tears as the panther cub became a naked baby boy, gazing up into Uzuri's face with adoration. She kissed him on the forehead.

"Fly free, Usafi, fly free at last," Uzuri said. The baby's soul felt the presence of life nearby. A new life barely begun, a home for him where he could start again. All that had been taken from him by Mauaji's knife would be his, and he slipped inside. The black idol, gone formless, crumbled to dust in Leila's hands.

Leila became herself, looking up at Betsalel. She had never seen him shed tears, did not know if he could; but the expression on his face intermingled joy and regret. Suddenly it came to her – Imbaso! "Master, Imbaso has been struck by a poison dart! You must heal him!"

Back at his usual six-foot height the god followed Leila around the altar. There they found Mauaji crouched over the body of his son – the dagger that had killed Nindao now planted in Imbaso's heart. "No!" she screamed, and kicked Mauaji in the chin again. "Bring him back, please bring him back!" she cried to her god as she rushed the fallen arch-priest. Priest of nothing, now.

The dagger that had most recently killed master Kifozi was in her hand in an instant, and as she knelt above Mauaji's supine form Leila plunged it into his forehead with all the strength in her arm. It penetrated the hard bone and went deep into the brain, killing him instantly.

Raging, tears flowing from her eyes in a torrent, Leila turned back to Imbaso where he lay on the floor behind the altar. The dagger was gone, as was the wound it had made. But Betsalel knelt beside her beloved, and his beautiful features were cast in a mask of unspeakable grief.

"I am so sorry, Leila," the Shadow God said, "his soul has gone to the One, and I cannot get him back." Leila fell full length across Imbaso's corpse, and sobbed until there was no more strength in her body. Then Betsalel sent her to sleep, and carried her in his arms to the palace.

Chapter 95

The status quo in Palambo proved more resistant than the new king and queen had expected. People were content with their reforms of the Council of Eight; but now the king was dead and no one – not even people Leila had thought were her friends and supporters – was willing to consider the idea of the country continuing under a reigning queen alone.

Leila must abdicate, they said. She would be provided with a dower house and supported for life by a populace grateful for her many contributions; but she could not remain as Palambo's monarch. And Leila really didn't care. Imbaso had become everything to her, and without him at her side her ambitions for the future of Palambo were so much dust.

It was almost more effort than she could muster to rise from bed in the morning, and she had refused to allow them to take away his clothes or wash the sheets. She lay there snuggled into them, smelling Imbaso's scent, and dreamed that she would open her eyes and find him beside her.

It was just not fair! She and Imbaso had given everything for Betsalel, and the only thing she wanted in return he had been unable to provide. Of course, he had warned her that resurrection would not always be possible. Oh Imbaso, why could you not have lingered near? Didn't you know I would bring you back?

Vandao, deeply saddened by the loss of his son-in-law and even more troubled by the despair he saw in the daughter he had come to love, spent most of his time running the country. Those who needed something from the crown quickly learned to come to him, as Leila spent most of her days in bed or crying before the idol of Betsalel she had put up in the royal suite.

Yet after a month the queen seemed to pull herself together. She bathed and dressed and came to see her father in his quarters near the royal residential wing, her gaunt face full of resolve. She had lost weight these past weeks, and her deep green eyes looked huge. One might have thought her a waif of twelve instead of a woman of eighteen.

"Father," she said, "I have made a decision. No one wants me to rule this kingdom, and I have no desire to stay where I am not wanted. I am going to abdicate the throne. Can I name you in my place?"

"Me?" he asked, surprised.

Leila almost smiled. "For Betsalel's sake, Father, who else has been running the country during most of my lifetime? Of course you!"

Vandao had to admit she had a point. He would make a good king for Palambo, possibly the best they had ever had. And Leila had discussed some of the innovations she'd hoped to put into effect during the long reign she'd anticipated with Imbaso. He could make those happen, where she clearly could not. "I don't think you can just appoint me to rule in your stead, Leila," he said. "People who deny that a ruling queen has legitimate authority would certainly claim you had no right to name your successor. It will have to go through the Council of Eight."

"Very well," Leila said, standing and embracing her father. "I'm off."

"Where are you going?" he asked.

"Imbaso has been dust for nearly a month, Father. I'm going to convene the Council of Eight and put in an application in your name."

The announcement was the talk of Iskand for days, and most people agreed that queen Leila was sensible and honorable and doing the right thing. She might have achieved amazing things and wiped out the pernicious cult that was spreading death across the land, but you could still not expect a young girl like that to rule a kingdom. Women who disagreed with their husbands on that score usually had the good sense to bite their tongues.

At last the Council of Eight opened its doors to receive applications for the post of king, as it had done close to a year before after the death of King Omali. That council had been ridden with corruption and operating under duress, but only two of the current council's members had sat on it then.

Yet when they met the next day to examine the applications, they reached a decision in little more time than it had taken to announce the election of King Imbaso. "I have never heard of such a situation before," said Mbala, who had won re-election as arch-priestess of Mulia by a landslide. "Twenty-three applications from twenty-three different individuals – and eighteen of them name Prince Vandao."

The announcement was made, and the man who had devoted his life to the running of Palambo was at last set to become its king in name as well as fact. Leila had him sit beside her at the last royal banquet over which she would preside. She had given Imbaso's necklace of protection to her father, as – things being as they were in Palambo – he was likely to need it.

She drank, she ate, she held hands with her father and there was a smile on her lips. Was not Leila the mistress of illusion? Leila cried herself to sleep that night, the last one she would spend sleeping in the royal suite. Tomorrow King Vandao would be crowned, and her life as Queen of Palambo would be over.

The king was crowned with pomp and circumstance considerably more ordinary than that which had put Imbaso and Leila on their thrones. There was but one throne and one crown (though it still bore the Rosette), and the Shadow God did not put in an appearance. But all there knew that the new king was allied with Betsalel as the last one had been, and that his reign would have divine backing.

There was a celebratory luncheon following the coronation, and this time Leila (no longer wearing a crown) sat beside the new king as his guest. "You had better get busy marrying and having children, Father," she remarked after the latest toast. He smiled at her, so glad to see her acting normally again. Her tale of the fate of her mother, his lost love Miriam, had saddened him – but it had also freed him emotionally. Over the past months he had begun meeting women with an eye to easing his lonely existence.

"I think I have a bride just about lined up," he replied with a wink. "There's a possibility she'll have me, now I've got my new job and all." Leila laughed.

When the luncheon was over she slipped away and went invisibly to the royal quarters, past the guards and into the suite where she and Imbaso had lived and loved, planned and dreamed. It was time to say goodbye. After walking around quietly, touching this piece of furniture, that carpet, smelling the flowers blooming in the garden, she returned inside and knelt before the idol of Betsalel.

This was the same idol she had carried with her in tiny size for so long, left large at her request so that she could look across the room and see him standing there, watching over her. The god bent to her and put a hand on her shoulder. "So, beloved," he said softly. "You are queen no longer?"

Leila rose to her feet. "I am free of Palambo, and Palambo is free of me," she said as quietly. She would never quite forgive the country for its ingratitude, even if most of the people in it had no idea all she'd done for them. "Master, I have but one request, a boon you can grant me."

"Whatever you want, little one, it is yours."

"Good," she nodded, then looked up into his face. "I want the boon you grant all those in pain. I want you to give me a kindly death." He looked down at her in shock. It had seemed that her grief was easing, her wounds healing. But this?

"I cannot. Never, that!" he said. And suddenly he was gone, the idol once again the six-foot statue of a man with eyes closed, hands forward and palms up as if in supplication.

"No, damn you, no!" Leila screamed, unmindful of who might hear. "You can't just abandon me, you bastard! You promised me I could have whatever I wanted, and I want to die! I want to start over, or join Imbaso in the One! Come back!"

Leila railed at the god, sinking gradually to the floor and sobbing as she clutched the idol's feet. Eventually, her cries unanswered, she curled into a fetal position and cried herself to sleep, lying on the cool stone floor of the royal parlor.

Some time later, Leila woke to the sound of someone calling her name. "Leila! Oh, Leila!" She got up into a sitting position on the floor and peered through bleary eyes. Betsalel stood there, and beside him, shorter by several inches, was… Tevo!

The young man who had been her first love, the man she had left in the lurch to love another and become a queen, stepped forward and gathered Leila tenderly into his arms. She buried her face in his shoulder, tears flowing again.

"Oh Tevo, I am so sorry!" she sobbed. "I… left you, and I thought it would just be for a while… But I was so lonely, and so weak… and I fell in love, Tevo!"

He stroked her hair and kissed her forehead, squeezing her tightly. "I know, Leila, I know. I was lonely too, and there were other women… but I've never stopped loving you, even though I thought I had lost you forever!" She blinked away tears and looked up into his warm brown eyes, saw the truth in them. And though Imbaso had become her dearest love and the center of her world, she had never, really, stopped loving Tevo.

He bent his head and kissed her, and a rush of joy flooded Leila's heart. She would never "get over" losing Imbaso, but that did not mean she had to die, or that she must live without love. Here it was before her, as it had once been, as it could be again. "Can we begin again, Tevo?" she asked hesitantly. "In Parat? Restoring Betsalel's church in the Dominion?"

"Yes, Leila, yes!" he cried, hugging her tight and then looking into her eyes with joy. "It is everything I want! You don't need to die to have a new life – we will make one together! Will you marry me?" For a moment a cold shudder passed through Leila. She had married Imbaso, and it had destroyed him. But then her good sense reasserted itself. It was Mauaji who had destroyed Imbaso, not his marriage to Leila. That had been what had made life worth living. And she and Tevo had no deadly enemies. They – and the children to come – would live safely and happily together in Parat.

She leaned up and kissed him. "Yes, Tevo, I will marry you. Does Gabriel Sforza still live?" He smiled at her warmly.

"The old High Archon will outlive us both, wait and see."

"I wouldn't count on that," Betsalel said. "I foresee a long, long life for both of you." Leila smiled at him, the first time she had done so since Imbaso's death.

"I want Gabriel to marry us in the Temple of the Eight in Parat. With bells on."

Tevo hugged her to him tightly, then let her go. "Are you ready to leave?" he asked, eager to begin the new life that was opening before his mind's eye like a glimpse of heaven.

"No!" she said, eyes wide. "I didn't pack anything because I wasn't planning on leaving here. And I need to say goodbye to the king!"

Hours later, Betsalel took Leila in one arm and Tevo in the other as they waved goodbye to Vandao, Lmambela, and a contingent of dignitaries. "You will let our master bring you to Parat for the wedding?" Leila asked, and Vandao smiled broadly. His heart was filled with joy to see her find happiness again.

"I wouldn't miss it for anything!" he said. "And you two are welcome here at the palace whenever you want a change of scenery. Might want to think about it this winter, eh?"

In moments Leila found herself looking down from a considerable height. They had departed via the large idol in the Library building, a place she had avoided since Imbaso had died there. But in Tevo's company, and with a bright future awaiting her, she had found that the place didn't bother her much at all.

They arrived in the Temple of the Eight in Parat on a lovely afternoon in late summer, and the twenty-foot Shadow God set his arch-priestess and arch-priest carefully on the floor. Gabriel Sforza, looking no older than the first time they had met him, stood nearby grinning. "Welcome home," he said.